# THE GRACE OF KINGS

## ALSO BY KEN LIU

THE PAPER MENAGERIE AND OTHER STORIES

# THE GRACE OF KINGS

BOOK ONE OF THE DANDELION DYNASTY

KEN LIU

LONDON SYDNEY NEW YORK TORONTO NEW DELHI

1230 AVENUE OF THE AMERICAS, NEW YORK, NEW YORK 10020

This book is a work of fiction. Any references to historical events, real people, or real places are used fictitiously. Other names, characters, places, and events are products of the author's imagination, and any resemblance to actual events or places or persons, living or dead, is entirely coincidental. ·  For information address Saga Press Subsidiary Rights Department, 1230 Avenue of the Americas, New York, NY 10020 · SAGA PRESS and colophon are trademarks of Simon & Schuster, Inc. · For information about special discounts for bulk purchases, please contact Simon & Schuster Special Sales at 1-866-506-1949 or business@simonandschuster.com. · The Simon & Schuster Speakers Bureau can bring authors to your live event. For more information or to book an event, contact the Simon & Schuster Speakers Bureau at 1-866-248-3049 or visit our website at www.simonspeakers.com. · Also available in a Saga Press hardcover edition · The text for this book was set in Palatino. · Manufactured in the United States of America · First Saga Press trade paperback edition August 2016 · 20 19 18 17 16 15 14 13 · The Library of Congress has cataloged the hardcover edition as follows: Liu, Ken, 1976– · The grace of kings / Ken Liu. — First edition. · pages : map ; cm. — (The dandelion dynasty) · Summary: "The Grace of Kings, the first book in this epic series, tells the story of two men who become friends through rebelling against tyranny and then turn against each other in defense of irreconcilable ideals. Wily, charming Kuni Garu, a bandit, and stern, fearless Mata Zyndu, the son of a deposed duke, seem like polar opposites. Yet, in the uprising against the emperor, the two quickly become the best of friends after a series of adventures fighting against vast conscripted armies, silk-draped airships, soaring battle kites, underwater boats, magical books, shape-shifting gods, and scaled whales who seem to prophesy the future. Once the emperor has been overthrown, however, the two find themselves the leaders of two sides with very different ideas about how the world should be run and the meaning of justice"—Provided by publisher. · ISBN 978-1-4814-2427-1 (hc) · ISBN 978-1-4814-2428-8 (trade pbk) · ISBN 978-1-4814-5186-4 (mm pbk) · ISBN 978-1-4814-2429-5 (eBook) · 1. Rebellion—Fiction. 2. Friendship—Fiction. I. Title. · PS3612.I927G73 2015 · 813'.6 —dc23 · 2014019957

*For my grandmother, who introduced me to the great heroes of the Han Dynasty. I'll always remember the afternoons we spent together listening to* pingshu *storytellers on the radio.*

*And for Lisa, who saw Dara before I did.*

# CONTENTS

## CLOUDS RACE ACROSS THE SKY

# A NOTE ON PRONUNCIATION

Many names in Dara are derived from Classical Ano. The transliteration for Classical Ano in this book does not use vowel digraphs; each vowel is pronounced separately. For example, "Réfiroa" has four distinct syllables: "Ré-fi-ro-a." Similarly, "Na-aroénna" has five syllables: "Na-a-ro-én-na."

The *i* is always pronounced like the *i* in English "mill."

The *o* is always pronounced like the *o* in English "code."

The *ü* is always pronounced like the umlauted form in German or Chinese pinyin.

Other names have different origins and contain sounds that do not appear in Classical Ano, such as the *xa* in "Xana" or the *ha* in "Haan." In such cases, however, each vowel is still pronounced separately. Thus, "Haan" also contains two syllables.

# LIST OF MAJOR CHARACTERS

## THE CHRYSANTHEMUM AND THE DANDELION

KUNI GARU: a boy who prefers play to study; the leader of a street gang; and much more.

MATA ZYNDU: a boy noble in stature and spirit; last son of the Zyndu Clan.

### KUNI'S RETINUE

JIA MATIZA: the daughter of a rancher; a skilled herbalist; Kuni's wife.

COGO YELU: a clerk in Zudi's city government; Kuni's friend in "high places."

LUAN ZYA: scion of a noble family in Haan; adventurer among the people of Tan Adü.

GIN MAZOTI: an orphan on the streets of Dimushi; seeker of fortune during the rebellion.

RIN CODA: childhood friend of Kuni.

MÜN ÇAKRI: a butcher; one of Kuni's fiercest warriors.

THAN CARUCONO: an old stable master in Zudi.

LADY RISANA: an illusionist and accomplished musician.

DAFIRO MIRO: "Daf"; one of the first rebels under Huno Krima; brother of Ratho Miro.

SOTO: Jia's housekeeper.

### MATA'S RETINUE

PHIN ZYNDU: Mata's uncle; his tutor and surrogate parent.

TORULU PERING: an old scholar; Mata's adviser.

THÉCA KIMO: a rebel also from Tunoa.

LADY MIRA: an embroiderer and songstress from Tunoa; the only woman who understands Mata.

RATHO MIRO: "Rat"; one of the first rebels under Huno Krima; brother of Dafiro Miro.

### THE XANA EMPIRE

MAPIDÉRÉ: First Emperor of the Seven Islands of Dara; named Réon when he was King of Xana.

ERISHI: Second Emperor of the Seven Islands of Dara.

GORAN PIRA: Chatelain of Xana; childhood friend of King Réon.

LÜGO CRUPO: Regent of Xana; a great scholar and calligrapher.

TANNO NAMEN: revered General of Xana.

KINDO MARANA: the empire's chief tax collector.

### THE TIRO KINGS OF THE SIX STATES

PRINCESS KIKOMI AND KING PONADOMU OF AMU: the jewel of Arulugi and her granduncle.

KING THUFI OF COCRU: once a shepherd; urges the Tiro kings to unite.

KING SHILUÉ OF FAÇA: ambitious but careful of self-preservation; interferes with Rima.

KING DALO OF GAN: oversees the wealthiest realm of the Six States.

KING COSUGI OF HAAN: an old king who may have lost his appetite for risk.

KING JIZU OF RIMA: a young prince who grew up as a fisherman.

## THE REBELLION

HUNO KRIMA: leader of the first rebels against Xana.

ZOPA SHIGIN: companion of Huno; leader of the first rebels against Xana.

## THE GODS OF DARA

KIJI: patron of Xana; Lord of the Air; god of wind, flight, and birds; his *pawi* is the Mingén falcon; favors a white traveling cloak.

TUTUTIKA: patron of Amu; youngest of the gods; goddess of agriculture, beauty, and fresh water; her *pawi* is the golden carp.

KANA AND RAPA: twin patrons of Cocru; Kana is the goddess of fire, ash, cremation, and death; Rapa is the goddess of ice, snow, glaciers, and sleep; their *pawi* are twin ravens: one black, one white.

RUFIZO: patron of Faça; Divine Healer; his *pawi* is the dove.

TAZU: patron of Gan; unpredictable, chaotic, delighting in chance; god of sea currents, tsunamis, and sunken treasures; his *pawi* is the shark.

LUTHO: patron of Haan; god of fisherman, divination, mathematics, and knowledge; his *pawi* is the sea turtle.

FITHOWÉO: patron of Rima; god of war, the hunt, and the forge; his *pawi* is the wolf.

# *The* ISLANDS *of* DARA

Écofi Island
Arulugi Island
Lake Toyemotika
Müning
Amu Strait
Tan Adü
Canfin
Napi
Dimushi
Dimu
PORIN PLAINS
GÉFICA
Kiesa
AMU
Zudi
Pan
COCRU
Er-Mé Mountains
Mount Kana
Thoco Pass
Wisoti Mountains
Caruza
Mount Rapa
Rana Kida
Farun
Tunoa
Gonlogi Desert
GÉJIRA
GAN
Sónaru Desert
Maji Peninsula
Nasu
Itanti Peninsula
Kishi Channel
Nokida
Toaza
0 75 150
Miles

Dasu
Daye
XANA
Gaing Gulf
Crescent Island
Mount Kiji
Rui Island
Kriphi
Big Island
Lutho Beach
HAAN
Ginpen
Damu Mountains
Mount Fithowéo
Zathin Gulf
RIMA
Na Thion
Silkworm Eggs
FAÇA
HIGHLANDS
Boama
Shinané Mountains
W
Rufizo Falls
S
N
Tazu whirlpool
Ogé
Big Toe
Wolf's Paw
E

# ALL UNDER HEAVEN

## CHAPTER ONE

# AN ASSASSIN

ZUDI: THE SEVENTH MONTH IN THE FOURTEENTH YEAR OF THE REIGN OF ONE BRIGHT HEAVEN.

A white bird hung still in the clear western sky and flapped its wings sporadically.

Perhaps it was a raptor that had left its nest on one of the soaring peaks of the Er-Mé Mountains a few miles away in search of prey. But this was not a good day for hunting—a raptor's usual domain, this sun-parched section of the Porin Plains, had been taken over by people.

Thousands of spectators lined both sides of the wide road out of Zudi; they paid the bird no attention. They were here for the Imperial Procession.

They had gasped in awe as a fleet of giant Imperial airships passed overhead, shifting gracefully from one elegant formation to another. They had gawped in respectful silence as the heavy battle-carts rolled before them, thick bundles of ox sinew draping from the stone-throwing arms. They had praised the emperor's foresight and generosity as his engineers sprayed the crowd with perfumed water from ice wagons, cool and refreshing in the hot sun and dusty air of northern Cocru. They had clapped and cheered the best dancers the six conquered Tiro states had to offer: five hundred Faça maidens who gyrated seductively in the veil dance, a sight once reserved for the royal court in Boama; four hundred Cocru sword twirlers who spun their blades into bright chrysanthemums of cold light that melded martial glory with lyrical grace; dozens of elegant, stately elephants from wild, sparsely settled Écofi Island, painted with the colors of the Seven States—the largest male draped in the white flag of Xana, as one would expect, while the others wore the rainbow colors of the conquered lands.

The elephants pulled a moving platform on which stood two hundred of the best singers all the Islands of Dara had to offer, a choir whose existence would have been impossible before the Xana Conquest. They sang a new song, a composition by the great imperial scholar Lügo Crupo to celebrate the occasion of the Imperial tour of the Islands:

*To the north: Fruitful Faça, green as the eyes of kind*
*Rufizo,*
*Pastures ever kissed by sweet rain, craggy highlands*
*shrouded in mist.*

Soldiers walking next to the moving platform tossed trinkets into the crowd: Xana-style decorative knots made with bits of colorful string to represent the Seven States. The shapes of the knots were meant to evoke the logograms for "prosperity" and "luck." Spectators scrambled and fought one another to catch a memento of this exciting day.

*To the south: Castled Cocru, fields of sorghum and rice,*
*both pale and dark,*
*Red, for martial glory, white, like proud Rapa, black, as*
*mournful Kana.*

The crowd cheered especially loudly after this verse about their homeland.

*To the west: Alluring Amu, the jewel of Tututika,*
*Luminous elegance, filigreed cities surround two blue lakes.*

*To the east: Gleaming Gan, where Tazu's trades and gambles glitter,*
*Wealthy as the sea's bounty, cultured like the scholars' layered gray robes.*

Walking behind the singers, other soldiers held up long silk banners embroidered with elaborate scenes of the beauty and wonder of the Seven States: moonlight glinting from snowcapped Mount Kiji; schools of fish sparkling in Lake Tututika at sunrise; breaching crubens and whales sighted off the shores of Wolf's Paw; joyous crowds lining the wide streets in Pan, the capital; serious scholars debating policy in front of the wise, all-knowing emperor. . . .

*To the northwest: High-minded Haan, forum of philosophy,*
*Tracing the tortuous paths of the gods on Lutho's yellow shell.*
*In the middle: Ring-wooded Rima, where sunlight pierces ancient*
*Forests to dapple the ground, as sharp as Fithowéo's black sword.*

Between each verse, the crowd bellowed out the chorus along with the singers:

*We bow down, bow down, bow down to Xana, Zenith, Ruler of Air,*
*Why resist, why persist against Lord Kiji in strife that we can't bear?*

If the servile words bothered those in this Cocru crowd who had probably taken up arms against the Xana invaders scarcely more than a dozen years ago, any mutterings were drowned out by the full-throated, frenzied singing of the men and women around them. The hypnotic chant held a power of its own, as if by mere repetition the words gained weight, became more true.

But the crowd wasn't close to being satisfied by the spectacle thus far. They hadn't seen the heart of the Procession yet: the emperor.

The white bird glided closer. Its wings seemed to be as wide and long as the spinning vanes of the windmills in Zudi that drew water from deep wells and piped it into the houses of the wealthy—too big to be an ordinary eagle or vulture. A few spectators looked up and idly wondered if it was a giant Mingén falcon, taken more than a thousand miles from its home in faraway Rui Island and released here by the emperor's trainers to impress the crowd.

But an Imperial scout hidden among the crowd looked at the bird and furrowed his brows. Then he turned and shoved his way through the crowd toward the temporary viewing platform where the local officials were gathered.

Anticipation among the spectators grew as the Imperial Guards passed by, marching like columns of mechanical men: eyes straight ahead, legs and arms swinging in unison, stringed marionettes under the guidance of a single pair of hands. Their discipline and order contrasted sharply with the dynamic dancers who had passed before them.

After a momentary pause, the crowd roared their approval. Never mind that this same army had slaughtered Cocru's soldiers and disgraced her old nobles. The people watching simply wanted spectacle, and they loved the gleaming armor and the martial splendor.

The bird drifted even closer.

"Coming through! Coming through!"

Two fourteen-year-old boys shoved their way through the tightly packed crowd like a pair of colts butting through a sugarcane field.

The boy in the lead, Kuni Garu, wore his long, straight, black hair in a topknot in the style of a student in the private academies. He was stocky—not fat but well-muscled, with strong arms and thighs. His eyes, long and narrow like most men from Cocru, glinted with intelligence that verged on slyness. He made no effort to be gentle, elbowing men and women aside as he forced his way forward. Behind him, he left a trail of bruised ribs and angry curses.

The boy in the back, Rin Coda, was gangly and nervous, and as he followed his friend through the throng like a seagull dragged along on the tailwind of a ship, he murmured apologies at the enraged men and women around them.

"Kuni, I think we'll be okay just standing in the back," Rin said. "I *really* don't think this is a good idea."

"Then don't think," Kuni said. "Your problem is that you *think* too much. Just *do*."

"Master Loing says that the gods want us to always think before we act." Rin winced and ducked out of the way as another man swore at the pair and took a swing at them.

"No one knows what the gods want." Kuni didn't look back as he forged ahead. "Not even Master Loing."

They finally made it through the dense crowd and stood right next to the road, where white chalk lines indicated how far spectators could stand.

"Now, this is what I call a view," Kuni said, breathing deeply and taking everything in. He whistled appreciatively as the last of the semi-nude Faça veil dancers passed in front of him. "I can see the attraction of being emperor."

"Stop talking like that! Do you want to go to jail?" Rin looked nervously around to see if anyone was paying attention—Kuni had a habit of saying outrageous things that could be easily interpreted as treason.

"Now, doesn't this beat sitting in class practicing carving wax logograms and memorizing Kon Fiji's *Treatise on Moral Relations*?" Kuni draped his arm around Rin's shoulders. "Admit it: You're glad you came with me."

Master Loing had explained that he wasn't going to close his school for the Procession because he believed the emperor wouldn't want the children to interrupt their studies—but Rin secretly suspected that it was because Master Loing didn't approve of the emperor. A lot of people in Zudi had complicated views about the emperor.

"Master Loing would definitely not approve of *this*," Rin said, but he couldn't take his eyes away from the veil dancers either.

Kuni laughed. "If the master is going to slap us with his ferule for skipping classes for three full days anyway, we might as well get our pain's worth."

"Except you always seem to come up with some clever argument to wiggle out of being punished, and I end up getting double strokes!"

The crowd's cheers rose to a crescendo.

On top of the Throne Pagoda, the emperor was seated with his legs stretched out in front of him in the position of *thakrido*, cushioned by soft silk pillows. Only the emperor would be able to sit like this publicly, as everyone was his social inferior.

The Throne Pagoda was a five-story bamboo-and-silk structure erected on a platform formed from twenty thick bamboo poles—ten across, ten perpendicular—carried on the shoulders of a hundred men, their chests and arms bare, oiled to glisten in the sunlight.

The four lower stories of the Throne Pagoda were filled with intricate, jewel-like clockwork models whose movements illustrated the Four Realms of the Universe: the World of Fire down below—filled with demons who mined diamond and gold; then, the World of Water—full of fish and serpents and pulsing jellyfish; next, the World of Earth, in which men lived—islands floating over the four seas; and finally the World of Air above all—the domain of birds and spirits.

Wrapped in a robe of shimmering silk, his crown a splendid creation of gold and glittering gems topped by the statuette of a cruben, the scaled whale and lord of the Four Placid Seas, whose single horn was made from the purest ivory at the heart of a young elephant's tusk and whose eyes were formed by a pair of heavy black diamonds—the largest diamonds in all of Dara, taken from the treasury of Cocru when it had fallen to Xana fifteen years earlier—Emperor Mapidéré shaded his eyes with one hand and squinted at the approaching form of the great bird.

"What *is* that?" he wondered aloud.

At the foot of the slow-moving Throne Pagoda, the Imperial scout informed the Captain of the Imperial Guards that the officials in Zudi all claimed to have never seen anything like the strange bird. The captain whispered some orders, and the Imperial Guards, the most elite troops in all of Dara, tightened their formation around the Pagoda-bearers.

The emperor continued to stare at the giant bird, which slowly and steadily drifted closer. It flapped its wings once, and the emperor, straining to listen through the noise of the clamoring, fervent crowd, thought he heard it cry out in a startlingly human manner.

The Imperial tour of the Islands had already gone on for more than eight months. Emperor Mapidéré understood well the necessity of visibly reminding the conquered population of Xana's might and authority, but he was tired. He longed to be back in Pan, the Immaculate City, his new capital, where he could enjoy his zoo and aquarium, filled with animals from all over Dara—including a few exotic ones that had been given as tribute by pirates who sailed far beyond the horizon. He wished he could eat meals prepared by his favorite chef instead of the strange offerings in each place he visited—they might be the best delicacies that the gentry of each town could scrounge up and proffer, but it was tedious to have to wait for tasters to sample each one for poison, and inevitably the dishes were too fatty or too spicy and upset his stomach.

Above all, he was bored. The hundreds of evening receptions hosted by local officials and dignitaries merged into one endless morass. No matter where he went, the pledges of fealty and declarations of submission all sounded the same. Often, he felt as though he were sitting alone in the middle of a theater while the same performance was put on every night around him, with different actors saying the same lines in various settings.

The emperor leaned forward: this strange bird was the most exciting thing that had happened in days.

Now that it was closer, he could pick out more details. It was . . . not a bird at all.

It was a great kite made of paper, silk, and bamboo, except that no string tethered it to the ground. Beneath the kite—could it be?—hung the figure of a man.

"Interesting," the emperor said.

The Captain of the Imperial Guards rushed up the delicate spiral stairs inside the Pagoda, taking the rungs two or three at a time. "*Rénga*, we should take precautions."

The emperor nodded.

The bearers lowered the Throne Pagoda to the ground. The Imperial Guards halted their march. Archers took up positions around the Pagoda, and shieldmen gathered at the foot of the structure to create a temporary bunker walled and roofed by their great interlocking pavises, like the shell of a tortoise. The emperor pounded his legs to get circulation back into his stiff muscles so that he could get up.

The crowd sensed that this was not a planned part of the Procession. They craned their necks and followed the aim of the archers' nocked arrows.

The strange gliding contraption was now only a few hundred yards away.

The man hanging from the kite pulled on a few ropes dangling near him. The kite-bird suddenly folded its wings and dove at the Throne Pagoda, covering the remaining distance in a few heartbeats. The man ululated, a long, piercing cry that made the crowd below shiver despite the heat.

"Death to Xana and Mapidéré! Long live the Great Haan!"

Before anyone could react, the kite rider launched a ball of fire at the Throne Pagoda. The emperor stared at the impending missile, too stunned to move.

*"Rénga!"* The Captain of the Imperial Guards was next to the emperor in a second; with one hand, he pushed the old man off the throne and then, with a grunt, he lifted the throne—a heavy ironwood sitting-board covered in gold—with his other hand like a giant pavise. The missile exploded against it in a fiery blast, and the resulting pieces bounced off and fell to the ground, throwing hissing, burning globs of oily tar in all directions in secondary explosions, setting everything they touched aflame. Unfortunate dancers and soldiers screamed as the sticky burning liquid adhered to their bodies and faces, and flaming tongues instantly engulfed them.

Although the heavy throne had shielded the Captain of the Imperial Guards and the emperor from much of the initial explosion, a few stray fiery tongues had singed off much of the hair on the captain and left the right side of his face and his right arm badly burned. But the emperor, though shocked, was unharmed.

The captain dropped the throne, and, wincing with pain, he leaned over the side of the Pagoda and shouted down at the shocked archers. "Fire at will!"

He cursed himself at the emphasis on absolute discipline he had instilled in the guards so that they focused more on obeying orders than reacting on their own initiative. But it had been so long since the last attempt on the emperor's life that everyone had been lulled into a false sense of security. He would have to look into improvements in training—assuming he got to keep his own head after this failure.

The archers launched their arrows in a volley. The assassin pulled on the strings of the kite, folded the wings, and banked in a tight arc to get out of the way. The spent bolts fell like black rain from the sky.

Thousands of dancers and spectators merged into the panicked chaos of a screaming and jostling mob.

"I *told* you this was a bad idea!" Rin looked around frantically for somewhere to hide. He yelped and jumped out of the way of a falling arrow. Beside him, two men lay dead with arrows sticking out of their backs. "I should never have agreed to help you with that lie to your parents about school being closed. Your schemes always end with me in trouble! We've got to run!"

"If you run and trip in that crowd, you're going to get trampled," said Kuni. "Besides, how can you want to miss this?"

"Oh gods, we're all going to die!" Another arrow fell and stuck into the ground less than a foot away. A few more people fell down screaming as their bodies were pierced.

"We're not dead yet." Kuni dashed into the road and returned with a shield one of the soldiers had dropped.

"Duck!" he yelled, and pulled Rin down with him into a crouch, raising the shield over their heads. An arrow thunked against the shield.

"Lady Rapa and Lady Kana, p-pr-protect me!" muttered Rin with his eyes squeezed tightly shut. "If I survive this, I promise to listen to my mother and never skip school again, and I'll obey the ancient sages and stay away from honey-tongued friends who lead me astray. . . ."

But Kuni was already peeking around the shield.

The kite rider jackknifed his legs hard, causing the wings of his kite to flap a few times in rapid succession. The kite pulled straight up, gaining some altitude. The rider pulled the reins, turned around in a tight arc, and came at the Throne Pagoda again.

The emperor, who had recovered from the initial shock, was being escorted down the spiraling stairs. But he was still only halfway to the foot of the Throne Pagoda, caught between the Worlds of Earth and Fire.

"*Rénga*, please forgive me!" The Captain of the Imperial Guards ducked and lifted the emperor's body, thrust him over the side of the Pagoda, and dropped him.

The soldiers below had already stretched out a long, stiff piece of cloth. The emperor landed in it, trampolined up and down a few times, but appeared unhurt.

Kuni caught a glimpse of the emperor in the brief moment before he was rushed under the protective shell of overlapping shields.

Years of alchemical medicine—taken in the hope of extending his life—had wreaked havoc with his body. Though the emperor was only fifty-five, he looked to be thirty years older. But Kuni was most struck by the old man's hooded eyes peering out of his wrinkled face, eyes that for a moment had shown surprise and fear.

The sound of the kite diving behind Kuni was like a piece of rough cloth being torn. "Get down!" He pushed Rin to the ground and flopped on top of his friend, pulling the shield above their heads. "Pretend you are a turtle."

Rin tried to flatten himself against the earth under Kuni. "I wish a ditch would open up so I could crawl into it."

More flaming tar exploded around the Throne Pagoda. Some struck the top of the shield bunker, and as the sizzling tar oozed into the gaps between the shields, the soldiers beneath cried out in pain but held their positions. At the direction of the officers, the soldiers lifted and sloped their shields in unison to throw off the burning tar, like a crocodile flexing its scales to shake off excess water.

"I think it's safe now," said Kuni. He took away the shield and rolled off Rin.

Slowly, Rin sat up and watched his friend without comprehension. Kuni was rolling along the ground as if he was frolicking in the snow—*how could Kuni think of playing games at a time like this?*

Then he saw the smoke rising from Kuni's clothes. He yelped and hurried over, helping to extinguish the flames by slapping at Kuni's voluminous robes with his long sleeves.

"Thanks, Rin," said Kuni. He sat up and tried to smile, but only managed a wince.

Rin examined Kuni: A few drops of burning oil had landed on his back. Through the smoking holes in the robe, Rin could see that the flesh underneath was raw, charred, and oozing blood.

"Oh gods! Does it hurt?"

"Only a little," said Kuni.

"If you weren't on top of me . . ." Rin swallowed. "Kuni Garu, you're a real friend."

"Eh, think nothing of it," said Kuni. "As Sage Kon Fiji said: One should always—ow!—be ready to stick knives between one's ribs if that would help a friend." He tried to put some swagger into this speech but the pain made his voice unsteady. "See, Master Loing did teach me something."

"That's the part you remember? But that wasn't Kon Fiji. You're quoting from a bandit debating Kon Fiji."

"Who says bandits don't have virtues too?"

The sound of flapping wings interrupted them. The boys looked up. Slowly, gracefully, like an albatross turning over the sea, the kite flapped its wings, rose, turned around in a large circle, and began a third bombing run toward the Throne Pagoda. The rider was clearly tiring and could not gain as much altitude this time. The kite was very close to the ground.

A few of the archers managed to shoot holes in the wings of the stringless kite, and a few of the arrows even struck the rider, though his thick leather armor seemed to be reinforced in some manner, and the arrows stuck only briefly in the leather before falling off harmlessly.

Again, he folded the wings of his craft and accelerated toward the Throne Pagoda like a diving kingfisher.

The archers continued to shoot at the assassin, but he ignored the hailstorm of arrows and held his course. Flaming missiles exploded against the sides of the Throne Pagoda. Within seconds, the silk-and-bamboo construction turned into a tower of fire.

But the emperor was now safely ensconced under the pavises of the shieldmen, and with every passing moment, more archers gathered around the emperor's position. The rider could see that his prize was out of reach.

Instead of another bombing attempt, the kite rider turned his machine to the south, away from the Procession, and kicked hard with his dwindling strength to gain some altitude.

"He's heading to Zudi," Rin said. "You think anyone we know back home helped him?"

Kuni shook his head. When the kite had passed directly over him and Rin, it had temporarily blotted out the glare of the sun. He had seen that the rider was a young man, not even thirty. He had the dark skin and long limbs common to the men of Haan, up north. For a fraction of a second, the rider, looking down, had locked gazes with Kuni, and Kuni's heart thrilled with the fervent passion and purposeful intensity in those bright-green eyes.

"He made the emperor afraid," Kuni said, as if to himself. "The emperor is just a man, after all." A wide smile broke on his face.

Before Rin could shush his friend again, great black shadows covered them. The boys looked up and saw yet more reasons for the kite rider's retreat.

Six graceful airships, each about three hundred feet long, the pride of the Imperial air force, drifted overhead. The airships had been at the head of the Imperial Procession, both to scout ahead and to impress the spectators. It had taken a while before the oarsmen could turn the ships around to bring them to the emperor's aid.

The stringless kite grew smaller and smaller. The airships lumbered after the escaping assassin, their great feathered oars beating the air like the wings of fat geese struggling to lift off. The rider was already too far for the airships' archers and stringed battle kites. They would not reach the city of Zudi before the nimble man landed and disappeared into its alleys.

The emperor, huddled in the dim shadows of the shield bunker, was furious, but he retained a calm mien. This was not the first assassination attempt, and it would not be the last; only this one had come closest to succeeding.

As he gave his order, his voice was emotionless and implacable.

"Find that man. Even if you have to tear apart every house in Zudi and burn down the estates of all the nobles in Haan, bring him before me."

CHAPTER TWO

# MATA ZYNDU

FARUN, IN THE TUNOA ISLANDS:
THE NINTH MONTH IN THE FOURTEENTH YEAR
OF THE REIGN OF ONE BRIGHT HEAVEN.

Few would have guessed that the man towering above the noisy crowd at the edge of the town square of Farun was only a boy of fourteen. The jostling townspeople kept a respectful distance from Mata Zyndu's seven-and-a-half-foot frame, rippling with muscle everywhere.

"They're afraid of you," Phin Zyndu, the boy's uncle, said with pride in his voice. He looked up into Mata's face and sighed. "I wish your father and grandfather could see you today."

The boy nodded but said nothing, looking over the bobbing heads of the crowd like a crane among sandpipers. Unlike the brown eyes most common in Cocru, Mata's eyes were coal-black, but each held two pupils that glowed with a faint light, a rare condition that many had believed was mythical.

Those double-pupiled eyes allowed him to see more sharply and farther than most people, and as he scanned the horizon, he lingered on the slender, dark tower of stone to the north, just outside of town. It stood next to the sea like a dagger stuck into the rocky beach. Mata could just make out the great arched windows near the top of the tower, whose frames were intricately decorated with carvings of the Two Ravens, black and white, their beaks meeting at the apex of the arch to hold up a stone chrysanthemum with a thousand petals.

That was the main tower of the ancestral castle of the Zyndu Clan. These days it belonged to Datun Zatoma, commander of the Xana garrison guarding Farun. Mata Zyndu hated to think about that commoner, not even a warrior but a mere scribe, squatting in the ancient, storied halls that rightfully belonged to his family.

Mata forced himself back into the present. He leaned down to whisper to Phin, "I want to get closer."

The Imperial Procession had just arrived in Tunoa by sea from the southern part of the Big Island, where rumor had it that the emperor had survived an assassination attempt near Zudi. As Mata and Phin made their way forward, the crowd parted effortlessly and silently before Mata like waves before a ship's prow.

They stopped just short of the front row, and Mata hunched down to his uncle's height to avoid drawing attention from the emperor's guards.

"They're here!" the crowd shouted as airships burst through the clouds near the horizon and the tip of the Throne Pagoda rose into sight.

While the townspeople cheered the beautiful dancers and applauded the daring soldiers, Mata Zyndu had eyes only for Emperor Mapidéré. At long last, he would set his eyes on the face of the enemy.

A wall of soldiers now stood in a circle on top of the Pagoda, arrows nocked, swords drawn. The emperor sat in their midst, and the spectators could only catch occasional glimpses of his face.

Mata had imagined an old man grown soft and fat from complacency, but instead, through the wall of soldiers, as through a veil, he saw a gaunt figure with hard, expressionless eyes.

*How alone he is, high above in his peerless splendor.*

*And how afraid.*

Phin and Mata looked at each other. Each saw in the other's eyes the same mixture of sorrow and smoldering hatred. Phin didn't have to speak aloud. Mata had heard from his uncle the same words every day of his life:

*Do not forget.*

Back when Emperor Mapidéré was still only the young King of Xana, and when the army of Xana routed the crumbling forces of the Six States across land, sea, and sky, one man had stood in its way: Dazu Zyndu, Duke of Tunoa and Marshal of Cocru.

The Zyndus came from a long line of great Cocru generals. But when Dazu was a young man, he was scrawny and sickly. His father and grandfather decided to send him north, far away from the family's fiefdom in the Tunoa Islands, to be trained under the legendary master swordsman Médo in the misty isles called the Silkworm Eggs, at the other end of Dara.

After one look at Dazu, Médo said, "I'm too old and you're too little. I taught my last student years ago. Leave me in peace."

But Dazu did not leave. He knelt outside Médo's house for ten days and ten nights, refusing food or drink except rainwater. On the eleventh day, Dazu collapsed to the ground, and Médo was moved by Dazu's persistence and accepted him as a student.

But instead of teaching the young man sword fighting, Médo used Dazu only as a ranch hand to care for his small herd of cattle. Dazu did not complain. In the cold and rocky mountains, the young man followed the herd everywhere, watching for wolves hiding in the mist and huddling for warmth among the lowing cows at night.

When a new calf was born in the spring, Médo told Dazu to carry the baby animal back to his house for a weigh-in each day so that the calf's legs would not be injured by the sharp stones on the ground. This involved walking many miles. At first the trip was easy, but as the calf gained weight, the trip became more difficult.

"The calf is capable of walking quite well now," Dazu said. "He never stumbles."

"But I told you to *carry* him back here," the teacher said. "The first thing a soldier must learn is to obey orders."

Every day, the calf grew a little heavier, and every day, Dazu had to struggle a little harder. He would collapse, exhausted, when he finally got to the ranch, and the calf would bound out of his arms, glad to be able to walk on his own and stretch out.

When winter rolled around again, Médo handed him a wooden sword and asked him to strike as hard as he could at the practice dummy. Dazu looked with distaste at the crude weapon with no edge, but he swung obediently.

The wooden dummy fell in half, cut clean through. He looked at the sword in his hand with wonder.

"It's not the sword," his teacher said. "Have you looked at yourself lately?" He brought Dazu to stand in front of a brightly polished shield.

The young man could hardly recognize the reflection. His shoulders filled the frame of the mirror. His arms and thighs were twice as thick as he remembered, and his chest bulged over his narrow waist.

"A great warrior trusts not his weapons, but himself. When you possess true strength, you can deal a killing blow even if all you have is a blade of grass.

"Now you're finally ready to learn from me. But first, go thank the calf for making you strong."

Dazu Zyndu was unmatched on the battlefield. While the armies of the other Tiro states succumbed like kindling before the fierce hordes of Xana, the men of Cocru, led by Duke Zyndu, held back the assaults of Xana like a steady dam against a raging flood.

Because his troops were outnumbered, Duke Zyndu placed them in strategically located forts and garrison towns across Cocru. Whenever Xana invaded, he directed his men to ignore the taunts of

Xana commanders and stay behind the walls like a turtle retreating into its shell.

But whenever the Xana army tried to bypass these well-defended forts and cities, the defenders would swoop out of their fortresses like moray eels erupting from their secret crevices and attack ferociously from the rear to cut off Xana supply lines. Though Gotha Tonyeti, the great Xana general, had at his disposal many more men and better equipment than Duke Zyndu, he was bogged down by Zyndu's tactics and could not advance.

Tonyeti called Zyndu "the Bearded Tortoise," intending it as an insult, but Dazu laughed and adopted the moniker as a badge of pride.

Unable to prevail on the field, Tonyeti resorted to plots. He spread rumors in Çaruza, the Cocru capital, of the ambition of Duke Zyndu.

"Why does Duke Zyndu not attack Xana, but only hide behind stone walls?" the people whispered to one another. "The Xana army is clearly no match for the might of Cocru, and yet the duke hesitates and leaves the invaders occupying our fields. Perhaps the duke has a secret agreement with Gotha Tonyeti, and Tonyeti is only pretending to be attacking. Could they be plotting to overthrow the king and set up Duke Zyndu as his replacement?"

The King of Cocru became suspicious and ordered Duke Zyndu to abandon his defensive positions and engage Tonyeti in field battles. This would be a mistake, Dazu Zyndu explained, but his arguments only made the king more suspicious.

Duke Zyndu had no choice. He put on his armor and led the charge. Tonyeti's forces seemed to melt before the fearsome Cocru warriors. The Xana troops kept on falling back, and back, and then collapsed into total chaos.

The duke pursued the defeated Tonyeti into a deep valley, where the Xana general disappeared into the dark woods. Suddenly, Xana troops, five times the number of men Zyndu had with him, emerged from the sides of the valley in ambush and cut off his path of retreat. Zyndu understood then that he had been tricked, and there was nothing to do but to surrender.

Dazu Zyndu negotiated for the safety of his soldiers as war prisoners and then took his own life, unable to live with the shame of capitulation. Gotha Tonyeti reneged on his promise and buried alive all the surrendered Cocru soldiers.

Çaruza fell three days later.

Mapidéré decided to make an example of the Zyndu Clan, who had resisted him for so long. Every male Zyndu within three degrees of relatedness was put to death and all the women sold to the indigo houses. Dazu Zyndu's oldest son, Shiru, was flayed alive in Çaruza while Tonyeti's men forced the capital's citizens to watch and eat bits of his flesh afterward to confirm their loyalty to Xana. Dazu's daughter, Soto, barricaded herself and her servants in their country estate and set fire to it to escape the worse fate that awaited her. The flames raged for a full day and night as though the goddess Kana was expressing her grief, and the heat was so intense that even Soto's bones could not be found afterward in the wreckage.

Dazu's youngest son, thirteen-year-old Phin, evaded capture for days by hiding in the maze of lightless storage rooms and tunnels in the basement of the Zyndu family castle. But in the end, Tonyeti's soldiers caught him when he tried to sneak into the kitchen for a drink of water. The soldiers dragged the young man before the great general.

Tonyeti looked at the kneeling boy before him, trembling and sniveling with fear, and laughed.

"It would be too shameful to kill you," he said in his booming voice. "Hiding like a rabbit instead of fighting like a wolf, how will you face your father and brother in the afterlife after this? You have not even a tenth of the courage of your sister. I will treat you just like your brother's baby because you behave the same."

Against Mapidéré's orders, Tonyeti had spared Shiru's newborn son from slaughter. "Nobles have to behave better than peasants," he had said, "even in war."

So Tonyeti's soldiers released Phin, and the shamed boy stumbled out of the family castle with only his dead brother's infant son, Mata, in his arms. Bereft of title, home, and clan, his life of ease and wealth stripped away like a dream, what was the boy going to do?

At the outer gate of the castle, Phin picked up a fallen red flag: singed, dirty, but still showing the embroidered gold chrysanthemum, emblem of the Zyndu Clan. He wrapped Mata in it, scant protection against the winter air, and uncovered the baby's face by lifting up a corner of the cloth.

Baby Mata blinked and stared, two pupils in each black eye. A faint light glowed from the pupils.

Phin sucked in his breath. Among the ancient Ano, it was said that those with double pupils had the special attention of the gods. Most such children were blind from birth. Barely more than a child himself, Phin had never paid much attention to the wailing bundle that was his newborn nephew. This was the first time he had realized Mata's condition.

Phin moved his hand in front of the baby, uncertain if he was blind. Mata's eyes did not move, but then the baby turned and focused his eyes on Phin's.

Among the double-pupiled, a rare few had the sight of an eagle, and it was said that they were destined for greatness.

Relieved, Phin held the baby against his chest, against his thundering heart, and after a moment, a teardrop, hot as blood, fell from Phin's eyes onto Mata's face. The baby began to cry.

Phin bent down and touched his forehead to the baby's. The gesture calmed the child. Phin whispered, "We have only each other now. Don't let what has been done to our family pass into oblivion. *Do not forget.*"

The baby seemed to understand. He struggled to free his tiny arms from the flag wrapped around him, raised them toward Phin, and clenched his fists.

Phin lifted his face to the sky and laughed into the falling snow. He carefully covered the baby's face with the flag again and walked away from the castle.

∽ ∾ ∽ ∾

Mata's frown reminded Phin of Dazu Zyndu's serious mien while deep in thought. Mata's smile was a replica of the smile of Soto, Phin's dead sister, when she ran around the garden as a child. Mata's sleeping face had the same serenity as Phin's older brother, Shiru, who had always told Phin to be more patient.

Gazing at Mata, Phin understood why he had been spared. The little boy was the last and brightest chrysanthemum blossom at the tip of the noble tree formed by generations of the Zyndu Clan. Phin vowed to Kana and Rapa, the twin goddesses of Cocru, that he would do everything in his power to nurture and protect Mata.

And he would make his heart cold and his blood hot, like icy Rapa and fiery Kana. For the sake of Mata, he would learn to become hard and sharp instead of pampered and soft. In vengeance, even a rabbit can learn to become a wolf.

Phin had to rely on occasional handouts from loyalist families who sympathized with the plight of the Zyndu Clan until he killed two thieves sleeping in a field and took their loot, which he then invested in a little farm outside Farun. There, he taught Mata to fish, to hunt, and to fight with a sword, after learning those skills himself under the severe tutelage of trial-and-error: The first time he shot a deer, he vomited at the sight of blood; the first time he swung a sword, he almost cut off his own foot. He cursed himself again and again for how he had luxuriated in his former life of ease and learned nothing of use.

The weight of the responsibility he undertook had turned his hair gray by the time he was twenty-five. Often, he sat alone at night outside their shack, after his little nephew had fallen asleep. Haunted by the memory of his weakness years ago, he brooded over whether he was doing enough, was even capable of doing enough, to set Mata on the right path, to pass on the courage and strength, and especially the yearning for glory, that was the boy's birthright.

Dazu and Shiru had not wanted the delicate Phin to follow the path of war. They had indulged Phin's love of literature and art, and look where that had gotten him. In a moment when the family needed him, Phin had been powerless, had been a coward who brought shame to the family name.

So he locked away memories of the kind words of Shiru and the gentleness of Dazu. Instead, he gave Mata a childhood that he thought they would have wanted. Whenever Mata hurt himself as all children did, Phin forced himself to refuse the boy any comfort until Mata learned that crying was useless. Whenever Mata fought with another boy from the town, Phin insisted that he press on until he emerged victorious. Phin never tolerated signs of weakness in the child and taught Mata to welcome every conflict as a chance to prove himself.

Over the years, Phin's naturally kind heart became so wrapped and concealed in the roles he assigned himself that he could no longer tell where family legend ended and his own life began.

But once, when five-year-old Mata was gripped by an illness that threatened to take away his life, the boy saw through a crack in his uncle's hard shell.

Mata had awoken from a feverish slumber and saw his uncle crying. The boy had never seen such a sight and thought he was still dreaming. Phin hugged Mata tightly—another gesture foreign to the child—and muttered many thanks to Kana and Rapa. "You're a Zyndu," he said, as he did so often. "You're stronger than anyone." But then he added in a voice that was gentle and strange, "You are all that I have."

Mata had no memory of his real father, and Phin *was* his father, his hero. From Phin, he learned that the Zyndu name was sacred. Theirs was a family born of noble blood rich with glory, blood blessed by the gods, blood spilled by the emperor, blood that had to be avenged.

Phin and Mata sold their produce and pelts from hunted animals in town. Phin sought out surviving scholars, family friends, and acquaintances. A few of them surreptitiously kept a cache of ancient books, written in the old logograms unique to Cocru and forbidden by the emperor, and Phin borrowed or traded for them and taught Mata to read and write.

From these books and from his memory, Phin told Mata stories and legends of Cocru's martial past and of the Zyndu Clan's glorious history. Mata dreamed of emulating his grandfather, to carry on the legacy of his prowess. He ate only meat and bathed only in cold water. Having no living calf to carry, he volunteered to help the fishermen at the wharf unload their catch each day (and earned a few coppers doing so). He filled small sacks with rocks and tied them around his wrists and ankles so that each step required more strength. If there were two paths to a destination, he picked the longer and more arduous one. If there were two ways to do something, he chose the harder and more strenuous method. By the time he was twelve, he could lift the giant cauldron in front of the temple in Farun over his head.

Mata did not have much time for play, and so he made no meaningful friendships. He treasured the privilege of noble and ancient learning, won with so much hard work by his uncle. But Mata had little use for poetry. Instead, he loved books of history and military strategy. Through them, he learned about the golden past that was no more and came to realize that Xana's sins were not limited to what had happened to his family. "Mapidéré's conquest had degraded the very foundations of the world," as Phin told him time and again.

The origin of the old Tiro system was lost in the mists of time. Legend had it that the Islands of Dara were settled long ago by a people who called themselves the Ano, refugees of a sunken continent far over the seas to the west. Once they had defeated the barbarians who were the original inhabitants of the Islands, some of whom intermarried and became Ano, they promptly fell to fighting among themselves. Their descendants, over many generations and many wars, separated into various states.

Some scholars claimed the great ancient Ano lawgiver Aruano created the Tiro system in response to the chaotic wars among the states. The Classical Ano word *tiro* literally meant "fellow," and the most important principle of the system was that each Tiro state was an equal of every other Tiro state; no state had any authority over another. Only when one state committed a sin that offended the gods could the other states band together against it, and the leader of such a temporary alliance was given the title *princeps*, first *tiro* among equals.

The Seven States had coexisted for more than a thousand years, and but for that tyrant from Xana they would have existed for a thousand more. The kings of the Tiro states were the ultimate secular authorities, the anchors from which seven parallel Great Chains of Being dangled. They enfeoffed lands to the nobles, who each kept the peace in his domain and administered it like a miniature Tiro state. Each peasant paid his taxes and labor to a lord, and each lord to his lord, and so on up the chain.

The wisdom of the Tiro system was evident in the way it reflected the natural world. In the ancient forests of Dara, each great tree, like a Tiro state, stood independent of the others. No tree held sway over another. Yet each tree was made up of branches, and each branch of leaves, just as each king drew his strength from his nobles, and each noble from his peasantry. It was the same with the separate Islands of Dara, each composed of islets and lagoons, of bays and coves. The pattern of independent realms, each composed from miniature copies, could be found in coral reefs, in schools of fish, in drifting forests of kelp, in mineral crystals, and in the anatomy of animals.

It was the underlying order of the universe, a grid—like the warp and weft of the rough cloth woven by Cocru craftsmen—formed by horizontal lines of mutual respect among equals and vertical lines of downward obligation and upward fealty in which everyone knew his place.

Emperor Mapidéré had eliminated all that, swept it away like the armies of the Six States, like fallen leaves in autumn. A few of the old nobles who surrendered early got to keep their empty titles and sometimes even their castles and money, but that was all. Their lands were no longer theirs because all land now belonged to the

Xana Empire, to the emperor himself. Instead of each lord giving the law in his domain, there now was but one law that governed all the Islands.

Instead of the scholars of each Tiro state writing with their own sets of logograms and arranging the zyndari letters in their own fashion, bound up with local tradition and history, everyone now had to write in the manner of Xana. Instead of each Tiro state determining its own system of weights and measures, its own way of judging and seeing the world, everyone now had to make their roads as wide as the distance between the wheels of a cart from the Immaculate City, their boxes as big as could be packed tightly into a boat from the port of Kriphi, the former Xana capital.

All sources of loyalty, of local attachment, were replaced with allegiance to the emperor. In place of the parallel chains of devotion forged by nobles, the emperor had put in a pyramid of petty bureaucrats—commoners who could barely write any logograms beyond those in their own names and who had to spell everything out in zyndari letters. Instead of ruling with the best, the emperor had chosen to elevate the craven, greedy, foolish, and low.

In this new world, the old orderly way of life was lost. No one knew his place. Commoners were living in castles while nobles huddled in drafty huts. Emperor Mapidéré's sins were against nature, against the hidden pattern of the universe itself.

As the Procession disappeared into the distance, the crowd gradually dispersed. Now they had to return to the struggle of daily life: fields to harvest, sheep to tend, and fish to haul.

But Mata and Phin lingered.

"They cheer for a man who murdered their fathers and grandfathers," Phin said quietly. Then he spat.

Mata looked around at the departing men and women. They were like the sand and mud stirred up by the ocean. If you scooped up a cup of seawater, it would be full of swirling chaos that obscured the light.

But if you waited patiently, eventually the common dross and dregs would settle to the bottom, where they belonged, and the clear water would allow the light through, the noble and the pure.

Mata Zyndu believed it was his destiny to restore clarity and order, as surely as the weight of history pulled everything down to its rightful place.

# THE PROPHECY OF THE FISH

CHAPTER THREE

# KUNI GARU

SEVEN YEARS LATER.
ZUDI: THE FIFTH MONTH IN THE TWENTY-FIRST
YEAR OF THE REIGN OF ONE BRIGHT HEAVEN.

In Zudi, many stories were told about Kuni Garu.

The young man was the son of simple farmers who had big hopes for their children to move up in the world, hopes that Kuni somehow dashed again and again.

Oh, as a boy, Kuni had shown hints of brilliance—he could read and write three hundred logograms before he had turned five. Kuni's mother, Naré, thanked Kana and Rapa every day and couldn't stop telling all her friends how brilliant her little boy was. Thinking that the child had a future as a lettered man who could bring honor to the family, Kuni's father, Fẹso, sent him at great expense to study at the private academy of Tumo Loing, a local scholar of great renown, who had served the King of Cocru as Minister of Grains before the Unification.

But Garu and his friend Rin Coda preferred to skip school whenever they could and go fishing. When he was caught, Kuni would apologize eloquently and profusely, convincing Master Loing that he was truly contrite and had learned his lesson. But soon he would be back to devising pranks with Rin and talking back at his teacher, questioning his explanations of the classics and pointing out errors in his reasoning until Loing finally ran out of patience and expelled him—and poor Rin Coda, too, for always following Kuni's lead.

That was just fine with Kuni. He was a good drinker, talker, and brawler, and soon became close to all sorts of disreputable characters in Zudi: thieves, gangsters, tax collectors, Xana soldiers from the garrison, girls from the indigo houses, wealthy young men who had nothing better to do than stand around all day on street corners looking for trouble—as long as you breathed, had money to buy him a drink, and enjoyed dirty jokes and gossip, Kuni Garu was your friend.

The Garu family tried to steer the young man into gainful employment. Kado, Kuni's elder brother, demonstrated an early instinct for business and became a local merchant of women's dresses. He hired Kuni as a clerk. But Kuni professed a disdain for bowing to customers and laughing at their stupid jokes, and finally, after Kuni tried to implement a harebrained scheme of hiring girls from the indigo houses as "models" for dresses, Kado had no choice but to fire him.

"It would have boosted sales!" Kuni said. "After the wealthy men saw the dresses on their favorite mistresses, they'd surely want to buy them for their wives."

"Have you no concern for the reputation of your family?!" Kado chased Kuni into the streets wielding a measuring ruler.

By the time Kuni was seventeen, his father had had enough of the idling young man coming home every night drunk and asking for dinner. He locked him out of the house and told him to find somewhere else to stay and ruminate on how he was wasting his life and breaking his mother's heart. Naré cried and cried and went to Kana and Rapa's temple every day, praying for the goddesses to set her baby on the right path.

Reluctantly, Kado Garu took pity on his little brother and took him in. Kado's generosity, however, was not shared by his wife, Tete. She took to serving dinner early, long before Kuni came home. And when she heard the sound of his steps in the entrance hall, Tete would bang empty pots loudly in the sink, indicating that there was no more food to be had.

Kuni quickly got the hint. Though he had thick skin—he had to when he hung out with the sort of friends he made—he was humiliated that his sister-in-law thought of him as only a mouth that she didn't want to feed. He moved out and slept on the floor mats in the houses of his friends, roaming from house to house as he wore out his welcome.

He moved a lot.

The smell of fried pot stickers and ginger-vinegar. The sound of glasses filling with warm ale and cold beer.

". . . so then I said, 'But your husband isn't home!' And she laughed and said, 'That's why you need to come in now!'"

"Kuni Garu!" Widow Wasu, proprietress of the Splendid Urn, tried to get the attention of the young man telling stories at the center of the crowd.

"Yes, my lady?" Kuni reached out with his long arm and draped it around her shoulder. He gave her a loud, wet kiss on the cheek. She was in her forties and accepted that she was aging gracefully. Unlike some of the other tavern keepers, she didn't slather herself with rouge and powder, and looked far more dignified as a result. Kuni often proclaimed to others how he was fond of her.

Wasu nimbly ducked out of Kuni's embrace. She pulled him away from the others, winking at the laughing and shouting crowd, who hollered appreciatively. She dragged him into her office in the back of the bar, where she deposited him in a pillow on one side of the desk, and she herself took the pillow on the other.

Kneeling upright and with her back straight in formal *mipa rari*, she composed herself and put on what she thought was a stern face—this discussion needed to be focused on business, and Kuni Garu had a way of changing the topic whenever one wanted something from him.

"You've hosted three parties at my place this month," Wasu said.

"That's a lot of beer and ale and fried pot stickers and fried squid. All the charges were put under your name. Your tab, at this point, is getting to be bigger than the lien on my inventory. I think you need to pay some of it."

Kuni leaned back on his pillow and stretched out his legs in a modified *thakrido* position, with one leg over the other, the way a man sat when he was with his mistress. Kuni narrowed his eyes, smirked at Wasu, and began to hum a song whose lyrics made Wasu blush.

"Come on, Kuni," Wasu said. "I'm serious here. The tax collectors have been hounding me for weeks. You can't treat me like a charity."

Kuni Garu curled his legs back under him and suddenly sat up in *mipa rari*. His eyes stayed narrowed, but the smirk disappeared from his face. Widow Wasu flinched even though she meant to stay firm with him. The man was a gangster, after all.

"Mistress Wasu," Kuni said in an even, low voice. "How often would you say I come to drink at your place?"

"Practically every other day," Wasu said.

"And have you noticed any difference in your business on the days when I'm here and the days when I'm not?"

Wasu sighed. This was Kuni's trump card, and she knew he would bring it up. "It's a little better on the days when you are here," she admitted.

"A *little* better?" Eyes as wide as teacups, he breathed loudly through his nose, as though his ego had been hurt.

Widow Wasu tried to decide whether she wanted to laugh at him or to throw something at the good-for-nothing young man. She settled by shaking her head and folding her arms across her chest.

"Look at the crowd out there!" he went on. "It's the middle of the day and this place is filled with paying customers. When *I'm* here, your business goes up by at least fifty percent."

This was a gross exaggeration, but Wasu had to concede that bar patrons did tend to stay longer and buy more drinks when Kuni was around. He was loud, told great dirty jokes, pretended to know something about everything—the man had no shame, and could get people around him to relax and enjoy themselves. He was like a bawdy troubadour, a tall-tale teller, and an impromptu gambling hall operator rolled into one. Maybe business didn't go up by 50 percent, but 20 to 30 percent? That was probably accurate. And Kuni's little gang also managed to keep the really dangerous men out of the Urn, the sort who would start fights and smash the furniture.

"Sister," Kuni said—now he was turning on his charm for her—"we need to help each other. I like coming to the Urn with my friends—we all have a good time. And we like bringing you more business. But if you can't see the benefits of this arrangement, I'll take my act elsewhere."

Widow Wasu gave him a withering look, but she knew she wasn't going to win this one.

"You better tell such good stories that all those Imperial soldiers get totally drunk and empty their pockets." She sighed. "And say something nice about the pork pot stickers. I need to get rid of them today."

"But you're right that we should reduce my tab a bit," Kuni said. "Next time I'm in here, I'm expecting that my tab will have already been cleared. Do you think you can make that happen?"

The widow nodded reluctantly. She waved Kuni away, sighed, and began to write off the drinks that Kuni and his gang were so happily consuming at the bar.

Kuni Garu stumbled from the Splendid Urn on unsteady legs, but he wasn't really drunk yet. Since it was early in the afternoon, his closest friends were still at work; he decided that he would kill some time by wandering the main market street of Zudi.

Though Zudi was a small city, the Unification had nonetheless changed its complexion substantially. Master Loing had lectured to the boys about the changes disdainfully, lamenting that his students couldn't appreciate the virtues of the simpler Zudi of his youth; but since this new Zudi was all Kuni had known, he made up his own mind about it.

Emperor Mapidéré, in a bid to keep the old Tiro nobles from plotting rebellions in their ancestral domains, stripped them of any real power and left them only with empty titles. But that wasn't enough for him. The emperor also divided the noble families and forced some members to relocate to distant parts of the empire. For example, a Cocru count's eldest son might be ordered to resettle—taking his servants, mistresses, wives, cooks, and guards with him—to Wolf's Paw, away in the old territories of Gan. And a Gan ducal clan's side branches might be told to pack themselves up and move to a city in Rui. This way, even if the hot-blooded younger nobles wanted to make trouble, they would have no influence with the local elites and could inspire no sympathy in the local populace to join their cause. The emperor did the same with many of the surrendered soldiers and their families from the six conquered Tiro states.

While the resettlement policy was very unpopular with the nobles, it did have the benefit of enriching the lives of the ordinary folk of the Islands of Dara. The resettled nobles craved foods and clothes from their homelands, and merchants traveled all over Dara, transporting products that seemed exotic to the local populace but were eagerly purchased by the exiled nobles, who yearned for a hint of home and their old ways of life. In this manner, the scattered nobles became teachers of taste for the commoners, who learned to be more cosmopolitan and ecumenical.

Thus Zudi played host to exiled noble families from all over Dara, and they filled it with new customs, new dishes, and new dialects and words that had never before been heard in the city's sleepy markets and sedate teahouses.

If you were going to give marks for Emperor Mapidéré's performance as an administrator, Kuni thought, the improvement in the diversity of Zudi's markets definitely had to be counted as a positive. The streets were filled with vendors selling all manners of novelties from across Dara: bamboo-copters from Amu—ethereal toys with revolving blades at the end of a stick that could be spun rapidly until the contraption took off into the air like a tiny dragonfly; living papermen from Faça—the paper cutouts would dance and leap like the veiled dancers on a tiny stage when you rubbed the glass rod in the ceiling with a silk cloth; magic calculators from Haan—wooden mazes with tiny doors at every branch that flipped as marbles rolled through them, and a skilled operator could use them to compute sums; iron puppets from Rima—intricate mechanical men and animals that walked down an inclined slope on their own power; and so on.

But Kuni paid the most attention to the food: He loved the fried lamb strips native to the Xana home islands, especially the hot and spicy variety from Dasu. He found the delicate raw fish served by the merchants from Wolf's Paw delightful—it went especially well with mango liquor and a dash of hot mustard grown in Faça's tiny spice estates nestled in the deep shades of the Shinané Mountains. He salivated so much as he admired the snacks on display from the various vendors that he had to swallow a few times.

He had a grand total of two copper pieces in his pocket, not even enough for a string of sugar-coated crabapples.

"Well, I really should be watching my weight anyway," he said to himself, and sadly patted his beer belly. He wasn't getting much exercise these days, what with all the partying and drinking.

He sighed and was just about to leave the market to find a quiet spot for a nap when a loud argument attracted his attention.

"Sir, please don't take him," an old woman dressed in the traditional garb of the Xana peasant—full of knotted tassels and the colorful, geometric patches that were supposed to be symbols for good luck and prosperity, though the only people who wore them had neither—begged an Imperial soldier. "He's only fifteen, and he's my youngest son. My eldest is already working at the Mausoleum. The laws say that the last child can stay with me."

The complexion of the old woman and her son was paler than most of the people in Cocru, but this didn't mean much by itself.

Though people from the various parts of Dara differed in their physical features, there had always been some steady migration and mixing of peoples, a process accelerated after the Unification. And the people of the various Tiro states had always cared much more about cultural and linguistic differences than mere appearance. Still, given the woman's Xana garb and accent, it was clear she was not a native of Cocru.

She was a long way from home, Kuni thought. Probably the widow of a Xana soldier stranded here after the Unification. Since the kite rider's assassination attempt seven years ago, Zudi had remained heavily garrisoned—the emperor's men never managed to find the rider, but they did imprison and execute many of Zudi's citizens on flimsy evidence and continued to rule Zudi with an extra level of harshness. At least the emperor's agents administered the laws without any favoritism. The poor from Xana were treated just like the poor of the conquered states.

"I've asked you for the birth certificates for the two boys, and you've produced nothing." The soldier brushed away the woman's pleading fingers impatiently. His accent indicated that he was from Xana as well. The man was bloated and flabby, a bureaucrat more than a fighting man, and he stared at the youth standing next to the old woman with a cold smirk, daring the young man to do something rash.

Kuni knew his kind well. The man had probably dodged out of having to fight during the Unification Wars and then bribed his way into a commission in the Xana army as soon as peace had been declared so that he could get assigned to one of the conquered territories as a corvée administrator. It was his job to raise up the local quota of able-bodied men to work on one of the emperor's grand infrastructure projects. It was a position with a little bit of power but a lot of room for abuse. It was also very lucrative: Families who didn't want to see their sons conscripted were willing to pay a high price.

"I know wily women like you," the man went on. "I think this story about your 'eldest' is a complete fabrication to get out of having to pay your fair share for the construction of a suitable palace for the afterlife of His Imperial Majesty, the Beloved Emperor Mapidéré. May he never leave us."

"May he never leave us. But I'm telling you the truth, Sir." The old woman tried flattery. "You are wise and brave, and I know you will take pity on me."

"It's not pity you need," the corvée administrator said. "If you can't produce the documents—"

"The documents are at the magistracy back home, in Rui—"

"Well, we aren't in Rui, now are we? And don't interrupt me. I've given you the choice to pay a Prosperity Tax so that we can forget this unpleasantness. But since you are unwilling, I'll have to—"

"I'm willing, Sir! I'm willing. But you have to give me time. Business has not been good. I need time—"

"I told you not to interrupt me!" The man lifted his hand and slapped the old woman across her face. The young man standing next to her lunged at him, but the old woman grabbed her son's arm and tried to position herself between the administrator and her son. "Please, please! Forgive my foolish son. You can hit me again for his faults."

The administrator laughed and spat at her.

The old woman's face trembled with unspeakable sorrow. It brought to Kuni's mind the face of his own mother, Naré, and the times when she would berate him for not making more of his own life. The drunken stupor evaporated.

"How much is the Prosperity Tax?" Kuni sauntered up to the three of them. Other pedestrians gave them a wide berth. No one wanted to draw the attention of the corvée administrator.

The man eyed Kuni Garu—beer belly, ingratiating smile, face still red with drink, and unkempt, wrinkled clothes—and decided that he was no threat. "Twenty-five pieces of silver. And what's that to you? Are you volunteering to take the boy's place on the corvée?"

Kuni's father, Féso Garu, had paid off corvée administrator after corvée administrator, and he did have the documents to show that he was exempt. He also wasn't afraid of the man. Kuni was a pretty good street brawler and thought he would acquit himself well if they came to blows. But this was a situation that called for some finesse, not force.

"I'm Fin Crukédori," he said. The Crukédoris owned Zudi's largest jewelry store, and Fin, the eldest son, had once tried to turn Kuni and his friends into the constabulary for disturbing the peace after Kuni humiliated him in a game of high-stakes dice. Fin's father was also known for being stingy and never spared a copper for any charity—but his son had a reputation as a spendthrift. "And I like nothing more than money."

"Then you should hold on to it and stay out of other people's business."

Kuni nodded like a chicken pecking in the dirt. "Sage advice, Sir!" Then he spread his hands helplessly. "But this old woman is a friend of my cook's mother-in-law's neighbor. And if she tells her friend, who tells her neighbor, who tells her daughter, who tells her husband, who might then not cook my favorite braised-eel-with-duck-eggs—"

The administrator's head spun as he tried to follow this story that was going nowhere. "Stop this senseless prattle! Are you going to pay for her or not?"

"Yes! Yes! Oh, Sir, you'll swear you have not had real food until you've tasted this braised eel. It is as smooth as a mouthful of jade. And the duck eggs? Oh my . . ."

As Kuni pattered on to the consternation of the Xana administrator, he gestured at a waitress at the restaurant by the side of the road. The waitress, who knew very well who Kuni really was, tried to keep from smiling as she handed him paper and brush.

". . . now how much did you say it was? Twenty-five? How about a bit of a discount? After all, I introduced you to the wonders of the braised eel! Twenty? . . ."

Kuni wrote out a note that entitled the holder to redeem it at the Crukédori family's house office for twenty silver pieces. He signed the note with a flourish and admired his own forgery. Then he inked a seal that he carried just for such occasions—it was so old and decrepit that the impression came out in a jumble and you could read anything you wanted in its lines—and pressed the seal against the paper.

He sighed and handed the paper over reluctantly. "There you go. Just go over to my family and present it to the doorman when you have time. The servant will bring the money to you right away."

"Why, Master Crukédori!" The administrator was all smiles and politeness when he saw the figure on the paper. A foolish and rich man like this Fin Crukédori was the best kind of local gentry to cultivate. "I'm always glad to make a new friend. Why don't we go and have a drink together?"

"I thought you'd never ask," Kuni said, and slapped the Imperial bureaucrat's shoulder happily. "I didn't bring any cash with me, though, since I'm just out to get some air. Next time I'll invite you home for the braised eel, but this time, maybe I can borrow some. . . ."

"No problem, no problem at all. What are friends for?"

As they walked away, Kuni stole a glance back at the old woman. She stood, mute and frozen, her mouth open and her eyes wide. Kuni thought she was probably too surprised and grateful to speak, and once more he was reminded of his mother. He blinked to clear his suddenly warm eyes, winked at her in reassurance, and turned around once more to joke with the corvée administrator.

The woman's son gently shook her by the shoulder. "Ma, let's get going. We should leave town before that pig changes his mind."

The old woman seemed to waken from a dream.

"Young man," she mumbled after the retreating figure of Kuni Garu, "you may act lazy and foolish, but I have seen your heart. A bright and tenacious flower will not bloom in obscurity."

Kuni was too far away to hear her.

But a young woman, whose palanquin had stopped by the side of the road while the bearers went into the inn to fetch her a drink, heard the old woman's words. By lifting a corner of the curtain on the palanquin window, she had taken in the whole scene, including Kuni's final look back at the old woman and how his eyes had grown wet.

She thought about the old woman's words as a smile broke out on her pale white face. She played with a lock of her fiery red hair, and her slender eyes, shaped like the body of the graceful dyran, the rainbow-scaled, ribbon-tailed flying fish, stared into the distance. There was something about this young man who tried to do good without seeming to *be* too good. She wanted to know him better.

## CHAPTER FOUR

# JIA MATIZA

ZUDI: THE FIFTH MONTH IN THE TWENTY-FIRST YEAR OF THE REIGN OF ONE BRIGHT HEAVEN.

A few days later, Kuni was back at the Splendid Urn to meet his closest friends—the band of young men had saved one another in bar brawls and gone to the indigo houses together.

"Kuni, when are you going to try to do something useful with your life?" Rin Coda asked. Still gangly and nervous, Rin made a living as a letter writer for the illiterate soldiers in the Xana garrison. "Every time I see your mother, she sighs and tells me to be a good friend and encourage you to get a job. Your father stopped me on the way here tonight and told me that you were a bad influence on me."

His father's comment bothered Kuni more than he wanted to admit. He tried to bluster through it. "I *do* have ambition."

"Ha! That's a good one," Than Carucono said. Than was the mayor's stable master, and sometimes his friends teased him that he understood horses better than people. "Every time one of us offers to find you a real job, you come up with some ridiculous objection. You don't want to work with me because you think horses are scared of you—"

"They are!" Kuni protested. "Horses are skittish around men of unusual character and high mind—"

Than ignored him. "You don't want to help Cogo because you think civil service is boring—"

"I think you're misquoting me," said Kuni. "I said I didn't think my creativity could be confined—"

"You don't want to go with Rin because you claim Master Loing would be ashamed to see you dropping allusions to the classics he taught you in soldiers' love letters. What *do* you want to do?"

In truth, Kuni thought he would have enjoyed peppering soldiers' love letters with Master Loing's pearls of wisdom, but he hadn't wanted to take away business from Rin, as he knew he was the better writer. But such reasons could never be spoken aloud.

He wanted to say that he yearned to accomplish something extraordinary, to be admired like a man riding at the head of a great procession. But every time he tried to come up with specific details, he drew a blank. From time to time, he wondered if his father and brother had been right about him: He was like a bit of floating duckweed, just drifting through life, good for nothing.

"I'm waiting—"

"—for the right opportunity," Than and Rin finished for him in unison.

"You're improving," said Rin. "You only say that once every other day now."

Kuni gave them a wounded look.

"I think I understand," Than said. "You are waiting for the mayor to come to you with a palanquin draped in silk, begging to present you to the emperor as the flower of Zudi."

Everyone laughed.

"How can mere sparrows understand the thoughts of an eagle?" Kuni said, puffing up his chest and finishing his drink with a flourish.

"I agree. Eagles *would* gather around when they see you," Rin said.

"Really?" Kuni brightened at this compliment.

"Of course. You look like a plucked chicken. You'd attract eagles and vultures from miles around."

Kuni Garu halfheartedly punched his friend.

"Listen, Kuni," Cogo Yelu said. "The mayor's throwing a party. Do you want to come? A lot of important people will be there, people you don't normally get to see. Who knows, you might meet your *opportunity* there."

Cogo was older than Kuni by about ten years. A diligent and studious man, he had passed the Imperial civil service examinations with high marks. But as he was from an undistinguished family not tapped into the network of patronage in the bureaucracy, being a clerk of the third rank in the city government was probably as high as he would ever rise in the civil service.

However, he liked his job. The mayor, a Xana man who had bought this sinecure but had no real interest in administration, relied on Cogo's advice for most decisions. Cogo was fascinated by matters of local governance and had a knack for solving the mayor's problems.

Others might see Kuni as a lazy, idle young man destined for the poorhouse or a life of crime, but Cogo liked Kuni's easy manners and his flashes of brilliance. Kuni was original, and that was more than could be said for most people in Zudi. Having Kuni there to joke with would relieve the monotony of the party for him.

"Sure." Kuni perked up. A party was something he was always interested in—free drinks and free food!

"The mayor's friend, a man by the name of Matiza, has just moved to Zudi. He's a wealthy rancher from up in old Faça who somehow got in trouble with the local magistrate. He's moving here to start over, but most of his assets are tied up in flocks and herds up there that can't be quickly converted to cash. The mayor is holding a welcoming party for him—"

"The real point of the party, of course, is to get the guests to bring lots of gifts for this Matiza in order to impress the mayor, and thus solve his cash flow problem," said Than Carunoco.

"Maybe you can come to the party as a servant hired for the occasion," Cogo suggested. "I'm in charge of the planning. I can get you a job as a waiter for the day. You'll get a chance to say a few words to the important guests as you deliver them their food."

"Nah." Kuni Garu waved the suggestion away. "Cogzy, I'm not going to bow and scrape for food and pay. I'll go as a guest."

"But the mayor wrote on the invitation that the suggested gift amount for guests is at least a hundred silver pieces!"

Kuni lifted his eyebrows. "I've got my wit and good looks. Those are priceless."

Everyone broke down in laughter as Cogo shook his head.

Bright-yellow lanterns hung in front of the mayor's house. Standing on both sides of the front door, young women dressed in traditional Cocru short gowns inhaled perfumed smoke sticks and blew soap bubbles at the arriving guests. The soap bubbles burst against them, releasing their fragrance: jasmine, osmanthus, rose, sandalwood.

Cogo Yelu acted as doorman and greeted the guests while recording their gifts in a ledger ("So that Master Matiza can properly write thank-you notes," he explained). But everyone knew that the ledger would be read by the mayor later. How easy it would be for someone to get things done in Zudi in the future might well depend on the size of the figure next to his name.

Kuni arrived by himself. He had put on a clean undershirt and his least-patched robe, and washed his hair. He wasn't drunk. This counted as "dressing up" for him.

Cogo stopped him at the door.

"I'm serious, Kuni. I can't let you in unless you've brought a gift. Otherwise you have to join the beggars' table over there." He pointed to a table set up against the outside wall of the estate, about fifty feet down from the gate. Even at this early hour, beggars and malnourished orphans were already fighting for seats around it. "They'll bring you the leftovers when the guests are done."

Kuni Garu winked at Cogo, reached into the folds of his sleeves, and took out a crisp sheet of paper, folded into thirds. "You've surely mistaken me for someone else. I'm Fin Crukédori, and I've brought with me a thousand silver pieces. Here's a note, to be drawn on my account at the house office."

Before Cogo could answer, a woman's voice interrupted. "Such an honor to see the famous Master Crukédori again!"

Cogo and Kuni turned their heads and saw, through the gate, a young woman barely in her twenties standing in the courtyard. She looked at Kuni with a mischievous smile. Her light complexion and curly, bright-red hair, common in Faça, stood out a little in Zudi, but Kuni was struck most by her eyes. Dyran-shaped, they seemed to be pools of dark-green wine. Any man who looked into them was doomed to lose his way.

"Miss," Kuni said, and cleared his throat. "Is something amusing you?"

"*You* are," the woman said. "Master Fin Crukédori came in not ten minutes ago with his father, and we chatted amiably while he paid me several compliments. Yet here you are again, outside, and looking so different."

Kuni put on a serious face. "You must have me confused with my . . . cousin. He's Fin, but I'm *Phin*." He pursed his lips, demonstrating the supposed difference in pronunciation. "You are probably not familiar with the Cocru dialect, which is subtle with such distinctions."

"Oh, is that so? You must be confused with your cousin often, what with Xana officials in markets also not being familiar with such subtle distinctions."

Kuni's face turned red momentarily, but he laughed. "Someone has been spying on me, it seems."

"I'm Jia Matiza, daughter of the man you intend to cheat."

"*Cheat* is such a strong word," Kuni said without missing a beat. "I had heard that Master Matiza's daughter is a great beauty, as rare as the dyran among fish." Jia rolled her eyes at this. "My hope was to have my friend Cogzy here"—he gestured in Cogo's direction, and Cogo shook his head in denial—"let me in under false pretenses so that I could have a chance to admire her. But now that I have accomplished my goal without having to go in, Cogo's honor and mine are intact. I shall take my leave."

"You really have no shame," Jia Matiza said. But her eyes were laughing and so the words did not sting. "You can come in as *my* guest. You are outrageous, but you are interesting."

When she was twelve years old, Jia stole some of her teacher's dream herbs.

She dreamed of a man who wore a plain gray cotton tunic.

"What can you offer me?" she asked.

"Hardship, loneliness, long-flowing heartache," he said.

She could not see his face, but she liked the sound of his voice: gentle and serious, but with a hint of laughter in it.

"That doesn't sound like a good match," she said.

"Good matches are not the stuff of stories and songs," he said. "For every pain we endure together, there will be a joy twice as great. They will still sing of us in a thousand years."

She saw that he had changed into a yellow silk robe. And he kissed her, and he tasted of salt and wine.

And she knew he was the man she was destined to marry.

The party from a few days ago lingered in Jia's mind.

*"I have never heard anyone claim that Lurusén's poem is about waking up in the middle of the night in an indigo house," Jia said, laughing.*

*"It's true that the traditional interpretation is all about high-minded politics and such," Kuni said. "But listen to the lines: 'The world is drunk; I alone am sober. The world is asleep, but I am awake.' This is clearly about the house watering down the liquor. I have research to back it up."*

*"I'm sure you do. Did you present this interpretation to your teacher?"*

*"I did, but he was too set in his ways to recognize my brilliance." Kuni grabbed two small plates off the tray of a passing waiter. "Did you know that you can dip pork dumplings in plum paste?"*

*Jia made a face. "That sounds disgusting. The two flavors are not compatible at all—you're mixing up Faça and Cocru cuisines."*

*"If you haven't tried it, how do you know it's no good?"*

*And Jia did try Kuni's invention; it was delicious. Surprisingly so.*

*"You have better instincts with food than you do with poetry," Jia said, and she reached for another pot sticker dipped in plum paste.*

*"But you'll never think of Lurusén's poem the same way again, will you?"*

"Jia!" Her mother's voice pulled her back into the present.

The young man who sat before her now was not ugly, Jia decided, but he seemed to have gone out of his way to make himself appear so. His eyes roamed all over Jia's face and body, eyes devoid of any sign of intelligence, and a tiny rivulet of spittle hung from the corner of his mouth.

*Definitely not the one.*

". . . his uncle owns twenty ships that ply the trade routes to Toaza," the matchmaker said. She reached under the table and poked Jia with an eating stick. Earlier, she had explained to Jia that that was the sign for her to smile more demurely.

Jia stretched her arms and did not bother to cover her mouth when she yawned. Her mother, Lu, gave her a warning look.

"Tabo, is it?" Jia asked, leaning forward.

"Tado."

"Yes, that's right. Tado, tell me, where do you think you'll be in ten years?"

Tado's face grew even blanker. But after a few awkward moments, his face wrinkled into a wide smile. "Ah, I understand the question now. Don't worry, sweet one. In ten years I expect to have my own mansion by the lake."

Jia nodded. Her face was unreadable. She stared at the young man's salivating mouth without saying anything further. Everyone else in the room squirmed. It felt like an eternity.

"Miss Matiza is an accomplished herbalist," the matchmaker offered, breaking the uncomfortable silence. "She studied with the best teachers in Faça. I'm sure she knows of ways to ensure her lucky husband's health and give him many beautiful children."

"We will have at least five children," Tado added magnanimously. "Maybe even more."

"Surely you see me as more than just a field for you to plow," Jia said. The matchmaker poked her under the table again.

"I hear that Miss Matiza is a skilled poet," Tado ingratiatingly offered.

"Oh? Are you interested in poetry too?" She twirled a lock of her red hair in a way that would appear coquettish to someone who did not know her, but her mother understood her mockery and eyed her suspiciously.

"I *love* reading poetry." He wiped away his saliva with the sleeve of his silk tunic.

"Is that so?" That mischievous smile appeared again. Jia was slightly sorry that the rivulet and her object of focus had disappeared. "I have a great idea! Why don't you write a poem right now? You may choose any subject, and in an hour I will come back and read it. I'll marry you if I like it."

Before the matchmaker could say anything, Jia was already up and away, retreating to her bedroom.

Her mother stood at her door, fuming.

"Did I scare him off?"

"No. He's trying to write a poem."

"Persistence! I'm impressed."

"How many eligible young men must you send off ranting and raving? We spoke to your first matchmaker back in the Year of the Toad, and it's now the Year of the Cruben!"

"Mother, don't you want your daughter to be happy?"

"Of course I do. But you seem determined to become an old maid."

"But, Mama, then I would get to stay with you forever!"

Lu stared at her daughter, eyes narrowed. "Is there something you're not telling me? A secret admirer perhaps?"

Jia said nothing but looked away. This had always been her habit. She would not lie, and so she would refuse to answer if what she had to say would not be welcomed. Her mother sighed.

"You keep this up, and soon no matchmakers in Zudi will want to work with you. You're gaining a reputation as bad as the one you left behind in Faça!"

When the hour was up, Jia returned to the living room. She picked up the sheet of paper and cleared her throat:

*Your hair is like fire.*
*Your eyes are like water.*
*I want you to be my wife.*
*Your beauty gives new meaning to life.*

She nodded thoughtfully.

The young man could barely suppress his excitement. "You like it?"

"It has inspired me to think of a poem as well."

*Your eyes are like empty wells.*
*Your drool like an inchworm.*
*I want you to have a wife.*
*How about this matchmaker? She's good at poking!*

The young man and the matchmaker stormed out of the Matiza residence as Jia laughed, long and very loud.

There was no way that Kuni could call at the Matiza house. No matchmaker would be so foolish as to suggest that a prospectless gangster could be a suitable match for a respectable, if unestablished, family striving to move up in society like the Matizas.

Fortunately, Jia had a perfect excuse to be away from the house unchaperoned: She took many trips to the countryside around Zudi to study the local herbs and gather them for her potions.

Kuni brought Jia to his favorite haunts: the best bend in the river for fishing, the best gazebo and tree under which to nap, the best bars and teahouses, places no respectable young ladies of good breeding should be found, places Jia found refreshingly honest, without the stifling conventions and desperate anxieties that always seemed to gather around those concerned with what was "proper." In these places, she enjoyed the company of Kuni and his friends, who did not care about how appropriate was her bow or how elegant her speech, but applauded when she drank with them and listened when she spoke her mind.

In turn, Jia showed Kuni a new universe that he had never paid much attention to: the grasses at his feet and the bushes lining the long country lanes. At first, his interest had been feigned—he thought her lips far more interesting than the flowers whose uses she tried to explain—but after she showed him how chewing ginger and evening primrose did wonders for his frequent hangovers, he became a true disciple.

"What is this?" he asked, pointing to a weed with white five-petaled flowers and two-lobed leaves shaped like praying hands.

"That is actually not one plant, but two," Jia said. "The leaves belong to a grass called mercy flax. The flowers are called crowsbane."

Kuni immediately got on his hands and knees to get a better look, careless about getting his clothes dirty. Jia laughed at the sight of this man behaving like a curious boy. Kuni acted as if the rules everyone accepted didn't apply to him, and that made Jia feel free too.

"You're right," Kuni said, wonder suffusing his voice. "But they really do look like one plant from a distance."

"Crowsbane is a slow poison, but the flowers are so pretty that the crows, as wise as the Blessed Kana and Rapa have made them, cannot resist their beauty. They pick them to decorate their nests with and over time die from their vapors and juices."

Kuni, who had been smelling the flowers, pulled back sharply. Jia's loud laughter echoed in the field.

"Don't worry, you're much bigger than a crow. You won't be harmed by such small quantities. Besides, the other plant, mercy flax, is a natural antidote."

Kuni picked a few leaves from the mercy flax and chewed them. "Strange that a poison and its antidote would grow so close together."

Jia nodded. "One of the principles of herbal lore is the prevalence of such pairings. The deadly seven-step snake of Faça nests in shady coves where the crying boy mushroom, which secretes an antivenom, likes to grow. The fiery salamander weed, a good, hot spice for cold winter nights, grows better next to the snowdrop, known for its power to relieve fevers. Creation seems to favor making friends of those destined to be enemies."

Kuni pondered this. "Who knew that so much philosophy and wisdom could be hidden among weeds?"

"You're surprised? Because the art of herbal healing is a women's art, beyond the notice of real scholars and doctors?"

Kuni turned to Jia and bowed. "I spoke in ignorance. I meant no disrespect."

Jia bowed back deeply in *jiri*. "You do not assume yourself to be better than anyone. That is the sign of a truly capacious mind."

They smiled at each other and kept on walking.

"What is your favorite plant?" Kuni asked.

Jia thought for a moment and bent down to pluck a small flower with a full yellow crown. "They're all dear to me, but I admire the dandelion the most. It is hardy and determined, adaptable and practical. The flower looks like a small chrysanthemum, but it's much more resourceful and far less delicate. Poets may compose odes about the chrysanthemum, but the dandelion's leaves and flowers can fill your belly, its sap cure your warts, its roots calm your fevers. Dandelion tea makes you alert, while chewing its root can steady a nervous hand. The milk of the dandelion can even be used to make invisible ink that reveals itself when mixed with the juice of the stone's ear mushroom. It is a versatile and useful plant people can rely on.

"And it's playful and fun." She picked up a puff ball and blew at it, scattering the tiny feathered seeds into the air, a few of which landed in Kuni's hair.

Kuni made no move to brush them away. "The chrysanthemum is a noble flower."

"That's true. It's the last flower to bloom in autumn, defiant against winter. Its fragrance is exquisite, and overwhelms all competition. In tea, it awakens the spirit; in bouquets, it dominates the arrangement. But it is not a flower that endears."

"You don't care much about nobility?"

"I think true nobility is shown in far humbler ways."

Kuni nodded. "Miss Matiza has a truly capacious mind."

"Ah, flattery does not suit you, Master Garu," Jia said, laughing. She turned serious after a moment. "Tell me, where do you think you'll be in ten years?"

"I have no idea," Kuni said. "All life is an experiment. Who can plan so far ahead? I just promise myself to do the most interesting thing every time there's an opportunity. If I can stick to that promise most of the time, I'm sure in ten years I won't have any regrets."

"Why do you have to make a promise like that?"

"It's very scary to do the most interesting thing when the chance arises. Most people don't dare to do it—like bluffing your way into a party you aren't invited to. But look how much more delightful my life is now. I got to know you."

"The most interesting thing is often not the easiest thing," Jia said. "There may be pain and suffering, disappointment and failure, for yourself and those you love."

Kuni became serious too. "But without having endured bitterness, I don't believe one will treasure sweetness as heartily as one should."

She faced Kuni and put a hand on his arm. "I believe you will do great things."

A warm feeling suffused Kuni's heart. Until Jia, he realized, he had never met a woman who truly became his *friend*.

"Will I?" he asked, a smirk curving the corners of his mouth. "How do you know you're not being fooled?"

"I'm too smart to be fooled," she answered without hesitation, and they embraced, careless who saw.

Kuni felt like he was the luckiest man in the world. He had no money to pay her father a proper bride price, but he had to marry her.

∽ ∾ ∽ ∾

"Sometimes the most interesting thing is also the most boring thing, the responsible thing," Kuni said to himself.

He went to ask Cogo to get him a job in Zudi's city government.

"You don't know how to do anything," Cogo said, his brows knit in a frown.

But a friend was in need, and Cogo inquired around until he found out that the Corvée Department needed a guard to watch the newly conscripted men and petty criminals sentenced to hard labor; they were kept in prison for a few nights until a full squad of them could be sent together to their work assignments. Once in a while, the guard might also be asked to escort the conscripts and prisoners on such journeys. This seemed a job that a trained monkey with a stick could do. Even Kuni shouldn't be able to screw it up.

"I never quite pictured myself serving the emperor this way," said Kuni, thinking of the corvée administrator who had, in a way, introduced him to Jia. He'd have to buy his future colleague a good meal to smooth over any hard feelings. "I'm not going to make up any 'Prosperity Tax,' though—well, not unless it's someone very wealthy."

"As long as you live frugally, you'll be fine," said Cogo. "The pay is very steady."

Steady enough for Kuni to go to the money lenders and pledge his future income for a present sum so that he could go to Jia's parents.

Gilo Matiza could not understand it. By all accounts, Kuni Garu was an indolent young man with no useful skills and no prospects. He had no money, no property, and until recently, no job—even his own family had thrown him out. He was also rumored to enjoy the company of loose women and had many girlfriends.

Why did his daughter, known to all the matchmakers as impossible to please, favor this man's suit?

"I prefer to do the most interesting thing," Jia said. And that was all the answer she would give him.

Nothing would dissuade her. Once her mind was made up, Jia's will was iron. So Gilo had to at least listen to the young man.

"I know I don't have a very good reputation," said Kuni, who was sitting up very straight in *mipa rari*, his eyes focused on the tip of his nose. "But as the sagacious Lurusén once said, 'The world is drunk; I alone am sober. The world is asleep, but I am awake.'"

Gilo was surprised. He did not expect a quote from Cocru classics. "What does that have to do with your suit?"

"The poet was speaking of the experience of sudden clarity after a life of doubt. Until I met Jia and you, I did not understand what the poem meant. Sir, a reformed man is worth ten men virtuous from birth, for he understands temptation and will strive the harder to not stray."

Gilo softened. He had wanted to make a good match for Jia—a wealthy local merchant or a young scholar who had a good future in government—but this Kuni seemed learned and respectful, and that was something. Perhaps all the rumors about him were wrong.

Gilo sighed and accepted Kuni's marriage proposal.

"I see you decided not to share your other reading of Lurusén's poem with my father. I'm impressed: I could almost believe that speech back there."

"It's just like they say in the villages: 'Howl when you see a wolf, scratch your head when you see a monkey.'"

"How many more of these readings do you have?"

"As many as the days we'll have together."

Kuni's brother Kado and his father Féso welcomed him again to their houses, believing that the prodigal son had finally returned.

Naré Garu was so happy that she embraced Jia and wouldn't let go, soaking the shoulder of Jia's dress with her tears. "You saved my son!" she said again and again, and Jia blushed and smiled awkwardly.

And so there was a big wedding—paid for by Gilo—that became the talk of Zudi for many days. Although Gilo refused to support the couple in a lavish lifestyle ("Since you picked him, you have to live within the means of his salary"), Jia's dowry allowed the couple to get a small house, and Kuni no longer had to calculate how long he had before he wore out a friend's patience and had to find another place to sleep.

He went to work every morning and sat in his office and filled out reports and made his hourly rounds to be sure that the listless men held in prison weren't up to any mischief while they waited to be sent to labor in the Grand Tunnels or the Mausoleum.

In no time at all, he hated his job—now he really felt he was drifting. He complained to Jia daily.

"Do not fret, my husband," said Jia. "They also serve who only stand and wait. There is a time for flight, and a time for descent; a time for movement, and a time for rest; a time to do, and a time to prepare."

"This is why you're the poet," said Kuni. "You even make paperwork sound exciting."

"Here's what I think: Opportunity comes in many forms. What is luck but being ready with the snare when the rabbit bolts from his hole? You've made many friends in Zudi over the years as a ne'er-do-well—"

"Hey, I resent that—"

"*I* married you, didn't I?" Jia gave him a light peck on the cheek to placate him. "But the point is, now that you're a member of Zudi's officialdom, you have a chance to make different kinds of friends. Trust yourself that this is only temporary. Take advantage of it to spread your circles. I know you like people."

Kuni took Jia's advice and made an extra effort to go out with fellow clerks to teahouses after work and to pay visits at the homes of senior officials from time to time. He was humble, respectful, and listened more than he spoke. When he found people he liked, he and Jia would invite them and their families to their little home for deeper conversation.

Soon, Kuni got to know the departments and bureaus of Zudi's city government as well as he knew its back alleys and busy markets.

"I had thought of them as the dull sort," said Kuni. "But they're not so bad once you get to know them. They're just . . . different from my old friends."

"A bird needs both long and short feathers to fly," said Jia. "You need to learn to work with different kinds of people."

Kuni nodded, glad of Jia's wisdom.

It was now late summer, and the air was filled with drifting dandelion seeds. Every day as he came home, Kuni gazed with longing at the tiny feathered seeds carelessly riding the wind, snowy puffs that danced about his nose and eyes.

He imagined their flight. They were so light that a gust of wind could carry one for miles. There was no reason that a seed couldn't fly all the way from one end of the Big Island to the other. No reason that it couldn't fly all the way over the sea, to Crescent Island, to Ogé, to Écofi. No reason that it couldn't tour the peaks of Mount Rapa and Mount Kiji. No reason that it couldn't taste the mist at the Rufizo Falls. All it needed was a little kindness from nature, and it would travel the world.

He felt, in a way that he could not explain, that he was meant to live more than the life he was living, destined to one day soar high into the air like these dandelion seeds, like the kite rider he had seen long ago.

He was like a seed still tethered to the withered flower, just waiting for the dead air of the late summer evening to break, for the storm to begin.

CHAPTER FIVE

# THE DEATH OF THE EMPEROR

ÉCOFI ISLAND: THE TENTH MONTH IN THE TWENTY-THIRD YEAR OF THE REIGN OF ONE BRIGHT HEAVEN.

Emperor Mapidéré had not looked into a mirror for weeks now.

The last time he had dared to look, a pallid, leathery mask had stared back at him. Gone was the handsome, arrogant, fearless man who had made ten thousand wives into widows and forged the crowns of the Seven States into one.

His body had been usurped by an old man, consumed by fear of death.

He was on Écofi Island, where the land was flat and the sea of grass stretched as far as the eye could see. Perched atop the Throne Pagoda, the emperor gazed at the distant herd of elephants strolling majestically across his field of view. Écofi was one of his favorite spots to pass through on his tours of the Islands. Miles and miles away from the busy cities and the intrigue of the palace in Pan, the emperor imagined that he was alone and free.

But he could not deny the pain in his stomach, the pain that now made it impossible for him to descend the Throne Pagoda on his own. He would have to call for help.

"Some medicine, *Rénga*?"

The emperor had said nothing. But Chatelain Goran Pira was, as always, observant. "This is prepared by an Écofi medicine woman who is said to know many secrets. It might ease the discomfort."

The emperor hesitated, but relented. He sipped the bitter beverage, and it did seem to numb the pain slightly.

"Thank you," the emperor said. Then, because only Goran could hear, he added, "Death catches up to us all."

"Sire, speak not of such things. You should rest."

Like all men who spent their lives in conquest, he had long turned his thoughts to the ultimate foe. For years, Pan had been filled with alchemists working on elixirs of eternal life and youth. Swindlers and con men had flooded the new capital and drained the treasury with their elaborate laboratories and research proposals that never seemed to produce anything useful; the clever ones always packed up and could not be found when it came time for an audit.

He had swallowed their pills, pills distilled from the essences of a thousand species of fish, some so rare that they were found in only a single lake in the mountains, pills prepared in the holy fire of Mount Fithowéo, pills that were supposed to protect him from a hundred diseases and make his body immune to the passage of time.

They had all lied. Here he was, his body ravaged by a disease that all the doctors gave different names to but were equally powerless against, a twisting, recurring pain in his stomach like a coiled snake that made him unable to eat.

*But this medicine really is very good,* the emperor thought.

"Goran," he said, "the pain is much better. This is a good find."

Chatelain Pira bowed. "I am your loyal servant, as always."

"You're my friend," the emperor said, "my only true friend."

"You must rest, Sire. The medicine is supposed to be a good soporific as well."

*I am sleepy.*
*But I still have so much to do.*

For centuries, back before the Xana Conquest, back when young Mapidéré was still called Réon, his hair still full and lush and his face unlined, the Seven States had vied for dominance of the Islands of Dara: rustic and arid Xana in the far northwest, confined to the islands of Rui and Dasu; elegant and arrogant Amu, fortified in rain-drenched and balmy Arulugi and the fertile fields of Géfica, the land between the rivers; the Three Brother States of woodsy Rima, sandy Haan, and craggy Faça, nestled in the northern half of the Big Island; wealthy and sophisticated Gan in the east, filled with big cities and busy trading ports; and finally, martial Cocru on the southern plains, famed for her brave warriors and wise generals.

Their web of shifting alliances and enmities was as confusing as it was dynamic. In the morning the King of Xana and the King of Gan might still call each other brothers, and by that night Gan's ships might already be sailing around the Big Island for a sneak attack, aided by fast cavalry from the King of Faça, who just that morning had sworn that he would never forgive Gan for past treacheries.

And then came Réon, and everything changed.

The emperor looked around.

He was in Pan, the Immaculate City, standing in the middle of the broad expanse of Kiji Square in front of the palace. Normally the square was empty, save for children who flew kites in spring and summer and built ice statues in winter. Occasionally an Imperial airship landed in it, and nearby citizens would gather to watch.

But today the square was not empty. He was surrounded by colossal statues of the gods of Dara. The statues, each as tall as the Throne Pagoda, were made with bronze and iron and painted with bright, lifelike colors.

Long ago, Thasoluo, the World Father, was called away by the King of All Deities, Moäno, never to return. He left behind his pregnant wife, Daraméa, the Source-of-All-Waters. Alone in the void, she cried hot, large tears of lava as she gave birth. The sizzling tears fell from the heavens into the sea and solidified into the Islands of Dara.

Eight children were born. As the gods of Dara, they staked out their claims to the Islands and watched over the native inhabitants. Daraméa, comforted, withdrew to the great ocean, leaving her children in charge of Dara. Later, when the Ano arrived and spread throughout the Islands, their fates also became inextricably bound with the doings and undoings of the deities.

The emperor had long dreamed of confiscating all the weapons of Dara, all the swords and spears, all the knives and arrows, and melting them down into their constituent metals so that they could be turned into statues honoring the gods. Without weapons, there would be eternal peace in the world.

He had always been too busy to convert his grand vision into reality, yet somehow here they were. Perhaps this was a chance for him to plead his case directly to the gods, to ask for long life and good health and restored youth.

Mapidéré knelt first before Kiji, the source of Xana's strength. The statue depicted a middle-aged man with white sideburns, a bald head, and a white cape on his back. Mapidéré admired the intricate designs on the cape, showing Kiji's mastery over wind, flight, and birds. On Kiji's shoulder sat his *pawi*, the Mingén falcon.

"Lord Kiji, are you pleased by this sign of my piety? There is yet much that I can do to glorify you, but I need more time!"

The emperor wished that the god would give him a sign that his prayer was heard. But he well knew that the gods preferred to work in obscure mystery.

Next to Kiji were the Twins, Kana and Rapa, patrons of Cocru. Kana wore a black dress and had brown skin, long silky black hair, and dark-brown eyes, while Rapa, with a face identical to her sister's, wore a white dress and had pale skin, snow-white hair, and light-gray eyes. Over the sisters' shoulders stood their *pawi*, a pair of ravens, one black, one white.

Mapidéré may have conquered all the Tiro states, but he sought the approbation of all the gods. He lowered his head to the goddesses next. "I honor you, Lady Kana, mistress of fire, ash, and death. I honor you, Lady Rapa, mistress of ice, snow, and sleep. I have taken away men's weapons and ended their strife so that they may all turn their hearts to thoughts of you. May you see fit to grant me many more years of life."

The statues of the goddesses shifted and came to life.

The emperor was too stunned to move or speak.

Kana turned her bronze eyes to the kneeling Mapidéré like a woman turning to gaze at an ant. Her voice was loud, harsh, discordant, recalling the scraping of rusty swords across an old sharpening stone.

"Even if Cocru lives on only in the heart of one man, it will bring about the fall of Xana."

Mapidéré trembled.

"Do you think I will stand by and do nothing?"

Mapidéré looked back and saw that the thunderous, sonorous voice belonged to Kiji, who had also come to life. The statue took a step forward and the ground quaked beneath Mapidéré. The Mingén falcon took off from his shoulder and circled over the statues of the gods; Kana and Rapa's ravens took off also and cried challengingly at the falcon.

"Have you forgotten our pact?" said Rapa, whose voice was mellifluous, cool, harmonious, but no less powerful than her sister's. She and Kana were as far apart as ice and fire, yet as close as sleep and death.

"I'm not the one agitating for further bloodshed," said Kiji. He lifted his left hand, which was missing a pinkie, placed the index and middle fingers into his mouth, and whistled. The Mingén falcon, still gazing balefully at the ravens, reluctantly returned to his shoulder. "Xana has emerged victorious. The time for war is over. Mapidéré has brought peace, however much you may dislike him."

The statue of Fithowéo of Rima, a lean, muscular man in leather armor carrying a long spear with an obsidian tip, shifted and spoke next. "Taking away men's weapons will not bring peace. They'll fight with sticks and stones, and tooth and nail. Mapidéré's is a peace supported only by fear, as secure as a nest built on a rotten branch."

Mapidéré despaired at the words of Lord Fithowéo, the god of the hunt, of metals and stone, and war and peace. The emperor looked into the god's eyes, the cold, dark obsidian from Mount Fithowéo, and saw no compassion. His *pawi*, the wolf, howled to accompany the end of his master's rumbling speech.

Fithowéo bared his teeth at Kiji and let out a bloodcurdling war cry.

"Do not mistake my restraint for weakness," said Kiji. "It has been eons since my falcon pecked out your eyes and you had to replace them with stones. Would you like to experience blindness again?"

"Listen to how you talk!" Kana's discordant laughter made Kiji wince. "The last time we fought I singed off all the hair on your head and your beard so that you now have to make do with these ridiculous sideburns. I'd be happy to leave you some deeper scars—"

"—or make you lose more than just your pinkie from frostbite," said Rapa. Her lovely, cold voice made the threat seem even more frightening.

Mapidéré fell to the ground and scrambled away on his hands and knees to the statue of Rufizo of Faça, lord of life, healing, and green pastures. He grabbed a big toe with both his arms, but the cold metal provided no comfort.

"Lord Rufizo," Mapidéré cried out, "protect me! Stop this strife among your siblings."

Rufizo was a tall, lanky young man wearing a cape of green ivy. His sad eyes came to life, and he shook his foot carefully, casting off Mapidéré like a dirt clod. He stepped between Kiji, Fithowéo, and the Twins and spoke in a voice as gentle and soothing as the pools fed by Rufizo Falls, whose water was hot year round, keeping nearby pastures green despite the cold climate of the Faça Highlands.

"Enough of this posturing, my brothers and sisters. After the

Diaspora Wars, during which all of us caused our mother much grief, we vowed that the gods would never again harm one another, as Moäno is our witness. During all the years of Mapidéré's wars, we kept peace among us. Today is not the day to break that promise."

Mapidéré, lying on the ground, was comforted by this speech. He remembered that in the aftermath of the mythical, bloody Diaspora Wars, when the gods had accompanied ancient Ano heroes onto the battlefield, the divine siblings had vowed to never again take up arms against one another. Henceforth they would only interfere in the affairs of men indirectly, by persuasion, trickery, inspiration, or prophecy. The gods also agreed to never again directly fight against the mortals, but to work through other men.

Emboldened by the thought that the gods were honor-bound to not harm him, a mere mortal, he stood up and croaked out to Rufizo, as loudly as his frail body could manage, "You, of all the gods, must understand how my life has been dedicated to a war to end all wars."

"You have spilled too much blood." Rufizo sighed, and his *pawi*, the white dove, cooed.

"I spilled blood to prevent the spilling of more blood," Mapidéré insisted.

Laughter, as wild as a tornado, as chaotic as a whirlpool, rose behind the emperor. It was Tazu, the shape-shifting god of Gan. He was a lithe figure in a fish-skin tunic decorated with a belt made of shark's teeth.

"I like your logic, Mapidéré," he said. "I want more of it." His *pawi*, a great shark, leapt out of the pool at his feet, its jaws opened in a deadly grin. "You have greatly increased my collection of drowned men and sunken treasures."

The swirling pool at Tazu's feet grew, and Mapidéré scrambled to back up out of its way. Although the gods had promised to not actively aim their wrath at mortals, the great Ano lawgiver Aruano had noted that the promise, like all the laws that bound men and gods, left room for interpretation. The gods were charged by their mother, Daraméa, the Source-of-All-Waters, with the running of the natural world: Kiji governed the winds and storms; Rapa guided the flow of glaciers across eons; Kana controlled the flashy eruptions of volcanoes; and so on. If mortals happened to be in the way of these forces of nature, like Tazu's famous whirlpool and raging tides, then their deaths would not be a violation. Mapidéré had no interest in testing how Tazu, the most unpredictable of the gods, interpreted his own promise.

Tazu laughed even louder, and the great shark sank back into the pool at his feet. But the pool of water stopped spreading as the ground beneath Mapidéré turned into quicksand as black as the famed sands at Lutho Beach. Mapidéré sank up to his neck, and he found that he could not breathe.

"I have always honored all of you," croaked Mapidéré, his voice almost inaudible as Tazu continued to laugh. "I have always tried only to make the world of men more perfect, closer to the world of the gods."

Lutho, the god of Haan, a stocky old fisherman whose skin was as dark as freshly solidified lava, lifted his foot off his *pawi*, a giant sea turtle, threw out the fishing net on his back, and pulled Mapidéré to safety. "There is often no line between perfection and evil."

Mapidéré struggled to breathe. Lutho's words made no sense to him, but that was to be expected of the lord of tricks, mathematics, and divination, whose domain was beyond the understanding of mortals.

"Tazu, I'm surprised," said Lutho. His old, hazel eyes twinkled with a brightness that belied his apparent age. "I had not expected you to take a side in this coming war. So it's Kiji against the Twins, Fithowéo, and you?"

Mapidéré, now forgotten, felt his old heart clench. *So it's to be war again? Has my life's project been in vain?*

"Oh, I can't possibly be bothered with something as restraining as picking a *side*," said Tazu. "I'm interested only in more treasure and bones for my underwater palace. I'll do whatever supplies me more of either. You can say I'm a neutral observer, like Rufizo over there.

Except he wants fewer people to die, and I want the opposite. What about you, old man?"

"Me?" asked Lutho in mock surprise. "You know I never had the talent for fighting and politics. I've always been interested only in Mapidéré's alchemists."

"Right," scoffed Tazu. "I think you're biding your time and waiting for a winning side to emerge, you trickster."

Lutho smiled and said nothing.

Tututika, the ethereal goddess of Amu, spoke last in a voice as calm and pleasant as the flat, tranquil surface of Lake Tututika. The speech of the golden-haired, azure-eyed goddess with skin the hue of polished walnut silenced the other gods.

"As the youngest of you all and the least experienced, I've never understood your appetites for power and blood. All I've ever wanted was to enjoy the beauty of my realm and the praise of my people. Why must we always end up as a house divided? Why can't we just promise one another not to be involved in the affairs of mortals at all?"

The other gods were silent. After a while, Kiji said, "You speak as if history does not matter. You know well how the people of Xana were treated by the other states before Mapidéré's wars. Looked down upon, cheated, taken advantage of, Xana suffered for years and lost blood and treasure until the insults could not be borne. Now that they're finally treated with respect, how can I do nothing when they're threatened?"

"Do not presume to speak of only your history," said Tututika. "The suffering of Amu was also great during Mapidéré's conquests."

"Exactly," said Kiji triumphantly. "If the people of Amu now cry out again for your help as they die, will you stand by and plug up your ears as you enjoy the sunsets on Arulugi Island, no doubt made even more beautiful by the smoke and ashes of burning cities?"

Tututika bit her bottom lip, and then sighed. "I wonder whether we're guiding the mortals or if the mortals are guiding us."

"You can't escape the weight of history," said Kiji.

"Leave Amu out of it, I beg of you."

"War has its own logic, Little Sister," said Fithowéo. "We can guide, but it cannot be controlled."

"A lesson that mortals have learned again and again—" said Rapa.

"—but it doesn't seem to take," finished Kana.

Tututika turned her gaze to the forgotten Mapidéré. "Then we should pity this man, whose work is about to be undone. Great men are always misunderstood by their own age. And *great* seldom means *good*."

The goddess glided toward Mapidéré, her blue silk gown spreading open like the calm sky. Her *pawi*, a golden carp whose sparkling scales dazzled the emperor, swam through the air before her like a living airship.

"Go," Tututika said, "you have no more time."

*It was only a dream,* thought the emperor.

*Some dreams are important: signs, portents, glances of unrealized potential. But others are mere meaningless creations of a busy mind. A great man must pay attention only to dreams that* can *become true.*

It had been the dream of generations of kings of Xana to win the respect of the rest of the Islands of Dara. The men of those other Tiro states, closer together and more populous, had always treated remote Xana with contempt: comedians from Amu mocked her accent, merchants from Gan cheated her buyers, poets from Cocru imagined her a land without manners, barely better than the savages who had once lived in Dara before the Settlement. The insults and slights became part of the memory of every Xana child who encountered outsiders.

Respect had to be earned by force. The men of Dara must be made to tremble before the might of Xana.

The rise of Xana was slow and took many years.

Since time immemorial, the children of Dara had been making paper-and-bamboo balloons, hanging candles from them, and then releasing the paper crafts to drift into the dark night sky over the endless ocean, tiny pockets of hot air floating like glowing jellyfish of the skies.

One night, as Mapidéré's father, King Dézan, observed children playing with flying lanterns near the palace, he had a flash of insight: Such balloons, properly scaled up, could change the tide of battle.

Dézan began with balloons made of layers of silk wrapped around a wire-and-bamboo framework. They floated on hot air generated by burning bags full of swamp gas. One or two soldiers, carried up in a gondola, could act as lookouts to spot potential ambushes or reconnoiter for distant fleets. Over time, the use of flame bombs—burning jars of sticky tar mixed with hot oil dropped from the gondolas—gave the balloons offensive capabilities. The other Tiro states quickly copied these Xana innovations.

But then came the discovery by Kino Ye, a Xana engineer, of an odorless, colorless gas that was lighter than air. The gas was found only at bubbling Lake Dako, on the side of Mount Kiji. When properly sealed up in airtight bags, the gas provided enormous lift, and could keep ships afloat in the air indefinitely. Propelled by enormous, winglike oars, these powerful airships made quick work of the passive, unreliable hot air balloons put up by the other states.

Moreover, the airships were deadly to navies, with their wooden hulls and cloth sails. A few airships could decimate an entire fleet caught by surprise. The only effective countermeasure involved long-range arrows propelled by firework rockets, but these were expensive and often proved even more dangerous to the other ships on the surface when they fell back down at the end of their long arcing flight, still burning.

King Dézan had contented himself with merely gaining the respect of the other Tiro states. His successor, the young and ambitious King Réon, decided that he preferred to dream a bigger dream, a dream that no one had dared to voice since the days of the Ano: to conquer all the Tiro states and unify the Islands of Dara.

Aided by the great airships, Xana navies and armies swept from victory to victory. It took thirty years of unceasing war for King Réon to conquer all the other six Tiro states. Even great Cocru, with its famed cavalry and skilled swordsmen, could not stand against him in the field. The last King of Cocru jumped into the sea when the capital Çaruza fell because he could not bear to be a naked captive in Réon's court.

So Réon declared himself Lord of All Dara and renamed himself Mapidéré, the First Emperor. He saw himself as the beginning of a new kind of power, a power that would transform the world.

"The time for kings is over. I am the King of Kings."

It was a new dawn, but the Imperial Procession remained where it was.

The emperor was still lying in his tent. The pain in his stomach was so intense that he could not get up. Even breathing seemed to take too much energy.

"Send our fastest airship, and bring me the crown prince."

*I must warn Pulo to prepare for the coming war,* thought the emperor. *The gods have prophesied it. But perhaps it can still be stopped—even the gods admit that they are not always in control.*

Chatelain Goran Pira held his ear close to the emperor's trembling lips and nodded. But there was a glint in his eyes, a glint that the emperor did not see.

The emperor lay, dreaming of his grand projects. There were still so many things to do, so many tasks unfinished.

Pira summoned Prime Minister Lügo Crupo to his own tent, a tiny, unassuming dome next to the giant Imperial pavilion, like a hermit crab sheltered next to a thirty-year-old conch.

"The emperor is very ill," Pira said. The hand holding the teacup was still. "No one knows the true extent of his sickness, yet, except for me—and now you. He has asked to see the crown prince."

"I will send *Time's Arrow,*" Crupo said. Crown Prince Pulo was away in Rui supervising the construction of the Grand Tunnels with General Gotha Tonyeti. Even *Time's Arrow*, the empire's fastest airship, oaring the air nonstop with shifts of conscripted laborers, would take almost two full days to get there and two more to return.

"Well, let's ponder that a bit," Pira said. His expression was unreadable.

"What is there to ponder?"

"Tell me, Prime Minister, who holds more weight in the heart of the crown prince? You or General Tonyeti? Who does he think has done more for Xana? Who does he trust?"

"That's a stupid question. General Tonyeti was responsible for the conquest of Cocru, the last and most defiant of the Six States; the crown prince has spent many years with him in the field, practically growing up in his company. It's perfectly understandable that the crown prince values him."

"Yet you have administered the empire for the better part of two decades, weighed and measured the fates of millions, made all the hard decisions, and did all you could to translate the emperor's dreams into reality. Don't you believe that your contributions are worth more than that of an old warrior who knows only how to fight and kill?"

Crupo said nothing in response and sipped his tea.

Pira smiled and pressed further. "If the crown prince accedes to the throne, the seal of the prime minister might be handed to Tonyeti. And someone would be looking for a new job."

"A loyal servant does not think of things outside of his control."

"But if young Prince Loshi, your student, were to ascend to the throne instead of his brother, things might be very different."

Crupo felt the hairs on his back stand on their ends. His eyes widened. "What you are saying . . . should not be said."

"Whether I say something or not, Prime Minister, the world will go on in accordance with its rules. *Ingaan pha naüran i gipi lothu*, as the Ano sages would say. Fortune favors the bold."

Pira placed something on the tea tray. He lifted his sleeves so that Crupo could take a quick peek. It was the Imperial Seal. Whatever document held its impression was the law of the land.

Crupo stared at Pira with his dark-brown eyes, and Pira stared placidly back.

After a moment, Crupo's face relaxed. He sighed. "This is a chaotic world, Chatelain. It can sometimes be difficult for servants to express their loyalty clearly. I will be guided by you."

Pira smiled.

As Emperor Mapidéré lay in his bed, he banked the embers of his vision for how Dara ought to be.

The first project that he had conceived of was the Grand Tunnels. He would chain Dara together by a system of undersea tunnels so that never again would the islands splinter into rival states. With the tunnels in place, commerce would flow between the islands and peoples would mix. The empire's soldiers would be able to ride from one end of Dara to the other without ever having to set foot in a boat or airship.

*This is madness!* declared the engineers and scholars. *Nature and the gods will not permit it. What will travelers eat and drink? How will they breathe in darkness, under the sea? And where will we find the men to do this?*

The emperor brushed aside their concerns. Didn't they also think that it was impossible for Xana to win? To conquer all the Islands of Dara? It was glorious to fight against men, but even more glorious to bend heaven, tame the sea, and reshape the earth.

Every problem had a solution. There would be side caverns dug every twenty miles or so, way stations for travelers bound between the islands. Glowing mushrooms would be cultivated in the dark to provide food, and water pulled out of the damp air with fog fences. If necessary, giant bellows would be installed at the tunnel entrances to pump fresh air throughout the system with bamboo pipes.

He decreed that every man chosen by lottery had to leave his profession, his fields, his workshop, his family, and go where the emperor wanted him to be, to labor under the watchful eyes of Xana soldiers. Young men were forced to leave their families behind for a decade or more, as they grew old under the sea, chained in permanent darkness, slaving away for a dream as grand as it was impossible. When men died, their bodies were cremated and the ashes sent home in tiny, unmarked boxes no bigger than the wooden tray for holding waste bones and fruit pits. And their sons would be conscripted to take their place.

Petty and shortsighted peasants could not understand his vision. They complained and cursed Mapidéré's name in secret. But he persevered. When he saw how little progress had been made, he simply drafted more men.

*The harshness of your laws is against the teachings of Kon Fiji, the One True Sage,* the great scholar Huzo Tuan, one of the emperor's advisers, said. *Yours are not the acts of a wise ruler.*

The emperor was disappointed. Mapidéré had always respected Tuan and hoped such an enlightened man could see further than the others. But he could not permit the man to live after such criticism. Mapidéré gave Tuan a grand funeral and published a collection of his writings posthumously, edited by the emperor himself.

He had many other ideas about how to improve the world. For instance, he thought all the people of Dara ought to write the same way, instead of each locale maintaining its own variant of the ancient Ano logograms and its own way of arranging the zyndari letters into word-squares.

Just remembering how the scholars of the conquered Tiro states had howled at the Edict on Uniformity of Speech and Writing brought a smile to the emperor's face. The edict had elevated the Xana dialect and the Xana script into standards for all of Dara. Virtually all the literati outside of the Xana home islands of Rui and Dasu foamed at their mouths and called the edict a crime against civilization. But Mapidéré knew perfectly well that what they were really objecting to was the loss of power. Once all the children had been educated under one standard script and one standard dialect, the local scholars no longer could dictate what thoughts could spread within their realm of influence. Ideas from outside—such as

Imperial edicts, poetry, the fruits of the culture of other Tiro states, an official history that superseded the local interpretations—could spread across all of Dara without the ancient barriers put up by seven incompatible scripts. And if scholars could no longer show their erudition by knowing how to write the same thing in seven different ways, good riddance!

Also, Mapidéré thought everyone should build their ships following the same specifications—ones he judged to be the best. He believed old books were fatuous and contained nothing useful for the future, so he collected them and burned every copy except one, and these last copies he stored deep in the bowels of the Great Library in Pan, the Immaculate City where everything was new, where only those who would not be corrupted by outdated foolishness could see them.

Scholars protested and wrote tracts denouncing him as a tyrant. But they were only scholars, with no strength to lift swords. He had two hundred of them buried alive and cut off the writing hands of a thousand more. The protests and tracts stopped.

The world was still so imperfect, and great men were always misunderstood by their own age.

*Time's Arrow* arrived in Rui. There, messengers led by bloodhounds carried the emperor's letter deep underground and followed the course of the Grand Tunnels, deep under the sea, until the hounds found the scent of Crown Prince Pulo and General Gotha Tonyeti.

The crown prince unrolled the letter and found a small sachet enclosed. He blanched as he read.

"Bad news?" General Tonyeti asked.

Pulo handed the letter to the general. "This must be a forgery," Tonyeti said after he was finished.

The crown prince shook his head. "The impression of the Imperial Seal is real. See how there's a chip in the corner? I saw the seal often as a boy. It's authentic."

"Then there has been some mistake. Why would the emperor

suddenly decide to strip you of your title and make your little brother the crown prince? And what is that packet?"

"It's poison," Prince Pulo said. "He's afraid that I might engage in a war of succession with my brother."

"None of this makes sense. You are the gentlest among your brothers. You have trouble even ordering these laborers whipped."

"My father is a difficult man to read." Nothing his father did shocked Pulo anymore. He had seen trusted advisers beheaded because of one careless comment. Pulo had defended them time and again, trying to save their lives, and for that his father had always considered him weak. That was why he had been assigned to this project in the first place: *You must learn how the strong make the weak do their bidding*.

"We must go to the emperor and ask him to explain this."

Pulo sighed. "Once my father's mind is made up, it cannot be changed. He must have decided that my little brother is more suited to being emperor than I am. He's probably right." Gently, respectfully, he rolled up the letter and handed it back to the messengers. He emptied the content of the sachet into his palm, revealing two large pills, and these he swallowed in one gulp.

"General, I'm truly sorry you chose to follow me instead of my brother."

The crown prince lay down on the ground as if to sleep. After a while he closed his eyes and stopped breathing. Tonyeti knelt down and held the young man's inert body. Through his tears, he saw that the messengers had all drawn their swords.

"So this is how my service to Xana is repaid," he said.

His cries of rage echoed in the tunnels long after they cut him down.

"Is Pulo here?" the emperor asked. He could barely move his lips.

"Soon. Just a few more days," Pira said.

The emperor closed his eyes.

Pira waited for an hour. He leaned down and felt nothing

emanating from the emperor's nostrils. He reached out and touched the emperor's lips. They were cold.

He came out of the tent. "The emperor is dead! Long live the emperor!"

PAN: THE ELEVENTH MONTH IN THE TWENTY-THIRD YEAR OF THE REIGN OF ONE BRIGHT HEAVEN.

Prince Loshi, a boy of twelve, ascended the throne and took on the new Imperial name of Emperor Erishi, a Classical Ano word that meant "continuation." Prime Minister Crupo was his regent, and Chatelain Pira took over as the new chief augur.

Pira announced an auspicious name for the new reign: Righteous Force, and the calendar was reset. Pan celebrated for ten straight days.

But many of the ministers whispered to one another that something was improper about the succession, that strange circumstances surrounded the emperor's death. Crupo and Pira produced documents proving that Crown Prince Pulo and General Tonyeti had been plotting with pirates and black-hearted rebels to seize Rui Island and found their own independent Tiro state, and when their plot was discovered, they committed suicide out of fear. But the evidence seemed to some of the ministers and generals flimsy.

Regent Crupo decided to ferret out the doubters.

One morning, about a month after the death of Emperor Mapidéré, as the ministers and generals gathered in the Grand Audience Hall to discuss the latest reports of banditry and famine with the emperor, Regent Crupo came in late. He brought with him a stag taken from the Imperial Zoo, one of Emperor Erishi's favorite places in the palace. The stag had huge antlers, and the ministers and generals milling about the hall backed away, giving them ample berth.

*"Rénga,"* Crupo said, bowing deeply. "I have brought you a fine horse. What do you and the assembled ministers think of it?"

The boy emperor's tiny figure seemed almost swallowed up by

the giant throne he sat in. He didn't understand what sort of joke the regent was playing. He had always had trouble following his old teacher's erudite, complicated lessons, and the boy did not feel close to the man, certain that his teacher found him lacking as a student. Crupo was also such a strange man—the regent had come to him in the middle of the night to explain that he would now be emperor, but then the regent had given him almost nothing to do, telling him to just enjoy himself and play games with Pira and be entertained by an endless stream of dancing troupes, acrobats, animal trainers, and magicians. The emperor tried to convince himself that he liked the regent, but in truth, he was more than a bit intimidated by him.

"I don't understand," Emperor Erishi said. "I don't see a horse. I see a deer."

Crupo bowed deeply again. "Sire, you are mistaken, but that is to be expected, since you are young and still have much to learn. Perhaps the other ministers and generals here can help enlighten you."

Crupo looked slowly around the room, and his right hand stroked the stag's back lightly. His gaze was cold and severe. No one dared to meet it.

"Tell me, my lords, do you see what I see? Is this a fine horse or a deer?"

Those who were more clever and sensitive to the winds of change caught on.

"An admirable horse, Regent."

"A very fine horse."

"I see a beautiful horse."

"*Rénga*, you must listen to the wise regent. That is a horse."

"Anyone who says that is a deer must face my sword!"

But some ministers, and especially the generals, shook their heads in disbelief. "This is shameful," said General Thumi Yuma, who had been in the Xana army for more than fifty years, serving even under Emperor Mapidéré's father and grandfather. "That is a deer. Crupo, you may be powerful, but you cannot make men believe or say what is not true."

"What is truth?" the regent said, enunciating his words carefully. "What happened in the Grand Tunnels? What happened on the Island of Écofi? These things must be written down in the history books, and someone has to decide what should be written."

Emboldened by General Yuma, more ministers stepped forward and declared that the regent had brought a deer to the Grand Audience Hall. But the pro-horse party refused to back down, and the two sides got into a shouting match. Crupo smiled and stroked his chin thoughtfully. Emperor Erishi looked from one side to the other and laughed. He thought it was yet another of Crupo's strange jokes.

As the months went by, fewer and fewer of those who stood up against Crupo on that day remained. Many were discovered to be coconspirators of the disgraced Prince Pulo, and from prison they wrote—after some convincing—tearful confessions of their crimes against the throne. They and their families were executed. That was the law of Xana: Treason was a taint in the blood, and five generations would pay for the crime of one.

Even General Yuma turned out to be one of the ringleaders in the failed plot—indeed, there was evidence that he had also tried to conspire with the emperor's other surviving brothers. Those other princes all swallowed poison just as the emperor's palace guards were about to seize them.

Unlike the other conspirators, though, Yuma refused to confess even after being shown incontrovertible proof of his guilt. The emperor was utterly devastated by the news of this betrayal.

"If he would just confess," the emperor said, "I would spare him, considering his service to Xana!"

"Alas," the regent said, "we tried to help him regain his conscience through the judicious application of physical pain, which cleanses the soul. But he is very stubborn."

"How can anyone be trusted if even the great Yuma thought to rebel?"

The regent bowed and said nothing.

The next time the regent brought his *horse* to the Grand Audience Hall, everyone agreed that it was a very fine *horse* indeed.

The young Emperor Erishi was at a loss. "I still see antlers," he muttered to himself. "How can that be a horse?"

"Don't worry about it, *Rénga*," Pira whispered next to his ear. "You still have much to learn."

## CHAPTER SIX

# CORVÉE

KIESA: THE EIGHTH MONTH IN THE THIRD YEAR OF THE REIGN OF RIGHTEOUS FORCE.

Because Huno Krima and Zopa Shigin were the tallest among the group of men sent from the village of Kiesa to fulfill the yearly quota of corvée laborers, they were made cocaptains. Krima was thin and bald as a polished river stone. Shigin had hair the color of straw, inherited from his Rima-born mother, broad shoulders, and a thick neck that reminded one of a reliable water buffalo. Both had the bronzed skin of Cocru peasants who labored long hours in the fields.

The corvée chief explained to the two their duties: "You have ten days to get the corvée team from here to the site of the Mausoleum of Emperor Mapidéré—may he rest his soul. The regent and the emperor are quite annoyed that progress has been so slow on the eternal house for the emperor's father.

"If you are late by one day, you will each lose one ear. If you are late by two days, you will each lose an eye. If you are late three days, you will each die. But if you are late by more than that, your wives and mothers will be sold to the brothels and your fathers and children will be condemned to conscripted hard labor forever."

Huno Krima and Zopa Shigin shivered. They looked up at the sky and prayed that the weather would remain calm as they led the corvée crew and began their journey west to the port city of Canfin, where they would get on a boat to carry them north along the coast and then up the Liru River to the site of the Mausoleum near Pan. A storm would mean delays.

The corvée laborers, thirty in number, piled into three horse-drawn carriages at dawn. The doors were then locked to take away the temptation for desertion. Two Imperial soldiers would ride with the caravan as escorts until they arrived at the next town, where the local garrison would take over and provide two more guards to the next stop.

The men looked outside the windows as the caravan made its way along the road to the west.

Though it was late summer, when the crops should be ripening, the fields were not golden with grain and few could be seen working. Typhoons this year had been worse than anyone remembered for years, and the crops in many fields had been ruined, rotting in the rain and mud. Women whose husbands and sons were away toiling for the emperor's grand visions struggled to manage the fields by themselves. What crops did survive had been claimed by the Imperial tax collectors. Though hungry men and women petitioned for reprieve, the answer from Pan was always a firm no.

Instead, the corvée quotas and taxes had been increased. The new Emperor Erishi had halted work on the Grand Tunnels, but he wanted to build a new palace of his own, and he expanded the design of the Mausoleum time after time to prove his filial piety.

The men stared blankly as they passed the corpses of starved men and women abandoned along the side of the road: skeletal thin, rotting, stripped of all their possessions, even the rags that constituted their clothes. There was famine in many of the villages, but the garrison commanders refused to open up the Imperial granaries, reserved for use by the army. Everything that could be eaten had already been eaten: some resorted to eating boiled bark and digging for grubs from the ground. Women, children, and old men tried to walk to where there was still rumored to be food, but sometimes they collapsed by the side of the road, their bodies without the strength to take another step, and their empty, lifeless eyes stared into an equally empty sky. Once in a while, a baby, still alive next to its dead mother, mewled with its last ounce of strength.

Young men, those who were not drafted for the corvée, sometimes escaped into the mountains to become bandits, and there they would be hunted down by the Imperial army like rats by exterminators.

The caravan rolled on, past the dead bodies, past the empty fields, past the desolation of abandoned huts, toward the port of Canfin and thence, the splendor of Immaculate Pan, the Imperial capital.

The caravan passed through the square in the center of a small town. A half-naked old man stumbled about, shouting at the carriages and pedestrians.

"Mount Rapa can be heard to rumble deep within for the first time in fifty years, and the Rufizo Falls have dried up. The black sands of Lutho Beach have turned red with blood. The gods are displeased with the House of Xana!"

"Is what he says true?" Krima asked. He scratched his bald head. "I had not heard of these strange signs."

"Who knows? Maybe the gods really are angry. Or maybe he's just mad with hunger," Shigin said.

The soldiers riding with the caravan pretended not to have heard the old man.

They had also come from peasant families, and they all knew people like that back in their home villages in Rui and Dasu. Emperor Mapidéré had left many widows and orphans across Dara, and even the home islands of Xana were not spared. Sometimes, the anger built up so much that people had to scream out their treasonous thoughts just to keep on breathing. Maybe not all of them were really *crazy*, but it was best for everyone involved to pretend that they were.

The Imperial Treasury may have paid their salaries, but that didn't mean that the soldiers forgot who they were.

The rain continued relentlessly for the fourth day. Krima and Shigin stared out the window of the inn and then put their faces in their hands in despair.

They were in Napi, still about fifty miles from the port of Canfin, but the roads were too muddy for the carriages. And even if they somehow made it to the coast, no ship would agree to set sail in this weather.

Yesterday was the last day when they still realistically had a chance of making it to the mouth of the Liru River and sailing up to Pan before the deadline. Each minute that passed meant a worse fate awaited them and their families. Whether the Imperial judges interpreted the laws in accordance with the letter or the spirit didn't matter—in neither was there mercy.

"It's useless," Krima said. "Even if we get to Pan, we'll end up as cripples or worse."

Shigin nodded. "Let's pool our money and at least get a good meal for today."

Krima and Shigin obtained permission from their guards to leave the inn to go to the market.

"There are so few fish in the ocean this year," the fishmonger told them. "Maybe even the fish are afraid of the tax collectors."

"Or maybe they are just scared of the hungry mouths of all the starving men in Dara."

But they paid the obscenely high price for the fish and then paid more for some wine. They used up all their money. Dead men had no use for copper coins.

"Come, come"—they gestured to the other men back at the inn—

"even sad men, even men who are about to lose their ears and eyes, have to eat, and eat well!"

The men nodded. This was true wisdom. As corvée laborers, life was simply one whipping after another, and you could only be scared for so long before you decided that filling your belly was more important than anything else.

"Who among you is a good cook?" Krima asked. He held up a large fish by the mouth: silver-scaled, rainbow-finned, as long as his arm. The men felt their mouths water. They hadn't eaten fresh fish in so long.

"We are."

The speakers were a pair of brothers, Dafiro and Ratho Miro, sixteen and fourteen, barely more than boys really. Pan kept on lowering the age when men would be available for the corvée.

"Your mother taught you how to cook?"

"Nah," said Ratho, the younger brother. "After Pa died in the Grand Tunnels, she spent a lot of time sleeping and drinking—" But his older brother shushed him.

"We're good cooks," said Dafiro, staring at every man around him and his brother in turn, daring anyone to make fun of what his brother had just said. "And we won't steal any of the fish for ourselves."

The men avoided his eyes. They had known too many families like the Miros. They were good cooks because they had to cook for themselves as children or starve.

"Thank you," Krima said. "I'm sure you'll do a great job. Be careful when you clean the fish. The fishmonger said that the gallbladder in this kind lies shallow."

The others remained at the bar of the inn and drank. They hoped to drink until they forgot what was going to happen to them when they did finally get to Pan.

"Captain Krima! Captain Shigin! You've got to come and see this!" the Miro boys shouted from the kitchen.

The men got up on their unsteady feet and stumbled for the kitchen.

Huno Krima and Zopa Shigin lingered behind for a moment and gave each other meaningful looks.

"This is it," said Shigin.

"No way out now," agreed Krima. And the two followed the rest of the men into the kitchen.

Ratho explained that he had sliced the fish's belly open to clean it, and what did he find in the fish's belly? A silk scroll filled with zyndari letters.

*Huno Krima Will Be King.*

The laborers stared at one another, their eyes and mouths wide open.

The people of Dara had always believed in prophecies and divination.

The world was a book in which the gods wrote, much as the scribes did with their brush and ink, wax and knife. The gods shaped the features of the earth and the seas much as the knife carved wax into logograms that could be touched and felt. Men and women were the zyndari letters and punctuation marks of this grand epic that the gods composed on the fly, changing their fickle minds from one moment to the next.

When the gods decreed that only Rui would possess the gas that made airships float, it meant that they wished to elevate Xana above all the other Tiro states and bring about the Unification. When Emperor Mapidéré had a dream of soaring above the Islands of Dara on the back of a Mingén falcon, that meant that the gods wished to glorify him above all men. It was useless for the Six States to resist the might of Xana, because the gods had already decided how the story would go. Just as wax clumps that refused to be shaped properly would be scraped away by the writer, to be replaced by new, pliant wax, so would men who resisted the fates be swept away, to be replaced by those sensitive to the shifts of fortune.

What did it mean that the typhoons were sweeping the coasts of the Islands more than ever before? What did it mean that strange clouds and strange lights were seen all over Dara? What did it mean that the giant crubens were sighted surfacing and breaching all over the western seas but not around Rui? What was the message brought by the famines and plagues?

Above all, what did the scroll in the belly of the fish tell the men who gawked at it, as Huno Krima and Zopa Shigin held it up to the light?

"We are dead men," Huno Krima said. "And so are our families. We've run out of time."

The men, packed into the kitchen, held their breaths and strained to hear. Krima wasn't speaking loudly, and the fire in the hearth cast flickering shadows across their faces.

"I don't like prophecies. They upset plans and make us into pawns of the gods. But it's even worse to resist a prophecy when it has been given. If we're already dead by the laws of Xana, and yet the gods tell us different, then I'd rather listen to the gods.

"There are thirty of us here in this room. Throughout the city are many other corvée crews just like us, marching to Pan without hope of getting there on time. All of us are the walking dead. We've got nothing to lose.

"Why should we submit to the words written in the Xana Codes? I would rather we obeyed the words of the gods. The signs are everywhere that the days of Xana are numbered. Men have been made into slaves, and women prostitutes. The old die of starvation and the young of banditry. While we suffer and know not why, the emperor and his ministers belch from a surfeit of sweetmeats fed to them by the soft hands of servant girls. This is not how the world was meant to be.

"Maybe it's time for a new story to be told by the wandering bards."

Ratho and Dafiro Miro, because they were the youngest and the smallest and seemed the least dangerous, were given the most difficult task. The brothers both had dark, curly hair, and small frames.

Ratho, being younger and more impulsive, accepted the assignment right away. Dafiro looked at his brother, sighed, and nodded.

Carrying two trays laden with wine and fish, they went to the room of the two soldiers escorting the corvée crew and explained that the men wanted to do something nice for their guards—perhaps the guards could then look the other way while the laborers tried to drink themselves into a stupor?

The soldiers ate and drank heartily. The warm rice wine and spicy fish soup made them sweaty, and they took off their armor and uniforms and sat only in their undershirts to be more comfortable. Soon their tongues grew heavy, and their eyelids drooped.

"More wine, Masters?" Ratho asked.

The soldiers nodded, and Ratho rushed to refill the cups. But these cups were never to be picked up again. The soldiers leaned back on their cushions, jaws open, and fell asleep.

Dafiro Miro took out the long kitchen knife he had hidden in his sleeve. He had butchered pigs and chickens, but a man was something different. He locked eyes with his brother, and they both stopped breathing for a moment.

"I won't be whipped to death like Pa," said Ratho.

Dafiro nodded.

There would be no stepping back from this.

Dafiro plunged the knife through the rib cage of one of the soldiers, right into his heart.

He looked across at his brother, who had done the same with the other soldier. The expression on Ratho's face, a mixture of excitement, fear, and joy, made Dafiro sad.

Little Ratho had always looked up to him, and he had always protected Ratho in fights with the other boys in the village. With their father gone early and their mother barely awake much of the day even when she was alive, he had practically raised Ratho. He had always believed that he would be able to protect his brother, and at this moment, he felt that he had failed.

Even though Ratho looked so happy.

∽ ∾ ∽ ∾

Two Imperial soldiers arrived at the Leaping Cruben, the largest lodging house in all of Napi. Clearly new recruits, their uniforms did not fit them very well.

The entire second and third floors had been requisitioned by the city as temporary holding cells for the corvée laborers and criminals sentenced to hard labor. The soldiers guarding them stayed in the suite on the second floor closest to the stairs and kept their doors open to prevent anyone in the other rooms from leaving without being noticed.

The two Imperial soldiers knocked on the open door and explained that they had been sent by the local garrison to look for a wanted criminal. Would the guards mind if the two just took a look through the men under their watch?

The guards, who were playing cards, waved dismissively at the two newcomers. "Look all you want. Your man is not here."

Huno Krima and Zopa Shigin thanked the guards, who went back to their liquor and game, and went to all the rooms one by one and explained their plot to the corvée laborers and criminals. This was their last stop. They had already visited all the other places in the city where men like them were held.

All over Napi, at midnight, the laborers and criminals rose up as one and killed their guards in their sleep. They set fire to the lodging houses and inns and congregated in the streets.

"Death to Xana!" they shouted. "Death to the emperor!" There was exhilaration in shouting the forbidden words, words that were on all men's minds. It made them feel invincible, just to say them aloud.

"Huno Krima will be king!"

Soon the men in the streets, the beggars and the thieves, the starving and the bankrupt, the women who had watched their husbands and sons taken away to be slaves under the sea and in the mountains, took up the same chant.

Brandishing only kitchen knives and bare fists, they rushed to the armory, broke in, and overwhelmed the soldiers guarding the doors. Now armed with real weapons, they attacked the army's granary, and soon bags of sorghum and rice and bundles of dried fish were traveling the streets, carried on the backs of men surging through the streets like flood currents.

They ran to the mayor's office and took over the building. Someone cut down the white flag of Xana, charged with a Mingén falcon spreading its wings, and hoisted up a sheet on which the crude figure of a leaping fish had been drawn—silver-scaled, rainbow-finned, with a scroll around it filled with letters: HUNO KRIMA WILL BE KING!

The soldiers of the local garrison, many of whom were from Cocru, refused to advance against their countrymen. The Xana commanders soon found themselves faced with the choice of surrender or being slaughtered by their own men.

Krima and Shigin were now in charge of a rebel force of a few thousand men—most of them desperate laborers, bandits, or soldiers in the Imperial army who had rioted along with the prisoners.

Those Imperial commanders who surrendered were promised rich rewards and paid immediately with money taken from the treasury of the city—tax money soaked with the blood, sweat, and tears of the people of Cocru.

Having secured Napi and sealed its gates against an anticipated counterattack from Xana troops stationed in cities nearby, Krima and Shigin set about the task of enjoying their spoils. The houses of merchants and nobles were looted, restaurants and brothels celebrated with special deals for the rebels, and contracts and debts were canceled. While the rich wailed, the poor celebrated.

"So we call ourselves kings now?" whispered Shigin.

Krima shook his head. "Too early. You and I need a symbol first."

To provide a measure of legitimacy to their rebellion, Krima and Shigin immediately dispatched a delegation to Faça to find the heir to the ancient Throne of Cocru, rumored to be a shepherd in exile. The two declared that they would restore the lost heir to his rightful place.

Couriers were sent to all corners of the Islands of Dara, calling for the nobles of the Six States to return to their ancestral domains and join the rebellion. The Tiro states would re-emerge from the ashes of the Unification, and together, they would topple the Imperial Throne in Pan.

A summer storm raged across the sky in the northwestern corner of Dara. The peasants of Rui and Dasu huddled in their houses, praying that the rage of Winged Kiji of Xana, god of winds and squalls, would not destroy the crops so close to harvest.

If one listened carefully, one might make out a voice amid the claps of thunder and sheets of rain.

*I never thought you, Lutho of Haan, would be the one to strike first. That bit with the fish and the scroll has your handiwork all over it.*

The reply, in the old and leathery voice of Lutho, the turtle-companioned god of calculation and tricks, was as gentle as flippers parting the waves, as soft as a shell scraping across moonlit sand.

*I assure you that I had nothing to do with it, my brother. It's true I have a knack for prophecies, but this one surprised me as much as you.*

*Then was it the Twins of Cocru, sisters of fire and ice?*

Two voices spoke together, discordant and harmonious, indignant and calm, like a river of lava flowing next to a glacier. It was Kana and Rapa, the raven-accompanied goddesses of fire and ice, death and sleep.

*The mortals find signs where they will. We had nothing to do with starting this—*

*But you can be sure we'll end it. Even if Cocru lives on only in the heart of one man—*

Kiji cut them off.

*Save your breath. You still have to find that one right man.*

CHAPTER SEVEN

# MATA'S VALOR

FARUN, IN THE TUNOA ISLANDS:
THE NINTH MONTH IN THE THIRD YEAR OF
THE REIGN OF RIGHTEOUS FORCE.

In Farun, on North Tunoa, the northernmost of the Tunoa Islands, Commander Datun Zatoma was troubled by news of the rebellion on the Big Island.

It was hard to get reliable information. Things were so chaotic. The bandits Huno Krima and Zopa Shigin claimed to have found the rightful heir to the Throne of Cocru, and this new "King of Cocru" had promised to make nobles of any Imperial commander who led his troops to join him.

The empire was in disarray. Ever since the suicide of General Gotha Tonyeti and the execution of General Thumi Yuma, the Imperial army had been without a proper commander-in-chief. For two years, the regent and the young emperor seemed to have forgotten about the army entirely, leaving all the regional commanders to their own devices. And now that a bona fide rebellion had broken out, Pan seemed stunned, and even after a month, no general had been put in charge of an Imperial force to put down the rebels. Each local garrison commander was trying to decide what to do.

*It's hard to tell which way the winds are blowing,* Commander Zatoma thought. *Perhaps it's better if I seize the initiative. The earlier I move, the greater my contribution. "Duke Zatoma" has a nice ring to it.*

But he was more comfortable behind a desk than on a horse. He needed good, capable lieutenants. In this he was lucky, being assigned to Farun. Tunoa had long been one of the most martial domains in all of Dara, as it was one of the last places in the Islands to be settled by the Ano, who had to pacify the warlike original inhabitants. In Farun, even the girls learned how to throw the javelin well, and every boy over five could wield his father's spear without disgrace.

If he approached the right men, they might be very grateful to get a chance to recover some of the honor of their disgraced families and serve him loyally. He would be the brain, and they would be his arms.

As Phin Zyndu walked through the cavernous halls and long corridors of his ancestral castle, he kept the turmoil in his heart off his face. He had not been back here since that day, a quarter of a century ago, when he had been driven away in the darkest hour of the Zyndu Clan. Coming back now at the behest of Datun Zatoma, a commoner in the garb of the conqueror, was not how he imagined his return.

Behind him, Mata hungrily took in the rich tapestries, the intricate iron latticework on the windows, and the paintings depicting the deeds of his ancestors. The heads of the figures in a few of the brush paintings had been torn out by Xana soldiers as souvenirs during the looting right after the conquest, and that lowlife Datun Zatoma had simply left the desecrated paintings in place, perhaps as reminders of the ignominious fall of the Zyndu Clan. Mata ground his teeth to keep the anger within from boiling over. All this, his rightful inheritance, had been soiled by the pig who had usurped his place and summoned them here.

"Wait here," Phin Zyndu said to Mata. Uncle and nephew exchanged meaningful glances, and Mata nodded.

"Welcome, Master Zyndu!" Datun Zatoma was enthusiastic and—in his mind, anyway—gracious. He clasped Phin Zyndu around the shoulders, but the man did not return the gesture. Awkwardly, Zatoma backed away after a moment and waved for the man to sit. Zatoma folded and crossed his legs, tucking each foot under the opposite thigh in *géüpa*, to show that they were speaking as friends, but Phin knelt stiffly on the sitting mat in formal *mipa rari*.

"You've heard the news from the Big Island?" Zatoma asked.

Phin Zyndu said nothing. He waited for the commander to go on.

"I've been thinking." This was a delicate matter, and Zatoma wanted to be careful so that his meaning would be unmistakable to Zyndu—and yet, should the emperor's troops prevail and crush the rebels, he would be able to explain his words satisfactorily. "Your family served the kings of Cocru faithfully and well for generations. Many great generals were Zyndus, a fact known to even a small child."

Phin Zyndu gave a barely perceptible nod.

"There is a war coming, and in war, men who know how to fight are rewarded. The Zyndus, it seems to me, may have interesting opportunities before them."

"We Zyndus fight only for Cocru," Zyndu said.

*Good,* Zatoma thought. *You are the one who said what needed to be said, not me.*

He went on, as if Zyndu had not just made the treasonous comment. "The troops under my command are either aged veterans who can no longer draw a strongbow or fresh conscripts who can't tell a parry from a thrust. They'll need to be whipped into shape, and quickly. I would be honored if you and your nephew would help me in this endeavor. In a time of change, we could rise together and taste glory side by side."

Phin looked at the Xana man, a supposed commander of the Imperial army. His hands were white, fat, and smooth, the color of a pearl on a woman's ring. These were not hands that knew how to grip a sword or swing an axe. *A bureaucrat,* he thought. *A man who knows only how to push beads on an abacus and to curry favor with his superiors has been put in charge of leading soldiers meant to defend the spoils of the Xana Conquest. No wonder the empire has stumbled so badly before a peasant rebellion.*

But as he smiled at Zatoma and nodded, his expression did not betray his disgust and contempt. He had already decided what he and Mata would do. "Let me get my nephew from the hallway. I think he would like to meet you too."

"Of course, of course! I always like meeting young heroes."

Phin emerged from the commander's room and nodded to Mata, who followed him back into the room. Zatoma approached, a big smile on his face and his arms opened wide to embrace the young man. But this welcome was a bit forced. The twenty-five-year-old Mata was over eight feet tall and quite intimidating. Also, his double pupils always made others look away. It was impossible to maintain eye contact with him: One didn't know which pupil to focus on.

Zatoma would never learn to get comfortable looking into those eyes. The first time he looked into them was also his last.

He looked down in disbelief. A dirk, thin as a needlefish and now red with his life's blood, was in Mata's left hand and being pulled out of his chest. All Zatoma could think about at that moment was how incongruous the tiny weapon looked in the hand of the giant man.

As he watched, Mata lifted the dirk again and slashed it across his neck, severing his windpipe and major arteries. Zatoma gurgled, unable to speak, and then collapsed to the ground, his limbs twitching as he choked on his own blood.

"And now, you will leave *my* house," Mata said. Datun Zatoma was the first man he had ever killed. He shuddered with the excitement of it, but he felt no regret or pity.

He stepped over to the weapons rack in the corner. It was full of beautiful ancient swords and spears and cudgels taken from the Zyndu Clan. Zatoma had seen them as decorations only, and there was a thick layer of dust over every weapon.

He picked up the heavy sword—by appearance, bronze—at the top. Its thick blade and long handle seemed to suggest that it was meant to be wielded by two hands.

He blew away the dust and pulled the blade halfway out of its scabbard, made of bamboo wrapped in silk. The metal's appearance was unusual: a somber bronze hue down the middle, as one might have expected, but edges glinting cold and blue in the filtered sunlight from the window. Mata turned it around in his hand and admired the intricate carvings—logograms of ancient battle poems—along both sides of the sword.

"This was the weapon of your grandfather for most of his career, a gift from his teacher Médo when he completed his studies," Phin said, pride in his voice. "He always preferred bronze because it was heavier than iron and steel, though it could not hold an edge as well and wasn't as hard. Most people could not even lift this sword with both hands, but he wielded it one-handed."

Mata pulled the sword all the way out of the sheath and swung it through the air a few times, with just one hand. The sword spun in front of him easily, reflecting light like a blossoming chrysanthemum, and he felt its chill wind on his face.

He marveled at its balance and heft. Most steel swords he had practiced with were too light, and their thin blades felt fragile. But this sword seemed to be made for him.

"You move like your grandfather," Phin said, his voice growing quiet.

Mata tested the sword's edges with his thumb: still sharp after all these years. He could detect no nicks or fractures. He gave his uncle a questioning glance.

"There's a story behind those sharp edges," said Phin. "When your grandfather was made the Marshal of Cocru, King Thoto came to Tunoa on an auspicious winter's day, constructed a ceremonial dais ninety-nine feet on each side and ninety-nine feet tall, and bowed thrice to grandfather Dazu on the dais so that all could see."

"The king bowed down to Grandfather?"

"Yes." Pride overflowed from Phin's voice. "That was the ancient custom of the Tiro kings. When a Tiro state designates a marshal, it is a most solemn occasion, for the king is entrusting the army, the most terrifying engine of state, to a pair of hands other than his own. The proper rites must be followed to show the great honor and respect the king places in the man he names his marshal. It is the only time that a king bows down to another man. Tunoa, the domain of our clan, has witnessed more of these ceremonies than anywhere else in all the Islands of Dara."

Mata nodded, feeling once again the weight on his shoulders, the history that ran through him. He was but a link in a long chain of illustrious warriors, warriors who had had kings bow down before them.

"I wish I could witness such a ceremony myself," he said.

"You will," Phin said, lightly clapping him on the back. "I'm sure of it. As a symbol of the marshal's authority, King Thoto gave Grandfather Dazu a new sword made of thousand-hammered steel, the strongest, sharpest blade metal known to men. But Grandfather did not wish to give up his old sword, for it was a mark of esteem from his teacher."

Mata nodded. He understood the duty of respect one owed to one's teacher, for the teacher was the model and mold of a man's skills and learning, as the father was the model and mold of a man's form and manners. These were ancient obligations, the kind that secured the world on top of its foundation. Though they were private bonds, they were as important and as unbreakable as the public duties one owed to one's lord and king. Mata keenly and vividly felt Dazu Zyndu's dilemma from decades ago.

Mapidéré had tried to suppress these private bonds and to elevate duty to the emperor above all, and that was why his empire had turned out to be so chaotic and unjust. Mata knew without having to ask that Mapidéré did not bow down to his marshals.

Phin continued, "Unable to decide which weapon to wield, your grandfather traveled to Rima to seek out Suma Ji, the best bladesmith in all of Dara, for help. Suma Ji prayed for three days and three nights to Fithowéo for guidance, and he was inspired to come up with a solution that also led to a novel method of compound blade making.

"The master bladesmith melted down the marshal's new sword. Keeping the old sword as the core, he wrapped it in layer after layer of hammered steel, forging it into a new blade that combined the weight and heft of bronze with the hardness and sharpness of steel. When the forging was complete, Suma Ji quenched it in the blood of a wolf, sacred to Fithowéo."

Mata caressed the sword's cold blade and wondered how many men's blood it had drunk over the years. "What is its name?"

"Suma Ji named it Na-aroénna," Phin said.

"The Ender of Doubts," said Mata, translating from Classical Ano.

Phin nodded. "Whenever Grandfather unsheathed it, in his heart, the outcome of the battle was no longer in doubt."

Mata gripped the sword tightly. *I will strive to be worthy of this weapon.*

Continuing his examination of the weapons rack, Mata let his gaze travel over spears, swords, whips, and bows, rejecting them all as unsuitable companions to Na-aroénna, but finally, his eyes stopped on the bottom rung.

He picked up the ironwood cudgel. The handle, as thick as his wrist, was wrapped in white silk, stained dark with years' worth of both blood and sweat. The cudgel grew thicker toward the other end, in which multiple rings of white teeth were embedded.

"That was the weapon of the Xana general Rio Cotumo, who was said to have the strength of ten men," Phin said.

Mata turned the cudgel this way and that, and the light glinted from the tips of the teeth. He could identify some of them: wolf, shark, even a few that might have come from a cruben. Some of the teeth were stained with blood. How many helmets and skulls had it smashed through?

"Grandfather and Rio Cotumo dueled for five days straight on the shores of the Liru without being able to determine a victor. Finally, on the sixth day, Cotumo stumbled because his foot slipped on a loose rock, and Grandfather was able to cut off his head. But Grandfather always thought his victory was unearned, and he honored Cotumo by giving him a lavish burial, and kept his weapon as a memento."

"Does it have a name?" Mata asked.

Phin shook his head. "If it did, your grandfather never learned it."

"Then I will call it Goremaw, companion to Na-aroénna."

"You will not use a shield?"

Mata gave a contemptuous laugh. "What need is there for a shield when my enemies will die before three strokes?"

He held the sword steady in his right hand and struck it sharply with the cudgel in his left hand. It clanged in a sweet, pure note that held for a long time, reverberating in the stone halls of the castle.

Phin and Mata Zyndu fought their way through the castle.

Having tasted his first blood, Mata was now possessed by the killing lust. He was like a shark set loose amongst a herd of seals. In the narrow halls of the castle, the Xana soldiers could not take advantage of their numbers, and Mata methodically dispatched them as they came at him in ones and pairs. He swung Na-aroénna with such force that it crashed through shields and arms held up vainly in defense. He smashed Goremaw down so hard that a man's skull was crushed into his torso.

There were two hundred men in the castle garrison. On that day, Mata slaughtered one hundred and seventy-three. The other twenty-seven were dispatched by Phin Zyndu, who laughed as he saw the image of his own father, the great Dazu Zyndu, reflected in the bloody young man fighting next to him.

Mata raised the flag of Cocru, a red field charged with a pair of ravens, one black and one white, over the castle the next day. And the chrysanthemum coat of arms of the Zyndu Clan was rehung over the castle door. News of his victory over the Xana garrison became a story, a legend, and then a myth, as it spread among the Tunoa Islands. Even children learned the names of Na-aroénna and Goremaw.

"Cocru has returned," the men and women of the Tunoa Islands whispered to one another. They still remembered Dazu Zyndu's tales of bravery, and his grandson compared favorably to him. Maybe there was hope to this rebellion after all.

Men began arriving at Zyndu Castle, volunteering to fight for Cocru. Soon, the Zyndus had gathered around them an army of eight hundred.

It was now the end of the ninth month, two months after Huno Krima and Zopa Shigin first saw the prophecy in the fish.

CHAPTER EIGHT

# KUNI'S CHOICE

OUTSIDE ZUDI: THE NINTH MONTH IN THE THIRD YEAR OF THE REIGN OF RIGHTEOUS FORCE.

The night before, Kuni Garu still had under his charge fifty prisoners—a few from Zudi, but most from far away, men who had committed some kind of crime and received sentences of hard labor in the corvée gangs.

The prisoners had been walking slowly because one of the men had a lame leg. Since they couldn't make it to the next town in time, Kuni had decided to make camp in the mountains.

In the morning, only fifteen prisoners were left.

"What are they thinking?" Kuni fumed. "There is nowhere to hide anywhere in the Islands. They'll be caught and their families will be executed or conscripted for hard labor to make up for their desertion. I treated them well and didn't have them chained at night, and this is how they repay me? I'm dead meat!"

Kuni had been promoted to head of the Corvée Department two years ago. Ordinarily, escorting a team of prisoners was something one of his underlings would do. But he had taken this particular assignment himself because he knew that the gang would probably not get to their destination on time because of the man with the bad leg—Kuni was sure he could convince the commander at Pan to let it go. Besides, he had never been to Pan, and he had always wanted to see the Immaculate City.

"I just *had* to do the most *interesting* thing," he berated himself. "Am I having *fun* now?" At that moment, he wished more than anything to be home with Jia, drinking a cup of herbal tea made from some recipe she was experimenting with, safe and bored.

"You didn't know?" one of the soldiers, a man by the name of Hupé, asked, incredulous. "The prisoners had been whispering and plotting all of yesterday. I thought you knew and were letting them go on purpose because you believed in the prophecy. They want to join the rebels who declared war on the emperor and pledged to free all prisoners and conscripted laborers."

Kuni did remember the prisoners whispering an unusual amount yesterday. And he, like everyone else in Zudi, had heard rumors about the rebellion. But he had been too distracted by the beauty of the mountains they were hiking through, and didn't connect the dots.

Abashed, he asked Hupé to tell him more about what he knew of the rebels.

"A scroll in a fish!" Kuni exclaimed. "A fish that they just happened to have bought. That con stopped working on me when I turned five. And people believe this?"

"Don't speak ill of the gods," Hupé, who was very religious, said stiffly.

"Well, this is a bit of a pickle," Kuni muttered. To calm himself, he took a plug of chewing herbs out of his waist pouch and put it into his mouth, letting it sit under his tongue. Jia knew how to make herbal mixes that made him feel like he was flying and caused him to see rainbow-haloed crubens and dyrans everywhere—he and Jia had fun with those—but she also knew how to make mixes that did the opposite: slowed things down and helped him see choices more clearly when he was stressed, and he definitely needed some clarity.

What was the point of bringing fifteen prisoners to Pan when the quota was fifty? He'd have an appointment with the executioner no matter how he tried to talk his way out of it. And most likely Jia, too. His life as a servant of the emperor was over; there was no longer any path back to safety. All the options he had were dangerous.

*But some choices are more interesting than others, and I did make a promise to myself.*

Could this rebellion finally be the opportunity that he had been seeking all his life?

"Emperor, king, general, duke," he whispered to himself. "These are just labels. Climb up the family tree of any of them high enough and you'll find a commoner who dared to take a chance."

He got up on a rock and faced the soldiers and the remaining prisoners, all of whom were terrified: "I'm grateful that you stayed with me. But there's no point in going any farther. Under the laws of Xana, we're all going to be punished severely. Feel free to go wherever you want or to join the rebels."

"Aren't you going to join the rebels?" Hupé asked in a fervent voice. "The prophecy!"

"I can't think about any prophecies right now. I'm going to hide in the mountains first and figure out a way to save my family."

"You're thinking of becoming a bandit then?"

"The way I look at it is this: If you try to obey the law, and the judges call you a criminal anyway, then you might as well live up to the name."

To his satisfaction but not surprise, everyone volunteered to stay with him.

*The best followers are those who think it was their own idea to follow you.*

Kuni Garu decided to take his band deep into the Er-Mé Mountains to minimize the risk of encountering Imperial patrols. The trail, winding slowly up the side of the mountain, was not steep, and the fall afternoon was pleasant. They made good progress.

But there was little camaraderie among ex-soldiers and ex-prisoners; they distrusted one another and were uncertain of the future.

Kuni wiped the sweat from his brow and stood still at a turn in the trail that gave him a good view of the verdant valleys below and the endless flat expanse of the Porin Plains beyond. He picked out another plug of chewing herbs from his pouch and bit into it with gusto. This one tasted minty and refreshing and made him feel like he should give a speech.

"Look at this view!" he said. "I had a pretty leisurely life"—those among the men who knew his history chuckled—"I never made enough money to rent a cabin up here and take my wife on a month-long vacation hiking in the Er-Mé Mountains. My father-in-law was wealthy enough to do it, but he was too busy with his business. All this beauty was here, but neither of us ever got to enjoy it."

The band admired the colorful fall foliage, a mosaic highlighted here and there by bunches of bright-red wild monkeyberries and late-blooming dandelions. A few of the men took deep breaths to fill their lungs with the mountain air, smelling of fresh-fallen leaves and loam that had been basking in the golden sun, so different from the air back in the streets of Zudi, which was dominated by the smell of copper coins and running sewage.

"So you see, it's not so bad being a bandit after all," Kuni said. And all the men laughed. When they went on, everyone's steps felt lighter.

Suddenly, Hupé, who was in the lead, came to a dead stop. "Snake!"

There was indeed a large white python in the middle of the road, as thick as a grown man's thighs and long enough that its tail was still in the woods even as its body completely blocked the trail. Everyone in Kuni's party scrambled back and tried to get as far away from the snake as possible. But the snake whipped its head around and wrapped its body around a gangly prisoner named Otho Krin.

Later, Kuni could not explain why he did what he did next. He didn't like snakes, and he wasn't the sort to rush impulsively into danger.

A surge of excitement coursed through his veins, and he spat out the herbs in his mouth. Before he could think, he had pulled a sword from Hupé and leapt at the giant white python. With one swing he lopped its head off. The rest of the body coiled and whipped around, and Kuni was knocked off his feet. But Otho Krin was safe.

"Are you all right, Captain Garu?"

Kuni shook his head. He was in a daze.

*What . . . what got into me?*

His eyes fell on a dandelion seed head by the side of the trail. As he looked at it, a gust of wind suddenly plucked the white puffs from it, and the seeds floated into the air, like a swarm of mayflies.

He tried to hand the sword back to Hupé, but the man shook his head.

"You keep it, Captain. I didn't know you were such a good swordsman!"

The men climbed on, but the susurration of voices grew among them like a breeze caressing the leaves of an aspen stand.

Kuni stopped and turned around. The whispers stopped.

In the eyes of the men, Kuni saw respect, awe, and even a hint of fear.

"What's going on here?" he asked.

The men looked at one another until, eventually, Hupé stepped forward.

"I had a dream last night." His voice was flat, as though he was still surrounded by illusions. "I was walking in a desert, where the sand was black like coal. Then I saw something white lying on the ground in the distance. As I came closer, I could make out the body of an enormous white snake.

"But as I approached the spot, the body disappeared. Instead, an old woman stood there crying. I asked her, 'Granny, why are you crying?'

"'Oh, my son has been killed.'

"'Who's your son?' I asked.

"'My son is the White Emperor. The Red Emperor has killed him.'"

Hupé stared at Kuni Garu, and the gazes of the others followed. White was the color of Xana, and red was the color of Cocru.

*Ah, prophecies again,* Kuni thought. He shook his head and laughed weakly.

"If this banditry business doesn't work out," he said, "you can try to become a wandering bard." Then he slapped Hupé's back. "But you need to work on your delivery, and you have to come up with more believable plots!"

Laughter echoed in the mountain air. Fear left the gazes of the men, but awe remained.

A hot breeze, as dry and gritty as volcanic ash, rustled the trees near the top of the mountain.

*What was that about, sister, my other self? Why have you taken an interest in this mortal?*

A cold breeze, as brittle and crisp as a shard from a glacier, joined the first.

*I know not of what you speak, Kana.*

*You didn't send in the snakes or give that man his dream? It seemed like your kind of sign.*

*I had no more to do with that than I did with that prophecy of the fish.*

*Then who? Fithowéo the Warlike? Lutho the Calculating?*

*I doubt it. They're busy elsewhere. But . . . now I* am *curious about this mortal.*

*He's a weakling, a commoner, and . . . not at all pious. We should not waste time with him. Ice-clad Rapa, our most promising champion is—*

*—young Zyndu. Yes, Flame-born Kana, I know you've liked him since the day he was born . . . yet, what strange things are happening around this other man!*

*Mere coincidences.*

*What is fate but coincidences in retrospect?*

Kuni Garu and his men took to banditry well. They made their camp high in the Er-Mé Mountains, and every few days they swept down to attack merchant caravans at dusk, when the drivers and their escorts were tired and sleepy, or at dawn, when they were just getting ready to set out on the road again.

They were careful to avoid deaths and serious injuries, and they always distributed a share of what they took to the scattered woodsmen living in the mountains. "We follow the virtuous path of the honorable bandit," Kuni taught his men to chant. "We are outlaws only because Xana's laws leave no room for honest men."

When garrisons in nearby towns sent detachments of riders to come after the desperadoes, the woodsmen always seemed to know nothing and to have seen nothing.

More and more runaway laborers and deserting soldiers came to join his gang, since Kuni had a reputation for treating his men well.

The attack on this particular caravan had gone wrong from the start.

Instead of scattering to the winds as soon as the bandits approached, the merchants had stayed where they were and huddled next to the campfires. Kuni cursed himself. That should have been a clue.

But his successes so far had made him arrogant. Instead of calling off the raid, he had ordered everyone to press on into the camp— "Knock them on the back of the head with your clubs and tie them up. Don't kill anyone!"

However, once the bandits were close enough, the oxcart curtains opened wide and dozens of armed escorts rushed out with swords drawn and arrows nocked. Whatever these merchants were carrying, they spent the funds to hire plenty of professional bodyguards. Kuni's gang was caught completely off guard.

Within minutes, two of Kuni's men fell with arrows sticking from their necks. Stunned, Kuni just stood there.

"Kuni!" Hupé shouted at him. "You've got to order a retreat!"

"Pull back! Abort! Tough marks! High fire! Tight wind!" All Kuni's notions about banditry had come from listening to storytellers in the markets and reading Kon Fiji's moral fables. He tossed out every bit of "thieves' cant" he could remember, having no idea what he was actually supposed to do or say.

Kuni's men milled about in confusion while the armed escorts for the merchants advanced. Another volley of arrows flew at them.

"They've got horses," said Hupé. "If we try to run for it, we're going to be cut down like vermin. Some of us have to stay behind and fight."

"Right," said Kuni. He felt calmer now that he was given a plan. "I'll stay behind with Fi and Gatha, you take the rest of the men and flee."

Hupé shook his head. "This isn't like a bar fight, Kuni. I know you've never killed anyone or practiced real sword fighting, but I was in the army, and so if anyone should stay, it's me."

"But I'm the leader!"

"Don't be foolish. You have a wife and a brother and parents still in Zudi, while I don't have anyone. And the others depend on you to have any hope of saving their families in the city. I believe in the dream I had about you, and I believe in the prophecy of the fish. Remember that."

Hupé rushed at the advancing escorts, holding high his sword—carved from a tree branch, since he had given his real sword to Kuni—and yelling fearsomely at the top of his lungs.

Another man fell next to Kuni, screaming and clutching at an arrow sticking from his belly.

"We have to leave! Now!" Kuni shouted. He did his best to rally the rest of the bandits, and they ran away from the merchants' camp toward the mountains, not stopping until their legs gave out and their lungs were on fire.

Hupé never came back.

Kuni stayed in his tent and refused to come out.

"You should at least eat something," said Otho Krin, the man who Kuni had saved from the great white snake.

"Go away."

Banditry wasn't at all how it was portrayed in bards' tales and Kon Fiji's fables. Real men died. Died because of his foolish decisions.

"There are some new recruits here to join us," said Otho.

"Tell them to go away," said Kuni.

"They won't leave until they see you."

Kuni emerged from his tent and blinked at the bright sunlight, his eyes red and puffy. He wished he had a jar of sorghum mead so he could retreat into oblivion.

Two men stood in front of him, and Kuni noticed that they were both missing their left hands.

"Remember us?" the older one asked.

They looked vaguely familiar to Kuni.

"You sent us to Pan last year."

Kuni looked closer at their faces. "You are father and son. You couldn't pay the tax, and so you both had to do corvée." He closed his eyes as he struggled to remember. "Your name is Muru, and you liked to play Two-Handed Rummy." As soon as the words left his mouth, Kuni wished he hadn't said them. The man clearly couldn't play his favorite game anymore, and he was sorry to draw attention to his loss.

But Muru nodded, a smile on his face. "I knew you'd remember, Kuni Garu. You may have worked for the emperor, and I may have been your prisoner, but you talked to me like we were friends."

"What happened to you?"

"Because my son broke a statue in the Mausoleum, they cut off his left hand. Because I tried to explain it was an accident, they cut off mine as well. After we finished our year of labor, they sent us back. But my wife . . . she didn't make it through last winter because there was nothing to eat."

"I'm sorry," said Kuni. He thought about all the men he had sent to Pan over the years. Sure, he had been kind to them while they were under his charge, but did he ever think, really think, about the fate he was consigning them to?

"We're the lucky ones. Plenty of others will never come back."

Kuni nodded numbly. "You have a right to be angry at me."

"Angry? No. We're here to fight with you."

Kuni looked at them, not understanding.

"I had to mortgage my land to give my wife a decent burial, but given the weather this year—it's like Kiji and the Twins are mad at each other—I'm certain I won't be able to redeem it. What path is open to my son and me but to become bandits? But none of the bandit leaders would take us because we're cripples.

"And then we heard that you've become a bandit too."

"I'm a terrible bandit," Kuni said. "I don't know a thing about leading men."

Muru shook his head. "I remember that when my son and I were in prison under your charge, you played cards with us and shared your beer. You told your men not to chain my legs because of a sore on my ankle. They say now you follow the path of the honorable bandit and protect the weak against the powerful. They say that you fight serpents to save your followers, and you're the last to retreat when a raid fails. I believe them. You're a good man, Kuni Garu."

Kuni broke down and cried.

Kuni put away his romantic notions about banditry and asked his men for advice, especially those who had been outlaws before being sentenced to hard labor. He became more cautious, scouted the targets carefully, and developed a system of signals. When he launched a raid, he divided his men into teams so they could support one another, and he always made plans for retreat before attacking.

Lives depended on him, and he would not be careless again. His reputation grew, and more men and women who had lost all hope flocked to him, especially people who were rejected by the other bandit gangs: those who had lost limbs, the too young or too old, widows.

Kuni took everyone. Sometimes his captains grumbled that the newcomers had to be fed without being able to do much, but Kuni figured out ways that the new recruits could contribute. Since they didn't look like bandits, they made ideal scouts and could ambush the caravans effectively—Kuni's gang managed to conduct a few raids without even drawing a sword simply by setting up tea huts next to the road into Zudi and feeding the merchants drinks laced with sleeping powder.

But Kuni's real goal had never been banditry alone. His failure to deliver the corvée team had placed his family in danger from official reprisal. Though the Zudi garrison seemed too distracted by the rebellion to enforce the emperor's laws—or perhaps they were waiting to see how the winds blew—he wasn't going to take any chances. Maybe the mayor would try to protect his friend, Gilo Matiza, and his daughter Jia, but who knew how long that protection would last? His parents and brother and Jia's family all had too much property to be able to leave it all behind, and he doubted he could persuade them to join him. But Jia, Jia he had to save as soon as possible.

When it was clear that he had built a stable base, Kuni decided to send someone to bring Jia to join him. It had to be someone who wasn't well known in Zudi and thus wouldn't bump into Imperials who might recognize him, and it also had to be someone he completely trusted. He settled on Otho Krin.

"Haven't we been here before?"

Until now, Jia had let the gaunt young man lead even when she doubted his competence. They had come to the same clearing in the woods for the third time and it was almost completely dark.

Otho Krin had hidden his face from Jia for the last hour by walking ahead. Now that he finally turned around to face her, the look of panic confirmed Jia's suspicion that they were lost.

"I'm sure that we're close," he answered nervously without looking into her eyes.

"Where are you from, Otho?"

"I beg your pardon?"

"Your accent tells me you're not from around Zudi. You don't know your way around, do you?"

"No, ma'am."

Jia sighed. It was useless to get angry at this pathetic bamboo stalk of a man. She was tired, even more so because she was pregnant. She and Kuni had been trying to conceive for a while without success, but just before he left, she had finally hit upon the right combination of herbs. This was a bit of news that she couldn't wait to tell Kuni—right after she gave him a good tongue-lashing for leaving her alone with no word from him for a month. She wasn't mad at him for turning into a bandit, exactly; it was more that she wished he had included her more in his plans. In truth, she was getting restless too; it was time for an adventure for both her and Kuni.

But first, she should take the lead here.

"Let's just camp here for the night. We'll continue in the morning."

Otho Krin looked at Jia. She was not much older than he. She never raised her voice, but the look in her eyes reminded him of his mother when she was ready to berate him. He hung his head and silently acquiesced.

Jia gathered some branches and leaves to make a bed for herself. When she saw Otho standing around helplessly, she gathered more branches and made a bed for him, too.

"Are you hungry?" she asked.

The young man nodded.

"Come with me."

Jia walked around with Otho tagging along behind her until she found some fresh droppings. She bent down and looked around until she found a patch of herbs next to the trail. She plucked the stalks and laid them out neatly. Then she took out a small bottle from her purse and sprinkled some powder over the herbs.

Holding a finger to her lips, she beckoned Otho to follow her. They backed away about fifty feet, ducked down in the shrubs, and waited.

A pair of hares hopped out onto the trail and suspiciously sniffed the pile of herbs Jia had left. But since nothing bad seemed to happen, after a while the hares calmed down and began to eat.

A few minutes later, the hares stuck up their ears, scented the air, and hopped away.

"Now we follow," Jia whispered.

Otho hurried to keep up with Jia. He was amazed by how fast this lady, by reputation a sheltered daughter of a wealthy man, could move through the woods.

They came upon a stream in the woods, and the two hares were lying next to the water, twitching but unable to run away.

"Can you take care of killing them quickly and without too much pain? It's bad luck for me to kill things right now . . . in my condition."

Otho nodded, not daring to ask what she was talking about. He picked up a large rock and smashed it down on the heads of the hares, killing them instantly.

"Now we have dinner," Jia said brightly.

"But . . . but the . . ." Otho struggled and his face grew red.

"Yes?"

". . . the poison?"

Jia laughed. "I didn't kill them with poison. The herb I picked was harenip, a sweet plant these creatures love to eat. The powder I put on it is my own creation, a mixture of natron ash and dried lemons. The mixture is harmless but gives off a lot of bubbles when it comes into contact with moisture, so the hares were very uncomfortable after eating for a while. They naturally tried to feel better by coming here to drink some water, but that only made things worse. They couldn't move because their bellies were so full of air that they couldn't breathe. The meat is perfectly safe to eat."

"How did you learn such a trick?" Kuni Garu's wife seemed to Otho a witch or a magician.

"Read a lot of books and try a lot of recipes," Jia said. "When you learn enough about the world, even a blade of grass can be a weapon."

Jia was just about to fall asleep when she heard Otho's sobs.

"Are you going to cry all night?"

"Sorry."

But the sniffles continued.

Jia sat up. "What's wrong?"

"I miss my mother."

"Where is she?"

"My father died early, and she was all I had. When famine struck our village last year, she mixed extra water into her porridge so that I wouldn't suspect that she was saving most of the food for me. When she died, I didn't know what to do, which is why I turned to thieving. I got caught and was sentenced to hard labor, and now I've become an outlaw. My mother would be so ashamed."

Jia felt sorry for the young man, but she did not believe in sentimentality or wallowing in sadness. "I don't think your mother would feel ashamed. She'd want you to survive because there's nothing she can do to help you now."

"You really think so?"

Jia sighed inwardly. Her own parents had cut her off when they heard that Kuni had become a bandit, fearing the consequences once he was caught. But she was trying to cheer this young man up, not bring him down. "Of course. Parents always want their children to run as far as they can on their chosen path. If you've chosen to be a bandit, be the best bandit you can be, and your mother will be proud of you."

Otho's face fell. "But I'm not a strong fighter. I'm not quick with figures. I can't even find my way back to camp. And . . . I had to rely on you to feed me!"

Jia wanted to laugh, but she also felt a wave of tenderness for the young man. "Look, we're all good at something. My husband must have seen something in you if he sent you to bring me to him."

"Probably because I don't even look like a bandit," Otho said. "And . . . one time I was part of a robbery that went bad, and everyone made fun of me because I wouldn't leave the dog behind."

"What dog?"

"I fed it jerky to keep it quiet while we snuck into the caravan campsite. But then the merchants woke up, and as we retreated, I heard one of the merchants say he was going to kill the useless dog. I felt bad for it and carried it back with me."

"You're loyal," said Jia. "That's not nothing."

She reached into her purse and brought out a small vial.

"Here, take this." Her voice was gentle. "I made it because I had trouble sleeping the last few weeks when I didn't know what had happened to Kuni. We have to sleep so we can be ready for tomorrow. Hey, you might even see your mother in your dream!"

"Thank you," Otho said, and accepted the vial. "You're nice."

"Everything will seem better in the morning." Jia smiled and turned away from him, soon falling asleep.

Otho sat by the fire and looked at Jia's sleeping figure long into the night, fingering the vial. He imagined that he could still feel the warmth of her hand on it.

Jia heard a faint voice calling *Mama, Mama*.

It must have been her child speaking to her through the womb. She smiled and patted her belly.

The sun had risen. A green-and-red parrot suddenly swooped in and landed next to her. It looked at her and cocked its head for a second before spreading its wings and rising skyward. Jia's gaze followed the bird. It flew into a giant rainbow that began in the clearing, riding its arch toward the other end.

Jia woke up.

"I heated some water for you," Otho said, and he brought her a pot.

"Thank you," Jia said.

*He looks a lot better than he did last night,* Jia thought. There was a kind of shy happiness on his face and in his posture. *Probably remembering his sweetheart.*

As Jia washed her face in the warm water and dried her face, she looked around the camp. Everything always did seem so much better in the morning.

She froze. The same enormous rainbow she dreamed of was hanging in the east. She knew they had to follow it.

Before long, she walked into Kuni's camp.

"Next time," Jia said, "make sure your lackeys know how to get back to you before you send them off. It would have been easier to send a dog."

But she gave Otho a gentle pat on the back of the hand to let him know she was joking. "We had a bit of an adventure," she said, smiling. Otho laughed as his face turned red.

Kuni embraced Jia and buried his face in her red curls. *My Jia can always take care of herself.*

"Well, we are in a bit of a mess, aren't we?" Jia said. "Your father and brother are so angry that you've turned into an outlaw that they won't even let me into their houses; they think I'm responsible for turning you to your old, irresponsible ways—am I? And my parents want nothing to do with me, claiming that since I insisted on marrying you, I have to live with the consequences. Only your mother tried to help me by sending me money in secret, and she wouldn't stop crying when she visited—and that made me cry too."

Kuni shook his head. "Yet they say blood is thicker than water! How can my father—"

"Being related to a rebel is a crime that can lead to the whole clan being punished, remember?"

"I haven't joined the rebels yet."

Jia regarded him carefully. "You haven't? Then what are you planning to do with this mountain base? I hope you aren't picturing me staying here for years as your bandit-queen!"

"I haven't thought through the next steps," Kuni admitted. "I just took the path that seemed open to me at the time. At least this way, I can keep you out of the hands of the Imperials."

"I'm not complaining, you know, but you certainly could have chosen a better time to do something *interesting*." Jia smiled and pulled Kuni's head down to whisper in his ear.

"Really?" Kuni said. He laughed and kissed Jia deeply. "Now that *is* good news." He looked down at her belly. "You'll have to stay in camp and not go anywhere."

"Right, I really need you to tell me what to do, just like you've done all these years." Jia rolled her eyes, but she stroked his arm affectionately. "Did you like that courage herb I gave you?"

"What are you talking about?"

Jia smiled mischievously. "Remember that pouch of calming herbs I gave you? I slipped in a plug for courage. You've always wanted to do the most interesting thing, right?"

Kuni thought back to that day on the trail up the mountain, and his strange behavior before the white python. "You have no idea how fortuitously things have worked out."

Jia kissed him on the cheek. "What you see as luck, I see as being prepared."

"So, if Otho was lost, how did you find me?"

She told Kuni about the dream of the rainbow. "It's a sign from the gods, surely."

*More prophecies,* Kuni thought. *Sometimes you can't plan things better than the gods—whoever they are—plan for you.*

The legend of Kuni Garu grew.

About a month later, two of Kuni's followers brought a burly man with his hands tied behind him into the camp.

"I'm telling you," the man shouted, "I'm a friend of your big boss! Treating me like this is a mistake."

"Or you could be a spy," his guards retorted.

The man had struggled the whole way and was out of breath. Kuni tried to not laugh when he saw the man's sweaty face, splotchy with exertion. He had a full, bushy black beard, and beads of sweat hung from the tips of the strands like dew from blades of grass in the morning. He was well muscled, and the guards had lashed the ropes about his arms very tight.

"As I live and breathe. Mün Çakri!" he said. "Are things so bad in

Zudi that you've come to join me? I'll make you a captain here." He directed the guards to loosen the ropes.

Mün Çakri was a butcher who had often drunk with Kuni and caroused about the streets of Zudi with him before he got his job as a jailer.

"Tight ship you run around here," Çakri said, stretching his arms to get the circulation back into them. "You've become notorious as the 'White Snake Bandit' for miles around. But when I asked about you, everyone on this mountain pretended to know nothing."

"It could be that you frightened them with those fists the size of copper pots and that beard—I really think you look more like a bandit than I do!"

Çakri ignored Kuni. "I guess I was asking too many questions, so a couple of woodsmen jumped me and brought me to your lackeys."

A boy brought out tea, but Çakri refused to touch his cup. Kuni laughed and then asked for two mugs of ale instead.

"I come here on official business," Çakri said. "From the mayor."

"Listen," Kuni said, "the only thing the mayor could want with me is to put me in jail, and I'm definitely not interested in *that*."

"Actually, the mayor is tempted by Krima and Shigin's call for Xana officials to defect. He thinks he might be able to get a title out of it if he presents Zudi to the rebels. And he wants you to advise him, since you're the closest thing to a bona fide rebel he knows. Because he knew I was your friend, he sent me to come and get you."

"What's wrong?" Jia asked. "Isn't this the opportunity you've been waiting for?"

"But all these stories people tell about me," Kuni said, "aren't really true. They're just exaggerations."

He thought about the deaths of Hupé and the others.

"Am I cut out to be a rebel? The real world is very different from adventures in stories."

"A little self-doubt is a good thing," said Jia, "but not excessive doubt. Sometimes we live up to the stories others tell about us. Look around you: Hundreds follow you and believe in you. They want you to save their families; you can only do that if you take Zudi."

Kuni thought about Muru and his son, about the old Xana mother in the marketplace trying to protect her son, about the widows whose husbands and sons would never return, about all the men and women whose lives the empire had destroyed without a thought.

"A bandit could still pray for a slim chance of being pardoned if enough money is paid," said Kuni. "But if I become a rebel, there's no way out."

"It's always scary to do the interesting thing," said Jia. "Ask your heart if it's also the right thing."

*I believe in the dream I had about you. Remember that.*

By the time Mün Çakri, Kuni Garu, and Kuni's gang arrived at Zudi, it was dusk. The gates of the city were closed.

"Open up!" Çakri shouted. "It's Kuni Garu, the mayor's honored guest."

"Kuni Garu is a criminal," the soldier atop the wall shouted. "The mayor has ordered the gates sealed."

"I guess he got cold feet," Kuni said. "Rebellion seemed good in theory, but when it came time to take the plunge, the mayor just couldn't do it."

His theory was confirmed as Than Carucono and Cogo Yelu emerged from the bushes by the side of the road to join them.

"The mayor has kicked us out of town because he knows we're your friends," Cogo said. "Yesterday he heard that the rebels were winning, and he invited us to dinner to discuss plans for his defection. Today he heard that the emperor was finally taking the rebellion seriously and would send the Imperial army shortly, and so he did this. That man is like a leaf dancing in the wind."

Kuni smiled. "I think it's too late for him to change his mind now."

He asked one of the men for a bow. He took a silk scroll from his sleeve and tied it around an arrow. Then he nocked it and shot it high into the sky. The men watched as the arrow traced out a high arc over the walls and fell into Zudi.

"Now we wait."

Anticipating that the vacillating mayor might change his mind, Kuni had sent a few men ahead earlier that day to sneak into Zudi before the gates were closed. They spent the rest of the afternoon spreading rumors that the hero Kuni Garu was leading a rebel army to liberate Zudi from Xana and return the city to the revived Cocru.

"No more taxes," they whispered. "No more corvées. No more killing whole families for one man's crimes."

Kuni's letter to the city asked for the citizens to rise up and topple the mayor. "You will be supported by Cocru's army of liberation," the letter promised. If one considered a band of bandits an "army," and if one ignored the fact that the King of Cocru had no idea who Kuni Garu was, the letter could be considered to sort of tell the truth.

But the citizens did as Kuni asked. Chaos erupted in the streets, and the people of the city, long resentful of the heavy hand of Xana rule, made quick work of the mayor and his staff. The heavy gates swung open, and citizens watched in amazement as Kuni Garu and his tiny band of bandits strode in.

"Where's the Cocru army?" one of the riot leaders asked.

Kuni climbed onto the balcony of a nearby house and surveyed the throng in the streets.

"*You* are the Cocru army!" he shouted. "Do you see how much power you have when you act without fear? Even if Cocru lives on only in the heart of one man, he will still overthrow Xana!"

Platitude or not, the crowd erupted into applause, and by acclamation, Kuni Garu became the Duke of Zudi. A few pointed out that titles of nobility really couldn't be handed out in such a democratic fashion, but these killjoys were ignored.

It was now the end of the eleventh month, three months after Huno Krima and Zopa Shigin first saw the prophecy in the fish.

## CHAPTER NINE

# EMPEROR ERISHI

PAN: THE ELEVENTH MONTH IN THE THIRD YEAR OF THE REIGN OF RIGHTEOUS FORCE.

In Pan, wine never stopped flowing. Fountains in the floor of the Grand Audience Hall of the palace sprayed and splashed wine of all colors into jade-lined pools. Ditches and ducts connected the pools so that the wines mixed together, frothing and intoxicating the air as those who approached the emperor gingerly picked their way around them.

Chatelain Goran Pira suggested to the young emperor that perhaps the pools could be shaped so that they represented the seas, and the parts of the floor that remained dry could be used to represent the Islands of Dara.

Wouldn't it be fun, he humbly offered, for the emperor to be able to survey his realm from his throne? Just by looking down, he would see the literally wine-dark seas and enjoy the sight of his ministers and generals island-hopping as they tried to walk up to present their reports and counsel.

The young emperor clapped his hands together in delight.

Chatelain Pira—really Chief Augur Pira, but he was so humble that he retained his old title, which he said made him feel closer to the emperor—always had such wonderful ideas! Emperor Erishi devoted many hours to drawing diagrams and directing the workmen as they dug up the golden bricks that tiled the floor of the Grand Audience Hall to put in sculpted models of the most important geographical features of the Islands: red coral for the cinder cone that was Mount Kana; white coral for the glacier-capped Mount Rapa; mother-of-pearl for the smooth sides of Mount Kiji, with a giant inlaid sapphire for Lake Arisuso and an emerald for Lake Dako; . . . culminating in a miniature garden of carefully cultivated bonsai trees that stood in for the towering oaks of old Rima. It was much too fun for the little emperor to pretend to be a giant striding across the land, dealing out life and death in this shrunken version of his realm.

When ministers and generals came up to him with reports of troubling rebels in remote corners of the empire, he impatiently brushed them away. Go talk to the regent! Couldn't they see he was too busy playing with Chatelain Pira, a wonderful friend who always warned him not to work too hard and not to neglect having fun while he was young? That was the whole point of being emperor, wasn't it?

"*Rénga,*" Pira said, "what do you think about a maze made of fine fish and tasty meats? We could hang all manner of delicious treats from the ceiling, and you could wear a blindfold and try to make a path through the maze by taste alone."

Now *that* was another brilliant suggestion. Emperor Erishi immediately set about planning for such a diversion.

If someone had informed him that men were dying every day in the Islands for lack of a cup of rice, he would have been surprised. "Why do they insist on eating rice? Meat is so much better!"

CHAPTER TEN

# THE REGENT

PAN: THE ELEVENTH MONTH IN THE THIRD YEAR OF THE REIGN OF RIGHTEOUS FORCE.

Regent Crupo did not enjoy his job.

Chatelain Pira was the one who had explained to the emperor that the best way to honor his father was to build the Great Mausoleum, a house for his eternal afterlife that would be even more splendid than the palace in Pan. Since the emperor's mother had died long ago after displeasing Mapidéré, his father was really the only parent he *could* celebrate. Didn't Kon Fiji, the Great Ano Sage, teach that a child should always honor his parents to the best of his ability?

But it was up to Lügo Crupo to make that dream real. He had to turn the emperor's childish drawings into real plans, draft the men to make the plans come to life, and order the soldiers to drive the lazy laborers to do their duty.

"Why do you fill the emperor's head with such foolish ideas?" asked Crupo.

"Regent, remember how we got to where we are today. Do you not feel the ghost of Emperor Mapidéré watching over us?"

Crupo felt a chill going up his spine. But he was a rational man, and he did not believe in ghosts. "What's done is done."

"Then feel the eyes of the world watching, scrutinizing us for signs of devotion. As you said, it can sometimes be difficult for servants to express their loyalty clearly. Think of the monument to Emperor Mapidéré as a complicated way for us to earn tranquility of mind and certainty in our places."

Crupo had nodded at the wisdom of Pira's words. He made thousands of men into slaves to the memory of the dead emperor and ignored their protests. Sacrifices were necessary in the pursuit of legitimacy.

That early exchange with Pira also established the pattern that would hold between them. He was the regent, holder of the Seal of Xana and the doer of deeds. Pira was the emperor's playmate, the voice that distracted the emperor. Together, they pulled the strings that moved the puppet that was Emperor Erishi. It had seemed like a good deal, one in which he got the better end of the bargain. But lately, he wasn't so sure.

He had craved power, yes, lots of it, and when Pira had come to him with that audacious plan, he had seized the chance. But actually exercising the power that came from the Throne of Xana was not nearly as enjoyable as he had imagined. Yes, it had been fun to watch the other ministers and generals cower before him and pay him obeisance, but so much of the work of being regent consisted of mere tedium! He did not want to hear about harvest numbers, petitions from starving peasants, reports of corvée desertions, and this latest plague, garrison commanders complaining about rebellions. Why couldn't they take care of the bandits in the areas they were responsible for? They were the soldiers, and that was *their* job.

Delegate, delegate. He delegated everything he could, and still, they came to him for decisions.

Lügo Crupo was a scholar, a man of letters, and he was sick of being bogged down by such petty concerns. He wanted to be the architect of grand visions, of new systems of laws, and new philosophies that would dazzle the ages. Who had time to philosophize, though, when people knocked on your door every quarter of an hour?

Crupo had been born in Cocru, back when it was still the strongest among the incessantly warring Tiro states. His parents, propertyless bakers in a small town, died during one of these border skirmishes. He was captured by bandits and taken to Haan, the most learned of the Tiro states, to be sold as a bonded servant, but in Ginpen, the Haan capital, the constables raided the bandits and freed Crupo into the streets.

Boys in Crupo's situation generally did not have much of a future. But he was lucky that as he begged for food in the streets of Ginpen as a refugee, the great scholar Gi Anji, famed lawgiver and adviser to many kings, passed by.

Gi Anji was a busy man and, like many who lived in Ginpen, had learned to harden his heart and ignore the many street urchins and beggars who shouted tales of woe—it was impossible to determine which were telling the truth. But on that day, he saw something in little Lügo Crupo's dark-brown eyes that moved him, a spark of yearning for something greater, not just hunger for food. He stopped and beckoned the boy to come closer.

And so Crupo became Anji's student. He was not one of those bright boys who mastered subjects effortlessly—like Tan Féüji, the precocious son of a famous Haan scholar and Gi Anji's favorite. And he had a hard time adapting to Anji's school.

Anji's favorite method of instruction was to engage in a group dialogue with his students, asking them carefully crafted questions that probed their understanding, challenged their assumptions, and led them down new avenues of thought.

Whereas Féüji could immediately come up with three different answers whenever Anji asked him a question, Crupo struggled to even understand the point Anji made by asking it. Crupo had to work hard for every bit of progress. It took him a long time to learn the zyndari letters and longer still to master enough logograms to read Anji's simpler treatises. Often the master grew impatient with the boy and threw up his hands in despair. Conversing with the bright Féüji was so much more pleasant.

Yet Crupo persevered. He wanted more than anything to please Master Anji, and if that meant that he had to read the same book three times to absorb the meaning, that he had to practice carving and writing the same logograms a hundred times, that he had to sit and work out a parable like a puzzle for hours, he did them all without complaint. He was the very definition of diligence as he squeezed every minute out of the day to study: He read while he ate; he did not play games with the other boys; he sat on sharp pebbles instead of sitting mats so that he would concentrate instead of becoming too comfortable and falling asleep.

Gradually, Crupo became one of Anji's best students. When speaking to kings, Anji often mentioned that of all the young men he had taught in his life, only Féüji and Crupo had understood everything he had to teach them and then gone on into the terra incognita of new ideas.

Once he left Anji's school, Crupo tried to become an adviser to the court of Cocru, his homeland. But while the king treated him with respect, he was never given an official position. Instead, he had to support himself by lecturing and teaching.

In addition to his lectures and pamphlets, Crupo's calligraphy was particularly admired by the literati. In contrast to his carefully constructed essays and tightly woven arguments, he shaped his wax logograms with the sensitivity of a child as well as the passionate abandon of a swordsman, and the zyndari letters from his brush leapt off the page like a flock of migrating wild geese captured in midflight over a still pond. Many imitated his calligraphy, but few could equal or even approach his artistry.

But there was a measure of condescension in their praise of Crupo that rankled. Some seemed almost surprised that a man of such humble origins could be the creator of such creative and artistic words. Behind the recognition there was also an implicit dismissal, as if Crupo's hard work could never measure up to Féüji's natural brilliance.

Crupo was never as famous as Tan Féüji. Tan became the Prime Minister of Haan at the age of twenty, and his essays on governance were more widely circulated and highly regarded than anything Crupo wrote. Even King Réon of Xana, the future Emperor Mapidéré, who had little good to say about scholars of the Six States, said he found Féüji's writing enlightening.

But Crupo thought Féüji's essays insipid. They were so flowery and illogical! All this concern about "the virtuous ruler" and the "harmonious society" and the "path of balance" nauseated him. They were constructed like castles in the air, with soaring rhetoric and lovely turns of phrase, but no care for the foundation.

Féüji's belief in a ruler who ruled but lightly, stepping out of the way of the people, who could better their own circumstances through hard work and their own initiative, seemed to Crupo hopelessly naïve. If the experience of living in the war-torn Tiro states taught men anything, it was that the common people were little better than animals who had to be herded and corralled by strong rulers advised by men with vision. What strong states needed were severe laws administered efficiently and without mercy.

And Crupo knew that all the kings and ministers, in their heart of hearts, agreed with *him*, not Féüji. Lügo was the one who said what they really needed to hear, yet they continued to heap praise and honor only on Tan. His many letters to the Cocru court in Çaruza, offering his services, went unanswered.

Crupo was despondent and consumed with jealousy.

He went to Gi Anji. "Master, I work so much harder than Tan. Why am I not as well respected?"

"Tan writes of the world as it ought to be, not as it is," Anji said.

Crupo bowed to his teacher. "Do *you* think I am the better writer?"

Gi Anji looked at him and sighed. "Tan writes without concern about pleasing others, and that is why men find his voice fresh and original."

The veiled criticism stung.

One day, while at the latrine, Crupo observed that the rats in the latrine were thin and sickly. He remembered that the rats he had observed in the granary earlier were fat and lively.

*A man's circumstances are not determined by his talents,* Crupo thought, *but by where he chooses to put his talents to work. Xana is strong and Cocru is weak. Only a fool goes down with a sinking ship.*

He defected from Cocru and went to the court of Xana, where he rose quickly because Réon thought having another student taught by Gi Anji was the next best thing to getting Tan Féüji himself.

But every time he was consulted, he heard behind the king's words an unvoiced regret: *If only Tan Féüji were sitting here with me instead . . .*

Crupo was enraged by the thought that King Réon valued what he could not have more than what he possessed. He was constantly racked by the pain of being deemed only second best, not quite good enough. He worked even harder, trying to come up with ways to strengthen Xana and weaken the other Tiro states. He wanted the king to acknowledge, one day, that *he* was much more valuable than Féüji could ever have been.

After the fall of the Haan capital, Ginpen, Tan Féüji was captured.

Réon was ecstatic. "Finally," the king boasted to his ministers, among whose ranks Crupo stood, "I will have a chance to convince a great man to join my cause. There are many in the Islands who admire his wisdom, and having him on the side of Xana would be better than a thousand horses or ten fearless generals. He is as exceptional among mere scholars as a cruben among mere whales or a dyran among mere fish."

Crupo closed his eyes. He would never be able to escape from the shadow of this mirage, this glib man who wrote of ideals instead of truths. Even when what he said was useless, King Réon wanted the prestige of the Féüji name.

Crupo visited Tan Féüji in prison that night.

Knowing how much the king valued this particular prisoner, the guards handled Féüji more like a guest. He was given the room of the prison warden, and the guards spoke to him with respect. He was free to do as he liked as long as he did not leave.

"It's been a long time," Crupo said, upon seeing his old friend. Tan's smooth, deep-black face was unlined, and Crupo imagined the life of ease he had led, toasted by kings and dukes, never having to scrabble for a living.

"Too long!" Féüji said, clasping Crupo by the arms. "I had hoped to see you at Master Anji's funeral, but I understand you were too busy. The master thought of you often during the last years of his life."

"Did he?" Crupo tried to clasp Féüji's arms with as much warmth. But he felt awkward, nervous, stiff. After a moment, he stepped back.

They sat down on the soft mats on the floor, a pot of tea between them. Crupo sat at first in the formal position of *mipa rari*, his back straight and tall and his weight on his knees.

Across the table, Féüji laughed. "Lügo, have you forgotten that we've known each other since we were schoolboys? I thought you were here to visit an old friend. Why do you sit as if we're negotiating a treaty?"

Embarrassed, Crupo shifted into the familiar *géüpa* to match Féüji, with his bottom on the floor and his legs crossed and folded so that each foot was under the opposite thigh.

"Why do you look so uncomfortable?" Féüji asked. "I think you're hiding something."

Crupo started and spilled some tea from his cup.

"I know what it is," Féüji said. "Old friend, you came to me because you wished to apologize for not being able to dissuade King Réon from his mad vision of conquest."

Crupo hid his flushed face behind his sleeves as he composed himself.

"And now you're embarrassed because you think an apology inadequate, when Haan has fallen and I am here, a prisoner awaiting execution. You don't know what to say."

Crupo set down his teacup. "You know me better than I know

myself," he muttered. He took out a small, green porcelain bottle hidden deep within his sleeves. "Our friendship is stronger than tea. Let us have something that fits better." He poured the liquor into the empty cup before Féüji.

"You feel responsible for the thousands slaughtered by Réon in his senseless wars," Féüji said. "You are kind, Crupo, but do not let your heart be troubled by a burden that isn't yours. I know that you've done your best to try to speak sense to the tyrant. I know you tried to save my life, but Réon won't allow me to live after having defied him for so long. I thank you, old friend, and I forbid you from feeling any guilt! It is the tyrant Réon who is responsible."

Crupo nodded, and hot tears flowed down his face. "You're truly the mirror of my soul."

"Let us be merry and drink," Féüji said, and drained the liquor in his cup in one gulp. Crupo drank too.

"Ah, you've forgotten to fill your own cup," Féüji said, laughing. "That's still tea."

Crupo said nothing but waited. Soon, Féüji's expression changed. He held his hands to his stomach and tried to speak, but nothing would come except gasps. He tried to get up but stumbled and fell, and after a while, he stopped writhing on the mat.

Crupo stood up. "I am no longer the second best."

After all these years, Crupo thought he had finally accomplished his dream. He was peerless, the most powerful man in the land. He finally had the opportunity to show the world that he was, all along, the one who deserved their admiration and praise.

He would be *respected*.

And yet his work was so unsatisfying, so *petty*.

"Regent, who should we appoint as commander-in-chief against the rebels?"

*The rebels? Those bandits? How can they withstand the might of the Imperial army? A trained monkey leading the army would win. Why are they bothering me with this? It's a transparent case of petty bureaucrats exaggerating threats to wheedle more money and resources from the throne. I will not be fooled.*

He thought about who at the court most annoyed him, who he would rather send far away from Pan, out of sight.

Glancing over at the small shrine to Kiji in the corner, he saw a pile of petitions marked urgent. No matter how hard he worked, there always seemed to be so much more for him to do. He had taken to piling the petitions next to the shrine, idly hoping that showing the god how much he had to deal with might arouse some sense of pity and bring about divine intervention to lessen his load.

All the petitions near the top of the pile were from one man.

Ah, he had it. Surely this was a sign from Lord Kiji himself. Kindo Marana, the Minister of the Treasury, had been hounding Crupo for days about some suggestions for improving the tax system. The sallow, small man was obsessed with trivial matters like taxes and finance; he could not understand the grand visions and the big picture that concerned the regent. Sending the chief tax collector, a bean counter among bean counters, to supervise the army against the bandits seemed deliciously absurd, and he was impressed with his own wit.

"Summon Kindo Marana."

*Maybe I will now finally get some peace to work on my treatise on government. It will be better than anything Tan Féüji ever wrote. Ten, no,* twenty *times better.*

CHAPTER ELEVEN

# THE CHATELAIN

PAN: THE ELEVENTH MONTH IN THE THIRD YEAR OF THE REIGN OF RIGHTEOUS FORCE.

A chatelain was just a glorified butler, Goran Pira often thought. There was a time, back in the early days of the old Tiro states, when a chatelain led the defense of a castle and was treated as a member of the nobility. Nowadays, his duties consisted of settling disputes among Mapidéré's wives, disciplining the servants, balancing the palace budget (though it *was* a very big budget), and being the emperor's playmate.

Pira had inherited the position from his father, who had served Emperor Mapidéré's father, King Dézan. Pira grew up in the old palace, back in the old Xana capital of Kriphi, on Rui, and played with young Prince Réon. The two often got in trouble for trying to peek into the windows of the bedrooms of the younger wives of Réon's father.

When they were caught, Pira always insisted that he was the instigator, the one who led the prince astray. He was the one who was spanked and whipped.

"That was very brave of you," Réon said. "You are a true friend."

"Ré," he said, grimacing with the pain from the spanking. "I'll always be your friend. But maybe next time you can be a little bit quieter."

The friendship survived Réon's ascension to the Xana throne. It survived the years of conquest and war, when Pira often comforted Réon when he was frustrated with the lack of progress or seethed because of some diplomatic insult. It even survived Réon's many pompous eccentricities after he conquered the Six States and became Emperor Mapidéré. He might make his ministers and generals tremble with the slightest movement of his pinkie, but away from the audience halls, back in the living quarters of the palace, he was still just Ré, Pira's childhood friend.

But the friendship could not survive Lady Maing.

Maing was from Amu, the daughter of a duke who refused to surrender to the Xana army. She was taken as a captive back to Pan, where Emperor Mapidéré built his new capital, and made to work as a serving woman in the palace kitchen.

Pira had never paid much attention to the women of the palace. It was a necessary part of surviving the job. A chatelain who could not resist the temptation of his lord's many beautiful wives and captives did not have a very long career.

Pira was married to a girl from Xana picked for him by his parents. They were polite to each other, but they rarely spent much time together since Pira was almost always by Réon's side. The woman bore him no children, but Pira did not care. He didn't think the life of the chatelain was so wonderful that he wanted to pass it on to a son. Long ago, Pira had learned to suppress his urges as a man.

But Maing awoke something in him. Was it the way she never lamented her fate, though she had been turned from a duke's daughter into a slave? Was it the way she never treated herself as a slave, holding her head high and looking straight at you? Was it the way she found joy in the simplest things, teaching the other serving women in the kitchen to turn the dripping of leaky faucets into music and to make finger shadow puppets dance against the wall in the light cast by the fire in the giant cooking hearths? He didn't know, but he knew he loved her.

They began to converse, and he felt that she was the only person who really understood him, who saw that he was more than the sum of his duties, who knew that he sometimes wrote poetry about watching the melting ice in spring and the summer stars spinning slowly overhead, about loneliness in a crowd, about the emptiness in the heart caused by touching too much silver and gold and not enough of a friendly hand.

"I am but a glorified slave," he said to her, and discovered that it was true. "Neither of us is free."

Finally, being with her taught him the meaning of real intimacy. Though he had thought he was close to Ré, they were, after all, not equals, and true intimacy required equality.

One night, Emperor Mapidéré held a banquet for his generals, and Pira wanted to wait until after the banquet, when the emperor would be in a good mood, to ask a favor of him. He would ask Ré, his old friend and playmate, to release Maing from her servitude and let him have her.

Maing served the swordfish steaks that night. She passed before the emperor's table, the platter of fish held high before her. The emperor had been bored, and he chose that moment to look for something to divert himself. He saw Maing's narrow waist. He saw Maing's flowing light-brown hair. He saw a thing that had long belonged to him but which he had been too busy to enjoy.

He summoned her to his bed that night, and she became Lady Maing, another of Mapidéré's many consorts. Mapidéré had never designated an empress, preferring the new to the old.

Pira's heart died that night.

Though this was a fate dreamed of by all the other slave women, when Pira came by to wake the emperor in the morning, Maing looked frightened, not joyful. She avoided Pira's gaze, and Pira carefully spoke in an even voice. In his dreams, he said good-bye to her again and again.

Lady Maing became pregnant, and the courtiers and servants congratulated her heartily. As the consort who brought another royal child, Lady Maing's place in the palace was secure.

But she said nothing to the well-wishers. As her belly swelled, she looked only more and more withdrawn.

The baby, a boy, was born two months early, and yet he was healthy and hale, and weighed as much as any other boy carried to full term. The doctor, suspicious, sent away the servants and nurses and interrogated the exhausted Lady Maing for an hour. When he finally got the truth out of her, he hurried to Pira with the news.

Since then, Pira had relived that day a hundred thousand times in his mind. Could he have saved his son? Could he have saved Maing? Could he have silenced the doctor with gold and jewels? Could he have thrown himself at the emperor's feet and pled for mercy? Was he such a coward that he could not even protect the one person in this world he loved? He imagined himself leaving everything behind so that he and Maing could have escaped in a small fishing boat, bound for ports unknown and a lifetime of looking over their shoulders—but she would be alive, alive.

Yet, every scenario ended with the same result: death to his entire family—his parents, his wife, his uncles and aunts. Treason was a taint in the blood, and a traitor's sin was borne by the whole family.

He could not think of what he could have done differently, but he blamed himself nonetheless.

He had gone to Emperor Mapidéré and told him what the doctor said.

"Who is the father?" the emperor raged.

"She wouldn't say," Pira said, his voice dead.

He wanted to try to reason with Réon, to explain that he had met her before Réon wanted her, and so they had not really committed treason. Yet, as chatelain, he knew the laws of the palace well. A slave girl belonged to the emperor, even if he never touched her, even if he didn't know her name, could not recall her face. They had indeed committed treason, starting with the minute that he looked at her as anything other than the emperor's possession.

And so he watched, and said nothing, as the boy was smothered in front of Lady Maing. He watched, and said nothing, as the Imperial Guards strangled her. Then he went to dispose of the bodies, and he strained to show nothing in his face as his hands touched her cold skin.

He did make a vow, though: He would avenge her and bring down the House of Xana. He would truly, spectacularly, really commit treason.

"Chatelain, they keep on pestering me with these reports of rebellion. What should I do?"

"*Rénga*, these are mere bandits and highwaymen, beneath your notice. You demean yourself by even wasting a second of your time to think about them. Announce that whoever brings you reports of such petty matters should be put to death. Let the regent take care of them for you."

"You are my only real friend, Chatelain. You always think of what's best for me."

"Thank you. Now, what shall we do today? Shall we go to the Imperial Zoo and Aquarium so you can pet the baby cruben? Or would you rather see the new virgins brought from Faça?"

# CHASING THE STAG

CHAPTER TWELVE

# THE REBELLION GROWS

THE BIG ISLAND: THE THIRD MONTH IN THE FOURTH YEAR OF THE REIGN OF RIGHTEOUS FORCE.

While wine flowed and gems sparkled in his toy empire, Emperor Erishi's real empire was in tatters.

By now, a force of twenty thousand men had rallied around the fish-prophesied flag of Huno Krima and Zopa Shigin. They had plucked the rightful heir to the Cocru throne, a twenty-three-year-old shepherd, from his quiet life in the northern countryside of Faça among his flocks and restored him to the throne as King Thufi.

Although the young man had spent his entire life so far having authority only over sheep, he soon took to the role of commanding men with grace and ease.

"See," Ratho Miro said to his brother, "the blood of the royal line *is* special. There's no other explanation for how a boy raised to be a shepherd could suddenly look so comfortable being in charge of a whole country! Such grace. Such command!"

Dafiro rolled his eyes. "If a bunch of well-dressed men came to me and told me that I was destined to be king, followed me around all day, and acted like I was so wise and clever and nodded at everything I said, and if they then gave me a big, heavy crown and a yellow silk robe to wear and put me on a golden throne, I'd probably also end up acting all confident and king-ish, as though my backside belonged on that throne all along."

"I don't know," Ratho said, looking over his brother skeptically. "You're good only at bossing me around. I think if you put on a silk robe you'd end up looking like a circus monkey."

At the grand old Temple of Fire and Ice in the middle of Çaruza, Thufi prayed to the goddesses Kana and Rapa, protectors of Cocru.

"The sins of Xana are many," he said to the assembled multitudes in the square. "But the day of reckoning is here. All the Tiro states have re-risen, and the world will be put aright."

Before a crowd throbbing with anticipation, King Thufi named Krima the Duke of Napi, Marshal of Cocru, and Shigin the Duke of Canfin, Vice Marshal of Cocru. They were given orders to attack Xana forces everywhere until all former Cocru lands had been liberated. Krima and Shigin marched out of Çaruza at the head of an army as the people showered them with flowers and fine white sand shipped from Çaruza's beaches.

"This is the life, eh?" said Ratho Miro. He smiled at the pretty girls cheering along the street.

"We haven't met Xana's real army yet," said Dafiro Miro. "Don't celebrate too early."

The seeds of rebellion spread wherever the wind blew, and soon the conquered Tiro states re-emerged like fresh bamboo shoots after a long winter.

In the northern part of the Big Island, a man named Shilué, the grandchild of the last King of Faça, reclaimed the throne in Boama. His troops soon numbered ten thousand.

To the east, a descendant of a side branch of the ruling house of Gan declared himself King Dalo of Gan, land of wealth and culture. The Xana garrison in Toaza, the old Gan capital on the island of

Wolf's Paw, surrendered without a single arrow being shot. The garrison promptly renamed itself the Royal Gan Guard, and the former Xana commander happily accepted the title of count. Gan also seized the ships of the Xana navy docked at Toaza Harbor, and King Dalo prepared for an invasion of the Big Island to recover the rich alluvial plains of old Gan.

Meanwhile, the cities of the Maji Peninsula, south of the Sonaru Desert, declared themselves members of an independent league. As Maji had been under both Cocru and Gan administration at different times in its history, the cities shrewdly pledged partial allegiance to both Tiro states.

In the west, Amu, known for its elegance and sophistication, re-established itself on the beautiful island of Arulugi, though the former Amu territories on the Big Island remained firmly under Xana control.

The resurrected Rima quickly reclaimed its territory north of the Damu and Shinané mountain ranges with the aid of Faça. Rima soldiers also pushed as far as they dared to the southern side of the mountain ranges. The hope was that should Xana fall, Rima would now have the first claim on territories it had always disputed with old Amu.

Of the Six States, only Haan remained completely under Xana occupation. But there was a Haan government in exile, and King Cosugi of Haan, who had surrendered to the emperor Mapidéré when he was a young man thirty years ago, now lived in Çaruza as a guest of the newly established King Thufi of Cocru.

"You'll soon see Ginpen again," Thufi promised Cosugi.

Cosugi nodded, his wiry gray beard swaying and a pair of cloudy eyes peering nervously out of a face as dark and wrinkled as newly hardened lava, hardly able to believe this recent turn of events. Just a few months earlier, Xana had seemed invincible and the dream of reviving Haan a fairy tale.

Thufi invited all the kings of the reborn Six States to join him in Çaruza for a Grand Council of War. They would elect a princeps, and decide on the best course of action.

## CHAPTER THIRTEEN

# KINDO MARANA

THE BIG ISLAND: THE THIRD MONTH IN THE FOURTH YEAR OF THE REIGN OF RIGHTEOUS FORCE.

Kindo Marana never dreamed that he would one day have to put away his abacus, wear a suit of armor, and strap a sword to his belt.

He preferred watching the emperor's treasury fill up with the money collected from all the Islands, not thinking about how to kill men in large numbers. He wanted to spend his time devising techniques for catching tax dodgers, not plotting strategy and examining casualty reports.

He had been a good student, showed a mind for figures, and worked his way diligently up the bureaucratic ladder. He enjoyed counting piles of coins and bushels of beans and bolts of cloth and jars of oil and bundles of dried fish and strings of shells and bags of rice and wheat and sorghum and sacks of wool and tins of fish scales. He found joy in classifying things, putting them in their rightful places, and checking their names off a list. He would have been happy doing that until he was old enough to retire.

But the regent was clear in his order. Somehow, a career bureaucrat who had never fought a single day in his life was now the Marshal of Xana, commander-in-chief of all of Xana's forces on land, at sea, and in the air.

Well, a servant's role was to discharge the duties of his post with diligence. He would begin with what he did best: an inventory of what he had to work with.

Nominally, Xana's forces on land numbered one hundred thousand. But just as Kindo Marana's yearly revenue projections for the treasury were never met, this number had to be discounted in several ways.

First, there was the matter of control. The only territories that the emperor still effectively held consisted of the Xana home islands of Dasu and Rui, Crescent Island in the northwest, Écofi Island in the southwest, and a butterfly-shaped slice of the middle of the Big Island, made up of the rich fields of Géfica and Géjira. The tall peaks of the Damu Mountains and the Shinané Mountains, and the broad expanse of the Liru River and the rapids of Sonaru River, for now, held the rebels at bay—and the deadly expanse of the Gonlogi Desert also helped.

Haan, in the northwest corner of the Big Island, was also still completely under Imperial occupation. But the garrisons of the other territories had either surrendered and joined the rebels or were sealed in their cities and cut off from his command. They couldn't be counted in the asset column of the ledger. The troops that he truly could command numbered only about ten thousand, consisting of the most loyal units around the Immaculate City.

Second, even in the areas that Xana still controlled, the situation was far from secure. The large number of prisoners and corvée laborers, forcefully conscripted from all over Dara to work on the Mausoleum and in the Grand Tunnels, could easily be turned into a rioting mob. They would welcome the rebels from their homelands as "liberators" if they should launch a coordinated attack on the Imperial heartland.

Third, the navy and the air force were in bad shape. The great airships were expensive to maintain and operate, as the lift gas leaked slowly but steadily from the silk gasbags, which had to be refilled periodically. Since there was only one source of lift gas in the whole world, scheduling the refill flights became a chore that many air force commanders avoided in peacetime. Except for the few airships that had accompanied Emperor Mapidéré on his constant tours, most of the Xana airships from the Unification Wars had been grounded for years. The navy was also barely a shell of its former self. Except for those patrolling for pirates in the north, the navy's ships had sat in docks for years, infested by shipworms and barely afloat. These were yet more liabilities.

Finally, morale was abysmal. Marana understood well how the way a man felt about something affected the way he went about doing it. Back when Xana was still only one Tiro state among seven, not an empire, the people of Xana had resented the way the other Islanders treated them as unsophisticated rubes, semi-barbaric poor cousins. When King Réon began his wars of conquest and the taxes had to be raised to support them, there was a palpable sense of purpose among the populace that Xana had to fight for its rightful place in Dara, and the people paid the tax collectors almost willingly. This changed quickly under the peace of the empire. And right now, that sense of hope and purpose belonged to the rebels of the Six States, while Xana soldiers were on the run, depressed, and uncertain about the justness of their cause.

Having tallied up the balance sheet, Marana methodically went about improving it. That was a task he was familiar with. During the later years of the Reign of One Bright Heaven, and especially now, the Reign of Righteous Force, the palace made many unreasonable demands of the Treasury. Yet, he had somehow always found ways to fulfill them.

He would begin by turning a liability into an asset. The corvée laborers could be impressed into the Imperial army, and the prisoners and slaves freed on condition that they distinguish themselves in battle. To train these men, the veterans of elite Xana units would be promoted into squad leaders, sergeants, fifty-chiefs, and hundred-chiefs in the new, expanded army. The inexperienced new conscripts would be organized and integrated in such a way that no squad would consist of too many soldiers with the same homeland. Thus divided, disciplined, and watched over by Xana veterans, they might yet prove effective at holding off an assault by the rebels on the Imperial heartland, at least temporarily. While debasing currency alone never solved a budget problem for the long term, it would work for a while.

But the real solution lay in Rui and Dasu, the Xana homeland. He would have to go back and raise up an army of dedicated believers in the cause of Xana and the empire.

Never mind the harshness of the empire's rules. Never mind that Xana's poor groaned under the Imperial yoke as loudly as the poor in other states. If he could inflame their love of country and manly pride, the fresh troops from Xana could and would reconquer the Six States one by one until Emperor Mapidéré's dream was complete again. It seemed a tall order, probably as challenging as his attempts to get the merchants and farmers of the empire to comply with the tax code—but he had done pretty well at that, hadn't he? Perhaps just as the tax code was a microcosm of all the policies that animated an empire, what he knew of administering the taxes was a microcosm of statecraft.

Maybe the regent had picked him for a reason.

Kindo Marana sighed. There was so much to do.

The Krima-Shigin Expeditionary Force met early success.

The Marshals Krima and Shigin decided to begin by clearing the southern shore of the Liru River of all remaining Xana garrisons. The Liru itself was patrolled by the Imperial navy, and crossing the wide river was not an option just yet.

City after city fell to the rebels, often after little fighting. The Imperial soldiers had no desire to resist and often simply opened the city doors, took off their uniforms, and tried to blend in with the civilian population as the rebels got close.

Krima and Shigin attributed the victories to their own genius and bravery. Who needed books of military strategy and tactics? These were simply more ways for the old nobles to make themselves sound important. The two of them, mere peasants, nonetheless made the fearsome Imperial soldiers run away at the mere sight of their banners.

The two newly minted dukes never ran drills or tried to assemble the troops into battle formations. What was the point? Theirs was an invincible army based on the righteous power and anger of the people!

They ignored all forms of discipline and the chain of command. Even uniforms were optional. Every rebel soldier dressed however he wished, and if a soldier really wanted a sign to prove his revolutionary zeal, he could tie a red bandanna around his head with the twin-raven insignia of Cocru. Everyone marched as fast or slow as he liked.

As for weapons, men could choose to wield swords taken from captured Imperial armories or stick with farm and kitchen implements if they felt more comfortable with them. There was no pay—except what soldiers could loot and take from civilians who were reported to have Imperial sympathies in conquered cities. The rebels laughed, joked, told stories, or even sat down to take a nap when they felt like it. When the Expeditionary Force approached a city, it was like a giant mob of peasants coming to market.

But woe to any unfortunate merchant, farmer, woodsman, or fisherman who was caught by the rebels in their sweeping march through northern Cocru. Goods, money, livestock, crops—the rebels took whatever they wanted. "We're requisitioning these for the liberation of Cocru," they would say to the owners. "You *do* want to do your part to bring down the tyranny of Xana and contribute to the glory of King Thufi, don't you?" Any owner not convinced by these eloquent arguments would soon be convinced by fists or worse.

The dazed victims were left on the ground, nursing their wounds and watching the dust kicked up by the mob-army fading into the distance. The country through which the rebel army traveled looked like a field picked clean by locusts.

"How are we different from bandits?" Ratho asked his brother. They each carried a sack laden with loot taken from the last merchant caravan they had passed on the road. "I don't feel like a liberator."

"Rat, don't worry about it," Dafiro said. He was richer than he had ever been. "Your job is not to ask why. Your job is to do what the marshals have told you to do. This has always been how wars are fought. Let wiser heads than ours philosophize about it and sort it out."

When Phin Zyndu heard about the exploits of the new Marshal and Vice Marshal of Cocru, he threw up his hands in disgust. "What is King Thufi thinking? We have been waiting for him to follow the proper ancient rites and come to Tunoa on an auspicious date and invest us with the leadership of Cocru's army, as was done in your grandfather's time. But he doesn't seem to understand what is expected of him."

"This will not end well, Uncle," Mata said. "We must cross over to the Big Island. If King Thufi will not come to us, then we must go to him. Cocru again needs the firm hand of the Zyndus, the real marshals of Cocru."

As the double-raven flags of Cocru and the chrysanthemum banners of the Zyndu Clan flapped in the cold breeze coming off the sea, eight hundred men lined up on shore in a tight phalanx. A fleet of fishing boats bobbed in the sea, waiting to take them to the Big Island.

Phin slowly paced before them, locking eyes with each soldier in turn.

"Thank you," Phin said. "*You're* the reason that Cocru lives again. I am honored to lead you."

A few soldiers began to chant. Soon, other voices joined in until eight hundred men were shouting as one.

"Zyndu! Zyndu! Zyndu!"

Phin nodded and smiled and tried to wipe away his tears.

Behind him, Mata leapt onto an anchor stone so that he towered even higher over the assembled men, and his voice rang out over their heads:

"You're the bravest men of Tunoa. Once we have stepped onto the boats, we won't come back until I take Emperor Erishi's head!"

"Zyndu! Zyndu! Zyndu!"

"And when we do come back," one of the soldiers shouted, "we'll all come back riding on tall horses and dressed in silk!"

All the men laughed, and Mata the loudest among them. Their laughter seemed to rise like a spear stabbing into the heart of the sky.

The men could feel the wind grow stronger and shift to the southeast, blowing toward the Big Island. Though it was only early spring, the wind felt as warm as the hot breath of smoldering Mount Kana.

"Lady Kana favors us," the men whispered among one another. "Mata is her champion."

The crater of Mount Kana in Cocru erupted and spewed forth thick plumes of smoke and fiery ash.

*Strange strategy, Kiji. You would match a tax collector against a true marshal?*

A strong gust of wind blew across the crater, and the dull lava within brightened.

*Looking down on Xana has never served you and your sister well.*

*I can't see how an abacus will prevail against the Doubt-Ender.*

*Don't forget that barbaric club with teeth. I know why you've chosen this bloodthirsty mortal bent on revenge.*

The glaciers of Mount Rapa, nearby, cracked and seemed to shift.

*Do enlighten us.*

*Because you think he is Fithowéo's type, and you hope you might draw the god of war onto your side with this ploy. If Fithowéo decides to make one side's blades stronger or another side's horses tire faster, he will technically not be in violation of our pact to not directly interfere.*

*And you picked your champion because you think you might get Lutho to help a fellow number cruncher. You're as transparent as those lakes on your mountain.*

*We'll just have to see who has offered the more tempting choice, won't we?*

Once they arrived on the Big Island, Phin Zyndu wanted to head for Çaruza right away.

But Mata had a different idea.

"I want to go see this Huno Krima myself," said Mata. "I don't know much about how to talk to kings and ambassadors, but I know how to talk with fighting men. Perhaps there is something that separates this man from his fellow commoners, and that is why King Thufi values him above us."

"I will wait with the eight hundred volunteers outside Çaruza until you're back," Phin said. "May the Twins speed your way." And when Mata was out of earshot, he sighed and shook his head. "You're wasting your time, child. Even a king cannot tell a diamond apart from a white topaz without a hard enough surface to test them against," he muttered.

And so Mata rode alone west through the broad plains and rolling hills of Cocru, following the path taken by the Krima-Shigin Expeditionary Force. He had always been too heavy and tall for most horses, and Phin had lacked the resources to train Mata in horsemanship during the time when he and Mata were living in exile from the family castle. For the young man, the long ride was an opportunity to practice. Purchased at great expense from the markets outside Çaruza, the horse he was on was of Xana stock, and so taller and stronger than most of Cocru's own breeds.

Mata found himself rather enjoying the company of horses. Horses had an inborn respect for authority, for fitting into the natural role meant for them in the scheme of things. As he rode farther and farther west, Mata thought of the complex dance between horse and rider, the coordination necessary to provide a smooth ride, as an analogue of the complex web of mutual duties and obligations between vassal and lord, between subject and king.

But even with the Xana horse's stronger and larger frame, Mata was just too heavy for it. After days of chasing after Krima and Shigin, the horse was exhausted despite Mata's attempts to care for it. Just outside of the city of Dimu, located at the mouth of the Liru River at the western shore of Cocru, the horse lurched and broke a leg, and Mata tumbled from its back. With great sorrow, he ended its life cleanly with Na-aroénna.

He blinked away the unexpected hot tears and reflected that he still had to find a suitable mount, just as he believed that Cocru still had to find her rightful marshal.

Back when Shigin had suggested that they find the heir to the Throne of Cocru to make the rebellion legitimate, it had sounded like a good idea, but now Krima wasn't so sure.

He and Shigin had been the ones to risk their necks to raise the banner against Xana. Theirs were the names that the soldiers recognized and followed, and they were the ones to chase the Imperial troops out of city after city. Yet it was that young man, that mere boy who had done nothing other than have the right father, who sat on the Throne of Cocru. He pointed here and there, said this and that, and Shigin and Krima had to *obey* him.

This did not seem right.

And the prophecy—well, the prophecy was indeed a trick that he and Shigin had cooked up, but Krima preferred to no longer think about it that way. Indeed, hadn't things mostly worked out the way the prophecy said they would? Weren't they winning? So, maybe it was the *gods* who decided to give him and Shigin the idea for the scroll in the first place. And maybe the gods had moved his hands and fingers and composed that message and rolled it up and pushed it into the belly of that fish. He was merely the gods' instrument.

Why shouldn't he think about it that way? Who knew for sure that the gods *didn't* work that way? Wasn't it all a mystery even to the wisest thinkers?

Shigin, always too shortsighted, made fun of him for these

thoughts. "You think my writing comes from the gods? Ha-ha, I cribbed it from a play I saw once."

But Krima now thought of the prophecy as something entirely external to himself, a true sign from the gods that he had been given. Shigin was the only one who might dispute that version of events. . . .

And the prophecy said that he would be king. King, not merely Duke of Napi, not merely Marshal of Cocru. King.

News that Huno Krima had declared himself King of West Cocru threw Çaruza into an uproar. Advisers to King Thufi demanded that the king immediately strip Krima of all his—imprudently granted—titles and send out a punitive force to seize the man and bring him back to face charges of treason.

"Bring him back?" King Thufi laughed bitterly. "How exactly do you propose I do this? Most of the army is in his hands, and his soldiers have followed him from day one. I can sort of see his point. He did all the work, so why should I get all the glory?"

The advisers turned silent.

"I should be glad that he has decided only to claim *West* Cocru, as opposed to the whole thing. There is no choice for me but to congratulate him."

"This sets a terrible precedent," the advisers murmured. "There is no such thing as 'West Cocru.'"

"Nothing we are doing right now has *any* precedent. Who could have seen that an empire would be quaking because two laborers decided that they had nothing more to lose?

"Why can't new Tiro states be created out of thin air? Many things in this world become real when enough people believe them to be real. Krima has declared that he is a king, and he has twenty thousand armed men who agree with him. As far as I can see, that is strong proof. Let us now do what we must and welcome him to the ranks of the Tiro kings."

A royal messenger was dispatched to congratulate King Huno on his coronation.

∽ ∾ ∽ ∾

"Just think, we knew the king back when he was just like us," Ratho said in wonder. "I was the one who cut open the fish with the scroll."

He gazed at King Huno sitting on his throne at the far end of the banquet hall—formerly the stable for the Xana cavalry here in Dimu, the great port city at the mouth of the Liru River.

The stable was the only building with the right shape and size for King Huno's purposes, though it was not exactly clean. So the surrendered Imperial soldiers had been put to work to make it ready for the coronation banquet. They had swept it and mopped it for three days, and the floor was sprinkled with water perfumed with sea rose to keep the dust down. All the windows were open to let in fresh air, despite the rain outside.

Yet, the odor of years of keeping horses in the place could be detected underneath the smells of sweaty bodies, cheap wine, and badly cooked food.

Tables from every restaurant in town had been requisitioned and hastily assembled into misshapen long banquet tables and then covered with crude tablecloths patched together from curtains and flags. It was dark in the hall with so many people squeezed in, so torches and candles were stuck into every nook and platform that could hold one. The mood was bright, warm, and festive, but not . . . regal.

"He was never like you and me," Dafiro said. "We don't dream of prophecies that would award us kingdoms. Actually, best you never mention that we were with him back when this whole thing started with that fish. I get the feeling that the king will not be interested in hearing much talk about his humble origins."

To ensure that the ceremony gained the favor of the gods, Huno Krima had rounded up all the masons and carpenters and sculptors and priests—dedicated to every god—in Dimu and ordered them to produce eight brand-new statues of the gods of Dara suitable for the coronation banquet in three days.

"Mar . . . er . . . Sire," the chief priest of Fithowéo in the city, bolder than the rest, had tried to object, "it's simply impossible to produce statues worthy of such an august purpose in so little time. The statue of Lord Fithowéo in my temple took ten craftsmen a full year's worth of work. It takes time to source the right materials; time to sketch a suitable likeness; time to rough cut, to carve, to smooth, to lay down gold foil, to paint; time to consecrate an auspicious day for the painting of the eyes and opening of the mouth. What you ask for is simply not possible."

Krima had looked at the priest contemptuously and spat on the ground. *I have made the emperor quake on his throne. I am an instrument of the gods. Who is this worm to speak to me of what is possible and what is not?*

"You say that ten men took a year to carve one statue. But I have given you more than one thousand men. Surely they can do in three days the same amount of work."

"By that logic," the priest had said, "if you have ten women, they will surely be able to produce a child for you in one month."

The insolent tone of the priest had sent Krima into an immediate rage. The priest was called a blasphemer—for he dared to claim that the work of gods could not be done quickly—and he was executed by having his belly sliced open publicly in front of the temple of Fithowéo so that all could see how tangled his entrails had become due to his obstinacy and internal blindness.

The other priests had all then assured King Huno that his logic was sound and pledged to work as hard as possible.

And so eight gigantic statues of the gods now lined the sides of the stable-turned-banquet-hall. Given the time pressure, the priests and workmen did not do work that they were proud of. The statue of Tututika, for instance, was made from stacked bundles of straw wrapped hastily with bolts of cloth. Pits in her skin were filled in with globs of plaster, and thick layers of garish paint were poured on with moplike brushes with little concern for refinement. The final result more resembled an oversized version of some farmer's attempt at creating a scarecrow than a solemn representation of the goddess of beauty.

The other gods looked, if possible, even worse. A hodgepodge of materials was used: stones and lumber left over from temple construction, broken bits of city walls, floating debris gathered off the Liru, stuffing from old winter coats—the desperate workmen had even forcibly removed a few nearby families and wrecked their houses to get more building material. All the statues had stiff poses designed more for ease of construction than appropriateness to character, and all the features were crude and patched over with glittering gold paint that was still wet to the touch.

The statue of Fithowéo was probably the worst of the bunch. After the old chief priest had been executed, the assistant priest decided that the safest thing to do was to break the old statue of Fithowéo in the temple into pieces and then carry the pieces here for reassembly. Never mind the sacrilege of such an act—the threat of further disembowelment had a way of making doctrines flexible. Transporting the pieces here, putting them back together, and patching over the seams with buckets of plaster and a new coat of paint had been a monumental undertaking and wasn't complete until the very last moment.

The men assigned to this task were lucky in that they were able to make use of a big packhorse. Captured by Krima and Shigin along with the rest of the occupants of the stable, this outsize equine specimen had been a wonder to the conquerors at first: Fully twice as long as the largest of Xana stallions and almost half again as tall, this gigantic, coal-black horse with flowing mane had seemed the mount of a great king, and Krima had claimed it for himself immediately.

But he soon found out why the horse had been kept in the darkest corner of the stable. Ornery and obstinate, the horse moved without grace and refused to obey orders. The Xana garrison commander explained that even the best horse-whisperers had been unable to do anything with the beast, for it was apparently too dumb to take to the reins properly. Unable to bear a rider safely, it was only useful for hauling heavy loads under constant whipping.

The disappointed Krima had assigned the dumb packhorse to help with the construction of the statues, and now it stood trembling and panting at the foot of the statue of Fithowéo, still trying to recover from a night and a morning of backbreaking labor. The human workers lying around it were in no better shape, trying to find safe places to doze off and stay out of the king's sight.

Now that King Thufi's congratulatory letter had silenced anyone who doubted the propriety of King Huno's claim, the captains and lieutenants got up in turn to toast the new king, who was already drunk—far beyond drunk. He could barely sit up on his makeshift throne—the mayor's old stuffed cushion painted in gold and set on four water barrels—and he simply touched the goblet to his lips and nodded each time someone toasted him again.

He was happy. Very happy.

No one seemed to notice anymore—or if they did, they said nothing—the absence of Duke Shigin.

Early on during the banquet, one of the king's lieutenants—one clearly about as smart as that big packhorse—had wondered aloud to his companions where Duke Shigin was on this festive occasion. His companions had pretended to not hear him and tried to cheer louder, but the man would not be dissuaded from his query.

The noise had drawn King Huno's attention, and he had glanced in the man's direction with a frown. In a minute, Huno's captain of the guards—a very clever man who seemed to always know what Huno wanted—had given the order. The foolish man's companions had instinctively ducked under the table, and the loudmouthed fool had found himself pierced through with a dozen arrows shot by the king's guards.

After that, Duke Shigin might as well have never existed, as far as the celebrants in the banquet hall were concerned.

Dafiro had the curious thought that he wasn't so much observing a king as looking at an actor playing the part of a king in a play. As boys, he and his brother had loved the shadow play troupes who toured the Islands with their colorful puppets, bright silk screens, and loud cymbals and trumpets. They would arrive at the brothers' home village in the afternoon and set up a little theater in the clearing in the middle of all the houses.

At dusk, the first spectators would arrive, having finished their work in the fields and eaten dinner, and the puppet troupe would put on a light comedy to keep the growing audience entertained. The players hid behind the elevated stage, and the roaring fire behind them cast colorful shadows of the articulated, intricate puppets against the screens, to the accompaniment of bawdy jokes punctuated by loud clashes of the cymbals.

And then, as night fell and most of the village gathered around the stage, the troupe would begin the main feature, usually a tragic old tale about star-crossed lovers, beautiful princesses and brave heroes, evil prime ministers and foolish old kings. The puppets would sing long, sweet, sad arias accompanied by the coconut lute and bamboo flute. Dafiro and Ratho often fell asleep, leaning against each other, as they listened to the haunting songs and watched the sky full of stars spinning slowly over their heads.

And in one of these plays, the one that Dafiro remembered now, a beggar had put on a whore's robes and a paper crown and pretended to be a king. He was ridiculous, and the villagers had howled with laughter as the puppet danced around the stage: a peacock, no, a rooster pretending to be a peacock.

After another flowery, barely literate speech cobbled together from clichés in history books, another captain sat down. He wiped his brow, happy that he hadn't inadvertently said anything to annoy the new king.

A new man stood up. Immediately, he drew the attention of everyone in the banquet hall: eight feet tall, a torso as thick as a wine barrel, and those eyes! Four dagger points glinted in the torchlight.

He stood there and did not lift up his cup to offer a toast, and the murmurs in the banquet hall ceased.

"Who . . . who are you?" demanded King Huno.

"I am Mata Zyndu," said the stranger. "I had come to study Huno Krima and Zopa Shigin, the heroes of the rebellion. But all I see is a monkey dressed up as a man. You're no different from any of the fools Mapidéré had elevated above their station. Neither Imperial fiat nor popular acclaim can make an ant into an elephant. A man can never fulfill a role he is not born for."

Deadly silence.

"You . . . you . . ." King Huno could not speak from rage. The captain of the guards whistled, and all the assembled guests around Mata ducked for cover. The guards pulled their bows full as the round moon. Mata flipped over the table in front of him so he could wield it as a shield, sending bowls and flagons and cups flying everywhere.

The great big packhorse by the statue of Fithowéo whinnied and leapt from where he was standing. As he leapt, his reins, still looped around the foot of the statue, broke. But the statue had not been on a secure foundation, and with a great groan, the statue of Fithowéo began to topple.

Everything seemed to slow down in the banquet hall. The arrows were let loose; the statue continued to fall; the horse arrived in front of Mata; Mata jumped onto the horse, whose height and stature seemed designed for his own; the statue crashed into the ground; the arrows thunked into the statue; dust and broken tables and dishes and cups exploded everywhere; men screamed.

And then Mata was gone from the banquet hall, riding on top of the all-black horse, whose movements were as fluid as wind, as sleek as water, as well matched to Mata's own as night is well matched to the lone wolf.

*I shall name you Réfiroa,* thought Mata as he rode back toward Çaruza. *The Well-Matched.* Wind whipped through his hair, and he had never felt such a sense of freedom or speed. He and the horse were parts of a greater whole.

*You're the mount I have been seeking, just as you have been seeking your rider. For too long we both languished in obscurity, away from our true roles on the world-stage. It is only when beings of true quality are matched to their stations that the world can prosper again.*

"That is what a real hero looks like," whispered Ratho to Dafiro.

For once, Dafiro had no wise comebacks.

*A dangerous precedent, Fithowéo, my brother.*

*Kiji, I've done nothing unusual. What mortal have I actively or directly harmed?*

*You shielded him with your statue—*

*To prevent harm is not the same as causing harm. Our agreement stands.*

*You argue like one of Lutho's paid litigators—*

*Leave me out of it, brothers and sisters. Though I do note that the distinction between acts of omission and commission has troubled philosophers for—*

*Enough! I will let this one go, Fithowéo. This one time.*

A week later, Duke Shigin's body was found floating in the moat outside the walls of Dimu. The king mourned the death of his friend publicly and loudly and cursed the drink that had caused Shigin to fall into the water and drown himself.

Everyone calibrated their grief by the king's. If King Huno cried for half a minute, no one dared to cry for longer. If the king never mentioned a certain name when he spoke of the discovery of the Prophecy of the Fish, then no one else was going to either. If the king reluctantly explained that he had worked hard to try to cover up for Duke Shigin due to their friendship even though the duke was always a bit cowardly and tended to exaggerate his own role in the rebellion—he was just a follower—and couldn't resist the drink . . . then the historians and scribes carefully edited their records to match the king's hints.

"Could you and I have remembered things so wrongly?" asked Ratho. "I could have sworn—"

Dafiro put his hand over his brother's mouth. "Shush, Little Brother. It's easy for men to be friends as close as brothers when they're poor and struggling, but much harder when things are going well. Friends are never as close as blood. Remember that, Rat."

And of course, no one ever, ever mentioned the faint red circle that had been found around the neck of Duke Shigin's corpse, which matched the impression made by a rope.

"You don't see anything wrong with this?" Mün Çakri asked gruffly, his eyes bulging from his round face. "You really don't see anything wrong with a King of West Cocru created out of thin air?"

Kuni Garu shrugged. "I am the Duke of Zudi by popular proclamation. How is that any more legitimate than his coronation by prophecy?"

"Once this is accepted, you're going to see kings and dukes springing up like mushrooms after the rain," Cogo Yelu said matter-of-factly. He shook his head. "We're all going to rue this day."

"Well, let them," Kuni said. "Getting a title is easy. It's keeping it that's hard."

While King Huno promoted many people, none of them were from the group of thirty corvée laborers who had started the rebellion with him. Indeed, after the death of Duke Shigin, none of the laborers would even admit to having been there with him. *Ah, the story of the fish. Yes, yes, it's a very good story. I heard it from someone else.*

King Huno slept more easily at night.

CHAPTER FOURTEEN

# KUNI, THE ADMINISTRATOR

ZUDI: THE THIRD MONTH IN THE FOURTH YEAR OF THE REIGN OF RIGHTEOUS FORCE.

Being the Duke of Zudi was probably the first job that Kuni Garu really enjoyed.

The only imperfection was that Jia's and his families still refused to have anything to do with him—they were sure that this victory was only temporary, and that the empire would be back at any moment.

"They know perfectly well how harsh Xana's laws are," Kuni fumed. "If the empire returns, they'll all be dead. Better go all in and bet everything on me."

But the elder Garu and Matiza hoped that Erishi would be more merciful than Mapidéré, and they thought it wiser to keep their distance from the doomed rebel and leave themselves some room to maneuver; Kuni obliged them by staying away. (Lu Matiza did manage to send word to Jia through friends that she was sure Gilo would come around, eventually, if Kuni continued to do well.)

But Naré Garu defied Kuni's father's wishes and came to visit him and Jia in secret a few times to give advice to the pregnant Jia and to cook Kuni his favorite meals.

"Ma, I'm a grown man now," Kuni said, as Naré insisted on filling his bowl with sweet taro rice.

"A grown man wouldn't give his mother so many heartaches," said Naré. "Just look at how many of my hairs have turned white because of you."

So Kuni kept on stuffing his mouth with sweet taro rice while Jia watched, smiling. He vowed to make his mother proud—like Jia, she was one of the only people in his life who never gave up on him.

He woke up with the sun, oversaw the morning drills of soldiers outside the city, came back for a quick brunch, and then reviewed civil and administrative matters until early afternoon—his time in the Zudi government came in handy, as he had good relations with the bureaucrats, his former colleagues, and he understood the importance of their unglamorous work. After a quick nap, he met with Zudi business leaders and elders from the countryside to hear their concerns. He invited them to stay for dinner and then reviewed more documents until it was time to go to bed.

"By the Twins, I've never seen you work so hard," Jia said. She stroked Kuni's hair and his back lovingly, as though she was petting a large, enthusiastic dog.

"Tell me about it," Kuni said. "I've cut my drinking down to only at mealtimes. I'm not sure this is healthy." He smacked his lips but refrained from looking around for a bottle. Jia wouldn't drink with him anymore, claiming that it wasn't safe given her very pregnant state. ("Surely a little drink wouldn't matter?" "Kuni, it wasn't easy for me to get pregnant; I'm not taking any chances.")

"Why do you have to meet with those old peasants?" Jia asked. "The mayor never bothered with them. So much of your work you impose on yourself."

Kuni's face turned grave. "People used to see me staggering around the streets, hollering and drunk with my friends. They thought I was a callow youth. Then they saw me go to work as a paid servant of the emperor, and they thought I was a boring bureaucrat with no ambition. But they were wrong.

"I used to think that peasants had little to say because they had no learning in their minds. I used to think that laborers were crude because they had no organ for fine feelings in their hearts. But I was wrong.

"As a jailer, I never got to understand my charges. But when I became a bandit, I spent a lot of time being close to the lowliest of the low: criminals, the enslaved, deserters, men who had nothing to lose. Contrary to what I had expected, I found that they had a hardscrabble beauty and grace. They were not mean in their nature, but made mean by the meanness of their rulers. The poor were willing to endure much, but the emperor had taken everything from them.

"These men have simple dreams: a plot of land, a few possessions, a warm house, conversation with friends, and a happy wife and healthy children. They remember the smallest acts of kindness and think me a good man because of a few exaggerated stories. They've raised me on their shoulders and called me duke, and I have a duty to help them get a little closer to their dreams."

Jia listened carefully and did not hear in Kuni's speech his habitual whimsy. She searched his eyes and saw in them the same sincere glint that she had seen when she asked him about his future years ago.

Her heart felt so full that she thought it might burst.

"Keep on working then." Her fingers lingered on his shoulder as she retired to sleep.

After Jia was gone, Kuni thought about sneaking out to share a few sips with Rin Coda at the Splendid Urn.

Rin had promised Kuni a great time if he came out tonight. "Widow Wasu has lined up some great entertainment for us. She's been telling people how you used to go there often and how she still has your ear. If you show up, you'll be doing an old friend a great favor."

Being the Duke of Zudi was very tiring work, and sitting in *mipa rari* all day long made his back ache. Kuni did yearn to go and be among his old friends, where he could lounge comfortably on the ground in *géüpa* without concern for his appearance, where he could say what was on his mind without worrying about every word being scrutinized, where he could be his old self, instead of being so *responsible*.

Yet he knew it to be an impossible wish. Like it or not, he was now the Duke of Zudi, no longer the gangster Kuni Garu. He could no longer be truly comfortable anywhere. Wherever he was, his new title was part of how people saw him.

The Widow Wasu wanted him there so that she could claim a bit of the magic of that title too and turn it into drunk customers and jangling copper pieces.

Rin was also happily running a business where he accepted people's money in exchange for "access" to the Duke of Zudi. And Wasu probably was one of his new clients.

Cogo Yelu disapproved of this whole business, but Rin answered him by quoting a Classical Ano proverb: "*Datralu gacruca ça crunpén ki fithéücadipu ki lodü ingro ça néficaü*. No fish can live in perfectly clear water."

Kuni agreed that it was important to keep some connections to the world of organized crime, and he also assured Cogo that he did not give the people who paid Rin any undeserved advantages.

But he had so much to do. The village elders he met earlier in the day had spoken of the need for repairs to the irrigation ditches. He wanted to review the bid budget from the masons Rin had recommended to be sure that it was fair. Maybe he'd just deal with a few more petitions. . . .

Before long he fell asleep at his desk, and a trail of saliva wet the paper under his face as he dreamed of sweet, hot bowls of sorghum ale.

"Lord Garu, we need to talk about our finances," Cogo Yelu said.

Kuni was both amused and annoyed whenever he heard his old

friends address him as "Lord Garu." Sure, he liked hearing it from former Imperial constables and soldiers who used to harass him and his friends, but it sounded wrong coming from someone like Cogo, who he always thought of as an older brother. There was no hint of joking in Cogo's tone, either. He was bowing slightly, his face turned to Garu's feet.

"Cut that 'Lord Garu' bit out, will you? We're old friends, but you're acting like a stranger."

"We *are* old friends," Cogo said. "But men have roles and masks that they wear, and these have a reality of their own. Authority is a delicate thing, and it must be carefully cultivated by proper ritual and action from the governing and the governed alike."

"Cogzy, I haven't even had a single drink yet today. It's much too early for your philosophy lessons."

Cogo sighed and smiled to himself. Kuni's lack of respect for conventions was both why he liked following Garu and was afraid of where it would all lead. He wanted to help the young man, who indeed seemed a fledgling eagle.

"Kuni, people won't take you seriously if they see your old friends treat you as an equal. It will confuse them. An actor playing a king on stage will make the audience believe that he really is king when all his fellow players behave as if he were king and follow the proprieties. But if one of the troupe winks at the audience, the illusion is broken. You're the Duke of Zudi now, and it's best if you make it clear that you are in charge, no matter who you're talking to."

Kuni nodded reluctantly. "All right, you can call me 'Lord Garu' in front of other people. But you are still Cogzy. I just can't call you 'Minister Yelu' and keep a straight face. Now don't object. You know how I get confused with new names."

Cogo shook his head but decided to let the matter drop. "The finances, Lord Garu."

"What about them?"

"The money we seized from the Imperial Treasury of Zudi has been exhausted. Much of it was sent to Çaruza when King Thufi called for funds for the Krima-Shigin Expeditionary Force. The remainder has been spent to pay the soldiers' wages and to, well, fund street parties and free food and clothes for the people of Zudi pursuant to your orders."

"And I'm guessing that you're about to tell me that the taxes aren't coming in fast enough."

"Lord Garu, your generosity is unmatched. You've abolished the multitude of heavy Imperial imposts, and the new taxes I drafted up at your request are quite fair and light. However, we have not been able to collect much on them. The businesses of Zudi are jittery. They aren't sure that the rebels will win, and if the empire comes back they think any taxes paid to you will be wasted. And so they are . . . dodging."

Kuni scratched his head. "The soldiers will have to be paid, of course, and I haven't forgotten your salary and everyone else who followed me through all the difficult times. I don't want to push the compliance issue too much, though—nothing gets people more riled up than overzealous tax collectors."

"Lord Garu is very wise. But I have a proposal."

"Let's hear it."

"We'll take the restaurant business as an example. The way bars and eateries have been able to avoid paying their full share is by keeping two sets of books. They might take in a hundred fifty silver pieces a night, but the books they show us contain only entries for fifty. We have to find a way to collect on the hidden entries."

"And how do you propose to do this?"

"I suggest that you announce the establishment of a new lottery game, to reward the lucky and free citizens of Zudi."

"I fail to see how this is related to the issue of tax dodging."

"It's linked, but only indirectly, as all money is fungible."

"That's your brilliant idea? We'll have to offer a huge prize for the lottery to get enough people interested. There's plenty of gambling parlors in the city already. How can we compete?"

"No, the lottery is only a cover for something better. You see, people won't be purchasing their lottery tickets directly. Instead, they'll get them only when shopping, as a kind of receipt. For each silver piece they spend, they obtain from the vendor a lottery ticket for free. The more they spend shopping, the more tickets they get."

"And where do the vendors get their tickets?"

"They have to purchase them from us."

Kuni thought about this. The scheme seemed preposterous, and yet . . . effective.

"Cogzy, you rascal!" Kuni slapped him on the back. "Under this scheme, the vendors won't be able to cook the books because their own customers will be hounding them for the right number of lottery tickets based on what they spend. And since the businesses have to buy the lottery tickets from us, they'll end up paying us fees in proportion to their real revenues."

"Just the way the taxes were supposed to work."

"You've just turned every customer in Zudi into a tax collector for us." Kuni imagined the look on Widow Wasu's face when she realized that she could no longer dodge his taxes and almost felt sorry. "Have you no shame?"

"I only learned from the best. When the lord is an honorable bandit, then the follower must come up with unconventional means to achieve his lord's goals."

Cogo and Kuni laughed together.

Kuni did not emulate the Krima-Shigin style of military preparation. The way his romantic notions of banditry had been dashed made him suspect that peasants swelled up by the momentary joy of having unexpectedly overthrown their Xana masters would be no match for trained Imperial troops. It was only a matter of time before the empire recovered from these stumbles and fought for real.

"Lord Garu!" Muru saluted smartly as Kuni showed up at the training grounds near the Zudi city gates.

Muru had turned out to be a decent swordsman, and by tying a shield to his left forearm, he could fight as well as any bandit in

Kuni's gang. Now that Kuni had taken over Zudi, Muru became the corporal in charge of one of the squads guarding its main gate.

Kuni waved for Muru to be at ease. He still felt guilty about what had happened to Muru, and having the corporal show such respect embarrassed him. "How's Phi?" he asked.

Muru lifted his chin in the direction of the training grounds. "He's in there, hard at work with Commander Çakri."

Kuni had to do what he could to turn former bandits and rioting citizens into some semblance of a real army. He began by assigning Mün Çakri to lead the soldiers in conditioning exercises.

He was stunned by the scene that greeted him now. A fence had been erected around a circular patch of ground about fifty feet in diameter. Inside, the earth had been doused with water to turn it into a mud pit. Five large pigs squealed and ran around, while ten men—every bit as muddy as the pigs—stumbled after them, struggling to pull their feet out of the thick mud with every step.

"What is going on here?" Kuni demanded.

"Seeing as I'm a butcher," Çakri said, puffing his chest out proudly, "my training methods may appear somewhat unconventional."

"This is *training*?"

"Wrestling pigs in mud will develop the men's agility and give them endurance, Lord Garu." As he surveyed the sweaty, mud-coated trainees and loudly squealing pigs, Çakri's bushy beard stuck out all around his mouth, like a hedgehog. "It will make them ready for the slick tricks of the Imperial pigs, too."

Kuni nodded and walked away before he broke down in laughter. He had to admit, Mün's madness did have its own logic.

The former stable master, Than Carucono, was put in charge of the cavalry—though this really meant fifty horses shared by two hundred men. "I need more horses." He began his habitual lament as soon as he saw the duke.

"And I need lots of things: more men, more money, more weapons and supplies, but you don't see me complaining about it. Than, you'll have to make do with what you've got."

"I need more horses," Than said stubbornly.

"I'm going to start avoiding you if you don't come up with a new theme."

For training in more formal tactics, siege craft, and infantry formations, he turned to Lieutenant Dosa, who had been the top-ranking Imperial officer of the garrison at Zudi. Dosa had surrendered after his men dropped their weapons before the rioting citizens of Zudi, and he seemed dedicated to the rebel cause. Kuni didn't exactly trust him, but he felt that he had no choice. No one else on Kuni's staff had gone to military school, after all.

Kuni sent his men on regular patrols of the surrounding countryside to clear it of bandits and highwaymen. By a combination of threats and promises, he recruited many of them into his own army—though Cogo and Rin had to persuade him to hang a few notorious leaders who had killed too often as examples. He might have plied the outlaw trade once, but that didn't prevent him from now becoming the bandit leaders' worst enemy. Again, it was simply a matter of economics: Merchants sold goods and made profits, which generated taxes, which paid for everything else the duke needed. And none of that would happen if bandits choked off the flow of commerce.

By the third month of the new year, merchants began to travel the roads to Zudi again, and the markets of the city once more bustled. The farmers outside the city also began spring planting. And even fish from the coast could once more be found in Zudi.

"For someone who has never been able to keep even a few prisoners in line, you're doing a pretty good job running the city," Jia said.

"I've just gotten started," Kuni boasted.

But he worried. Everything had been going well for him—too well. He felt sure that this was just a momentary lull before the dam broke. The empire was going to make its move soon.

CHAPTER FIFTEEN

# THE KING OF RIMA

A HAMLET, RUI AND NA THION, THE BIG ISLAND:
THE THIRD MONTH IN THE FOURTH YEAR OF
THE REIGN OF RIGHTEOUS FORCE.

Tanno Namen was old.

He had been a soldier all his life. Heeding the call to serve the homeland and to bring Kiji glory, he had begun his career as a lowly pikeman under General Kolu Tonyeti, the father of General Gotha Tonyeti. He had risen through the ranks steadily by dint of his bravery and unflinching dedication. By the time he finally retired as a general of the Xana Empire, he had spent more than fifty years on the battlefield.

Then, he had gone to the northern coast of Rui Island, to his home village, where he purchased a large estate next to the sea. He planted olives and wolfberries, and he kept a dog named Tozy, who had a limp and would fall asleep next to Namen as he dozed off on the patio overlooking the star-speckled sea at night.

Namen spent his days lolling about the turbulent waters of the Gaing Gulf in his tiny fishing boat. Sometimes, when the sea was calm, he would stay out for a few days and drift with the currents, sleeping in the shade of the sail when it was noon to keep cool, sipping rice wine when it was night to keep warm. When the mood struck him, he would stop, drop anchor, and take out his fishing rod.

He enjoyed catching marlin and sunfish. There was nothing like a meal of raw fresh fish.

Sometimes, on these long sails by himself, he would see the graceful dyrans leaping out of the ocean at sunrise, their scales shimmering like rainbows in the sun, the long, silky tails tracing out parallel arcs in front of his boat. He would always stand up, put his hand respectfully over his heart, and bow. Though he had slept with a sword by his side all his life and never married, he had a great deal of respect for the power of the feminine, symbolized by the dyran.

Namen's one great love in his life was Xana. He had fought for her and bled for her until she was elevated above all other Tiro states. He was sure that his fighting days were over.

"Look at me," Namen said. "My limbs are stiff and slow. My sword hand shakes when I try to raise it. I'm most of the way to the grave. Why have you come for me?"

"The regent"—Kindo Marana hesitated, being careful to select the right words—"has removed many generals he suspects of disloyalty. I cannot comment on what I think of these charges. But it has left me with few senior commanders with experience or skill. I need, indeed I'm desperate for, someone to help stem the tide of the advancing rebels."

"Younger men will have to stand up and be counted." Namen leaned down to stroke Tozy's back. "I have done my duty."

Marana looked at the old man and his dog. He sipped his tea. He calculated in his mind.

"The rebels say that Xana has grown indolent," Marana said, his tone contemplative and his voice low, as though he were speaking to himself. "They say that we have gotten used to lives of ease and forgotten how to fight."

Namen listened without showing any sign that he had heard.

"But some say that Xana has not changed at all. They say that the Unification happened only because the Six States were divided and weak, not that Xana was ever strong and brave. They ridicule tales of the bravery of General Tonyeti and General Yuma and call them exaggerations or mere propaganda."

Namen smashed his cup against the wall. "Ignorant fools!" Tozy's ears stood up as he turned to see what had angered his master so. "They are not fit to kiss the feet of Gotha Tonyeti, much less speak his name. There is more courage and honor in General Tonyeti's little toe than in a hundred Huno Krimas."

Marana continued to sip his tea, keeping his face impassive. Motivating a man was about finding the right tender spots to push until he couldn't wait to do what you wanted, just like defeating a tax dodger involved finding the one thing he cared about and squeezing it until he opened his purse and willingly, tearfully, offered up everything he owed.

"The rebels are really doing that well, then?" Namen asked, after he was calmer. "Reliable news is hard to come by."

"Oh yes. They may not look like much, but our garrisons run for the hills as soon as they see the dust thrown up by the rebel mobs over the horizon. The people of the Six States want the blood of Xana to flow, to satiate their hunger for vengeance. Emperor Mapidéré and Emperor Erishi have not ruled . . . with a gentle hand."

Namen sighed and unfolded his legs from *géüpa*. Holding on to the table, he stood up with some difficulty. Tozy came closer and leaned against his legs as he bent down to scratch the dog's back, but his spine ached and he had to stand back up.

He stretched his stiff back and ran a hand through his silvery hair. He could not imagine getting up on a horse again or swinging his sword with even one-tenth of his former strength.

But he was a Xana patriot through and through, and he realized now his fighting days were not over.

While Marana stayed on Rui to raise up an army of volunteers, young men yearning for adventure and willing to die to defend the spoils of Xana's conquests, Namen set sail for the Big Island. He would assume command of the defenses around Pan and see if the rebels had any weaknesses that could be exploited.

Along the northwest coast of the Big Island lay the former territory of Haan, curled around the shallow and cold Zathin Gulf and still firmly under Imperial occupation. The floor of the gulf was rich with clams, crabs, and lobsters, and seasonally, herds of seals came to feast.

Moving away from the coast, the land rose gently and turned into a dark forest. The Ring-Woods, ancient, primeval, roughly diamond-shaped, formed the heart of the resurrected Tiro state of Rima. Land-locked and sparsely populated, it was the smallest and weakest of the Seven States prior to the Unification. It seemed a bit of a paradox that Fithowéo, the god of war, weapons, the forge, and slaughter, chose his home here in ring-wooded Rima.

While the towering oaks of Rima formed the masts and hulls of many ships in the navies of the other states, Rima herself never had ambition for the seas. Indeed, her armies were famed for their ability to mine and tunnel deep under the camps of opposing forces and then blow them up with fireworks, an art that Rima craftsmen had perfected from working the rich veins in the Damu and Shinané Mountains.

An old folk song from Xana before the Conquest went something like this:

*Power abhors a vacuum, need demands complement.*
*Cocru and Faça draw their strength from solid land;*
*Deep miners of Rima wield fire in either hand.*
*With ships, Amu, Haan, and Gan rule the watery element,*
*But he who masters air, the empty realm,*
*Seizes the vantage point, holds the world's helm.*

The song purportedly explained why Xana, once it mastered the airships, achieved victory over all the other Tiro states. But in truth, the description of Rima in the song was a bit exaggerated. The fiery miners of Rima had indeed once been fearsome, but that was a long time ago, and they were only the last embers of a dying glory.

There was a time, long before the Xana Conquest, when Rima's heroes, wielding weapons made by the best bladesmiths in all of Dara, had dominated the Big Island. The Three Brother States of Haan, Rima, and Faça had made an alliance that combined Haan's sleek and advanced ships, Rima's superior weaponry, and Faça's rugged, terrain-defying infantry into an unstoppable force. And of the three, Rima's warriors had by far the most renown.

But that was when armies were small, steel was rare and expensive, and battles were waged by individual champions dueling mano a mano. Under such a system, Rima's small population was no disadvantage. Fueled by the wealth of her mines, the Rima kings could afford to train a few elite swordsmen and hold sway among the other Tiro states. And Fithowéo's favor for the domain was understandable.

But once the Tiro states began to field large armies, the prowess of the individual warrior became less important. A hundred soldiers fighting with brittle iron spears in formation could still bring down a champion clad in thick armor and wielding a sword of thousand-hammered steel. The martial prowess of someone like Dazu Zyndu was mainly symbolic, and even Dazu himself understood that battles were won and lost as a result of strategy, logistics, and numbers.

Under such a system, Rima's decline was inevitable. It became dominated by Faça, the far more populous state to its northeast, and its once illustrious past became merely a distant memory. The Rima kings turned for solace to ritual and ceremony, keeping alive a dream of greatness that was long dead.

Such was the Rima that had been conquered by Xana, and the Rima that was revived.

"Rima is hollow," the spies sent out by General Namen told him. "Faça troops drove away our garrisons and re-established Rima a few months ago. But Faça has recalled them to help in a dispute with Gan. Rima's own soldiers are untrained and the commanders full of fear. They can be easily bought with gold, women, and the promise of clemency from the emperor."

Namen nodded. Under cover of darkness, three thousand Imperial troops from Pan quietly ferried across the Miru River, marched stealthily around the tip of the Damu Mountains, and disappeared into the dark woods of Rima.

With the help of Faça's King Shilué, King Jizu, the grandson of the last King of Rima before the Unification, had reclaimed the throne in the ancient capital of Na Thion.

Young Jizu was bewildered by the change in his circumstances. He had been just a boy of sixteen trying to make a living as an oysterman on the shores of Zathin Gulf, and his biggest concern was winning the heart of Palu, the prettiest girl in the village.

And then soldiers of Faça came into his hut, knelt down before him, and told him that he was now the King of Rima. They draped a robe of silk woven with gold and silver threads over his shoulders, handed him an old cruben bone inlaid with coral and pearls by the jewelers in misty, salt-kissed Boama, and whisked him away from the sea and from the dark but lively eyes of Palu, eyes that said so much without making a sound.

So here he was in Na Thion, where the streets were paved with strips of sandalwood laid on a bed of crushed volcanic pumice, and the palace, built from the hard ironwood of Rima's mountains, seemed as foreign as a palace on the moon. On every street corner there seemed to be a shrine dedicated to one of Rima's ancient heroes, back when the name of Rima still inspired respect and fear on the battlefield.

"This is your ancestral home," men who called themselves his ministers said. "We watched your father grow up here. We watched him cry before the Double-Tree Gate as the rest of your family was cut down by Xana soldiers for refusing to surrender. Oh, how straight were their backs as they looked at their executioners with equanimity!"

The ministers refrained from criticizing his father, the crown prince. He had been the only member of the royal family to kneel down to the Xana general and to offer up the Seal of Rima. He had then been exiled to the shores of the Zathin Gulf, in old Haan, where he became a fisherman and brought up his boy to be an ordinary man, a man with no concerns other than hauling in a good day's catch and settling down with a good woman.

But Jizu could tell that the bowing ministers wished, perhaps without themselves being clearly aware of it, that his father had followed the example of the rest of his family and allowed himself to be killed rather than submit to the Xana conquerors. In their eyes, his father was not the quiet, thoughtful man that Jizu had known all his life, a man who enjoyed grilling oysters on hot stones, a man who only ever drank dandelion tea flavored with a bit of crushed rock sugar, a man who was so gentle that he never raised his voice.

"There is far more happiness in a life that is your own," his father had said to Jizu, "than a life in which you are handed the lines to say and shown the gestures to make. Do not ever be ambitious." His father had always been reluctant to speak of his former life in the Palace of Na Thion, a reticence that lasted until his death from a lingering sickness caused by an injury from the poisonous spines of sea urchins.

But in the eyes of the ministers, his father was a mere symbol, a symbol of Rima's humiliation.

Jizu wanted to tell them that his father was a good man, a man who decided that enough blood had been shed, that being king was not as important as being alive, as waking up every morning to see the sun dappling the waves and the dyrans leaping across the bow of a fishing boat. He wanted to defend his father's honor against the contempt that he saw in their faces.

But he said nothing as he listened to his ministers recount the haughty words of his grandfather, the last King of Rima, as he defied the Xana conquerers.

*Even when every last man of Rima has died, we will continue to fight you as spirits.*

*You have not seen the last of me. I will await you on the other side.*

The story seemed to him the account of a family that lived only in fairy tales and shadow plays.

He did as his ministers directed him to do. Knowing nothing of the rituals of kingship, he gave himself up to be their puppet. He followed their orders and then parroted back what they told him to say, as if he were the one giving the orders.

But he was not stupid. He could tell that King Shilué had helped him reclaim the throne not simply out of the goodness of his heart. Rima was weak and dependent on Faça. It served as a buffer between the Imperial heartland in Géfica and Faça itself. Should the new Tiro states successfully overthrow the empire, there would be a new contest for dominance, and King Shilué would enjoy an advantage in such a contest if he could run things in Na Thion by pulling on invisible strings attached to Jizu. Were his ministers really *his*? Or did they also listen to orders coming out of Faça? He could not tell.

He imagined a giant pair of scissors cutting the strings away. But who could wield such scissors? Not him.

He prayed for guidance from Fithowéo, but the god's statue in the temple simply stared back at him, giving him no signs. He was on his own.

He did not like this new life, but he felt compelled to accept it. He wished he could return to his days as an oysterman in love with another oysterman's daughter, but his royal blood made that dream impossible.

Three thousand Imperial soldiers slipped through the woods of Rima like ghosts. Rima commanders, fearful or paid off by Xana spies, dismissed reports from their scouts and refused to leave their oaken-walled fortresses to engage the invaders. Some soldiers, hardy woodsmen of Rima who believed that they were free of the emperor's cruelties forever, defied the treachery and cowardice of their commanders and fought on their own. They were cut down quickly by the Imperial army.

A week later, on a foggy, cold morning, the Imperial army emerged from the woods into the clearing around Na Thion and laid siege to the capital.

The defending soldiers soon exhausted their meager supply of arrows. Jizu's ministers ordered the houses of the common people disassembled so that shingles, beams, and broken pieces of building materials could be used as weapons to be hurled at the Xana soldiers trying to scale the walls. The people of Na Thion, their homes destroyed, slept in the streets and shivered at night in the chilly air of spring.

Messenger pigeons sent to seek aid from Faça went unanswered. Perhaps they were hunted down by trained falcons that the defecting Rima commanders had offered up to General Namen. Or perhaps King Shilué had decided that aid would be wasted because Faça's young army could not stand against General Namen and his battle-hardened veterans. In any event, no help would be forthcoming for Rima.

The ministers begged the king to consider surrender in the face of certain defeat.

"I thought you did not approve of my father's decision."

The ministers had no response to this. But a few snuck out of the city on their own and headed for the Xana camps. Their heads were sent back to Na Thion in sandalwood boxes.

General Namen's men shot arrows with letters wrapped around the shafts into Na Thion. Xana was not interested in the surrender of the city. An example had to be made to the other rebel Tiro states that insurrection would not be tolerated. Traitors to the empire must pay. Na Thion would be slaughtered to the last man, and all the women sold.

Their hope for mercy from Xana or salvation from Faça gone, the ministers became desperate. They now wanted the king to order the citizenry to resist to the utmost. Perhaps if they put up enough of a fight they could convince Namen to reconsider.

But Namen stopped attacking the city. He ordered his men to dam up the river flowing into Na Thion and to wait until starvation, thirst, and disease did his work for him.

"We are running out of water and food," King Jizu said, and licked his parched lips. He had given the order that the palace and all officials must follow the same rationing regimen imposed on the rest of the city. "We must think of a way to save the people."

"Your Majesty," one of the ministers declared, "you are the symbol of the will of the people of Rima. The people should be happy to die for you. The glorious expiration of their bodies will preserve the rectitude of their spirit."

"Perhaps we should order some of the citizenry to commit suicide to demonstrate their loyalty to Rima," another of the ministers suggested. "This will conserve supplies for the rest of us."

"Perhaps some of the women and children can be organized into a siege-breaking unit," yet another minister offered. "We can open the city gates and herd them to rush at the Imperial forces. The emperor's soldiers, faced with so many feminine and childish faces, may hesitate, unable to cut them down in cold blood. If they allow the women and children to escape, we can wear disguises and mingle into their number to reach safety. And if they do start killing the women and children, we can retreat and make another plan."

King Jizu could not believe what he was hearing. "Shameful! You have lectured me all these months about the honor of the House of Rima and the duties the king and the nobles owe to the people. But now you suggest the people of Rima make meaningless sacrifices to save your worthless lives. The people offer up their treasure and labor and maintain all of us in luxury with the single expectation that we will protect them in times of danger. Yet this one obligation you wish to shirk by sending women and children to die. You disgust me."

∽ ∾ ∽ ∾

King Jizu stood on the walls of Na Thion and asked to parley with General Namen.

"You care for the lives of the young men who fight for you, General."

Namen squinted up at the young boy, saying nothing.

"I can tell because you have not attacked Na Thion. You're unwilling to let even one soldier die if victory could be obtained another way."

The Xana soldiers looked at their general, who stood tall and kept his face still.

"The city is close to death now. I can give the order for a desperate counterattack. We will surely lose, yet some of your men will die, and your name will be despised among the people of the Six States for generations as a killer of women and children."

Namen's face twitched, but he continued to listen.

"Rima is poor in arms and men but rich in symbols. I am perhaps the best symbol of all, General. If you wish to make an example to the other rebelling Tiro states, it is enough that you have me. The people of Na Thion have resisted you only at my orders. If you spare them, you may win future battles with less resistance and less loss of life. But if you slaughter them, you will only make every city you attack in the future more determined to never surrender."

Finally, General Namen spoke.

"You may not have grown up in a palace, but you're worthy of the Throne of Rima."

The terms of the surrender were very clear. Jizu and all his ministers would pledge complete obeisance to Emperor Erishi and cease all resistance. In exchange, General Namen would not harm the population of Na Thion.

Jizu knew that Namen planned to take him back to Pan as a war captive. There, he would be paraded, naked, through the city's broad avenues, filled with jubilant citizens celebrating victory over a rebel king. More strings; more puppetry. Then, he might be executed in public after long torture, or he might be spared. It was up to the whims of Emperor Erishi.

It was now night. As the gates of Na Thion opened, King Jizu knelt in the middle of the road. He held up the Seal of Rima in one hand and a torch in the other. He looked very alone in that circle of light surrounded by darkness.

"Remember what you promised," he said to the approaching General Namen. "I have ceased all resistance and I am at your mercy. Do you agree that this is so?"

General Namen nodded.

Jizu looked to his ministers, kneeling on the two sides of the main street of Na Thion. They were dressed in their finest formal clothing, as if it were the day of his coronation. The bright colors and fabrics made a sharp contrast against the tattered rags on the commoners arrayed behind them, like the contrast between the calm dignity on the faces of the ministers—they were witnessing a ceremony, a matter of ritual and politics—and the fear and anger on the faces of the emaciated crowd.

The king laughed quietly. "And now, my loyal ministers, you'll get the symbol you wished for. I will await you on the other side."

He dropped the torch and lit himself on fire. His clothes had been doused with fragrant oil, and the flames quickly consumed his body and the Seal of Rima. He screamed and screamed, and all the men around, from both Xana and Rima, stood as if frozen in their places.

By the time they finally doused the flames, King Jizu was dead, and the Seal of Rima damaged beyond recognition.

"He hasn't lived up to his promise," one of Namen's lieutenants said. "We can't bring this charred body back to Pan as a trophy and parade it in triumph. Should we slaughter the city?"

General Namen shook his head. The smell of burned flesh nauseated him, and he felt very old and tired at that moment. He had liked Jizu's pale face, his curled hair and thin nose. He had admired the way the boy held his back straight, and the way he looked at him, the conqueror, with no fear in his calm gray eyes. He would have liked to sit and have a long talk with the young man, a man he thought very brave.

He wished again that Kindo Marana had not sought him out. He wished he were sitting in front of the fire in his house, his hand stroking a contented Tozy. But he loved Xana, and love required sacrifices.

*There are enough sacrifices for now.*

"He has lived up to a promise greater than the one he made to me. The people of Na Thion are safe from the sword of Xana today."

The densely packed people of Na Thion greeted his announcement with silence. Their eyes were focused on the kneeling ministers, now trembling like leaves in a breeze.

Namen sighed. *War is like a heavy wheel that spins with its own momentum.*

He continued in a toneless voice. "But load all of Jizu's ministers into prison carts; we'll bring them back to Pan and feed them to the emperor's menagerie."

And the crowd broke into wild, barbaric cheers; their dancing, pounding feet sent tremors through the ground under the feet of the Xana army.

CHAPTER SIXTEEN

# "YOUR MAJESTY"

DIMU: THE FOURTH MONTH IN THE FOURTH YEAR OF THE REIGN OF RIGHTEOUS FORCE.

At Dimu, where the great Liru emptied into the sea, the channel of the river was almost a mile wide. On the north side of the river mouth, across from Dimu, was the city of Dimushi, Dimu's younger, richer, more sophisticated sister. While ships departing from Dimu were laden with the produce of the farms of the Cocru heartland, Dimushi's docks were filled with ships carrying the thousand-hammered steel, lacquerware, and porcelain made by the skilled craftsmen of Géfica, part of the old Tiro state of Amu.

After the Unification, taxes, goods, and people from all over the Islands arrived at Dimu and Dimushi before sailing up the Liru to Pan, the glittering heart of the empire. On both shores, countless water mills churned, powering millstones and workshops that drove commerce along the watery highway. More money flowing through the mouth of the Liru meant more of everything, good and bad. Travelers to the twin cities said that if you wanted good food and honest merchants, you went to Dimu, but if you were in search of beautiful women and nights that never ended, you went to Dimushi.

These days, Dimu and Dimushi stared across at each other like two angry wolves across a ravine. Dimu was where King Huno set up his court, and his ten thousand rebels waited for the chance to cross the river and march on Pan. Dimushi was where Tanno Namen waited with ten thousand Imperial troops, looking for an opportunity to crush the rebels. The Liru itself was patrolled by the great ships of the Imperial navy, a moving wooden wall that separated the two sides. Once in a while, one of the ships would launch a flaming bucket of oil at Dimu, and as the men on shore scattered, cursing, the catapult operators on the ships laughed uproariously.

As the Imperial forces in Dimushi seemed content to do nothing except offer up a low level of constant harassment of the defenses at Dimu, Huno Krima decided to ignore them. After all, he was now King Huno, and he had more important matters to attend to.

Such as his new palace.

Huno Krima might not have known much about being king, but he held as an article of faith that a great king had to have a great palace. A Tiro state would not be properly respected unless it had a palace as grand as—no, grander than—those of the other Tiro states.

And so the soldiers of West Cocru spent their days not in drills, but in hauling wood and stacking brick, in digging foundations and shaping stone.

*Faster, higher, bigger!* King Huno berated his ministers and architects. *Why is the progress on the palace so slow?*

*Faster, faster, faster!* the ministers insisted to the captains and lieutenants, now acting as construction foremen. *You must make the men work harder.*

*Faster, faster, faster!* the foremen screamed at the soldiers, now pressed into service as laborers. And they were liberal with the use of whips and canes and other methods of amplifying their message.

Some of the soldiers began to wonder why they were "rebels" if what they were doing was pretty much the same as what they had been doing for Emperor Erishi at the Mausoleum or in the Grand Tunnels.

The soldiers' grumbling reached King Huno's ears.

The king thundered and raged at the ungrateful men, who refused to see the difference between laboring unwillingly for a tyrant like Emperor Erishi and fervently contributing to the glory of their liberator and their new country. The men who were whispering such things were clearly spies of the empire, here to sow the seeds of dissatisfaction and dissent and to spread lies and propaganda. They must be rooted out.

Trusted officers, led by the captain of the guards, were assigned by the king to form a special secret unit whose members would walk through the camps at night, listening for those who dared to speak against the honor of King Huno and West Cocru. They wore black kerchiefs tightly fastened by a knot in the back of the head as an addition to their uniforms, and those that the Black Caps accused of treason were never heard from again.

The more traitors the Black Caps caught, the more afraid King Huno became. It seemed that the empire had spies everywhere. He would stare for minutes at trembling ministers who had forgotten to properly address him as "Your Majesty." He would ask one man to spy on another, only to tell the other one an hour later to spy on the first. How could he be sure that the Black Caps themselves had not been infiltrated by Imperial spies too?

The solution was obvious. He gathered a few men that he especially trusted and gave them the authority to spy on the Black Caps. These men wrapped white kerchiefs knotted at the backs of their heads to signify their elevated level of trust. The first man they accused of treason was the former captain of the guards, leader of the Black Caps—the result disappointed King Huno, but he thought it made perfect sense. Just as a fish rots from the head down, corruption started at the top. Of course the captain of the guards would betray him.

So the Black Caps watched the people, while the White Caps watched the Black Caps. But who was going to watch the White

Caps? This troubled King Huno greatly. He thought and thought and came up with the Gray Caps.

Every solution seemed to create a new problem, and King Huno fell into despair.

During the nights, men began to run away from the camps in Dimu—first a trickle, and then, gradually, a flood.

"Maybe we should run away too, Rat," Dafiro whispered to his brother. He was careful to do this out of the hearing of anyone else. One could never be sure who was a Black Cap in disguise. "Before we are also called traitors."

But Ratho shook his head. He still remembered the thrill of the moment he plunged the knife into the Xana soldier, the first man that he ever killed. King Huno was the one who showed him that he could stand up like a man and take back the life that the empire was going to grind into dust with the same carelessness as the empire crushed stones for the foundation of the Mausoleum. King Huno promised that men like Ratho would be able to bring down the empire and avenge his mother and father.

Ratho would not forget that.

The camps at Dimu still had room for ten thousand men, but more than half the bunks were empty at night.

"Why is the palace still not done?" King Huno raged. "I told you to hurry. Hurry!"

None of the ministers dared to tell him that there were now not enough soldiers to maintain the construction schedule. Press gangs roamed the surrounding countryside, forcefully conscripting any men who still hadn't run away. Deserters who were caught were executed in front of those who remained to instill lessons in loyalty, but this seemed to only make the problem worse, not better.

Finally, even the sentries posted on the banks of the Liru had to be pulled back into the city to work on the construction of the palace, the only project the king cared about.

∾ ∾ ∾ ∾

"General, lookouts sent aloft in battle kites report counting smoke from cooking fires in front of only one out of every ten tents at dinnertime."

"It's time," General Namen said.

In the dead of the night, while King Huno's soldiers slept the sleep of exhaustion and fear, five thousand Imperial infantry silently floated across the Liru on shallow-bottomed transports, landing a few miles up the river. As they marched toward Dimu, the Imperial navy began to bombard the shore with an intensity never before seen by the defenders. The bright arcs traced out by the tumbling buckets of flaming oil were like meteors that lit up the sky, and in their flickering light, swarms of arrows screamed toward the camps where King Huno's last soldiers lay sleeping.

It was a rout, pure and simple. Half of West Cocru's soldiers died before they were even fully awake or had put on their armor. The other half tried to put up some resistance and found that they should have spent their days practicing with swords and bows, not chiseling stones and sawing lumber. But it was too late for regret.

King Huno grabbed his scepter and the smooth new jade Seal of West Cocru. He leapt into his carriage and screamed at his driver to hurry. They had to get out of Dimu right away and go back to Çaruza, where King Thufi would have to give him command of the rest of the rebel forces so that he could avenge this humiliating defeat.

*It's not fair,* he fumed. The righteous hatred that his men shared for Xana should have made them invincible. The only explanation was that his troops had been betrayed by cowards hidden within their ranks. He lost only because the Imperial general, that decrepit and crafty Namen, had too many dirty tricks and spies. He needed not only the Black Caps and the White Caps and the Gray Caps, but also caps of every hue of the rainbow.

"Faster, faster, *faster*!" he barked at his driver.

The driver was a man in his thirties. The tattoos on his face showed that he had been a convicted felon under the laws of Xana. Instead of whipping the horses as King Huno had expected, he let the horses trot along leisurely and turned around to face the king.

"My name is Théca Kimo, from the Tunoa Islands."

Huno looked at him blankly.

"I was one of the first to heed the call for rebellion in Napi, to join you and Duke Shigin," said Théca. "You and Zopa Shigin shared a drink with me that night, after we won."

"Do not speak of Shigin as though he were my equal—"

But Théca interrupted him. "My brother fell sick ten days ago, but his hundred-chief wouldn't let him rest because everyone had to work on your palace. He fainted in the noon heat, and a foreman whipped him until he died. Did you know about this?"

King Huno had no idea what this man was babbling about, but he caught another mistake in his manners. "You must say 'Your Majesty' when you speak to me. Now hurry up and get me out of here."

"I don't think so, *Your Majesty*," Kimo said. He yanked on the reins so that the carriage lurched to a sudden stop, tumbling King Huno out of his seat. Then with a swift stroke of his sword, Kimo severed Huno Krima's head from his shoulders.

"And now you can dream of a palace as grand as you like." Kimo released one of the horses from the carriage harness and jumped onto its back without a saddle. "But as for me, I'm going to follow a real hero."

He turned east and rode toward Çaruza, where Mata Zyndu, another son of Tunoa and already a legend, had ridden with Réfiroa.

*We concede this first round, Kiji. We've clearly underestimated both Marana and Namen.*

*That seems to be a pattern with you two and Fithowéo, always looking down on Xana.*

*Gloat all you want, brother, puff up like one of your airships. The one laughing the last will be the one laughing the loudest.*

"My heart is gladdened to see you," King Thufi said, as he welcomed Phin and Mata Zyndu at the gates of Çaruza. "Cocru desperately needs a true marshal."

## CHAPTER SEVENTEEN

# THE GATES OF ZUDI

ÇARUZA AND ZUDI: THE FOURTH MONTH IN THE FOURTH YEAR OF THE REIGN OF RIGHTEOUS FORCE.

Tanno Namen's surprise attack on Dimu marked the beginning of a grand Imperial sweep along the southern shore of the Liru River. Within weeks, most of the towns and cities that had surrendered to the Krima-Shigin Expeditionary Force were back under Imperial control, and the Imperial army began an inexorable march south for the reconquest of Cocru.

The Grand Council of War in Çaruza, convened by King Thufi of Cocru, had been debating for weeks without coming to a resolution.

King Thufi glanced around the meeting hall and saw that the ambassadors of Amu, Faça, Rima, and Gan, along with King Cosugi of Haan, were all present. Each man sat in formal *mipa rari* on mats in their respective Tiro colors on the thick and smooth straw paper floor, keeping their backs tall and straight while spreading their weight evenly between their knees and toes.

"We must begin by properly honoring the memory of King Jizu, the bravest monarch of the Islands of Dara," said the Rima ambassador. He dabbed at the corners of his eyes with his sleeves.

Everyone in the hall nodded in assent, and each rose in turn to offer an elaborate speech praising the brave life and even braver death of King Jizu. King Thufi glanced at the descending level in the water clock and tried to hide his impatience. It was doubtful if any of these men, including the Rima ambassador, could have picked King Jizu out of a group of beggars three weeks ago. But now they all acted as if they had known the man since he was a child.

The Faça ambassador gave the longest speech of all and emphasized again and again the "special relationship" between Faça and Rima. King Thufi tried so hard not to give in to the temptation to roll his eyes that he found himself suffering from a headache. The Faça ambassador finally sat down, an hour later.

"Thank you for the honor shown Rima today," the Rima ambassador said, his voice almost cracking. "I suppose I am now the head of the Rima government-in-exile," he added in a voice that was just loud enough to be heard by everyone in the meeting hall without being considered indecorous.

Just as King Thufi was about to raise the main issue he wanted the council to discuss, the Faça ambassador got up again. "We should also mourn King Huno of West Cocru. Though his manners might have been rough"—the ambassador winked at the ambassadors from Gan and Amu, who tittered—"he was nonetheless honored by King Thufi and elevated into the ranks of the great Tiro states."

*You might think Huno Krima was a country bumpkin, but without him, this rebellion wouldn't have even started. The least you could do is to honor the man's memory with some sincerity.*

But Thufi had to suppress his anger. There were more important things that he wanted to discuss, and he needed the cooperation of this idiot who spoke for Faça.

One by one, the others in the hall stood up again to offer disingenuous tributes to King Huno. Thankfully, their speeches were brief this time.

*Finally,* thought King Thufi. "My *tiro* Lords, we must discuss the urgent matter of Tanno Namen's invasion of Cocru—"

But King Cosugi interrupted him. "Thufi, if you would indulge an old man for a minute."

With great effort, King Thufi swallowed the rest of his speech and nodded at Cosugi to go on. He already knew what Cosugi was going to say. Though Haan wasn't even free of Imperial occupation, Cosugi was obsessed with preserving Haan's "territorial integrity." The man had one tune, and he sang it constantly.

Yet, he couldn't just tell Cosugi to shut up. All the Tiro states were, in theory, equals. So despite the fact that Haan had contributed absolutely nothing to the rebellion so far, Thufi had to let Cosugi have his say in the Grand Council.

"I've heard some distressing news that Faça's troops are taking advantage of Namen's focus on Cocru to occupy lands that by ancient and natural right belong to Rima and Haan," King Cosugi said.

"Your Majesty, I'm certain you're mistaken," the Faça ambassador said. "The maps given to the Faça commanders have been scrupulously examined to correct those old errors that might have mistakenly enlarged Haan at the expense of Faça. But you've reminded me of something else. I *do* need to lodge a protest with Gan. Gan ships have been harassing Faça fishermen around the Ogé Islands. Those islands have always belonged to Faça, not Gan, as I'm sure everyone here can attest."

"I don't think the Annals of Gan agree with you," said the ambassador of Gan. "Indeed, the illegal occupation of those islands by Faça occurred only because Gan had been too busy dealing with Xana more than a hundred years ago. And while we are talking about correcting old errors, I think it's high time for Cocru to finally do the honorable thing and return the Tunoas to Gan."

King Thufi rubbed his temples in a vain attempt to alleviate the sharp stabs of pain that threatened to break his skull.

"My *tiro* Lords," he finally said, and he almost had to spit out the honorific. "You seem to be operating under the impression that the empire is already history and that we're already back to the old days of the squabbling Seven States. But you're forgetting that the Imperial army is marching closer with each passing minute, and either we put aside our differences and stand together, or else we'll each again suffer the fate of Rima and fall under the yoke of Xana."

The ambassadors and King Cosugi were silent for a moment, but soon the meeting hall was again filled with their incessant bickering.

King Thufi rubbed his temples harder.

Phin Zyndu, listening in the corridors outside the meeting hall, shook his head and said nothing as he turned to leave. There was real work to be done, and he could no longer afford to waste time.

Since it was spring and the weather warm and pleasant, Kuni Garu decided to take Jia, Rin, Cogo, Mün, and Than on a picnic. All the reports said that Namen and the Imperial army were still miles away to the west, and a picnic would take people's minds off the anxiety of how to defend Zudi against an Imperial assault.

"I do *not* want to hear anything about needing more horses today," Kuni said as soon as Than Carucono arrived with horses for the party.

Than smiled. "Not a word."

They kept the pace slow for Jia's benefit. She was due any day now, but she enjoyed the fresh air and the hills full of wildflowers. From time to time she stopped and asked others to dig up interesting-looking herbs that she sniffed and then put away in her pouch.

Jia had also prepared a picnic lunch of fresh steamed pork buns (these she flavored with some of the new herbs she picked up on the way; "As fresh as they get," she said), bamboo shoots soaked with sugar and vinegar, crab cakes sprinkled with Dasu hot pepper, and bubbly wine taken from the collection of Lieutenant Dosa, the former commander of the Imperial garrison at Zudi who had rebelled and joined Kuni. Instead of using eating sticks, everyone just picked from the dishes with their hands.

"That was a good meal," Kuni said, and burped in satisfaction. The six of them were lying on the side of a sun-warmed hill, having eaten and drunk their fill, and tired from hunting hares and pheasants. They let the horses wander and graze at will. It was such a lovely day, and it would be a shame to go back to the city and do actual work.

Than got up to stretch and to make sure the horses didn't go too far. "Why are they flying white flags over the city?" he said.

The others lazily got up, shaded their eyes, and gazed at the walls of Zudi in the distance. Than was right. Instead of the red flags charged with black and white ravens, white flags now flapped over the city gates, and Kuni had the unpleasant suspicion that the bird on the flags was a Mingén falcon.

Suddenly sober and worried, Kuni and his retinue rode hard and rushed back to the gates of Zudi. Unsurprisingly, the gates were closed and locked.

"I'm sorry, Duke Garu." The man shouting from the top of the walls was a former Imperial.

"Where's Muru?" Kuni shouted. Muru was normally in charge of raising and lowering the gates.

"He wouldn't betray you and tried to fight, and Lieutenant Dosa had to kill him."

Kuni felt as if he had been punched hard in the gut. "Why are you doing this?"

"While you were out, Lieutenant Dosa asked the city elders to pledge allegiance to the emperor again. We hear that General Namen will spare any city that ejects the rebels and surrenders right away. But if we resist, the punishment will be harsh. I really like you, Duke Garu, and I think you're a fine prince. But I have a wife and a little girl, and I want to watch her grow up and get married."

For a moment, Kuni was racked by his old doubts. His face clouded over, and as his horse backed up, he almost fell off.

"Damn," he muttered. "Damn."

"You started with nothing," said Jia. "Why can't you start again?"

Kuni reached for Jia's hand and squeezed, hard.

When he looked up again, his face was filled with determination.

"It's all right," he shouted up at the walls. "Tell everyone that I understand their decision, even if I don't agree. But you haven't seen the last of Kuni Garu."

As the sun set in the west, six horses carrying six dejected riders stopped by a small stream to camp for the night. After some deliberation, Kuni decided that the most sensible course was to head for Çaruza and see if he could convince King Thufi to accept this "duke by proclamation" and lend him some troops to get Zudi back.

They cooked the hares and pheasants they had caught earlier on the open fire, but the dark mood around the fire contrasted sharply with the lighthearted festivities earlier in the day.

A tall man emerged from the woods next to the river and approached the group. Than and Mün were wary and lifted their hands to the hilts of their swords. The man smiled disarmingly, held up his empty hands, and walked slowly toward the fire. As he came closer, into the circle of light cast by the fire, they saw that he was lean and gaunt, and his skin was as black as the famed sands of Lutho Beach. His bright-green eyes sparkled in the flickering light.

"I am Luan Zya, a man of Haan. Would you be willing to share your food with a stranger? I would be happy to offer my wineskin."

Kuni stared at the stranger. This Luan Zya—something about his figure stirred his mind and recalled a memory from almost a dozen years ago: that day when he and Rin Coda had admired the Imperial Procession of Emperor Mapidéré just outside of Zudi.

"You are the kite rider," he blurted out. "You are the man who tried to kill the emperor."

## CHAPTER EIGHTEEN

# LUAN ZYA

GINPEN: BEFORE THE XANA CONQUEST.

In high-minded Haan, scholarship had been not just a luxury, but a way of life.

Before the Xana Conquest, in the countryside, next to the broad, reedy tidal flats and rocky beaches, countless learning huts used to sprout up like sand castles; the tutors in these huts, paid for by the state, instructed the children of the poor in reading, writing, and basic proficiency with numbers. More talented and wealthy students went to Ginpen, the capital and home to Dara's most renowned private academies. Many of Dara's greatest scholars spent their formative years within the lecture halls and laboratories of Ginpen's academies: Tan Féüji, the philosopher who elaborated governance into an art form; Lügo Crupo, regent of the empire and a peerless calligrapher; Gi Anji, who taught them both; Huzo Tuan, who defied death to criticize Mapidéré to his face; and many others.

In old Haan, a traveler could stop any farmer walking through the fields and have a conversation about politics, astronomy, agriculture, or meteorology and learn something. In Ginpen, even a common merchant's assistant clerk could calculate cube roots and fill out magic squares with no assistance. In teahouses and wine bars—though the food was plain and the drink merely passable—one could encounter the most brilliant minds of Dara debating matters of political and natural philosophy. Though Haan wasn't the most industrious of the Tiro states, her engineers and inventors created the most sought-after designs for water mills and windmills and made the most accurate water clocks.

But all this changed after the Conquest. Compared with other Tiro states, Mapidéré's book-burning and scholar-burying had dealt a harsher blow to Haan's spirit. The learning huts were no longer funded and fell into disuse; many of the private academics in Ginpen closed; and the few that survived were mere shadows of their former selves, where the scholars were afraid to give true answers and more afraid to ask real questions.

Every time Luan Zya thought of giving up his life's mission, he would remember the dead scholars, the burning books, and the empty lecture halls where accusations from ghostly voices seemed to echo without cease.

The Zyas had served the House of Haan since time immemorial. Just in the last five generations, the Zyas had produced three prime ministers, two generals, and five royal augurs at the Haan court.

Luan Zya was a brilliant boy. At five, he could recite from memory three hundred poems by Haan poets who composed in Classical Ano. At seven, he managed to perform a deed that stunned the Royal College of Augurs.

Divination was an ancient art in the Islands of Dara, but no Tiro state was more dedicated to its practice than scholarly Haan. After all, Haan was the favored land of the god Lutho, divine trickster, mathematician, and seer. The gods always spoke ambivalently, and sometimes they even changed their minds in the middle of your asking them a question. Divination was a matter of ascertaining the future through inherently unreliable methods.

To improve the accuracy of predictions, it was thus best to ask the same question multiple times and see what came out as the most common answer. For example, suppose the king wished to know whether the harvest and fishing this year would be more bountiful than last year. To answer the query, the College of Augurs would gather and formulate the question in prayers to Lutho.

Then they would take the dried shells of ten great sea turtles—the messengers of Lutho—and line them up on the black sands of Lutho Beach. Ten iron rods would be heated in a brazier full of hot coals fanned by a furnace, and when the rods were glowing red they would be taken out and pressed against the turtle shells until they cracked. The augurs would then gather and tabulate the directions of the cracks. If six shells cracked in a more-or-less east-west direction and four shells cracked in a more-or-less north-south direction, that meant that the year's harvest and fishing had a three-in-five chance of being better than last year's. This result could be refined further by measuring the precise angle each of the cracks formed relative to the cardinal directions.

For the augur, geometry and other branches of mathematics were important tools.

Luan's father was chief augur, and Luan observed his father's work with great interest as a child. One day, when he was seven, Luan accompanied his father to Lutho Beach, where the College of Augurs was to consult on the answer to an important question from the king. While his father and the other gray-bearded augurs did their work, Luan wandered away by himself and began to play a game of his own devising.

He drew a square in the sand and inscribed within it a circle. He closed his eyes and tossed pebbles in the general direction of the figure and then marked down on a piece of paper the number of times the pebbles managed to land inside the square and the number of times the pebbles also landed inside the circle.

His father came to get him after the ceremony was over.

"What game are you playing, Lu-*tika*?"

Luan replied that he was not playing a game at all. He was calculating the value of Lutho's Number, which is the ratio of a circle's circumference to its diameter.

The circle's area, Luan explained, was Lutho's Number times its radius squared. The square's area, on the other hand, was the square of twice the circle's radius, or four times the radius squared. So the ratio of the circle's area to the square's was equal to Lutho's Number divided by four.

If enough pebbles were thrown, the ratio of the number of pebbles that fell in the circle and the number of pebbles that fell in the square approximated the ratio of the figures' respective areas. Multiplying the ratio by four gave Luan an estimate of Lutho's Number itself. The more pebbles thrown, the more accurate the estimate.

And so, from chance, Luan derived certainty; from chaos, order; from randomness, a pattern that reached evermore for meaning, perfection, and beauty.

Luan's father was stunned by his precocious son. It was a sign of his intelligence, of course, but also of his piety. Surely the god Lutho watched over this one especially.

In the normal course of events, Luan Zya would have succeeded his father as the chief augur of Haan, and he would have devoted his life to numbers and figures, to calculations and theorems, to proofs and mystical conjectures, to the endlessly fascinating task of approximating the elusive will of the gods.

But then came Emperor Mapidéré.

The Zyas threw themselves into the defense of Haan. His father invented the Curved Mirrors that set aflame Xana ships sighted off the shore of Haan with nothing but the power of the sun. His grandfather designed crossbows augmented with firework rockets that brought down Xana airships that flew too low. Luan himself, merely twelve years old, came up with the idea of layering leather with fine mesh wire to create lighter, better shields that protected many Haan soldiers against Xana arrows.

But none of it ultimately mattered. Xana forces made costly but steady gains on the seas, over land, and in the air, until only the capital of Ginpen was left of Haan. Xana laid siege to it, wrapping it in ring after ring of determined Xana troops, like the women of Haan wrapped their bodies in layers of long silk cloth for the winter dances. Still, Ginpen had its own deep wells and full storehouses. King Cosugi planned to wait out the siege until the other Tiro states sent help.

But the court of Haan was corrupt and rotten from within. Education proved to be no match for avarice. A prince, seduced by the promise of Xana's support in his bid for the Throne of Haan, agreed to open the city gates in secret, and overnight Ginpen fell. King Cosugi surrendered, but not until the Xana invaders had made blood flow all over Ginpen, turning the black-sand-paved streets as red as blood corals, as fresh lava, as the western skies behind the setting sun.

Enraged by the successes of the ingenious military inventions of the Zya Clan, General Yuma, the conqueror of Ginpen, sent a detachment of troops specifically toward the Zya estate as the rest of his soldiers looted and slaughtered the city.

"Lu-*tika*," Luan's father whispered as he leaned down and touched his forehead to his son's. "Today the Zya Clan will give up many lives to show our loyalty toward Haan, our piety toward the gods, and our contempt for that tyrant, Réon. But for our deaths to be meaningful, a seed of the Zya Clan must be preserved and given a chance to grow. Do not return here until you have driven out the Xana invaders and restored the glory of Haan."

He called over a loyal old family servant and instructed him to make himself look like a Xana soldier.

"Put a servant girl's dress on Luan and take him away from here. In the chaos out in the streets, everyone will think that you are just another Xana invader with a captive. Get out of Ginpen and keep my son, the last of the Zyas, safe. Now go!"

Luan screamed and cried and begged to be allowed to die with his family as the servant dragged him through the streets. Other Xana soldiers saw a fellow soldier with a tearful, hysterical captive and ignored them. Later, the boy would realize what a great augur his father had been—he had picked a disguise where Luan's terror and loss of control would not give them away.

His father's trick worked, and the pair escaped to safety. But later, that night, in the rural countryside, Haan villagers who thought they were rescuing a captured young girl from a Xana brute killed the servant as they slept.

As the sun rose on the first day of Haan's long captivity, Luan found himself alone among strangers and miles from everything he had ever known.

None of the rest of the family survived the fall of Ginpen.

Luan grew up as the Six States fell, one by one.

Always running, hiding, staying out of sight of the emperor's numerous human bloodhounds, who were eager to sniff out those harboring treasonous thoughts, Luan vowed to avenge his family and the House of Haan. He pledged to fulfill his father's last wish. He swore he would carry out the will of Lutho, and restore balance to this upside-down world.

He was not a man who could lead a charge on the battlefield. He was not a man who could rouse a crowd with impassioned words. How would he fulfill his dream of vengeance?

He prayed fervently and tried, again and again, to ascertain the will of the gods.

"Lord Lutho, is it your will that Haan should rise again and Xana should fall? What must I do to accomplish your will?"

Every day, every hour, every waking moment, he asked the same questions and sought answers in signs.

What did it mean that the field of wildflowers he passed through had more Queen Naca's Lace than butter-and-eggs? Since the former were white and latter were yellow, the respective colors of Xana and Haan, did that signify that the gods favored the empire?

Or perhaps the key was in the shapes of the flowers: Whereas butter-and-eggs reminded one of the curving beak of a Mingén falcon, Kiji's *pawi,* delicate Queen Naca's Lace put one in mind of Lutho's fishing net. In that case, the gods must have meant to show their favor for Haan.

Or—and Luan had to stop in the middle of the road because he was thinking so hard—perhaps the answer was hidden within a mathematical puzzle. While it was easy to calculate the area of the petals that made up the flower of the butter-and-eggs, it was not at all clear how to determine the exact area of an umbel of Queen Naca's Lace. From a common center, the stalks branched and subbranched, like blood vessels dividing into capillaries, until they terminated in tiny white florets that were barely visible. Luan could already see that calculating the area of such a thing, made up more of holes and edges than solid presence, would be like computing the circumference of a snowflake. It required a new kind of mathematics, one that could account for the infinitesimal and fractal.

So was that a hint from the gods that the road to Haan's resurrection would be long and winding, requiring hard work to discover new paths that could surmount difficult odds?

For all his skill in divination, all that Luan could determine was that the gods refused to speak clearly, leaving the outcome in doubt.

Unable to find out how to proceed from the gods, Luan focused on matters in this world. His knowledge of mathematics was not limited to the realm of divination alone. He understood how to calculate force and resistance, tension and torque, how to combine levers and gears and inclined planes into intricate machines. Could such a machine, an engine, allow a lone assassin to succeed where the armies of the Six States had failed?

Alone, secreted in dark basements or abandoned storehouses, he plotted and replotted schemes for the death of Emperor Mapidéré. He carefully made contact with old Haan nobles, now scattered around the Islands, and tested their loyalty to the new regime. When he found a sympathetic soul, he demanded their help: money, letters of introduction, a place to let him build his secret workshop.

He settled on a daring plan. The Xana Conquest was largely symbolized by the great oar-propelled airships powered by the lift gas from Mount Kiji. So, in a gesture of poetic justice, he would bring death to Emperor Mapidéré from the air. Inspired by the great albatrosses and cliff-dwelling eagles found along Haan's bleak coastline, who stayed aloft for hours without flapping their wings, he designed a stringless battle kite that would take a rider and a few bombs aloft. He experimented with larger and larger prototypes in test flights in remote, uninhabited valleys and passes in the Wisoti Mountains along the border of old Cocro and Gan, out of sight of the emperor's spies.

Several times, after his prototypes had crashed and left him at the bottom of some valley, days from the nearest village or town, disoriented and nearly dead, bones broken and blood oozing from a dozen wounds, he wondered whether he was mad. He watched the stars spin slowly overhead, listened to wolves howl in the distance, and thought about the brevity of life compared to the eternal indifference of the natural world.

Could it be, he thought, that the gods always spoke so ambivalently and were so hard to understand because they experienced space and time at a different scale than mere mortals? For Rapa, rivers of ice that moved inches a year flowed as fast as torrential floods, and for Kana, lava thawed and froze as regularly as mountain streams. Lutho, the old turtle, had lived for a million millennia and would continue to live for millions more, and all the generations of men in the history of Dara would be gone in a few blinks of his leathery, salty-teared eyes.

The gods did not care who was sitting on the throne in Ginpen, he thought. The gods did not care who died and who lived. The gods did not have a stake in the affairs of men. It was foolish to think that one could divine their will. It was foolish to think that his vendetta against Emperor Mapidéré meant anything to them other than a balm for his aching, raging heart.

And then he blinked and realized that he was back in the world of men again, the world dominated by Xana, the world where so many were content to live with tyranny, the world where his promises were still unfulfilled.

He had a job to do. He bandaged his legs and closed his eyes to lie wearily until he could limp his way out of the valley, until he could fix the errors in his calculations and try again.

The attempt on the emperor's life from the Er-Mé Mountains, on the road north of Zudi, was the culmination of years of work.

The Porin Plains, basking in the steady sun, generated the rising air currents that could keep the stringless kite aloft.

He strapped himself in, checked everything one last time, and then launched himself over the Imperial Procession, a slow-flowing river of barbaric splendor in the flat expanse below.

And yet he had failed. His aim had been true, but the emperor's Captain of the Imperial Guards had been brave and quick-thinking, and he would never have such a chance again. He was now a wanted man, and throughout the empire they hunted for him, the man who came closer than anyone to assassinating Emperor Mapidéré.

Was it the will of the gods that had saved the emperor? Was it Kiji who had bested Lutho and thus preserved Xana? It was impossible to know what the gods wanted.

There was nowhere safe in the empire for him. All his old friends and the Haan nobles who had once helped him would not hesitate to turn him in now that sheltering him meant death for five generations.

He could think of only one place to go: Tan Adü, the remote southern island where the savage natives kept the Islanders away. Poised between a known terror and an unknown one, he chose to wager his life. After all, Lutho was also the god of gamblers.

He drifted onto the shores of Tan Adü in a raft, half-dead with thirst and hunger. As he crawled up the beach, out of the reach of the tides, he fell into a deep slumber. When he came to, he realized that he was enclosed in a circle made of pairs of feet. He looked up from the feet, up the legs, up the naked bodies, and stared into the eyes of the warriors of Tan Adü.

The Adüans were tall, lanky, and very muscular. They had brown skin like many men of Dara, but it was covered in intricate dark-blue tattoos. The ink patterns glowed with a rainbow sheen in the sunlight. Blond haired and blue eyed, they held spears whose tips seemed to Luan sharp as shark's teeth.

He fainted again.

The Adüans were rumored to be brutal cannibals who killed without mercy—this was the explanation for the failure of the various Tiro states, especially Amu and Cocru, to conquer Tan Adü over the years. The civilized people of Dara simply could not be as savage as the Adüans.

But they did not kill him and eat him, as Luan had feared. Instead, when he woke up, the Adüans were gone. They left him to fend for himself on the island, unmolested.

Luan built himself a hut on the beach, away from the Adüan village. He caught his own fish and cultivated his own taro patch. Nights, he sat in front of his hut and watched the flickering fires in the distant village, around which young men and women with lithe bodies and sweet voices sometimes danced and sang and at other times sat still to listen to old tales being told in new ways.

But he could not believe his good fortune. He was certain that he needed to prove that he was useful to the Adüans to justify their strange mercy. When he caught a particularly large fish or found a bush loaded with more juicy berries than he could eat, he would bring the excess to the village and leave an offering at the border.

Curious Adüan children began to visit his hut. At first, they acted as if they were approaching the lair of some dangerous animal, shrieking in laughter and running away if Luan showed signs that he had seen them. So he pretended to be oblivious until the children were so close that the pretense was no longer possible, at which point he would look up and smile at them, and a few of the boldest would smile back.

He found he was able to communicate with the children through a set of gestures and signs—it was impossible to feel self-conscious when faced with their open smiles and infectious laugh.

They made him understand that the villagers found him peculiar, with his habit of leaving them gifts.

He spread his hands open and put on an exaggerated look of confusion.

The children pulled at his clothes—now little more than rags—and made him come with them back to the village. There was a dance and a feast, and he was made to join in the eating and drinking as though he were already one of them.

In the morning, he moved into the village and built himself a new hut.

Only months later, after he had acquired some facility with their language, did he finally understand how strange his behavior had seemed.

"Why did you hold yourself apart," Kyzen, the chief's son, asked, "as though you were a stranger?"

"Wasn't I?"

"The sea is vast and the islands few and small. Before the power of the sea, all of us are helpless and naked like newborns. Anyone who drifts onto shore becomes a brother."

It was odd to hear such a note of compassion from a people reputed to be savage, but by then Luan Zya was finally ready to accept that he really knew nothing about the Adüans at all. So much received wisdom was not wisdom at all, just like so much of what men imagined as signs from the gods were only wishes in their heads. It was best to attend to the world of what *was*, rather than what he *had been told*.

The Adüans called him *Toru-noki*, which meant "long-legged crab."

"Why did you name me that?" he finally asked.

"That's what we thought you looked like, when you crawled up from the sea."

He laughed, and together they drank bowls full of strong, sweet arrack, fermented from coconuts and with a kick that made one see stars.

Luan Zya wanted to be happy living the rest of his life as an Adüan, never again having to concern himself with the mysterious signs of the gods or impossible promises he made as a boy.

He learned the secrets that the Adüans knew: to see the sun-dappled ocean not as a featureless expanse, but as a living realm criss-crossed with currents as neatly laid out as roads; to comprehend as well as imitate the calls of colorful birds, clever monkeys, and fierce wolves; to make useful implements out of everything one laid eyes on.

In return, he showed his friends how to predict eclipses of the sun and the moon, how to track the passage of the seasons with precision, how to divine the weather and estimate the coming year's taro harvest.

But his nights began to be filled with dark dreams that left him drenched in sweat. Old memories surfaced and refused to sink. The sight of burning books and the voices of dying scholars seized his mind. His heart yearned for the task he thought he had left behind.

"The aspen wishes to stand still," his friend Kyzen said as he saw the look in Luan Zya's eyes. "But the wind does not stop."

"Brother," Luan said, and then the two men stopped and drank arrack together, which was better than any sad speech.

And so, seven years after Luan Zya became *Toru-noki*, he said goodbye to his new people and left Tan Adü in a coconut raft headed for the Big Island.

Slowly, he made his way across the Big Island. It was true that after so many years, the hunt for him had slackened off. But he continued to live in disguise, wandering through the fishing towns of Zathin Gulf as a storyteller, biding his time.

The sights that greeted him depressed him. The empire had been able to get its fingers into every nook and cranny of life in old Haan. The people were now used to writing in the Xana way, dressing after the Imperial fashion, and imitating the accents of the conquerors.

It pained him to hear children mock his old Haan accent, as though he were the strange one. Young girls in teahouses played the coconut lute and sang the songs of old Haan, songs composed by court poets to celebrate the fragile beauty of a way of life: learning huts, stone-halled academies, men and women debating earnestly the methods of knowledge gathering. But the girls sang as though the songs were from another land, a mythical past, with no connection to them. Their laughter showed no understanding of the ache of losing their country.

Zya was lost. He didn't know what he was supposed to do.

One day, as he walked next to the beach outside of a small town in Haan, still enveloped in the fog of early morning, he saw an old fisherman sitting on the pier, dangling his feet over the water and fishing with a long bamboo rod. As he walked by, he saw that the old man's shoes fell from his feet and splashed into the sea below.

"Stop," the old man said to him. "Get down there and pick them up."

There was no *please,* no *would you*, no *could I ask you a favor*. Luan Zya, still a son of the noble Zya Clan, bristled at the old man's tone. But he forced himself to relax, and dove into the water, retrieving the old man's dirty, ragged shoes.

As he climbed onto the pier, the old man said, "Put them on my feet." His hazel eyes were impassive, staring out of a wrinkled face whose color was even blacker than Luan's own.

There was no *thank you*, no *I'm grateful*, no *sorry, but could you*. Luan was now curious rather than angry. He knelt down, still dripping with seawater, and put the shoes back on the old man's feet. The skin on his feet was calloused and full of cracks, Luan saw, and reminded Luan of the leathery skin of a turtle.

"You are not so arrogant as to be unteachable," the old fisherman said. He smiled and revealed two rows of crooked yellow teeth full of holes. "Come here first thing tomorrow morning, and I might have something for you."

Luan showed up at the pier the next day, before the first strike of the temple bells. The sun was barely up, but the old man was already sitting in his place, dangling his feet over the sea and fishing. He looked, Luan thought, not so much like a fisherman, but like a tutor in one of the old learning huts waiting for his pupils to show up at dawn to squeeze in an hour of study before the day's labor.

The old man did not look at Luan. "You are the youngster while I'm the elder. You are the student while I'm the teacher. How could you show up *after* me? Come back in a week, and do better."

During the week that followed, Luan thought several times of leaving the town—most likely, the old man was nothing but a fraud. But *what if* gnawed at him, and *hope* told him to stay. On the appointed day, Luan showed up at the pier before the sun had even risen. Yet there the old man was again, dangling his feet and fishing.

"You'll have to try harder. One last chance."

After another week, Luan decided to camp out at the pier the night before. He brought a blanket, but the chill night air from the sea made it impossible to sleep. He sat, shivering under the blanket, and again thought he ought to be put in a madhouse.

The old man showed up two hours before sunrise. "You made it," he said. "But why? Why are you here?"

Luan, cold, tired, and hungry, was about to give the crazy old man a piece of his mind. But he looked into the old man's eyes and saw that they glinted warmly in the starlight. They reminded him of his father's eyes, when he used to quiz Luan under a starry sky about the names of constellations and the paths of the planets.

"Because I don't know what I don't know," Luan said, and bowed deeply.

The old man nodded, satisfied.

He handed Luan a book, a very heavy one. While scrolls filled with wax logograms were used for poetry and song, books like this one, dense codices made from thin sheets of paper bound together, were packed with zyndari letters and numbers, suitable for note taking and the passing on of practical knowledge.

Luan flipped through it and saw that it was filled with equations and diagrams for ingenious machines and for new ways to understand the workings of the world—many of them elucidations and amplifications of ideas that he had already been aware of, but only dimly.

"Understanding nature is as close as men can get to understanding the gods," the old man said.

Luan tried to read a few pages and was overwhelmed by both the text's density and its elegance. He could spend a lifetime studying these pages.

Continuing to flip through the pages, he saw that the second half of the book was blank. He looked at the old man in confusion.

The old fisherman smiled, and mouthed, *Watch*.

Luan looked down and was astonished to see that figures and words began to appear on the formerly blank page. Logograms rose out of the paper as indistinct blobs but gradually gained sharp edges, smooth faces, and intricate details. They seemed solid enough, but when Luan tried to touch them, his fingers only moved through airy phantasms. The zyndari letters wriggled onto the page as faint traces, milled about and danced, and settled into tight, beautiful formations. Drawings began as blurred, black-and-white outlines and slowly became filled with vibrant colors.

The writing and illustrations took shape like islands rising out of the sea, like mirages gaining substance.

"The book grows as you grow," the old man said. "The more you learn, the more there is to learn. It is an aid to your mind, an extension of your capacity for seeing order in chaos, for invention. You shall never exhaust its knowledge, for it is replenished by your curiosity, and when the time is right, it will show you what you already know, but daren't yet think."

Luan knelt down. "Thank you, Teacher."

"I'm leaving now," said the old man. "If you should succeed in your task—your *true* task, not that which you now think is your task—meet me in the small courtyard behind the Great Temple to Lutho in Ginpen."

Luan did not dare to look up. He touched his forehead to the wooden slats of the pier as he listened to the footsteps of the old man moving away, like an old turtle shuffling down the beach.

"We care more than you know," the old man said, and then disappeared.

Because the magical tome given to him was without a title, Luan decided to call it *Gitré Üthu*, a Classical Ano phrase that meant "know thyself." It was a quote from Kon Fiji, the great Ano sage.

As Luan traveled around the Islands, he took notes on geography and local customs in *Gitré Üthu*. He sketched the giant windmills in fertile Géfica, which tamed the mighty Liru for irrigation; he bribed engineers in industrious Géjira to learn the secrets of the intricately geared water mills that powered the weaving and textile workshops; he compared the designs of the battle kites of the Seven States and elucidated their advantages and disadvantages; he spoke to glassmakers, blacksmiths, wheelwrights, clockmakers, and alchemists and wrote down everything he learned; he kept a diary of weather patterns, the movements of animals, fish, and birds, and the uses and virtues of plants; he constructed models based on the diagrams in the book and verified its teachings with experiments.

He wasn't sure what he was preparing for exactly, but he no longer felt purposeless. He understood now that the knowledge he was gathering would be put to use in some great task when the time was right.

Sometimes the gods did speak clearly.

## CHAPTER NINETEEN

# BROTHERS

ÇARUZA: THE FOURTH MONTH IN THE FOURTH YEAR OF THE REIGN OF RIGHTEOUS FORCE.

"I haven't thought about that day in a long time," Luan Zya said. His eyes focused far beyond the firelight.

"On that day, you showed me that one man *can* change the world," Kuni said. "There are no impossible odds."

Luan smiled. "I was young and rash. Even if I had succeeded, it wouldn't have done much good."

Kuni was taken aback. "Why do you say that?"

"When Mapidéré died, I felt a momentary panic. He was responsible for the deaths of my family, of my promising future, of Haan. I berated myself for losing forever the chance to exact vengeance.

"But then I saw how things only got worse as Emperor Erishi and the regent turned the empire into their playpen. Mapidéré was but one man—and indeed, judging by rumors of his decrepit state near death, a weak, sickly man—but his creation, the empire, had taken on a life of its own. Killing the emperor would not have been enough. We have to kill the empire.

"I'm on my way to Çaruza now to offer my services to King Cosugi. It's time to bring Haan back and carve up the carcass of the empire."

Kuni hesitated. "Yet, is it really better for us to go back to the days of the warring Tiro states? The empire was harsh, but sometimes I wonder if Krima and Shigin were any better for the ordinary people. There must be a better way than these two rotten choices."

Luan Zya appraised this strange young man. He had never met a rebel who so openly questioned their cause, and yet, he found himself liking Kuni Garu.

"I think the rebellion is only the beginning," Luan said. "It's like the start of a deer hunt: Many are in the field, brandishing their bows and spears, but as for who will bring down the stag, there is no way yet to know. How the hunt will end is up to all of us."

Kuni and Luan smiled at each other. They shared the roasted hares and pheasants, flavored to perfection by Jia's herbs, and drank the sweet arrack from Luan's wineskin.

They stayed up and talked long into the night, after the others were asleep, after the fire had died down to mere embers, after the awkwardness of new friendship had given way to familiar sincerity.

"It seems that good friends are always parting too quickly," Luan Zya said, and he clasped his hands together and raised them toward Kuni Garu in the traditional Haan formal gesture of farewell.

They were standing in front of the Second Wave, a comfortable but not ostentatious inn in Çaruza. Kuni had just gotten his retinue settled.

"I've learned much from you even after only talking for one night," Kuni said. "Again, you've shown me how large the world is, and how little I know of it."

"I have a feeling that before long, you will see more of it than I," Luan said. "Lord Garu, I believe you're a sleeping cruben about to waken."

"Is that a prophecy?"

Luan hesitated. "I'd call it a hunch."

Kuni laughed. "Ah, it's too bad you aren't saying this in front of my relations and friends. A lot of them still don't think I'll amount to much. But no, I don't think I want to be a cruben. I'd rather be a dandelion seed."

Luan was startled for a moment, but then slowly broke into a smile. "Forgive me, Lord Garu. I should have known better than to speak in a way that could be mistaken for flattery. You may not be born noble, but you have a noble mind."

Kuni blushed and bowed back. Then he lifted his eyes and grinned. "My friend, I want you to know that there is always a place for you at my table, no matter what happens in the future."

Luan Zya nodded solemnly. "Thank you, Lord Garu. But my heart is set on serving King Cosugi. I must go to him and fulfill my duty to Haan."

"Of course, I meant no disrespect. I only wish we could have met earlier."

King Thufi had no idea what to do with this "Duke of Zudi." There was no such traditional title or domain, and he didn't remember creating one. But with the same tact that he handled the news about the King of West Cocru, he graciously allowed this stocky young man, who looked more like a gangster than a duke, to introduce himself that way to everyone.

With the king's apparent acquiescence, Kuni Garu was amused to find that he now had to take his title more seriously. If even the king treated you as a duke, then you most definitely had to act like one.

"Your Majesty," he said. "I came here not only to pay my respects to you, but also to bring you important news. Tanno Namen's forces are coming south, and many of the cities taken by Krima and Shigin may flip back to Namen since he has a fearsome reputation. Indeed, Zudi itself has already done this."

*So you are a "duke" without anything to offer,* King Thufi thought. *A swindler, in essence. I like how you kept this bit of news to yourself till I'd introduced you.*

"I need troops to take back Zudi, and we should make a stand there to hold back the Imperial forces."

*Ah, a beggar and a bold one at that!*

"Matters concerning military strategy must be discussed with Marshal Zyndu," King Thufi said. He wanted to get this character out of his sight as soon as possible.

"Mata, I won't permit it. It's too much of a gamble," Phin Zyndu said. "If Théca Kimo's version of the fall of Dimu is to be believed, Namen comes well prepared. It's better to wait for him to come to us."

His nephew was about to argue some more, but the guards reported that Kuni Garu, Duke of Zudi, was here to see Marshal Zyndu.

"Who is this Duke of Zudi? Have you ever heard of the fief?" Phin asked Mata, and Mata shrugged.

Kuni came in and immediately sucked in his breath. Standing in the middle of the tent was the most amazing specimen of a human being he had ever seen. Mata Zyndu was over eight feet tall, and each of his arms seemed as thick as both of Kuni's thighs put together—and Kuni wasn't exactly *slender*, to put it mildly. Mata's long and thin eyes angled up at the outer corners like a dyran's body. And in each eye, there were two pupils.

But Kuni had spent so many hours in gambling parlors that he knew exactly how to put on his card-playing face. He clasped Mata by both arms, looked up into his eyes—he decided to just focus on the pupils closest to Mata's nose—and explained heartily how glad he was to finally meet the legendary Duke Phin Zyndu of Tunoa, Marshal of Cocru.

"That would be my uncle," Mata said, amused by the boldness of the small man. Well, Kuni Garu wasn't really small. He was of average height, just a bit under six feet tall, but everyone looked small in comparison to Mata. And that beer belly meant that he probably wasn't the most skilled fighter—a fault in Mata's view. But Mata did like the fact that Kuni didn't appear intimidated by his height or his unusual eyes.

Kuni showed no sign of embarrassment at his mistake. He turned to Phin Zyndu and continued without missing a beat. "Of course. I see the resemblance most clearly. I must congratulate you, Marshal Zyndu, on having such a wonderful successor. Cocru is lucky to have two such great warriors defending her."

The three sat down on plain mats on the floor. Kuni went straight into *géüpa* for comfort, crossing and folding his legs and settling his bottom on the floor. After a moment of hesitation, Phin and Mata followed suit. For some reason, Kuni's informal manners did not bother Mata. There was a warmth and enthusiasm radiating from Kuni that made Mata feel an instinctive respect for the man, even though he didn't behave at all like a noble.

Kuni quickly explained what he came for, and his plan for making a stand at Zudi.

Mata Zyndu and Phin Zyndu glanced at each other and both burst out laughing.

"Duke Garu, you won't believe this," Phin Zyndu said after he recovered. "Right before you came in, my nephew had been debating military strategy with me. My view was, and remains, that we should stay on this side of the Porin Plains, fortify our positions, and wait for Namen to come to us. We should be prepared to give up all the cities in north Cocru. By the time Namen reaches us, his supply lines will be overextended and his men exhausted. We'll have a better chance of crushing him."

"And my view is just the opposite," Mata said. "I think we should strike Namen right now. So far, he has met no meaningful resistance—that fool Krima had no idea what he was doing. He will be arrogant, and his men overly confident. If Uncle Phin and I take a company of our best troops and go meet Namen head on at one of the cities on the plains, we'll be able to defeat him before he gets very far into Cocru. The victory will give a much-needed boost to the confidence of the other rebels after the death of King Jizu."

"I think Zudi sounds perfect for what you have in mind," Kuni said, catching Mata's drift.

"As I said, it will be a gamble." Phin paused to do the calculation in his head. "You'll need at least five thousand men to stand a chance against Namen, which we can ill spare at this time. Should you fail to hold Zudi and lose the five thousand, you'll have greatly weakened our defenses here near Çaruza, perhaps enough to turn the tide of war."

"All life is a great game," Kuni said. "In war, there are no certainties. If you aren't willing to gamble, you'll never win."

Mata Zyndu nodded. Kuni said exactly what was on his mind.

"But there is a moral dimension as well," Kuni continued. "If you cede all of north Cocru to Namen, the people of all the cities of Porin Plains will suffer greatly under Xana reoccupation for having supported Krima and Shigin and King Thufi. If we abandon the people for the cold calculus of abstract strategy, we'll chill the people's hearts.

"They rose up under the banner of Krima and Shigin, and then of King Thufi, because of the promise that life will be better without the empire. Some of us have worked hard to make that vision come true, and I think we should try to do what we can to stop Namen from ripping that dream to shreds."

Phin thought over the situation. He had been worried that Mata was too hot-blooded to be given his own command. But this Kuni Garu seemed to have good sense and would complement Mata's courage and battlefield prowess.

He nodded. "I'm giving Mata five thousand men. You will go with him as co-commander. Don't let me down.

"Meanwhile, I'll continue to recruit and train here to build up our forces. The longer you can hold out against Namen, the more likely it is that I'll be able to come and lift the siege."

Jia decided to stay behind in Çaruza, in light of her condition. Phin Zyndu promised to look after her as though she were a daughter.

"Be careful," she said to Kuni, and tried to put on a brave face.

"No need to worry. I never take unnecessary risks—ahem, as long as I haven't been given certain herbs."

She laughed at this, and Kuni thought Jia looked especially beautiful with tears still not dried on her face, like a pear tree after rain.

His voice turned tender. "Besides, you'll soon have a Little Garu with you."

They held hands and said nothing for a long time, and they only let go of each other when the sun rose and the sound of men and horses mustering grew too loud to ignore. He kissed her hard, once, and then did not look back as he left the little hut that Jia was staying in.

The trip back to Zudi took much less time than the trip down to Çaruza. Five thousand horses could really move.

Kuni smiled at Than, riding next to him. "I'm hoping that I won't have to hear about needing more horses for a while."

But Than did not respond. His attention was entirely occupied by Réfiroa, Mata's otherworldly mount. He couldn't believe that such a horse existed, much less that it could be ridden. He longed to get to know the horse better when he got a chance.

As soon as the red banners of Cocru could be seen amidst the dust kicked up by the horses, the soldiers manning the walls of Zudi had a change of heart. Maybe General Namen would still win, but the Imperial army was still nowhere to be seen, whereas King Thufi's forces were right at the gates. Lieutenant Dosa was quickly arrested and tied up, and the flags flying over the walls switched to match the banners flapping over the horses coming up the road. (The soldiers on the wall, however, carefully folded and hid the white Imperial flags. One never knew if they might become handy again in a few days—*always be prepared*.)

Mata Zyndu was in full chain armor, with Na-aroénna, the Doubt-Ender, and Goremaw, its companion, on his back. Before they set out, Kuni had asked to see his unusual sword, but it was so heavy that he could barely lift it with both hands, and he stuck out his tongue and laughed at himself as he asked Mata to take it back.

"I could practice for a hundred years and not be one-tenth the warrior you are."

Mata had nodded at the compliment but said nothing. He could see that Kuni was sincere and not merely trying to curry his favor. *A man who willingly acknowledges his own weakness is strong in his own way.*

Mata's great black stallion, Réfiroa, dwarfed all the other horses just as Mata dwarfed their riders. He strained at the reins, impatient with having to keep pace with lesser horses. Kuni Garu, wearing a traveling tunic, rode next to Mata on an old white mare who had been a draft horse all her life—next to Réfiroa, she resembled a pony or a donkey. Her chief virtue was steadiness, as Kuni was no great horseman.

The odd couple rode side by side and led the Cocru army into Zudi. The Zudi garrison lined up at the gates to welcome them, acting as if they had not been flying Imperial colors just hours earlier. A few of the Zudi soldiers brought over Lieutenant Dosa, trussed up like a sheep bound for the market, and threw him at the feet of Mata and Kuni's horses.

Lieutenant Dosa closed his eyes, resigned to his fate.

"Is this the man who betrayed the Duke of Zudi?" Mata Zyndu asked. "I think we'll have him drawn and quartered. And then we'll send the bits to Namen as a welcome present."

Dosa shuddered.

"That might be an easy end for him," Kuni Garu said. "But General Zyndu, would you give me the pleasure of dealing with this man?"

"Of course," Mata said. "He insulted you, so it's only proper that you decide his punishment."

Kuni got off his horse and walked to the tied-up man.

"You really thought that we had no chance against Namen?"

"Why ask a question whose answer you already know?" Dosa's voice was bitter.

"And you figured that there was no point in wasting soldiers and people's lives."

Dosa nodded wearily.

"You didn't have much confidence in my ability to defend Zudi."

Dosa laughed. "You're nothing but a bandit and a gangster! You don't know the first thing about fighting a war!" There was no point in lying. He might as well let this idiot know what he really thought.

"I can see your point. If I were in your position, I might have done the same." Kuni knelt down and untied Dosa. "Since you were trying to save the lives of the people of Zudi, including the lives of my parents, brother, and in-laws, according to the teachings of Kon Fiji, it would be wrong for me to punish you harshly, even if you did betray me. But I assure you that we'll beat old man Namen and his Imperial thugs. As for your punishment, I'm leaving you in charge of the men who had followed you, so that you can now teach them faith and courage."

Dosa could hardly believe his ears. He looked at his freed arms. After a moment, he knelt before Kuni Garu and touched his forehead to the ground.

Mata Zyndu frowned. This was surely a mistake. The Duke of Zudi seemed to have a woman's mercy and little sense of discipline. To be so lenient to a traitor would only invite more betrayals in the future, but since he had already said that the man's fate was up to Kuni, he couldn't intervene.

He shook his head and decided not to worry about it for now. There was still much to be done. Namen's forces could arrive at any moment.

During the time Dosa was in charge of Zudi, he had left Kuni's and Jia's families alone. Kuni was grateful when he heard this and even more certain that he made the right decision to spare Dosa.

Kuni first went to visit Gilo Matiza, Jia's father. Gilo received him politely, but he was cold and distant, and Kuni understood that the man still didn't trust that Kuni's position was secure; he quickly left.

The reception at Féso Garu's house was rather different. Mata had come along with Kuni to pay his respects to the co-commander's parents.

Kuni ducked as a shoe was thrown at his head.

"How many more times do you want to put your mother and me in danger with your reckless ways?" Féso shouted from the doorway. Anger made his eyes round as plums, and his bushy white beard floated up like the whiskers of a carp as he labored to catch his breath. "I just wanted you to find a nice girl and settle down with a real job; instead, you've gone and made it so that the whole clan could lose our heads at any minute!"

Kuni ran away, wrapping his arm protectively around his head as another shoe sailed past.

"Kuni, I know you're trying to do the right thing," shouted Naré as she struggled to hold back Féso. "Stay away for a bit while I try to talk some sense into your father."

Mata was stunned by this display. Having grown up an orphan, he had always wondered what it might be like to have a father. The scene between Féso and Kuni was not something he ever imagined.

"Your father is not proud of your achievements?" asked Mata. "But you've become a duke! That's surely the highest honor in at least ten generations of Garus?"

"Honor is not everything, Mata," said Kuni as he nursed the spot on his shoulder where the first shoe had struck. "Sometimes parents just want their children to be safe and ordinary."

Mata shook his head, unable to understand such common sentiments.

In contrast to his relatives, Garu's old followers, those who had gone into the Er-Mé Mountains with him to become bandits and who had then come with him to Zudi to become rebels, were ecstatic to have Kuni back. During his absence, some had obeyed Dosa only reluctantly, while others resisted outright and had been imprisoned.

Otho Krin, the awkward youth who had brought Jia to Kuni in the mountains, was one of these. Kuni went to the city jail right away and unlocked the door to the dank cell himself. Otho blinked at the sudden appearance of light.

"I'm sorry for how much you've endured on my behalf," Kuni

said, and he helped Otho stand up from his straw mattress. Then he bowed down to Otho. Wiping the corners of his eyes with his sleeves, he added, "I'm ashamed that all of you who have followed me have suffered so much. I vow today that I will never consider this debt I owe you repaid until I have brought you, my brothers, all the riches and honor that you deserve."

All of his old followers who had come to the prison with him knelt and bowed back.

"Lord Garu, do not speak in this way! We cannot bear it!"

"We will follow you to the top of Mount Kiji and the bottom of the Tazu whirlpool!"

"We're blessed by the gods to have a generous lord like you, Lord Garu!"

Mata frowned at this breach in etiquette—he could not understand how a superior like Kuni could bow to a servant like Otho Krin, and now these lowly peasants were speaking in such foolish ways.

A momentary smile appeared on Cogo's face before fading away. No matter how many times he saw it, he was still amazed by how Kuni's sincerity shaded into an instinct for political theater. He was, of course, moved by the loyalty of a man who would rather be in jail than betray him, but he also knew to play it for all it was worth to cement even more loyalty.

"Is . . . Lady Jia here?" Otho asked, his voice trembling.

Kuni held him by the shoulders. "Thank you, Otho, for caring about her so much. Lady Jia remained behind in Çaruza because it's too dangerous for her to be here . . . in her condition."

"Oh," Otho said, and he could not hide his disappointment.

"Cheer up," Kuni said, and laughed. "Why don't you write to Lady Jia? You were friends in the Er-Mé Mountains, right? I'm sure she'll be glad to hear from you."

Kuni and Mata let it be known that any survivors from the Krima-Shigin Expeditionary Force were welcome to join them at Zudi. Small bands of straggling soldiers wandering the Cocru countryside after the fall of Dimu heeded the call, and soon the five thousand men at Zudi swelled to more than eight thousand.

"Rat, you really want to go back into the army?" Dafiro asked his brother. "We could just stay in the mountains and be bandits, and let the nobles fight their own war."

They were still a few miles from Zudi. The hill they stood on was the same hill that Kuni and his friends had picnicked on several days earlier.

The escape from Dimu had been a nightmare. Dafiro and Ratho fought as well as they could in the darkness and confusion of the rout. When it was clear that all was lost, they had hidden in the basement of a wealthy merchant's house and waited until the looting of Dimu was over before sneaking out by hiding in a cart hauling corpses away from the city for burial. They had both gotten very good at playing dead in the last few days.

"Ma and Pa would not want to see us as bandits," Ratho said stubbornly.

Dafiro sighed. His brother had fonder memories of their mother than he did. After their father died in the Grand Tunnels, the emperor's tax collectors had hounded the family to pay more taxes as "compensation" for depriving the emperor of the use of their father's labor. Driven by grief and despair, she had turned to alcohol as her only solace. Many times she broke Dafiro's heart as she tearfully apologized to him in the sober morning only to fall back into a drunken stupor by nightfall. Dafiro had tried his best to shield Rat from some of her worst drinking episodes.

All the boys had were each other now.

"I want to see Emperor Erishi and ask him why our pa never came back and why his men wouldn't just let Ma and us be. We weren't bothering anyone, just staying out of people's way and trying to make a living," Ratho said. His voice grew fainter as he swallowed, hard.

"All right," Dafiro said. He thought his brother very foolish, but also very brave. He wished he were as brave. "Let's go join the Duke of Zudi and General Zyndu."

"Hey, didn't we see General Zyndu once? I know! He was that mystery rider at King Huno's coronation—the one who made fun of the king and called him a monkey!"

Dafiro chuckled as the brothers remembered that day.

"Now *that* is a lord worth fighting for," said Ratho. "He was afraid of nothing, and when the king's men tried to shoot him, Fithowéo himself stepped in."

"Don't repeat foolish superstition," said Dafiro. The admiring tone in Ratho's voice made him feel a twinge of sorrow. Ratho had always only spoken that way about their father or Dafiro. Maybe Ratho was finally growing up, and he was going to get his own heroes.

After a pause to collect himself, Dafiro continued, "I hear that they are pretty fair and pay their men on time. At least we'll be fed and maybe we'll even get to see Emperor Erishi someday. But if anything goes wrong, you and I are running away. Only fools would die for these nobles. By the Twins, they wouldn't even blink if they could get a copper piece for our lives. So we have to watch out for ourselves. You hear me?"

CHAPTER TWENTY

# FORCES OF THE AIR

RUI: THE FIFTH MONTH IN THE FOURTH YEAR OF THE REIGN OF RIGHTEOUS FORCE.

Kindo Marana, like most in Xana, had great pride in the Imperial airships. But he never thought that one day he would have to become as familiar with their operation as the mechanics with hands full of calluses who maintained them at the Mount Kiji Air Base.

Mount Kiji, a snow-peaked giant stratovolcano that rose high into the sky, dominated the landscape of Rui. It had several craters, two of which were filled with lakes: Lake Arisuso, higher, bigger, evening-sky blue, and Lake Dako, lower, smaller, emerald green. Seen from on high, the two lakes were like two jewels worn against the pale-white bosom of proud Mount Kiji.

The mountain was home to the giant Mingén falcons. With a wingspan of about twenty feet, these fearsome and majestic raptors were bigger than any other predatory bird found on the Islands of Dara.

But what truly distinguished these birds was their extraordinary powers of flight. Not only were they able to stay aloft for days, circling slowly over one spot on the ground, but sometimes they took as their prey small cattle and sheep or even the lone shepherd. The feat seemed impossible, even considering their larger-than-average size.

For years, the amazing flight of the Mingén falcons was simply treated as an aspect of Kiji's power, but during the reign of Emperor Mapidéré's father, King Dézan, a few inquisitive men and women who were willing to commit sacrilege and risk their lives dissected some of the birds and finally discovered their secret.

Most Mingén falcons nested around the shores of pristine Lake Dako and fed their young on the meaty white icefish found in its waters. Lake Dako, however, had a peculiar feature. Streams of large bubbles constantly rose from its depths and broke on the surface. The gas in the bubbles did not smell sulfuric, could not be lit, and indeed had no taste or smell at all. No one had ever paid much attention to it.

But the gas turned out to be very special. It was lighter than air.

Within the body of each Mingén falcon was a network of large hollow sacs. These they filled with the strange gas of Lake Dako by dipping into the stream of bubbles, and just like a fish expanded and contracted its swim bladder to rise or sink in water, the Mingén falcons used these gas sacs to create buoyancy in air. This was the source of their marvelous lifting ability.

The brilliant Xana engineer Kino Ye derived the design of the great winged airships of Xana from the anatomy of the Mingén falcon. Although the graceful airships could not compete with sea vessels in carrying capacity for soldiers or goods, they were fast, mobile, and very valuable as intelligence-gathering vehicles. They also wreaked havoc with enemy navies: While ships could do little against threats from on high, a few airships could drop bombs filled with sticky burning tar and devastate an entire fleet.

Their most important military use, however, was psychological. The presence of airships intimidated opposing soldiers and told them that there was no escape as their every maneuver would be known by the Xana commanders.

∽ ∾ ∽ ∾

It took Marana a month just to get the air base at Mount Kiji restaffed and properly running again. The place was in bad shape: the bamboo pipes broken; the leather valves dry, brittle, and cracked; the docks and ships in disrepair. The old base administrator had been diverting the funds allocated for the base's maintenance into his own purse, though a small amount was saved to construct luxurious, recreational two-person airships for his friends and their mistresses.

But the administrator was well versed in the ways of being a good bureaucrat. He had been diligent in sending intricately carved model airships to Pan, much to the delight of Emperor Erishi, who loved to have courtiers and maids steer the ships by means of fans and blowing tubes as he ordered them to engage in pretend battles over the model empire. Pleased with his toys, the emperor had been effusive in his praise of the administrator to Chatelain Pira and Regent Crupo.

Marana immediately arrested the administrator, his friends, and their mistresses, stripped them naked, and brought them to the shores of Lake Dako. There, they were strung up in trees as offerings to the Mingén falcons. The baby chicks feasted well that day on corrupt flesh.

Worst of all, the former administrator had let most of the skilled engineers go. But the timely reconquest of northern Cocru generated the necessary funds for Marana to offer attractive wages.

Now the former chief tax collector walked through the base, examining the hulls of old airships undergoing repairs and new ships being constructed. He listened and nodded as engineers explained the hubbub of activity around him.

Giant hoops and longitudinal girders made of bamboo formed the semirigid skeleton of the airships. Within this frame, silk gasbags were hung. These would be filled with the lift gas collected from Lake Dako. The gasbags were also girded with a network of ropes that could be winched from the gondola so that their volume could be contracted or expanded to change the amount of lift—when the bags were compressed, the pressurized lift gas took up less volume, resulting in less buoyancy; when the bags were allowed to expand, the lift gas took up more volume, resulting in more buoyancy. The entire frame was then covered with a layer of lacquered cloth to provide protection from enemy arrows. Inside, along both sides of the airbags, were seats for the engine crew—mostly conscripted men little better than slaves—who would row the giant wings that propelled the airships through the sky. These wings were made from the molted feathers of the Mingén falcons, which were light, strong, and pushed hard against the air.

The gondola, built partly within the hull of the airship and protruding partly below it, was where the battle crew and officers lived and stored their munitions and supplies. The biggest airships had a complement of fifty, thirty in the engine crew and the rest with battle duties.

"How many ships would be ready for duty in a month?" Marana asked.

"We already have men working around the clock, Marshal. And we can't hurry the collection of the lift gas—it comes as it likes, the same as it has done for a thousand years. In a month, we should be able to prepare ten, maybe twelve, airships of the line."

Marana nodded. That might be enough. With the aid of the airships, the Imperial navy should be able to sweep through Arulugi and bring all of Amu back under Imperial control, and then, with its back secure, the empire could begin the assault on the rebel strongholds in the south of the Big Island.

CHAPTER TWENTY-ONE

# BEFORE THE STORM

ZUDI: THE SIXTH MONTH IN THE FOURTH YEAR
OF THE REIGN OF RIGHTEOUS FORCE.

"Another round?" Kuni asked. Before anyone could answer, he was already waving at the serving girls.

Mata groaned. He did not enjoy the bitter beer or the cheap, hard sorghum liquor they served here at the Splendid Urn: It was like drinking the stuff they used to strip paint from old houses. And the food was greasy and heavy, though necessary if one didn't want the liquor to burn a hole through the stomach. Sometimes the sight of everyone licking their sauce-coated fingers nauseated him—they didn't provide eating sticks here.

Growing up, Phin had kept him away from alcohol so that he could focus on his studies, and then he had been exposed only to the fine wines stored in the dry and cool cellar of the Zyndu Castle back in Tunoa. He longed for them now.

But he sighed and forgave Kuni's unrefined taste in drinks, like he forgave his informal manners and crude speech. After all, Kuni was not a noble by birth—Mata still could not wrap his head around the concept of "dukedom by acclamation"—but Mata put up with it all because being with Kuni was just . . . *fun*.

Since Jia was away in Çaruza, and by custom, the birth of a child could not be announced unless the baby survived for one hundred days, Kuni had heard nothing and was filled with anxiety. In order to not affect morale and to also take his own mind off the guilt of not being with her, Kuni held drinking parties every night, to which Mata was always invited.

At these gatherings, Kuni treated his subordinates more like friends, and Mata could tell that these men, Cogo Yelu the civil administrator, Rin Coda the personal secretary, Mün Çakri the infantry commander, Than Carucono the cavalry specialist, and even that flip-flopping Lieutenant Dosa, had great affection for Kuni. Theirs was a loyalty founded on more than duty.

They told dirty jokes and flirted with the pretty waitresses, and Mata, who had never in his life been to such parties, discovered that he enjoyed them. They were much more interesting than the stiff, formal receptions that the hereditary nobles back in Çaruza held, where everything was done properly and nothing impolite was ever said and each smile felt plastered on and each compliment disguised an insult and every word had to be parsed for a second and even third meaning. They had given him headaches and made him think that he was unfit for company, but among Kuni's friends, he wished the nights would never end.

And the man actually took the work of being the Duke of Zudi seriously—indeed, probably *too* seriously. Mata still couldn't believe how happily Kuni delved into the minutiae of governance. He even looked into how to *collect taxes*, by Kana and Rapa's lustrous hair!

Mata had never met anyone quite like Kuni, and he felt that it was a cosmic injustice that he wasn't born a noble. Compared to some of the hereditary nobles Mata knew, Kuni was far more worthy of admiration.

*Except that he's just a bit too forgiving sometimes,* Mata thought, eyeing Dosa critically.

But Kuni and he shared a vision of the big picture, of freeing the land from the yoke of Xana once and for all. *Kuni has greatness of spirit*, Mata decided. It wasn't poetic or eloquent, but that was the most sincere compliment Mata ever paid anyone, noble or common.

The girls brought over trays filled with flagons overflowing with more of that throat-burning liquor. Mata gingerly took a sip from his—alas, it was every bit as bad as he had remembered.

"Let's play a game," Than Carucono said. The others noisily assented. Drinking without games was like drinking alone.

"Shall we play Fool's Mirror?" Kuni suggested. He looked around the room and rested his eyes on a vase containing a bouquet. "I'll pick flowers as the theme."

This was a game popular among nobles and commoners alike. A category would be chosen—animals, plants, books, furniture—and everyone took turns comparing himself to an object from the chosen category. If the others judged the comparison apt, they would drink. If not, the player who made the comparison would drink.

Rin Coda chose to go first. He stood unsteadily, supporting himself by hugging a column.

"That's a stout girl you've got in your arms," Than said. "I prefer them with a bit less girth and more curves, myself."

Rin threw the chicken leg he was holding at Than. Than dodged out of the way, almost fell, and laughed.

"Friends," Rin announced seriously. "I am the night-blooming cereus."

"Why, because you get lucky only one night a year?"

Rin ignored the jab. "The cereus is not much to look at during the day, and most people think it's a just a dead-looking stick in the ground. But below the ground, it gathers the moisture and sweetness of the desert and hoards them into a large, juicy melon, which is delicious and has saved many a desert traveler's life. Only the fortunate can see it bloom, once a year in the middle of the night, a great white flower like a ghost lily bathed in starlight."

The others were momentarily stunned by this flowing disquisition.

Than broke the silence. "Did you pay a schoolteacher to write that speech?"

Rin threw another chicken leg at him.

"Your virtues are indeed hidden," Kuni said, smiling. "I know that you've done a lot to get the more—let's call them 'unorthodox businessmen'—of Zudi to cooperate with me and Mata in this time of crisis. Others may not always appreciate what you do, but know that I see and remember your efforts."

Rin waved at him nonchalantly, but everyone could see that he was moved.

"The comparison is apt," Kuni said, "I'll drink to it."

Next up was Mün Çakri, who immediately compared himself to the prickly cactus.

Everyone drank without debate.

"It's that beard, my good man Mün," said Than Carucono. "I really think if you tried to kiss anyone, you'd stab a dozen holes in their lips."

"That's absurd!" said a scowling Mün.

"Why do you think that young man over by the city gate tries to hide every time you go over with your presents? You ought to try shaving sometime."

Mün's face turned bright red. "I don't know what you're talking about."

"Half of Zudi can tell you like him," said Than. "I know you're a butcher, but do you have to look like it every moment?"

"Since when are you the sage of love?"

"All right," Kuni said, laughing. "Mün, why don't I make a formal introduction between this young man and you? Surely he wouldn't run away at the invitation of the duke?"

Mün's face remained flushed, but he nodded in thanks.

Cogo Yelu then compared himself to the calculating and patient snapping flytrap.

"No, no," Kuni said, shaking his head like a rattle. "I can't have you denigrate yourself that way. You're the stout bamboo that holds up Zudi's civil service—strong, flexible, yet with a heart that is hollowed of selfish thoughts. You have to drink."

Now it was Kuni Garu's turn. He stood up, grabbed Widow Wasu—who was passing by with a tray of drinks—around the waist, and while she laughed and ducked out of the way, he plucked a dandelion from behind her ear and held it up for everyone to see.

"Lord Garu, you compare yourself to a weed?" Cogo Yelu frowned.

"Not just any weed, Cogzy. A dandelion is a strong but misunderstood flower." Remembering his courtship with Jia, Kuni felt his eyes grow warm. "It cannot be defeated: Just when a gardener thinks he has won and eradicated it from his lawn, a rain would bring the yellow florets right back. Yet it's never arrogant: Its color and fragrance never overwhelm those of another. Immensely practical, its leaves are delicious and medicinal, while its roots loosen hard soils, so that it acts as a pioneer for other more delicate flowers. But best of all, it's a flower that lives in the soil but dreams of the skies. When its seeds take to the wind, it will go farther and see more than any pampered rose, tulip, or marigold."

"An exceedingly good comparison," Cogo said, and drained his cup. "My vision was too limited to not have understood it."

Mata nodded in agreement and drained his cup as well, suffering silently as the burning liquor numbed his throat.

"Your turn, General Zyndu," Than prompted.

Mata hesitated. He was not witty or quick on his feet, and he was never good at games like this. But he glanced down and saw the Zyndu coat of arms on his boots, and suddenly he knew what he should say.

He stood up. Though he had been drinking all night, he was steady as an oak. He began to clap his hands steadily to generate a beat, and sang to the tune of an old song of Tunoa:

*The ninth day in the ninth month of the year:*
*By the time I bloom, all others have died.*
*Cold winds rise in Pan's streets, wide and austere:*
*A tempest of gold, an aureal tide.*

*My glorious fragrance punctures the sky.*
*Bright-yellow armor surrounds every eye.*
*With disdainful pride, ten thousand swords spin*
*To secure the grace of kings, to cleanse sin.*
*A noble brotherhood, loyal and true.*
*Who would fear winter when wearing this hue?*

"The King of Flowers," Cogo Yelu said.

Mata nodded.

Kuni had been tapping his finger on the table to follow the beat. He stopped now, reluctantly, as if still savoring the music. "'By the time I bloom, all others have died.' Though lonely and spare, this is a grand and heroic sentiment, befitting the heir of the Marshal of Cocru. The song praises the chrysanthemum without ever mentioning the flower by name. It's beautiful."

"The Zyndus have always compared themselves to the chrysanthemum," Mata said.

Kuni bowed to Mata and drained his cup. The others followed suit.

"But, Kuni," said Mata, "you have not understood the song completely."

Kuni looked at him, confused.

"Who says it praises only the chrysanthemum? Does the dandelion not bloom in the same hue, my brother?"

Kuni laughed and clasped arms with Mata. "Brother! Together, who knows how far we will go?"

The eyes of both men glistened in the dim light of the Splendid Urn.

Mata thanked everyone and drank himself. For the first time in his life, he didn't feel alone in a crowd. He *belonged*—an unfamiliar but welcome sensation. It surprised him that he found it here, in this dark and sleazy bar, drinking cheap wine and eating bad food, among a group of people he would have considered peasants playing at being lords—like Krima and Shigin—just a few weeks ago.

CHAPTER TWENTY-TWO

# BATTLE OF ZUDI

ZUDI: THE SIXTH MONTH IN THE FOURTH YEAR OF THE REIGN OF RIGHTEOUS FORCE.

When Krima and Shigin began the rebellion in Napi, many did flock to join them, but many also decided to become robbers and highwaymen and make the best of the ensuing chaos. One of the most ruthless and feared robber gangs was led by Puma Yemu, a peasant who lost everything when the emperor's bureaucrats requisitioned his land to build an Imperial hunting resort without paying him a single copper piece.

Yemu's men preyed on the merchant caravans on the highways crossing the Porin Plains until the pickings became slim. Trade was dying and fewer and fewer merchants took to the roads. It was just too risky, what with the Imperials and the rebels marching back and forth and armed men defecting every which way and no one able to keep the roads safe. Yemu's gang had to go farther and farther to search for good targets, and then they discovered that trade was still going strong at the formerly sleepy town of Zudi.

Apparently the Duke of Zudi took his job seriously enough that he was keeping the area free of robbery, and all the bold merchants who still wanted to make a profit were taking their goods there. Just like wolves followed sheep to new oases in the desert, Yemu immediately took his gang and resettled in the Er-Mé Mountains.

He wasn't afraid of the Duke of Zudi. In his experience, the rebels were not as disciplined or well trained as the Imperials, and usually Yemu could defeat their commanders easily in single combat. Sometimes, a rebel detachment would even join his gang after he killed their leader. He was going to "tax" the stupid merchants going to Zudi as much as he could and live richly off the spoils.

It was afternoon, and Yemu's gang of thieves hid inside a copse near the top of a small hill.

They were watching a slow-moving caravan wind its way along the road south of Zudi. The carts moved so slowly that they were clearly weighed down by goods of great value. Yemu let out a great ululating cry that his men took up, and the gang rushed down the hill on their horses like a wind blowing across the plains, certain that they were going to be well rewarded.

The carts stopped. The drivers unhitched their horses, abandoned everything, and ran away as the robbers approached. Puma Yemu laughed. It was too easy being a robber in this age. Far too easy!

The abandoned carts sat still on the road, like a bunch of wild geese caught napping by the shore.

But just as the robbers reached the caravan and pulled up in the middle of the carts, the walls of the carts collapsed like folding paper screens, and soldiers in full armor spilled out.

While some began to fight the robbers on foot, the rest pulled the carts into a circle around the gang to cut off their avenues of escape. A few quick-witted robbers, sensing trouble, kicked their horses hard and escaped before the circle could be completed, but the rest, including Puma Yemu himself, were boxed in by the carts and trapped.

A gigantic man, with arms muscled like horse legs and shoulders broad as an ox's, strode into the center of the circle. Yemu looked into the giant's eyes and shuddered. Each eye had two pupils, and it was impossible to hold his gaze.

"Thief," the giant spoke solemnly, like a spirit-judge out of a nightmare. "You fell right into Duke Garu's trap." He unsheathed a sword as huge as himself from his back. "Meet Na-aroénna. There is no doubt your outlaw days are over."

*Well, we'll see about that,* Yemu thought. He was confident that he could win any fight. This giant might look impressive, but he also had the air of a high-born noble. Yemu had defeated plenty of arrogant but useless nobles before. They fancied themselves brave warriors but knew nothing about fighting dirty.

He kicked his horse and rushed at Mata Zyndu, raising his sword high overhead to cut the man down in one stroke.

Mata stayed still until the last minute, when he dodged aside quicker than Yemu believed was humanly possible. Mata reached out with his left hand and grabbed the reins of Yemu's horse. His right arm rose up to block Yemu's overhead strike with his big sword.

*Cliiiiinnnnng!*

Yemu found himself lying on the ground, the breath knocked out of him. Through the dazed fog and the ringing in his head, he could pick out only two thoughts.

First, somehow Mata had pulled the galloping horse to a standstill with his left arm alone, and he had managed this without even shifting his feet. While the horse had been stopped, Puma had kept on moving, tumbled over the horse's head, and flipped once in the air to land on his backside.

Second, Mata's right arm had effortlessly blocked Yemu's downward swing, despite the fact that Yemu was higher and that his blow had the combined strength of his arm and the momentum of his horse.

Yemu raised his right hand and saw that the part between the thumb and the forefinger was bloody. He couldn't feel his hand. The swords had clashed with such force that the fine bones in his right palm had been shattered and his sword had flown out of his hand.

He looked up, and there was his sword, still tumbling, high in the sky. It reached the apex of its flight, hung for a second, and dove straight down.

Yemu rolled without thinking, and the sword plunged into the ground right next to him, buried to the hilt, missing his leg by inches.

"I surrender," Yemu said, and there was indeed no doubt in his mind as he stared into Mata Zyndu's cold eyes.

Mata Zyndu wanted to hang Puma Yemu from a post over the city gates as a warning to other robbers who might think of Zudi as easy hunting grounds.

But Kuni Garu disagreed.

Mata looked at him askance. "Feeling compassionate again? He's a robber and murderer, brother."

"I was a robber once too," Kuni said. "That doesn't *automatically* mean he deserves to die."

Mata stared at Kuni, incredulous.

"Just for a brief while," Kuni said. He gave Mata an embarrassed smirk. "And we always tried to avoid hurting anyone. We even left the merchants enough money to get home. I had to pay my followers somehow, you know?"

Mata shook his head. "You really shouldn't have told me that. Now I'll always have this image in my head of you wearing prisoner's garb and banging on bars in a jail."

"Fine," Kuni said, laughing. "I think I'll refrain from telling you what I used to do for a living before I was a robber. But now we are getting far afield.

"My point is this: Yemu is a great horseman and a proven leader. He knows how to run and hide from a superior force and wait for the chance to strike. We have all these horses, so we can use him; as our scouts say: Namen is on his way."

∽ ∾ ∽ ∾

Namen's army poured over the Porin Plains like a hungry tide; bands of defeated rebels fled before it, crying for mercy. Many fell, and, in a moment, disappeared under trampling hooves and marching feet. As Kuni surveyed the cloud of dust on the horizon, glinting with occasional flashes from bright armor and unsheathed swords, his gut tightened and his mouth felt dry.

Kuni kept the gates of Zudi open for as long as he dared to allow more of the refugees to enter, but in the end, he had no choice but to order the doors shut before Namen's army were at the walls. His soldiers had to beat back the flood of refugees with swords and spears to close and bar the gates. More than a few broke down and cried as they listened to the screams and pleas on the other side of the wall.

"Lord Garu! They're using fire wagons on the gates!"

"Lord Garu! We've run out of arrows in the guard tower. They're about to breach the top of the walls!"

But Kuni stood as if frozen. The pleas of the refugees kept out of Zudi echoed in his head and would not leave. He thought of Hupé and Muru. Once again, men were dying because of his decisions; once again, he felt overwhelmed and did not know what was the right thing to do.

Zudi's soldiers, seeing the state of their lord, began to panic.

Namen's men had erected long ladders against the outside of the wall, and under cover of volleys of arrows from their archers, swordsmen climbed up. A few had already reached the top of the walls and were fighting with Zudi's defenders. The Zudi soldiers, who had never fought except in training exercises, swung their swords hesitantly and stumbled back before the ferocious assault of Xana veterans.

A Zudi soldier's arm was severed; he screamed as he fell down, trying to grab for his lost limb on the ground. The faces of the other defending soldiers around him drained of blood. Xana soldiers stepped forward and silenced the screaming soldier, and a few of the defenders dropped their weapons and turned to flee.

Soon, dozens more of Namen's soldiers joined their comrades. If they established a position on top of the walls and took the guard tower, they could open Zudi's gates, and all would be lost.

Mata Zyndu took the stairs to the top of the walls in a few great, long leaps. Na-aroénna in his right hand, Goremaw in his left, he plunged into the middle of the small group of Xana soldiers.

Goremaw smashed into a soldier's head, and brains and blood splattered everywhere. The Xana soldiers fell back, momentarily stunned. Mata opened his mouth and licked some of the gore from his club.

"Tastes the same as everyone else's blood," Mata said. "You're all mortal."

And then Na-aroénna spun like a chrysanthemum of slaughter, and Goremaw rose and fell like the beating heart of death. The blocking swords and shields of Xana soldiers broke or spun out of their hands, and in a moment, dozens of dead bodies lay around Mata Zyndu.

"Come," Mata said to the cowering soldiers of Zudi around him. "Is it not glorious to fight?"

And the Zudi soldiers, emboldened by this display, rallied around Mata Zyndu and hacked at the hooked tops of the ladders until they broke and they pushed the ladders away from the walls, delighting in the terrified cries of the Xana soldiers still on them.

Kuni looked at Mata, standing atop the walls like some arrogant hero of the Diaspora Wars, careless of the volleys of arrows that flew around him, and his heart was filled with admiration. Indeed, everyone was mortal in a terrifying world, but one could choose to live like Mata Zyndu and fight with no doubt, or cower in fear and indecision and let error compound on error.

He was the Duke of Zudi, and his city depended on him.

Kuni rushed up the stairs. Behind Mata, another Xana soldier was trying to climb onto the wall. Kuni pulled out his sword and rushed ahead, batting aside the blocking stroke from the soldier and plunging it deep into his neck. A crimson gush. Then Mata was beside him and helping him break the top of the ladder and pushing it away from the wall.

Kuni felt something warm on his face. He reached up, touched it, and looked at his fingers. Blood. From the first man he had killed.

"Taste it," said Mata.

Kuni did. Salty, thick, a bit bitter. With Mata next to him, he felt courage flow through his veins as though he had consumed a dozen of Jia's courage herb plugs.

"Lord Garu, the fire wagons have set the gates on fire!"

Kuni looked over and saw that hide-covered wagons were amassed at the base of the city gates. The covering prevented the defenders' arrows from reaching the men underneath, who had succeeded in setting the thick oaken doors aflame.

Inspired by Mata and Kuni's example, the defenders on the guard towers rallied and succeeded in destroying the wagons by dropping heavy stones, but the fire raged on.

"We should have prepared more water and sand," Dosa muttered.

Kuni cursed himself for lack of experience. He had been so focused on preparing for the siege by gathering food and weapons that he had neglected other basic preparations.

Namen's men pulled back from the foot of the walls. Everyone watched the rising smoke and the flickering tongues of the flames. Soon, the gates would crack and then break open.

"We should line up our troops in the square before the gates," said Mata. "Once the doors are gone, we'll fight them to the death in the streets."

Kuni shook his head. No matter how brave and fierce Mata was, he could not stand against ten thousand. He licked his lips. *Water, should have prepared buckets of water.*

"Come with me!" he shouted, and ran up to the guard tower above the flaming gates. He began to loosen the belt around his robes.

"What are you doing?" Mata asked, following close behind.

"Shield me," Kuni yelled. And he climbed onto the ramparts, turned around, squatted down, and began to urinate against the outside of the wall.

The other soldiers immediately got the idea. Some began to loosen their belts as well; others leaned out over the ramparts and raised shields to protect the squatting figures of their comrades. Namen's men, also catching on, loosed volleys of arrows at them. The thunking of arrow against shield sounded like a summer hailstorm.

Streams of urine flowed down the wall and dripped onto the burning gates. Flames hissed and clouds of steam rose.

"Come on, brother, you've got to contribute!" Kuni shouted at Mata, laughing. Then he coughed from the smoke and piss-smelling steam around him. "This will be a real pissing contest."

Mata didn't know whether he should laugh or get mad. This hardly seemed like the right way to fight a war.

"What, you can't go in front of other people?" Kuni asked. "Don't be shy. We're among friends here."

Mata sighed, climbed onto the ramparts, squatted behind another pair of raised shields, and let his bladder go.

For two weeks now, Tanno Namen had laid siege to Zudi with an army numbering more than ten thousand.

He had not anticipated the fierce resistance. The defenders of Zudi were unlike the ragtag mob that he had routed at Dimu. This Duke of Zudi, whom he had never heard of, and General Mata Zyndu, a grandson of the famous Cocru marshal Dazu Zyndu, seemed to know what they were doing. They had evidently stockpiled supplies before the siege and now waited patiently behind the walls, like turtles in their shells.

Namen would have preferred to leave Zudi and march on to Çaruza, where the rebel king was. But scouts he had sent aloft in battle kites informed him that Zudi was packed with soldiers, their flashing swords and battle banners filling the streets. They probably equaled his forces or even exceeded them. If Namen tried to bypass Zudi, they could attack him from behind on the way to Çaruza.

To his regret, Namen had brought little siege machinery, relying on his experience of the rebels abandoning the cities and running for the hills as soon as his army approached. The defenders of Zudi made quick work of the few ladders, fire wagons, and battering rams he did have. Now Namen was left without options for taking Zudi quickly: Mining would take a long time, and constructing ballistae and catapults on the deforested Porin Plains was impossible without transporting lumber from the Er-Mé Mountains.

Namen furrowed his brows. An extended siege seemed his only option, but he was confident that he would prevail. After all, he could resupply himself from the Imperial warehouses in Géfica, while the defenders didn't even have access to the surrounding countryside. No matter how much Zudi had in its storehouses, the food would eventually run out.

"Kuni, why are we making such a big deal over a few soldiers?" Mata asked.

Kuni had insisted on holding "victory banquets" every day in the markets of Zudi, where soldiers and civilians who had performed particular deeds of bravery the day before were feted. There was drinking, dancing, and platters of hearty roasted pork and fresh-baked flatbread.

"Everyone's jittery in a siege," said Kuni in a low voice. He stood up and made another toast, recounting the brave deeds of the soldiers being celebrated that day. His particular retelling added a lot of details that Mata deemed only semitrue, and the soldiers who were its subject blushed and laughed and shook their heads. But the crowd seemed to love it.

Kuni drank and sat down as the crowd cheered. He smiled, waved at them, and continued to whisper to Mata. "It's important that we keep the mood confident and optimistic. The public celebrations also show that we're not concerned about our supplies—important to prevent hoarding and profiteering."

"Seems to be a lot of effort aimed at keeping up appearances," Mata said. "Show, not substance."

"Show *is* substance," Kuni said. "Look, by having civilians dress up in paper armor and wave around wooden swords in the streets, we've been able to convince Namen's scouts that we have many more armed men here than we actually do. That's why he's still here instead of heading for Çaruza. Every day we keep him here is another day that the marshal can gather strength for the counterattack."

Mata had disapproved of Kuni's plans, thinking them more akin to theater than warfare, but he had to admit that the results of Kuni's tricks were desirable.

"How much longer can our provisions hold out?" Mata asked.

"We will probably need to start rationing soon," Kuni admitted. "Let's hope that Puma Yemu does his job."

Namen's plan for an extended siege wasn't working as well as he had hoped.

While Garu and Zyndu shut the doors of Zudi and refused to come out of the city to face the Imperial forces on the plains in front of the city, Namen found himself constantly harassed by bands of roaming bandits on horseback.

These bandits, or "noble raiders" as they preferred to style themselves, sabotaged the long Imperial supply lines leading from the Liru River. They followed no law of war and caused Namen no end of headaches.

Whenever Namen sent a platoon of cavalry after them, they simply ran away, taking advantage of their speed due to the lack of heavy armor. But whenever Namen's men rested, often in the middle of the night, the raiders would make a great deal of noise and feign attacks *without* actually attacking. They did this repeatedly to keep Namen's men from sleeping and exhausted their alertness.

After a few rounds of this wolf crying throughout the night, Namen's soldiers let down their guard and no longer responded with alacrity to new alarms. But that was when the raiders would *actually* attack. They rode through the camps like a tornado, setting everything on fire, cutting loose all the horses, and generally wreaking havoc and sowing confusion everywhere. But they wouldn't linger to fight. Their only aim was to loot from the carts loaded with food and provisions and spoil what they couldn't take by dousing it with excrement and poisoned water. They also made it a practice to ransack the treasury carts intended to pay the Imperial soldiers' wages.

An army marched on its stomach, and soldiers mutinied without pay. Namen became concerned about how much longer he could maintain such a large army in hostile territory. He had so far resisted forcefully taking supplies from the locals, believing it would make the pacification of reconquered Cocru difficult if the Imperial army imposed too much hardship on the peasants. But as his supplies dwindled, he worried that in a few more days he might have no choice.

Morale sank, and desertion became rampant. The platoons dispatched to chase the raiders down were always a step behind. And since the raiders took care to distribute some of their loot to the peasants in the surrounding areas, the result was that when Namen's men came to the villages to ferret out the raiders, not a single person would help the Imperials. When Namen's frustrated soldiers took out their anger on the recalcitrant villagers, they only managed to swell the ranks of the "noble raiders."

The raiders infuriated Namen. But he had to admit that whoever came up with this tactic was a worthy opponent.

"Hit-and-run tactics are the province of the weak." Mata had dismissed Kuni's proposal contemptuously at first. "True warriors do not resort to such dirty tricks. We must confront Namen on the open field and best him fairly and squarely."

Kuni had scratched his head. "But our job is to protect the people of Zudi. Despite your excellent training, we're outnumbered and our soldiers are too green compared to the Imperial veterans. Fact is, we *are* weak, as you put it, and I don't want our men to die needlessly. What's 'dirty' about winning?"

It took hours of persuasion, but in the end Kuni wore Mata down. Mata agreed to forgive Puma Yemu for his past acts of banditry—on condition that he convert his gang into auxiliary fighters for Cocru.

"Let's sweeten the pot a little bit," said Kuni.

"It's not enough that he gets to keep his life?"

"Yemu is like a proud donkey. We have to use both the stick and the carrot to motivate him."

Reluctantly, Mata wrote to King Thufi to recommend Yemu for the title of Marquess of Porin, with a hereditary march of his own to be specified by the king later.

So that was how Puma Yemu became the Marquess of Porin, Scourge of Xana, Commander of the Whirlwind Riders of Cocru.

"Meeting Kuni Garu was the best thing that ever happened to me," Puma declared to his followers as he generously divided the spoils of the noble raids among them. "Follow me closely, boys, and there'll be plenty more where that came from. Look at me, a marquess! A lord who knows how to wield men is ten times more fearsome than one who knows only how to wield a sword."

Namen decided that he had to put an end to the siege of Zudi before his army lost the will to fight. He studied reports of the two commanders of Zudi with care and came up with a plan. If he couldn't get the crafty Duke of Zudi to face him on the battlefield, he would try to provoke the young, hot-blooded Mata Zyndu into playing by his rules.

He began by launching battle kites over the walls of Zudi and dropping pamphlets filled with pictures depicting Kuni Garu and Mata Zyndu dressed in women's clothing and cowering in fear.

*Kuni Garu and Mata Zyndu are too scared to fight from within their boudoir,* the pamphlets declared. *Cocru is a nation of cowards with feminine hearts.*

The kite riders jeered and shouted more insults:

"Kuni Garu is the Duchess of Zudi, and Mata Zyndu is her servant girl."

"Kuni Garu loves to wear makeup! Mata Zyndu prefers perfume!"

"Kuni and Mata squeal in fright even at shadows!"

"Let them say what they want," Kuni said. He admired the pamphlets and laughed. "I look pretty good as a girl, though I think they are suggesting I lose a few pounds. I have to send some of these to Jia; she could probably use the laugh as I imagine the baby—may the Twins protect the child—is making her life very stressful."

"What is wrong with you?" Mata Zyndu roared and tore the pamphlet in his hands into pieces. He smashed the table in front of him; then, for good measure, smashed the table in front of Kuni as well. He stomped and ground the broken pieces of wood into even smaller pieces against the stone floor.

But his rage was not assuaged. Not even a little bit. He paced back and forth in front of Kuni, kicking the wooden splinters every which way. Servants scattered to distant corners of the room, away from the barrage.

"What is so bad about being compared to women?" Kuni said. "Half the world is made of women."

Mata glared at him. "Have you no sense of shame? Where is your honor? These insults cannot be borne."

Kuni didn't change his tone at all. If anything, he grew even calmer. "These cartoons are very amateurish. I could show Namen many more tricks about how to insult people artfully. For example, the drawings could have been made much more subtle and also much more lewd."

*"What?"* Every part of Mata's body shook with rage.

"Brother, please calm down. This is a good sign. Namen is clearly frustrated that we're not going out there to meet his superior force on the open field. We are dug in, well provisioned, and he's jumping around like a dog trying to deal with a hedgehog, having nowhere to bite. Puma Yemu is straining his supplies, and he's getting desperate. That's why he's using this trick to try to get you to fight on his terms."

"It's working, though," Mata said. "I *have* to fight him. I can't stay cooped up like this. If you do nothing, I will order the city gates open and lead a cavalry charge on the morrow."

Kuni saw that Mata was serious. He pondered and pondered, and then he began to smile.

"I have an idea. You *will* get your satisfaction."

∽ ∾ ∽ ∾

Mata felt like an eagle who owned the skies. Had he known how wonderful flying would feel, he would have done this a long time ago.

Far below him, the streets and houses of Zudi appeared as miniature toys. On the other side of the city walls—from this high up, they looked like low mud ridges dividing rice paddies—Namen's camps spread out like a big painting. He noted their arrangement and layout and counted the tiny dots that were the soldiers.

It was as if he had sprouted great wings made of bamboo and silk on his back, and the sound of the wind whipping against them to lift him aloft was glorious. By leaning this way and that, he could turn, roll, dive, and soar. He felt weightless, free in all three dimensions, and able to fly across all of Dara.

He laughed with the joy of flight.

The only thing that marred the illusion was the long silk rope attached to his harness, which went down to the ground, where Théca Kimo and a few soldiers worked the winch that put tension on the rope and kept him aloft. He waved at the tiny figures below, and one of them, probably Kimo, waved back. The winch crew let out more rope and Mata rose even higher. He turned back to surveying the Imperial camps.

"Is there anyone in old lady Namen's camps willing to fight me?" he shouted, and brandished his sword, still bloody from the last ten kite riders he had cut down in midair.

The giant battle kite strapped to his back—three times the size of regular reconnaissance kites—was Kuni's idea, as was the idea of air duels.

Kuni had sent a herald to the walls of Zudi and announced that they accepted Namen's challenge. But there would be a twist.

"Since General Namen has insulted the honor of Duke Garu and General Zyndu, it's only fitting that the affront be settled in the ancient ways," the herald called out. "From the Diaspora Wars to the glorious exploits of Marshal Dazu Zyndu, our annals tell us great heroes have always dueled man-to-man. How can we rely on ordinary peasant soldiers to protect the dignity of great nobles? General

Zyndu wishes to fight General Namen, one-on-one, and settle this personally."

"Now that's the sort of thing I wish the nobles said more often," Dafiro whispered to Ratho. "While they resolve all their disputes this way, the rest of us can go back to planting our harvests and enjoying our lives. Let the kings and dukes get in an arena and fight all their wars with their own two hands. We'll watch and cheer them on."

"Daf, how can you continue to be so *common*?" Ratho stared at the flying Mata, enraptured. "Aren't you inspired by General Zyndu? I wish you and I could be as brave."

"They're more stupid than brave, in my opinion. All one of them has to do is aim for the rope, and down the other guy goes."

Ratho shook his head. "Not even a Xana dog would resort to such a dishonorable trick for victory, and certainly not General Zyndu. Weren't you paying attention during the old shadow puppet plays? Dueling is all about honor, whether on the ground or in the air."

Dafiro wanted to say more but finally shook his head and held his tongue.

The herald explained that in consideration of General Namen's great age, General Zyndu was willing to duel any champion of Xana in his stead. Since General Namen might be tempted to try to rush General Zyndu with his greater numbers if the duel took place on flat ground, the Duke of Zudi suggested that the duels take place in air, over the walls of Zudi. What could be more fair and honorable?

Namen was stuck and cursed this shameless trick from Kuni Garu. Dueling was not at all what he had in mind. He had hoped that Mata Zyndu and Kuni Garu would be taunted into opening the city gates and agreeing to a field battle between their armies in front of the city, in which case they would surely be crushed. But Kuni had twisted his words around to invoke the outdated ancient ritual of a personal duel between two commanders. If Namen refused, he would be the one to be seen as cowardly, and it would be a blow to the morale of the already depressed Imperial forces.

He gritted his teeth and asked for volunteers from among the strongest soldiers and officers to be designated as the Champion of Xana. One after another, the volunteers rose into the skies, strapped to battle kites, to duel Mata Zyndu in the air.

*Cling! Clang! Cliiiiinnggggg!*

The kites dove and rose like a pair of great Mingén falcons, and whenever they approached each other, there was a flurry of strikes and blows that rang out in the air. Soldiers from both sides craned their necks and raptly followed the circling fighters in the sky. It was dizzying just watching them turn and dodge like birds.

Mata Zyndu's heart was filled with joy. *This is how all battles ought to be fought! Kuni truly understands my soul.* His sight, sharper than that of any man who had only one pupil in each eye, seemed to capture his opponent in slow motion. He parried the ineffectual blows casually, and as his strength sent the sword flying from his opponent's hand, he quickly ended the poor man's life with a graceful strike from Na-aroénna against the neck or a quick bash from Goremaw on the skull.

Ten Champions of Xana rose into the air. Ten lifeless corpses fell to the ground. The cheers from within the city of Zudi grew louder and louder, while Namen's camp fell silent.

"He's like Fithowéo coming to life," Ratho said.

Dafiro did not respond with a joke. For once he was awed into silence. General Mata Zyndu was indeed a god among mere men.

While Mata fought in the air, Kuni stood next to Théca Kimo and watched anxiously. He trusted Mata's prowess and bravery, but he couldn't help the way his heart almost leapt out of his throat as Mata executed one daring maneuver after another, defying death each time.

"Pull it tight!" Kuni muttered to Théca and his men, knowing perfectly well that the winch crew did not need his instructions. They understood that they had to winch the rope tight whenever there was a slack—lest the kite crash to the ground—and then gradually let the line out. Kuni felt like he had to say something anyway to make himself feel useful.

Though they had not known each other long, Kuni was beginning to think of Mata as one of his closest friends—almost family. There was something about Mata's stiff, formal, outdated ideas that endeared him to Kuni. Being with Mata made Kuni want to be better, to rise to Mata's estimation, to be more *noble*. He couldn't bear the thought of losing him.

Seeing that no more Xana champions took to the air, Kuni and Mata's men jeered at Namen's camp from atop the walls:

"Who's the girlie *now*?"

"Tanno Namen is an old lady more skilled with the embroidery needle than the sword!"

"Namen, what's for dinner?"

"Maybe the girls from Xana should go back to Pan before it's too late."

Some of the women hauling stones and logs onto the wall cringed.

Above them, Mata chuckled, though he was slightly embarrassed to be enjoying such humor, but Kuni waved for the men to be quiet.

"I've seen the bravery of Xana's women firsthand," Kuni said. He wasn't shouting, but his voice could be heard clearly even by Mata, soaring high overhead. Soldiers of both sides waited, hanging on his words—Kuni seemed to have that effect on people.

Mata looked at Kuni in consternation. *Is Kuni preparing another one of his jokes?* But his tone and expression were too solemn, with not even a hint of mockery.

"I know a mother from Xana who was willing to bear a corvée administrator's lash to save her son. I know a wife from Cocru who hiked miles through mountains filled with bandits even while she was pregnant and managed to save the man who was sent to save *her*. While we stand here mocking each other like two gangs of schoolboys, who has farmed our lands and kept us fed, who has sewn our tunics and made our arrows, who has carried up the siege stones and carried down the wounded? Have you forgotten how the women of Zudi fought alongside you in this rebellion? By custom, we wield the sword and wear the armor, but who among you does not know a mother, sister, daughter, friend, who exceeds you in courage and fortitude?

"So let us no more think of being compared to women as an insult."

It was so quiet—both on and below the walls of Zudi—that only the creaking of the battle kite's winches could be heard.

Mata did not wholly agree with Kuni's speech—women's courage was not comparable to men's at all!—but he noted that even Namen's men, below him, seemed subdued. Perhaps they were thinking of their mothers and sisters and daughters back in distant Xana and wondering what they were doing here. *If that's part of Kuni's plan for corroding the morale of Namen's troops, it's devious.*

"But I will say that it's not surprising that Namen is so scared." The familiar mocking tone and swagger had returned to Kuni's voice. "Why, it's sometimes hard to tell Namen apart from Erishi—both of them need bedtime stories!"

Wild laughter broke out on top of the walls of Zudi, and Kuni and Mata's men took up this new theme with creativity and vigor.

Ten dismembered bodies falling from the sky had a way of discouraging more Imperial troops from volunteering to rise up into the air against Mata, still brandishing Na-aroénna and Goremaw. Namen's officers shrank away from him, trying to avoid the old general's pained and furious eyes.

After waiting as long as it took a cup of tea to cool, Kuni signaled the drummers and trumpeters to play the victory song. Namen's camp remained silent, conceding the point.

As the men in Zudi gradually winched Mata's kite back down to a soft landing in the city, a shout went up everywhere: "The Marshal of Cocru!"

Indeed, to the south appeared a great dust cloud obscuring the road to Zudi. Through the dust, as through a fog, one could barely make out the galloping figures of horses and the bloodred ensign of Phin Zyndu, Marshal of Cocru.

"The cavalry is here," Kuni shouted to Mata, as the latter unlashed himself from the kite. "Your uncle has come with more troops to relieve the siege of Zudi. We did it!"

Mata grabbed Kuni by the arms and pulled him into a fierce hug. For a moment he didn't know what to say, surprised by the depth of his feelings. "Brother," he said finally, "we have stood together and held back the tide of the empire."

"Brother," Kuni said, his eyes tearing up, "I'm honored to fight beside you."

"Open the gates," Mata shouted. "We'll attack together with the marshal and drive Namen back to Pan!"

It was indeed a rout. The Imperials collapsed like a flock of sheep caught between two packs of wolves. The soldiers abandoned everything—weapons, gold, armor, extra boots—as they whipped their horses to go faster, back to the north, to safety.

Hundreds drowned as they tried to cross the Liru River in overloaded transports. Leaving Cogo Yelu in charge of Zudi, Kuni and Mata led their men to join the chase, and the cities along the southern shore of the Liru again flew the banner of the rebellion.

CHAPTER TWENTY-THREE

# THE FALL OF DIMU

DIMU: THE SEVENTH MONTH IN THE FOURTH YEAR OF THE REIGN OF RIGHTEOUS FORCE.

The Cocru army now laid siege to Dimu, the last Imperial stronghold south of the Liru River.

As memories of King Huno's disastrous occupation of the city were still fresh in the minds of the inhabitants, the city elders decided that they would take their chances with the empire, and citizens volunteered to help the Imperial troops defend its walls.

Mata Zyndu announced that for each day Dimu continued to resist, he would permit his troops to loot the city for one more day and to execute an additional one hundred prominent citizens once the city fell. Unfortunately, this announcement did not have the intended effect of diminishing Namen's popular support in Dimu. If anything, it seemed to increase the zeal of the citizen volunteers resisting the rebels.

There was also news that Marshal Marana was sailing toward the Amu Strait with a great armada. If the defenders held out long enough, the siege of Dimu would be relieved.

"The threat was unwise," Kuni said. "It's understandable that the people of Dimu would be leery of joining the rebellion again after what Krima put them through."

"Brother," Mata said, "Dimu has always been a Cocru city. That these men would now side with the empire against us, liberators from their motherland, shows that they have been corrupted by the occupation. Traitors must be purified with their own blood."

Kuni sighed. It was difficult to argue with Mata when he got into these moods where he launched into pretty speeches full of abstractions. Mata could be proud and unrelenting in his hatred. Sometimes, he saw the world in terrifying, bloody clarity.

Since they had arrived at Dimu by marching over land, Kuni and Mata were not prepared for a naval battle and had no warships. They had no choice but to cede control of the coast and the mouth of the Liru River to the Imperial navy. Their siege of Dimu was thus incomplete. Namen continued to bring supplies and provisions into the city's wharfs, and Imperial ships patrolled the Liru River constantly, taunting the rebel soldiers on shore.

"If I had fifty thousand men," Mata muttered, "I'd have each carry a bag of sand and march upriver. We'd be able to dam up the Liru River in one afternoon. Then we'd walk right up to those ships, stranded in the dry riverbed like flopping fish, and teach those sailors some manners."

"If you had fifty thousand men," Kuni said, "they'd be able to climb over the walls of Dimu just by standing on one another's shoulders. I don't think you need such an elaborate damming plan." He grinned at Mata.

Mata laughed. "You're right. Keeping it simple and direct is best."

So day after day, Mata directed his forces to attack Dimu in waves, giving the defenders no chance to rest. He also conscripted peasants from miles around to join the miners digging under the walls of Dimu.

∽ ∾ ∽ ∾

"By the Twins, my back is screaming." Dafiro stood and stretched. "I need a rest from all this digging. Rat, sit with me a bit." He dumped the basket of earth he had carried out of the mine in the pile near the opening and sat down.

Ratho dumped his load, looked at his brother, said nothing, and went straight back into the mine.

"What's the matter with you?" Dafiro asked the next time Ratho emerged with another full load. "You're working so hard you'll kill yourself. Listen, Baby Brother, Krima isn't our boss anymore. Duke Garu isn't going to whip us if we take a little break."

"I'm not resting until General Zyndu rests."

Dafiro shaded his eyes and gazed at the walls of Dimu. He could see Mata Zyndu's tall figure at the head of a ladder crew rushing at the wall, holding up a giant pavise to protect the men behind him from the arrows raining down from the ramparts. Zyndu had been at it all morning and all afternoon, not taking a single break through two shifts of soldiers.

"Doesn't that man ever get tired?" Dafiro wondered aloud.

"General Zyndu is like a hero from the old stories come to life."

"These days with you, it's always General Zyndu *this* and General Zyndu *that*. Maybe you should make *him* your older brother."

Ratho laughed. "Come on, Daf, don't be silly."

"He's a noble like the rest of them," Daf said. "Have you forgotten what it was like when Krima became king?"

"General Zyndu is nothing like Huno Krima." Ratho's voice was fierce and hard, and Dafiro knew better than to argue. "He leads by example, and I would rather die than disappoint him. I'm going to keep on mining until the walls fall or he tells me to stop. We've got to take Dimu before the armada gets here."

Dafiro sighed and reluctantly went back to digging.

On the tenth day, the mines succeeded in collapsing Dimu's city walls.

The rebels showed no mercy as they poured into the city like a flood and overwhelmed the remnants of the Imperial army. Namen and a few hundred of his most loyal men fought like trapped wolves all night and managed to make their way to the docks, where they were picked up by an Imperial transport and brought to safety in Dimushi.

Out of the ten thousand Imperial soldiers Namen had brought with him across the Liru, only three hundred made the crossing back with him.

Over Kuni's strenuous objections, Mata carried out his threat.

"A threat is like a promise. We will lose men's respect unless we follow through," Mata said.

"You would have won more hearts by being merciful."

"Being compassionate to one's enemies means being cruel to one's own soldiers."

Kuni had no response to this. He stood by and watched helplessly as Cocru soldiers rounded up one thousand prominent citizens of Dimu, denounced them as Imperial sympathizers, and made them dig their own grave.

"Brother, this is a mistake."

But Mata gave the order, and Cocru soldiers pushed and shoved the crying men and women into the mass grave, and then began to bury them alive.

"You do not ever want to have General Zyndu against your side," Ratho said. He and Dafiro plugged up their ears, but the screams of the dying men and women could not be blocked out.

*My Dearest Husband,*

*Please excuse the brevity of this letter. I'm still very tired and our little boy is taking up all my time.*

*There, that was the big news. You are a father now!*

*It's been one hundred days since his birth, and he's healthy as can be. I'm calling him Toto-*tika *for now, until he reaches the age of reason and we decide on a formal name.*

*He looks like a shrunken-down version of you, which, unexpectedly, actually makes him look extremely cute—I hope he does not get that belly of yours any time soon, though. The ladies at King Thufi's court cannot keep their hands off him. But unless he's held by me, he starts crying within minutes. I have been imbibing some lovely dream herbs so that the baby can have some as well through my milk. I think it's working. He smiles in his sleep!*

*I pray that Kana and Rapa protect you, and that you and Mata are doing well. You must promise to not take any unnecessary risks. Come back safely to me and to our Toto*-tika.

*Your loving wife,*
*Jia*

"Congratulations, brother! A son is a wonderful miracle, and now we know who'll be the next Duke of Zudi. I cannot wait to meet him."

"Since he's born in the Year of the Chrysanthemum, you'll have to watch over him as his uncle!"

Mata and Kuni drained their cups of mango liquor. Jia's happy news was indeed welcome amidst all the death and slaughter.

The two men stood on the docks of Dimu and gazed at the Imperial ships sailing up and down the Liru River, well out of range of Dimu's arrows and catapults. After Mata's rage was spent, Kuni had quickly reestablished order in Dimu and ordered their troops to prevent acts of looting. It was going to be a while before the city would recover, but at least the citizens were no longer utterly terrified of the "liberating" force.

Beyond the ships, they could see the brightly colored buildings of Dimushi, across the Liru's mouth, and they imagined going still farther, past Dimushi, past the rich farmlands of the Karo Peninsula, until they arrived at the roiling waves of the Amu Strait, beyond which lay Arulugi Island, with its floating cities and suspended palaces, its imposing docks and graceful ships, its elegant customs and haughty manners immortalized in ten thousand poems and a hundred thousand brush paintings.

"Amu has a good navy," Mata said. "It will be up to them to stop Marana's armada and then help us cross the Liru and bring this war to the emperor's doors."

"Let's pray for their success," Kuni said.

CHAPTER TWENTY-FOUR

# BATTLE OF ARULUGI

ARULUGI: THE SEVENTH MONTH IN THE FOURTH YEAR OF THE REIGN OF RIGHTEOUS FORCE.

The Island of Arulugi—whose name meant "beautiful" in Classical Ano—lived up to its name: wide, white beaches; gentle, lazy dunes held down by tufts of beachreed; verdant hills covered by *pili* grass; and deep valleys full of forests of banyan and looking-glass mangrove, the aerial roots of the former hanging down from branches like a woman brushing out her hair, and the platelike roots of the latter rising up like lacquer screens imported from sophisticated Gan.

Everywhere, orchids of all descriptions and sizes bloomed: the white ones whiter than seashells and the red ones redder than coral. Golden hummingbirds hovered from orchid to orchid during the day, only to give way to gentle, ethereal moths at night, their wings silvery in the moonlight.

And the crown of Arulugi was Müning, the City in the Lake. Built on a series of tiny islands in shallow Lake Toyemotika—Lake Tututika's baby sister—the city resembled a diadem floating over the water: the delicate spires of its temples and the graceful, thin towers of the palace were connected by a network of narrow, arching bridges that defied gravity.

The houses and towers of Müning were built to make the most of the limited space on the islands. Narrow, tall, and built from flexible walls, they swayed and flexed with the wind like bamboos in a grove. Having run out of space on land, some houses had to be built like water striders hovering above the lake, supported by long pylons sunk into the lake bed.

Floating gardens drifting around the islands of Müning provided its inhabitants with fresh fruits and vegetables. Platforms made of ropes and sweet sandalwood planks hung between the buildings, on which the lords and ladies of Arulugi danced at night in silk slippers and sipped tea as they admired the moon slowly rising over the sea and the port of Müningtozu, on the seashore just a few miles to the east of the lake.

But the jewel of Müning was undoubtedly Princess Kikomi.

At seventeen, her olive-colored skin, rich, light-brown hair that fell in cascades of curls, and bright-blue eyes that shone like two deep, calm wells were the stuff of legends and bards' songs. She was the granddaughter of King Ponahu, the last King of Amu before the Conquest, and his only surviving descendant. But as the laws of succession in Amu did not permit women to accede to the throne, the restored Amu was led by King Ponadomu, the half brother of Ponahu, and Kikomi's granduncle.

In the suspended teahouses of Arulugi, out of the earshot of Ponadomu's soldiers and spies, sometimes you could hear the people whisper to one another that it was a pity that Kikomi was not born a boy.

Alone in her chamber, Kikomi looked at her reflection in the mirror, putting the last touches on her makeup. She had sprinkled gold dust in her light-brown hair to give it the appearance of being blond, and she had brushed blue powder around her eyelids to highlight her blue eyes. The goal was to push her appearance closer to Tututika, the goddess of Amu.

She didn't sigh. Tonight, she would be a symbol, and she understood that whatever else symbols did, they did not sigh and complain about their fate. She would smile and wave and stand silently by the side of her granduncle as he stumbled his way through an insipid speech meant to rally the troops. She would remind the sailors and marines of why they were fighting, of the ideal of Amu womanhood, of the favor of Tututika, of the pride that Amu took in being the epitome of grace and beauty and taste and culture, far superior to the brutality of backward Xana.

But she could not deny that she was unhappy.

As long as she could remember, she had been told incessantly that she was beautiful. It wasn't that her adoptive parents—a couple loyal to her poor executed grandfather who had raised her as one of their own—didn't praise her cleverness when she learned to read and write before all the other children, or that they didn't think it noteworthy that she could jump higher and run faster and lift more weights than her adoptive brothers and sisters; rather, it was that everyone seemed to treat these other accomplishments as mere ornaments on the crown that was her physical beauty.

And as she grew older, that crown had grown heavier. She was no longer allowed to spend her summer days running wild next to the shores of Lake Toyemotika with her companions until, hearts pounding, throats parched, their skin glistening with sweat, they stripped off their clothes and jumped into the cool, refreshing lake for a swim. Instead, she was told how the sun could damage her flawless skin, how running barefoot would lead to unsightly calluses on the bottoms of her feet, how diving into the lake recklessly could risk her getting a permanent scar from the jagged rocks hidden underwater. The only summer activity permitted to her was dancing: in sedate, calm studios where the sunlight was filtered through silk screens and the floor was lined with soft woven-grass mats.

Her plans, nurtured since childhood, of traveling to Haan to study with the masters of mathematics and rhetoric and composition, and of going to Toaza in distant Gan afterward to set up a trading house of her own, were put on hold. Instead, teachers were hired at great expense from the fashion houses in Müning to instruct her in the color and cut and fabrics of different dresses, suitable for different occasions, emphasizing different aspects of her body, which was described to her again and again as beautiful. The teachers also gave her lessons in how to walk, how to talk, how to hold the eating sticks to indicate her mood with grace, how to apply makeup to achieve a thousand different looks, each as elaborate as a painting.

"What use is this?" she asked her adoptive parents.

"You're not a plain girl," her mother answered. "But beauty must be enhanced to reach its full potential."

And so instead of rhetoric she studied elocution; instead of composition she studied how to compose her face—with powder and paint and jewelry and dye and frowns and smiles and pouts—to be more beautiful.

It was a cliché for a beautiful woman to complain about being cursed with beauty, Kikomi knew, but just because it was a cliché didn't mean it wasn't true, for her.

When the rebellion happened and the court of Amu was restored, she had thought she would finally earn a reprieve. In a time of revolutions and wars, the raising of armies and navies and the promulgation of new policies, what was the use of beauty? As a member of the ruling house of Amu, Kikomi thought she would be working by the side of her granduncle the king, perhaps becoming one of his trusted advisers. She was intelligent and she wasn't spoiled; she knew the value of hard work. Surely the king and his ministers could see that?

But instead, her body was draped in beautiful dresses and her face painted until she could barely feel her skin move; she was told to stand here or move—gracefully, remember, like dancing, like floating—over there, always displayed prominently, but always told to say nothing, to look serene and demure, to *inspire*.

"You're a symbol of the revival of Amu," her granduncle, King Ponadomu, said. "Of all the Tiro states, we have always been known for our dedication to the essence of civilization, of grace and refinement. Being beautiful is the most important thing you can do for the nation, Kikomi. No one else can remind the people of our ideals, our self-image, and our goddess as well as you."

She glanced at the dress hanging from the stand next to the window, the blue silk cut in a classical style meant to evoke more of Tututika. She prepared herself for another night of playing a well-draped and well-painted statue.

"You are like Lake Tututika," a voice said.

Kikomi whipped her head around.

"Calm on the surface, but full of conflicting currents and shadowy caves underneath." The speaker was standing in the shadows next to the door to her bedchamber. Kikomi didn't know her, but she was dressed in a fern-green silk dress cut in the modern style worn by all the ladies-in-waiting at the court. Perhaps she was the wife or daughter of one of the king's trusted advisers.

"Who are you?"

The woman took a step forward so that the light from the setting sun illuminated her face. Kikomi marveled at her: golden-haired, azure-eyed, with skin as flawless as a polished piece of amber. She was the most beautiful woman the princess had ever seen, and she looked at once a maiden, a mother, and a crone—ageless.

The woman didn't answer her question, but said, instead, "You wish you would be valued for what you can say and think and do; and you think if you were plain it would be easier."

Kikomi flushed at the presumptuous statement, but something in the woman's blue eyes, open, kind, placid, made her decide that the woman meant her no ill will.

"When I was younger," Kikomi said, "I would get into debates with my brothers and their friends. They could seldom win, for their minds were dull, and they did not apply themselves to their work. But often, when it was clear that I had the better argument, they would laugh and say, 'It's impossible to argue with such a pretty girl,' and thereby deny me my victory. Life has not changed much since then."

"The gods give us different talents and different endowments," said the woman. "Do you think it profits the peacock to complain that he is hunted for his feathers, or the horned toad that she is valued only for her poison?"

"What do you mean?"

"The gods may make one plain or pretty, stocky or thin, dull or clever, but it's up to each of us to make a path for ourselves with the gifts we're born with. A toad's poison may take away the life of a tyrant and save a country, or it may become the murder weapon of a street gang. A peacock's feather may end up adorning the helmet of a general, rallying the hearts of thousands, or it may end up in the hands of a servant fanning a foolish man who has inherited his wealth."

"Mere sophistry. The peacock does not choose where his feathers may go, nor does the toad her poison. I am but a mannequin that the king and his ministers dress up and put on display. They might as well use a statue of Tututika."

"You seethe and simmer because you think your beauty traps you, but if you're truly as strong and brave and intelligent as you think you are, you'll understand how dangerous and powerful your beauty can be, if you wield it properly."

Kikomi stared at her, at a loss for words.

The woman continued. "Tututika, youngest of the gods, was also considered the weakest. But during the Diaspora Wars, she faced the hero Iluthan alone. Dazzled by her beauty, he let down his guard, and she was able to slay him with her poisoned hairpin. That act prevented Amu from being overrun by Iluthan's army, and generations of Amu's people praise her for that intervention."

"Must a beautiful woman always be a seducer, a harlot, a mere bauble put on display as a *distraction*? Is that the only path open to me?"

"Those are the labels men have put on women," the woman said, an edge coming into her voice. "You speak as though you despise them, yet you're merely parroting the words and judgments of historians, who should never be trusted. Consider the hero Iluthan, who stole into the bed of the Queen of Écofi, who played with the hearts of Rapa and Kana, who showed his naked body to the gathered princes and princesses of Crescent Island, claiming himself to take equal delight in men and women. Do you think the historians call him a seducer, a harlot, a 'mere bauble'?"

Kikomi pondered this, biting her bottom lip.

The woman went on. "A seducer is one who wins through deception rather than force, a harlot is one who wields sex like a sorcerer wields a staff, and a 'mere bauble' may yet *decide* to put herself on display to guide the hearts and minds of thousands into an unstoppable force.

"Amu is in danger, Kikomi, a danger that may reduce this Beautiful Island to rubble. If your head is clear and your heart stout, you may yet see how difficult a path you have ahead of you and how you must choose to make your beauty serve you and your people, rather than curse it."

Kikomi stood on the docks of Müningtozu and watched the fleet departing the harbor. She was dressed from head to toe in blue, the color of Amu, and from a distance she looked like a manifestation of Lady Tututika.

She waved at the sailors, young men whose faces still held the wonder and naïveté of boys as they stood at attention in rigid lines along the decks. Some smiled at her and waved back. Officers standing on the foredecks saluted the king and assembled ministers on shore. Below them, the great oars dipped into the water in unison and propelled the ships away, like graceful water striders.

In the distance, ten glowing oval shapes, the empire's airships, floated over the horizon. The tiny orange blobs seemed to possess light, feathery wings, like some hybrid moth-firefly that would be at home in the orchid-strewn forests of Arulugi.

*How can something so beautiful be so deadly?* Kikomi thought.

∽ ∾ ∽ ∾

In the cockpit of *Spirit of Kiji*, flagship of the Imperial armada, Marshal Kindo Marana gazed at the glowing lights of Müning on the horizon. Closer to him, flickering over the dark sea, he could make out the faint lights of the torches on the decks of the Amu fleet oaring out to meet him.

He had visited Müning on holiday in the past and enjoyed its beautiful classical architecture and the hospitality of the Amu people. Nowhere else in the Islands did they make orchid-bamboo-shoot tea as fragrant as in Müning. A hundred varieties of orchids led to ten thousand combinations, and one could spend an entire life sampling the hanging teahouses of Müning and still never taste all the flavors Müning had to offer.

It was tragic that he might have to destroy something so beautiful.

Below him, sailing in formation, were eighty ships of the Imperial navy, and in the air around him were the other nine airships of the Imperial air force. The airships were propelled by giant battle kites, and the naval ships were rigged with full sails to conserve the arm strength of the oarsmen. During battle, they would need the agility and speed that only muscle could provide.

Behind the ships, down on the dark sea, the slow, bulky transports rode the waves, filled with ten thousand fresh troops from Rui and Dasu, the newest recruits of the Imperial army.

He continued to watch as the Amu fleet approached the armada. News that Namen had suffered a crushing defeat in Cocru meant that they had to win a victory here quickly to quell the rising rebel sentiments in Haan, Rima, and the rest of Dara.

As the Imperial armada came into range, Admiral Catiro of the Amu fleet gave the order to assume battle formation by releasing two orange lanterns. The tiny lanterns, made of paper stretched over a woven grass frame, floated into the sky, propelled by candles hanging below them.

The fleet extinguished all torches, reefed their sails, opened their oar ports, and dipped their long battle oars into the water.

Admiral Catiro cautiously allowed himself to smile at his luck. It appeared that this Imperial tax collector wearing the armor of a marshal knew nothing about naval tactics. He was a fool to pack his ships in such a dense formation and to attempt a risky night assault on Arulugi.

Given the reduced visibility, the heavier Imperial ships would have to move slower lest they run into one another. The lighter, faster Amu ships could neutralize the Imperial advantage in numbers by quickly driving between the tightly packed ships of the armada, breaking their oars and flinging burning tar bombs onto their decks.

The Imperial captains seemed to sense the foolishness of their tight formation. The ships slowed and then began to reverse their oars, backing away from the approaching Amu fleet.

"You have nowhere to run, Marana." Admiral Catiro launched a quartet of bright-red lanterns, the signal for all-ahead assault. All forty Amu ships began to oar furiously, chasing after the retreating Imperial ships.

But the ten great airships continued to move forward and were soon on top of the Amu fleet. As they drifted over the Amu ships, they began to drop flaming bombs.

Catiro was prepared for this. The flammable sails had all been stowed away, and his sailors had cleared the decks of all obstructions and covered them with a layer of wet sand before ducking belowdecks. These were old tactics developed during the Xana Conquest. With the sand in place, the flaming tar bombs splashed and fizzled, but the fire could not spread far. After a while, the airships seemed to exhaust their supply of bombs and began to oar back as well, following the retreating armada.

The Imperial ships, predictably, ran into trouble in their hasty retreat. The ships, not having time to turn around, were unable to steer effectively. As they backed up, they bumped into one another and slowed down. They were sitting ducks for the bow rams and catapults of the Amu fleet. As the Amu ships got closer and closer, some impatient captains began to launch tar bombs and rocks at the Imperial ships, but most of the projectiles fell harmlessly into the water.

"Patience," Catiro whispered. But it didn't matter. The Amu ships were going so fast that they would ram into the Imperial armada soon. The seas would soon be strewn with broken oars and the dead bodies of Xana sailors and marines.

The ship next to Catiro's flagship suddenly lurched to the right, its oars an uncoordinated jumble. Something had fouled the oars and turned the ship into a centipede with half of its legs no longer obeying, and it was spinning in place on the sea. It began to careen toward Catiro.

"Move out of the way!" Catiro shouted. But the rowers on the left side of the flagship cried out in surprise. Their oars were also mysteriously out of control. The oars seemed stuck in some thick, heavy medium, and the more the oarsmen pulled, the more they refused to obey. The two ships crashed into each other with a thunderous thud. Some oars were broken in the chaos, others ripped out of the oarsmen's hands.

As panicking Amu marines lit torches to examine the damage, Catiro looked over the side of the ship and saw small boats full of men hacking at his ship's oars.

Only now did Catiro understand what Marana had been up to.

As the Imperial armada retreated, they left behind small boats with men dressed in dark clothing and holding nets studded with hooks. As the Amu fleet passed by them, completely unaware of their existence, the crew on the small hidden boats had thrown their nets onto the banks of oars of the Amu ships and tied them into jumbled messes. The Amu ships spun out of control and crashed into one another.

The airships again approached overhead, dropping a fresh salvo of deadly tar bombs that caused the marines on deck to duck for cover or scream and jump into the sea. The great warships of the Imperial armada now advanced on the disabled Amu fleet, ready for slaughter.

∽ ∾ ∽ ∾

Kikomi closed her eyes. She did not want to see the Amu ships, now distant flaming arks adrift on the sea, or to imagine the desperate cries of drowning men.

King Ponadomu, her granduncle, said nothing as he began the walk back to Müning. It was time to prepare for the surrender.

Ponadomu was stripped naked and put into a cage. He would be taken by airship to the Immaculate City, where he would be paraded around the streets to the jubilation of the capital crowds. But Marana was far more interested in Kikomi, the Jewel of Amu.

"Your Royal Highness, I regret that we have to meet under such circumstances."

Kikomi regarded the thin man and his humorless face. He looked like a bureaucrat, the same as hundreds of others she had known in her life. And yet this man was responsible for the deaths of thousands.

While he held in his hands the reins of the killing machine of the empire, she had nothing but herself.

But she knew the effect that she had on men.

"I am your captive, Marshal Marana. You may do with me as you wish."

Marana caught his breath. Her voice seemed to have fingers in it, fingers that caressed his face and lightly stroked his heart. Her bold tone made the implication of her statement unambiguous.

"You are a very powerful man, Marshal. I do not believe that there's another like you in all of Dara."

Marana closed his eyes and savored her voice. He could fall asleep to it and dream beautiful dreams. It was like the orchid-flavored tea of Amu: sweet, lingering, ever-refreshing. He wanted to listen to her forever.

She came up to him and placed her arms around his neck. He did not resist.

∽ ∾ ∽ ∾

"What's next?" Kikomi combed her hair in front of the mirror. The morning light, filtered through the curtains, seemed to Marana to turn her tresses into a glowing golden halo.

"I will have to take the captives back to Pan," he said from the bed.

"So soon?"

Marana chuckled. "I can hardly tarry. The other states are still in rebellion." He mused for a while. "But it might make sense to leave someone the population trusts in charge here. Someone who's more sensible and willing to collaborate with the emperor."

The princess's hand slowed for a moment, but she resumed combing her hair.

"How would you like to be the Duchess of Amu?" Marana asked. "It is said that you are far more suited for this throne than your uncle."

The princess continued to comb her hair, making no reply.

Marana was surprised. He had just shown this girl more respect than her own family and people did. He expected some . . . gratitude.

"What are you thinking?"

Kikomi stopped moving the brush. "You."

"What about me?"

"I'm picturing you back in Pan, where you have to bow and scrape to men who have not done one-hundredth of what you have done for the glory of Xana. A boy who owes everything to you will pat you on the head and tell you to go away while he celebrates your victory."

"Take more care with your speech." Marana looked around to be sure there were no servants who might have overheard.

"You said I'm more suited for this throne than my uncle. Perhaps. The world is not always fair or just. Honor does not always flow to the deserving. It's a pity."

Her bold words awakened something in him. Marana imagined himself flying back to Pan in the cockpit of *Spirit of Kiji*. He imagined his troops marching into the capital. He imagined himself approaching the palace, his home, and by his side was his consort, the beautiful Princess Kikomi.

He looked at the mirror and Kikomi's reflection. Her eyes gazed back, poised between boldness and submission, lively, ambitious, seductive.

"But can we not make the world fairer, more just?" she asked. Again, her voice seemed to wrap itself around him, to lead him to places he had not dared to visit.

He looked at the small stand next to the bed, upon which his tunic lay, neatly folded—he had taken the time to do this before embracing her last night. A few coins were scattered on the stand as well; he reached out to stack them in a neat column. He disliked disorder.

The coins struck one another and made a familiar sound. In a distant corner of his mind, he heard the sound of clarity, of meticulous accounting, of neatly sorted ledgers where each entry made sense. He shivered, and the spell she wove faded.

With great reluctance, he turned back to her. "That's enough."

He took a deep breath. She'd almost had him.

*She is very clever and brave, and she can be useful.*

"I had thought you ambitious," Marana said. "But I was wrong."

She turned to look at him, and her face fell as she realized that she had failed.

"You're not *just* ambitious," Marana said. "You love this land and her people. You crave their approval."

"I am a daughter of Amu."

"Your Royal Highness, I will make you a proposal. If you agree, I will leave Arulugi as it is. Life here will go on much as it was before, save for proper taxes and the renewed duty of loyalty the people will owe to the emperor. The teahouses of Müning will continue to be filled with sweet aromas and lovely songs, and men and women will still marvel at the grace and elegance of this filigreed island. You will be remembered in song and story as the protectress of your people."

"I thought I was going to be the Duchess of Amu."

Marana laughed. "That was before I understood how dangerous it would be to leave you in charge of Amu."

Princess Kikomi said nothing. Her fingers absentmindedly stroked her blue silk dress, and she seemed to be admiring the large sapphire she wore on her finger.

She wished that she had been a little more patient, a little less obvious. She'd had a chance to set this man on a path to betray Erishi, to march on Pan, and she had let it slip through her fingers because she had overplayed her hand.

"But if you refuse, I will have you brought to the lowliest brothel of Pan, where I will sell you for a single piece of copper. You will always be remembered as a whore."

Now it was the turn for Princess Kikomi to laugh. "You believe that would frighten me? You already think of me as a whore."

Marana shook his head. "There's more. I will also order Lake Toyemotika drained and Müning burned to the ground. I will spread salt in the fields and order one in ten inhabitants of Arulugi executed. I have already killed so many men that a few more will not matter. But most of all, I will let it be known that you, you alone, were responsible for the fate of Arulugi. You had the chance to save your people, and you said no."

Princess Kikomi stared at Marana. She had no words for how she felt about this man. *Hate* seemed inadequate.

A light airship was dispatched to bring Princess Kikomi and King Ponadomu to Pan. Transported along with them were a few other Amu nobles and important prisoners, including the captain of the palace guards, Cano Tho.

Only a skeleton crew traveled along with the captives. In the section of the gondola inside the frame of the airship, along a short corridor, were several rooms used for storage and as sleeping quarters for the crew. In one of these rooms, Kikomi and Ponadomu were naked and kept in cages. The other prisoners were tightly bound with rope and held in the room across the corridor.

Once the flight was under way, Cano Tho tested the rope binding his wrists. The guards were lazy and did not do a very good job, and the rope was old and had lost its tension.

He waited a few hours, until he thought the guards had dulled some of their alertness. He worked at the ropes, stopping whenever the single Imperial guard assigned to the room walked by. He rubbed against the rope until his skin broke and blood seeped out. He grimaced but kept on going. The blood lubricated the ropes and made the work easier.

There. His hands were free.

He had stood helplessly on the docks and watched as the men of Amu died in the dark, leaping from burning ships into the cold waters of the Amu Strait to die. But now the arrogant Imperials had made a mistake, and he was going to make them pay.

When the guard's back was turned, Cano quickly untied the binding around his ankles.

The next time the guard passed by him, Cano leapt up and wrestled him to the ground. Quickly pulling the dirk from the guard's belt, he slit the man's throat.

He freed the other prisoners around him. The freed men took what weapons they could find in the room and carefully peeked into the corridor. They were lucky: The corridor was empty. All the other guards were asleep in their bunks.

The men moved quickly. The few Imperial guards were killed in their sleep, and within minutes, the prisoners had taken over the cockpit, and the pilots and oarsmen, conscripted laborers, put up little fight before surrendering.

Cano walked into the room holding King Ponadomu and Princess Kikomi. He averted his gaze so as not to humiliate them in their nakedness. He opened the cages and handed them clothes and linens taken from the quarters of the Imperial guards.

"It is a miracle, Your Majesty and Your Royal Highness! We are free and we now have control of an Imperial airship."

Princess Kikomi, proud and elegant even in her nakedness, thanked Cano and wrapped a rough cotton sheet around herself. She was without her silk dress, her diadem, her makeup and her sparkling jewels, and yet Cano found her more beautiful than any woman he knew. He had admired her from afar for a long time. She was indeed the Jewel of Amu.

Cano saw joy and relief in Princess Kikomi's face, no doubt because he had helped her escape whatever degrading fate Marana had planned for her. Cano was almost glad that events had transpired to put him in this place. She looked at him now with tenderness in those icy blue eyes, so cold and warm at the same time. He would have gladly died for her if she asked for it.

"Where shall we go now?" the king asked. He was lost without his ministers, away from the comforting security of the palace. He had not yet adjusted to life as a man without a country.

"To Çaruza. King Thufi will help us." The princess's tone was calm and cool. Cano saw that she was already putting the humiliation of her captivity behind her. She was again Her Royal Highness, the Jewel of Amu. People were looking to her now for decisions, and she would rise to the occasion and lead them, the laws of succession be damned.

The airship adjusted the trim of the kite sails and the rudder and began to fly south, toward Cocru.

CHAPTER TWENTY-FIVE

# "IT IS A HORSE"

PAN: THE EIGHTH MONTH IN THE FOURTH YEAR OF THE REIGN OF RIGHTEOUS FORCE.

Chatelain Pira was concerned.

Against all odds, Regent Crupo's appointment of the Minister of the Treasury as the Marshal of Xana had turned out to be an ingenious move. The meticulous, calculating man had exceeded all expectations.

The victory at Arulugi was all anybody talked about. Some of the Tiro states were even sending secret emissaries to discuss the terms for a surrender. Certainly there were setbacks along the Liru River, but the rebels were unable to cross the river and come into Géfica, the heartland of the empire.

Crupo crowed about his insightful personnel decision every day and strutted about the palace as though he were the second coming of Aruano, the great lawgiver. He was quickly becoming insufferable, apparently forgetting how, without Pira, he would have been nothing.

It was no secret that Crupo was ambitious. He was already the most powerful man in Pan, but Pira could see that one day, Crupo might decide that he no longer needed Erishi. With the backing of Marana—whose commission depended on Crupo's pleasure—he would simply step into the Grand Audience Hall and ask the assembled ministers who they believed was really the emperor.

And the assembled ministers, all of whom had once agreed that the regent brought a horse into the Grand Audience Hall, would nod sagely and affirm that the emperor was standing in front of them, had just asked them a question.

*Who is that boy sitting up in the throne then?*

*Who knows? He must be an impostor.*

*And who is that man standing beside the boy?*

*A mere butler, the boy's playmate. A corrupter of Xana's ancient virtues. Off with his head!*

Pira shook his head. He could not let that happen. He would have been content, once, merely to see Xana fall, but now he wanted more. He had suffered the idiots Erishi and Crupo long enough.

*He*, not Crupo, should be the one to seize the throne from the House of Xana. Maing must be properly avenged.

"I need to see the emperor," Crupo said.

"*Rénga* is busy," Pira said.

"Busy playing, you mean." Crupo was getting more and more annoyed with the way things were being run. He made all the decisions and kept the empire humming along, and yet every week he had to come and report to the spoiled boy like a mere servant.

The boy emperor's high-handed decree that any audience with him had to be approved first by Chatelain Pira—who actually *was* a servant—only added to the load of indignity he suffered under. *Maybe it's time to change things.*

"The emperor is young and easily distracted," Pira allowed. "But I will keep a close eye on *Rénga*'s moods and tell you to come when he's in a more suitable frame of mind."

"Thank you," Crupo said. Chatelain Pira was a silly man, just the sort of companion that the emperor liked. But he and Pira were bound together by that unspeakable conspiracy at the time of the old emperor's death. He still needed Pira, for now.

"Come now. Come quickly. The emperor says he's interested in learning about the details of governance. You must go see him right now."

Crupo straightened his formal robes and hat, from which hung the jade and amber beads, the symbols of his authority, and rushed along the halls of the palace to the emperor's private garden. Pira ran behind him to keep up.

They turned the corner and went into the garden. The emperor was sitting on a bench; he seemed to be fondling a bundle of clothes piled along the bench, spilling into his lap; he was talking and laughing.

Crupo came closer. "*Rénga*, you called for me?"

Startled, the fifteen-year-old looked up. The bundle of clothes along the bench rustled, and a red-faced girl sat up in his lap, trying vainly to cover her breasts. She bowed quickly to the regent, the chatelain, and the emperor and ran along the path and disappeared behind some bushes.

"I most certainly did not." Emperor Erishi was blushing, furious. "Get out. Get out! *Get out!*"

Crupo backed away as quickly as he could.

Pira fell to the ground and touched his forehead to the cold stone. "I'm sorry, *Rénga*. He just burst in. I couldn't stop him!"

The emperor nodded and waved him away impatiently. He got up to follow the path the girl had taken.

Pira smiled to himself. There was nothing that humiliated and annoyed the boy more than to be interrupted during such moments. Now every time the emperor saw the regent, this indelible memory would rise in his mind.

Next, Pira bribed Crupo's butler to save all the scrap scrolls that Crupo used to practice his calligraphy.

"I'm a great admirer of the regent's art," Pira said humbly. "I just want to save some of this beauty that he throws out as trash."

The butler saw no harm in this, and he even pitied the chatelain. What a sad life he led. All day long his only work was to keep a teenager entertained, and for his hobby, he begged to be allowed to collect scraps from another's refuse pile. He was a far cry from Regent Crupo, a truly great man.

Pira had to wait a while to collect enough scrolls with the logograms he needed. He took them and carefully rubbed a hot kettle against their backs until the wax logograms were soft enough to be pried off. Then he selected and arranged the logograms he needed on a new scroll, and again he heated the scroll from the back until the logograms melted just enough to adhere to their new locations.

Now he had in his possession a new poem in Crupo's beautifully sculpted, flowing script: a poem that the regent did not write and yet could not prove to be a forgery.

He left it, carelessly, on the steps leading up to the Grand Audience Hall, where it would be discovered and brought to the emperor.

*I am the eagle who must carry a mouse.*
*I am the wolf who must obey a vole.*
*But one day I will assume my rightful place,*
*And then the foolish child will beg me for his life.*

"You remember the deer, *Rénga*?" Pira whispered to the frightened and furious Emperor Erishi. "I hope you have finally learned what you needed to know."

*Treason!* Crupo could hardly believe it. The palace guards had come to his quarters in the middle of the night, woken him up, and placed him in shackles. Here he was in the emperor's dungeon, and no one would even tell him the evidence against him.

Well, he would prove his innocence. If there was anyone who knew how to write persuasive essays, it was he. He would save himself by his brush and ink, his knife and stick of wax.

He wrote petition after petition to the emperor, letter after letter, but no answer ever came.

Chatelain Pira came to visit his old friend.

"What have you done?" Pira said, shaking his head sadly. "Does your ambition have no limits?"

Crupo admitted nothing. Pira gestured, and the men behind him came forward.

Crupo had never experienced such pain in his life. The bones in his fingers were broken one by one, and then the broken pieces were each broken again. Crupo fainted.

They poured cold water on his face to wake him up and hurt him some more.

He admitted everything. He signed whatever paper Pira put in front of him, holding the brush with his teeth, as his fingers were now soft as melted wax.

Three palace guards came to visit Crupo in his cell.

"*Rénga* sent us here to be sure that your confession is true," one of the guards said. "He's concerned that Chatelain Pira might have been overzealous. Have you been tortured?"

Crupo lifted his head and looked behind the guards through his swollen eyes. Pira was nowhere to be found.

*Finally, a chance for justice!*

Crupo nodded frantically. He tried to speak but could not—Pira's men had burned his tongue with hot pokers. He held up his hands to show the guards what he had been put through.

"The confession—it wasn't true, was it?"

Crupo shook his head.

*Pira, you lowly slave. You cannot get away with this.*

The guards left.

"I had some of my men dress up as palace guards to test you," Chatelain Pira said, his voice cool. "They found out that you weren't sincere in your confession. You still seem to be laboring under the impression that you're looking at a deer, instead of a horse, and I'm telling you it is a horse. Do you understand?"

Pira's men tortured him all night.

Pira had the best doctors come care for Crupo. They bandaged his hands and salved his tongue. They fed him healing soup and applied herbal paste to his bruises. But Crupo shrank at their touch, terrified that it was but a trick from Pira to hurt him more.

One day, more palace guards came to visit Crupo in his cell.

"The emperor wishes to ascertain the truth of your confession. Have you been tortured?"

Crupo shook his head.

"The confession—it wasn't true, was it?"

Crupo nodded vigorously. He mumbled and croaked and tried to indicate with every gesture that it was all true, every single word. He was a traitor to the emperor. He wanted the emperor dead. He was very, very sorry for it, but he deserved what he got. He hoped that his performance, this time, would pass muster.

Emperor Erishi was filled with great sorrow as he listened to the report of the captain of the palace guards. Somewhere deep inside himself, he had refused to believe that the regent really wanted to commit treason against him.

But the captain of the palace guards recounted his men's visit with Crupo. In a safe room where Chatelain Pira was nowhere to be found, Crupo had insisted to the interrogating guards that he had not been tortured. He was very contrite, but the confession was true.

The emperor was distraught.

Chatelain Pira came to comfort him. "It's hard to see inside men's hearts, no matter how well you think you know them."

Emperor Erishi ordered Crupo's heart cut out of his chest and brought to him so he could see whether it was red with loyalty or black with betrayal.

But when the heart was brought to him, the boy lost his courage; he ordered it fed to his dogs without looking.

Chatelain Pira now also had the title of prime minister, and he turned his attention to the rebellion.

Someday, he would enjoy watching the boy emperor beg him for his life: the day that he took away the empire from the House of Xana. But for now, he had to get rid of the rebels first.

Directing armies from afar did not seem very difficult to him. If Crupo could do it, so could he.

With the fall of Amu, only three Tiro states remained in rebellion: rugged Faça in the north, with its strength of ten thousand beyond the dark woods of Rima; rich Gan in the east, with ten thousand more foot soldiers and the rebels' only remaining navy on the island of Wolf's Paw; and martial Cocru in the south, which faced off against General Tanno Namen across the Liru River.

Kindo Marana did not think much of King Shilué of Faça, who was opportunistic and weak, nor did he have much respect for King Dalo of Gan, who was content to stay on Wolf's Paw and forget his ancestral claims to Géjira on the Big Island. Marana's plan was to combine his forces with Namen's for a coordinated general assault on Cocru, the only Tiro state that posed a real threat to the empire.

But before he could put his plan into operation, a messenger arrived from the Immaculate City with the news that Regent Crupo had been caught in a treasonous plot and executed, and Prime Minister Pira now ordered all Imperial forces be amassed for a general assault on Wolf's Paw.

"Pacify the Outer Islands first." The messenger read the words of Goran Pira. "And the Big Island will come to heel by itself."

This seemed to Marana the wrong strategy, but he suppressed his annoyance before the Imperial messenger. The emperor and the new prime minister seemed to think war a game they played on that model of the empire in the Grand Audience Hall. He might be the

Marshal of Xana, but ultimately he was just a token, to be picked up and put down wherever his superiors wished.

For a moment, he almost wished he had given in to the temptation of Princess Kikomi.

But that opportunity was past, and the path of treason would remain for him only a thing of the imagination. He was too meticulous, too attached to beliefs about order and a man's proper place.

Marana sighed and sent out the new deployment orders. The Imperial armada and its twenty thousand soldiers would sail north around the Big Island, bypassing Faça for Wolf's Paw.

Simultaneously, Namen was to leave a small number of defenders at the Liru River and the edge of the Rima woods. He would then take another twenty thousand men through Thoco Pass, through gentle Géjira and its wealthy garden cities and peaceful rice paddies, and meet the armada at the point where the Shinané Mountains ran into the coast. From there, the empire would launch an all-out assault on Wolf's Paw.

CHAPTER TWENTY-SIX

# THE PRINCEPS'S PROMISE

ÇARUZA: THE NINTH MONTH IN THE FOURTH YEAR OF THE REIGN OF RIGHTEOUS FORCE.

King Thufi thundered at the gathered ambassadors and kings of the Tiro states.

He was sick of how *pettily* everyone behaved. The debates had raged on for months, and yet nothing was ever decided. Rather than coming together with a plan to march on Pan, the assembled dignitaries preferred to squabble over how to divide up the spoils of an imaginary victory.

Rima and Amu were gone, and Haan never managed to free itself, even temporarily. The empire was going to reconquer the Tiro states one by one, a repeat of Emperor Mapidéré's feat decades earlier. The rebellion was teetering on the abyss of failure.

*The fiction of the equality and independence of all Tiro states is nice,* Thufi thought, *but now we must face reality.*

"No more debates," King Thufi declared. "I'm nominating myself as princeps."

The room fell into stunned silence. There had not been a princeps for hundreds of years.

But no one objected, at least not openly. Cocru, after all, had the largest army, and it was the only Tiro state to have won any victories in the field against the empire.

"Marana and Namen are throwing everything they have into an assault on Wolf's Paw, and we have to put aside our differences and do everything we can to help Gan"—the Gan ambassador nodded vigorously at this—"Faça and Cocru will send every man who can be spared, and the rest of you must do what you can to help—money, weapons, intelligence. The Six States will make a collective stand at Wolf's Paw."

In truth, this wasn't a mere platitude. All the Tiro states *could* help. The remnants of Rima's army had made their way into Cocru, bitter men who longed for vengeance. A few Amu ships had escaped from the Battle of Amu Strait and limped their way to Çaruza, along with King Ponadomu and Princess Kikomi—though it was too bad that the airship they escaped in had mysteriously sprung a leak shortly after landing and had to be scuttled. And wealthy nobles from all the conquered Tiro states had fled to Çaruza, laden with national treasures that could be converted into military funds.

Even Haan had something to offer. King Cosugi had sent Luan Zya on a secret mission into Haan, where he had managed to start an underground movement among dissatisfied young men willing to make trouble for the empire in the heartland.

"Should we fail at Wolf's Paw, then the Islands of Dara will again sink back into barbarism and tyranny. But if we succeed, we will have extinguished the empire's last glimmer of hope. Kindo Marana will not be able to find more men willing to die for the empire in Rui and Dasu. The people of Xana have suffered almost as much as we have.

"We will rise or sink together, as one."

Thufi did not trust the kings and ambassadors, who had their own agendas. To inspire the men to fight, he had to speak to them directly.

"Should we succeed, we will push on through the fields of Géjira, through Thoco Pass, and bring the war to the emperor in his palace in Pan. As princeps, I decree now that whosoever, be he churl or earl, captures Emperor Erishi will be made the king of a new Tiro state encompassing the richest parts of Géfica."

The assembled ambassadors and kings offered halfhearted cheers at this announcement, but their applause grew louder as Marshal Phin Zydnu stared coldly at each of them in turn.

Words always seemed so much more convincing when backed by swords.

King Ponadomu muttered that the princeps was making promises with land that by right belonged to Amu, but considering he and Princess Kikomi were living on handouts from King Thufi, he kept his voice very low.

The house that Jia rented was outside Çaruza, in a tiny village right on the beach. It had been the summer home of a Cocru noble family now fallen on hard times. The house was large but not ostentatious, and the rent was affordable.

To the east, below the horizon, were the Tunoa Islands. Mata Zyndu stood for a while on the beach, tossing broken shells and pebbles into the waves, thinking about home. Then he ducked his head and walked through Kuni's front door.

"Brother Kuni and Sister Jia!" he shouted. "I hope this is not an inconvenient time for a visit."

Mata and Kuni had returned to Çaruza a month ago, after it was clear that Marana and Namen were not going to attack Dimu. Kuni stayed with Jia and enjoyed being a father while Mata helped his uncle with his duties managing the Cocru army. They were both getting a little antsy, though, waiting for the kings and ambassadors to decide on a strategy for the rebels.

"Ah, it's Brother Mata," Kuni said, standing up with Jia. "You know that there is no inconvenient time where you're concerned. You're family."

Otho Krin came in bearing a tray of snacks and a tea set.

"How many times have I told you that you don't need to act like a servant?" Jia said. "You came here as Kuni's bodyguard, not to carry things for me."

"I don't mind, Lady Jia," Otho said, his face red. "I begged Lord Garu to bring me here, and I told him that I would make myself useful, whether it's protecting him or helping you with anything you need around the house. There's nothing I wouldn't do for Lord Garu . . . and you."

"You're like a child who never grows up," Jia said, but she was also smiling. "Thank you, Otho." The awkward young man bowed and left.

Jia and Kuni welcomed Mata and they sat on the floor in *géüpa*. Jia poured tea while Kuni handed the baby to Mata. Mata, unsure what to do, held the baby gingerly in his big palm like a coconut. The baby didn't cry, but looked up at the giant man curiously. Kuni and Jia laughed.

"He has your figure, Kuni," Mata said as he looked at the baby's chubby legs and round belly. "But he is much better looking."

"You've clearly been spending too much time with my husband," said a smiling Jia. "You're even learning his low style of humor."

While they drank tea and snacked on dried mango chips and cod strips with bamboo eating sticks, Mata told Kuni about King Thufi's announcement.

"King of Géfica!" Kuni marveled. "That is certainly going to excite the officers and soldiers."

"Indeed it will."

"My brother, how can you remain so calm? Surely you see it as a promise meant for you to fulfill!"

Mata grinned. "There are many heroes in the rebellion. Who can say whom the gods will favor with such a prize?"

Kuni shook his head. "You do not need to be so humble. Strive for your destiny."

Mata laughed, happy at Kuni's confidence but also feeling embarrassed. "Right now, I just hope King Thufi will make me commander-in-chief of the alliance forces at Wolf's Paw so that my uncle can stay in Çaruza—he deserves a rest, and King Thufi would feel safer with the marshal around in charge of homeland defense."

"I'll go with you. We fight well together."

Mata smiled. He did enjoy having Kuni Garu by his side. Kuni might not be much of a warrior, but he always had clever ideas.

Kuni and Jia then looked at each other and shared a smile. Kuni leaned toward Mata. "There might be another Little Garu soon."

"Congratulations again! Well, you two certainly aren't wasting any time." Mata toasted the happy couple.

"We Garus are like the dandelions: We multiply no matter how difficult things are." Kuni gently stroked Jia's back, and Jia looked contentedly into the eyes of the baby in her arms. The walls around them were bare and drafty, yet Mata thought it felt warmer here than in the stone halls of King Thufi's palace, full of luxurious tapestries and hurrying servants.

He had never thought much about children. But these days, in the company of Princess Kikomi, his mind was drifting to things other than war strategies and battle tactics.

CHAPTER TWENTY-SEVEN

# KIKOMI

ÇARUZA: THE NINTH MONTH IN THE FOURTH YEAR OF THE REIGN OF RIGHTEOUS FORCE.

While the army prepared to set out for Wolf's Paw, Çaruza was consumed with gossip about Princess Kikomi.

The glamorous princess was often seen in the company of young General Mata Zyndu. The two made a striking couple: Mata was like Fithowéo come to life, and Kikomi was as beautiful as any vision of Tututika. There was no better match that could be conceived.

Mata did not consider himself a man of fine sensibilities, but Kikomi caused his heart to flutter and his breath to quicken in ways that he had always thought existed only in old poems. Looking into her eyes, he thought time stopped, and he longed to sit all day just watching her.

But it was listening to her that Mata most enjoyed. Kikomi spoke in such a low voice that he often had to lean in to hear her, and he could then breathe in her flowery scent—tropical, lush, luxurious. She seemed to caress him with her voice: lingering on his face, combing through his hair, stepping gently through his heart.

She spoke of her childhood on Arulugi, of the contradictions of growing up as a princess who had been deprived of her realm.

She had been brought up in the family of a loyal retainer of her grandfather, and though she longed to think of herself as a wealthy merchant's daughter, just like her adopted sisters, she was taught that she had to remember the duties that came with her royal blood.

The people of Amu still thought of her as their princess, even if she no longer had a throne or palace. She led the dances at the great festivals, reassured the nobles who commiserated with her about their lost glory, and went to the fine schools of Müning with her brothers and sisters, where she read the Ano Classics and learned to sing and play the coconut lute. She wore the title of princess like an old sentimental cloak, too shabby to keep her warm, but too dear to shed.

Then came the rebellion, and overnight she came to live the life she had only encountered in fairy tales. Ministers bowed before her, and men with lowered eyes carried her into the palace at Müning, and all the old rituals and ceremonies became real again. An invisible wall rose up around her. Being Princess Kikomi was a great privilege, but it was also a great burden.

Mata understood that weight, the weight of privilege and obligation, of lost ancient glory and fresh, heavy expectation. This was an experience that someone like Kuni Garu, who was not born noble, who had not been deprived of his birthright, could not possibly understand. For Mata, Kuni was like a brother, but Princess Kikomi could *see* into his heart. He could not imagine feeling any closer to another person, not even Phin.

"You are like me," she said. "All your life, others have told you how you should be, given you an image to strive for. But have you ever thought about what you wanted? Just you, simple Mata, not the last son of the Zyndus?"

"Not until now," he said.

He shook his head and woke from this dreamlike state he often fell into in the presence of Kikomi. He was a believer in propriety, and he wanted to honor his pure intentions. He would bring her to meet his uncle, the Duke of Tunoa and Marshal of Cocru, and secure his blessing, and then he would approach King Ponadomu to ask for her hand.

Kikomi stood up from a deep *jiri* and watched as Mata's figure disappeared down the hall.

She closed the door and leaned against it, her face falling into an expression of deep grief. She mourned her freedom, mourned the loss of her self.

How foolish of Captain Cano Tho, thinking that his bravery had engineered her and King Ponadomu's "miraculous" escape.

*I made a deal.*

What pained her most was that she did like Mata, liked his awkward, stiff demeanor; his sincere, unadorned speech; his open face that could not hide how he felt. She even saw his faults in a forgiving light: his hot temper, his fragile pride, his overweening sense of honor—with time, these could be tempered into aspects of true nobility.

*Can you not see through my painted smiles? Can you not see through my false devotion?*

She did not know the art of seduction well—had always scorned it, in fact, and she had moved too fast with Kindo Marana. But now, now she was succeeding so well. The cause was so obvious that she tried to deny it whenever it surfaced in her mind: Perhaps she wasn't feigning it at all. That made what she was doing so much worse.

She clenched her fists, and her nails dug into her flesh. She thought of Amu in flames, of Müning being put to the sword.

She could not lay bare her heart to Mata.

*I made a deal.*

Phin Zyndu had always thought of women as diversions. He would bed a servant girl now and then to sate his urges, but he did not permit them to distract him from his real task: restoring the honor of the Zyndu Clan and the glory of Cocru.

But this woman was different, this Princess Kikomi, who came in the company of his nephew.

She was strong, like a young jujube tree. Though he commanded twenty thousand men, and even King Thufi deferred to him on all military matters, she was not cowed by him. She was a princess without a land, and yet she behaved as if she were his equal.

She did not ask for his protection with her eyes or attitude, the way so many women seemed to. This only made him feel even more protective of her. He yearned to reach out and pull her into his embrace.

She spoke of her admiration of him and of her sorrow at the sacrifices made by the young men of Arulugi. So many noblewomen in Phin's experience were silly creatures, their minds confined to the walls of their boudoirs and the schedule of balls and parties. But the princess cried genuine tears for the men who died, each alone, in the dark waters of the Amu Strait. She understood what moved men who went to the battlefield to seek glory, but whose dying thoughts always turned to mothers and wives, daughters and sisters. She was worthy, indeed, of the men who died for her.

And she was beautiful, so beautiful.

Kikomi smiled demurely.

Inside, she wanted to scream.

The marshal simply assumed that she wanted and needed to be protected, had been surprised to hear her speak of Amu's naval defeat with knowledge and sense. She noted how Phin had condescendingly praised her education, had chuckled when she expressed wonder at Çaruza's library. He had not paid much attention when she spoke of the suffering and hardship of the women who worked the docks of Müningtozu to prepare the ships for war, but his eyes had lit up when she turned the conversation to the sailors on those ships.

He had truly meant to pay her a compliment when he told her how different she was from "those silly young noblewomen," had truly believed that she would be flattered to be thought extraordinary from her sex.

It was men like him who had made her into a symbol, had put her into this impossible position.

But, in a way, that made the task easy. She knew exactly what she needed to say and do, and she even enjoyed the challenge of playing the role of his ideal: She was worthy only insofar as she oriented herself to men, like a sunflower adoring the sun.

*I made a deal.*

What was the meaning of those glances between Kikomi and Phin? Mata thought. What was the meaning of the way she lowered her head, and the way he reached out to touch her shoulder? Was that how an uncle greeted the intended of his nephew?

Somehow all three of them skirted around the purpose of the meeting. It was confusing. Nothing concrete or improper was spoken, and yet too much seemed to have been said.

Was it right that he was feeling this way for a woman so much younger? Phin thought. Was it proper that he was preempting the claim of his nephew? He had always treated Mata as a son, and yet, now he felt jealous of him, of his youth, of his strength, of his unjust claim on *her*.

But Kikomi had given him permission to feel this way about her, had she not? Those looks, those sighs—they spoke volumes.

He could tell she appreciated his maturity, the steadiness of feeling brought on by the accumulation of years. Mata was young and impulsive, and he was infatuated with her, like a puppy. But she could see through it. She wanted a love more manly, more lasting and real.

Mata asked Kuni to come and visit.

Morose and dejected, Mata said nothing as he filled two cups with sorghum liquor. An open fire burned in a bronze brazier next to the table. Kuni sat down across from his friend and took a sip from his cup. The liquor was cheap, strong, and made Kuni's eyes water.

Kuni had heard the same gossip as everyone else, and, tactfully, he said nothing.

"He's sending me away," Mata said. He drained his cup and immediately fell to great heaving coughs that disguised his tears. "He has decided that Pashi Roma, that decrepit old man, fit only to sit by the gates of Çaruza, will be commander-in-chief at Wolf's Paw. I'm in charge of the rear guard only, and I must leave within the week to begin preparations for the crossing over the Kishi Channel. But I won't even get to cross with the main force. My duty is to play harbor-master and guard the Maji Peninsula in case there has to be a retreat."

Kuni continued to say nothing. He simply refilled Mata's cup.

"She said that she would not choose between us. And so *he* decided to make the choice for her and get me out of the way. It's his way of demonstrating how much power he has over me, to belittle me. He's taken away my chance for glory." Mata spit into the fire.

"It's not good to speak this way, brother. You and the marshal are two pillars holding up the sky over Cocru. Discord, like termites in the foundation, is an infestation that must be plucked out, lest it bring ruin upon all of us. You have a duty to focus on the task at hand. The lives of men depend on you."

"I am not the uncle who *stole* a nephew's woman, Kuni! I am not the one who betrayed a bond of trust! He's a weak old man, and he has always relied on me to fight his wars for him. Maybe it's time I stopped."

"Enough! You are drunk and know not what you say. I'll go with you, Mata, to the Maji Peninsula. Forget about the fickle woman. She has played with both of your affections, and she is not worthy of your anger."

"Do not speak ill of her." Mata got up and tried to strike at Kuni, but he stumbled and missed. Kuni deftly dodged out of the way and then held Mata up, looping one of his thick arms over his own shoulder.

"All right, brother. I'll shut up about the princess. But I dearly wish neither of you had ever met her."

But Kuni could not go with Mata to war after all. Cogo Yelu sent news from Zudi: Kuni's mother had died. Kuni had to go to Zudi and stay in mourning for thirty days as was the custom. Kuni did offer to delay the mourning until after the present crisis, but Mata strenuously shook his head. Even in war, such proprieties had to be respected.

Since Jia was pregnant again, and it would be difficult to travel with the baby, she decided to remain in Çaruza. Mata promised that he would send reliable men to look after her.

Otho Krin offered to stay behind to protect Jia, and Kuni immediately agreed. He felt better about leaving Jia behind if he knew she had someone loyal she could call on.

"It's slightly inconvenient to have a man stay in the house with me when my husband isn't around," Jia said. "While I don't much care about Çaruza's gossip, it's best not to give them fodder."

"I could become your steward and thus be a proper part of your household," Otho suggested.

Though Jia protested the idea, Kuni decided that it would be for the best. "Thank you, Otho. I'm honored that you'd be willing to do this just to protect Lady Jia. Your loyalty will not be forgotten."

Otho mumbled his thanks.

Meanwhile, although most of Kuni's soldiers had been incorporated into the expeditionary force to Wolf's Paw, Mata assigned a platoon of five hundred veterans out of Kuni's and his old unit to accompany him back to Zudi.

Kuni thanked him and began to prepare for the trip home.

"Be careful, brother. Focus on our only concern: defeating the empire. Remember your song, the song about our golden-hued brotherhood. One day, I expect to see you parade in triumph in Pan as the King of Géfica. The crowd will praise your name into the sky, and I promise to be there by your side, cheering the loudest."

But Mata said nothing. His eyes seemed very far away.

∽ ∾ ∽ ∾

"Daf," the hundred-chief said. "Wake up and start packing. You're going with Duke Garu back to Zudi."

Dafiro and Ratho looked at each other, yawned, and began to pack up.

"What are you doing?" the hundred-chief said to Ratho. "Just your brother, not you. You're still coming with us to Wolf's Paw."

"But we've always been together."

"Tough. General Zyndu said to pull fifty men from Third Company for Duke Garu, and that's what I'm doing. Daf goes, and you stay." The hundred-chief, a young man with an arrogant face, smirked. He fingered the shark's-teeth necklace around his neck, as if daring Daf or Rat to defy his petty authority.

"I told you we should never have come back into the army," Dafiro said. "I think we have to desert."

But Ratho shook his head. "General Zyndu gave the order. I won't disobey him."

There was nothing to do then but for the Miro brothers to say good-bye to each other.

"This is because they think I'm lazy," Dafiro said. "Now I wish I had worked as hard as you. Damn this wind. It's making my eyes water." There was only a very light breeze.

"Hey, look at it this way: If I don't come back from Wolf's Paw, you'll be able to stop worrying about taking care of me. Then you can marry a nice girl and keep the Miro name alive. Ha, who knows, maybe you'll even get to be the one to capture Emperor Erishi. Duke Garu is full of tricks."

"Take care of yourself, you hear? Don't always rush to be at the front. Stay back and watch carefully. If things aren't going well, run."

At night, the glowing crater of Mount Kana could be seen for miles around.

It rumbled.

*What are you doing here, Tazu of Gan, dressed up like a hundred-chief?*

A wild laughter, as chaotic as sea wreckage, as amoral as a shark gliding through the unlit ocean.

*You're about to bring your damned war to my island, and I'm not allowed to play some games?*

*I thought you weren't going to take sides.*

*Who said anything about taking sides? I'm here to have fun.*

*You consider it fun to divide brother from brother?*

*The mortals are always dividing uncle from nephew, husband from wife. I'm doing no more than adding a bit more randomness to their lives. Everyone can use a bit of Tazu now and then.*

Phin told himself that he did it to protect both Mata and Kikomi.

Mata had been behaving more and more erratically, and Kikomi had been frightened by what Mata might do if she rejected him outright. It was up to Phin to cure Mata of his infatuation and to protect the fragile, delicate Kikomi.

He asked her to stay the night with him. She sat still for a moment but then nodded silently.

She poured him cup after cup of mango liquor, and her beauty complemented the drink so well that he couldn't stop drinking. She made him feel so young again, and he felt that he could take on the whole empire all by himself. Yes, it was definitely the right decision. She belonged with him.

He pulled her to him, and she smiled and demurely lifted her face for a kiss.

The moon was very bright. The silvery light spilled through the window onto the woven-grass-matted floor, onto the bed where Phin Zyndu snored loudly.

Princess Kikomi sat on the edge of the bed. She was naked. The night air was warm, but she shivered.

*You will practice your womanly arts on the Zyndus.*

She replayed Kindo Marana's words in her head for the hundredth time.

*Phin and Mata Zyndu are the heart and soul of castled Cocru's martial might. But you will divide uncle and nephew from each other with your feigned affections until jealousy and suspicion have paralyzed the Cocru army. And when the time is right, you will assassinate one of the two: with either of Cocru's two arms gone, Namen and I will make short work of the other.*

*This is my offer, Your Royal Highness: Dedicate yourself to this task, or the people of Amu will pay the price for your failure.*

Kikomi got up. Silently, gracefully, she slid across the floor in the way her dance teachers had taught her. She stopped at the folding screen on the other side of the room, where her dress was draped. Reaching inside a hidden fold within her belt, she retrieved the thin dagger. She felt the rough handle digging into the skin of her palm.

*This is called Cruben's Thorn. Once, an assassin from Gan tried to use it on Emperor Mapidéré, back when he was still called King Réon. I'll leave it for you in your cabin. The Thorn is carved from a single cruben's tooth, and so, unlike other weapons made of metal, it cannot be detected by magnetic doors or probes, a common precaution of paranoid Tiro kings. It's the perfect weapon for assassins.*

She touched the tip with a finger. A drop of blood, a black pearl in the silvery moonlight, grew on her finger. The marshal's guards had required her, like all visitors to the marshal's private quarters, to pass through a short corridor constructed from strong lodestone, apologizing to her all the while. If the dagger had been made of metal, the part of her body attached to it would have stuck to the lodestone, exposing her true intentions.

Marana had thought far ahead.

Silently, gracefully, she slid back next to the bed.

She smiled bitterly. Marana thought she was a peacock's feather, thought she was a drop of poison from the horned toad's sac. Yet she had a choice: Narrow and confined though it was, she would make the most of it.

She had thought long and hard. Mata was younger, but he was

on the rise, just coming into full awareness of his own potential. Phin, on the other hand, was past his prime.

If she killed Mata, Phin might be accelerated on his arc of long and inevitable decline. But if she killed Phin, hot-blooded Mata might be so filled with rage and thoughts of vengeance that the empire would be forced to face a monster it had created.

She hoped that her decision was rational, wasn't influenced by her real feelings for Mata.

She looked at the naked body of Phin, at his balding head, at his muscles, just starting to lose their definition. How she wished she did not have to do this. How she wished she was not a princess, but only the daughter of a wealthy merchant. With privilege came duty, and sometimes one had to choose between one life and the lives of an island.

"I'm sorry. I'm sorry. I'm sorry."

She lifted Phin's chin, and as he stirred in his sleep, she plunged the dagger deep into the soft hollow of his neck. Holding the handle by both hands, she slid the dagger left and right, and blood spurted everywhere.

With a gurgle, Phin came awake and grabbed both of her hands. In the moonlight she could see his eyes, as wide as the wine cups. Surprise, pain, fury. He could not speak, but he squeezed until the dagger fell from her fingers. She knew that her wrists were broken. She would not be able to end her own life, as she had wanted to.

With all her strength, she grunted and pulled herself free and backed out of his reach.

"I do this for the people of Arulugi," she whispered to him. "I made a deal. Forgive me. I made a deal."

Marana had promised that she would be remembered in the hearts of the people of Amu. That generation after generation would sing songs about her sacrifice and tell stories about her heroism.

Did she deserve such praise? Yes, she had saved the people of Amu. But she had also cut down the Marshal of Cocru in cold blood and endangered the rebellion and the lives of countless others. She did not exactly regret it: She was a daughter of Amu, and for her the people of that island would always come first. Between two great evils, she chose the lesser.

Yet how could she bear to face Phin Zyndu and all those who were about to die under the sword of Marana in the afterlife? She must steel her heart for the accusing stares.

The writhing of Phin's body became slower and less vigorous.

In the cold moonlight, Kikomi's vision, momentarily obscured by the pain of her broken wrists, cleared. She shuddered as she finally understood the deviousness of Marana's plan: If Xana were to spare Amu in the subsequent wars and her name were then celebrated, Cocru would suspect an alliance between Amu and Xana and consider her act proof of Amu's treachery. Müning, that beautiful, fragile floating city, might yet be put to the torch by Mata's army.

*A seducer is one who wins through deception rather than force, a harlot is one who wields sex like a sorcerer wields a staff, and "a mere bauble" may yet decide to put herself on display to guide the hearts and minds of thousands into an unstoppable force.*

Marana was counting on her vanity, on her desire to be a great hero to her people, to be remembered for her sacrifice. But her glory would bring endless strife between Cocru and Amu and doom the Beautiful Island.

There was only one way to thwart his plan: She would have to desecrate her own memory to ensure the safety of Amu.

As Phin's body stopped moving, she began to shout. "I have killed the Marshal of Cocru! Oh, Kindo Marana, know that I have done this for you out of love."

The sound of heavy running footsteps in the hallways and the clanging of swords came closer and closer. She stumbled to where Phin's body was and sat down.

"Marana, my Marana! I would rather be your slave girl than the Princess of Amu!"

*They will cut me down,* she thought. *Cut me down as a whore of the Marshal of Xana, a silly girl who was blinded by love to betray her people and the rebellion. And that is how they will remember me. But Amu will be safe. Amu will be safe.*

She continued to shout, until they silenced her with their swords.

*I'm truly sorry, Little Sister. . . .*

Though the Mingén falcons occasionally flew to every island of Dara, from that day on, they never approached Arulugi, the home of Tututika, last born of the gods.

CHAPTER TWENTY-EIGHT

# LUAN ZYA'S PLAN

ZUDI: THE TENTH MONTH IN THE FOURTH YEAR OF THE REIGN OF RIGHTEOUS FORCE.

After paying his respects to Féso Garu, Luan Zya stopped in the mourning hall to offer a prayer for the repose of Lady Garu's soul and to light a candle.

He had ridden nonstop from Haan to Çaruza, and thence to Zudi. For much of the journey, when he was in Imperial territory, he had had to ride at night and hide during the day to avoid the emperor's spies. Living for so many days in the saddle thinned his already-gaunt body and coated his robe in a thick layer of mud and dust. But his eyes were brighter, more feverish, and filled with more excitement than ever.

Naré's death had finally softened Féso's heart and caused him to rescind his order that Kuni was never to be allowed in his house.

Kuni Garu got up as Luan Zya entered his room. Kuni was dressed all in white, and wore ashes on his face and draped rough sackcloth around his shoulders. His eyes were red and tired. The two men grasped arms and shared a moment of silence.

Luan sat down, back straight, knees bent in *mipa rari*. "A mother's love is the strongest thread in the tapestry of life. My heart rings in tune with your loss."

Instead of replying with an equally flowery cliché, as most cultured men would, the duke simply said, "I've been a great disappointment to my mother. But she loved me no matter what."

"I've often thought the pleasure that parents take in their children is like the pleasure a man gets from releasing a wild bird. I would venture to guess that Lady Garu had plenty of joy, though she had seen but a little of how high you would fly."

Kuni Garu bowed his head. "Thank you."

"Lord Garu, you and I do not know each other well, and yet I have often thought of you in the months since we met. I believe you to be among the few who will one day stride across this world like a colossus and drink with the gods."

Kuni laughed lightly. "Even in mourning, I enjoy such flattery. What a strange beast is Man."

"I come not to flatter you, Lord Garu, but to offer you an opportunity."

Luan Zya had been in Haan on a secret mission to rouse up hot-blooded young men who would be willing to risk their lives and perform acts of sabotage in the Imperial heartland. It was dangerous work that held little promise, but Luan took to it without complaint. When a man loved his homeland enough, even the slimmest hope was worth pursuing, contrary to prudent calculation and careful forethought.

But one night he was awakened by the sound of paper rustling. As he sat up, he saw in the starlight that the pages of *Gitré Üthu*, the tome given to him by that old fisherman by the sea, fluttered by themselves on his desk.

He got up from bed, sat down next to the desk, and saw that the book had opened itself to a new section he had never seen before. Slowly, the blank pages were being filled with a new landscape of words and pictures.

There was a map of the Islands of Dara, filled with tiny black and white symbols that he recognized as representing the armies that the empire and the rebellion respectively commanded. Below the map was the beginning of what appeared to be a long treatise.

He read. The sun rose and set and rose again. He continued to read, forgetting hunger and thirst.

Three days later, he got up, closed the book, and laughed.

The book had simply shown him what he had learned in his years of travel among the Islands. It was as if his mind had been poured out onto the pages—but systemized, made orderly, and presented in one place. And the new way of seeing what he already knew gave him a new idea. All his life, he realized, had been a prologue to this moment.

It was time to fulfill his promise to his father.

Luan Zya had first presented his plan to King Cosugi.

"I'm an old man, Luan. Such risks are for men who have seen seen little enough of the world to retain faith in themselves. I am content to be King Thufi's guest and let others perform the great deeds that you dream of."

Luan then went to visit Mata Zyndu at Nasu, on the Maji Peninsula. But the general, still brooding over the deaths of his uncle and Princess Kikomi, turned away all visitors, and Luan never even got to speak to Mata.

Kuni Garu was his last hope. Garu was no great warrior, and he was born only a commoner. But Luan Zya had felt something stirring in the depths of the man's heart, a willingness to be persuaded and to gamble.

"King Thufi has promised to make anyone who captures Emperor Erishi the king of a new Tiro state."

Kuni nodded. He thought of Mata Zyndu. If anyone had the bravery and prowess to march into Pan, it was his friend.

"Tanno Namen left Pan with minimal defenses when he departed for Thoco Pass to join Marana at Wolf's Paw. He thought it enough for the Imperial navy to hold the Liru River and the Amu Strait, with the Alliance focused only on Wolf's Paw."

"Namen is right. We have no navy to speak of on the west coast of the Big Island."

"A navy does not mean only ships."

Kuni looked at him, his expression a question.

Luan explained his plan to Kuni in a few broad strokes, striving to keep his voice even. He had to appear to be sane, in control, even if what he proposed was madness. He ended by saying, "To defeat a gang of thieves, you must seize the leader. To kill a great python, you must cut off its head."

Kuni sat in silence for a while. "A bold plan," he said finally. "And exceedingly dangerous."

Luan locked gazes with Kuni. "Lord Garu, you must now choose: Will you soar as high as a Mingén falcon though you might die trying, or will you spend a lifetime safely pecking at grains of rice scattered under someone else's eaves?"

Kuni's face was unchanged. Luan could not tell if he had succeeded in kindling the man's ambition—in all his calculations, predicting Kuni's reaction had always been the hardest part.

"Even if I succeed, how will I hold the Immaculate City? It will be like trying to parry a sword with a sewing needle."

"Lord Zyndu, your friend, will surely come to your aid. But only after—this plan cannot work unless it's known by as few people as possible ahead of its execution."

"And then we will be kings together," said Kuni. "Brothers in arms, brothers on the throne."

Luan nodded. "You will be as well matched together as you were here at Zudi."

"Provided I succeed," said Kuni, after a pause. "You offer me nothing but a gamble."

Luan was prepared for disappointment. Though Kuni had once been a gambler, he had already accomplished much. And achievement had a way of lowering a man's tolerance for risk.

"Tell me," Kuni said, "what does Lutho think of your plan?"

Luan kept his gaze steady. "My father was chief augur to Lutho, and I have a bit of a reputation as a master of divination. But the truth, Lord Garu, is that the will of the gods cannot be ascertained. I have never witnessed a sign that cannot be interpreted multiple ways. I've always believed that the gods are like the wind and the tides, currents of great power that may be ridden only by those willing to help themselves."

Kuni smiled at him. "An ignorant man might think such words from an augur's son impious."

"It's a common sentiment among those who have studied long in Haan. It isn't by coincidence that Ginpen's schools, though small, have produced a disproportionate number of Dara's mathematicians, philosophers, lawgivers: We strive to calculate that which is knowable in favor of that which is not."

"I apologize for my feigned surprise," said Kuni. "It was a test. Had you promised the aid of Lutho's favor for your mad plan, I would have known not to trust you."

Luan laughed. "You're a good actor, Lord Garu."

"I learned my skill in a life of petty crime and street wagering. You probably know that among gamblers, there is a divide. Half of us pray to Lutho, and the other half to Tazu. Do you know why?"

Luan did not hesitate. "Those who prefer Lutho favor games of skill, believing that with sufficient knowledge and calculation, the future is predictable; those who prefer Tazu favor games of chance, believing that the world is as random as the path of his whirlpool and the future as likely to delight as to disappoint."

"I have always prayed to both," said Kuni. "And so, Luan, tell me again of your plan and the knowledge behind the madness."

Luan proceeded to explain his reasoning, laying out detailed figures and maps and intelligence of troop movements and profiles of Xana commanders. Kuni listened intently, asking questions from time to time.

By the time Luan was done with his explanations, he looked at the pile of paper scraps in front of him in despair. His plan seemed preposterous, an impossible dream. The odds of success were so slim as to be nonexistent. By forcing Luan to explain himself, Kuni had succeeded in showing him that the plan was impossible.

"I'm sorry to have wasted your time," said Luan, and he began to pack up.

"Even in games of skill," said Kuni, "there is no guarantee of winning. In the end, there is always a gap that cannot be bridged by knowledge. Once you have worked out all the odds, you still have to toss the dice, to take that leap of faith."

A passing breeze filled the courtyard outside with floating dandelion seeds.

Kuni turned to look at them. He wished he had a plug of Jia's special chewing herbs like he did in the Er-Mé Mountains or Mata by his side on the walls of Zudi. But this time, he had to decide on his own.

*Is this the particular moment when the breeze I have awaited all my life has arrived? Is this when I am to be plucked from my home and take flight?*

"I've always promised myself an interesting adventure," Kuni said, smiling. "There should be a little bit of Tazu in everyone's life."

Then he went to say good-bye to the spirit of his mother and to apologize for having to leave early.

Dafiro Miro yawned. The road out of Zudi was still cold in the predawn darkness. He looked up at the stars and sighed.

He had no idea where they were going, only that it promised to be days of quick marching and nights spent on hard ground. The great lords never told the foot soldiers what was happening, and Dafiro was used to being sent hither and thither with no explanation. But Dafiro noticed that no messengers had been dispatched to Çaruza and King Thufi—he had made sure to befriend the couriers, knowing that they were like the antennae on an insect, the first to know anything worth knowing. Curious. Whatever Duke Garu had planned, it was to be a secret from King Thufi and General Zyndu and everyone else.

Dosa was left in charge of Zudi while all of Duke Garu's advisers came along. This would be important, that was clear.

His life was about being fed, being paid, and being bored for long stretches, interspersed with brief flashes of terror and extraordinary exertion. War was not good for anyone except those in charge.

Still, if one had to be a soldier, Duke Garu was a good lord to follow. He really seemed to make it a point not to risk his men's lives unnecessarily, and Dafiro thought this made him a better man than General Zyndu. Rat was obsessed with Zyndu's arrogant bravery and his deeds of valor, but Dafiro could see that Zyndu didn't really care about death. He wasn't afraid of anything, and that was not a virtue, as far as Dafiro was concerned.

The five hundred foot soldiers marched along the road, disguised as a merchant caravan. Always, they headed southwest. Duke Garu rode at their head on a horse, and only the gods knew where they were going.

They arrived at the port city of Canfin. Duke Garu's new adviser, the mysterious Luan Zya, went to the docks alone while the company made camp just outside the city.

Dafiro gazed at the city walls and reflected on the strange path of his life. More than a year ago, he and his brother were headed here to board a ship bound for Pan, where they had expected whips and chains and endless toil to build Emperor Mapidéré's Mausoleum. But they never made it to Canfin because their captains, Huno Krima and Zopa Shigin, changed their lives forever.

And here he was, finally. But where were they headed now?

The Imperial navy harassed ships up and down the Cocru coast, and there were few ships that dared running the blockade. But with enough money, people could be persuaded to attempt any kind of risk. Luan Zya showed the shipmasters at the docks a great deal of money.

Duke Garu's men boarded three merchant ships at night. Dafiro tried to go to sleep in the dark cargo hold. The soldiers were packed in very tightly, like dried fish or bundles of cloth, and the rocking of the ship over the waves made so many men dizzy that the smell of sickness was everywhere.

Once they were at sea, they could go up to the deck to take in fresh air in shifts. Dafiro tried to guess where they were headed by looking at the sun, the moon, and the stars. There was no land in sight, so they weren't hugging the coast. Were they headed for wild Écofi, where elephants roamed the sea of grass and much of the land was uninhabited? Was Duke Garu going to start a new settlement? Dafiro had never left the Big Island, and he wondered what he would find there.

But the sun always set to the right of the ship as they sailed ever southward.

"Land ho!"

Dafiro gazed at the dark trees on shore, the virgin forest that had never been cut down and turned into ships, houses, siege machines, and palaces.

They were at Tan Adü, the land of savage cannibals. Dafiro put his hand on the hilt of his sword. Why had Duke Garu taken them here? This was not a place for civilized men. Over the years, various Tiro states had made countless attempts to settle and subdue this island, attempts that had always failed.

The ships anchored in a shallow bay, and men were ferried ashore in small boats. Then the merchant ships pulled up their anchors, turned around, and sailed away, leaving Duke Garu and his company alone in the wild.

It was twilight, and Cogo Yelu and Mün Çakri directed the men to make camp right on the beach. Luan Zya went to the edge of the camp and took out a small hot-air lantern. He filled the hanging fuel pouch with dried grass, lit it, and launched it into the air. As the small orange flickering dot floated away into the dark sky, he followed it with his eyes until it disappeared among the stars.

Then he began to ululate, much as he had done on that long-ago day when he had tried to assassinate Emperor Mapidéré, and his cry, like the cry of a wolf, rode the winds to the dark interior of the forbidding woods.

Dafiro shivered.

In the morning, the camp was surrounded by hundreds of Adüan warriors. Their bowstrings taut and their spears raised over their shoulders, the bronze-skinned, blond men watched the Cocru soldiers impassively.

"Drop your weapons!" Luan Zya shouted at the tense soldiers. "Hold your hands up."

The soldiers hesitated, but Duke Garu repeated the order. Dafiro reluctantly put down his sword and lifted his hands. He examined the hostile-looking Adüans around them. Their naked bodies and elaborate tattoos—even on their faces, which made reading their expressions difficult—frightened him. He remembered all the stories that he had heard about Tan Adü. He hadn't had breakfast yet—and he certainly didn't want to *become* breakfast.

The warriors parted their ranks to make a path, and an old fighter, who had so many tattoos that he seemed to be more ink than skin, walked through the forest of spears and arrows into the clearing.

He looked around at Duke Garu and his advisers and then at the individual soldiers. His eyes stopped when he saw Luan Zya. The ink lines on his face shifted and shimmered, and he showed his white teeth. With a start, Dafiro realized that he was smiling.

*"Toru-noki, xindi shu'ulu akiia skulodoro, nomi nomi,"* he said.

*"Nomi, nomi-uya, Kyzen-to,"* Luan Zya said. He was smiling too.

Then they both stepped forward, and the two put their foreheads together and grabbed each other around the shoulders.

While Chief Kyzen negotiated with Luan Zya and Kuni Garu, the men of Cocru and Tan Adü tried to get to know one another.

Mün Çakri invited one of the big Adüans, Domudin, to a wrestling bout. Everyone gathered around and placed small items on the ground as bets. It was a good match. Domudin outweighed Mün by at least forty pounds, but years of wrestling muddy pigs gave Mün an advantage in skill. After he finally pinned the bigger man to the ground and Domudin placed his hands palms up on the ground to indicate that he yielded, both sides cheered. Mün pulled Domudin up, and coconut husks filled with arrack were passed all around.

Dafiro won a sharkskin pouch that he admired and happily tied it to his belt. He felt bad for the man who lost it to him, though, and he handed two copper coins over. The man, whose name sounded like "Huluwen" to Dafiro, nodded and smiled back. Dafiro tried to get him to explain his tattoos, which the man proceeded to do by drawing on the ground.

*Ah, it's all about women,* Dafiro thought as he puzzled over Huluwen's drawings. He took a stick and began to also draw a female figure on the ground, exaggerating the breasts and butt. The other men gathered around to appreciate Dafiro's artistry, and he basked in the Adüans' admiring looks.

*For a bunch of cannibals, they aren't too bad.*

It was dinnertime, and some of the Adüan women came to camp to prepare the meal. The Cocru soldiers were warned by Duke Garu to stay on their best behavior, and they gaped at the women, as tattooed as their men, without making any gesture or noise. Dafiro suddenly remembered his artwork and was relieved to find that Huluwen had already discreetly wiped all traces of it away. The two looked at each other and laughed.

There was baked wild taro. There were boars wrapped in banana leaves and roasted underground with heated stones. There were wild bird eggs and meat from sharks and whales. Little spice was used except sea salt, but the food was fresh and strange and very delicious. And everyone drank plenty of arrack.

Mün Çakri pulled Dafiro aside after dinner as the Adüans danced and some of the drunken Cocru soldiers joined them.

"Are you a good swimmer, lad?"

Dafiro nodded. Both he and Rat had spent many hours in the

small river that flowed through the village of Kiesa, and they sometimes spent the idle months after harvest hiring themselves out on fishing boats along the Cocru coast. He knew his way in water.

"Good. Duke Garu is a landlubber, and so am I. I'll need you to stay close to the duke tomorrow and keep an eye on him."

"Are we setting out to sea?"

Mün nodded, a happy twinkle in his eye. "After tomorrow, you are going to have some real stories to tell."

"So you wish to overthrow this tyrant, the All-Chief of the Islands?" Luan Zya translated Chief Kyzen's question.

Kuni nodded.

"And you will become All-Chief in his place?"

Kuni smiled. "Probably not. The men of Dara love freedom, and we do not want one All-Chief to rule over us all. But we will probably have several Big Chiefs again, and I may end up as one of them."

"I can understand that. There are many tribes here on Tan Adü as well, and we certainly do not wish to obey only one man." Chief Kyzen's eyes narrowed. "But to say you love freedom? That seems strange when the men of Dara love to make war on us and make us follow your ways."

"Not all men of Dara think the same, just as not all fish swim in the same direction."

Kyzen grunted. "What will you offer in return, if we help you?"

"What do the people of Tan Adü want?"

"If you become one of the Big Chiefs, will you and the others promise to leave us alone forever? To never permit any man of Dara to come to Tan Adü?"

Kuni Garu considered this. Over the years, the dream of conquering Tan Adü never died. The kings and dukes of Cocru, Amu, and Gan had all tried, at one time or another, to pacify this island. Even Emperor Mapidéré sent two expeditions, though nothing ever came of them. He could see why the Adüans were tired of it.

Luan Zya had told him that King Sanfé of Cocru, King Thufi's great-grandfather, had once sent an army of ten thousand to conquer Tan Adü. The Cocru army managed to secure a colony of about fifty miles square and tried to teach the captive Adüans the arts of writing, farming, and weaving, hoping that by showing them the benefits of civilization, they would be convinced to give up their struggle. But the Adüans, while conceding that Cocru's methods and tools produced more food, kept their bodies comfortable against the weather, and allowed them to pass their wisdom on to future generations more securely than talk-story, refused to adopt them, even at the point of the sword. These were men and women who treasured freedom.

"I can promise that, but it won't mean much."

Chief Kyzen's face hardened. "You're saying your word is worthless?"

"If I become a Big Chief, I can make decrees, and I can perhaps try to persuade the other Big Chiefs to do the same. But I cannot expect everyone to obey an unreasonable decree, not unless I put them all in prison. As long as Tan Adü is here, the men of Dara will want to come. I cannot take that desire to see what has not been seen out of their hearts."

"Then it is useless to talk to you."

"Chief Kyzen, it would be easy for me to lie and tell you what you want to hear, but I won't do that. Can you swear that no boy in your land ever wondered what it might be like to live as one of the men of Dara? To dress in fine clothes, to eat from porcelain dishes, to court women who look like no others they had seen? Can you swear that no girl in your land ever thought about what it might be like to live as one of the women of Dara? To wear silk and dyed cotton, to sing and write poetry, to be married to men who are of another race, of another country?"

"There is no such foolishness in the hearts of our children."

"Then you do not know young people at all, Chief Kyzen. The young often want that which the old detest and fear. The yearning for the new, for something different glimpsed but faintly through legends and shadows, cannot be taken from them—not unless you freeze their hearts and imprison their minds. Yet, you say you wish Tan Adü to remain free."

Chief Kyzen scoffed at this, but Kuni could see that the chief understood what he was getting at.

"I cannot stop traders from stopping by your shores—they will always risk anything for more profit. I cannot stop men from setting sail for your land—if they believe that just going somewhere that no other men of Dara have been is reward enough. I cannot stop men from coming here and preaching—if they believe that they have a duty to tell you what they think is right and just and to teach you a better way of life.

"But I *can* promise that if I become one of the Big Chiefs, I will not permit my people to come here and perform these acts accompanied by the accoutrements of war. And I will do my utmost to urge the other Big Chiefs to follow my example. If men of Dara come here, they will come to persuade, not to coerce. And so long as you do these visitors no injury, no army or navy of Dara will intercede on their behalf."

"The soft invasion of your traders and preachers may do far more damage to us than your arms ever would. The lure of your wealth and novel ways and your fantastical *possessions* may prove irresistible to those who are too young to understand their danger. If your men poison and corrupt the hearts of our young, then we are doomed. As you say, the young often want that which is harmful because they lack experience. Many thoughts I had as a young man I would now forswear, and many desires that consumed me as a young man I would now disown."

"If the freedom and way of life that you so treasure are worthy of your love, then you will win the hearts of your young far more easily than the visitors of Dara can. But the young must be allowed to make their own choices, to live their own lives as grand experiments. They must *choose* to become you. That is the only hope for Tan Adü."

Chief Kyzen drained his arrack in a single gulp. Then he threw his coconut bowl down and laughed. "It would have been easier for you to just lie to me, Kuni Garu. And if you had promised me exactly what I asked, I would have known that you were unworthy of our help."

*A test.* Kuni glanced over at Luan Zya, and the two men shared a smile of understanding.

Even after Luan retired to sleep, Kuni Garu and Chief Kyzen continued to drink together late into the night, their eyes bright with the recognition of kindred spirits.

They rowed out into the sea in the early morning, before sunrise.

Carved out of a single trunk with outriders, the long wooden canoes of the Adüans each held about thirty people and were surprisingly steady. Dafiro was barely awake and baffled. Were they going to row all the way back to the Big Island?

After two hours of steady rowing, the sky in the east turned fish-belly white. Chief Kyzen raised his hand, and the canoes stopped. To the men of Cocru, it looked just like any other part of the sea.

Chief Kyzen took out a long whalebone trumpet and placed the bell under water. Then he blew into it, and the trumpet produced a surprisingly loud sound that could be felt through the hull of the canoes. The music was like whale song, mournful and majestic. A few of the Adüans in the other canoes began to beat the surface of the water with their oars in rhythmic accompaniment.

Just as the sun peeked over the eastern horizon, a great black shadow, shaped like the sleek shell shuttle favored by Gan weavers, rose out of the water a mile to the east, arced across the rising sun, and fell back into the water. A moment later the thunderous boom of the breaching creature reached the men in the canoes.

It was a cruben, the great one-horned scaled whale of Dara and sovereign of the seas: two hundred feet long and as large next to an elephant as an elephant would be next to a mouse. Its eyes were so dark that they sucked in all sunlight like deep wells, and when the great fish exhaled through its blowhole, the fountain shot as high as a hundred feet.

More crubens breached nearer to the canoes: one, two, five, ten. The canoes rocked and the Adüans struggled to keep them from tipping over.

"I'm guessing our ferry has arrived," said Mün Çakri, and Dafiro realized that his own jaw had been hanging open without his notice.

The Adüans rowed the canoes next to the great floating islands of heaving flesh and glistening armored scales. Duke Garu's men, shocked into silence, sat very still.

As the Adüans scrambled up the sides of the great animals and affixed saddles to the scales on top and attached two reins to the flaps over the crubens' great eyes, Mün explained to Dafiro what he had learned from Luan Zya.

The Adüans believed that the crubens were as intelligent as men, but their long lives, passed in the limitless ocean rather than on tiny dots of land, had almost nothing in common with men. They had their own civilization, as sophisticated as any Tiro state, but their concerns were foreign to mankind's minds and their sensibilities alien to mankind's hearts. The inhabitants of Dara, awed by the crubens' physical presence, only admired them from afar, but the men of Tan Adü had learned to speak to them, after a fashion, over a hundred generations.

The Adüans asked the crubens to perform a small favor for their guest, this Kuni Garu. The great fish considered the request and assented. They sought no reward. What could men give them? They needed nothing. They would do this for their own amusement.

Before Dafiro climbed onto the leading cruben's head to take up the reins, he handed his sword to Huluwen, who sat in the same canoe. "A gift in case I don't survive today," Dafiro said, hoping that the Adüan understood.

Huluwen picked up the sword, felt its heft, and handed Dafiro his war club, whose thick end was studded with sharp bits of bone and razor-sharp stone flakes. It reminded him of Goremaw, Mata Zyndu's cudgel.

Dafiro held the club tightly in his hand. He wished his brother were around to witness this. Rat would not believe his retelling, but the club would at least corroborate some aspect of his story.

"I'm going to call you Biter," said Daf. Sure, it wasn't an impressive allusion from Classical Ano, but at that moment, Dafiro Miro felt every inch a hero from the old tales.

Every time Dafiro thought he was dreaming, he bit his tongue and the pain told him that he was not. Every time Dafiro thought he was not dreaming, he looked around, and the sights that greeted his eyes were impossible.

Before him, jutting into the sky like the bowsprit of a great warship, was a twenty-foot-long horn. It was so thick at the base that two men together could not have wrapped their arms around it. The tip of the horn was sharper than the point of a spear, threatening destruction to anything that stood in its way.

Roaring waves dashed against the horn and the barnacle-encrusted forehead below it, breaking into a violent mist that soaked his clothes and sometimes made it hard to open his eyes. Everywhere he looked, sunlight was refracted into rainbows in the salty mist.

The waves divided themselves around the creature they rode on, and from where Dafiro was sitting, he could barely feel them. He felt only the gentle and slow undulating motion of the great mass heaving beneath him, ponderous, forceful, four hundred tons of muscle and sinew.

He was sitting in a saddle clipped to the two scales directly under him, each a foot across. The scales were dark blue and shimmered like rain-slicked obsidian, like the night sky just after twilight. Identical scales paved and covered the heaving, powerful body below him, forward to the brow and the horn, and behind him, for two hundred feet, until they reached the tail, twin flukes fifty feet across. The flukes reared out of the water and then beat down, slapping against the surface with the thunderous roar of a tsunami.

Behind him, in another saddle, sat Duke Garu. He was drenched in water too, and he held on to Dafiro with his arms so that he would not slip from the saddle. Though Dafiro could feel the duke's fear in his tight grip, he also saw on the duke's face the biggest smile Dafiro could remember.

"Aren't you glad you came with me, lad?" he shouted when he saw that Dafiro was looking back.

Dafiro nodded and bit his tongue again to be sure he was not dreaming.

They were riding on the back of a cruben, and around and behind them, twenty other crubens swam along. Duke Garu's force was sailing up to the Amu Strait on the backs of the sovereigns of the sea.

They moved faster than any ship, than any airship, than any creation of mankind.

As the great cruben fleet approached the Amu Strait, the riders raised the red flags of Cocru charged with double ravens.

To the patrolling Imperial fleet, what they saw was a scene out of myths, legends, descriptions of mirages. The great cruben was the symbol of the princeps or the emperor, and yet Cocru soldiers were riding them. It was impossible. It could not happen.

One of the Imperial ships was slow to get out of the way, and a cruben decided to ram it with its horn. The ship's solid ironwood hull and oaken masts snapped like twigs stepped on by a giant, and men were thrown into the air as the ship under their feet exploded into a million pieces of splinter and wreckage.

The crubens arrived at Rui, one of the home islands of Xana. They swam close to shore, slowly making a counterclockwise circuit of the island.

The men on their backs waved the flag of Cocru and shouted that the empire had fallen, that Mata Zyndu had already marched into the Immaculate City and was burning down the palace at this very moment. Duke Garu of Zudi had come to seek the surrender of Rui, and any who refused would be struck down by the sovereigns of the sea.

The men of Rui stood mute at the sight of crubens ferrying Cocru soldiers. No one had ever even heard of people riding on crubens, much less seen it with their own eyes. Surely this meant that the gods were on the side of the rebels.

Xana soldiers did not approach as the crubens beached themselves, and their riders climbed down. They stood at attention as the great fish backed into the water, turned, and swam away. They set down their weapons as Duke Garu walked solemnly down the streets, the bloodred ensign of Cocru waving over him.

Kuni Garu arrived at Mount Kiji Air Base, where the engineers and the administrators lay prostrate on the ground to welcome the conqueror of Rui.

"We've come a long way," said Luan Zya, a smile on his face.

"Just a little farther," said Kuni, smiling back.

Then the five hundred ascended into the air in ten great airships and winged their way back toward the Big Island, to Pan.

As the airships floated over the fields and towns of Haan and Géfica, people stopped, looked up, and then went back to their work. Marshal Marana was preparing to crush the rebels on Wolf's Paw, and these new airships were no doubt going to provide additional reinforcements. The empire would triumph, as everyone had always known it would.

The airships slowed as they approached Pan and descended toward the palace. The palace guards looked at the ships with little concern. Had the emperor, perhaps, decided that he would ride one of the airships to the front so that he could witness the death throes of the rebels personally?

They landed in the middle of the Great Court, the wide-open space before the Grand Audience Hall where Emperor Erishi reviewed the palace guards and sometimes played hunting games with horses and animals drugged to be docile and easy to shoot.

"Leave twenty men with me," Luan said. "We will guard one of the airships. If you don't succeed in an hour, fight your way back and we'll retreat."

"Do you always plan for failure even when success is within reach?" Kuni asked.

"It's the prudent thing to do."

"If you hadn't thought of the possibility of failure, I wonder if your attempt to assassinate Mapidéré might have worked out differently. Because you thought of escaping to Zudi, you did not want to burden your flying machine with too much weight. You could have carried bigger bombs, or flown lower before launching them."

Luan stood still as he pondered this.

"Sometimes prudence is not a virtue," said Kuni. "I gambled a lot when I was younger. I can tell you that Tazu is more fun than Lutho. If you're going to gamble, you'll have more fun if you don't hold anything back."

Luan laughed. "Then let's make this wager count. I will fight by your side today, and no one will stay behind."

Armored soldiers jumped out of the ships and rushed into the palace, Luan and Kuni in the lead.

Luan guided Kuni and the others away from the main doors, constructed of lodestone. Mapidéré had been paranoid about assassins, and those who came to see the emperor were required to be disarmed. If, by chance, someone managed to come into the palace armed, the magnetic doors would pull the swords out of their hands. Instead, Luan pointed to the side doors, reserved for the emperor's own guards and servants.

They ran over the model of the Islands in the Grand Audience Hall, the model that Emperor Erishi had taken such care to construct. Wine splashed everywhere, and the fountains finally ceased to flow as Kuni Garu's soldiers crushed the delicate pipes underfoot, casually, almost as an afterthought, on their way to the rest of the palace.

The palace guards woke from their slumber and rushed onto the

Great Court. But it was too late. Fire was burning everywhere, and the wailing and screaming of dying ministers and servants filled the halls.

To search the vast palace effectively, Luan and Kuni divided their forces in half. Luan would cover the western side while Kuni took the eastern side.

Dafiro Miro followed the duke closely. Mün Çakri had told him that his job was to *protect* the duke. Sure, maybe Mün only meant that he needed to keep the duke from falling off the cruben into the sea since the duke didn't know how to swim. But Dafiro was going to take the instructions very literally and stay right by the duke's side.

The duke didn't want to die, and others would always try to save him if things went wrong. *Therefore, the safest place to be in battle is right next to the duke.* Dafiro was always very practical.

They rushed through the halls, following every twist and turn, dividing into halves where the paths branched. Kuni seized a servant and forced him to lead the way. Dafiro and the others set fire to everything they could see. They wanted to create as much confusion and chaos as possible.

Then they were rushing down a corridor, which terminated in thick golden doors. Kuni Garu pulled on the doors, but they were locked from within. Dafiro and the others lifted up a heavy stone statue of Kiji found in one of the alcoves in the corridor and began to use it as a battering ram.

*Tum, tum, tum.*

They could hear frightened shouts and desperate whispers from behind the doors. The people inside had nowhere to run.

*Tum, tum, tum.*

Shouting and heavy steps echoed up the corridor. They looked back and saw that some palace guards had found them and were closing fast. A few of the soldiers dropped the statue/battering ram to hold off the guards, while the duke and Dafiro continued to batter the door.

There were many guards, too many for the few soldiers that Kuni had with him. Farther up the corridor, Mün Çakri, Than Carucono, Rin Coda, and their men hacked at the guards, trying to join up with Kuni. But they were too far away.

The door gave way.

Kuni and Dafiro tumbled through. They were inside a huge bedroom, and a crying boy was on the bed, trying to hide himself by piling blankets around himself. He wore a silk robe embroidered with the figures of leaping crubens.

An old man stood at the foot of the bed, wearing an expression that was a mixture of pity and triumph. He turned around to face the men who had burst through the door. "I am Prime Minister Goran Pira. Now if you will put down your weapons and listen—"

Dafiro bashed in his skull with one strike from Biter. He had no time to waste on anyone who stood in the way of his prize. He was going to get his hands on the boy emperor.

*Whichever man, be he churl or earl, captures Emperor Erishi will be made the King of Géfica.* Dafiro's lips curled up in a smile. Of course he didn't expect to be really made a king, but surely Duke Garu would reward him handsomely for paving his way.

But Kuni had moved even faster. He was on the bed in one leap, pulled the boy in front of himself, and pushed the blade of his sword up against the boy's throat.

"Tell your guards to stop fighting," Kuni said, and brushed the boy's neck with the edge of the sword so that a thin trickle of blood formed against the pale skin.

"Stop, stop, stop fighting!" Emperor Erishi shouted as tears and mucus covered his red face.

The guards hesitated, uncertain what to do.

*Too bad that the boy wasn't closer to this side of the bed,* Dafiro thought. *Ah well, you can't ever win a race against the duke. He's too clever.*

"I'm going to bash your head in just like the old coward's, if you don't get them to stop." Dafiro waved Biter at the boy.

The boy was so frightened that he could not speak. The entire room fell silent.

Then, everyone heard the sound of water trickling against the marble floor.

Emperor Erishi had let his bladder go.

The guards dropped their swords.

CHAPTER TWENTY-NINE

# BATTLE OF WOLF'S PAW

WOLF'S PAW: THE TENTH MONTH IN THE FOURTH YEAR OF THE REIGN OF RIGHTEOUS FORCE.

Wolf's Paw stood across the Kishi Channel from the Itanti Peninsula. Its northern and eastern sides, facing the endless ocean, were dominated by rugged cliffs that provided few safe harbors. On the other hand, its western and southern coasts, facing the channel, sloped gently down to the sea and offered many inviting ports. This was the heart of old Gan, which, besides Wolf's Paw, also claimed the rich alluvial plains and the bustling cities of Géjira on the Big Island.

The most prominent port on Wolf's Paw was Toaza, the Port That Never Slept and capital of old Gan. Deep, sheltered along the island's southern shore, and warmed by hidden currents, Toaza's waters never froze even in deepest winter. From here, Gan's intrepid merchants sailed to all the Islands of Dara and built a maritime trade network unrivaled by any of the other Tiro states. In every major port city of Dara, one could find quarters filled with sailors and merchants speaking in the accent of Gan, which had been described by scholars, disdainful for lucre, as "jangling with the sound of filthy coins."

The Gan merchants smiled at this and took it as a compliment. Let Haan be high-minded and continue to philosophize, and let Amu be alluring and hang on to its elegance and sophistication, the people of Gan understood that only gleaming gold gave one security, gave one power.

But shipping across the Kishi Channel was a hazardous endeavor because of the god Tazu.

It was said that Tazu manifested himself as a ten-mile-wide maelstrom of roiling water that sucked everything within its orbit into the bottomless deep. It wandered up and down the channel like an angry child tumbling around its room. No one had ever been able to predict its pattern of movement, capricious like the will of Tazu, the legendary rogue. Vessels captured by the whirlpool had no chance of escaping, and over the years, countless ships, some laden with treasure, some filled with lives, were sacrificed to the god's insatiable hunger.

The only year-round safe shipping lanes to Wolf's Paw involved long detours that avoided the channel by approaching Wolf's Paw from the the south. This meant that most of the ports in Wolf's Paw, save for Toaza, were unusable for long-range shipping, though daring shippers, lured by the draw of shorter trips and quicker profit, sometimes risked crossing the channel by betting against the movement of Tazu. Occasionally, they succeeded.

Mata Zyndu sat brooding in his camp at Nasu, on the eastern shore of the Maji Peninsula.

Kikomi's betrayal had infuriated him and then left him drained of feeling, like the Kishi Channel after Tazu passed through—a calm surface strewn with wreckage, and in the depths underneath, death.

He blamed his own foolishness and that of his uncle. They were taken in by a woman, one blinded by love.

How could she rebel against her noble birth? Act contrary to her duty to her people? Amu needed a leader who would give them strength to resist the empire, and yet she had willingly become an assassin for Kindo Marana because she had fallen for him.

As he thought about what she had done, Mata's hands shook with rage, and he believed that he would strangle her himself if she were still alive.

And yet, he could not deny that even knowing the falsity of her words and pretended feelings, he missed her. He had taken something of great value hidden in his heart and willingly handed it to her. And she had torn it to pieces and scattered it to the winds so that it was gone forever. Yet he did not want to have it back. He wanted only to be able to give it to her again. And again.

At the same time, he was racked with guilt for how he had behaved toward his uncle. Phin had been the only surviving member of Mata's family, the closest thing he had to a father. He was the source of all Mata's dreams about the glorious past of the Zyndu Clan and the force that propelled him to emulate the martial deeds of his illustrious ancestors. Phin Zyndu was the template against which Mata had always measured himself, the one man whose opinions on duty and honor he valued above all others. He was Mata's sole connection to the past and his most trusted guide for the future.

And yet, over Kikomi, he had almost been willing to come to blows with his uncle, like a madman or a lowly peasant consumed with jealousy. Mata's shame weighed so heavily on him that he could not lift his head.

He yearned to redeem himself on the battlefield, to wash away his shame in blood and glory.

After Phin's death, he was the Duke of Tunoa, and the last man to carry the proud Zyndu name. He had expected that he would now be made Marshal of Cocru and put in charge of the battle on Wolf's Paw. But as the days passed, neither King Thufi nor General Roma, commander-in-chief at Wolf's Paw, sent for him to offer him a role befitting his station.

He was still merely the commander of a rear guard of two thousand to remain at Nasu. His only job was to wait and guard the rebels' retreat should they fail to overcome the emperor's most puissant strike.

He saw the silence from Toaza and Çaruza as an insult, a rebuke. He sulked and drank and brooded.

Théca Kimo, now acting as his aide-de-camp, came every hour to give him the latest military reports on the situation on Wolf's Paw, but he barely paid any attention.

Torulu Pering, rebel tactician and adviser, entered the audience hall and knew right away that something was wrong. General Pashi Roma, commander-in-chief of the Alliance on Wolf's Paw, was staring at a scout's report on the tea table in front of him, his brows knit in a tight frown and his fingers tapping nervously.

Pering decided to get right to the point. "Bad news from the Ogé Islands?"

Roma started and looked up. "Terrible."

"How many ships were lost?"

"Nearly all. Only two made their way back."

Pering sighed. Roma had ordered the rebel navy to intercept the Imperial armada in the Ogé Islands, the archipelago to the north of Wolf's Paw, supposedly formed from the sweat drops of the god Rufizo, a plan Pering had objected to from the start.

An old teacher of the Classics who had impressed both King Thufi and Phin Zyndu with his knowledge of ancient books of military strategy—most of which had been burned by Emperor Mapidéré after the Conquest—Pering had actually begun his career as a merchant who plied the trade routes between the Big Island and Wolf's Paw. He knew the sea and the unique challenges of fighting upon it.

Roma, who had spent his entire career in the pre–Conquest Cocru army in the logistics and supply divisions, had little exposure to the battlefield except the defense of Çaruza. He thus tended to think of all military endeavors as variations of city defense. Viewing the Ogé Islands as analogous to the gates to Wolf's Paw, he had believed that a hodgepodge of rebel ships could hide among the tiny islands to disguise their true strength and surprise the Imperial armada, much as the appearance of undefended city walls could lure attackers into coming too close before being surprised by a shower of falling rocks and buckets of burning oil.

But Pering knew that hiding ships was nothing like hiding men. Without air support, naval ambushes were impossible under the gaze of Marana's airships. This, however, was not the time for *I told you so*.

"As we speak, the armada is sailing around the eastern shore of Wolf's Paw to assault Toaza." Roma's voice was morose. "We're done for!"

"We still have half of our fleet left in Toaza Harbor," offered Pering. "If we keep them close to shore, batteries of catapults and ballistae on land could support them, and the shallow waters and hidden reefs will give the armada's larger and deeper-drafting ships less room to maneuver."

"What good are these tricks when Marana has airships?" Roma snapped.

Pering suppressed the urge to grab Roma by the neck of his robe and shake him. The old general was swinging wildly from overconfidence to despair. Before, he had ignored the power of airships; but now, he was convinced they were invincible.

Keeping his voice calm, Pering said, "Airships may be useful, but they're hardly unbeatable. The navies of the Six States had all developed techniques for dealing with them. For example, our ships could cover their decks with a layer of armor made from rawhide stretched tight across wooden frames like drums, so that the tar bombs from the airships would bounce harmlessly off them."

Roma looked at Pering skeptically. "But then they can still bomb Toaza. We can hardly cover the whole city with armor."

"If they try, they won't be able to sustain the bombing campaign for long. Airships are very limited in their armament capacity, and a few raids will hardly cause much damage."

"But if they concentrate on the palace, King Dalo will lose all will to fight."

"True. But I have a plan for taking care of the airships."

The Imperial armada arrived at the southern shore of Wolf's Paw.

In the Battle of Toaza Harbor that followed, the rebel ships, supported by land-based batteries, managed to hold out for three days against sustained air-and-sea assaults from the armada, sinking six ships of the line.

As Roma predicted, Kindo Marana changed tactics and ordered an aerial bombardment of Toaza, focusing on King Dalo's palace.

As the airships approached the Toaza, thousands of floating bamboo-and-paper lanterns rose into the air from the city.

"Have you seen anything like these before?" Marana asked the pilot in the cockpit of *Spirit of Kiji*, his flagship.

The pilot shook his head.

"Better order the fleet to avoid them."

"But there are too many for us to maneuver around them. Besides, they're so small, I don't think the tiny flames powering them will do any damage to our hulls."

But out of caution, Marana ordered *Spirit of Kiji* to stop while the other ships pressed on.

The airships sailed into the swarm of floating lanterns like a whale amongst a school of minnows. The lanterns seemed to stick to the airship hulls like remoras.

Then, Marana heard the sound of an explosive *pop*, followed by hundreds more. Bright flashes of light sparkled over the hulls of the other airships, and the sunlit air between them also filled with the showering sparks of unattached lanterns exploding.

"Retreat! Order a general retreat!" Marana shouted, and his officers waved the signal flags from the gondola frantically.

But it was too late. The oars of some of the great airships dangled uselessly, the oarsmen having been killed by shrapnel; others began to lose altitude, the gasbags having been punctured; fires spread on hulls and gondolas.

The lanterns were Pering's invention. He had collected what little firework powder could be gathered from King Dalo's royal warehouses—a luxury reserved for important ceremonies and New Year's celebrations—and had the powder packed into bamboo tubes along with many sharp metal spikes to increase their kill capacity. These bombs were then attached to floating lanterns with a slow-burning fuse, and the lanterns themselves slathered with a coat of sticky pine tar.

*Spirit of Kiji* escaped from the swarm of deadly floating lanterns back to the safety of the sea, the rest of the surviving aerial fleet limping along behind. Altogether, four Imperial ships were lost, and two more lost so much gas that they could barely keep afloat and were no longer useful except as reserve float gas containers.

Although Marshal Marana believed that the Imperial armada could ultimately prevail—the rebels' supply of firework powder must be limited—the victory would have been achieved at heavy cost. He decided to withdraw from Toaza Harbor.

Toaza celebrated the victory wildly, and General Roma and King Dalo heaped praise upon Torulu Pering, the Savior of Wolf's Paw, as a master tactician, a Lutho among mortals.

But Roma refused to give pursuit to the retreating armada. All remaining rebel ships would stay in Toaza Harbor. Despite this victory, the might of the Imperial armada had deeply impressed Roma. He wanted to have plenty of ships around to be used as transports to evacuate the rebel troops from Wolf's Paw, if it came to that.

General Pashi Roma summoned all rebel commanders and advisers.

"Marana's latest plan appears to be an attempt to land along the less well defended north shore of Wolf's Paw and then advance to Toaza over land," Roma said. "What is your counsel?"

The commanders from the various Tiro states looked at one another, but none spoke up.

Torulu Pering regarded them contemptuously. These men were unwilling to speak because they treated this council of war as some kind of political game, a jostling for positions. Whoever spoke up first was sure to be criticized by others, and unless he had a perfect plan, he'd lose face for the Tiro state he represented.

Pering stepped forward. "The north shore of Wolf's Paw is sparsely populated and has no good harbors, and so Marana would have to land his troops with small transports vulnerable to warships. Traditional tactics would suggest a naval engagement to prevent a landing."

Some of the other advisers were about to object, but Pering held up his hand to silence them. "However, since there are no batteries or coastal forts, our ships cannot match the armada at sea."

Roma nodded. "Exactly. We seem to have no good options."

Pering shook his head. "Just because some options are closed to us doesn't mean that we don't have even better ones. I propose that we cede the beaches to them and fight them on land—this was King Thufi's plan from the start."

"Cede them the beaches!" roared Huye Nocano, the Gan commander. "What gives you, a man of Cocru, the right to dictate the disposition of Gan territories?"

"Besides, Kindo Marana has twenty thousand troops with him, and Tanno Namen will soon bring more," said Owi Ati, commander of the allied troops from Faça. "The advantage of numbers is overwhelmingly with them. Master Pering, just because you won an aerial and naval victory at Toaza Harbor doesn't mean you know everything there is to know about fighting a war on land. Allowing them to land is not a decision to be made lightly. Strategies in books are not the same as conditions in the real world."

Pering smiled. These theatrical outbursts were exactly what he had expected—these men had no ideas of their own, but they were ready to shoot down others' proposals. Patiently, he said, "I didn't say we should just allow them to land wherever they want. We should station troops along the northern and eastern shores but leave Big Toe open."

Big Toe was the northernmost peninsula of Wolf's Paw, which jutted forth from the main part of the island.

"But Big Toe is large enough to comfortably hold all of Marana's troops," said Pashi Roma. "Why give them such a good base?"

"That is the point, General. Big Toe appears ideal to Marana, and if we leave it undefended, he will not be able to resist taking the bait. But from Big Toe, the isthmus would neutralize the empire's numerical advantage and force both sides to fight across a narrow strip of land. If we set up our defenses in layers, the hills of the isthmus will be impregnable. Big Toe will become a trap for Marana and Namen, and we will grind their troops down until the demand for supplies by their large army forces them to retreat."

As predicted by Pering, Marana landed on Big Toe. By then, Namen's twenty thousand veterans had made their way across the Big Island to the end of the Shinané Mountains on the coast. Marana's supply ships worked nonstop to transport all of them over to Big Toe. Added to the twenty thousand fresh recruits originally carried there by the armada, the empire now had forty thousand troops camped on Big Toe, ready for the final assault.

In the hills of the isthmus south of them, ten thousand troops from Cocru were dug in behind heavy defensive fortifications. Faça had sent five thousand men, and they were stationed behind the Cocru troops as a second line of defense. Remnants of the armies of Gan, Rima, and the other Tiro states made up the final defense around Toaza, Gan's capital.

"What are they waiting for?" General Roma asked his advisers. "It has been a month since Marana and Namen landed, and they're just camped there on Big Toe, day after day, doing nothing except consuming their provisions. Even the empire surely cannot afford such expenditures for long."

Again, Torulu Pering was the one who spoke up. "Marana's supply lines are long, and his soldiers are fighting far from home. There is no reason to wait unless he is working at some plot or trick, as is his wont. We should not wait but attack first and drive them into the sea."

But Roma was a cautious man. For most of his career, he had risen through the ranks of support and logistics, more an engineer than a soldier. He had been in charge of repairing Çaruza's walls, maintaining the dikes and levees along the Liru, building sturdy bridges and smooth roads for the Cocru army—and after the Xana Conquest, for the Imperial garrisons. This was a man who had little instinct for the shifting vagaries of the battlefield.

Roma preferred to react rather than act. He deliberated for hours, asking for the opinions of each adviser and then asking them to give yet more advice. Hours became days, then weeks.

Three times he almost decided to give the order to attack the Imperial camp, but each time he changed his mind.

He continued to wait.

To King Shilué of Faça, Marana's secret messenger presented this argument: The emperor understood that the rebellion had largely been the doing of Cocru. Faça and the other Tiro states had been coerced into joining, or, at worst, jumped onto the bandwagon only as minor participants.

The emperor was willing to contemplate granting Faça some measure of autonomy after the inevitable defeat of the rebellion *if* Faça's troops would remain neutral in the coming battle on Wolf's Paw.

"Why should Faça's boys die for Gan and Cocru?" Marana's messenger whispered to King Shilué. "Indeed, even now Gan is arguing that the Ogé Islands belong to them rather than Faça. If you were amenable to the offer, the emperor may be willing to support Faça's claim once the battle is over."

King Shilué nodded, deep in thought.

Just outside of Toaza, King Dalo of Gan met Marana's secret emissary. The two men, disguised as merchants, huddled over plum wine and fried squid dipped in hot pepper sauce in a cheap inn, out of the sight of General Roma's spies.

"Your Majesty, permit me to speak bluntly. Your country is already under Cocru occupation. Although the coming battle will be fought on Gan territory, the largest contingent of armed men on Wolf's Paw belongs to Cocru, and General Roma of Cocru is in charge.

"Even if the rebels were to achieve the impossible and win the coming battle against far superior Imperial troops, do you imagine that Roma or Thufi will leave Wolf's Paw willingly? It's easy to invite a foreign army onto your soil, but far harder to get them to leave peacefully."

King Dalo had already been uneasy when he heard that King Thufi had appointed himself princeps in that mockery of an election. Gan was the only Tiro state to win a naval victory over the supposedly invincible Imperials in Toaza Harbor—even Marana showed Dalo enough respect to humble himself and send an emissary to negotiate with him. Yet, the Cocru commander, General Roma, simply dictated plans for the defenses of the island without consulting him. His ministers had already warned him multiple times about the cost of feeding and providing for the armies from Cocru and Faça, and Roma never once mentioned that Cocru would help with the bill.

There was much truth in what Marana's man had to say.

The messenger pressed on. "Only the madmen of Cocru believe that they can thwart the emperor's will and the tactical genius of Marshal Marana. The marshal understands that it isn't possible for Gan to formally withdraw from the alliance and pledge fealty to the empire right now. But in the coming battle, if Gan's troops would simply pull back to Toaza without engaging us, then Marshal Marana can take care of the Cocru problem for Your Majesty, and the marshal would speak on Gan's behalf before the emperor.

"Who knows, perhaps Gan may even be rewarded for her act of bravery by being granted the Ogé Islands."

~ ~ ~ ~

"I am not the commander-in-chief," said Mata Zyndu.

"Yet the fate of Cocru and all the Tiro states now rests with you," said Torulu Pering. "I've come to Nasu because I believe Roma is too old and timid, and every day he waits is another day that Marana's chance of victory grows."

"What is that to me? If King Thufi and General Roma believe that I should play ferryman, then that is what I will do."

Torulu Pering sighed. Mata sounded like a petulant child.

"I'm an old man, and I'm no warrior. But during my years watching the rise and fall of those in power, I've learned that great men do not wait for their greatness to be recognized.

"If you wish to have the respect that you yearn for, then you must grab it and fight off anyone who would say otherwise. If you wish to be a duke, you act like a duke. If you wish to be commander-in-chief, then act like a commander-in-chief."

This was not the sort of speech that a younger Mata Zyndu, certain that each man had a proper place assigned to him in the chain of being, would have believed in. But he realized with a start that his thoughts had changed.

Didn't Kuni Garu become a duke simply by acting as one? Didn't Huno Krima become a king simply by declaring that he was one? He, Mata Zyndu, heir of the proudest name in all the Islands, was a greater warrior than either of them, and yet here he sat, unhappy that people had not come to beg him to lead them.

As he imagined himself at the head of the rebel army, he realized that he no longer missed Princess Kikomi and was no longer torn by guilt over Phin. This was what he was meant to do: to be astride Réfiroa, to swing Na-aroénna and Goremaw, to write the story of his life in blood and death. Men would fall at his feet, and women would fight for a glance from him, a touch.

*How silly it is for me to sulk here, when there is a war to be fought.*

~ ~ ~ ~

One minute all was stillness and silence in the Imperial camps, the next minute the hills were filled with waving white ensigns charged with the Mingén falcon.

The Cocru soldiers scrambled to their barricades, to the packed-earth ramparts and wooden palisades, and hastily launched volleys of arrows at the Imperial attackers.

But Marana and Namen had wisely exploited General Roma's month-long indecision. From deep within their own camps, hidden behind tents and fences, they had secretly mined under the Cocru fortifications. Marana, ever resourceful, had leveraged the expertise of conquered Rima's miners by his usual mix of threats against their families and promises of future rewards.

As some Imperial soldiers pulled away the supporting beams deep in the tunnels, hundreds of Cocru soldiers fell into the gaping holes in the ground, where they were cut down before they even knew what was happening. The defensive structures that the rebels had taken so much care to build fell apart within seconds.

The collapsing mines revealed swarms of Imperial soldiers rushing out of the ground. This, combined with the sudden general assault aboveground, shocked the Cocru troops into utter confusion. Though General Roma valiantly tried to rally his men, the defensive lines crumbled before the Imperial onslaught.

"Fall back!" General Roma ordered. They would pull back to the secondary defenses, where the Faça army was stationed, and try to stem the Imperial tide.

Imagine their surprise when they reached the Faça camp and found that their allies had already abandoned their positions. They had moved east, out of the path of the Imperial advance, and were camped on a hill.

General Roma sent a rider with orders for the Faça army to join him and hold the line, but the rider returned with the news that Owi Ati, the Faça commander, thought it more prudent to wait and see how the situation developed.

Roma knew then that the battle was lost. The Tiro states would fall like dominoes, one after the other, because they could not fight as one.

Despairingly, he gave the order for a general retreat back to Toaza, where they would try to make a last stand.

But Toaza had already been abandoned. Even as the first rumors of General Roma's defeat arrived at the capital, King Dalo was at work stripping the naval ships of their armament and converting them into transports. The ships rode low in the water, heavy with treasure from the king's palace.

The Gan soldiers hurried aboard, driving away the crowds of civilians begging for a berth. They commandeered every merchant vessel and fishing boat. The desperate crowd then constructed rafts from doors and bits of furniture and launched them into the harbor with no thought on how such unseaworthy "vessels" would survive the long southward detour to the Big Island. Minor nobles who were not lucky enough to be taken on the king's ships promised the soldiers untold riches if they would just be allowed to climb onboard. Some jumped into the water and began to swim to the ships and rafts that were pulling away from the docks, and as they begged those aboard to pull them up, the men on the ships pushed them away with their oars.

Then someone shouted that a fleet had been sighted coming toward Toaza Harbor—the armada!—and the confusion and chaos in the harbor boiled over into utter panic.

General Roma watched King Dalo's betrayal with a mixture of anger and regret. He wished that he had listened to Torulu Pering and attacked before Kindo Marana had a chance to pry the alliance apart. There was no stratagem left now. Only brute force, terror, and the desire to run away.

The "armada" turned out to be Mata Zyndu with his two thousand men aboard twenty ships.

Mata observed the confusion in the harbor with disgust. He spread his ships out in an arc and sealed the harbor. All the ships clamoring to leave were ordered to go straight back to the docks.

The royal transport carrying King Dalo dared to test Mata's resolve, and Mata promptly ordered Théca Kimo's ship to ram it.

"You dare to attack a royal transport?" the Gan sailors shouted at Kimo in a mix of bravado and fear.

"I've already killed a king," Kimo said. His tattooed, laughing face terrified the Gan sailors. "I'm happy to send yours to meet King Huno."

The sailors did not resist as Kimo's men boarded the royal transport, brandishing their weapons. They chained the royal transport to Kimo's ship and dragged it back to Toaza.

The other escaping ships followed.

The Gan soldiers amassed on the docks shouted in confusion, while the empty ships that had ferried Mata's troops floated right next to them. They could hear, dimly, the noise of the approaching Imperial army, and the Imperial airships could be sighted far in the east, escorting the armada coming around Wolf's Paw to Toaza. It was only the experience of Pering's floating needle-bombs that kept the airships so cautious—if they were to fly over Toaza Harbor now and strafe it with a salvo of firebombs, the rebels would be completely done for.

"Excellent work," General Roma said. He was ecstatic to see Mata Zyndu, the man in charge of the rear guard, who had come to do his duty and save the commander-in-chief. "Let's evacuate our men and leave the Gan traitors to face Marana alone."

Mata shook his head. "We must counterattack immediately."

Roma stared at him in disbelief. "There is no counterattack, you fool! The battle is lost."

Mata shook his head again. "We haven't even begun to fight."

Roma looked into young Mata's eyes. He remembered the rumors about Mata's cruelties at Dimu. He remembered the tales about his recklessness and hot temper. He wanted blood, only blood.

*This is why King Thufi and Marshal Zyndu made me commander-in-chief instead of this man.*

Roma tried to straighten his back and make his voice as authoritative as possible. "I'm ordering you to retreat. Your only job is to ferry us back to the Big Island safely."

Mata unsheathed Na-aroénna and in a single motion lopped off Roma's head. The Doubt-Ender would not tolerate a commander who vacillated and had no heart for battle.

Silence and stillness gradually spread out from where Mata stood like a ripple until everyone on the docks of Toaza Harbor stared at the towering man in wonder.

As they watched, Mata ordered his soldiers to set fire to all the rafts, boats, and ships—including those they had arrived on. Within minutes, the water was a sea of roaring flames.

"All the ships have been burned, and along with them all provisions. There is now no way to retreat. You have only the food that is already in your bellies. If you want to eat, you'll have to kill an Imperial soldier and take his rations from him."

From his perch atop Réfiroa, Mata lifted his sword high overhead so that all could see the bloody tip. "This is Na-aroénna, the Doubt-Ender. I will not sheathe my sword again until the outcome of this battle is no longer in doubt. We will be victorious today, or we will all die today."

He turned toward the Imperial army and began to ride. He rode alone, shouting at the top of his lungs.

Ratho was one of the first to start running after him, shouting just like General Mata Zyndu. *All life is a gamble,* wasn't that what Tazu, god of this realm, would say?

A few soldiers began to follow, then a few more, and eventually the trickle became a flood like the tide coming in, and the two thousand that Mata had taken to Wolf's Paw now rushed in a writhing mass to meet the far bigger wave of Imperial soldiers.

Mata Zyndu laughed, and so did his men.

The odds were impossible against them, but so what? There was no need for strategies and tricks now. In their minds, they were already dead, freed from the hope of retreat or rescue. They had nothing to lose.

Ratho Miro rushed at an Imperial soldier and made no attempt to parry or protect himself. He simply *attacked*.

He severed the sword arm of the man even as the other man's sword bit into his shoulder. But in his bloodlust, he felt nothing. Ratho roared, pulled his sword out, and cut another Imperial soldier down.

He knew Daf would think he was foolish, but he also thought that his brother would be proud of him.

*I'm fighting just like General Zyndu,* he thought, remembering the time when General Zyndu had flown high over the walls of Zudi and fought until no man from Xana dared to face him. Now he knew just how General Zyndu must have felt, and it was indeed glorious.

They tore into the Imperial ranks like an arrow into flesh. The tip of the arrow was Mata Zyndu himself.

Réfiroa leapt; Mata swung Na-aroénna, and men fell like weeds. Réfiroa dashed and dodged; Mata bashed and crushed, and Goremaw tore into whatever stood in the way. Réfiroa, seized by a battle lust of his own, opened his mouth wide and tore out chunks of flesh from the flood of infantry, shaking the red foam from his mouth. Mata was soon completely covered in crimson gore. Every so often he would have to wipe the blood from his eyes so that he could see again.

*More, more, more death!*

To the Imperial soldiers, the men of Cocru seemed inhuman. They were oblivious to pain and showed no interest in defending themselves. Every strike from their swords felt as if they put all their strength into it. They did not want to survive, only to kill. How could you fight men like that? The sane could not withstand the insane.

Slowly, the tide began to turn. The Imperial advance slowed, stopped, and then reversed. The two thousand soldiers led by Mata Zyndu were now completely surrounded by the forty thousand

Imperial soldiers, but it was as if a python had swallowed a hedgehog who did not know what it meant to die or to give up. The Imperial soldiers began to back up, break ranks, and then flee from the blood-crazed fury in their midst.

The remaining Cocru soldiers standing by the shore seemed to finally wake from the shock of General Roma's death. With a shout, they followed their brothers. The rout was on.

Now that it was clear that the Imperial army was going to lose, Huye Nocano, the Gan commander, rediscovered his rebel heart. He gave the order for his men to join the chase.

"Our Cocru allies need us!"

Now that it was clear that Marshal Marana's promises could not be kept, Owi Ati, the Faça commander, reawakened his hatred for the empire. He gave the order to join the fray and cut off the retreating Imperial forces.

"Faça will strike her blow against the empire!"

Twenty thousand soldiers of the emperor died during the Battle of Wolf's Paw. Twenty thousand more surrendered. Nine times the Imperials tried to rally and make a stand, and nine times Mata Zyndu's berserkers broke through. The battle lasted ten days, though its outcome had been determined on the first.

The Imperial ships could not enter Toaza Harbor, filled with burning ships. They milled about in confusion for a while until it became clear that the battle on land was lost. The armada retreated back up the eastern shore of Wolf's Paw, hoping to regroup near Big Toe.

The airships made attempts to land and rescue some of the senior army officers, but Zyndu's berserkers were always so close on the heels of the fleeing Imperials that such attempts failed time after time. Five airships were even captured as they struggled to lift off, dragged down to the earth by panicked Imperial soldiers hanging on to the gondola and one another's feet like anchor chains made of men.

By the time the armada reached the Imperial camps at Big Toe, it was too late to salvage anything. The young men of Xana who had followed Marana and Namen across the empire, filled with hope and dreams of martial glory, were all either dead or kneeling as prisoners of the rebels.

The Imperial ships, now light and empty, sailed aimlessly into the northern waters. The surviving airships, after dropping a few salvos of tar bombs on the triumphant rebels below—hollow, useless gestures—left Wolf's Paw and followed the armada.

Tanno Namen and Kindo Marana had hoped to enjoy their greatest triumph close up and were thus not aboard the airships.

They regretted that decision now. The rebels surrounded the last detachment of Imperial soldiers, and Namen and Marana looked longingly at the distant silhouettes of fleeing Imperial ships.

Namen thought about Tozy at home on Rui and wondered how the old dog was getting on in the cold weather with his limp.

"Old friend," Marana said, "it would have been better if I had never come to your house on the shores of Gaing Gulf. Now instead of pruning wolfberry shrubs and sailing your fishing skiff, you will spend your last years as a prisoner. I do not understand why we lost today. . . . I am truly sorry."

Namen brusquely brushed off Marana's apology. "I spent my life fighting to see Xana exalted above all other Tiro states. To have the chance to serve the empire again in my old age is an honor.

"But we live at the mercy of the gods. The race goes not always to the swift, nor the battle always to the strong. We have fought as well as we were able, and the rest is mere chance."

"You're kind to lay no blame on me." Marana looked around and sighed. "We should prepare to surrender. There's no sense in letting more men die needlessly."

Namen nodded. Then he said, "Marshal, before you give the order to surrender, would you do me a favor?"

"Anything."

"If you get the chance, look in on my old house, and see that Tozy, my hound, is provided for. He likes to have a lamb's tail to chew on once in a while."

Marana saw the smile on the old warrior's face. He tried to find something to say to delay the moment, but he knew it was too late.

"Thank you for indulging my last bit of vanity. I have never surrendered."

Namen unsheathed his sword and wiped its sharp edge across his gaunt neck. He fell like a great oak tree. For minutes, his strong heart continued to pump the blood out of his body into a spreading pool around him.

Marana knelt next to the body and mourned until the heart that so loved Xana finally stopped beating.

Marana and his men left Namen's body where he last stood. They would come and retrieve it later, after the formal ceremony of surrender.

A great shadow passed over them. Marana looked up. The sky was filled with the wings of Mingén falcons: dozens, no, hundreds of them. No one could ever recall hearing of so many falcons appearing together away from the shores of Lake Arisuso, on Mount Kiji back in Rui.

The falcons swooped down. They moved not like the solitary predators that they were, but like a flock of starlings, each a component of a greater whole. The flock dove as one and picked up the body of Tanno Namen. Then the flock turned and flew westward over the sea, eventually disappearing over the horizon.

Marana and his men bowed to the west. Legend had it that the sons of Xana who fell after great deeds in battle would be taken away by Lord Kiji, god of all birds, to eternal rest in the heavens.

Mata stood in the midst of what remained of the Imperial camp at the tip of Big Toe. He enjoyed a bowl of porridge made from the provisions captured from the Imperial stores. He was still covered in blood, as were his men. None of them had bothered to clean themselves.

"You were the first to follow me," Mata Zyndu said to Ratho Miro.

Ratho nodded.

Mata Zyndu reached out to grab Ratho by the arms. "You'll stay by me in the future, as my personal guard."

Ratho knew that later, when his heart finally slowed down, and the hazy glow of battle lust finally wore off, he would be awed again by this man. But for now, he felt like an equal of the great general, and he cherished that feeling.

His only regret was that Dafiro was not around to see this moment.

Marana was brought before Mata. The Marshal of Xana knelt, lifted his sword with both hands, and lowered his eyes to the ground. He waited for Mata's decision on his fate and the fate of all the other prisoners.

Mata gazed at him, disappointed. This was a bureaucrat who was no more skilled with the blade than a common farmer-turned-soldier; Namen was an old man who dared not face him in a duel. They had fought well with their minds, but they did not match his ideal. Was this the best Xana had to offer? Where was an opponent clothed in martial splendor equal to his own?

Behind Marana, Owi Ati and Huye Nocano, the commanders of the Faça and Gan armies, also knelt, as did King Dalo. All eyes, full of awe, were focused on Mata, as if they were watching Fithowéo himself.

There was no man greater among all the rebels than Mata Zyndu, not even King Thufi.

CHAPTER THIRTY

# MASTER OF PAN

PAN: THE ELEVENTH MONTH IN THE FOURTH YEAR OF THE REIGN OF RIGHTEOUS FORCE.

Emperor Mapidéré had chosen the site for his capital, the Immaculate City, not because he wanted to live there, but because he wanted to die there.

He wanted the Imperial Tombs, planned around his Mausoleum, to tap into the ground energy of the great volcanoes: Mounts Kana, Rapa, and Fithowéo. He thought that the vitality of the mountains, forever young because they constantly remade themselves with fresh lava in violent explosions, would similarly renew the strength and vitality of the Imperial family and therefore the empire itself.

Mapidéré's spirit, if it still was around, must now be wondering why his plan had not worked out.

Kuni Garu accepted Erishi's surrender as the latter was curled in his bed in the fetal position, the sheets and his clothes soaked with his urine.

∽ ∾ ∽ ∾

Luan Zya came to say good-bye.

"You won't stay with me?" Kuni asked. "I would not be the master of Géfica without you."

Kuni had admired Luan even as a boy, when he saw the assassin soar through the air. And he doubted that there was another mind in Dara that could have come up with such a daring plan to capture Pan.

Collecting talented friends was one of Kuni's favorite hobbies, and Luan Zya was one of Kuni's most prized acquisitions.

"Lord Garu, you have achieved what the gods had intended for you. Didn't you slay the great white python in one strike in the Er-Mé Mountains, as I hear in the legends of the common people? Weren't you surrounded by rainbows even when you were a fugitive? Today you have ridden on a cruben and made the Emperor of All the Islands tremble at your feet. You are a good lord and master, but you have no further need of my assistance. I wish to go serve Haan, a small and weak state and the last of the Six States to be free, but nonetheless *my* home."

Kuni and Luan toasted each other with bowls of sorghum liquor before Luan went on his way. Both attributed their tears to the burning drink.

Luan returned to Ginpen, capital of old Haan.

News of the fall of Pan had already reached the city, and the streets were filled with young men of Haan milling about, excitedly talking of a new era. Soldiers from the Xana garrison were holed up in their barracks, fearful of the mood of the volatile citizenry.

Unmolested, Luan returned to the site of the ancestral estate of the Zya Clan, where he had last seen his father and made the pledge that drove his life.

There were no more marble-floored halls tiled with marvelous geometry, no more study rooms where the walls were covered in slates on which he and his father had written out equations and debated proofs, no more private library stocked with antique books collected from all corners of the Islands of Dara, no more sunlit laboratories filled with instruments to investigate the stars and the tides and time and the natural world.

Instead, the estate was a burned-down wreckage of broken stones overgrown with weeds.

"Father," Luan said, kneeling in the middle of the ruins. "I have returned because the Xana Empire is no more. King Cosugi will return soon, and I will help him rebuild Haan, our homeland, and restore her to her rightful place. I have fulfilled my pledge. Are you pleased? Will your soul now have rest?"

A breeze rustled the weeds. A lonely bird cried out in the distance.

Luan knelt there for a long time, listening, until the sun sank and the moon rose, trying to divine the will of the gods and the ambiguous answers of dead ancestors.

Kuni was worried about the thousands of surrendered Imperial troops in Pan. He had only five hundred men with him, and if Imperial loyalists decided that they were willing to sacrifice the life of Emperor Erishi, they could easily overwhelm his tiny contingent.

Kuni gathered all his advisers for counsel.

"We can't let news of the fall of Pan get out just yet," said Cogo Yelu. "If Imperial commanders in the rest of Géfica knew just how small your army is, they'd converge on Pan, and we'd be dead."

"Then we must seal the city immediately," said Kuni. "But what if some Imperial had already sent out a messenger pigeon?"

"I already took care of it," said Rin. "Roasted pigeons are delicious, especially if salted appropriately."

Kuni laughed. "Good thing I have all of you thinking for me. The first priority now is to get word out to my brother, Mata Zyndu, and ask him to send aid as soon as possible."

"It would have been best if we still had the airships," said Cogo. "But, unfortunately, since you didn't want Luan Zya to stay behind to guard them, the palace guards destroyed them."

"I'll take care of getting word out to General Zyndu," said Rin.

"I have ways of sending messages that won't be intercepted by Imperial patrols."

Kuni nodded, thankful that he had had the foresight to have Rin maintain his connections to the less savory aspects of society.

"But water from afar won't save the fire that's burning down the house," fretted Kuni. "How will we ensure that the surrendered soldiers of Pan won't turn on us?"

Rin Coda whispered a suggestion. It was thuggish and dishonorable, and Mün Çakri and Than Carucono both objected. Kuni Garu was about to say no, but Cogo Yelu spoke up in support of Rin.

"The possibility of mutiny is great, Lord Garu, and we must do what we can to preserve the fruits of our gamble."

Still, Kuni hesitated. "Cogzy, you believe that we must purchase the loyalty of the surrendered Imperial soldiers at such cost?"

"Those who would be great must be great in all measures, including cruelty."

Cogo's reasoning troubled Kuni, but he was always willing to listen to counsel. Reluctantly, he agreed to Rin's plan.

Pan lived up to its status as the capital of the empire by the size of its population, by the wideness of its streets (sixteen carriages could pass over them side by side), by the splendor of its architecture, by the variety of goods offered for sale in its markets, indeed, by any measure you cared to invent. Traders and opportunists of all stripes came to make their fortune at the feet of the emperor, and it was often said that it was better to be a mouse in Pan than an elephant in Écofi.

It was whispered among the surrendered Imperial troops that they would be allowed to loot Pan as a reward for their submission to Duke Garu—as long as they did not kill anyone. A few bold soldiers went into the streets to test out the rumor. Kuni's men watched them but did nothing. By afternoon, the former Imperial barracks were empty.

The soldiers had free rein of the entire city. Pan was treated as though it had been conquered, except that the conquering army was composed of the men who had sworn to defend it. They broke into the wealthy mansions lining the streets, took whatever they fancied, and did as they liked to the men and women they found inside them—the soldiers did take care not to kill anyone, but there were many forms of suffering short of death.

For ten days the streets of Pan became a living hell, and families huddled in basements and shuddered while they listened to the cries and screams of the less fortunate. The Immaculate City became stained with terror, blood, avarice, and cravenness.

During this time, Kuni Garu kept his own men in the palace, away from the chaos in the streets. Cogo Yelu, however, took a few men and went to the Imperial Archives, where the empire's census and tax records, and all other administrative papers of the civil bureaucracy, were kept.

"Lock the doors and don't let any of the looters come in," Cogo ordered.

"Why do we care about these old scrolls and papers?" asked Dafiro. Then he whispered, "Is this where the emperor kept his most valuable treasure? Clever to hide it where no one would be looking. Maybe . . . you and I can take a peek later?"

Cogo laughed. "You won't find gold or gems here."

"Some kind of art?" Dafiro was a bit disappointed. He knew that art could be valuable, but he didn't care particularly for paintings unless they were of beautiful ladies.

"In a manner of speaking," said Cogo. "Politics is the highest of the arts, and perhaps someday you will understand it."

While the former Imperial soldiers rampaged in the streets of Pan, Kuni had to get away from the horrors he had unleashed. He chose to wander thorough the silent corridors and empty halls of the palace.

The splendor around him was breathtaking. The ceiling in every room was at least fifty feet high. Every wall was covered with intricate carvings and golden filigree. On the floor lay pillows covered in silk and damask, stuffed with the soft downy feathers of thousands of ducklings and the baby wool of yearling sheep. Priceless paintings and calligraphy scrolls taken from the conquered Six States hung on the walls.

Everywhere Kuni looked, his eyes were met with elaborate furnishings, toys, decorations: pearl and coral murals from Gan, sandalwood carvings from Rima, jade statues from Faça, turtle-bone tables from Haan, feathered tapestries from Amu, and gold, ingots and ingots of gold, squeezed from the dead laborers of Cocru. The objects spoke of power, power that Emperor Mapidéré had wielded over the empire, power palpable to Kuni as he caressed them.

He remembered how he had felt as a young man watching Mapidéré's procession through the road near Zudi: that mixture of awe and fear, the trembling one felt in the presence of so much power. He marveled at the change in circumstances.

"Emperor, king, general, duke," he whispered to himself. "These are just labels." Yet the labels changed how one behaved. He had already become used to the idea of himself as the Duke of Zudi, and now he was growing used to the idea of himself as the King of Géfica. Might he grow used to yet another label? Might he grow used to being the object of awe and wonder and . . . perhaps fear and hatred?

The animals in the Imperial Zoo and Aquarium moaned for food. They were beautiful and lonely, caged things that had no control over their own fates.

In one of the cages was a beautiful and proud stag who paced back and forth impatiently. Yet, the label in front of its cage declared it to be a horse. Puzzled, Kuni stared at the creature, who stared back.

"Who will bring down the stag?" Kuni asked himself. "Is the hunt almost over?"

Kuni came to the small houses at the back of the palace, the hidden women's quarter. Here, the wives and consorts of Emperor Mapidéré and of young Emperor Erishi lived. They were frightened and uncertain of their future. But when they saw Kuni, they painted their faces and came out—each to stand in front of her own house—clad only in seductive smiles. Luscious, pitiful creatures, they seemed to him not very different from the animals in the zoo.

Kuni was tired. He had been fighting and running, it seemed, for years. Away from Jia, he had never yielded to the temptation of the company of other women. But he had physical needs, and having come so close to death sharpened his appetite. The palette of tantalizing shades of flesh before him would not, could not, should not be resisted.

Didn't he deserve some rewards? Didn't he deserve to relax just a little?

"A brave man deserves a great beauty," one of the women said. She was lovelier than any women Kuni knew, and she wore nothing except a necklace made from shark's teeth. The strange, barbaric jewel somehow seemed fitting to Kuni. And her smile pulled him in—he thought, for a moment, he could see her face flicker into the image of a skull, but then he blinked, and the vision went away.

He stayed in the women's quarter for that night, and then the next. He did not leave for ten days.

Rin Coda came to find Kuni.

He had known Kuni before he was Duke Garu, before he was even a prison guard, before anyone thought Kuni would amount to anything.

A friend like that sometimes could say things that would not be tolerated if they came from other subordinates.

"Kuni," Rin said. "It's time to stop."

Kuni heard him but promptly put Rin out of his mind. He was enjoying a massage from two women who he had decided were his favorites. One of them was from Haan, and her dark skin was smooth as polished lacquer, warm as a cooking stone. Her thighs were so strong and supple that he constantly felt the need to test them. Her eyes held such promises of pleasure and compassion.

The other woman was from Faça, and she had skin so pale that you could see the blood flowing in her veins as she blushed and laughed. Her hair was bright red, like the passion of an exploding volcano (not unlike Jia, come to think of it). Her breasts were so ripe and full that Kuni felt as though he were caressing peaches, peaches full of honey nectar.

"Kuni," Rin said again, louder. "Look at me. Have you forgotten what we came to do?"

Kuni frowned in annoyance. Rin was intruding on his daydream. He imagined living here forever. He could now see why Emperor Erishi did not want to leave his palace, did not care about what happened outside of it.

He would live like the emperor. He would eat out of golden bowls with jade spoons. He would smoke, in coral pipes, ethereal tobacco that had been cured and sifted a hundred times by specially trained monkeys who could climb the cliffs where the tobacco was grown, fed by dew. He would drink tea that consisted of the tenderest leaves, plucked by young children whose fingers were nimble enough to not break the buds prematurely and release their flavor. He would have a new woman to bed every night, but these two he would always keep for comfort when he had had a surfeit of the new.

"You should address me as 'Lord Garu,'" Kuni Garu said. "Or maybe even 'Your Majesty.'"

*The dandelion seed has finally found the right soil. The eagle has finally soared as high as he should.*

Desperate, Rin tried one last time. "Kuni, imagine how Jia would feel if she were to see you now."

"Silence!" Kuni was out of the bed in a single motion. "You are too bold, Rin. Jia lives in my heart. But it is my appetite that needs comfort right now. Do not forget who you're speaking to."

"*I* am not the one who has forgotten who you are."

"I do not wish to see you anymore, Rin."

Rin Coda shook his head. He left to find help.

Cogo Yelu came in with a large basin. He directed Mün Çakri and Than Carucono to pry the two women from Kuni's grasp and pull them out of the bed, and then he emptied the basin, full of water and ice taken from the winter cellar, onto Kuni's naked form.

Kuni howled and jumped out of bed. He was fully awake for the first time in ten days, and he had a good mind to order Cogo Yelu's head chopped off right then and there.

"What is the meaning of this?" he roared.

"What is the meaning of *this*?" Cogo pointed at the bed, now a sodden mess of silk sheets and lace covers, the empty wine goblets on the floor, the piles of art and treasure that Kuni had hoarded from all over the palace and then strewn carelessly around the room.

"Cogzy, I want to enjoy myself for a bit. By the Twins, I deserve it!"

"Have you forgotten the men who died in the Grand Tunnels? Have you forgotten the children fallen by the roadside from starvation? Have you forgotten the mothers and sons forcefully separated by corvée administrators so that the emperor could add another stone to his Mausoleum? Have you forgotten all the men who have died to fight for an end to all of this, and the women who will mourn them forever? Have you forgotten your wife, who prays for your safety daily, dreaming that you will achieve greatness and bring relief to the people of Dara?"

Kuni had no reply to this. He felt as though he was waking from a dream, a dream that made him vaguely disgusted with himself. He shivered as he felt the ice water on him again.

"I am ashamed to see this, Lord Garu," Cogo said, and he averted his eyes from Kuni Garu's nakedness. Than Carucono and Mün Çakri did the same.

Kuni stared at him. "How dare you lecture me? You are the one who counseled me to allow the surrendered Imperial soldiers to turn Pan into a lawless hell. You urged me to be great in all things, cruelty and appetite, so that I can keep the reins of power. I am simply enjoying the role you designed for me."

Cogo shook his head. "You are very much mistaken, Lord Garu. I counseled you to seize power so that you may use it to do good, not so that you can indulge in its exercise as its own end. If you cannot see the difference, then I have indeed been blind."

Kuni Garu sat down on the bed and covered himself with a sheet. *It was a nice dream while it lasted.*

"I'm sorry, Cogo. Please bring me some clothes." He waited a moment and then added, "Do not speak of this to Jia."

But Rin Coda came into the room and handed Kuni his old robe; it had been sewn by Jia and was now full of sweat stains and patches.

"Thank you," Kuni said. "And I'm sorry for how I behaved. Old friends are like old clothes: they fit the best."

Duke Garu announced that the looting of Pan would stop immediately and henceforth he would govern Pan with a gentle hand: All the cruel and complicated laws of the empire would be abolished and the profession of paid litigators eliminated—the people cheered wildly at this. There would be no more corvées, and taxes would be reduced to one-tenth of what they were before.

From this point forward, only three criminal laws would be enforced in Duke Garu's Pan: first, a murderer would be executed; second, one who physically injured another had to pay compensation; third, thieves must return their loot and pay a penalty.

There was wild celebration in the streets, and the people now cheered Kuni Garu as the Liberator.

"Lord Garu, now you see how Rin's suggestion has worked out," Cogo said. "Not only did the period of looting give us the loyalty of the surrendered Imperial soldiers, but it turned the people of Pan permanently against them. Even if those men were to plot a mutiny now they would have no support among the populace. The former Imperial soldiers, knowing that the people of Pan hate them, have no choice but to support and defend you. You have trapped them into throwing in their lot with you without them being any the wiser.

"And by ruling Pan now with a gentle hand, you are like the spring breeze after a winter of frost, a stream of fresh water after a wild fire.

Had you been gentle with them from the start, the people would have treated your compassion as weakness. But now that they have suffered for ten days, they appreciate your kindness ten times more."

"You are a cruel and manipulative man, Cogo," Kuni said. He smiled and waved at the people as he and his followers paraded down the street, but the smile did not reach his eyes.

"The common people are like unruly children. If you give them candy always, they will think they should be given even more. But if you slap them hard and then hand them candy, they will come crawling to you and lick your hand."

"You're comparing me to men who treat their wives like dogs, to be beaten and then caressed."

"It sounds harsh and unpleasant," Cogo said. "But the world is full of harsh and unpleasant things that must be done, especially if you would like to soar as high as an eagle."

Kuni paused. "You're probably right, Cogo. But enough has been done in my name that I do not wish to look into a mirror for a while."

Cogo Yelu sighed. He noticed that the duke no longer called him *Cogzy*, and he found that he missed the endearment. Speaking about the world as it was did not always endear you to those you served.

Kuni administered Pan with the same care he had managed Zudi.

Every day, he spent hours dealing with the minutiae of getting the city back to some semblance of normalcy after the chaos of the conquest and the ensuing looting. He reorganized the surrendered soldiers and began to get to know their commanders. He met with the elders of the city and the surrounding villages to take measure of their thoughts and concerns.

Rin Coda, meanwhile, put his feelers out to the unsavory criminal underside of Pan, as was his wont.

"The king and I will need the support of all the business interests of Pan, especially yours," Rin said, toasting the men assembled in the private dining hall of Pan's most luxurious inn. They were leaders of smuggling gangs, heads of secret societies, even "legitimate" businessmen who made most of their profits in other, darker ways.

"As long as the king is reasonable, we will be reasonable," the man who called himself Scorpion said. He claimed to be the owner of Pan's most lucrative underground gambling dens. Two earrings made of shark's teeth dangled from his earlobes. "But why has the king not made an effort to secure Thoco Pass?"

Rin nodded at him, indicating that he should continue.

"In my line of business," Scorpion said, keeping his voice low so that everyone held their breath and strained to hear him, "much of my profit comes from promises being kept. For example, a man might promise that he would pay everything back within a day if the house would just spot him another thousand gold pieces for the next bet."

Rin nodded, trying to determine if this story was going anywhere.

"I like to believe that people keep their promises, but it's always better if you can be sure. And the best way to be sure is to make sure the man understands that I have the power to hurt him a great deal if he tries to renege."

Rin tried to keep the impatience out of his voice. "A charming bit of advice, Master Scorpion. The king and I will keep that in mind."

Scorpion smiled. "King Thufi, the princeps, has promised that anyone who captured Emperor Erishi would be King of Géfica, a new Tiro state. But it seems to me that if King Kuni wants to be sure that the promise is kept, he ought to show others that he has teeth. Any claim becomes more legitimate when it is backed up by arms.

"And any army that wants to come into Géfica must pass through Thoco Pass."

The next day, Rin Coda secretly dispatched an army to Thoco Pass.

Sure, Kuni had asked him to send messengers to Mata Zyndu as soon as possible and invite him to come to Pan to share in the victory and help defend it, but Rin always believed in self-reliance: Why ask for others to help when you were capable of taking care of everything yourself?

Besides, Pan was already secure, thanks to his own plan, and why should Mata share in a glory that belonged to Kuni and his loyal followers alone? Wouldn't it be better if just Kuni became King of Géfica? A man who didn't think of himself first was not someone the gods favored.

He was sure Kuni would agree.

*Did you enjoy sleeping with Kuni Garu, Tazu the Unpredictable?*

*Ah, so you saw, Lutho. I looked lovely, didn't I?*

*He's harder to tempt than you thought, isn't he? I note that he didn't pick you as a favorite.*

*A matter I blame on his taste. Well, I had my fun, and that's what matters.*

*Where are Kiji the Storm-Bringer, the Twins of Ice and Fire, and Fithowéo the Warlike? I thought they're the ones most invested in this war?*

*Those three birds and the wild dog are sulking. While their champions are engaged elsewhere, this nobody came in and stole the show.*

*Such is the danger of guiding mortals.*

*Don't act so innocent, you tricky old turtle. You've been plotting this move for years. I was wondering when your man was going to make his move.*

*When you want to catch a big fish, you have to let out a long line.*

*This isn't over, you know? Winning is easy; staying as the winner, now that's hard.*

*Well said, but it all depends on what you mean by winning.*

*I'm heading home to Wolf's Paw; there's more fun to be had.*

## CHAPTER THIRTY-ONE

# THE SLAUGHTER

WOLF'S PAW: THE ELEVENTH MONTH IN THE FOURTH YEAR OF THE REIGN OF RIGHTEOUS FORCE.

Admiral Filo Kaima of the Imperial armada had only one thing on his mind: put as much distance between his ships and that madman Mata Zyndu as possible. Images of berserking rebels coming over the horizon like a swarm of bloody demons haunted him, awake or asleep.

It was a few days before he realized that he actually held the upper hand.

Since Zyndu had burned all the ships in Toaza Harbor, the rebels now had no navy left and no way to get off Wolf's Paw. What were the rebels going to do, swim out to fight him on the seas?

Kaima, now the highest-ranking military officer of the empire, gathered the dejected Imperial ships and airships and reversed course. He would set up a blockade around the northern and southern shores of Wolf's Paw. Since the great whirlpool that was Tazu made the Kishi Channel unnavigable, this would ensure that no ship could go to or from Wolf's Paw.

The empire might have lost on land, but they could lay siege to the whole island and trap Mata Zyndu and all his rebels here until Pan sent another army.

*Zyndu wants to gamble with all the lives of his men? Well, let him.*

Mata Zyndu began to call himself the Marshal of Cocru. Torulu Pering drafted a proclamation, and none of the kings and nobles on Wolf's Paw made a peep of objection.

Mata didn't wait for an order from King Thufi. That shepherd boy would be nothing without him and his uncle. Réfiroa alone was worth ten Thufis. *He*, not Pashi Roma, had saved the rebellion from certain defeat. *He*, not Thufi, had conquered the invincible Kindo Marana. *He*, and no one else, had overcome an army of forty thousand with two thousand berserkers. He had not resorted to tricks or strategems; he had won by pure courage and battle lust.

It was the fairest and therefore the sweetest victory in the world.

Thufi was a figurehead, and Mata didn't need him. Torulu Pering was right: Whatever he wanted and thought he deserved, Mata had to take for himself. Wallowing in self-pity had been foolish; the world respected a man who respected himself.

The weak and sniveling men around him disgusted him. Traitors and cowards, they did not deserve to be called noble at all. Though they might have been born with the right names, they did not have even one-tenth the courage of his guard, Ratho Miro, a peasant boy, or one-hundredth the spirit of his brother, Kuni Garu, a farmer's son.

Mata evicted King Dalo from the palace in Toaza and took it over. Owi Ati and Huye Nocano, the Façu and Gan commanders who had come to Mata's aid during the Battle of Wolf's Paw only when it was clear that he would be victorious, were put under house arrest until he could try them as traitors. He was not fooled by their halfhearted support after he had already won the day.

But Namen and Marana he treated with respect. They were not great warriors in his estimation, but he respected their stations. There was no shame for men who strove to carry out their duties but were denied victory due to the limitation of their abilities—and how could anyone expect to win against *him*, Fithowéo incarnate? He gave Namen's sword—since the body was not available—a burial befitting a duke, and he even allowed Marana to keep his sword. Marana's small frame had surprised him, and he could not understand why Kikomi had chosen this sallow, weak man over him—more evidence of her lack of judgment and true nobility, perhaps. Faced with such an inferior specimen of manhood, Mata found himself unable to even summon feelings of jealousy at this "rival" for Kikomi's affections—it was beneath him. He might even magnanimously ask Marana to serve him one day like the ancient heroes did with their defeated foes—he hadn't thought that far yet.

*I am the princeps,* he thought, *first among equals.* No, that was not quite right. What other mortal man could compare to him in valor and strength of arms? He would march into Pan and put his foot on the neck of Emperor Erishi. He would be the foremost hero of the rebellion. He was the Conqueror, the *Hegemon*, a title of legends and myths.

Only then would the Zyndu name be finally redeemed.

But first, he had to get his army off Wolf's Paw and into Géjira, from where he would march through Thoco Pass and into the Immaculate City.

The blockade of Wolf's Paw by the armada presented only a minor difficulty. He set his army to the task of building new ships, and the island's verdant hills were soon denuded of trees.

An old woman came to see the new Marshal Zyndu. She walked with the aid of a cane, and her hair was all white. But her face glowed with health and vigor above her shawl of shark skin and necklace of shark's teeth.

"I can speak to Tazu," the old woman said in a trembling, piercing voice that made listeners wince.

The priests of Tazu shouted in outrage.

"We're the messengers of Tazu."

"She's nothing but a fraud, a witch who fools the gullible villagers!"

"Throw her off the cliffs, and let her speak to Tazu directly!"

But Mata silenced them with a dismissive wave. He took perverse pleasure in seeing these men howl like young children at the smallest hint that their authority was challenged. To Mata, the priests seemed of a kind with the effete and greedy nobles and kings that he now found so contemptible.

This old woman, on the other hand, had courage. She stood without trembling in front of the most powerful man in the rebellion and looked him straight in the eyes. Mata liked that.

"What message from Tazu do you bring me?" he asked.

"Tazu can help you leave Wolf's Paw. But first, he must be given sacrifices."

The old woman refused to tell him any specifics until Mata dismissed all others from the audience hall. Then she whispered in his ear.

Mata's eyes grew wide. He shrank back. "Who *are* you?"

"That is a foolish question," the old woman said. But she didn't sound like an old woman anymore. Her voice was deep and sonorous, and the walls of the audience hall shook as she spoke. She sounded like waves striking against the sea wall and strong currents swirling in the deep.

She stood with her back straight and held her cane like a weapon. She smiled, and her face was as fierce as a shark's. "You already know the answer."

Mata stared at her. "You ask for much." Though he tried to keep his voice steady, he trembled.

"No, *you* ask for much," the old woman said. "I'm merely hungry."

Mata continued to stare at her. He shook his head. "I can't. I won't."

The old woman chuckled. "You're wondering what Kuni Garu would think of you if you did as I asked?"

Mata said nothing.

The old woman shrugged. "I've said my piece. Do as you will." And suddenly, she was frail and ancient again as she shuffled her way out of the audience hall.

A whole fleet of ships was constructed within twenty days. With steady keels and tightly joined, smooth hulls, they bobbed gently in Toaza Harbor, gleaming with fresh paint. Mata's army had worked as hard and well as they had fought.

"Marshal Zyndu is a master shipwright! Is there anything on earth that Marshal Zyndu does not do a hundred times better than any other man?"

"How dare you compare Marshal Zyndu merely to other men? He is a general sent to us by the gods!"

"How dare you suggest the Marshal Zyndu is merely a mortal? He is Tazu incarnate, master of the seas and waves!"

Marshal Zyndu only half listened to the nobles and courtiers vying to outdo one another in their flattery. He knew that they were foolish, but he couldn't help how good he felt as they talked. Their words tickled his heart and made him feel like he was floating on clouds.

"Enough," he said. The chattering voices around him stopped immediately. "We set sail for the Big Island tomorrow. Let Kaima come to us on the sea, and we will crush him as easily we crushed Namen and Marana on land!"

And everyone cheered.

That night, the greatest storm in living memory swept through Toaza Harbor.

The howling of the winds clashing against one another caused those living closest to the sea to go deaf. The waves smashing against the coast were so high that they flooded the palace. The streets of Toaza turned into canals, and sharks swam through them in the morning, as dazed as the citizens watching them from third-story windows.

The fleet of new ships disappeared. Only a few broken masts and smashed boards were left. A thousand men who had already boarded the ships to break them in and keep watch were killed.

When he heard the news, Mata Zyndu ordered everyone to search for the old woman who had come to see him. But though Toaza was turned upside down, no trace of her could be found.

"Is this the price for defying the gods?" Mata talked to himself rather than the cowering courtiers. "Or perhaps this is a reminder of the weight of history?"

Then he raised his voice. "If our ships are destroyed, then we must build more."

He issued new orders.

There were simply too many surrendered Imperial soldiers to keep all as prisoners. They would be freed—provided that they agreed to join Mata Zyndu's army.

The prisoners jumped at the chance.

The first task of the new, bigger army was to build more ships to replace those that had been lost.

Many of the former Imperial soldiers had served as supervisors on the emperor's grand construction projects, where they wielded whips on the corvée laborers. Many of the Cocru soldiers, on the other hand, had worked as corvée laborers or had family and friends who did.

Now that they were supposed to be comrades with their erstwhile tormentors, the men of Cocru exacted revenge in ways big and small. Latrine duty was always assigned to the former Imperials, as was cooking, cleaning, and standing guard at night.

And during the day, as the former Imperials toiled at shipbuilding, the men of Cocru stood around and taunted them to work harder and faster. Morale among Mata's men rose despite the loss of the first fleet: Tormenting the Xana soldiers offered a concrete form of justice.

Ratho, among others, took great pleasure in ordering the Imperial scum about. As far as the surrendered men were concerned, the word of the marshal's personal guard was law.

Ratho's favorite game was to order these men to carry the great oak trees cut from the mountains down to the harbor. He would assign sixteen men to each tree and tell them that they had to walk all the way down from the mountain without ever setting the tree on the ground for a break. When the exhausted men inevitably dropped the tree before reaching their destination, he would make them leave the tree where it was and go back for another one. This was a diversion he never tired of.

"After what you Xana bastards put my father through"—he whipped them—"I'm practically giving you massages."

"There's a lot of complaining among the surrendered soldiers," Ratho said. "Many officers think that a mutiny is likely."

"Let them complain," Mata Zyndu said, his voice quiet.

"You spared their lives! They should be on their knees every day thanking you," Ratho said.

"Rat, sometimes it can be both too late to curse the gods and too early to thank men."

Ratho didn't know what Marshal Zyndu meant. All he knew was that the surrendered Xana soldiers were ungrateful. He muttered, "You can't get pigs to stop loving mud."

With great effort, Marshal Zyndu's army-of-former-prisoners managed to construct a new fleet in half as much time as before: ten days.

But this time, the sullen efforts of these abused men resulted in heavy, slow, and crude transports. Experienced Gan sailors looked at these ships in dismay. They resembled large boxes hammered together hastily with no thought about seaworthiness, stability, or maneuverability.

Torulu Pering spoke. "It would be a miracle if these ships didn't fall apart on their own once they were in the open ocean. I cannot see them posing a challenge to the blockading armada."

Mata impatiently waved for him to be quiet. "I have heard enough of words of doubt."

Fearing Marshal Zyndu's wrath more than the sea, no one else said anything.

"And hasn't he already snatched victory from the jaws of certain defeat?" the soldiers whispered. "Perhaps his will for success alone is enough to intimidate the gods into granting miracles. Even Tazu would not dare to fight our Marshal Zyndu."

When Mata gave the order to board, no one objected.

The huge holds of the ships seemed designed to transport grain and fish rather than men. As soldiers filed in, guards stationed at the steps leading down into the holds pushed them until the holds were packed so tight that it was impossible for anyone to even turn around. When the guards were satisfied that the cargo holds were really, truly full, they closed the doors.

The ships sailed out of Toaza Harbor, and men held their breath in the darkness, waiting for the armada to strike. But nothing happened, and the ships sailed on. Did Marshal Zyndu's fearsome reputation keep the Imperial ships at bay?

Gradually, the men in the suffocating dark were lulled to sleep by the gentle rocking motion of the ships, still standing and leaning against their comrades.

Hours passed, and with a jolt, some woke from their slumber. It was very quiet. The decks above their heads creaked, but there was no sound of footsteps. Shouldn't the cargo holds be opened to allow some of the men to go above to take in fresh air?

Those near the doors banged against them. No answer.

"They didn't just bar the doors. They sealed us in!" someone who peeked through cracks in the doors shouted. There were heavy boxes stacked against the outside of the cargo hold doors so that the men inside could not push them open no matter how hard they tried.

"Is anyone here from Cocru? Anyone who had served under Marshal Zyndu from before?"

No one answered. The whole cargo hold was filled with surrendered Imperial soldiers.

"Who's sailing the ship? Is there anyone up there?"

More silence.

The sailors had long ago left on lifeboats. The rudders of the ships had been jammed to fix their course. The creaking, leaky ships, filled with twenty thousand surrendered Imperial soldiers, sailed northward into the Kishi Channel.

Tazu's hungry maw opened in front of them.

Tazu, now happily fed and strengthened by this sacrifice, grew even more violent and powerful. He careened north, shot out of the Kishi Channel, circled around the Big Toe, and sucked half of the Imperial armada into his bottomless maw.

Without a break, he now moved down the eastern coast of Wolf's Paw and within a few hours completed the circuit of the island. South of Toaza, within sight of those on shore, Tazu caught up to the other half of the armada. Admiral Filo Kaima and all his men went to join their dead companions at the bottom of the ocean.

Great plumes of water shot out of the center of Tazu and reached high into the sky like the flicking tongues of toads aiming for dragonflies. The last of the lumbering Imperial airships tried to escape, but they were caught and pulled down into the great whirlpool and disappeared in silent puffs as they collapsed against the torrid sea like soap bubbles.

Tazu moved back into the Kishi Channel. His work was done.

In the gray and oppressive light of dusk, lightning bolts shot from the clouds, striking the tempest-tossed water in deafening blasts. Kiji, the stormy god of Xana, raged across the sea to the north of Wolf's Paw.

*Come and fight me, Tazu! You have broken the pact among the gods. The blood of Xana must be avenged! I will pull out every one of your teeth.*

But Tazu's whirlpool stayed out of the reach of the lightning bolts. It danced across the sea, careless as a well-fed shark.

*Brother, your rage is misplaced. It is in my nature to wander these seas daily. If the mortals wish to stand in my way, I'm well within my rights to do as I did.*

*I will not hear of such sophistry!*

The soothing, gentle voice of Rufizo, the healing god of nearby Faça, interceded.

*Kiji, you know that Tazu is right. Much as I abhor his methods, he has stayed within the letter of our pact. He only persuaded Mata Zyndu to make this sacrifice.*

For hours, the storm continued to rage, but eventually, as the sun rose, it dissipated.

"You disapprove," Mata said to his advisers. He kept his voice deliberately low and calm so that everyone strained to hear.

Except for Torulu Pering, who smiled coldly, all the other advisers lowered their eyes, not daring to meet his gaze.

"You think it was wrong to kill so many men who had already surrendered."

The assembled men continued to say nothing, striving to breathe quietly through their noses.

"When we were merciful and allowed the prisoners to live, we were trapped on this island. A storm came and took away the lives of our soldiers, young men who deserved to die in glory, not at sea.

"But our victory became assured when I decided to listen to that old woman, who was truly Tazu's messenger, and offer him a sacrifice commensurate with his appetite. The gods were speaking to us, don't you see?

"I had been too merciful. Perhaps I had allowed Kuni Garu, my gentle brother, to affect me too much. After all, he's no great warrior. I had to remember that being merciful to one's enemies is the same as being cruel to one's own men. Tazu wanted blood, and I had to give it to him.

"Some of you may flinch at the thought of killing so many Xana prisoners, but know that there is divine justice in this. Years ago, my grandfather, Dazu Zyndu, lost his war against Xana due to treachery. The Xana dog Gotha Tonyeti then buried alive the surrendered Cocru soldiers. Only now has that blood debt been repaid."

With the armada gone, a fleet of merchant and fishing ships came from Cocru to pick up Mata and *his* army—it no longer seemed necessary to pretend that the soldiers owed their allegiance to anyone but Mata.

King Thufi sent along congratulatory messages, which Mata threw away without even opening.

He was Mata Zyndu, the Butcher of Wolf's Paw. He had killed twenty thousand men with his sword and twenty thousand more with water. He was beyond the opinion of mere mortals like King Thufi. He was a god of death, and he made his own laws of war.

He would now go back to the Big Island and march through Thoco Pass into Pan, where he would crush Emperor Erishi and take what rightfully belonged to him.

## CHAPTER THIRTY-TWO

# THE HOUSEKEEPER

OUTSIDE ÇARUZA: THE TWELFTH MONTH IN THE FOURTH YEAR OF THE REIGN OF RIGHTEOUS FORCE.

Lady Jia felt overwhelmed.

Not being of noble birth, she never could seem to break into the social scene at Çaruza. Kuni was too coarse and practical-minded for most of the *real* hereditary nobles and kings and ambassadors, and that was reflected in the way she was treated. While Phin had been alive, his special regard for her had elevated her status somewhat, but after his death, the few noble ladies she had thought were her friends soon grew cold and distant.

Though Mata called on her from time to time and made sure she and the children lacked nothing materially, his care didn't help much with her social life—Mata was stiff and aloof and more feared than liked by the lords and ladies of the court.

She gritted her teeth and tried to venture out to some of the parties in Çaruza on her own a few times, but she couldn't shake the feeling that the stately, great ladies looked down on her and made fun of her too-loud laughter, her homely merchant's-family phrases, her loose and easy and unrefined manners.

So she stayed away from the court and tried to find solace in her son.

But Toto-*tika* had a weak constitution and was often sickly, and he would cry and cry until he fell asleep from exhaustion. It had taken all her skill and knowledge of medicine to nurse him back to health and to keep him alive. She was also pregnant again, and the new baby inside her seemed equally demanding, as it kept her up at night and made her feel irritable and drained. *I suppose it makes sense,* thought Jia, *the baby is going to be born in the Year of the Deer, and it's already bounding around inside me like a high-spirited fawn.*

The children seemed to require so much of her attention that she sometimes thought of them as akin to those legendary wraiths in the Gonlogi Desert who sucked travelers' blood until they fell down as empty husks.

Jia knew such thoughts were unbecoming in a mother, but she was beyond caring.

She had a sizable household staff, but most of the servant girls were war orphans who she had taken in out of pity. They were young and needed looking after themselves. Sometimes, Jia felt like one of those women who took in baby birds that had fallen out of their nests and stray cats who meowed for milk—she was happy they were around, but sometimes her compassion became a burden.

Thank goodness for Steward Otho Krin, who was solicitous and kind and seemed to crave her approval in everything he did. . . . Oh, who was she kidding? Jia understood what she really yearned for and was flattered by the attention. Truth be told, she sometimes admired his lanky form and shy but pretty eyes and imagined a secret tryst—but she'd quickly berate herself, blushing guiltily.

But he *was* very good at keeping the footmen and stablehands busy and useful so that all the household repairs and maintenance got done, so at least she didn't need to worry about that. Still, he was a man and could not help her with the thousands of little things that besieged her daily.

It was night. The baby was asleep and the house finally quiet. Jia felt the empty space next to her in bed and the ache in her heart. She closed her eyes and tried to reach across the miles and miles between herself and Kuni with her thoughts.

Letters from Kuni were sporadic and rare, like any reliable news from the front; she had heard nothing from him after he suddenly took off from Zudi without telling anyone where he was going. She realized this was the norm, not the exception, in their life: though they had married for a future of shared excitement, most of the time, Kuni went away and had adventures while she stayed behind with the children and the tedious weight of the quotidian. Where was "the most interesting thing" for her?

*What are you up to, my husband? Are you thinking of me?*

In a few hours she had to get up again and smile and keep up a stream of cheerful chatter all day. Everyone needed her; everyone depended on her; she was the one who had to be strong and sensible—one day, she was sure she was going to be sucked dry and fall down where she stood.

She felt so alone. And a heated thought rose into her mind that she resented Kuni for leaving her behind like this. She felt bad immediately and tried to push the thought away, but that only made it linger and hurt worse.

*I knew this was going to be hard. But this is the path I've chosen.*

She began to cry, at first quietly, and then louder. She bit down on her pillow to stop the sounds from spilling out into the hallway.

*Why do I feel so helpless?*

She punched the pillow hard, hard enough that her knuckles hurt from the muffled contact with the solid coconut husk core buried in the seeds and herbs she had stuffed the pillow with to give herself better sleep. The pain, surprisingly, *did* make her feel better.

She punched the pillow a few more times, targeting where she could feel the sharp edges of the coconut husk; she winced. She shifted her punches to the sides a bit so that her fist fell into the seeds and crushed herbs; she felt better. At least she was in control of this, she smiled bitterly, tears on her face. She could control how much pain she got from punching her pillow.

Her smile froze.

*I've been allowing myself to lose control.*

She was in the middle of a maelstrom, and she was at risk of drowning. But she had to find a spar, a piece of driftwood, to hang on to. Then she would climb up and navigate her way out.

She needed to make choices again, to feel she was the master of her own fate.

The door slid open, and she stepped out of the room quietly. Noiselessly, she made her way down the hall, around the corner, to the front wing, and then she slid open another door with a barely audible creak.

She tapped the figure in the dark on the shoulder. It stirred, mumbled, and turned to go back to sleep.

She tapped the shoulder harder and whispered in the dark, "Wake up, Otho."

Otho Krin rolled over and rubbed his eyes. "What . . . what time is it?"

"It's me, Jia."

Otho sat up immediately. "Lady Jia! What are you doing here?"

Jia took a deep breath and wrapped her arms around him in a deep embrace. Otho stiffened.

"Don't be alarmed," said Jia, her voice gaining confidence as she continued to speak. "I have decided on something that will make me happy, something I choose for just myself."

"You have?" came Otho's muffled response.

Jia laughed quietly. Paradoxically, perhaps insanely, she no longer resented Kuni. She felt alive, in control; she felt she was swimming toward a spar, a glimmer of hope.

She sat back and began to undress Otho in the dark.

"No!" Otho protested. But then he stopped struggling. "Surely this is a dream," he mumbled. "Is Lady Rapa rewarding me with a lovely dream?"

"This is no dream," said Jia. "We will justify it another time. It's enough for now to know that sometimes we need to hang on to each other as tightly as possible simply to remember that we are still alive, that we choose our fates, whatever the gods have planned for us."

And they lay down together in the darkness, their bodies sliding against each other hungrily, desperately, their mouths meeting in urgent kisses that sought time and timelessness in equal measure.

"Let it be known that I am looking for a housekeeper," Jia said.

"A housekeeper?" Steward Otho Krin asked. He could sense there was something different about her this morning—further evidence that last night had not been a dream.

Jia looked at him in the eyes—there was no awkwardness, no embarrassment in her gaze. She smiled. "I've been feeling too isolated. I want a companion: someone who can help me with women's tasks and be my friend."

Otho Krin nodded. This was the Jia he had fallen in love with, the woman who had awed him and showed him what was possible in the world. He would always be loyal to her and be discreet, of course, but he had shared a night with her. He had. The joy in his heart was indescribable.

He bowed and left.

At the door stood a middle-aged woman who radiated efficiency from the top of her hair knot—not a single strand out of place—to the uppers of her embroidered cloth shoes—the hand stitches tight and neat like a line of marching ants.

"My name is Soto," she said.

"You have experience with large households?"

"I grew up in a very large house," Soto said. "I know some tricks." She appraised Jia.

Though she tried to speak like a commoner, Jia noted the refined accent and the formal way Soto held herself: There was none of the ingratiating bowing and scraping a real servant would have used to her potential mistress.

She liked Soto immediately.

"Çaruza is filled with many noble houses," Jia said. "Many of them look on me with contempt. It's not a good stepping-stone to a better position in the future."

"If I wanted to live in houses run by spoiled children who are too old to spank," replied Soto evenly, "I would have knocked on those doors."

Jia laughed, and the hint of a smile appeared on Soto's face. Soto's contempt for Çaruza's aristocrats made Jia guess she was the daughter of a minor Cocru noble family who had fallen on hard times.

"Welcome to the house of Duke Garu. I hope you and Steward Otho Krin get along. I'm just about at my wit's end."

Soto turned out to be an efficient but kind housekeeper, and soon Jia's house hummed along like a well-oiled machine.

She took the most responsible servant girls and had them take turns taking care of the baby during the day so that Jia could be freed up. The servant girls learned useful domestic skills from her that would stand them in good stead for future employment, while the stablehands and footmen appreciated her gentle touch and eye for details. She took care of things that Steward Krin never bothered with—such as making sure to give everyone an extra egg on the festival days.

And Soto told such wonderful stories about the old days before the Conquest! Even Jia sometimes was mesmerized when Soto spun one of her yarns about the old Cocru aristocracy for the entertainment of the servants in the kitchen. Jia thought most of the stories Soto told were probably made up, but she sprinkled them with so many delicious and scandalous details that she wished they were true.

They took walks together in the Cocru countryside: along the beach, over the plains, up and down the hills. Soto was interested in Jia's herbal collection and asked intelligent questions as Jia happily showed her the various seaweeds, flowers, grasses, and shrubs and explained their diverse virtues. She also asked after the history between Jia and Kuni, and Jia happily told her all about Kuni's less well-known exploits.

In return, Soto told Jia many stories of Cocru's past that were tragic, serious, and romantic—like the one about Prime Minister Lurusén, the famous poet, who had drowned himself in the Liru River because King Thoto refused to listen to his counsel to not trust Xana's overtures of peace.

*The world is drunk; I alone am sober.*
*The world is asleep, but I am awake.*
*My tears are not wept for you, King Thoto,*
*But for the men and women of Cocru.*

"What a loyal and good man he was," Jia said, sighing. She remembered Kuni's creative interpretation of the poem, and a smile curled the corners of her mouth.

"You know he had not wanted to go into politics at all?" said Soto. "He wanted to be a hermit poet in the mountains."

"What changed his mind?"

"His wife, Lady Zy. She was far more of a patriot than he was, and she encouraged him to use his gift with words for some higher purpose than entertainment. 'Politics is the highest of the arts,' she used to tell him, and eventually, he listened and wrote those passionate pleas for Cocru to go to war against Xana before it was too late. When King Thoto dismissed Lurusén from his post to sign the peace treaty with Xana, Lurusén and Lady Zy plunged into the Liru together to voice their protest."

Jia was quiet for a while. "Had he not listened to her, perhaps they both would have lived out full lives in the mountains."

"And died in obscurity," said Soto. "But today every child of Cocru can recite the poems of Lurusén and revere his name. Not even Mapidéré dared to ban his books, though the poet had cursed the name of Xana on every page."

"So you think he might be thankful to his wife?"

"I'd like to think they made their decisions together and were happy to face the consequences together," said Soto.

Jia was thoughtful. Soto said no more and they continued their walk in peace.

Once more, Jia wondered just who Soto was—she was skillful at dodging questions about her past, and Jia hated feeling like she was prying.

Still, Jia liked Soto because she seemed to understand that sometimes all Jia wanted was for someone to be there, walking companionably next to her, so that she knew she was not alone. And in her presence Jia could complain, pettily and selfishly, or laugh, loudly and unladylike, and Soto never seemed to think there was anything wrong with what she did.

"Lord Garu has been away for a long time," Soto said one morning, as she came to get Jia's instructions for the day.

Jia felt the ache in her heart again. "It *has* been a long time. And he probably won't be here when the new baby is born either."

Speaking the fact out loud seemed to give it substance, make it real. When Kuni first sent word that he was leaving Zudi on a mission he could not speak about, she had been angry that he would be so reckless—though, hadn't the dream herbs always told her that some measure of heartache was inevitable with Kuni? She shouldn't really have been surprised.

As the days went by with no further messages, she grew more and more worried. Since Phin was dead and Mata was away at Wolf's Paw, Jia had no source for reliable news. King Thufi and the other nobles barely knew who she was.

"I understand that he and Marshal Zyndu are good friends," Soto said.

"Yes. Marshal Zyndu and Lord Garu fought together, and they are as tight as brothers."

"Friendships among men tend to not survive great rises or falls of fortune," Soto said. She paused, seeming to hesitate over whether to go on. "What do you think of this Mata Zyndu?"

Jia was taken aback by Soto's tone. Zyndu was the Victor at Wolf's Paw, Bane of the Empire, the Greatest Warrior of Dara. Right now, he was sweeping through Géjira and mopping up the scattered bits of Imperial resistance in the old cities of Gan. Even King Thufi seemed to speak of the marshal with deference. Yet Soto spoke his name carelessly, as though he was a child. Was there some history between Soto's family and the Zyndus?

Jia answered carefully. "Marshal Zyndu is without a doubt the most important member of the rebellion. Without him, we would never have achieved victory over the crafty Marana and the stout Namen."

"Is that so?" Soto seemed amused. "That sounds like what the town criers keep on telling us every day, as if they're afraid we'll stop believing the minute they stop. I only know that he killed a lot of people."

Jia didn't know how to respond to this, so she stood up. "Let us speak no more of politics."

"That may not be possible forever, Jia. You're a political wife, whether you want to be or not." Then Soto bowed and left.

Soto's room was just down the hall from Jia's, and she was a light sleeper.

She heard Jia's door open after everyone had gone to bed, and she knew she would hear the door open again right before dawn.

She had seen the way Steward Otho Krin looked at Lady Jia when he thought no one was watching. She had seen the way he lingered near her when he held the reins of her carriage. She had also seen the way Lady Jia furtively returned his smiles and carefully listened as he gave the reports on household finances.

More than anything else, the scrupulous way they avoided being too close to each other when others were around told Soto everything she needed to know.

Soto lay awake in the darkness, thinking.

She had come to the Garu household because she was intrigued by the wild tales of Mata Zyndu and Kuni Garu, the Marshal and the Bandit, the unlikeliest of friends who had become the most faithful of companions, whose exploits against Tanno Namen had inspired thousands in the rebellion. There were folk operas composed about them, and many spoke confidently of their favor in the eyes of the gods.

She wanted to see for herself the truth behind the legends, to understand Kuni the way his wife understood him. No matter how large a man grew in the eyes of the world, in the eyes of his wife he would always be life-size, or maybe even smaller-than-life. Unexpectedly, she had come to like Jia, the woman who was once only a means to an end for her. She saw a measure of the man Kuni was by the woman he loved.

Jia could become a force to be reckoned with, a shaper of the path of the rebellion so that its fruits might taste sweet for more than just men like Mata Zyndu, men who looked to an ideal past but were blind to messy realities. Soto hoped to nudge Jia along the path that she was meant to take, which would require Soto to reveal the truth of her own past. But now that she knew of this wrinkle in Jia's life, she had to consider what it meant.

There was a tendency by some to romanticize love, to make a fetish out of it. The poets made love seem like a bar of iron coming out of the furnace at the blacksmith's, red hot and staying so forever. Soto did not think much of such notions.

A man fell in love with a woman, married her, and the passion would cool. He would then go into the world, see other women, fall in love again, marry them, and feel the new passion cool in turn. After all, in all the Tiro states, a man was allowed to have multiple wives, if he could persuade all the wives to agree.

But if he was a good man, the passion would cool into a smoldering ember, ready to be fanned aflame again. As the great Kon Fiji wrote so long ago: A good husband remained in love with all his wives, but being good took hard work, and most husbands were lazy.

It was no different from how a lonely wife, away from her husband, would seek comfort in a lover. Yet, for the most part, she would not be lying to say that she still loved her husband.

For both women and men, Soto believed that love was more like food. The same dish tired the palate, and variety was spice.

The world did not tolerate such betrayals by the wives, if betrayal was what they were, as it tolerated the same betrayals by husbands. But the world was wrong. Accommodations for the vagaries of the heart should be made for women as well as men.

So Jia was not a woman bound by conventions when it came to matters of the heart. Soto hoped Jia would be as bold in making use of her position and influence as she was in her passions. She hoped it for Jia's own happiness as well as the happiness of the men and women of Cocru—and all of Dara.

Soto went back to sleep, and said nothing of what she knew.

CHAPTER THIRTY-THREE

# THE REAL MASTER OF PAN

GÉJIRA: THE FIRST MONTH IN THE
FIRST YEAR OF THE PRINCIPATE.

Now that the empire was without a leader like Marshal Kindo Marana or General Tanno Namen, the remaining pockets of Imperial resistance in Géjira collapsed before Mata Zyndu like empty husks. Many garrisons surrendered without a fight.

But a few cities *did* fight, and the other rebel commanders vied to present Mata with stratagems for conquering them to prove their worth. A scrawny little man named Gin Mazoti, in particular, insisted on seeing him at every opportunity.

"If you give me fifty men, we can enter cities as disguised merchants long before your arrival and open the gates for you when you do."

"There is a drainage pipe that empties out into the sea here; we may be able to enter the city through the sewers."

"It is exceedingly strange that Pan has been completely silent. Why has the regent not appointed a new leader to rally the troops in Géjira? Marshal, something is afoot, and we must redouble our efforts to spy in Géfica."

Mata dismissed him contemptuously. Men like him wanted to rely on tricks rather than real mettle. Unworthy.

After he conquered each recalcitrant city by brute force, Mata gave his troops three days to do whatever they liked to the inhabitants. For good measure, he decided to wreck Géjira's industry to ensure the conquered territories would not rise up behind him. Water mills along the Sonaru were smashed, and windmills irrigating the fields burned like giant torches.

King Dalo, whom Mata Zyndu dragged along as a prisoner, sometimes tried to intercede on behalf of Géjira, which had belonged to Gan before the Conquest. Even Marana, now a "guest" of Marshal Zyndu in the rebel army, occasionally joined King Dalo in calling for mercy.

People were so eager to give Mata advice. He was tired of it.

"You understand, of course, that by making examples of these cities, I discourage further resistance in the rest of Géjira and so save more lives in the long run, especially the lives of my men?"

Dalo had no answer to that. Marana had the grace to sometimes blush, as he had once used the very same logic.

But in Zyndu's mind, the people of Géjira were also cowards and traitors because they had not risen up against the empire back when the rebellion could have used their help. In a way, he thought the soldiers' brutality toward the conquered Géjira cities was just.

After Wolf's Paw, he did not ever want his own mercy to cost the lives of those who followed him.

Although the fiction that the armies of the other Tiro states remained under independent command was still maintained, Owi Ati and Huy̌e Nocano, the Faça and Gan commanders, increasingly became more like puppets. Their troops were tightly incorporated into Zyndu's own chain of command. King Thufi sometimes also tried to send messengers with "suggestions" for Marshal Zyndu, but Mata only glanced at them and then threw them away.

For all intents and purposes, Mata Zyndu was now the real princeps—no, more than a princeps, a hegemon—and all the Tiro states understood this.

Géjira was finally pacified after a month. But reliable news of happenings in Géfica, the heart of the empire on the other side of the mountains, were hard to come by. The caravan traffic through Thoco Pass had ceased, and none of Mata's spies came back. The remaining Imperials seemed to huddle in the Immaculate City and sent no reinforcements to Géjira.

Mata's messengers to Zudi also returned empty-handed: Duke Garu was missing, and no one knew where he had gone. Mata wasn't overly concerned; he had wanted to have Kuni by his side as he prepared for his final assault, but he knew that Kuni was wily and could take care of himself.

As the new year arrived, Mata brought his rebel army to Thoco Pass, from where they would begin the march on Pan and the boy emperor Erishi.

*Finally,* he thought, *the dream of freeing Dara is about to come true.*

He felt as light as a feather, as giddy as a child.

The snow-topped peaks and sheer cliffs of the Shinané Mountains and the Wisoti Mountains formed two walls impenetrable to all but birds and mountain goats.

The only place to pass from Géjira, on the east side of the two mountain ranges, to Géfica, on the west side, was through Thoco Pass, a twenty-mile-long valley between the towering Mounts Kana and Rapa, to the south, and Mount Fithowéo, to the north. Thoco Pass was narrow, dark, and covered by towering trees that stretched as high as they could to catch the bits of light that filtered down through the gap between the steep mountains. Rumblings from the great volcanoes on both sides set off occasional rockslides that blocked the pass until the debris could be cleared. It was the perfect place for an ambush.

Over the years, the various Tiro states around the junction fought over the series of walled forts that guarded Thoco Pass. Whoever controlled them controlled the spine of the Big Island.

Coming from the eastern end, the first fort in Thoco Pass was Goa, a massive stone citadel built more than two hundred years ago.

∽ ∾ ∽ ∾

Marshal Zyndu's army approached Goa cautiously and sent out several scouting parties. As the last barrier before Pan, Thoco Pass was likely heavily defended.

Doru Solofi, the captain of the scouts, came back with the surprising news that the red flags of Cocru were flying from the walls of Goa.

Mata Zyndu took a few personal guards and rode up to Goa's gates.

"Open up!" Ratho called out. "We're with Marshal Zyndu, commander-in-chief of all rebel forces. Who's your commander?"

The soldiers peeked carefully over the wall. "Without Lord Garu's orders, we won't let anyone through."

"Lord Garu? You mean Kuni Garu, the Duke of Zudi?"

"The very same. Though now that he's captured Emperor Erishi, he's going to be King of Géfica!"

Mata rode forward. "He's done *what*? Open up the gates now and let me speak to him!"

The defenders of Goa, being former Imperial soldiers who had surrendered to Kuni, wanted to show their zeal for their new lord. They shot volleys of arrows at Mata Zyndu and his guards and laughed at this presumptuous man who thought he could just strut in and talk to their king.

Ratho lifted his shield in front of Mata, but Mata struck it out of his hand and tossed it away. An arrow struck him in the shoulder, but he didn't even seem to feel it.

But Ratho felt as if his heart were bleeding—how could Lord Garu take up arms against his friend? And after all he and the marshal had been through together, too.

"There must have been some mistake," Mata Zyndu said.

*Didn't Kuni tell me once that only I had the courage and strength to conquer Immaculate Pan, to take the prize promised by King Thufi?*

*Had I not spoken to Kuni of my dream of the Imperial capital covered in a tempest of gold, a tide of chrysanthemum, and, I had hoped, dandelion?*

*Are we not brothers who pledged to support each other in everything, to fight for the same goals and not for selfish gain?*

Mata Zyndu could not understand it. How could Kuni have snuck into Pan like a thief while he was struggling for the very life of the rebellion on Wolf's Paw? And how could Kuni now raise swords against *him* like a gangster protecting his turf? It was impossible. It had to be some impostor.

"Everyone betrays me," he muttered. "There is no honor in a woman like Kikomi or a man like Kuni Garu." No matter how much he trusted people, they always ended up betraying him in the most despicable manner.

But Torulu Pering informed him that a follower of Kuni Garu, a man by the name of Ro Minosé, had escaped from Goa and come to surrender to him. He had seen the size of Mata Zyndu's army and decided that joining Mata made more sense.

"Tell me about Lord Garu's successes," Mata Zyndu said. He worked hard to keep his face impassive and his voice calm.

Ro spoke to him of Kuni Garu's ride to Rui on the back of a cruben, of his surprise attack on Pan, of his careful manipulation of the surrendered Imperial troops, of his gentle administration afterward, and of the esteem in which he was held by the people of Géfica.

"The people love Lord Garu. They think that the gods blessed them when they made him the conqueror of Pan rather than . . ."

"Go on."

"Than you, Marshal. Lord Garu's men often speak of what happened at Dimu, and Imperial deserters have spread rumors of what happened at Wolf's Paw and in Géjira. Some wish that Lord Garu would not only be their king, but perhaps the new emperor."

Mata Zyndu's fury was sudden, scorching, and all-consuming.

He paced like a caged animal inside his tent. Everything inside the tent was already broken, and as he paced, he ground the broken pieces into the muddy soil.

*While I and my soldiers used our lives to hold back the empire's greatest army on Wolf's Paw, Kuni snuck through an unguarded back door like a thief.*

*While I, by pure valor and strength, earned the greatest victory this world has ever known, Kuni stole the honor and reward that belonged to me.*

*And now, now? The thief does not even have the decency to face me and explain himself. Kuni Garu, who was like a brother, has locked the door against* me, *like a robber trying to keep a bigger portion of the loot.*

"I'll die before I let *him* become King of Géfica!" Mata Zyndu roared. He was more outraged for his soldiers, young men, barely more than boys, who had followed him from Tunoa and fought for him fearlessly. They deserved to have their bravery recognized by the world.

*To have people think of Kuni Garu as the one who finished the empire would be intolerable.*

The other nobles and commanders, keeping their heads bowed submissively, gradually eased themselves step by step to the entrance of the tent, mumbled their excuses, and hastily retreated.

Torulu Pering was the only one who remained. "Marshal, be calm and think this through."

"*Think?* We have to act! We must attack Goa immediately so we can get to Pan and catch the trickster Kuni Garu. I want to see the traitor's face—though he's probably too shameless to even understand that he's done me wrong."

"Marshal, Kuni Garu might have snatched up Emperor Erishi like a sly vulture while you fought the empire like a lone wolf. But he *has* fulfilled the literal terms of King Thufi's promise, and it would appear poorly in the eyes of the world for you to fight him like a jealous child. Though the empire has fallen, open warfare among the great lords of the rebellion so soon after will bring all of us dishonor."

"*He does not deserve it!* He stole a title that belongs to me!"

"It might be better to allow him to think that he has won it," said Torulu Pering, "and that you acquiesce in his usurpation. Approach him. When his guard is down, and he away from his men, you can seize him and lay bare his trickery for the world to see. Then and only then can you properly claim the throne of the new Tiro state in Géfica for yourself."

Marshal Zyndu sent messengers to Goa to congratulate the men in the fort for serving such a great lord as King Kuni of Géfica. Might the soldiers be willing to bring a message to their king?

> *Marshal Zyndu would like to congratulate his old friend on his amazing victory in Pan, and he very humbly requests that His Majesty, King Kuni, grant him the boon of an audience.*

Of course Mata Zyndu could not stand to write the words "His Majesty, King Kuni." He tried to do it because Torulu told him he had to, but he was so angry that he squeezed the wax stick until it melted in his hand.

He jumped up and told Torulu Pering to finish the message for him.

"I'm going hunting," Mata said. "I have to kill someone or something right now."

Kuni blanched as he read the sarcastic message from Mata.

"Whose idea was it to block Thoco Pass against Marshal Zyndu?" he asked. His voice trembled. "What happened to the messengers I dispatched to my brother to invite him to share my victory in Pan?"

Rin Coda stepped forward. "Marshal Zyndu is known for a streak of cruelty. I kept news of our victory here from spreading east and fortified Thoco Pass. I thought it might give us more time to secure our position in Pan and gain the support of the people."

"Oh, Rin, what have you done?" Cogo Yelu shook his head in frustration. "You've openly challenged the marshal as though we were enemies rather than allies! Now even if Lord Garu's message gets out, no one will believe his good faith.

"Mata Zyndu has more than ten times our soldiers, and his reputation is as high as the midday sun. All the Tiro states revere him, and Lord Garu's claim to Géfica would not stand without Zyndu's support. Had we openly welcomed him into Pan, we could have made Lord Garu's surprise attack seem all along part of Marshal Zyndu's plan and gotten his support that way—"

"Not just *seem*," interrupted Kuni. "Sharing the victory with my brother *was* all along my plan."

"But that's no longer possible now," lamented Cogo. "This is a mistake that will be hard to rectify."

Fast riders were immediately dispatched to Haan to fetch Luan Zya. Kuni needed his counsel.

"Victory has not turned out to be as sweet as I hoped," said Kuni to Luan.

Luan nodded, thinking of the loneliness and listlessness he experienced in the ruins of his ancestral estate in Ginpen as he waited for comfort from his father's soul. "The vagaries of the human heart are as hard to divine as the will of the gods."

Philosophy aside, they still had to take care of the immediate problem. Kuni's forces had pulled out of Goa, and Mata's army followed close behind.

Luan Zya and Cogo Yelu carefully planned the retreat of Kuni Garu's forces from Pan. They sealed up the palace and put all the treasures that could be recovered back in their places. Cogo loaded the records from the Imperial Archives into oxcarts and brought them back to Kuni—Dafiro was now convinced that some secret treasure was hidden among them, but Cogo just shook his head sadly when Dafiro probed.

Then Kuni took the men he brought from Cocru and any surrendered Imperial soldiers who wanted to follow him ten miles west of the city and made a new camp by the shores of Lake Tututika.

The elders of Pan accompanied Kuni for miles. They had enjoyed Duke Garu's gentle rule, which was far preferable to Emperor Erishi's heavy levies and cruel enforcement. Marshal Zyndu's reputation—colored by the blood of Dimu, Wolf's Paw, and Géjira—made them reluctant to embrace the new conqueror. They begged Kuni Garu to stay.

"There has been a misunderstanding between Marshal Zyndu and me," Kuni Garu said. "If I stay, it would make things worse." But he remembered the death cries of the citizens of Dimu, and he could not drive away the pangs of guilt.

Kuni stared at the wide expanse of Lake Tututika. The water stretched all the way to the sky, like the sea, only calm and flat like a mirror.

"Now we have to wait and see how Mata will deal with us. I hope he can still remember our friendship and forgive the perceived insult."

Once he arrived in Pan, Mata Zyndu ordered a general cleansing of the city by looting. His men had been promised the riches of the Imperial capital, and he wasn't going to deny them their pleasure. He did not exactly encourage the slaughter of Pan's citizens, who tried to welcome him as best as they could, but he didn't exactly forbid it either.

Cold, wintry rain fell, and as panicked people ran through the slick, slippery streets ahead of drawn swords, the rivulets in the city's gutters gradually turned red.

The boy emperor Erishi had been left behind in the palace when Kuni and his men left Pan.

"Please take me with you," the boy had begged. "I don't want to face that butcher."

Kuni had sighed and said that there was nothing he could do. Mata Zyndu was now the self-proclaimed Hegemon of All Tiro States. The emperor's fate was in his hands. Kuni pried the child's fingers from the sleeves of his robe and took his leave, but Erishi's piteous cries echoed in Kuni's head long after.

Mata Zyndu's men carted away all the treasure that could be

removed from the palace. The soldiers then sealed the palace doors with the emperor and his few loyal servants inside.

Aloud, Mata Zyndu proclaimed the sins of the Xana Empire against the people of the Six States and set the palace on fire. The boy emperor was last seen jumping from the top of the tallest tower in the palace, having run out of places to hide from the rising flames. The fire raged on and on, and the people of Pan were forbidden from trying to put it out, however it spread. All of Pan eventually burned, and the flames smoldered for three months. The ashes and smoke from the destruction could be seen from as far away as Haan, rising like a black spear stabbing into heaven.

The Immaculate City was no more.

"With the death of Erishi, the empire is at an end," Mata announced. "It is now the first year of the Principate." The cheers from the crowd seemed to him subdued and lacking in enthusiasm. This irked him.

Mata Zyndu also sent his men after Emperor Mapidéré's Mausoleum. Almost every rebel soldier had known family or friends who were forced to work on it at some point—many of them dying on their corvée stints. Everyone, it seemed, wanted to destroy Mapidéré's final resting place for vengeance, and Mata thought it perfectly fitting.

The Mausoleum was an underground city built deep inside a hollowed-out mountain in the Wisoti Mountains.

Mata Zyndu's men quickly smashed the entrance to the city, a gate made of the whitest, purest marble. Beyond the gate, dug into the mountain, was a maze of twisty tunnels covered in intricate carvings. Many of the tunnels led to traps or dead ends, and a great number of men rushing in with torches and pickaxes without knowing which paths were safe were injured or even killed.

Only a few of the tunnels led to the underground city itself, where mercury-filled, jade-lined trenches and pools emulated the seas and rivers of Dara, and sculpted piles of gold and silver mirrored the Islands of Dara. On the model islands, their chief geographical features were re-created with jade, pearls, coral, and gems.

In the middle of the model of the Big Island was a raised dais, on which Emperor Mapidéré's sarcophagus rested. Around the sarcophagus were placed smaller coffins, containing some of the emperor's favorite wives and servants who had been strangled and buried along with the emperor to keep him company in the afterlife. More bright jewels were set into the ceiling of the underground city to re-create the patterns of constellations and stars, and lamps fed with slow-oozing oil drawn deep from the earth were supposed to keep the underground city lit for thousands of years.

After the rebel soldiers pried out all the gemstones and smashed everything that could not be taken, they dragged Emperor Mapidéré's body from the tomb and whipped it in Kiji Square, the empty space in the middle of Pan. Then the frenzied mob set upon the body and tore it into a thousand pieces.

Meanwhile, Mata Zyndu's soldiers continued to prey on the citizens of Pan and the peasants in the surrounding countrysides. There was much suffering and crying for mercy that fell on deaf ears.

Mata Zyndu rode through the streets, surveying the destruction of Pan. The sweetness of exacting vengeance was soured by the disappointment of a string of betrayals he had suffered: Phin Zyndu, Princess Kikomi, and now Kuni Garu, whom he had thought of as a brother.

The joy of being the master of Pan felt hollow. The city, after all, had been handed to him by Kuni, not conquered by his own arms. Nothing felt as good as he had imagined.

He slowed down as he heard a woman singing a dirge by the side of the road. The sound of grieving women was common in the streets of Pan these days, but this mourning song was different because it traversed familiar paths from his ears to his heart: He had heard it often as a child.

Ratho Dafiro, who always rode with Mata, went over to investigate and brought the grieving woman back to face Mata Zyndu.

"Woman, you are from Tunoa?"

The woman, slender and tall, parted her dirty and stringy hair to gaze at Mata. Mata found her dark complexion curious—she looked like someone from Haan, but her speech was pure Tunoa.

"My name is Mira," she said. "And I am indeed a woman of Tunoa." She looked at him defiantly, as if daring him to challenge her on this assertion. "My parents made their living by fishing in Haan until, one day, my father's nets accidentally caught a dyran. The local Xana garrison commander claimed that my father had committed sacrilege because the dyran was sacred to Lady Datha, the emperor's late mother. To propitiate the gods, my father had to pay him ten gold pieces. To escape that debt, my family ran to Tunoa, where they weren't exactly welcomed. But my brother and I were both born on the Isle of Vines, smallest and farthest of the Tunoa isles."

Mata nodded. The fishermen of Tunoa, like the tradition-bound Cocru farmers on the Big Island, were suspicious of strangers and no doubt contemptuous of a family who ran from a debt—even one that was unjust. He could imagine that the children were picked on by others in their village as they grew up in their adopted homeland.

"How did you come here, and whose death do you mourn?"

"My brother had come over the sea with you," she said. "He was called Mado Giro." When she saw no sign that Mata recognized the name, her dark eyes, which had momentarily shone with the light of hope, dimmed. "He was the first from our village to heed the call to rebel. Going from house to house, he told all the parents that they should send their sons to join him because you were an even greater man than your grandfather, and that you would bring glory to Cocru. Sixteen young men went with him to Farun."

Mata nodded. So the woman's brother was one of the original Eight Hundred who had crossed over the sea with him and his uncle to join Huno Krima and Zopa Shigin. They had believed in him back when he was nobody, when the rebellion had seemed certain to fail.

"I waited at home, but his letters were few and far between. He was proud of what you had done, but he didn't seem to have risen much in your estimation, though I was sure he fought as bravely as all the times he had protected me from the other children when we were little."

It seemed that he ought to remember something about this man, who must have stood out in his army given his Haan ancestry. But he could recall nothing about his face, his rank, or his name.

He had been so focused on his own valor, on his own deeds of might, on the glory he could accrue to the Zyndu name that he had not taken the time to get to know most of those who trusted him and put their lives in his hands. Ashamed, he avoided Mira's eyes.

"I stayed home to care for our parents, but Kana took them both last winter. I lived alone until I received another letter from Mado, saying that you had finally entered Pan and that the war was over. I packed and came to seek him."

But instead of a happy reunion, she found her brother just another body wrapped in a shroud in a mass grave. He had been one of the soldiers intent on breaking through the Mausoleum. A set of booby-trap crossbow bolts took his life, though his error allowed his companions to pass deeper and retrieve some treasure from a side burial chamber.

"Fortune is unfair," Mata Zyndu muttered.

He pitied this woman in a way that surprised him. Maybe it was her accent, which brought to him memories of simpler times at home. Maybe it was her face, which he found beautiful despite the mixture of dirt and dried tears that covered it. Maybe it was a sense of duty born from his embarrassment at having no memory of a man who had loyally followed him for so long. Maybe it was the way he empathized with the dead soldier, who had been courageous and took a great risk only to have other men receive the benefit of his labor.

He felt hot tears welling up.

"Woman, you shall stay by my side. I will take care of you, and you will never lack anything. Your brother was one of the first to follow me, when it was far from clear that I would be victorious. I shall give him a proper burial."

Mira bowed deeply and then followed silently behind the men all the way back to Mata's camp.

In an alcove to the side of the street, a beggar and a nun had silently observed the exchange between Mata and Mira.

No one paid them any attention. With so many dead in Pan, itinerant monks and nuns had flocked to the city to perform last rites, and Mata's soldiers had made many homeless, with begging their only choice.

The nun wore the black habit of an itinerant of indeterminate denomination, and the face that peeked out from under the cowl seemed ageless. Behind her, a big, black raven stood on the wall on top of the alcove, imperiously surveying the street.

"I like the new look," she said to the beggar. "You're in mourning for your empire?" The voice was unpleasant, sharp, doleful, raspy.

Though grime covered every visible inch of the beggar's skin—including his bald head—he incongruously wore a spotless white traveling cape. If anyone passing by the alcove paid attention, they would have noticed that the beggar's hand holding the walking stick had only four fingers. He backed up a step and regarded the nun with cold, pale-gray eyes.

"The war has not gone my way," he conceded. "But your champion is not the one who struck the decisive blow. We've all been tricked."

The nun's face seemed to flush momentarily, though it was hard to tell in the shadow of her cowl. "Garu may be a son of Cocru, but I wash my hands of him. It's my sister Rapa who seems to have taken a liking to him."

The corners of the beggar's mouth turned up in a smirk. "Do I detect discord among the Twins and Fithowéo? Perhaps the war is not over yet."

She refused to take up his bait. "Stay away from Mata," she said. "I know you hunger for vengeance for those men of Xana who died at Wolf's Paw, but Mata had his reasons."

"If blood for blood were all that mattered, history would be easy to write. But don't worry, I won't be the first one to break our pact."

"You may refrain from directly harming a mortal like Mata, but who knows when a gust of wind may decide to topple a weakened flagpole near him? Or when a passing eagle may mistake his head for a rock and drop a turtle on it?"

The beggar chuckled mirthlessly. "Sister, I'm disappointed that you think I will resort to such low tricks. I'm not Tazu. Keep on hovering around Mata like a mother hen if you want."

The beggar walked away, but before disappearing around the corner, he turned back and said, "I have learned much from watching the mortals."

# THE CAGED WOLF

CHAPTER THIRTY-FOUR

# THE BANQUET

PAN: THE THIRD MONTH IN THE FIRST
YEAR OF THE PRINCIPATE.

Now that Mata Zyndu had put an end to the empire, it was time to hand out the proper rewards for all the rebel leaders. Marshal Zyndu announced that he would hold a banquet.

"This is your opportunity to confront the Duke of Zudi," Torulu Pering said.

Kuni's advisers studied Mata Zyndu's invitation carefully.

"You can't seriously be thinking of going to this," Than Carucono said. "Marshal Zyndu has refused to see you all this time, so he's clearly still angry about you taking Pan before him. This banquet is a trap. If you go, you won't come back."

"Lord Garu has no choice," Cogo Yelu said. "If he doesn't go, his refusal will be seen by everyone as an insult to Marshal Zyndu and an admission that he has done the marshal injury. If Zyndu then declares Lord Garu a traitor, all the Tiro states will support him."

"I just don't see why we're wringing our hands here. Lord Garu was the one who got into Pan first and captured Emperor Erishi. Why shouldn't the terms of King Thufi's promise be carried out?" Rin Coda said.

"Do you think you can best Mata Zyndu on the battlefield?" Luan Zya asked.

"No."

"Then King Thufi's promise means nothing. In this world, the only currency is force of arms. Lord Garu has to go because he's in a weak position, and Mata Zyndu gets to declare the terms.

"But, if we can come up with a way to present our case at the banquet to the assembled nobles, Lord Garu will appear to be so good and loyal in the eyes of the world that Zyndu will have to forgive him. Otherwise, we're finished."

Kuni listened to the debate without speaking. Eventually, the advisers quieted.

"Mata and I are brothers," said Kuni, his voice low and somber. "I have done nothing wrong. Why are you speaking as though I must make up a story to justify what has been done? Surely I can simply speak the truth."

"What is this truth you speak of?" asked Cogo Yelu. "Actions may be interpreted multiple ways, and it is how they're seen that matters, not what was intended."

"And can you truly say that you have never thought of being King of Géfica yourself?" asked Luan Zya. "You have never been tempted, even once?"

Kuni thought back to his actions in the palace and sighed.

"Luan Zya is right," Kuni said. "I have no choice. I'll go humbly and apologize to Mata Zyndu, and let's pray for the best."

To show that he was seriously contrite and posed no threat whatsoever to Mata, Kuni took only Luan Zya and Mün Çakri with him.

"You picked the brains and the brawn," Mün said, laughing. "You don't need anyone else."

Kuni left Cogo Yelu in charge of the camp by Lake Tututika with instructions to take all his followers and head for Zudi if Kuni didn't return by that evening.

Mata's camp was right outside Pan, on a hill by the stream that fed into the city. The great fire in Pan continued to billow smoke over the camp, which dampened the celebratory mood.

Soldiers in brand-new uniforms lined the entrance of the camp, their bright spears and rigid new bows fresh from the captured Imperial Armory. They stared at Kuni and his two followers with contempt. Kuni felt the hairs on the back of his neck stand up, and his instinct was to run back to Lake Tututika and tell everyone to get on their horses and take off immediately.

But Luan Zya put a hand on his shoulder. Kuni took a deep breath and continued the long walk into the camp of Mata Zyndu.

The largest tent in camp had been transformed into a banquet hall. Low tables were placed in rows, with seats for all the nobles and commanders of the Six States. At one end of the tent, on a raised dais, was the special table for Marshal Zyndu and his most honored guests. King Thufi had sent an ambassador to attend the banquet on his behalf, but this ambassador was pointedly not seated at the table on the dais.

Kuni saw that he and Luan had been assigned seats near the entrance to the tent, as far away from the honored guests as possible. Mün, on the other hand, didn't even get a seat. He was supposed to sit outside, with bodyguards and other low-ranking followers of the various nobles and officers.

"Mata Zyndu doesn't speak subtly, does he?" Luan observed.

Kuni gave a helpless smile and sat down on the ground in *thakrido*. He was worried, but he was not a man who ever let anxiety get in the way of enjoying good food and wine. Soon, he was toasting the other nobles and enjoying the juicy meats, just as he would have at a party hosted by himself in Zudi.

"Most Honored Lords of Dara." Mata raised a goblet for the first toast. "For a year and a half we've lived in our saddles and slept under the stars. But we have brought down the evil that was the Xana Empire, a task once deemed impossible!"

"Hear! Hear!"

Mata drained his goblet in one gulp and threw it to the ground. "Yet not all of us fought with one heart. While my brothers and I bore the brunt of the empire's most mighty strike, others among us behaved as mice who steal from the banquet while guests are engaged in conversation. What shall we do with men such as these?"

The assembled lords fell silent. No one dared to look at Kuni Garu.

Kuni stood up. "Brother, let me congratulate you on your great victory. Wolf's Paw will live on in men's memories as a byword for valor, a day when a god walked the earth. Your glory will never be matched. My heart overflows with joy to remember that once you and I stood on the walls of Zudi together."

A servant brought a new goblet of wine to Mata, but Mata did not take it. A few of the guests had begun to raise their goblets at Kuni's words, but put them down when they saw which way the wind was blowing. Kuni stood and waited awkwardly, and then he drank by himself.

"Kuni Garu," Mata Zyndu said. "Do you understand your error?"

"If I have given offense, brother, let me humbly apologize to you before all the assembled lords. Your strength at Wolf's Paw gave me an opportunity to stab the heart of the empire in a surprise strike, and I did what I did in aid of the rebellion, of you."

"Do not call me 'brother'! Tempted by fame and treasure, you took advantage of the empire's preoccupation with my army and stole into Pan by a dirty trick. You claimed the riches of the palace as your own and manipulated the hearts of the people of Pan and Géfica to support your dream of ascending to the throne. You wished to keep the fruits of the rebellion for yourself, depriving others, far braver and worthier men, of their just deserts. And then you had the temerity to station troops in Thoco Pass to keep out the forces of other rebel leaders, as though you were first among equals of the lords of our rebellion. Do you deny any of these charges?"

Torulu Pering had made this list. Mata's original plan was to arrest Kuni as soon as he arrived and to ask him in a one-on-one conversation for the cause of his betrayal. But Pering explained that it was best to make the case against Kuni Garu in front of the assembled leaders of the rebellion and persuade the world of Marshal Zyndu's righteousness and Kuni Garu's guilt. After all, he did capture Emperor Erishi, and everyone still remembered King Thufi's promise. Kuni's claim had to be made to appear illegitimate.

Kuni looked over at Luan Zya, who pointed to his eyes. *It is how actions are seen that matters, not what was intended.*

Kuni understood then that he had no choice but to perform, though the performance might cost his friendship with Mata forever. He wouldn't exactly lie, but the dream of sharing Mata's glory was dead. His heart ached as though a knife twisted in it.

"Marshal Zyndu, I'm afraid that you have been ill-counseled." Kuni's voice was calm and his demeanor remained humble and sorrowful.

Torulu Pering had told Mata to not bother listening to anything Kuni had to say, but Mata couldn't help but be curious. "How so?"

"To punish me for what I did would chill the hearts of all men of daring. The truth is that I knew what was in your heart, and I listened to your dreams. My actions were aimed at procuring the greatest glory for you. I am but a dandelion, softening the hard and bare soil in preparation for the dream of the chrysanthemum."

Mata's heart softened at this. "Explain yourself."

"I came into Pan with five hundred men not to take advantage of your sacrifice at Wolf's Paw, but to give it greatest effect.

"Consider, Pan and Géfica were garrisoned with the cream of the Imperial army, the best of the best. Valiant as you are, Marshal Zyndu, do you not think it would have taken you much time and cost the lives of many of your men to pacify the region?"

Mata thought about this and nodded almost imperceptibly.

"My gambit was designed to cut off the empire's head in one swift stroke and lessen the number of good men who might have to die.

Though I knew well that you could have vanquished the Imperial army on your own, yet was it not a good thing to try to preserve the lives of your loyal followers from Tunoa? If I could, by my actions, prevent one mother from losing a son, one wife from losing a husband, one sister from losing a brother, would it not have been my duty to act?"

Mata remembered the mourning song from Mira, and anger drained out of his face.

"Once we were in Pan, we guarded the treasures of the palace—after some inevitable small-scale looting that could not be denied to men in the throes of victory—as temporary custodians anticipating your arrival.

"My retainer, Cogo Yelu, took care to protect the Imperial Archives so that when you came to Pan, you'd be able to administer effectively. We took nothing from the Imperial Treasury, nothing from the Imperial Armory, nothing at all from the people of Pan, in order to prepare the place to welcome you in a proper triumph. We pulled out of Pan as soon as we heard that you were coming.

"We did everything in your name and paved the path for your glory. If you think I am ambitious, then you have sorely misunderstood me."

Kuni Garu's voice cracked, and he made an effort to swallow and to wipe his eyes discreetly.

Torulu Pering rolled his eyes. This Kuni Garu was a consummate actor and liar. To claim that he did what he did in Pan for the benefit of Mata Zyndu was preposterous. Kuni was buying up the hearts of the people, laying the groundwork for comparison with Mata Zyndu's high-handed and brutal occupation later. Garu was banking on the fact that Zyndu wasn't as good as he at these political games.

Pering knew that Kuni Garu had a reputation as a talker. He was almost like a paid litigator in his ability to turn black to white, to make specious arguments about wrong and right. Mata Zyndu would be no match for Kuni Garu's verbal tricks. Pering berated himself for not foreseeing how this public spectacle could be turned to Kuni's advantage.

Kuni continued. "The troops stationed at Goa in Thoco Pass had orders to prevent scattered Imperial detachments from coming back to Pan. In their zeal to defend the fruits of the rebellion—fruits that we all know you deserve more than anyone else—they misunderstood and failed to welcome you properly. For this error I have already punished those responsible."

Marshal Zyndu was unconvinced. "But your man, Ro Minosé, came to me and said that you were preparing to declare yourself king, perhaps even emperor. Your men were spreading malicious rumors, poisoning the hearts of the people against me."

Torulu Pering wished he had some way of telling Mata Zyndu to be quiet. To bring up the name of Ro Minosé was like painting a target on Ro's back, inviting retaliation from those loyal to Kuni. And after that, who in the future would want to defect from Kuni's camp and join Mata, knowing that Mata didn't even care enough about them to protect their names?

"If Ro Minosé would betray me, why would he not betray you?" Kuni spread his hands and pleaded. "One should never give heed to the words of traitors, for they would lie to gain themselves any advantage."

Torulu scoffed at this, but Mata Zyndu seemed to reconsider.

"You swear all that you've said is true?"

"I swear it on all the books of Kon Fiji."

"Then I apologize, Lord Garu, for doubting your heart. Now will you drink with me?"

A servant handed a goblet filled to the brim to Mata, and Mata lifted it in Kuni's direction.

Kuni gulped the drink down. *He still won't call me brother*. Though the wine was of the highest quality, he felt his throat burn as he swallowed. He understood that he would never again be able to truly bare his heart to Mata. *It is how actions are seen that matters, not what was intended.*

The other guests were relieved that tension seemed to be dissipating and eagerly joined in. Soon wine flowed freely, and merriment again filled the tent.

Kuni sat down and wiped his brow. "That was close," he said to Luan Zya.

Luan nodded. He wasn't sure that the danger was past yet. He kept his eye on Torulu Pering. Among Mata Zyndu's retinue, Pering seemed the only one who had his eyes on the bigger picture.

Pering kept on trying to catch Mata Zyndu's eye. When Mata finally looked at him, Pering grabbed the centerpiece from his table, a great three-legged jade ritual vessel called a *kunikin* in Classical Ano, and made as if to smash the vessel against the ground.

Mata shook his head and looked away. Pering waited until Mata was looking his way again, and again raised the *kunikin* over his head and pretended to smash it. Mata again looked away. This went on a few more times, and Mata Zyndu always shook his head.

Pering sighed. He could not make himself any clearer. Having seen the man in action, he could tell that Kuni Garu was the most dangerous challenger to Mata's authority. He had to be killed right now, or else he would become an unmanageable threat. Pering would have preferred it if Zyndu could make Garu appear to be a traitor before the eyes of the others, but since Garu's slippery tongue had saved him from that fate, Pering was willing for Zyndu to resort to outright murder.

Pering had examined carefully the tactics that Kuni Garu employed in Pan, and there was no question that the man was ambitious and would not be satisfied until Mata Zyndu was ruined. But since Mata was unable to put aside his compassion, Pering had to make the hard decision for him.

Pering got up and made his way gradually to Ro Minosé, toasting the other guests along the way. He pulled Ro aside and whispered to him, "Marshal Zyndu has a special mission for you. Because you betrayed him, Kuni Garu now hates you more than any man alive.

Marshal Zyndu desires you to prove the truth of your accusations with a demonstration of loyalty."

Ro, who had been pondering his fate morosely, shuddered at this. "Marshal Zyndu wants Kuni Garu to die?"

Pering nodded. "Kuni Garu has deceived the guests here with his clever words, so openly killing him is not an option. Can you make it look like an accident?"

Ro hesitated. He did not like the position he was in. Marshal Zyndu had exposed him to reprisal from Kuni Garu's men. But Kuni's words seemed to make the marshal distrust Ro as well. He was caught between two sides and had to do something to secure his own future.

"If I do this, won't the marshal preserve his own honor by leaving me to shoulder all the blame? I need some reassurance."

"Don't you dare to bargain!" Pering whispered harshly. "A servant cannot have two masters. You must make a choice and stick to it. You have to trust the marshal to take care of you, or you'll be on your own to face Garu's wrath."

Ro gritted his teeth and nodded glumly.

As Pering made his way back to his seat, Ro got up and pretended to stumble. "Honored Lords, it's boring to eat and drink without something more to delight us. The men of Cocru have often enjoyed the art of sword dancing at a banquet. If you would excuse my lack of refinement, I'd like to entertain all of you with a sword dance today."

The assembled guests clapped and whistled, and Pering called for music. As the coconut lute and whale-skin drums created a syncopated and rousing beat, Ro unsheathed his sword and began to dance. He leapt, parried, swung his blade overhead in bright circles of flashing light like blossoming chrysanthemums, and slowly made his way toward Kuni Garu's table.

The guests cheered while Pering whispered in Mata Zyndu's ear. Mata's face was filled with uncertainty, but he said nothing as the chill wind from Ro's sword moved closer and closer to Kuni.

~ ~ ~ ~

Ratho watched Ro's dance and furrowed his brows.

He was familiar with sword dancing, but Ro was dancing so close to Lord Garu that the blade of the sword often passed within inches of the man. Lord Garu's smile was forced, and he was already up, out of his seat, dodging left and right and awkwardly jumping out of the way of Ro's swings.

Something was not right about this. Ratho had served under Lord Garu at Zudi and liked the man. Daf and he often spoke about how Lord Garu seemed someone who genuinely understood what the common soldier wanted, and he was glad that Lord Garu's speech had convinced Marshal Zyndu. He never believed that Lord Garu would betray the marshal.

But now Ro Minosé, a known traitor, seemed to be trying to kill Lord Garu. If he succeeded, some foolish people might even whisper that Marshal Zyndu authorized it out of petty jealousy for his good friend's bravery—imagine, capturing Pan with only five hundred men!

Ratho had to protect Mata Zyndu's reputation.

He got up and unsheathed his own sword. "I'm also from Cocru," he said. "One man dancing is not fun at all. Why don't I help by joining in?"

He swung and twirled his blade to the music, and within seconds he moved next to Ro. Their swords clashed, swung apart, and clashed again, and Ratho did his best to keep Ro's sword from coming near Lord Garu.

But Ratho was only a common soldier, and Ro was a far better swordsman.

Luan Zya got up and excused himself. He quickly left the big tent and found Mün Çakri outside.

"You've got to do something. Lord Garu is going to die in an 'accident' unless we intervene."

Mün nodded, wiped the grease from his mouth with his sleeve, and picked up his shield with one hand and his short sword with the other. Mün's shield was unique, designed by himself. The outside of the shield was studded with a set of butcher's meat hooks, the better to catch his opponents' swords and twist them out of their hands.

With Luan Zya running behind to catch up, Mün rushed to the great tent. The guards at the door tried to stop him, but Mün stared at them, his eyes full of fury. The guards hesitated for a moment, and Mün was past them.

Mün entered the tent and stood right next to Kuni Garu's table. Planting his feet in a wide-open stance, he roared at the top of his lungs—the way he used to make himself heard above the squealing of pigs—"Stop!"

The assembled guests thought they had gone deaf temporarily. Both Ro and Ratho stumbled and leapt away from each other. The music stopped. The tent was completely silent.

"Who goes there?" Mata Zyndu, the first to recover, asked.

"Mün Çakri, a lowly follower of Lord Garu."

Mata recalled their days at Zudi. "I remember you. You're a brave man and a good fighter." He turned to an attendant. "Come, bring this man some meat and drink."

Mün did not sit but took the platter of food from the servant and stood where he was. He grabbed the steak from the plate and hooked it onto the outside of his shield, and began to carve pieces from it with his sword. He ate heartily and washed it down with gulps of wine from another guest's goblet. The assembled guests were amazed by the vitality of the man. He was like a barbarian from another age, and he made all of them feel effete, weak, and small.

"Marshal Zyndu, I'm surprised that you still remember me. I thought you forgot all about your friends from Zudi."

Mata Zyndu flushed and said nothing.

"Lord Garu may have come into Pan before you, but we were all on the same side, fighting against the empire. He's done everything he can to honor you and to explain his actions, and yet you keep on pressing him, even permitting others to do him harm. If I didn't know better, I might have thought you were jealous of Lord Garu's favor among the people."

Mata Zyndu forced himself to laugh. "You are a good man, and I always appreciate a loyal retainer who speaks from the heart in defense of his lord. Lord Garu and I have come to an understanding, and you need not be concerned."

He gestured for both Ro and Ratho to sit, and the banquet resumed. The air of merriment felt very forced, however.

Luan Zya whispered to Kuni, and Kuni nodded.

After a few minutes, Kuni got up, held his stomach, and asked an attendant for directions to the toilet. Mün Çakri followed him out.

"Lord Garu feels unsafe even going to the toilet alone?" Pering sneered, and those sitting near him tittered.

"Lord Garu ate and drank too quickly," Luan Zya said evenly. "Mün just finds it hard to sit in a tent. He prefers to be outside with other fighting men."

Pering whispered directions to Ro and a few other guards. They left to make preparations.

Mata Zyndu was too softhearted to believe that his old friend posed a danger, but Pering wasn't going to let Kuni Garu slip away. This was the best chance to get rid of him, away from his loyal followers and soldiers. Once Kuni Garu's head was on a stake, his men would have no choice but to surrender.

Half an hour later, Pering became agitated. Kuni Garu and Mün Çakri had not come back. And Ro, who had left to check up on the two, was also nowhere to be seen.

"Luan Zya, where is Lord Garu?" Mata Zyndu asked.

Luan stood up and bowed deeply. "I must apologize for Lord Garu's rude departure. But he's feeling unwell and has already returned to his camp. He left gifts for Marshal Zyndu, and I will present them now."

Luan Zya brought up trays of jewels and antiques, and Mata

smiled and thanked Luan Zya. Inwardly, he was quite annoyed. Kuni's departure smacked of fear, as though he didn't trust Mata to not harm him. After Mün's speech, Mata was afraid that others might really think he was jealous of Kuni.

Torulu Pering could no longer contain his frustration. He jumped up and grabbed the *kunikin* in front of him and smashed it into pieces at his feet. "It's too late!" he said, to no one in particular. "This is a mistake that will haunt us all."

Luan Zya bid the assembled lords farewell and left.

Two days later, soldiers clearing the latrines found the body of Ro Minosé. He had evidently been too drunk when he went to the toilet and fell into the dirty water and drowned himself.

As soon as Kuni Garu and Mün Çakri returned, Kuni's men moved their camp along the shoreline of Lake Tututika until they were on a hill so that they could see the approach of any pursuit from far away. The horses were readied, and everyone prepared to evacuate at the first clear sign that Mata Zyndu would attack.

But the attack never came. Marshal Zyndu was apparently satisfied with Kuni's apology, and Torulu Pering's outburst was treated as merely an embarrassing lapse in decorum from an old, drunk man.

CHAPTER THIRTY-FIVE

# A NEW WORLD

PAN: THE FIFTH MONTH IN THE FIRST YEAR OF THE PRINCIPATE.

Mata Zyndu sat in his tent, contemplating the new seals that he was supposed to hand out.

He picked one up and caressed it, running his fingers over the cool jade surfaces and the intricate patterns that could be pressed into wax to make the logogram of power, the symbol of a new Tiro state's authority. He held on to it as though it were a part of himself.

He sighed and put it down, and picked up another seal.

King Thufi gave his view of the matter in a letter to the marshal: In spite of the relatively puny contributions made by Kuni Garu to the success of the rebellion, given that he *did* fulfill the terms of King Thufi's promise, the king hoped that Marshal Zyndu would honor the original promise and create a new Tiro state in Géfica to be awarded to Kuni.

Mata threw Thufi's scroll onto the ground in disgust and ground his foot against it until all the wax logograms had fallen off and were illegibly mixed into the mud. He was finished with listening to that shepherd boy. Henceforth he was done with the old title of Marshal of Cocru. He had defeated the empire, and that made him the hegemon. So he would reward people as he saw fit.

Indeed, if one new Tiro state was going to be created, why not two? Why not ten or twenty?

On Wolf's Paw, the kings of the Six States had shown themselves to be unworthy of the respect accorded them, so why should they benefit from what Mata Zyndu had achieved? The ranks of nobility had become polluted over the years, Mata realized, and that was why so many men and women of noble birth had behaved so ignominiously.

He was in charge of the fate of Dara now, and he would cleanse their ranks and restore honor to the old titles. He would remake the world to be more perfect. As for justification? Wasn't it enough that he had the largest army? If anyone was unhappy, let them speak to him on the battlefield.

The heads of the Six States had sat around in endless debates while their countries burned and their people died. He would not make that mistake. He would not hesitate to act.

To begin with, he would divide the world into new pieces and hand them out to people he thought more deserving. Mapidéré's error had been to trust people who lacked the necessary qualities. In contrast, he would hearken back to ancient times, when the foundations of the world were laid. Like the great Ano lawgiver Aruano, he would also create a new world order that would last millennia. He would measure the world against the rigid grid of his heart and put each man in charge of a domain no more and no less than his just deserts.

"You should hold on to Géfica," Torulu Pering said. "It has the richest farms in all of Dara, and Lake Tututika gives plenty of fresh water for irrigation. It's easy to defend, given Thoco Pass and the Miru and Liru Rivers, and yet easy to attack from if you can dominate the sea. Whoever controls Géfica would be able to feed a larger army, and by that means gain an upper hand over the other Tiro states."

But Mata felt that might lower his esteem among the others. He didn't want Kuni to have Géfica, so taking it for himself might appear too greedy. He wanted the power to draw lines on a map, but he also wanted to be seen as a wise and generous lord.

"I'm from Cocru," he said to Pering. "The whole point of leaving home to accomplish great deeds is so that one day I could *return* home to receive the adulation of my homeland. Géfica is too far from Tunoa."

Pering sighed. Advising Zyndu was often frustrating. He cared so much about honor and display and so little about the real foundation of power.

Mata decided that instead of keeping Géfica, he would divide it into three pieces—North, Central, and South Géfica—and hand them out to Théca Kimo, who was also from Tunoa and fought well at Wolf's Paw, Noda Mi, who was in charge of provisions for the army and had always done a good job, and Doru Solofi, who had led the scouting party that first discovered Kuni Garu's treachery at Goa.

"That makes no sense, Lord Zyndu," Pering objected. "None of these men have much experience with governing, and it seems that you are rewarding them for their personal loyalty to you, rather than weighing the contributions of the commanders from all the Tiro states fairly. Rebel leaders of the other Tiro states will not like this."

Mata Zyndu ignored Pering. If they didn't like it, too bad. The people who meant the most to the rebellion were the people who helped him, and that was that.

On the other hand, the Xana home island of Rui was also made into a new Tiro state, and as its king, Mata Zyndu settled on Kindo Marana. Granting the empire's greatest commander and the man Kikomi loved such a boon would be seen as a grand gesture and cement his own reputation for compassion and forgiveness. He felt this was right and just—Torulu Pering was always telling him how Kuni was trying to win the hearts of the people; this would show the people just who was the more honorable lord.

"That cannot be," Pering said. "Marana is associated with the hated empire, and he would be despised by the people of Rui for losing the war, especially since so many of the young men who heeded his call are now at the bottom of the sea feeding Tazu's sharks."

"That's his problem, not mine."

As for the kings of the Six States, Mata Zyndu decided to shrink their territories and reduce their power. He still seethed at the treachery of Princess Kikomi, but he also felt some measure of sentiment for her, and after all, it seemed wrong to punish Amu for what she had done out of her own misguided, foolish feminine love. He compromised by restoring King Ponadomu to the throne in Müning, except that Amu would be deprived of all her territories on the Big Island and be confined to Arulugi.

Likewise, King Dalo of Gan was a coward, and his kingdom would be reduced to just Wolf's Paw. And to add insult to injury, the isles of Ogé would be taken away from Gan to be made into a new Tiro state, to be administered by . . . ah, Huye Nocano, the Gan commander who finally decided to join the Battle of Wolf's Paw only after it was clear Mata had won. He made a small contribution, so he would get a small domain. That was fair. And the assignment would annoy Gan to no end, which would be delicious.

Mata laughed at his own joke.

Torulu Pering shook his head but held his tongue.

On and on Zyndu went, redrawing old borders and rewarding whoever he pleased.

When the results were revealed, many whispered that his decisions seemed odd, whimsical, nonsensical.

But Mata saw a deeper order, an order that others simply did not appreciate.

For example, some scholars shook their heads as they saw that although the rebellion had only begun because of the courage of Huno Krima and Zopa Shigin, the hegemon refused to grant their families or their followers any title or fief.

But Mata understood that to do so would be to encourage further rebellions against the established order. Sometimes those who lit the spark that began a conflagration must be consumed by it lest the fire burn on indefinitely.

Others complained that despite the bravery of King Jizu of Rima, the hegemon carved Rima into six tiny new Tiro states all clustered around Na Thion like pigs feeding at a trough.

But Mata understood that Jizu had been made into something like a saint, a symbol around which people could rally. Such symbols were the most dangerous because they could be made to say whatever those who held the symbol wished. He had to prevent the cult of Jizu from getting out of hand and maintain order.

And as far as Mata was concerned, Haan had done nothing during the rebellion. Indeed, worse than nothing—Luan Zya had been instrumental in the thievery of Pan. So he decided to install King Cosugi in a new Haan composed of only Ginpen and a crescent-shaped slice of land fifty miles around it. Even parts of Lutho Beach were now no longer encompassed in this tiny Tiro state, but incorporated into one of the three new Tiro states he made out of Géfica.

*This is madness,* Pering thought. *These fanciful borders will cause endless trouble.*

As for Faça, King Shilué, ambitious yet cowardly, greedy yet indecisive, had long recognized that Mata Zyndu was a man of hot passions and quick impulses. Flattering him could guarantee no favor. The best strategy, Shilué had decided, was to stay out of his way and out of his sight.

Therefore, ever since the Battle of Wolf's Paw, King Shilué had kept a low profile, though he gave Mata Zyndu whatever he wanted when Zyndu's emissaries came to demand more aid—troops, money, food—in the war against the empire. This strategy now paid off, as nothing the man had done stuck out in Mata's mind as either particularly good or bad. He decided to leave Shilué in charge of Faça as it was.

But many knew of Shilué's numerous plots and betrayals against his nominal allies. He had orchestrated the politics of Jizu's Rima from Boama, his fair, foggy capital. He had sought to snatch Ogé from Gan when the very survival of the Six States was uncertain. To these observers, it now seemed as if Shilué was being rewarded for his crafty ways. Pering explained that not punishing Shilué would chill the hearts of friends and breed further discontent among the allies.

But Mata was in no mood for counsel. He saw men like Shilué as undistinguished and therefore harmless.

Mata Zyndu reserved most of Cocru for himself as the new King of Cocru and Hegemon of All Tiro States. To compensate Thufi, he decided to install the man as the king of the remote and barely populated Écofi Island. Since King Thufi began as a shepherd, why not send him somewhere where he had plenty of land to open up new ranches? He laughed at his own wit.

Of course it was a bit awkward for the former Marshal of Cocru to now dictate terms to his old king and lord, but Hegemon Zyndu decided that once King Thufi moved out of Cocru, no one would remember who he was.

That still left the problem of Kuni Garu, however. The man who had actually entered Pan and captured Emperor Erishi. Mata had to give him something more than Zudi, but what?

Mata Zyndu's eyes roamed over the map until he saw the island farthest from the Big Island.

Tiny Dasu had nothing to offer but spicy foods and unsophisticated fishermen and peasants, barely better than savages. Not only was it far away, it was also blocked on the way to the Big Island by Rui, where Kindo Marana would be king and could keep an eye on Kuni Garu's every move like a watchdog. It was perfect. Dasu would be the jail for the former jailer, and Kuni Garu would stay on his minuscule island prison until the day he died.

And Mata would keep Jia and Kuni's children near Çaruza. Oh, Mata Zyndu wouldn't mistreat them, but they would act as excellent hostages to guarantee Kuni's good behavior. There would be no more tricks out of Kuni, no more surprise attacks.

Torulu Pering had gone on and on about the threat posed by the ambition of Kuni Garu. Well, with this bit of "reward," Kuni Garu's ambition would no longer pose a problem.

Pering had to agree that at least on this point, the hegemon was indeed very clever.

Though Mata had told her that she needn't feel obliged to do anything, Mira couldn't just be idle.

She felt awkward sitting all day in the small tent that Mata had installed her in, next to his own. On the day he had brought her back, he had sent her a box filled with gold and silver and jewels, more wealth than she had ever seen, but he had then left her alone, busy with his own affairs.

The servants and maids all treated her as though she were already Mata's woman, speaking to her with exaggerated courtesy and serving her elaborate meals. When she asked to help around the camp, the servants responded by kneeling and asking her in terrified voices whether their service had been unsatisfactory in some manner. It was suffocating.

So she simply decided to start doing things around the camp. She didn't know what Mata's intentions were, but she wasn't going to be a kept woman. She would make herself useful.

"Let me help out in here, at least," she pleaded with Mata's personal cook in the kitchen.

The cook bowed deeply and backed away from the stove, gesturing that he was at Mira's command.

Though he had once prided himself on being able to appeal to a palate as jaded as Erishi's, the former palace chef found Mata leaving most of his carefully prepared creations untouched. Ever since the time he spent in Zudi by the side of Kuni Garu, Mata had preferred the same rough rations and throat-burning liquor that were the common soldiers' fare. The former palace chef had been worried about his own future, and Mira's offer of taking over cooking for the hegemon pleased him greatly. If the mercurial Mata continued to be displeased with the cooking, he thought, at least now he had someone to share the blame with.

The only dishes Mira knew how to make were from Tunoa: salted fish paste on twice-boiled rice; pickled vegetables wrapped in flatbread made from rough sorghum flour; fresh southern char grilled on planks made from scholar's trees, spiced with nothing but smoke from the wood and sprinkles of seawater—this last really a mix of Haan and Cocru traditions. The former palace chef looked at these homely dishes and wrinkled his nose. Erishi would have gagged on such food, and he could not imagine how a man who was said to be almost a god would deign to eat such peasant fare.

But the servants who served Mata's meals on trembling knees came back, astonished. "The hegemon finished everything. And he asked for the portions to be bigger next time."

This only confirmed the belief held by everyone in camp that Mira knew the secret path to the hegemon's heart. Mata had left all of Erishi's wives and concubines untouched, but asked Mira to live right next to his own tent—though she didn't seem particularly pretty and was not of noble birth, she had somehow gained the favor of the most powerful man in the world. Everyone was envious.

But Mira had simply remembered the momentary look of longing when he had gazed at her on that day when they first met, when he had asked her if she was a woman of Tunoa. She understood that it was not desire for her, but for home.

Mira went out to Kiji Square, bringing with her the food that the former palace chef had prepared as a backup in case her own food found no success with the hegemon. The chef had wanted to throw it all away, but Mira had intervened and asked that the food be distributed to the beggars of Pan. The servants and courtiers scurrying around Mata's camp hurried to obey.

She watched as they ladled out the rich, exotically spiced dishes and filled the bowls of the line of beggars, and she felt a pang of guilt—so little food, so many mouths to feed. Had she not encountered Mata, she would probably be in their ranks by now.

A beggar in a strangely clean white cape—he probably hadn't been on the streets for long—approached her.

"Thank you for the food, miss. It's very kind of you."

The accent indicated that the man was from Xana. Mira nodded at him coldly. She understood that most of the Xana soldiers were also poor and had suffered much, just like her and her brother, but years' worth of animosity was hard to push aside.

"You're close to the hegemon," the beggar said. It wasn't a question.

Mira's face felt hot. "I am simply a woman he pitied." *Does everyone in Pan already know of my awkward position?* "Do not believe the gossips."

"I know nothing of gossip," the beggar said.

Mira found the beggar odd. He was surprisingly bold, as if he fancied himself a lord, her superior. And there was something about his air that compelled her attention.

"But perhaps I misspoke. I should have said that you *will* be close to him."

"Is that a prediction or a command?" Mira asked. The beggar's impudence was making her angry. She considered calling for some of the courtiers—they were always so eager for her to tell them something to do.

"Neither. Prophecies are funny things—they don't tend to come out the way I want. And so I will stick to history instead: Mata Zyndu is responsible for your brother's death."

Mira blanched. "Who *are* you? I have borne more than enough of your insults!"

"Listen to your heart. You know my charge is true. Your brother would still be alive now, strong and brave, had he not been seduced by Mata Zyndu's promise. And what has he gained after marching a thousand miles and living on the edge of a sword to build up Mata's reputation? The hegemon does not even remember his name!"

Mira turned her face away.

"Men like your brother brought the empire down and secured the victory to which Mata lays claim. He is no better than that Kuni Garu, whom he despises."

"That's enough," said Mira. "I . . . don't want to speak with you anymore." She turned and fled from the square.

"I just want you to remember your brother," called out the beggar. "Just remember him when you are with the hegemon."

The next day, Mira decided to tidy up Mata's tent.

The legends surrounding Mata had grown to the point where the maids whispered to one another that he was so temperamental that a single misplaced pillow could cost the one responsible her head, and none dared to take up the duty, though being so close to a powerful man seemed a good way to curry favors. But Mira was unafraid: Her brother had left home to follow this man, believing that he would make the world right again, freeing it from injustice. She would not dishonor Mado's memory by being frightened of Mata.

The tent was a mess, she saw. Papers were piled on multiple desks haphazardly arranged around the tent, as though new ones were brought in as soon as old ones had been filled; pillows and cushions for sitting were scattered around, the detritus of ad-hoc meetings with his advisers; the bed where he slept looked like it hadn't had its sheets changed in weeks.

Mata was sitting at one of the desks, his back to her, his legs folded under him in *géüpa*. He did not turn as she entered, perhaps thinking that she was one of his personal guards who had come in to help him get ready for bed, as none of the maids dared to come in.

Quietly, she went about her business: collecting the pillows and cushions into one corner of the tent; rearranging the desks into rows so that their papers could all be accessed; stripping off the sheets and putting on new ones; sweeping up the accumulated trash on the floor.

*In his presence, fear and cowardice disappear like darkness before light*, Mado had written to her after the Battle of Wolf's Paw. *He will sort this upside-down world out and put everything in its rightful place.*

*Mado died because he believed*, thought Mira. *He had no regrets as he laid down his life. I cannot tarnish his memory with doubt.*

But the hegemon evidently had difficulty putting everyday objects in their rightful places. And Mata's personal guards, it seemed, were ignorant of the basics of housekeeping. A small smile appeared on Mira's face.

She looked up from her tasks from time to time, and saw that Mata had not moved. Even in repose, his presence was powerful, otherworldly. Mira could see why he had exerted such a pull on her brother—she could feel the pull herself.

Mata continued to admire something in his hand, rubbing, caressing it obsessively.

She couldn't help but speak up. "If you keep on rubbing that thing, you'll make all the corners on it rounded and smooth."

Mata turned around and paused. He had not been expecting her.

He put the seal he was admiring down. The remark, if it had come from one of his advisers, especially that doddering Pering who seemed to disapprove of everything he did, would have enraged him. But he wasn't going to get angry at Mira. What did she know of the affairs of the world?

"I'm observing the reward I'm about to bestow upon those who do not really deserve it. There are so few worthy of being called noble."

Nobility had been important to Mado, Mira remembered. He had written to her of Mata Zyndu's peerless nobility, a quality that overflowed and inspired those around him. *I cannot describe to you how it felt,* Mado had written. *But for a moment I was touched by the gods, transported into a higher realm of existence as we charged behind him. He is the ocean that lifts up all of us.*

The beggar's words seemed to do battle with Mado's in her head. She bit her bottom lip and shook her head. *Mado was not stupid. He saw the good in this man, and so will I.*

Mira continued to sweep the floors. When she was done, she left with the sweepings and a tray of empty dishes and bowls that had held Mata's dinner. Then she came back with a pitcher of water that she sprinkled on the uncovered part of the tent floor to keep the dust down, humming an old Tunoa folk song.

*Come for me, my darling, come for me in your fishing boat;*
*Come before dawn, for I don't wish to marry the duke's son.*
*I'll come for you, my sea rose, 'fore the rise of the sun;*
*We'll never be apart, so long as ships remain afloat.*

She looked up and saw that Mata had been staring at her. She blushed. Trying to find something to say, she saw that the thing Mata held in his hand glowed with the soft light of precious green jade.

"It's hard to give up a treasure, isn't it?" she blurted out. Then she silently cursed herself for saying something so foolish, and she went back to her work with redoubled effort.

Mata frowned. Suddenly it seemed very important to him to make this woman admire him. Her implied accusation made him ashamed, as though he himself was not worthy either.

"I kept very little of the treasure taken from the emperor's palace," he said stiffly. "Much of it I gave away to the families of soldiers who died fighting for me." He did not add that he had done this after meeting her, after realizing how little he had done for his men.

Mira paused. "You're a generous lord." The silence grew awkward again, and she tried to cover it up by more humming and quicker work.

"Would you like to touch it?" Mata Zyndu held up one of the seals.

Mira knew that this was a symbol of kingship, whose impression on wax could launch a hundred ships, ten thousand men, a hundred thousand arrows, and endless slaughter.

The beggar's words came to her again. *The hegemon does not even remember his name.*

She saw Mado's body again, wrapped in a shroud like thousands of others, at the bottom of the pit that was to be their final resting place. *Is this what you called nobility? Is this what you died for?*

Mira shook her head and backed away from the seal, as though it were a hot lump of coal. "It's beautiful," she said. "But I do not think it as beautiful or worthy as my brother's life."

She finished her work, bowed, and left the tent.

Mata Zyndu stared at her departing figure in silence. Then he put the seal down, gently.

"Are you sure you don't want to come with me?" Kuni asked.

"Your Majesty," Luan Zya said, "I'm a man of Haan, and now that the hegemon has made it even smaller and weaker, King Cosugi will need all the help I can give him."

They drank their parting cups of arrack and smiled at the memory of Tan Adü.

"Mata Zyndu has made Dasu my prison," Kuni said wistfully. "Come and visit me from time to time."

"You will not disappoint Chief Kyzen, King Kuni. I'm certain of it. A caged wolf is a dangerous creature. Dasu won't hold you for long."

Kuni wasn't sure he shared Luan Zya's optimism. The chips were stacked against him. One, Dasu was tiny and poor. Two, Jia and the children, as well as his father and brother, were still back in Cocru, and Mata made it clear that he intended to keep them there as hostages to ensure Kuni's loyalty. Three, Mata was going to send ten thousand troops under the command of Kindo Marana to "escort" Kuni and his entourage to Dasu and to guard them from Rui. It would take a miracle for Kuni to escape from his predicament.

"I have one last bit of advice to you, King Kuni. Burn all your ships after your arrival in Dasu."

"But then I'll have no way of ever leaving it."

"Your priority is to clear the hegemon of suspicions about your ambition. Burning the ships will let him know that you are no threat. Focus on the administration of Dasu and being a good king for now, and let time take care of other matters."

Ratho and Dafiro finally got a chance to meet for the first time since they parted ways in Çaruza. Kuni's men had been confined to his camp, and Mata's soldiers had certainly not been allowed to visit.

But this was King Kuni's last day in Pan, and his soldiers were finally allowed to roam the streets freely for one day. Although both brothers worked hard to not shed any tears, they had wet eyes and noses that suddenly became stuffed up.

"I heard about you on Wolf's Paw. Could have gotten yourself killed!"

"You're one to talk. You held the reins of a cruben!"

"I'm the older brother. I'm allowed to do foolish things."

Daf showed Biter to Rat, who admired it and swung it through the air a few times.

"You will not leave Lord Garu?" Rat asked.

Daf shook his head. "Even if I leave, I know you won't leave the hegemon. I might as well make the best of my career with a lord who appreciates strategic laziness."

"Ah, and here I thought you had finally learned something of honor and would feel bad about desertion."

They embraced and laughed.

"I wish Lord Garu and the hegemon had remained brothers."

They drank until the last light of dusk, and then parted ways.

## CHAPTER THIRTY-SIX

# DASU

DASU: THE SIXTH MONTH IN THE FIRST YEAR OF THE PRINCIPATE.

Marana and his soldiers watched from the sea in surprise as Kuni Garu's men set the transports that had carried them to Dasu on fire. The sight brought to mind Mata's gambit at Wolf's Paw, and Marana frowned.

But Kuni's words dispelled the association. "These large ships will be too expensive to maintain, and I'm going to stay here for a while," Kuni shouted, his hands cupped around his mouth. Smiling ingratiatingly, he waved at Marana's men. "Bring my good wishes to the hegemon, Your Majesty. Don't be a stranger!" He bowed repeatedly to Marana, like a servant trying to curry favor with his master.

Marana looked away contemptuously. Why was the hegemon so worried about this man? He was no better than a common gangster, a petty criminal more than satisfied with a tiny island and some hovels. Marana decided that Kuni's one "victory" must have been the result of plain good luck.

He had faced far worthier adversaries. Princess Kikomi, for

example. A complex set of feelings fought in Marana's heart whenever he thought of her. Though he was a masterful schemer, he had met his match in her. Kikomi had, in the end, stayed one step ahead of him and thwarted his plot. Just as she had *almost* succeeded in ensnaring him with a vision of rebellion, he had *almost* succeeded in seducing her with promises of eternal glory. The princess was willing to live in abiding infamy in the pages of history to save her people—Marana had to admire such grandness of spirit. He also wondered if, in a way, his own current position could be attributed to Mata's own surely complicated feelings about Kikomi. Fortune was indeed a strange thing.

He gave the order to set sail for the northern coast of Rui, where Tanno Namen had lived. He had a promise to fulfill. "Do we have any lamb's tails?" he asked. Even Namen's dog seemed to have more ambition and honor than the groveling Kuni Garu.

Now that he was settled in Dasu, King Kuni handed out titles to his followers. Cogo Yelu and Rin Coda were made dukes, and Than Carucono and Mün Çakri were made into marquesses. He distributed to his followers the few treasures he had kept from Pan—he had been a robber once, after all—and held a lavish banquet for the three thousand soldiers who had followed him to Dasu.

"Now I'm as poor as every one of you." He lifted his empty purse and let go, and the wind took the silk pouch from him and blew it into the sea. He shook his wide sleeves in the wind to show that they were also empty. The soldiers laughed.

"Since I have so little treasure, I can only hand out lavish titles. Hopefully they'll mean something one day." Then he turned serious, inclining his head in apology. "You've followed me and suffered a great deal of hardship. I'm sorry I can't give you more."

His followers uttered murmurs of consolation, but they felt warm in their hearts.

Kuni and his advisers went to Daye, the largest town on the northern coast of the tiny rocky isle. This would be the capital of Kuni's little kingdom. His "palace" was actually just a two-story wooden house not much bigger than the other houses in town.

"Lord Garu, you look weary," said Cogo.

Now that he wasn't performing in front of a crowd, Kuni allowed his exhaustion and despair to show on his face.

"What am I doing, Cogo? Have I made a mistake from which I cannot recover? What kind of future can I give to my family or the men who have followed me? My domain is about the size of a sheep pen, as far away from the centers of power as possible. Mata will likely never allow me to return home or to bring Jia here unless I give up my territory—am I doomed to die in obscurity, having risked everything with nothing to show for it?"

Cogo had never seen Kuni so morose since he became the Duke of Zudi. "Strength comes from inside the heart, Lord Garu. If your heart has no center, then you will drift without purpose."

Kuni was silent for a while, and then he nodded.

Jia took the letter from the Cocru soldier but kept her face as frosty as a statue of Rapa.

The soldier waited awkwardly for a moment, realized that no "thank you" would be forthcoming, and scrambled away.

Jia closed the door. The address on the envelope was written in Kuni's unmistakable flowing scrawl. The flap of the envelope had been opened, of course.

Ever since Mata had sent the squad of men to camp outside her house, they had insisted on following her around everywhere she went and examining everything that came into and left the house "for her protection."

"I once called Mata Zyndu brother!" Jia had screamed at the Cocru captain. "Tell him to come here in person and explain to me why I have been made into a prisoner in my own home."

The captain had muttered that the hegemon was busy with official business and then ducked out of the way as Jia threw a teapot at his head.

Looking at the letter in hand, she was filled with both joy and rage. The zyndari letters in the script, full of soaring ascenders and wide, expansive loops, threatened to break out of their word-squares and reminded her of Kuni's careless, open smile. But the letter was also a tangible reminder that Kuni wasn't here, with her and their children, but stuck on a distant island where he could play at being a king.

She wished Kuni were in front of her so she could hug him and kiss him and then punch him a few times, really hard.

News of what had happened in Pan had left her bewildered. How could Kuni and Mata, the heart and soul of the rebellion, have come almost to war against each other? And when would he and Jia see each other again?

> *My Beloved Jia,*
>
> *Everything is lovely. Please send my regards to Mata.*
>
> *Your Loving Husband*

The rest of the page was blank.

Jia had to stop herself from ripping the letter into pieces. After all the weeks of worry and lack of reliable news, *this is it?*

Then she saw that Kuni had drawn the picture of a dandelion in the upper left-hand corner of the letter, which was written on thick, rough paper. She pulled the letter closer and inhaled—yes, now that she was looking for it, the trace of dandelion fragrance was faint, but to her trained nose, easily detectable.

*Kuni must have known that his letters would be read,* Jia realized.

She smiled. *He remembered what I told him about the uses of the dandelion.*

Quickly going to her workshop, she took a cup of dried stone's ear mushroom, mixed it with water, ground up the mixture until it was a thin paste, and brushed the paste all over the thick page. Then she waited until the paper had been soaked through before dipping it into a thin dish of water, gently washing away the paste.

Zyndari letters emerged in the blank space on the page, fading into view like ships coming out of the fog. Kuni had written the real letter in dandelion milk, invisible until now.

*I'm coming home, my beloved, center of my heart.*

## CHAPTER THIRTY-SEVEN

# A VISIT HOME

OUTSIDE ÇARUZA: THE SEVENTH MONTH
IN THE FIRST YEAR OF THE PRINCIPATE.

A rumor spread in Daye that King Kuni was sick and bedridden. When Kindo Marana's envoys came to Dasu to inquire after Kuni's health, a harried Cogo Yelu received them.

"Our poor king thinks of the hegemon every day," said Cogo. "He has spoken to me often of how he wishes they had parted on better terms, and he thinks of this illness as an opportunity from the gods for him to reflect on his own circuitous path."

Marana sent his report to Mata Zyndu in Çaruza: "Kuni is in seclusion. No signs of ambition. The lowly weed has decided to settle."

On a cool summer morning, a beggar arrived at the house outside of Çaruza.

He had gray hair, and his face was scarred. Dressed in rags and straw shoes, he walked with a limp. A straw rope was cinched tight around his belly.

Lady Jia had instructed Steward Otho Krin that all beggars who came to the house should leave with full stomachs, and so he brought out a hot bowl of porridge for the man.

"My lady made this porridge from a special recipe," explained Krin. "It's hearty and spiced with potent herbs that will not only fill your belly but fortify your body against diseases. You won't be hungry for the rest of the day."

But instead of thanking him profusely, the beggar only looked at Krin, a twinkle in his eye. "Do you not recognize me?"

Krin stared at the beggar carefully, and then gave a little cry. He looked around to be sure that the hegemon's soldiers down the road were not looking and hurriedly let the beggar into the house. Then he bowed deeply.

"It is good to see you, Lord Garu!"

A warm bath washed off the mud on Kuni's body and the fake scars on his face. His hair had been bleached gray, and it would take time for it to grow out and be restored its natural black color. He was happy to be free of the cinched straw rope that had disguised his beer belly.

He emerged into Jia's bedroom to change. A small vase filled with fresh dandelions stood on the small table by the window. Hanging on a stand nearby were a few new robes she had sewn for him with her own hands, he saw. He buried his nose in them and smelled the fresh herbs that she always used to do their laundry. Tears, unbidden, came into his eyes.

He sat down on their bed and caressed Jia's pillow, thinking of the nights she had spent alone, not knowing what had happened to him. He would have to make it up to her somehow, he vowed.

There were a few strands of hair on the pillow. He picked them up affectionately, and froze.

They were not Jia's red curls, but the straight, black hair of a man.

"I signed on as a seaman on a merchant vessel at Dasu," explained Kuni. "That was the only way to evade Kindo Marana's spies. Once

I got to the Big Island, I had to make my way here slowly, switching disguises every few days."

Toto-*tika* did not recognize Kuni and cried when he tried to hold the boy, and Rata-*tika*, the new baby, joined her brother in wailing. This made both Kuni and Jia cry as well. In a house full of weeping people, only Soto managed to get things done. She got food on the table and took away the crying babies.

Otho Krin stood nearby, unsure what to do. Kuni noticed him and, especially, his straight, black hair.

He patted Otho Krin on the back. "Otho, you were a scrawny young lad when I last saw you. I appreciate your taking care of my family. I know that you've always been faithful and true, in your own way."

Otho flinched and Jia's face was frozen halfway between joy and terror. There was a moment of awkwardness before Soto gave Otho a gentle nudge. Kuni seemed to notice nothing.

"It is . . . my pleasure to serve," Otho replied, and bowed. Discreetly, he and Soto left the room, closing the door after themselves.

Once they were alone, Jia broke down and cried in Kuni's embrace.

"Oh, I'm so sorry, Jia," Kuni said, stroking her hair. "I can only imagine what you think of all that has happened, and you've had to endure the cold gazes of everyone in Çaruza all by yourself."

"It's hopeless, isn't it?" Jia wiped her eyes. "I was so angry when I heard what you did and how Mata responded. How can you ever get anywhere when you're holed up on that little island? And whatever you try, Mata still has me and the kids under his thumb here. My family will not talk to me at all, terrified of what the hegemon might think."

Kuni held tightly to Jia. Everything she said felt like daggers twisting in his heart.

On an impulse, she seized his hands and looked into his face with feverish eyes. "Kuni, what about begging Mata for forgiveness? Give up your title. Let him make you into one of his ministers or even a commoner. We can live a happy life back in Zudi with our children. My family and yours would be so happy to have us back. Maybe you're thinking of flying too high."

Kuni looked away. "I've thought about it."

Jia waited, and when nothing seemed forthcoming, she nudged. "And?"

"I think about other families."

"Other families?"

"On my way here, I had to travel away from the major cities and big roads, and I got to see a little of how bad things have become. Mata may be a great warrior, but he's not a good ruler. The old Tiro states were forced to work together only because they feared the empire more than one another, but now all the old enmities are resurfacing; Mata made things worse with his childish map-drawing, and the new Tiro kings he created have no legitimacy. All the states are preparing for war: Taxes have increased to boost the sizes of armies, and prices in the markets keep going up. Though the rebellion is over, the lives of the common people have not grown better."

"What does any of this have to do with you and me and our children?"

"This is *not* why you and I risked our lives. The people deserve better."

Despair and anger warred within Jia as she listened to this speech. "You'd rather be loved by the fickle crowd than be a good husband to me and a good father for our children? How can you neglect us while you blather on and on about 'saving' the people? The world is not your concern, *we* are. Have you thought that maybe the suffering you see is bound up with the very warp and weft of the world? No matter who is emperor or hegemon, war and death are inevitable? That makes you think you'll be better at ruling the world than him?"

"I *don't* know, Jia. That is why I've come to you to hear your counsel. But what has happened to you? You were once so willing to challenge the world, to imagine how things could be different."

"Life happened, Kuni! I'm just an ordinary person, a mother. Why is it wrong for me to want my children to be safe, to care about them more than other people's children? Why is it wrong for me to want to live with the man who promised to share my life by my side, to not have him risk death and limb every day?"

*"The man by your side?"* Kuni blurted out. "You dare to speak of the man by your side?"

Jia took a deep breath. Then she looked Kuni in the eyes. "You were not here, Kuni. I did what I did to survive, to know that I could still master my fate. But I have never stopped loving you."

"I never thought faith would be such a difficult thing between us." Then Kuni stood there, stunned. He had not meant to voice his suspicions; he had come home to seek refuge and encouragement, but this wasn't going at all the way he imagined.

There was now an invisible wall between them, they both saw. They had felt closer to each other in their dreams and yearnings than they did now in person. When they had been apart, each had striven to fulfill an idealized vision they thought the other had of them. But the truth was that they had both changed.

Jia's time of isolation and deprivation had made her treasure the stability and charm of an ordinary life. But Kuni's ambition, now stoked, had made him impatient with concerns he deemed petty. The passion that had united them early on now seemed to have been reduced to embers.

"Drink, husband," said Jia, and she served Kuni a bland tea that calmed nerves and dulled hearts. She had given the mix to many couples who were too tired to continue fighting.

Kuni drank it willingly.

The visit was drained of its pleasure, as Kuni and Jia behaved like guests sharing a house.

Both focused on the children, anchors for two kites that rode different winds.

∽ ∾ ∽ ∾

"You and Jia are having a hard time," said Soto.

Kuni was working on improving Jia's workshop. Ceramic jars and glass bottles filled with preserved herbs filled every shelf, and there was barely room to move inside. He was nailing new shelves to the wall, installing ladders for her to access the higher shelves more easily, and adding a low gate to the door so that the children would not be able to get inside as they toddled and crawled.

"We've been apart for too long," he acknowledged.

Though he still didn't know Soto very well, Kuni felt comfortable talking to her. The kids loved the serious but kind housekeeper, and she made the household function as smoothly as Cogo did Dasu. Soto didn't cower before him like some of the other servants, awed by his status as a king and the legends that had grown up around his complicated history with the hegemon. Instead, she treated him as an equal, and was sometimes even gruff and impatient, especially when he was clumsy with the children. In her presence, Kuni felt more like his old self, careless and free.

"You've both grown more used to the image of each other than the reality," said Soto. "That's the danger with ideals. We're never as perfect as how others wish us to be."

Kuni sighed. "You're right about that."

"But I've always found that true happiness must take into account our imperfections. Faith is stronger when it acknowledges and embraces doubt."

Kuni looked at Soto and made a decision. "I'm not blind, Soto. I can guess what happened. Otho has always liked Jia, and I decided long ago to trust them rather than act the part of the jealous lord of folk operas. But perhaps I have been a fool."

"Not at all. You haven't raged or been petulant, which speaks well of you. You know that you've never been absent from Jia's heart."

Kuni nodded. "I haven't reacted the way you might have expected because . . . I've done things while I was away too, things that I'm not proud of."

"It is the rare man who would be as severe with himself as he is with his wife," said Soto. "I'm glad to see I was not wrong about you. The sages and Ano Classics tell us that faith means one thing for a husband, and another for a wife, but you are clearly not a man who accepts received wisdom."

Kuni gave a little chuckle. "I've always thought it nonsense to believe something true simply because it was written in a book long ago. Mata is the one who thinks the past was perfect, but I think we must perfect the present for the future. I believe she did what she did because she thought it necessary, and I would not act the hypocrite."

"Great men and women are not constrained in the forms their loves may take," said Soto. "You and Jia may love others, but in each other's estimation, you'll always be first among equals."

"But it will never be smooth sailing and all sunshine, will it?"

"What would be the fun in that?"

"You're angry at your husband," said Soto.

She and Jia were embroidering in the shade of the dining alcove while Kuni played with the children in the courtyard. Kuni was looking for dandelion seed clusters and helping little Toto-*tika* to blow them. Rata-*tika*, too young to participate, hung on to her father's neck and watched, crying out in delight.

"I am angry that he takes being a king more seriously than being a husband," said Jia.

"Do you think you have been taking being a wife more seriously than anything else? I have heard your bedroom door open and close at night."

Jia stopped her needle. She looked over at Soto. "Be careful of your words." Her hands trembled.

But Soto continued her needlework, precise, meticulous, each stitch straight and tight, as though measured by the flight of an arrow. Her hands were steady. "You misunderstand me, Lady Jia. Do you love your husband?"

"Of course."

"How do you reconcile your lover to this love then?"

"It's completely different." Jia kept her voice low, but her face was flushed. "Otho was something I needed . . . for myself, to stay sane, to stay alive. I did it to feel in control again, to be able to be the Lady Jia that those around me needed me to be. I don't regret it, even if the Ano sages may frown on what I've done. And I don't consider it an act of betrayal because Kuni was never displaced from the center of my heart."

"Do you think Kuni understands?"

"I . . . don't know. But if he's the man I think he is, he should. I never claimed to be perfect, but I have always tried to do the right thing."

"That is my point, Jia. The heart is a complicated thing, and we're capable of many loves, though we're told that we must value one to the exclusion of others. You can be a good wife at the same time that you're a good mother, though sometimes the needs of your husband may seem to conflict with the needs of your children. You can be loyal to your husband at the same time that you take a lover for your own sake, though the poets tell us this is wrong. But why should we believe that the poets understand us better than we do ourselves? Do not retreat into conventionality because you're afraid—as you already suspect, your husband may understand you better than you think."

"You're a strange one, Soto."

"No more than you, Lady Jia. You're angry at Kuni because you perceive a conflict between his duty to provide a safe home for you and his desire to make Dara a better place for all. But can his heart not contain both? And can you not see how you might help him achieve both?"

Jia laughed bitterly. "Whatever I think, what can I do about it? I'm not a man, just the wife of a man trying to seek his fortune in war."

"You cannot take refuge in toothless platitudes when it suits you, Jia. Your husband is a king, an equal of the other Tiro kings. Do you really think you're as helpless as the widows in the Cocru farmlands whose husbands were ordered to fight and die for your husband and Mata?"

"Kuni is the one who decides these things, not me."

"Because you don't wield a sword or wear armor, you believe it absolves you of responsibility for how things turn out."

"What is the alternative? I do not wish to be known as a woman who manipulates her husband to satisfy her hunger for power; I am not going to be called a pillow-whisperer who obtains in the bedroom what should only be won on the battlefield or through legitimate study. I've studied the Ano Classics—I know well the dangers of women meddling in the affairs of the state."

"What of Lady Zy?"

"I would not presume to compare myself to a woman of legend."

"Yet she was once but a woman who loved a man and who believed she could move her husband to do the right thing. No matter how diligently you study, can you ever become an official? No matter how brave you feel, can you ever charge onto a battlefield? We live in a world in which these paths are closed to you, as a woman, and yet you will not explore other paths by which you may alter your own fate and the fates of others because you fear the wagging tongues and sharp writing knives of scribes who manufacture history for their own purposes.

"The conventional life of a 'good wife'—as defined by the scribes of the court—is closed to you. You're the one who defied your family's wishes and married a ne'er-do-well because of a dream, who followed a bandit into the mountains, who believed in him when no one else would—"

"It's not . . . not that . . . I just want things to be safe for me and my family. . . ."

"But it's too late for that, Jia. Some believe that the world is a fate-shaken sieve where men and women are sorted out by their innate qualities; others believe that we carve out our own destinies by luck and skill. Yet, either way, those in high places have a duty to do more because they're more powerful. If you value safety so much, you should never have said yes the day Kuni asked you to yoke your fate to his.

"A marriage is a carriage with two sets of reins, and you must not let him do all the driving. Accept that you're a political wife, and perhaps you will not feel so helpless."

When they embraced again, it was raw, awkward, like the first night they had been together.

"It's never going to be easy with you, is it?" she asked. "You'll keep on changing, as will I."

"Would you have it any other way?" he asked. "Safety is an illusion, as is faith without temptation. We're imperfect, unlike the gods, but in that imperfection we may yet make them jealous."

And they both felt their hearts expand, large enough to contain a multitude of loves.

Afterward, they lay in darkness, their limbs entwined.

"You must go back to Dasu," said Jia. "And never speak of surrender to Mata again."

Kuni could feel his heart speeding up to match the rhythm of Jia's. "You're certain?"

"Even if you give up the little that you have, there's no guarantee that Mata will leave us in peace. But as long as you're a king, you have room to maneuver. A bandit who rose up to become a duke and who seized the emperor from an airship is never without possibilities."

Kuni held her tighter. "I knew I would find what I needed from you."

Jia kissed him. "And you must take on another wife."

Kuni froze. "What? If this is your misguided way of 'balancing' things—"

"Kings are supposed to have multiple consorts to ensure many heirs—"

"Since when am I supposed to be like other kings—"

"Oh, please, Kuni, stop being childish. I know my place in your heart is as secure as yours is in mine. Since I'm the mother of your firstborn, Mata will never imagine that you'd dare do anything as long as he controls me. But you also have to convince him that you're content with your lot, happy, maybe even overjoyed, to be the king of a tiny, faraway island. There is no better way to do this than to take on another wife, to show him that you're settling in like a true, greedy, lustful Tiro king, ready to make your home in your nook like a weed. If you're sufficiently convincing, he may even eventually agree to allow me to go to join you."

"But Jia, I can't just marry another girl like some stage prop—"

"I'm not asking you to do anything of the sort—I know you can't marry someone as a cold, political act. But you'll be far from me, and I know well how loneliness eats away at affections and passions. You must marry someone you love, someone who'll be your companion and trusted adviser. You need such a voice by your side, especially in moments of doubt."

Kuni was silent for a while. "If I do this, someday she may become your rival in the palace."

"Or my replacement, should Mata decide that I am no longer useful alive."

Kuni sat up. "What!? I will never permit that to happen."

But Jia's voice remained calm. "You cannot be without an heir. Who can predict the direction of the winds for sure? What we're plotting is dangerous, and before success, we must plan for failure. When Lady Zy persuaded Lurusén to denounce Mapidéré, she knew that she might have to pay for it one day with her life."

"I know not whether to admire you or to be afraid of you."

Jia placed her hand on his. "I speak only from prudence. It may be that Mata will be persuaded that your affections lie with your new wife, and paradoxically, the shift will make me safer."

"You speak of a wager of your life as though we're discussing the weather."

"I'm not so naïve as to think it will be easy," said Jia. "But our faith is not the kind bound by conventions. No matter who pleases your senses and takes up residence in your heart, I know you'll never be happier than when you can share your flight with me."

Kuni kissed her. "And I know no matter who you take to your bed when I can't be around, you'll always be happiest when you soar with me as high as we did in your dream."

"My husband is a man of truly capacious mind."

CHAPTER THIRTY-EIGHT

# RISANA

OUTSIDE ÇARUZA: THE SEVENTH MONTH IN THE FIRST YEAR OF THE PRINCIPATE.

Kuni asked Soto to take him with her into Çaruza.

"You need someone to carry groceries for you," he said.

"I'm not sure it's a good idea for you to show your face in Çaruza," Soto said. "You're supposed to be ill and in Dasu."

But Kuni would not be dissuaded. The reconciliation between him and Jia had re-energized him. He felt ready to take on the world; he wanted to see Çaruza and to observe the nobility in Mata's capital up close. It was a way to thumb his nose at Mata and the little island prison the hegemon had set up for him. And so, disguising himself as a servant, he followed Soto to the city.

Soto bought rice, fish, vegetables, pork ribs. . . . The basket of goods strapped to Kuni's back grew heavier and heavier, but Kuni didn't complain. The sights and sounds of bustling Çaruza, so much more cosmopolitan and sophisticated than Daye, made him realize how much he missed the Big Island.

"Get up, you worthless, lazy dog," a Cocru army officer, a fifty-chief, shouted as he whipped a thin, young boy on the ground. The boy tried to get up but collapsed back down from weakness. It was clear that he was underfed and abused. The crowd parted around them, giving them plenty of space.

"What's going on there?" Kuni pushed closer and asked.

Soto shrugged. "The hegemon made many of the Xana prisoners into bonded army laborers—essentially slaves."

"That boy looks no older than fourteen."

"The hegemon said that the prisoners deserve whatever happens to them because they served the emperor. Most people agree with him."

"There's never going to be an end to suffering if 'he deserves it' is all the justification people need for inflicting pain."

Soto appraised Kuni and nodded, thoughtfully.

Kuni looked at the half-dead young man lying on the ground. His face twitched.

Then he laughed and strode up to the angry officer.

"Sir! Sir! Can I ask you a favor?"

The officer paused and wiped the sweat from his brows. "What do you want?"

"I hate these Xana dogs as much as the hegemon. I like to devise ingenious games to torment the simple brains of Xana slaves. Since this one is clearly useless for more work, can I buy him from you? I have some new games I want to try."

His voice was oily and smooth, and his eyes radiated pleasure at the anticipation of inflicting torture. Even the fifty-chief shuddered. But he nodded when Kuni whispered his offer in his ear.

"Ah," Kuni said, making a face. "I don't have enough cash. Here's ten silver pieces, which is all I have with me." He frowned, patted his sleeves, and then his eyes lit up. "But I did bring my seal."

Kuni went to a stationer by the side of the road and came back with a piece of paper that he handed to the soldier. "Just present this to the doorman at the house of Lord Pering and tell him that Master Kunikin—that's me—owes you. I'm the private tutor in his household and the house office will pay you out of an advance on my salary. That's my seal down there."

The fifty-chief thanked him and unrolled the paper to look at it. He was not a quick reader and puzzled out the letters and logograms with his lips slowly.

"Let's bring the boy home and clean him up," Kuni whispered to Soto.

"You and Jia are a lot alike," Soto whispered back. "You can't help but want to help people. Do not underestimate the potential of that quality."

Kuni was thoughtful for a moment. "Thank you."

The Cocru officer froze as he got to the impression of the illegible seal.

"It's you!" he shouted. "Fin Crukédori!"

Kuni, Soto, and the boy were not even twenty steps away. Those in the crowd closest to them turned to stare.

"What is he talking about?" Soto asked.

Kuni smiled bitterly. "My past catching up with me."

The fifty-chief rushed at Kuni. A young woman selling iced sour-plum soup tripped as she was trying to get out of his way, and the ice blocks she carried on her tray scattered on the ground; the soldier slipped on the ice blocks, fell, tried to get up, and fell again.

Kuni said to Soto. "I have to go."

"Wait!" she said. "Now that I know what manner of man you are, I will tell you my secret." And she pulled him close to whisper in his ear. Kuni's eyes widened. Then he looked at Soto, and understanding dawned on his face.

"Do what you have to out there in Dasu," said Soto. "When the time comes, I will be here."

He turned around and disappeared into the confused crowd.

*Why, Sister, why have you helped that slippery eel slip away? Can't you see he plots against the favored son of Cocru?*

*He's your favorite. I rather like Jia. She's got . . . character. This isn't the time for her to mourn.*

*I think you've been taken in by the pretend virtues of her trickster husband. He's an actor, a fraud.*

Kuni whipped the horse he had stolen to put as much distance between himself and Çaruza as possible. But the horse was old and frail and already was foaming at the mouth. He could see the figures of his pursuers and the cloud of dust they raised behind him.

He cursed his luck. Of all the soldiers in the Cocru army, he had to run into one who had been in Zudi. And of all the soldiers from Zudi, he had to run into one who had seen him using his old trick.

The fifty-chief had called for backup right away. Mata Zyndu had made it clear to the world that Kuni Garu was not allowed off of Dasu. And all of the hegemon's men knew that a reward came with catching Kuni if he returned from exile without permission.

In front of Kuni, now, was a small farmer's cottage. He jumped off the horse, whipped it hard to keep it running down the road, and rushed to the door of the cottage, where a young woman was shelling peas.

"Sister, I need your help." Kuni was aware of the impression he must have made: The roots of his dark hair were growing out under his bleached hair, and he was dressed like one of Jia's servants. The fake scars on his face and the sweat from his escape made him look like a desperado on the run—which he was.

The young woman, whose olive skin and light-hued hair and eyes suggested that her ancestors were from Amu, not Cocru, stood up, looked at him, and glanced up the road at the approaching dust of Kuni's pursuers. "If you're running from the hegemon, you're probably not that bad."

Kuni sighed inwardly with relief. Mata never cared much about how the peasants thought of him and saw no point in being their friend. Kuni could just imagine how Mata's nobles, generals, and tax collectors had been treating the populace. But the people were like the sea: They could float a heavily laden ship, or they could make it sink.

"Come with me." The young woman led Kuni to the well behind the cottage and had him slowly winch himself down into it with the rope and pulley over the well. Once Kuni was in the water, she told him to hold on to the rope and wear the bucket over his head like a helmet. If someone took a quick look down the well, it would look like the bucket was just floating.

She went back into the cottage and built up the fire in the hearth. But she soaked the wood in water first, and then there was a great deal of smoke. Soon, smoke filled the cottage, spilling out the open door.

The Cocru soldiers in pursuit slowed down as they passed the cottage. The fifty-chief thought he had seen the rider getting off near here. He sent half of his men down the road after the cloud of dust they could still see in the distance. The other half walked up the path to the smoking cottage.

They were greeted by a young woman whose face was covered with soot and tears.

"Have you seen a fugitive?" the fifty-chief asked. "He's a dangerous man, an enemy of the hegemon." He hadn't told his men they were looking for Kuni Garu, specifically, just in case he turned out to be wrong.

The woman shook her head. Agitated, she waved her arms to clear the air around her. But as she did so, the smoke followed her movements, thickened into heavy swirls of dense fog, and soon enveloped both her and the fifty-chief and his soldiers. Everyone began to cough in the smoke, and tears streamed down their faces.

The fifty-chief strained to look around the cottage, but it was hard to see anything. He pushed past the woman and walked deeper into the small cottage. Shadows seemed to leap out of the thick smoke, indistinct shapes and monsters with eyes of fire. The fifty-chief became frightened and confused. His head felt very thick and slow for some reason. It was as though the smoke filled his head.

"The man you are seeking is not here," the woman's voice said.

"Not . . . here," the fifty-chief repeated.

He shook his head. He just couldn't think with all this smoke.

He backed out of the dark interior of the cottage, and his head instantly cleared.

*Of course the man I'm seeking isn't here. How silly of me. Why would Kuni Garu try to hide in a peasant's cottage? Every man in Cocru knows that Kuni Garu betrayed the great Hegemon Zyndu, and no one would dare to help him.*

He mumbled an apology to the young woman and led his men on down the road. If they couldn't catch the fugitive, he decided that he would say nothing. The hegemon would not react kindly if one of his officers found Kuni Garu and let him get away—he might even be suspected of having helped Kuni.

The water in the well was cold, and Kuni shivered as the young woman winched him out. As he emerged into the light, he looked into her face, now bathed in the soft light of the setting sun. Kuni saw that under the streaks of soot and ashes, she was very beautiful.

"What, you've never seen a woman of Cocru before?" she said, laughing.

"I'm Kuni Garu," he said. He had no idea why. Something about her, about the way she subtly moved her hands and arms to clear away the smoke that still lingered in the yard, compelled him to speak the truth.

"I'm Risana," she said, "a simple smokecrafter."

Risana laid out some sweet snacks and bitter tea on a tray and set it on the table between them. Kuni thanked her.

"What is this thing you do with . . . smoke?"

She got up and lit a stick of incense and set the burner down also on the table.

"Watch."

She moved her hands through the air, trailing the long, oversized sleeves behind them. The air currents in the room changed and shifted, and the smoke, rising in a straight line, began to curl into a spiral. She stopped moving, but the spiral stayed in place, as though it were solid.

"That's amazing," said Kuni. "How did you do that?"

"My family was from Arulugi, the Beautiful Island. I don't know who my father was; it was just me and my mother. She was an herbalist who discovered the secret of creating smoke that can be sculpted. It requires certain ingredients in the incense that, when burning, do not follow the expected patterns of normal smoke.

"We traveled from town to town and made a good living entertaining in the teahouses. My mother improved on the technique and devised ever more elaborate smoke displays. She could create labyrinths out of them, and guests would pay to be lost in them and laugh and scream and feel the thrill of danger that is not really danger."

He heard a trace of sorrow in her voice. "But something happened, didn't it?"

She nodded. "My mother realized that the smoke also had an effect on the minds of men and women, made them more compliant, willing to follow suggestions. It was part of what made her labyrinths so effective: She could give the suggestions of monsters moving behind the smoke, and those within would believe they were real."

Kuni nodded. He had heard of such things, street entertainers who offered to put volunteers into a semi-asleep state in which they would do all kinds of silly things that they would not do normally: The shy would give a rousing oration, the bold would cower at shadows, dignified men and women would cluck like chickens and bark like dogs. It was close to madness.

"One day, a prince famed for his bravery came to experience her smoke labyrinth. Trying to give him a thrill, my mother enclosed him in a thick fog and suggested that he was beset by monsters wielding tongues of fire. She had intended to make the monsters back off when the prince defended himself with his sword, so that he could feel the satisfaction of battling mythical creatures.

"But the prince, despite his reputation as a skilled fighter, turned out to be a coward. As the monsters my mother put into his mind began to appear, he dropped his sword and ran screaming from the labyrinth, having soiled his clothes in the process.

"King Ponahu of Amu was not amused and arrested my mother for witchcraft. She was scheduled to be executed, but she convinced her guards to slip her some herbs—for her womanly troubles, she claimed—and then used them to create a smoke screen that enveloped the guards. She had them open her cell under the influence of the smoke, and she escaped. And then she came to Cocru, and we've tried to live here inconspicuously since then."

"That is a sad story," said Kuni. "King Ponahu thought your mother's smokecraft witchery, but isn't authority itself a form of smokecraft too? It relies on performance, stage management, and the power of suggestion."

Risana tilted her head and stared at him, until Kuni felt awkward and embarrassed under the gaze of those light-brown eyes.

"What? Did I say something wrong?"

"No, but I wish my mother were still alive. She would have liked you."

"Oh?"

"She always said that the world would not be set aright until the powerful vied to entertain the powerless, rather than the other way around."

Kuni laughed, but then, after a moment, looked serious. "There's much truth worth following in your mother's words."

"That was her motto as a smokecrafter: to delight and to lead."

Being with Risana reminded Kuni of his childhood days when life was simple, and it put him at ease.

He had not realized how much *politics* there was in his daily life. Every word, every gesture, every expression had layers of meaning that he had to be attentive to. Cogo had drilled into him the belief that a king was always on display, and always speaking, even when he was silent. People were always watching, inferring meaning from how he held his hands, how he seemed to listen or not listen, how he stifled a yawn or drank his tea. In the minds of those around him, there were plots and plots upon plots.

He had to admit that a part of himself enjoyed this, and he was good at it.

Jia, in her own way, was master of the same art. She had long been the center of attention, the one others looked to for approval, for strength, for signs of one kind or another. Though their hearts were connected in a way that made them understand each other like few others could, when they were together, they couldn't help but continue to play the game, put on a performance, parse each other's words and acts for clues.

But with Risana, Kuni felt no pressure. She spoke what was on her mind and saw through whatever evasions he put up. She waved her hands, and fog seemed to clear from his mind. There was no need for any flattery, deceit, lies. She was not interested in the kind of mental games that he and Jia were trapped in. Because she saw through layers of guile in men so easily, she seemed to have no guile herself.

Being with Risana made Kuni realize how tiring his life was. There was no longer room in the life of *King Kuni* for the young man who once felt such pure elation at the sight of a lone man flying across the sky.

Risana had not told Kuni the whole truth about her talent, which was similar to, but also different from, her mother's.

Whereas her mother had been skilled in planting suggestions in an audience while smoke dulled their senses, Risana was best at the opposite: clearing the minds of those in thrall to the smoke. She was the one who would lead them out of the labyrinths after they'd had their fun, the one who would show them that the monsters they thought they saw were not real.

If she wished, she could also manipulate the smoke in people's hearts and behind their eyes, making them see visions where there was nothing, to have doubts where there was clarity. But she far preferred to do the opposite.

Even without the aid of her herbal smoke, she had always found it easy to speak with people—she had a talent of seeing what was in their hearts through the fog and smoke of their self-deception and their wish to seem other than they were. Most of the time, she chose to go along with the deception; indeed, that was often what it took to be well-liked.

But sometimes, when she thought the person needed it, she did something different. With a word, a song, a judiciously enforced bit of silence, she showed them what she had seen, giving them that most precious of gifts: acceptance of the truth.

When men and women realized what she was capable of, often they pulled away in fear. They did not like to be so naked.

There was, however, a limit to her skill.

She discovered that some hearts were opaque to her sight, like sealed boxes. She could not tell what their owners wanted or what they feared, and she knew not whether they were friend or foe.

"I'm afraid for you," her mother had said, when Risana tried to explain this particular blindness.

"What for?" Risana had asked.

"You've never learned to navigate the darkness, as the rest of us must."

And then she had pulled Risana into an embrace, and would explain no more.

At first, Risana had thought Kuni was just such a man, a man whose heart was sealed against her sight. And then she realized that it was simply because she didn't look hard enough.

Kuni was such a complicated man. There were so many layers in his heart that it appeared opaque. He was like a cabbage, one leaf nestled inside another, each half-formed idea enclosed by another, desires and suspicions and regrets and ideals wrapped tightly lest they spread too far. There was a growing ambition in him and an overwhelming desire to be liked. Yet there was also sorrow and a gnawing sense of doubt, of not being as good a man as he thought he was, of not being as certain of the right path as he wished.

He intrigued her. Powerful men, in her experience, were usually not so full of doubt. Kuni was consumed by the desire to do good for others, but uncertain what "good" might be and whether he was the right man for the job.

Kuni was the sort of man, Risana realized, who, rather than deceive himself, was so full of self-doubt that he could no longer see himself.

*And what should I do?* Risana asked herself. *What is my role when I see a king in need of counsel?*

*To delight and to lead.*

Kuni stayed with Risana for two weeks. At first he told himself that it was because he was still hiding from Mata's men. But it was impossible to lie to himself with Risana around.

So he asked her to come with him. And she agreed, as she already knew she would.

And that was how King Kuni married his second wife, Lady Risana.

# CHAPTER THIRTY-NINE

# LETTERS

DASU AND OUTSIDE ÇARUZA: THE NINTH MONTH IN THE FIRST YEAR OF THE PRINCIPATE.

My Beloved Jia,

As usual, forgive me for writing only in zyndari letters like a schoolboy—a problem we'll have to endure until you figure out how to form solid logograms from invisible ink; though given my handwriting, perhaps it's best I can't use logograms here.

Do you have everything you need? If you need money, let me know—I'm sure I can send you some, and Mata would be too proud to interfere with something like that. It can't be easy to keep everything running, even with Soto and Otho's help. I pray that Toto-*tika* and Rata-*tika* are not giving you too much trouble.

I'm overjoyed to have received your gifts and the letter of congratulations for me and Risana. She asked me to tell you that she very much loves the box of herbs you sent her, though she would not tell me what they are, only smile mischievously.

Imperfect as we are, I can only resolve to never again make assumptions and cling to ideals and to be honest and reveal to you everything in my heart. She is different from you, and I love you both.

The wedding was a lavish affair, though I think our wedding in Zudi was more fun—I had more freedom then to say outrageous things. Tiro kings from across Dara sent gifts, which will certainly help the Dasu treasury. Even Mata sent a case of fine wines from Zyndu Castle.

Kindo Marana came himself, and I made an elaborate show of how much I enjoyed the pleasures Dasu had to offer: fresh sea air, spicy foods, a population who considers me refined, a new wife.

"Do you not miss home, Lord Garu?" he probed, as he waved his eating sticks to refuse my offer of more spicy dumplings—he has a sensitive stomach.

"Home is where the heart is," I said, looking over at Risana.

I hope my performance was convincing.

What a game we're playing, Jia, and may the gods protect us all.

Your Husband, performing the role of his life

Kuni,

Don't worry about money. Though we are kept under watch by Mata, we are given all that we need materially. Since your departure, Toto-*tika* is now able to say a few words and walk on his own, and Rata-*tika* is just as cute as can be. They miss their father, as do I.

I am indeed curious about Risana. Another woman who has captured your heart . . . well, interesting. I can't wait to meet her.

Mata came to see me—just himself this time, and unarmed.

"Kuni seems to prefer his new home," he said. "Loyalty comes harder to some than others."

"I suppose some men think of women like clothes," I said, dabbing at my eyes. "Newer is better."

He looked at me, and for a moment it seemed as if he was the Mata I knew, the man who held my son in his palm and joked with you. And then his face hardened, and he left.

I hope you've looked over the other gifts I sent you carefully. The maps you asked for and engineering plans for water mills and windmills were hidden in the lining of the wedding blankets; a wedding is indeed a good opportunity for smuggling—Rin came up with that idea, didn't he? I hope he has enough now to do his work properly.

Courage, my husband, and faith.

Your Jia, learning to spy, which is indeed
one of the most interesting things

My Beloved Jia,

Now that I've been back in Dasu for a while, I've given much thought to what others call my ambition. The misunderstanding between Mata and me may appear to be a matter of competition for honor, for credit and empty fame. But the roots go far deeper than that. Now that I have seen the larger world, I wish to change it, as does Mata. But while he wishes to restore the world to a state that never was, I wish to bring it to a state that has not yet been seen.

I may not be much of a fighter, but I have always tried to do the best for those who have followed me, who have been put in my charge, who are dependent on me. I have seen the poor suffer when nobles seek the purity of ideals. I have seen the powerless die when princes believe in the nostalgia of their dreams. I have seen the common people torn from peace and thrown into war when kings yearn to test the clarity of their vision.

I have come to think that Emperor Mapidéré was misunderstood.

Let me finish, Jia.

In Pan, I saw with my own eyes the horrors of Mapidéré's madness, the bones of those he had killed were embedded in every wall, and the widows and orphans he had made cried in the streets. Yet there was also something else, something I found in the documents saved by Cogo from the Imperial Archives and which he secretly brought here.

The minutiae of administration show that for all that the emperor had done wrong, he had also gotten some things right. He had promoted the flow of commerce, the migrations of peoples, the exchange of ideas; he brought the wider world to each isolated corner of Dara; he had done all he could to destroy the nobility of the Seven States, the old centers of power, so that all of Dara could be one people.

Why should there be so many Tiro states, Jia? Why should there be so many wars? The ever-shifting lines between the Tiro states are drawn by men, not gods, and why can we not erase them altogether?

I don't yet know what the right answer is, but I believe that returning to the past is not the answer. I feel the heavy weight of a new responsibility. For the rebellion's promise of succor to the common people to not be betrayed, I must find a new path forward.

Meanwhile, I'm stuck on this island and must keep myself busy.

Now, contrary to what you might have heard, Dasu is actually a very nice place. There are so few nobles here except the ones I've made myself that there are no boring parties or ridiculous gossip. I'm working on getting everyone to stop calling me "Your Majesty." I don't like the way people stumble over it, and I don't much feel like a king. Cogo hates how I'm so careless with protocol, and you know how stubborn he can be. Well, I can be stubborn too.

Daye is really just about the size of Zudi, though much poorer and with far fewer people. As a capital, I'm afraid it's not going to stand up to Çaruza.

Few traders make their way here, since all we have is fish. Well, if you ever come here, be prepared to eat lots of raw fish and shrimp. The crabs and lobsters here are not as big as the ones they catch in Zathin Gulf, but far tastier.

But my favorite thing about Daye is the view. Because we are on the northern coast, away from Rui and the other islands, we face the endless open ocean. The water is pristine, and we rarely see any trash drifting in. I've taken to swimming in the mornings in the cold water, before the sun comes up. It really wakes you up, and you're ready for the whole day. At night, we build bonfires on the beach and drink and tell stories. Yes, entertainment opportunities in Daye are a bit limited.

The locals say that beyond the ocean, beyond the scattered isles where the pirates hide, below the horizon, there are other islands, filled with other people far different from us. Elders speak of strange flotsam and wreckage washing up on shore years ago, bearing designs never seen in all of Dara. We repeat these stories around the bonfire and scare one another, but I do wonder. Wouldn't it be exciting, Jia, to find other lands out there that we've never seen?

Cogo, as always, has come up with some great ideas for improving the people's lives—but he's generous enough to let me take credit for them so that the people will think I'm a wise ruler. Ha!

For example, he thinks we should make the best of what Dasu is most famous for: our cuisine. Emperor Mapidéré had forced people to relocate all over Dara, and the most cosmopolitan inhabitants of the other islands have acquired a taste for Dasu's spicy cooking. Now Cogo is offering restaurateurs a special banner they can buy after completing a course here in Daye so that they can call themselves Authentic Dasu Cooks.

I came up with the design for the banner: a little leaping whale, which happens to be also on the new flag of the Tiro state of Dasu. So far we've already had fifty or so restaurant owners from Arulugi and the Big Island take up our offer, and it's a good source of revenue. Cogo tells me that one other benefit to this program is getting people all over Dara used to the sight of Dasu flags flying everywhere and associating them with good things—delicious Dasu food. That Cogo, always thinking.

He's also introduced some new crops—like the taro they grow over on Tan Adü—that seem to do better than the traditional varieties. The farmers who have tried them are very impressed.

Cogo is also experimenting with a new, simpler tax code—though it still seems plenty complicated to me. But when I speak to the business leaders in Daye and the elders in the countryside, they tell me that Duke Yelu is a genius. (And I remind them that I'm an even *bigger* genius for letting Cogo do what he wants.)

He has also managed to win over Kindo Marana, the man supposedly watching our every move, by humbly going over to Rui on a little fishing boat to seek advice on taxation. Only Kiji knows how they can spend weeks talking taxes, but Marana seems now disinclined to treat us as a threat. His ships used to patrol close to our harbors, menacing the fishermen, and his airships used to circle over Daye daily, which got all the children very excited. But more recently he's scaled back these spy missions.

On the recruiting front, things aren't as good. Though Rin has spread the rumor through our network of spies on the other islands—mainly recruited through his connections with smuggling gangs—that I'm looking for able men to join us, few have shown up. Dasu is simply too remote and too poor to be really attractive.

Indeed, every day, a few of my soldiers desert because they miss home or because they don't see much of a future here. They steal fishing boats at night and row over to Rui, where they board the bigger ships bound for the Big Island. Others have left to go join the pirates up north. It's all a bit dispiriting.

But I keep on telling myself that this is just a temporary setback. Mata doesn't have the patience for the boring details of administration, and the new Tiro states are already squabbling over the arbitrary borders he drew and fighting for advantages. Maybe I'm just fooling myself, thinking that I still have a chance to escape from my island prison, but hope is a good dish, even better than Dasu spices.

Above all, don't worry. I'll figure it out. I promise.

Your Loving Husband

Kuni,

I must ask you to stop treating me like a delicate flower you must protect and stop thinking that you must come up with solutions for everything on your own. I fell in love with you not only because I knew you'd fly high one day, but also because I knew you'd always listen to my counsel and not dismiss me for "meddling," the way the scribes and ministers are alway warning the noble ladies of Çaruza to not interfere in the serious affairs of their husbands, brothers, and sons.

Oh, I'm sure this will come as no surprise to you, but I've decided to no longer attend any parties among the nobles in Çaruza. It's insulting, and frankly, I don't feel like I'm accomplishing much. At the last party I went to—Mata actually sent the invitation himself: I guess he wanted to feel out your ambition by observing the way I conducted myself—a stupid man, some count or other from Gan, pretended to not know where Dasu was and called you the "king of a lobster pot." And the other guests laughed like it was so witty. I had to go home before I did something I'd regret. Sorry, your wife is not much of a diplomat—I hope Risana will do better, for both our sakes—and I can never make my face say that which I do not feel.

It's hard being here on my own. I had hoped my family would finally be reconciled with us after you and Mata made a name for yourselves—and indeed, for a while distant cousins and grand-uncles I had never met wrote to me, speaking of plans for visits. But now all the cousins and clan elders are pressuring my parents to stay away from me since you're the hegemon's least favorite person. Oh, I could scratch out the eyes of these distant "relatives."

Soto has continued to be a great companion and the children love her. Despite her clear interest in politics, I find it odd that she goes out of her way to avoid the nobles of Çaruza. She disappears whenever any member of the nobility stops by—pretending to inquire after me and the children, but in reality just here to gather material for gossip. Even when Mata stopped by personally the other day—a very awkward visit, let me tell you—she hid herself in the kitchen and wouldn't come out. There must be a secret in her past.

But I enjoy talking with her . . . and though I'm no Lady Zy, I want to tell you a few things, my husband, that I think you may be neglecting.

You mention that it's hard to find and retain capable men who will serve you; but what about the ladies, Kuni? Remember that you're in a position of weakness, and those with clear paths to success will want to wager on the hegemon and his new Tiro kings. But Mata is a man who believes in traditions, in proven ways of doing things. Those who cannot compete for his attention—the desperate, the poor, those without lineages or formal learning—may be far more willing to gamble with you. It's not our custom or practice to look to women for talent, so who is to say that you may not have more success there?

Don't be shocked by my suggestion. I'm not saying you should turn the world upside down and do everything that the Ano sages warned against in their ancient books. But think about what I have said, and perhaps you may find an opportunity you have overlooked.

Oh, I have some news about one of your old followers. Remember Puma Yemu, Commander of the Whirlwind Riders? He did so much to aid you and Mata back during the Battle of Zudi. But Mata has never liked him because of his criminal past and didn't reward him after he took Pan from you. In fact, when he drove King Thufi away, he also stripped Marquess Yemu of his title and made him a lowly hundred-chief. Yemu was so mad that he quit the army and became a bandit again!

Just the other day, he came to see me in secret and brought me some very good tea that he had seized from a caravan going into Çaruza. Can you believe it? Such a great warrior reduced to banditry again. It's hardly what he deserved. I dropped some hints about serving you again, and he is very much interested.

Take care of yourself.

Your Jia, Tired But Happy

My Beloved Jia,

You're indeed the wisest, my better half. I told Cogo about your ideas, and he immediately agreed that they were brilliant. We've been trying to think of ways to get our message out to women of hidden talent.

And your note about Puma Yemu made me think about who else might have lost favor with Mata—if you can keep in contact with them, that would be a great help, but do be careful and don't make Mata suspect you.

But I'm afraid that I also have some horrible news. Cogo Yelu has left me. Excuse me if this letter doesn't make much sense. I can hardly think straight.

Cogo didn't show up this morning for our usual meeting. I sent Dafiro Miro, captain of my palace guards (which consist of him and two other soldiers, but I'm not skimping on titles, since titles are all I have to hand out), to retrieve him. He came back and gave me the bad news: Prime Minister Cogo Yelu was last seen leaving his home at night on a horse headed toward the southern coast of Dasu.

Fearing some mishap, I sent riders immediately after him, and I then spent the rest of the morning pacing around my room like an ant running around on a hot stove. They've now returned, Cogo-less. No one knows where he's disappeared to.

I'm devastated. If even Cogo has decided that following me is a lost cause, then I'm doomed, positively doomed. Ever since I became a rebel, Cogo has been like my right hand. I hardly know how to get home on my own after a night of drinking without him. How am I going to manage his new crops? How am I supposed to certify Authentic Dasu Cooks? How am I to collect taxes without making the people unhappy?

I'm going to be trapped on this little rock in the sea forever.

Many other soldiers and even officers have left me in the past few months, but this betrayal by Cogo feels different. I'm too upset to even be mad at him.

Your Kuni, in Desperate Times

My Beloved Jia,

Disregard that prior letter. Cogo has returned!

It has been a week since he left, and I haven't been eating or sleeping well. But this morning, just as I was out using the latrine, I saw Cogo ambling up the street, like nothing had happened.

I didn't even bother doing up my robes properly. I ran out into the streets in bare feet and grabbed his arms. "Why, oh why did you leave me?"

"Decorum, Lord Garu, remember decorum," he said, and he was smiling as if this was all very amusing. "I didn't run away. I was trying to chase down someone who you couldn't afford to lose."

"Who were you chasing?"

"Gin Mazoti, a corporal."

I threw his hands down in disgust. "Cogo, now you're just lying. At least twenty corporals have deserted in the past months, and who knows how many hundred-chiefs and even captains. And you went away for a whole week to chase down this Gin Mazoti? What's so special about him?"

"Gin Mazoti is the secret to the rise of Dasu."

I was very skeptical. I had never heard of this man. But just as Than Carucono can always tell when a colt will grow up to be a great horse, Cogo is very good at recognizing talent in obscurity. I knew that he must have had good reasons to chase after this man, and I should see him.

But instead of bringing the man to me, Cogo said I should go visit him at Cogo's house, where he was staying temporarily.

"Gin doesn't believe that he'll be given enough respect here in Dasu. He used to follow Mata Zyndu, but Mata never listened to any of his suggestions or gave him much to do. So when we departed for Dasu, Gin defected and joined us. But now that he's been here a few months and hasn't been promoted, he decided to leave even though I told him to be patient and wait for me to present him to you. So I had no time to tell you anything. I had to chase after him by moonlight."

"By moonlight!"

"Indeed. I was in my slippers, not even having had the chance to put on good walking shoes."

"And how did you catch him?"

"Ah," said Cogo, stroking his chin and smiling until his eyes practically disappeared. "It's quite a stroke of luck. Gin was going to hire a fishing boat and head for Rui before dawn, and had he succeeded in his plan, it would have been impossible for me to catch him—I'd have to put on a disguise or else Marana's spies would know something was up. But before Gin could get on the boat, a doctor stopped Gin to get his help."

"What kind of help?"

"Gin told me all about it afterward. The doctor wanted Gin to hold on to a pair of doves while he wrote out a long prescription describing the ingredients and method of preparation for a patient."

"Doves!"

"Just so. I got to see these doves myself, and they were extraordinary: thrice as big as the pigeons you normally see, and with eyes so intelligent you'd swear they were about to talk. The doctor, a lanky young man in a green traveling cloak, told Gin that the cooing of the doves made it hard to concentrate.

"'Just hold on to my doves and keep them happy and quiet so I can think. When I'm done, they'll fly the prescription to my patient.'

"So Gin waited and waited, while the doctor took his sweet time. He'd write one zyndari letter, pause, think hard, and then write another. Finally, Gin said, 'Doctor, I'm in a hurry. How much longer are you going to take?'

"'You've already waited this long,' said the doctor. 'Why not wait a little longer? You don't want the patient to get nine-tenths of a prescription, do you? That's not going to do him any good at all.'"

"What kind of doctor *is* this?" I asked. "He sounds like a fraud."

"Fake or not, Lord Garu, you and I have much to thank him for. Due to this unexpected delay, Gin remained at the village by the sea until I got there. I immediately begged him to come back.

"At first he was adamant about not coming back. 'Lord Garu hasn't seen me after all these months of waiting. It would be madness to continue to wait.'

"But the doctor broke in. 'Would you stop drinking medicine after a week when it takes ten days to show results?'

"Gin looked at him and narrowed his eyes. 'Who *are* you?'

"The doctor put down his brush and paper and smiled at Gin. 'I think you already know.'

"Because Gin was staring at him, I looked too. And I realized that the doctor was uncommonly good-looking. Otherworldly, almost. Gin asked, 'What do you want with me?'

"'I've always regretted what was done to you in my name,' the doctor said. 'So I've kept an eye on you, though I've tried to stay out of your way because you can take care of yourself, and a doctor's first rule is to do no harm.'

"'Why are you showing yourself to me now?' asked Gin.

"'I'm afraid that if you leave Dasu, you'll never return,' said the doctor. 'And that would be a harm.'"

"'If that is all true,' said Gin, 'then you must know the truth about me. What chances can a person like me have with a lord of great repute like Kuni Garu?'

"'Lord Garu is hungry for talent,' said the doctor. 'He is seeking everywhere: among bandits, pickpockets, scholars who never passed the Imperial examinations, deserters, even women.'"

"'Is this true?' asked Gin, turning to me. And I nodded."

I was so confused, Jia, that I had to interrupt Cogo. "They know each other? Who is this doctor, really?"

Cogo shook his head. "I don't know. After this speech, the doctor took back his doves from Gin and walked away, and Gin looked very thoughtful. When the doctor disappeared down the beach, he turned to me and agreed to come back."

"That's certainly an interesting story. But Cogo, just how did you come to the conclusion that this Gin is so great?"

"He told me of a way to get you off this island."

Well, Jia, as you can imagine, we went to Cogo's house right away.

Gin Mazoti is a small man, thin and wiry. He has leathery, dark-brown skin, black hair cropped close to the skull, and dark-brown eyes that dart around, taking everything in.

Cogo had told me that I needed to be respectful, so I didn't act like the king, just a man in search of a great warrior. That was easy—I'm always doing that anyway. So I bowed down to him and asked if I had the honor of meeting the famed Master Gin Mazoti.

"It's Miss Gin Mazoti, actually." And she bowed back in a woman's *jiri*, her hands folded across her chest. "I came back in part because I heard that you're even willing to consider the talents of the weaker sex. But if you're going to pay me the honor of an audience, I should at least let you know the truth about myself."

Well, imagine the expressions on Cogo's and my faces. (And how prescient of you, my Jia!)

Kisses for Toto-*tika* and Rata-*tika*.

Your Kuni, Ecstatic

CHAPTER FORTY

# GIN MAZOTI

DIMUSHI: A LONG TIME AGO.

No one ever called her Gin-*tika*. Her mother was a prostitute who died giving birth to her, and she didn't know who her father was. "Mazoti" was just the name of the indigo house where she was born.

Growing up in a whorehouse meant that Gin was the property of the house. She fetched water and welcomed the guests, mopped the floors and rinsed out the chamber pots. She was beaten because she was too slow ("Do you think I'm feeding you to crawl around like a snail?"), and she was beaten because she was too fast ("What makes you think you can just loll about because you finished your chores?"). When she was twelve she overheard the madam speak of auctioning off her virginity. During the night she cut her way out of the closet that the madam locked her in, took all the money that was in the house, and escaped into the streets of Dimushi.

The money didn't last long, and she was faced with a choice. She could sell herself, or she could steal. She chose to steal.

A gang of thieves took her in.

"When it comes to being a thief, young girls like you have certain advantages," said Gray Weasel, the leader of the gang.

Gin said nothing because her attention was entirely taken up by the feeling of warm porridge filling her belly. It had been three days since she had eaten.

"You are quick, and you don't look threatening," continued Gray Weasel. "Many people instinctively cross the street when they see a group of boys, but they pity a lone girl begging for food and let their guard down. You can relieve them of their possessions while smiling and pestering them to buy a flower."

Gin thought his voice sounded kind. Perhaps this was because he was the first man who had ever looked at her as a student, as a colleague, as a *person*, not just a piece of flesh.

It wasn't always that easy, of course, and Gin also learned to fight—sometimes others tried to steal from her, sometimes she was caught and the constables had no pity. The gang taught her that because she was a girl, she had to learn to make the best of her meager advantages.

Her greatest asset was that people didn't *expect* her to fight, though this only conferred a fleeting opportunity that she could make use of, once. She could not posture and taunt and boast and display the way the boys did. She had to behave as though she was helpless and then unleash her strike in one overpowering burst of fury. She went for the eyes, the soft tissue under the lump in men's throats, the groin. She had no qualms about sharp nails, teeth, hidden daggers. She could choose not to fight and yield, or she could choose one flash of deadly force. There was nothing in between.

One day, the gang robbed a caravan making a stop at a cheap inn. Their haul consisted of gold and jewels and a carriage filled with a dozen frightened boys and girls, none older than six years.

"Looks like this 'merchant' is a child trafficker," Gray Weasel said, looking at the children thoughtfully. "Probably snatched from their parents in faraway lands."

The children were brought back to Gray Weasel's home, which

was also the thieves' den. They were fed and put to bed. Gin stayed in the room and told them stories until the last boy sank into an uneasy sleep.

"Good job calming them down," Gray Weasel said to her, a toothpick dangling from the corner of his mouth. "I was sure some of them would try to run away the first chance they got. You've got a way with these kids."

"I'm an orphan too."

In the morning, Gin awoke to the sound of children screaming. She rushed out of the house. In the backyard, a few of the children lay on the ground crying. One had a bloody bandage wrapped around his right shoulder, his arm gone. Another sat with gauze wrapped around her head, two spreading red stains marking where her eyes had been. A third had lost his feet, and he crawled slowly, trailing blood on the grass. The other children, still uninjured, were held by members of the gang against the back wall. They screamed and kicked and bit, but the men stood as still as statues, not loosening their iron grasp.

In the middle of the backyard was a stump used for splitting firewood. A girl was tied to it, her left arm laying across the stump. She was so frightened that her voice no longer sounded human, but like the cries of some wild animal. "Please, please! Don't. No!"

Gray Weasel stood next to the stump, a bloody axe dangling from his hand. His expression was as calm as his voice, as though this was the most routine of mornings. "It won't hurt for very long, I promise. I'll just take off your arm from the elbow down. People can't resist giving money to a pretty, maimed little beggar girl."

Gin ran up to him. "What are you doing?"

"What does it look like? Making enhancements. I'll drop them off around the city every morning and collect them in the evening. They'll bring in a lot of money from begging. Compassion can be a valuable thing to steal too."

Gin moved to stand between him and the girl. "You never did anything like this to me."

"I thought I saw in you the potential of becoming a good thief." Gray Weasel's eyes narrowed. "Don't let me regret my decision."

"We saved them!"

"So?"

"We should return them to their parents."

"Who knows where they're from? The traffickers didn't keep records, and these kids are too young to give precise directions. And how do you know their parents didn't sell them because they couldn't afford to feed them?"

"Then you should let them go!"

"And allow another gang to snatch them up and make use of what ought to be *my* property? Are you going to suggest next that I feed them and board them with me for free? Should I abandon my profession and take up Rufizo's work of doing charity?" He laughed, pushed Gin aside, and swung the axe.

The girl's scream seemed to go on forever.

Gin jumped on him and tried to scratch out his eyes. He yelped and threw her to the ground. But it took two men to finally subdue her. Gray Weasel slapped her across the face and then made her watch as the rest of the children were, one by one, maimed in various ways. Afterward, he had her whipped.

That night, Gin waited until all the men fell asleep, then she got up and tiptoed her way into Gray Weasel's room. Through the window, the moonlight cast a pale white pall over everything. Next door, she could hear the pained murmurs of the children.

Slowly, very slowly, she reached into the bundle of clothes next to the bed and retrieved the thin dagger Gray Weasel always kept on him. In a single lightning-quick thrust, she plunged it into his skull through his left eye. He screamed, and Gin pulled out the dagger and thrust it into the soft spot under the lump in his throat. With a bloody gurgle, the scream stopped.

She kept on running until she fell down by the docks next to the Liru River from exhaustion.

That was the first man she ever killed.

Being on her own made it much harder. She had to avoid the gang of thieves, who had let it be known that they were looking for her. She hid in the basements of old temples and only came out when she had to eat.

A couple caught her trying to cut the purse of the wife in the markets one evening. But the husband, a devout follower of Rufizo, decided that rather than turning the young thief in to the constables, he would perform a good deed. They would take the young girl in and try to give her a home.

But the reality of raising a street urchin and rehabilitating a young criminal was far different from how the man had envisioned it. Gin did not trust the couple and tried to escape. They shackled her and read her sacred texts with her meals, hoping that she would open her heart and repent. But she cursed at them and spat in their eyes. So they beat her, proclaiming that it was for her own good because evil had gotten into her heart, and pain was necessary to pry open her heart to Rufizo.

Finally, the couple tired of their experiment in charity. They took her from their house, blindfolded her, and pushed her off their carriage in the countryside far away from Dimushi, far away from their home.

During her stay with them, they had shaved her head (to cure her of her vanity, they said) and dressed her in plain cotton rags that hid her young, lithe figure (to cure her of her lust, they said). Gin was mistaken at first as a boy by those she encountered, and she found that there were advantages to pretending to be a boy. By looking tough as a boy, and by prominently displaying on her belt a short sword that she stole from a hunting lodge, she could avoid a great deal of unpleasant attention.

She stole food at night from the fields, and during the day she wandered down to the Liru River to try to catch some fish.

All day long, laundresses worked next to the river, beating sheets and shirts against the rocks with a cleaning stick. Gin sat a little above the river from them and fished. She caught nothing, so after a while she gave up and just watched the washerwomen. When the women took their lunch break, she looked at them hungrily and swallowed.

An old woman saw the pair of hungry eyes peeking out from behind a tree and offered to share her lunch with the emaciated, dirty boy in rags. Gin thanked her.

The next day, Gin showed up again, and the old laundress shared her food with the boy again.

This went on for twenty days. Gin knelt down and put her forehead against the ground. "Granny, if I ever make it, I will repay your kindness a hundredfold."

The old woman spat on the ground. "You foolish child! You think I share my food with you because I expect a reward? I do it only because I think you are a sorry sight, and Tututika said all living things have a right to food. I would do no different for a stray dog or cat." She softened her voice. "I feed you so that you don't have to steal. A man who steals is a man who has lost all hope, and you're too young to have no hope."

Gin cried for the first time that she could remember when she heard this speech, and she refused to get up from her knees for many hours, no matter how much the old woman coaxed her.

The next day, Gin did not go back to the Liru River. She made her way back to the port of Dimushi, where the docks were perpetually busy. There, she found work as an errand boy for the dockmaster and shipping companies. Her thieving days were over.

Gin treasured the freedom that a boy's disguise brought her. She always kept her breasts tightly bound and her hair closely cropped.

She was also aggressive and quick to anger, sensitive to every slight, every perceived insult. Rumors of her skill with the sword became more exaggerated with every retelling, and so she kept herself safe without having to fight often—but when she did have to fight, she struck without warning and was often deadly.

Once, the dockmaster and a captain had trouble fitting all the captain's cargo into a ship's tight hold. Gin, who happened to be there, offered some suggestions that allowed all the boxes to be arranged so as to fit into the small space. From then on, the dockmaster and captains often consulted her for similar matters. She found that she had a talent for seeing the arrangement of things, for designing patterns and shapes and fitting oddly contoured bundles into tight spaces.

"You have a way of holding the bigger picture in your head," the dockmaster said. "You might be good at games."

He taught her to play *cüpa*. The game was played with formations of black and white stones on a grid, and the object was to surround the other player's stones with one's own and take over the board. It was a game of patterns and spaces, of seeing potentials and seizing opportunities.

Though Gin learned the rules quickly, she never could beat the dockmaster.

"You play well," the dockmaster said, "but you're impatient. Why do you immediately challenge me on every move, attacking before you have uncovered my real weakness? Why do you fight tenaciously for every tiny open space before you, to the neglect of the larger prize of a dominant board position?"

Gin shrugged.

"You play *cüpa* like you strut around the docks, as if you can't bear to be considered weak for even a moment. You play like you have something to prove."

Gin avoided the dockmaster's eyes. "Because I'm small, everyone has always acted as if they can push me around."

"And you hate that."

"I can't afford to appear soft—"

The dockmaster's voice took on a stern tone. "You dream of someday standing tall before men who're bigger than you, but you have not learned to bide your time. If you insist on fighting every fight that comes your way, you're simply letting them push you around in a different way. You will die young and foolish."

Gin sat still, thinking. Then she nodded.

After two weeks, Gin started winning against the dockmaster.

∽ ∾ ∽ ∾

The dockmaster, impressed, gave her some classical books on *cüpa*.

"These books explain the origin of *cüpa* as a simulation of war. If you study them, you will also understand how the game is entwined with military history and military strategy."

"I can't read," Gin said, embarrassed.

"Then it's time to learn." The dockmaster's eyes and voice were gentle. "My sister never learned to read, and she didn't understand that she had been betrayed by the man she married when he had her sign a contract that deprived her of her right to dower. You must learn to read to protect yourself. I'll teach you."

One day, while Gin was walking about the docks, a large man, a stranger, stopped her.

"I hate the sight of a scrawny little man like you strutting around with a sword. People here tell me you're a fighter, but I don't believe it. Either fight me and I'll bleed you out like a dirty piglet, or crawl between my legs and I'll let you live."

For a man of Géfica, crawling between another man's legs was a humiliation that could not be borne. Other men on the docks soon surrounded the pair, anticipating a show.

Gin looked at the man: He was tall and broad-shouldered, and he had arrogant eyes that told her he was used to bullying others to make himself feel good. But his face was smooth and his arms scarless, which mean that he hadn't spent much time in the dark alleys of Dimushi. He didn't know how to really fight. She could kill him before he even knew what was happening.

But then she would have to leave behind this life she had just started to build for herself. She would not be able to finish learning how to read from the dockmaster. She could take the insult or kill the man. These were the only choices. There was nothing in between.

Slowly, Gin put her sword on the ground and began to crawl between the man's legs.

The crowd booed, the man laughed, and Gin felt her ears grow red.

A darkness rose in her heart, urging her to unsheath her sword and plunge it into the soft belly of the man standing over her. But she forced the darkness down.

*If you insist on fighting every fight that comes your way, you're simply letting them push you around in a different way.*

Afterward, Gin read the books on *cüpa* and military strategy in every free moment and dreamed impossible dreams.

Then came the rebellion, and all the world was turned upside down. The docks at Dimushi filled with naval ships and profiteers and smugglers, crowding out the regular merchants. There was less and less work.

One day, the dockmaster called Gin to his room.

"I'm too old for this chaos. I'm retiring to my home village." He paused, and smiled at Gin. Then he handed Gin a small pouch of loose gold. "This should be enough to get yourself a better sword and some armor. Take care of yourself, daughter."

Gin looked at him. *Daughter*. She tried to speak, but no words came.

"I always knew," he said. "Your disguise is very good, but I grew up with many sisters. I hope someday you can live in a world where you don't have to be afraid to be a woman."

Gin got herself a better sword and leather armor. To avoid impressment by the Imperial navy, she left Dimushi to join a roving gang of bandits. They roamed through the countryside and waved whatever flag was convenient. When the Imperial army showed up, they became loyal Xana militias taking arms to support the emperor. When rebels showed up, they became brave Amu or Cocru warriors fighting for freedom.

After a while, she found that she had a knack for leading men. Limited by her small frame, she was not a great fighter on the field, but she was careful and calculating, and men who followed her won many victories in surprising ways.

Yet, because she was so unimposing physically, men attributed the success of her plans to luck rather than skill. She was forever being brushed aside when the bandits struggled for power.

Gin drifted through Haan, through Rima, through Faça, serving briefly in various armies and hoping that she could rise through the ranks. But the officers of the various armies did not take suggestions from this small-statured man seriously. Commanders assumed that she couldn't know anything about military strategy because she didn't kill many men with her own hands.

Even the great Marshal Zyndu, whose gambit at Wolf's Paw she greatly admired, did not give her a chance. She had bribed the guards to give her an audience with him and presented a strategy for how to quickly eliminate the empire's last bits of resistance in Géjira without killing many more people. But Marshal Zyndu had called her ideas dishonorable.

Gin then joined Kuni's ragtag army as they set off for Dasu. She had heard that Lord Garu was a good master who thirsted for men of talent, but she could think of no way to see him. In her frustration she got into a drunken rage at a restaurant in Daye and smashed the tables in that place. This was against the strict discipline that Than Carunoco and Mün Çakri maintained in Kuni's army. Gin was imprisoned and scheduled to be flogged publicly.

Cogo Yelu happened to be walking by the whipping post that morning.

"Does King Kuni want a great warrior?" the man being punished shouted at him.

Cogo Yelu stopped and looked at the man tied to the post. He was in his undershirt only, and the uniform at his feet told Cogo that the man was a lowly corporal. "You do not look like a great warrior."

"A man who can kill several people with a sword is merely a living weapon. A great warrior can kill thousands of men with just his mind."

Cogo was intrigued. He ordered the prisoner, a man by the name of Mazoti, released.

∽ ∾ ∽ ∾

A *cüpa* set sat in Cogo Yelu's front hall. The stones on the board were laid out in a famous pattern. It was the final formation of a game concluded two hundred years ago between two great *cüpa* masters: Count Soing, the great Amu strategist, playing with white stones, had conceded the game to Duke Fino, the famed adviser to the Cocru court, playing with black stones.

"Do you play?" Cogo asked.

Mazoti nodded. "I've always thought that Soing should not have given up. There was hope yet."

Cogo was not a great player, but he was a connoisseur of *cüpa* history and strategy. Mazoti's statement made no sense. Most of the board was occupied by black stones. The white stones, clustered in the center, had few breaths left.

Every student of *cüpa* knew that there was no way for Soing to escape from his hopeless situation.

"Care to show me how?" Cogo asked. They sat down to play.

Cogo immediately sent the black stones on attack.

Mazoti placed a stone far away from his army, in a corner of the board. Cogo evaluated the position. There was no threat. It was a pointless move.

The white stones seemed to retreat before the black stones. Instead of engaging, Mazoti only made the situation more hopeless.

"You're certain?" Cogo asked.

Mazoti nodded again, his face unreadable.

Cogo placed a new column of black stones to cut off Mazoti's retreat. Mazoti's only choice was now a battle of attrition at the center, where Cogo had an overwhelming advantage.

Confidently, Cogo placed another stone.

Mazoti's next stone choked off one of his own breaths. It was a mistake that even a rookie would not have made.

Cogo sighed and shook his head. He struck the final blow and took half of Mazoti's stones prisoner. Where Mazoti's army had been, there was now an empty expanse on the board, testament to Mazoti's blunder.

Cogo prepared to accept Mazoti's surrender. No player could recover from such a large loss.

But Mazoti said nothing and placed another stone in the corner. The two white stones there were like two lonely scouts with no support.

There was nothing else to do but for Cogo to take over the center, and fill in the empty expanse vacated by Mazoti with his own stones.

Mazoti placed one more stone in the corner. The three white stones looked less lonely than two. But it was still hopeless.

As he took over the empty space in the middle, Cogo frowned and hesitated. Somehow, with his old white stones arranged into rigid ranks and columns gone, Mazoti's new white stones achieved a kind of nimble, loose formation that defied analysis. Every time Cogo thought he had figured out a way to choke off Mazoti's new army, the corporal managed to force a new opening. Gradually, the little group of white stones in the corner connected with one another and coalesced into a growing force.

Too late, Cogo realized that he had been too greedy and intent on claiming the middle. Mazoti's army began to thrust into the soft underbelly of Cogo's formations, and whenever Cogo patched up one vulnerability, Mazoti seemed to find two more. Now it was the black stones, locked into unwieldy ranks and rows with no life, that were on the run.

*Clink.* Mazoti placed another stone onto the board. Cogo watched helplessly as Mazoti's army completed the march to the other corner of the board, dividing his black stones into isolated groups. Now it would only be a matter of time before the black stones would be driven into even more disarray and eliminated from the board.

Cogo put down his bowl of stones. "Lord Garu must meet you."

## CHAPTER FORTY-ONE

# THE MARSHAL

THE TENTH MONTH IN THE FIRST YEAR OF THE PRINCIPATE.

Kuni Garu closed his mouth and acted as if nothing was out of the ordinary.

He bowed again. "I apologize. Miss Gin Mazoti, I'm all ears for your advice on my state."

They sat down on the ground around the low table in *mipa rari*. Kuni Garu took care to pour tea for Gin.

Gin was touched. A king was serving her. Even though he knew she was a woman, he treated her just like the great strategist that she claimed to be. Perhaps this was a lord that she could serve, and serve well.

But first, she would test him again.

"Lord Garu," she said, in the familiar manner that she knew his followers used with him. "What position will you give me?"

"How many soldiers can you lead?"

"If you give me ten men, I can make them fight like fifty. If you give me a hundred men, I can make them fight like a thousand. If you give me a thousand men, I can conquer Rui in five days."

Kuni Garu hesitated. There was a thin line between arrogant delusion and genius, and he was inclined to think that this madwoman was closer to the former. But Cogo Yelu had never been wrong, and Kuni had learned to listen to the counsel of those he trusted.

"The more the better then?"

Gin nodded.

"Then I must make you the Marshal of Dasu."

Gin sucked in her breath. A woman marshal was an idea that did not even exist in fairy tales. Lord Garu really was different.

"Lord Garu, I will be frank. I believe you are in a weak position. Your family is held hostage by the hegemon. You have no more than three thousand soldiers under your command, while the hegemon can call on his own fifty thousand men and fifty thousand more allied troops from the other Tiro states. You have brave commanders following you, but none of them have the capacity to make your vision come true. Most would think that you have no chance."

Kuni Garu nodded. "Yet you believe you can defeat Mata Zyndu?"

"I cannot match him on the battlefield in single combat, and I will never be able to repeat his feat of daring in the air over Zudi. Yet Mata Zyndu is impulsive, emotional, and he relies on brute valor rather than sound tactics. He has no understanding of the art of drawing power from men's hearts: politics.

"He can shed tears when a prized horse dies, yet he doesn't understand how forcefully requisitioning provisions from the peasantry weakens his support.

"He has set up the new Tiro states in a haphazard fashion, rewarding the undeserving and passing over the worthy. He is like a crossbow bolt near the end of its flight: seeming strength disguising terminal fall."

Kuni and Mazoti stayed in Cogo's house for three days and three nights. They shared food from the same plate as they debated and slept on mattresses placed next to each other on the floor as they discussed strategy, and Kuni held the reins of the carriage personally as he drove Mazoti around Daye when they both wanted a breath of fresh air.

The palace issued a formal proclamation that King Kuni had decided to name the Marshal of Dasu. The whole army was abuzz with rumors about who it would be. Mün Çakri and Than Carucono both had supporters, and betting pools were set up.

As the army on Dasu assembled outside Daye on the auspicious day, they faced a dais with the blue-whale-on-red-sea banner flying high over it. King Kuni led the ministers and soldiers in prayer to Kiji, patron of this island, and then asked the new Marshal of Dasu to stand up.

The soldiers strained to get a good look at the new supreme commander of all Dasu forces. But they rubbed their eyes and looked again. Could it be? How was this possible?

There, on the dais, in a bright-red dress, was a woman. Not a very good-looking woman to be sure, with her shaven head and thin figure, but there could be no doubt. The new Marshal of Dasu was not a man.

King Kuni bowed down to her three times, as was dictated in the ancient rites of Tiro kings.

"I entrust the army of Dasu to you, Gin Mazoti," said Kuni. "From this day forward, whatever you have decided about the affairs of the army, let no man, not even me, gainsay."

He untied his sword from his belt and handed it to Gin. "I am not a noted swordsman, but this sword is a gift from a dear friend. I once slew a great white serpent with it, and it was the first weapon to make Emperor Erishi cower in fear. May this blade be as lucky in your hands as it has been in mine." Gin bowed in *jiri* and accepted.

The soldiers below the dais watched the ceremony in stunned silence, but now they could no longer stay quiet.

"Soldiers of Dasu." Gin Mazoti raised her voice to be heard above the rising murmurs. "The world will be as confused as you when they see me. And in their confusion, we will strike them down."

ᔕ ᔓ ᔕ ᔓ

Kindo Marana almost spit out his tea as he heard the news that Dasu's new marshal was a woman.

"What's next? Will the soldiers of Dasu now hold needlepoint classes and put on makeup before battle?" He laughed, tried to drink, and had to stop to laugh some more.

He could not imagine how this foolish Kuni Garu ever managed to get into Pan and capture Emperor Erishi. He had been lucky once, but luck would not favor him again. Kuni Garu was doomed to die on the tiny island.

Than Carucono and Mün Çakri seethed as they sat around the table.

"Gentlemen," Gin began the meeting. "I am not so stupid as to not understand that you are unhappy with my elevation."

Than and Mün had pressed Kuni Garu in private to explain the decision.

"We've followed you since the days you were a bandit!"

"What has she *done*? Nothing!"

But Kuni had demurred, saying only that he did not think that talent cared whether it was found in one Tiro state or another, or in men of noble or common birth, or even whether it wore a robe or a dress. This was as hard to argue against as it was unhelpful.

Than found it hard to look at and address the new marshal properly. Even sitting down, he and Mün towered over her. She looked like a woman and also not like a woman: her shaved head, her scarred face, the muscles in her arms and calloused fingers—they contrasted with her silk dress, her low voice, and her . . . breasts.

And she looked straight at them instead of lowering her eyes demurely.

"A woman is often weaker than a man physically," Gin continued. "And that means she must use a different set of techniques when she wishes to overcome a stronger opponent. She must turn his strength against him, let him defeat himself by overexertion, throw him off balance. She must not be ashamed to benefit from every advantage available to her and break the rules of warfare established by men."

Mün and Than nodded reluctantly at this. Her words, at least, did make sense.

"Dasu is far weaker than the other Tiro states and certainly than Zyndu's Cocru. Yet our king dreams of victory and of one day, perhaps, ascending to the Imperial Throne. It seems to me that being a woman, I may have a better sense of the hard decisions that must be made to bring about Dasu's rise from its present weakness. I cannot inspire the soldiers by my personal valor and deeds of strength, and so I will need your support and faith to put my plan into action."

Mün and Than drank their tea. They found that they were not as angry as they had thought.

"The history books are full of examples of young commanders establishing their authority with the common soldier through terror and discipline. They would put the troops through some silly exercise and then flog or behead those judged insolent. Yet, because I'm a woman, if I were to do this I would be called a petty castrating harpy, a shrew in need of a man's firm hand. Instead of respect I would only create resentment. Such is the way of the world.

"So, I will need your ideas and help, gentlemen, on earning the hearts of our soldiers."

On the advice of Mün and Than, Marshal Mazoti immediately abolished the marching drills. "Being able to parade around in synchrony is useless on the battlefield," she declared, and the assembled soldiers cheered.

Instead, training now primarily took the form of war exercises. The Dasu army was divided into operating units of various sizes. Then they were put through simulated battles involving different scenarios: assaulting a beachhead, defending or taking a fortress, preparing for an ambush in hills and forests. During the war exercises, sword blades and the tips of spears were wrapped with heavy cloth to reduce the chances of serious injury, but other than that, the officers and soldiers were encouraged to make the exercises as realistic as possible.

The new marshal told her officers that their job was not only to carry out the orders of the chain of command, but to improvise on the basis of changing battlefield conditions. Every officer, Mazoti explained, from herself all the way down to a lowly corporal leading a squad, needed to think of themselves as the head of a living organism fighting for survival, and every advantage must exploited. If that involved unorthodox tactics that broke written or unwritten laws of war, so be it. "In war, our only goal is to win."

Mazoti held *cüpa* lessons and promoted the game throughout the army. Whether playing the game really improved strategic thinking or not, the effort sent a message that valor and strength alone were not enough, and had to be accompanied by tactical thinking at all levels.

The war exercises, due to their realism, took a heavy toll on the soldiers. Everyone had bruises, and more than a few men suffered broken bones as they fell into pit traps set by the opposing side. Sometimes mock battles were lost when one side was fooled by "enemies" who dressed up as civilians.

For the most part, the soldiers did not complain; they were rewarded for quick thinking and bravery during these exercises. Soldiers received bonuses or had their pay docked depending on how well they performed, and officers were promoted or demoted based on their display of tactical brilliance.

Even the most realistic war games could only do so much. To further the soldiers' training, Mazoti sent small detachments on raiding missions to pirate havens in the islets to the far north. These skirmishes gave the men experience of real warfare that could not be obtained any other way. Whatever booty they captured they got to keep.

She wasn't just teaching the officers and foot soldiers; she was also teaching them *how* to teach. The Dasu army was going to have to grow a lot if the snake was going to swallow an elephant, and she needed to install values and practices that would scale.

But training was not the only thing Mazoti focused on. The marshal also held meetings with small groups of ordinary soldiers to hear their concerns. These meetings, suggested by Than and Mün, were based on the administrative experiences of Lord Garu and Prime Minister Yelu, and they were as effective with the fighting men as they were with ordinary citizens in Zudi and Dasu. Mazoti improved the food served in the mess halls and asked Kuni to increase the pensions that would be paid to the families of those who died or were wounded in battle. After one man complained that he did not have good shoes for marching in tough terrain, Mazoti spent months studying various designs for shoes used by the other Tiro states—her army, after all, was composed of deserters from all over Dara—and made the best one standard equipment for Dasu.

Many veterans of the rebellion had come to Dasu because the other Tiro states rejected them: They had lost hands or limbs in war, and most commanders deemed them no longer useful. But thinking of Muru and the others, Kuni accepted these men into his army—if they wanted to continue their military careers—and he was prepared to debate Gin if she objected; he didn't want to interfere with the marshal's authority in military affairs, but this, he felt, was a matter of principle.

Somewhat to his surprise, Mazoti simply nodded when he brought up the topic.

"You're not concerned about their less-than-perfect bodies?" he probed.

"We all have experiences that shape us," Mazoti replied, and would say no more.

She worked with the craftsmen and inventors Cogo had recruited to Dasu to create new harnesses and mechanical devices that could replace some of the functionality of lost body parts. The tension in mechanical hands made of bamboo wrapped in cloth could be adjusted with ox sinew until the owners could wield spears effectively, and soldiers who lost a leg could recover some field mobility with spring-loaded peg legs that adjusted to the terrain automatically. These devices were expensive and had to be custom-made for each, but Mazoti considered it money well spent to extend the careers of battle-hardened veterans. In return, the veterans admired the marshal and pledged their lives to the cause of Dasu.

Lady Risana came to see the marshal.

Gin wasn't sure what to make of the visit. She knew that Kuni's new wife was one of his trusted advisers, and it was said that Kuni relied on her judgment when he received conflicting counsel. But Gin had only seen her dance with Kuni sometimes, after dinner. She had certainly never heard Risana express much interest in war.

To her relief, Risana did not attempt the kind of small talk that Gin dreaded. She simply stated her purpose.

"Marshal, I think you should make use of the women of Dasu."

A large number of women had come to Dasu to seek their fortune at Kuni's call, many with specialized skills: herbalists, cosmeticians, dancers, weavers, dressmakers, entertainers, and other tradeswomen. Some had come with husbands; others were independent and single, either by choice or having lost their families during the rebellion.

Gin was confused. "I will. A marching army draws them naturally, like carrion drawing vultures." She was thinking of the unofficial camp followers that every army needed and had to tolerate: laundresses, cooks, prostitutes, and so on.

But Risana shook her head. "I don't mean that."

Gin regarded her coolly. "Few women have the strength to draw a standard bow or to wield a five-pound sword effectively. What would be the point?"

Instead of answering her, Risana walked over to the corner of Gin's room, where a bamboo flagpole leaned against the wall. She took the pole and laid it across the gap between Gin's desk and the windowsill. Then she leapt onto the pole, as graceful as a siskin alighting on a branch. She twirled in place on the tips of her feet; the slender bamboo pole barely dipped.

"Lightness can be an advantage," said Risana, "especially if you need to be in the air."

A fog seemed to dissipate from Mazoti's vision. She imagined slender frames and lighter bodies on battle kites that soared higher, on balloons that stayed aloft longer, on airships that sailed farther and carried more weapons. . . .

She bowed to Risana in *jiri*. "You have opened my eyes to an advantage that all the Tiro states have been blind to. It is inexcusable that I, of all people, could not see it."

Risana leapt off the bamboo pole, landed, and bowed back. "Even a brilliant mind sometimes needs a dull stone to sharpen itself."

Gin smiled at her. "But only some women will qualify for these tasks. I think you have still more suggestions."

"The women of Dasu have many skills. An army does not need only to fight; there's also what happens before and what happens after."

Gin pondered this for a while. Then she nodded. "Dasu is lucky to have you as her queen."

Besides calling for nimble and agile women who craved adventure to serve in Dasu's air force—for now limited only to kite riding and ballooning—Marshal Mazoti also began recruiting women to serve in an auxiliary corps within the army itself.

Herbalists and dressmakers made excellent nurses and field surgeons—the herbal remedies were effective at dulling pain, and sewing silk and lace trained steady fingers for stitching wounds; cosmeticians and weavers improved battlefield camouflage; and entertainers and dancers devised new marching songs and battle hymns that would raise morale and spread the message of Kuni's vision. Adding women meant more hands to repair and maintain armor, more fingers trained as bowyers and fletchers, more bodies and minds to take up the endless tasks that needed to be done in an army.

The women auxiliaries also took part in and advised on other tasks that men carried out: the herbalists made suggestions to the cooks so that a healthier diet could be adopted to prevent diseases common to marching armies; the dressmakers and weavers shared tips with the armorers to improve the production of armor, leggings, shoes, and so on.

Besides these noncombat duties, Gin also gave the women auxiliaries basic combat training so that they could protect themselves or act as emergency reinforcements in a pinch. If others did not expect them to be capable of fighting, that would give Dasu an advantage.

Slowly but surely, jokes about Marshal Mazoti became affectionate rather than dismissive. When officers saluted her, there was now real respect in their eyes.

CHAPTER FORTY-TWO

# THE DANDELION RIPENS

DASU: THE SIXTH MONTH IN THE SECOND YEAR OF THE PRINCIPATE.

Now that it had been a year since Kuni Garu had come to Dasu, Cogo was finally beginning to see the fruits of his efforts at attracting men (and women) of talent to the island. Rumors spread all over Dara that in Dasu, a hardworking man could count on light taxes and fair laws and that interesting ideas would get a fair hearing, and even a woman would be treated with respect and given a chance to prove the worth of her thoughts.

Many came: inventors with new contraptions, warriors of great strength, magicians claiming new knowledge, herbalists with novel recipes, entertainers with fresh acts—Cogo welcomed them all and tried to sift through the charlatans for nuggets of gold.

"A method for converting base lead into gold," an alchemist with white hair and a beard that hung to the ground proclaimed. "But I'll need a great deal of funding to build a laboratory."

Cogo nodded and politely invited the alchemist to stay in Dasu and raise money from private sources. Next.

"A mixture of potent herbs that will soften stones so that they crumble at the touch," an old woman from Faça explained. "I've been putting on magic shows with it for years."

"Have you tried to approach miners with this?" asked Cogo.

The old woman nodded. "The mine owners tell me they're not interested since they can find plenty of men willing to break their backs wielding the pickax and hammer."

"Not to mention firework powder," said Cogo.

"But firework powder requires saltpeter, the supply of which is limited, not to mention that firework powder is extremely dangerous. I know there's potential in this, if developed properly."

Cogo wasn't sure what potential she was thinking of, but at least it didn't sound completely useless. "We would be honored to have you stay with us as the king's guest."

"A method for extracting energy from volcanic heat," a middle-aged man with only one arm said. "I have a prototype that draws on the heat of the earth to boil water, and the resulting steam can be directed to turn a wheel."

Cogo wasn't sure how this could be useful, but it seemed interesting. He politely invited the man to stay in Daye and build a prototype for demonstration.

"A treatise on the relationship of the gods to mankind, and how the proper model for the state may be derived from the pattern of rivers and winds," a young scholar with eyes full of zeal declared. "I will require the king's undivided attention."

Cogo's eyes glazed over as he unrolled the manuscript scroll. The raised logograms were elaborate and painted in color, and the zyndari letters were as dense as flies on honey. He rolled up the manuscript carefully and offered the man a free meal. "King Kuni is somewhat preoccupied with lesser matters," he said. "But I have a feeling that the hegemon would be extremely appreciative of such a work. I can write you a letter of introduction."

It was a very busy time in Daye.

∽ ∾ ∽ ∾

Luan Zya came to Dasu dejected and tired.

"I have some things I'd like to discuss with King Kuni," he said to Cogo, who welcomed him. "But don't tell him I've arrived yet."

"It's just as well. The king is away temporarily with Lady Risana to speak with some of the elders on the eastern tip of the island."

"I see the king is as interested as ever in the details of administration. Would that the other Tiro kings were as diligent."

"But you and the king are old friends," Cogo said. "Why don't you want to go see him right away?"

"It is true that we're old friends," Luan said. "But this time, I come not for friendship."

"Ah," said Cogo, finally understanding. "You have decided that you may wish to serve him."

"And what better way to judge a lord's worth than to get to know his followers first?"

"Then I will introduce you to the marshal."

Luan appraised Gin's clean-shaven head, the scars on her face that matched his own, her thin but strong arms. Her clean and simple dress fit her sleek and muscular frame well. She was like a wild lynx, all energy and fury under tight control. He liked her.

"Yes, I'm a woman," Gin said, since Luan was staring. "You're surprised?"

Luan chuckled. "Forgive me. I had heard the rumors, but it's difficult to know how much to believe of such reports. Though considering how long I've known King Kuni, nothing should surprise me. When I told him my plan to ride the crubens through Amu Strait, he was the one who assured *me* that the plan wasn't crazy."

They grabbed each other by the elbows, and each felt the heat of the other's hands through the thin sleeves. Gin was pleased that Luan's grip was strong. He did not condescend to her.

Over the next few days, Gin took him to observe some of the war exercises, and Luan was impressed. He had never seen training done this way in any of the armies of Dara.

He showed Gin some plans he had devised for constructing siege machinery with more portable components for ease of assembly and transportation; Gin immediately pointed out their flaws—Luan might be intelligent, but designing machines on paper was very different from making them real and useful in the field.

Luan looked dejected.

"Well," Gin said gruffly. "The basic ideas are not bad. I can probably help you make them work."

Then Cogo took Luan to see some of the more interesting inventions he had saved for Kuni to evaluate, and Luan grew excited also and discussed their virtues with Cogo.

Evenings, the three stayed up late conversing, drinking, and singing in the little house that passed for a palace in Daye. Their laughter and voices were harmonious, the sound of people who admired and respected one another as consummate craftsmen in their distinct realms. The torches cast their flickering shadows against the paper window of the little house, and it seemed sometimes as though they were three spirits, three dancing pillars that held up the roof of the palace.

"Lord Garu, in a thousand years, how do you think people will remember Emperor Mapidéré?"

Coming from someone else, it would have been an invitation to repeat the universal condemnation of a tyrant. But Luan Zya was not an ordinary man.

"I've changed my mind many times on this question," Kuni admitted. "It's easy to say that he was a tyrant who did nothing good. But it would also be untrue. I was a provincial boy, and yet I got to see some of the wonders of all the old Tiro states because of his forceful resettlement of people all across Dara.

"We talk often of the hundreds of thousands who died in Mapidéré's wars, but we rarely speak of the many lives that might have been lost had he not stopped the incessant petty wars between the Tiro states. We talk often of the many who were forced to labor in his

Mausoleum, but we rarely speak of the many who would have died from diseases or starvation without the reservoirs and roads he built. Only the gods know if the emphases and omissions in our histories will sway the opinions of men down the ages. A man's legacy is a hard thing to foresee, especially when passions still run hot, and it is so much easier to speak ill than well."

Luan nodded. They sat next to each other, and before them was a great bonfire on the beach of Daye and the endless darkness beyond of the open ocean. Above them the stars blinked in the pristine sky like the eyes of the gods.

"Things are rarely simple when it comes to judging a man who did much to change the world." Luan took a long puff on his pipe, collecting his thoughts. "You're right that the passage of years has a way of changing minds. When the first Ano settlers, refugees of the sunken Western Continent, arrived in Dara, all these islands were inhabited by natives like the people of Tan Adü. To the Adüans, our founding fathers were murderers and tyrants of no redeeming value. Yet today we walk on land they conquered and celebrate festivals that they brought with them. And few of us stop to reflect on the blood debt all of us owe.

"Emperor Mapidéré justified his wars by arguing that he would unify all the squabbling Tiro states under one throne and turn all swords into plowshares. Indeed, he even sought to confiscate all weapons after the Unification, melt them down, and construct from the metal eight statues of the gods to be placed at the center of Pan. That effort was abandoned in the end as too difficult, though many thought he merely wanted to remove the ability of the populace to resist the state with force.

"But the emperor's words were not mere self-serving propaganda. Many scholars in Xana and the other Tiro states supported his vision of peace through unification and conquest. The bloody, endless wars between the Tiro states, spurred by the invention of ever more powerful weapons and larger armies, frightened many, and it was thought that a war to end all wars might be preferable to the interminable attrition due to a balance of powers.

"Had Mapidéré patiently spent more time on consolidating his rule, rather than pursuing the mirage of immortality; had he focused more effort on just administration and lasting institutions, rather than megalomaniacal engineering projects—it's possible that the empire would have survived more than two generations. Had that been the case, in another hundred years, men who remember the old Tiro states would have all passed into death, and the new generations would have known nothing but a unified peace under Xana. Memories of the death and suffering caused by wars do not last beyond three generations, and people would remember Emperor Mapidéré fondly, as a visionary, a lawgiver who gave us peace."

Kuni Garu threw more wood on the fire. "You are a heretic, Luan. Few dare to think such thoughts."

"Sometimes I wonder if I'm mad. I spent my entire life seeking revenge against Mapidéré, trying to restore the independent Tiro states, to break apart what he fused together. But when the moment of victory finally arrived, I found myself mourning him because I had spent so much time studying him that I understood him better than his own ministers and children. I may have helped to bring about the fall of Xana, but Mapidéré, in some way, managed to bring about the fall of my convictions.

"After you came to Dasu, I went back to Haan to help King Cosugi to rebuild. I worked tirelessly to build up Haan's strength, but everywhere I looked, there was only the rise of old conflicts and ancient enmity. When Emperor Mapidéré conquered Haan, he had deposed the old nobles and elites from power, and in their place he had put in a new elite of bureaucrats and merchants who prospered. When King Cosugi returned, he took the new elites out and moved the old elites in. Those who were politically astute profited, while others lost all they had. Yet, for most people—the fishermen, the peasants, the prostitutes and beggars and longshoremen—life did not change. They went on suffering as they had before: Officials remained corrupt, tax collectors stayed cruel, the corvée assignments were still onerous, and the threat of war ever present.

"I heard a children's song in Haan:

*When Haan falls, the people suffer.*
*When Haan rises, the people suffer.*
*When Haan is poor, the people are poor.*
*When Haan is rich, the people are poor.*
*When Haan is strong, the people die.*
*When Haan is weak, the people die."*

"Whatever the nobles and kings say they believe in, they always treat the people as mere stones on the *cüpa* board," Kuni said.

There was no irony in his speech. In his heart, he still thought of himself as a commoner, a man who had nothing to his name and had to beg his friends for a place to sleep.

Luan looked directly at him, his eyes blazing in the reflected light of the bonfire. "King Cosugi did not see anything wrong with the new draft to raise an army to reconquer old Haan territories from North Géfica, the new corvée to rebuild the Palace of Ginpen, the new taxes to pay for a grand coronation.

"I went to the ruins of my ancestral estate and prayed to the soul of my departed father. Though I thought I had accomplished what I promised him on the day of his death, my heart was not at peace.

"As the moon rose, I saw the light illuminate an ancient quote from the Ano Classics, carved into one of the broken lintels: 'All life is an experiment.'"

"A fitting quote for a scholar of Haan," said Kuni.

Luan smiled. "A fitting quote for any man or woman of Dara. I understood then that I had been lacking in my vision. I thought my duty was to restore Haan, but Haan is not King Cosugi or the burned-down palace or the ruins of the great estates or the dead nobles and their descendants pining for glory—these are but parts of an experiment at a way of life for the people of Haan, her true essence. When the experiment has proven to be a failure, one must be willing to try new paths, new ways of doing things.

"I could not bear to walk on my old path, a path that did not serve the people of Haan, any longer. That is why I came to you.

"For Mata Zyndu, there is no law but the use of force, no higher ideal than martial glory. And the world he created is a mirror of his mind. When King Thufi died 'mysteriously' on the way to Écofi, rumor had it that his last words were: 'I should have remained a shepherd.'

"The rebellion was supposed to usher in a more just world, and yet nothing really changed."

Kuni looked back at Luan, his heart quickening. "Do you think we are words written on a page by the gods, and that there will always be rich and poor, the powerful and the powerless, noble and commoner? Do you think that all our dreams are doomed to forever fail?"

Luan stood up and walked steadily toward the ocean. His dark figure shimmered through the dancing flames, and his voice blended with the roar of the fire. "I refuse to believe in the futility of change, because I have seen how the lowly dandelion, with time and patience, can crack the strongest paving stone. Lord Garu, will you complete the dream of Emperor Mapidéré, but avoid his mistakes? Can you unite the Islands of Dara under one crown and bring about lasting peace, while lessening the burden of the people?"

Lady Risana had quietly appeared out of the dark night to join them by the fire. Noiselessly, she sat by Kuni and put her hand on his shoulder. Her hands flickered in the firelight, and Kuni again felt a clarity of mind and a willingness to speak difficult truths. He was not perfect; he was not a god; he would accept that.

"I don't know how to answer you, Luan. I've always told myself I loved the people, but how can I speak of love when I can't even raise my own children? I've always told myself I'm a compassionate lord, but how can I speak of compassion when I've killed so many and betrayed so many others?

"I cannot say that I'm a good man, only that I'm a man who tried to do good. I like to believe that the people will remember me fondly, but I also know that the legacies of men cannot be foreseen during their lifetimes. I do not know if I'm the man who will complete the task you dream of, for that is a question that must be asked of our descendants in a thousand years."

Luan laughed. "Lord Garu, this is why I serve you. The right path is not revealed to us by the gods or ancient sages, but must be found by ourselves through experimentation. You are uncertain, and in your uncertainty you will always seek to ask questions rather than believing yourself to possess all the answers. An ant who rides a dandelion seed will land wherever the seed lands. Men of talent will be judged in the light of the legacies of those they served."

"*Géüdéü co loteré ma, pirufénrihua nélo*. All life is an experiment," Kuni said. "We are all swallows flying in the storm, and if we should land safely, it will be due to equal measures of luck and skill."

In the silence, Risana began to sing an old Classical Ano song:

*The Four Placid Seas are as wide as the years are long.*
*A wild goose flies over a pond, leaving behind a voice in the wind.*
*A man passes through this world, leaving behind a name.*

The three of them sat quietly around the fire, until the flame burned itself out and dawn arrived.

## CHAPTER FORTY-THREE

# FIRST STRIKE

RUI: THE SEVENTH MONTH IN THE THIRD YEAR OF THE PRINCIPATE.

For more than a year now, the reports from the airships' surveillance flyovers of Dasu remained much the same. Gin Mazoti went on holding her strange war games instead of drilling the soldiers, and Cogo went on building new fisheries, roads, bridges, and other meaningless things that had no military use.

As far as Kindo Marana could tell, Kuni Garu was content to remain on Dasu, more like a gardener cultivating his plot than an ambitious warlord plotting military adventures.

But recently, his spies reported that Mazoti seemed to be up to something. On the southern coast of Dasu, right across the Dasu Channel from Rui, two hundred men were seen building ships. Their progress was slow, as they were shorthanded and among them there was no skilled shipwright. Marana intensified surveillance flights over the site. Mazoti seemed to be pushing her workers hard, and the airships reported witnessing workers being whipped.

A Dasu soldier even defected to Rui by stealing a tiny fishing boat and rowing over. Kindo Marana interrogated the man himself.

"Gin Mazoti is a cruel and heartless woman," the soldier, whose name was Luwen, told Marana. "She's ordered us to build twenty transport ships within three months. When I told her that this was impossible, she had me strung up by my thumbs and whipped until I fainted." Luwen lifted his shirt to show the whipping scars on his back, and even Marana winced at the sight.

"She said that if her orders were not carried out, I would be executed on the last day of her three-month schedule. I had no choice but to desert."

Marana shook his head. Just like a woman, full of wishful thinking and no understanding of the scale of things. Did she think that building a heavy transport ship was like raising a barn? Two hundred men in three months would not even finish two transport ships, let alone twenty. Kuni Garu was a fool to trust his army to this woman, and it appeared that she was capable only of venting her rage on hapless soldiers, not planning logically.

He ordered Luwen be given a good meal and be seen by a doctor.

It was midnight, and the people of the tiny village of Phada, on the northern coast of Rui, were asleep.

A great explosion woke them. As they scrambled out of their houses, they saw a sight that seemed to come out of a myth. A great crater had opened in the ground, and out of the hole, men in full armor emerged, their swords drawn.

Kindo Marana was awoken by his chatelain. The sound of alarm was everywhere.

"Sire, the Dasu army has surrounded Kriphi."

Marana could not understand what he was being told. How could Mazoti have constructed so many ships so quickly? And even if she managed to do so, how could they have crossed the Dasu Channel unchallenged, as the channel was patrolled by Marana's ships?

He dressed and ascended the city walls to see for himself.

"Kindo Marana!" Gin Mazoti shouted up at him in the torchlight. "Surrender. We have taken over the air base at Mount Kiji. All the other garrisons on Rui have surrendered, and you're alone."

SIX MONTHS EARLIER.

While Marana's airships crisscrossed the skies of Dasu and his navy patrolled the Dasu Channel, men were hard at work below them, under the sea, beneath the seafloor.

Emperor Mapidéré's vision of the Grand Tunnels had been long abandoned. The half-finished tunnels, deep holes into the earth that terminated at dead ends, could be found all over the islands. Over the years, weather, erosion, and flooding turned most of them into deep wells, mute relics of a bygone age.

The entrance to the aborted tunnel from Dasu to Rui was located several miles down the shore from Mazoti's makeshift shipyard, where two hundred men put on a show that drew the attention of Marana's airships.

Meanwhile, a grain storage depot had been built over the abandoned shaft of the tunnel, and carriages could be seen pulling into the depot and then leaving, apparently to gather more goods from the rest of the island. Marana's airships took note of the activity but attributed it to merely another effort to stockpile grain against a lean year.

The airships could not see that the carriages entering the depot were much lighter than the ones that left it. They were not carrying things *into* the depot but *away* from it. Instead of grain, the carts carried dirt, rocks, and earth excavated from under the sea.

Luan Zya had combed through the strange inventions gathered by Cogo Yelu and found a few of particular interest. One was a method of splitting stone. Water mixed with certain salts extracted from herbs gathered and prepared by the inventor, an old Faça herbalist, could be poured onto stone surfaces, where the paste would seep into the cracks, large and small. After the rock had been stewed in this brine for a while, a second, different solution of salts would then be poured over the rock, and where the two mixtures came into contact, crystals formed.

Like ice in winter, millions of tiny crystals growing in the cracks exerted a force that pried granite and schist apart, and made solid walls of rock as soft as cheese.

The second invention that Luan Zya selected was a way to pump air with a hand-cranked bellows into a sealed tank of water until the water, under great pressure, shot out of a hose. The pressurized stream of water could be focused to strike at any surface with great force. When this water was brought to bear on the rocks softened with the mixture of salts, the rocks crumbled like wet sand.

The combination of these two inventions allowed tunneling through deep rock at speeds that were impossible to conceive. Best of all, it required no use of firework powder, and so was safe and undetectable by surveying airships.

For six months, the Dasu army toiled in secret, completing the dream of Emperor Mapidéré to build a path between Dasu and Rui that went under the sea.

RUI: THE SEVENTH MONTH IN THE THIRD YEAR OF THE PRINCIPATE.

*The shipyard was only a decoy,* Kindo Marana thought. *I was fooled by a simple trick.*

He had always been a careful man, but he was too focused on what could be seen and measured, what could be marked down in the notebooks of scouts flying over Dasu. He had been caught by what lay beneath the numbers, hidden by the appearance of superficiality, under the ocean waves.

He imagined the Dasu army emerging from beneath the sea, an endless stream of men erupting onto the surface like a fresh lava flow. It was a trick that he himself had used on Wolf's Paw against the hesitating General Roma. Mazoti was not above copying her enemy's successes.

It felt like an unworthy loss, as though someone had taken advantage of a loophole in the tax code.

Luwen, the surrendered Dasu soldier, made his way next to Marana.

"We were both fooled," Kindo said. "You were just a pawn in her game. She whipped you not because she needed you to work harder, but to hide her real plans."

Luwen grinned at him. Marana looked back, and his face fell as he finally understood.

With one quick stroke, Luwen lopped off Marana's head. Then he leapt from the wall, holding aloft the head by its hair.

The Dasu soldiers below the wall had been prepared and caught Luwen safely with a taut cloth stretched out on poles. Mayhem and confusion reigned on the walls of Kriphi, and commanders still recovering from the shock of King Kindo's death debated whether to immediately surrender or try to negotiate for better terms.

Marshal Mazoti walked up to the man getting off the stretched canvas trampoline.

"Welcome back, Daf."

Daf cracked a smile. "How hard it is to foresee how life will turn out. Back when our corvée gang joined the rebellion, my brother and I thought we'd never be whipped again."

Mazoti clasped him by his arms. "Lord Garu and I will not forget your sacrifices. I hope your wounds have healed."

News of the conquest of Rui by Dasu ripped through the Islands of Dara like a tsunami. Mazoti was only the second opponent to ever triumph over the great Kindo Marana. The other Tiro states, already craving war, began to fight, intuiting that the hegemon would be distracted by the Dasu victory and not pay attention while they fought over more territories.

Zyndu immediately ordered King Cosugi of Haan and King Théca of North Géfica to increase their vigilance and send out their navies to aid the remnants of Marana's navy in a blockade of Dasu and Rui. He did not bother sending out a messenger to demand an explanation from Garu. What was there to explain? Garu, the man he once thought of as his brother, had rebelled against the hegemon. It was proof of his original treachery at Pan; he was a betrayer through and through.

Dasu still had no navy to speak of. Rui was also much farther away from the Big Island than Dasu was from Rui, so Mazoti's tunneling trick would not work a second time. Just like Mata Zyndu was once trapped on Wolf's Paw, he would now trap Kuni on Rui. It was still an island prison, just a bigger one.

But he would go visit Kuni's family.

Mira wandered the streets of Çaruza aimlessly. She browsed at the market stalls—she had enough money to buy anything she wanted, but nothing appealed to her. She was simply stalling for time, not willing to go back to the palace. At least here, in the streets, with the right dress, she could be anonymous and pretend to be just another Cocru lady of sophistication, instead of—

*Instead of what?*

She was angry with herself, with Mata, with the courtiers and ladies-in-waiting and the countless servants who surrounded the hegemon. Since coming back from Pan to Çaruza, her position had grown only more awkward. What was she? She still oversaw the preparation of Mata's meals and tidied his bedchamber, but ministers and couriers called her Lady Mira. Mata had not asked her to come to his bed, and yet everyone seemed to assume that she already visited it with regularity.

*I suppose I should ask to go home.*

But she never made such a request. Now that she had seen the world, had become used to being in the company of kings and dukes and generals, she wasn't sure if she could tolerate the cold glances of the villagers back home, who would still speak of her as being "from away."

It was true that, as she walked through the streets of this metropolis, Mata's men followed her from afar, keeping her in sight, but she knew it wasn't because she was their prisoner. Mata had said that he would take care of her, and he would keep that promise wherever she wanted to be. They were there to protect her, because they believed that the hegemon's enemies might try to harm him through injury to her.

*Are they right? Is that how he feels about me?*

In truth, she wasn't sure how she felt about Mata either—indeed, she wasn't sure if she knew him at all, even after all this time. He was unfailingly polite to her and inquired after her well-being every day. Whatever she wanted, he tried to satisfy her.

Once, she mentioned that she missed her old home, and a few days later, she found her old hut—which her parents and Mado and she had shared back in the Isle of Vines—in the palace courtyard in front of her chambers: every foundation stone, every wooden slat, every layer of wall-mud was in place, and the roof had been freshly thatched. Inside, every piece of furniture, every dented pot, every chipped cup and bowl and plate had been moved over and placed exactly the way she had left them on the day she set out to search for Mado.

Another time, she made an offhand remark that she found the singing of birds pleasant, and the next day, she awoke to a magnificent chorus of birdsong. Walking out, she found her little courtyard filled with hundreds of cages hanging from tree branches, in which songbirds from every corner of the Islands of Dara were guided by dozens of handlers to sing in harmony.

"When will the announcement of the auspicious day be?" The ladies-in-waiting tittered and giggled. "Do not forget us when you've been formally elevated!" They were sitting around Mira's guest hall, keeping her company as they did their embroidery.

Mira refused to pretend that she didn't know what they were talking about. "The hegemon has been kind to me out of consideration for the service my brother provided to him. I would ask you to not to dishonor him or me with gossip of nonexistent things."

"So you're the one holding out? Why? Do you want him to promise to make you First Consort?"

Mira put down her hoop. "Do not continue in this vein. I have not been plotting or scheming, as you seem to think. There is simply no fire where you imagine smoke."

"You should seize an opportunity that all the women of Cocru pray for. The hegemon is in love! Everyone can see that. "

*But am I?*

She had left the palace in a foul mood. Everyone seemed to want to tell her what she should be doing. She tried to clear her mind by walking about the streets.

Sometimes she thought she saw him as her brother must have seen him: a man elevated above others by his own qualities, a dyran among mere fish. Sometimes she thought she saw him as just a lonely man, peerless, but also friendless. Sometimes she thought her heart ached for him, and if he asked her to join him, she thought she would.

But then she would remember her brother's body wrapped in the shroud. She would remember that Mata had not even recognized her brother's name.

She had dreams in which Mado was alive again:

*Sister, has General Zyndu now made the world just and right?*

She tried to avoid having to answer, tried to hide from him the fact that the world was still at war, that Mata had not made the lives of men and women in Tunoa better, that Mata had not even known who he was.

But of course, in the end, she had to tell him everything, and as his face fell into stony disappointment, she would wake up, her heart so weighed down with pain and sorrow that it was hard to breathe.

She had come to the end of the row of stalls, and she sighed, thinking she would cross the street and browse aimlessly through the other side.

"Lady Mira, a moment, please."

Mira saw that the speaker was a beggar wearing a bright-white cape. He smiled at her. "It's been a while."

She backed up a step. "What are *you* doing here?"

He didn't move. "I have something for you."

"I don't want it."

"Mata's guards are watching us from a distance," the beggar said. "If I move up to you, they'll interpret it as a threat, and I may never get a chance to see you again. Please, for Mado's sake, step closer."

The mention of her brother's name softened her. She took a step toward the strange beggar. He handed her a small bundle wrapped in cloth.

"What is it?"

"It's called Cruben's Thorn. Mata once almost died from it; I'm hoping you'll succeed where the first owner failed."

Mira almost dropped the bundle. "Get away from me."

"Mata is too skilled to be killed on the battlefield," said the beggar. "And so he must die from a blade he does not expect. I ask you to consider this not because of the thousands who have died needlessly in his wars or the thousands more who will die if he is not stopped. I ask you to consider only your brother and whether the Mata you know is the Mata he thought he knew."

"How can I dishonor the memory of my brother by plotting against the man he died for?"

The beggar chuckled. "Lady Mira, your answer gives me hope, for you have not denied me by recourse to any of the qualities of the hegemon, but by appealing to the memory of your brother. Your heart is not his, despite what others may think."

"If you don't leave immediately, I'll cry out for help."

The beggar took a step back. "Peace. Permit an old man just a few more words.

"I always thought your brother the braver man. He was afraid, and yet he fought. He risked his life without the promise of certain glory and the arrogance of long, distinguished lineage. He thought he was fighting for a better world, not one in which a new tyrant simply replaced an old one. Think of your dreams—oh, yes, I know of your dreams, even if you haven't told anyone. Think about what dishonors his memory more: that Mata dies or that Mata sits comfortably on his throne, a throne built on the bones of your brother and others like him.

"See him for who he really is, Mira. That is all I ask."

And the beggar turned and disappeared into the crowd, leaving Mira alone with the bundle. Without unwrapping it, she could feel the rough handle and the sharp, thornlike blade.

*Some want me to marry him; others want me to kill him. They all think they can use me. My only worth to them is my proximity to* him.

*But I don't even know who he is. How can I decide what* I *want?*

Mata led his guards to the house of Jia, just outside of Çaruza. He would avenge this act of rebellion and treachery by the ruthless Kuni, whose ambition couldn't even be contained by the threat to his family. Jia and the children would pay for Kuni's sins.

But a middle-aged woman stood at the door of Jia's house and refused to let the guards in. She held up a jeweled pin in the shape of the chrysanthemum arms of the Zyndu Clan and asked to speak to Mata Zyndu. As the pin was clearly old and precious, the guards did not force their way past her but sent a report back to the hegemon.

Mata went up to the madwoman.

"Do you recognize me, Mata?"

Mata Zyndu stared at her. In her lined face he could see shades of Phin Zyndu and of himself.

"I am your aunt, Soto Zyndu."

Mata cried out in joy and opened his arms to embrace her. Since the death of Phin, he had been plagued by dreams where his uncle rebuked him for his failure to give family loyalty its proper place. He was the last of the Zyndus, alone and filled with guilt. The sudden appearance of his aunt seemed to him a sign from the gods, a second chance for him to do right by his family.

But she pushed him away.

"There has been far too much killing, Mata. You're consumed by aggrieved pride. All your life, you've held to certain ideals about loyalty, honor, just deserts. When the world turned out not to be quite as black and white as you would like, you decided that the world must be remade.

"You are, in your own way, a lot like Emperor Mapidéré. You are both men who, because one path is not smooth, declare that the entire garden must be paved over with flagstones."

Mata Zyndu was stunned. "What kind of comparison is this? Have you forgotten our family's history?"

Soto shook her head emphatically. "You're the one who misunderstands history. Because decades ago Gotha Tonyeti buried alive twenty thousand men of Cocru under your grandfather's command, you believed you had to drown twenty thousand men of Xana, men who were not even born when that atrocity happened—"

"I had to appease an angry god—"

"Excuses! Do you think your grandfather never killed an innocent? Do you think his father fought only honorable wars? Do you want to see your outrage repeated in twenty more years on the boys of Cocru? Blood always begets more blood—"

"The joy of our reunion is spoiled by your harsh words, Aunt! How did you survive?"

"When Grandfather Dazu died, I locked the doors of our house in the country and set fire to it so that I could follow him to the afterworld. But the gods had other plans for me, and I survived, unconscious, in a space formed by falling stone beams and columns. I have hidden all these years, living in obscurity, trying to atone in some small measure for the sins of the men of the Zyndu Clan.

"I came to serve this family because of the compassion of its lord and lady. I wanted to see if the great lords can take another path.

"You once called Kuni your brother, yet now you would do violence to his wife and children. Ambition has made you mad. Stop this, Mata. No more."

"Kuni Garu has killed just as I have," Mata Zyndu said, his voice equal parts grief and rage. "I've done what I could to restore order to the world and to bring glory to the Zyndu name. Kuni is a mouse who steals my table scraps. He is unworthy of your protection. Come back to the palace with me, Aunt, and live in splendor again."

But Soto shook her head. "If you harm a woman and her children in vengeance, then no valor will ever cleanse you of that bloody stain. I'll not allow you to soil the Zyndu name in such a manner. If you wish to harm them, you must kill me first."

Soto gently closed the door in Mata Zyndu's face. It would have been easy for Mata to smash the door open with his bare hands, but he stood in front of the door for a long while without moving.

He thought back to his childhood with Phin, to the tales Phin told of his heroic ancestors. He thought of Princess Kikomi and the death of his uncle. He thought of the happy drinking parties he had with Kuni and his friends. He thought of Mira and Mado.

Finally, he turned around and gazed across the beach, across the dark sea, to the invisible isles of Tunoa beyond the waves. He sighed and walked away with his guards.

"Lady Soto, would you come and have some tea with the mistress?" Steward Otho Krin asked.

Once she had revealed her identity, of course Jia could no longer permit Soto to be treated as a servant. Soto had tried to ignore Jia and continue her work in the house, but the other servants treated her as a great lady, and Soto had to concede defeat. She now lived as a guest of the Garu household, Jia's companion.

Soto followed the steward through the halls. The children were taking a nap, and it was pleasant to sit in the courtyard, filled with the sweet smell of plum flowers and the buzzing of industrious bees.

Otho brought the tea set. He knelt, placed the tray on the table, gently touched Jia on the shoulder, and whispered to her. Jia put her hand on his for a moment. He stood up, smiled at her, and respectfully backed away from the two.

"Soto, did Mata reply to your request that I be allowed to visit my parents and my father-in-law?"

"Not yet. Right now, he's preoccupied with the wars between the Tiro states."

"But we can both guess that the answer is probably going to be no. The smart thing to do is to continue to keep me and the children as prisoners and bargaining chips right here."

Soto sipped her tea. "True. Though your plan was worth a try. You're getting to be as crafty as your husband."

Jia laughed. "I can't hide anything from you. It did seem to me that I might be able to connect with more of Kuni's old followers in Zudi if I was allowed to leave."

"You would have had a better chance if you had gotten your parents or Kuni's father to manufacture some sickness or death in the family—Mata respects the old traditions and would have probably permitted you to go in mourning. If you want to succeed in future palace politics, you're going to have to think through your moves more."

Jia blushed. Soto had a sharp eye and a sharper tongue, but Jia actually found her to be a kindred soul. Jia had abandoned life as a wealthy merchant's daughter to marry a man who seemed to have no future, and Soto had left a life as a great hereditary lady to live as someone else's maid. They both knew something about adapting to the vagaries of life. Soto's criticism was well meant: She had decided to become a political wife, hadn't she? Then she needed to adapt to its requirements, both pleasant and unpleasant.

Soto had saved her life and the lives of the children, and Jia was grateful for that. But Soto was also full of secrets. Today, Jia was determined to dig into them.

"Do you sometimes wish," Jia said, "that Mata would win instead of Kuni? He's family, after all."

"I don't know what it means for someone to *win* in this, Lady Jia. Whatever happens, a great many people will suffer. But I do think that Kuni will be gentler on this world than Mata."

"Is that all? Do you not wish to gain an advantage for yourself?"

Soto put down her teacup. "Speak plainly, Lady Jia."

"You told Kuni who you were before he left, didn't you?"

Soto gazed at Jia, utterly amazed.

"Kuni is a gambler, but he's not reckless, and he would not endanger me or our children with an invasion of Rui unless he knew of a way to keep us safe. He must have known who you were before he went to war. Did you make some kind of bargain with him? Mata would not take kindly to women meddling in politics, but Kuni is far more flexible."

Soto chuckled. "I see that I've been trying to give advice to a mind already subtle. You're right that I told Kuni my secret so that he would feel free to make his move when the time was right."

"And you kept the secret from me because you weren't sure I could continue to act the part of the proper hostage. If I grew too confident or bold in my dealings with the hegemon, he might have suspected that I was no longer afraid of him, and thus deprived Kuni of the cover of my being essentially at his mercy."

Soto nodded. "Forgive me for my deception, Lady Jia. I had always hoped you would be a force, but I wasn't sure if you were ready. I assure you, though, that I do not wish to become a puppeteer behind Kuni's throne. What I said to Mata is the truth: I believe there must be an end to the killings, and Kuni is far more likely than Mata to achieve that vision."

"How did Kuni win you over?"

"You won me over *for* him; and during his visit, his actions and words confirmed that he's a lord worthy of my loyalty."

"You didn't suspect us of just acting? Great lords are often good at theater, as in the stories you tell the children."

Soto considered this. "If it's a mask, it's a very good mask. How can you ever truly know the heart of someone? You and your husband are both natural actors, but if you're performing, you've kept up that performance for your servants, for the powerless, for the low and base. Sometimes there is no distinction between the role and the player."

Jia gazed at her. "No more secrets, Lady Soto. I want at least one real friend in the palace. As you said, I have much to learn about politics, and there will be more of it in the future."

Soto nodded. She and Jia continued to drink tea, talking of inconsequential things.

CHAPTER FORTY-FOUR

# THE CRUBEN IN DEEP SEA

ÇARUZA: THE FIRST MONTH IN THE
FOURTH YEAR OF THE PRINCIPATE.

By throwing out everything that added weight—armor, weapons, extra provisions and water, even the mattresses in the sleeping quarters for the crew—Marshal Mazoti turned a few of the airships captured from Mount Kiji into sleek speedsters. True to the vision she and Risana had shared, Mazoti staffed them with all-women crews.

Unmatched in speed and maneuverability, these airships evaded the hegemon's airships and flew all over the Islands of Dara; their heavier pursuers were slower and could not stay aloft for as long.

As they flew over the cities, Dasu airships dropped leaflets denouncing Mata Zyndu for his sins: the Massacre at Dimu, the Slaughter of Prisoners at Wolf's Paw, the Destruction of Surrendered and Peaceful Pan, the Betrayal of the Promise of Just Rewards for Rebel Leaders, the Usurpation of the Throne of Cocru, the Murder of King Thufi . . .

The self-righteous tone, the lurid language, the manipulative illustrations—these had troubled Kuni when Cogo Yelu first presented them.

"The facts in these accusations may be true, but why do we have to tell them as if they are stories whispered in teahouses?"

"Sire," Cogo said, "this is the only way to get the common people to be interested."

"I know that. But this seems . . . too much. We've done some things that we are not proud of either, and we may yet commit more sins in the future. If we denounce Mata like this, people will think us hypocrites."

"Hypocrisy troubles only the unrighteous," said Rin Coda.

Kuni was unpersuaded, but he always listened to counsel.

He nodded reluctantly.

Torulu Pering, who had more than a little experience fighting against airships, came up with a plan.

As one of the Dasu ships headed for Çaruza, Pering ordered Cocru airships near the capital to lay a trap. They took off from the airfield at the last possible minute and plotted an intercept course from the east. This allowed them to take advantage of the rising sun that temporarily blinded the Dasu ship's pilot. By the time the Dasu ship realized the danger, the Cocru ships would be too close. They'd have to engage in an air fight, and the Dasu airship, lightly armed and outnumbered, would be no match.

But it was deep winter, and just as the ships were about to let loose their volleys of flaming arrows, a heavy, punishing storm of freezing rain began to fall. As the ice sheets thickened on the hulls, the weight gradually pulled all the ships down. The Dasu ship was going to have to land, even though it wasn't being shot out of the sky.

However, Luan Zya, who had studied the weather patterns around the Islands of Dara during his extensive travels, had been prepared. He had advised Gin to equip the crew with long-handled pikes that they now used to loosen the sheets of ice as they leaned out of the gondola. The Dasu ship rose, unscathed, and for good measure, dropped a full load of pamphlets on the capital of Cocru.

ᔕ ᔓ ᔕ ᔓ

*Rapa, my other half, are you really going to work now against a son of Cocru?*

*Kuni is also a son of Cocru; as was Thufi, and countless others who have died. You have picked your favorite, and I have mine.*

*I never thought we'd see the day when sister works against sister among the gods.*

*I'm sorry, Kana. But our hearts are as varied and tumultuous as those of the mortals.*

Mata Zyndu read through the pamphlet and grew angrier with each line.

*Lies, all the words are lies.*

When he killed, he killed only cowards and traitors and enemies. He was always forgiving and generous to his real friends.

Kuni Garu the betrayer, despite his dirty tricks and dishonorable band of hooligans, preened and paraded like a saint before the ignorant masses. Meanwhile, even Mata's own aunt treated him as some tyrant. There was no justice in the world.

His own room was too confining. Mata strode into the courtyard to get some fresh air.

There was Mira, sitting under the shade of a sweet olive, embroidering. Clusters of pale-yellow flowers hung from the evergreen branches over her, giving off a sweet, pungent fragrance that lingered in the lungs. He walked closer to see what she was making.

It was a picture of him. The needlework was very fine. Mira had used only black threads so that the result was like an ink painting.

She did not faithfully reproduce his face or figure. His body was represented by a rough, elongated diamond, and his head an oval with two triangular patches for his eyes. Yet, with ragged lines and these bold geometric patterns, somehow Mira managed to suggest Mata Zyndu in flight, brandishing his sword while hanging from a kite. It was not a picture that hewed close to nature, with its soft curves and shades of light, but seemed to somehow supersede it, as though showing the skeleton beneath the world's flesh. The Mata Zyndu in her picture was all spirit and energy.

"It's very good," he said, his anger momentarily forgotten.

"I've made several of these," she said. "But none of them *feels* right. I can't seem to fully capture the idea of you."

Mata Zyndu sat down. He felt relaxed in her quiet presence, like a cool breeze in early autumn. She never talked to him about matters of state, never plotted to gain some advantage from him for one faction or another. When she expressed a longing for something, it was simple: a house, a flower she remembered seeing once, the song of birds in the morning.

He wished he could be so easily satisfied as well.

"What's it like?" he asked idly. "To make pictures like that? It seems to require so much effort, one stitch after another. And it's so . . . small."

Mira went on embroidering, not lifting her eyes. "I imagine it's not very different from what you do."

Mata Zyndu laughed. "I am the hegemon of all of Dara. When I stomp my foot, thousands tremble. Comparing what I do to your idle feminine pursuits is like comparing the path of a cruben in the sea to that of an ant beneath my foot." As he spoke, he put his boot down on an ant crawling nearby and crushed it into a smear.

Mira glanced at the ant and then looked up at him. Something seemed to change and shift inside her. When she spoke again, her tone was different.

"When you lead an army into the field, you make a picture. I use a needle; you wield a sword. I make stitches; you make bodies. I leave behind a figure on fabric; you leave behind a new arrangement of power in the world. In the end you work on a larger canvas, but I do not think the satisfaction we get from our respective work is very different."

Mata had no answer to this. Mira's words infuriated him, yet he could not say why. It would be easy to dismiss her as a woman unable to understand the grandeur of his vision, but he stubbornly tried to get her to *see*. He had always been able to make her happy, hadn't he?

"It's silly to compare how you feel to what I feel. I change the lives of every person in these Islands. You are confined to a woman's narrow circle: a few feet in front of you."

"That's true," Mira said. "Yet in the eyes of the gods, you and I are not much different from that ant. But I do have the consolation that my enjoyment brings no death and suffering; when I die no one will jump up and down in joy; and I remember all the names and faces that matter to me."

Mata stood up and lifted his hand. If he used his full strength, she would be dead in a moment.

He had been in this position many times on the battlefield, poised to strike a final blow against a foe with Na-aroénna or Goremaw. Always, he had seen something in their eyes: despair, terror, defiance, disbelief.

But she stared back at him with perfect equanimity; there was not even a hint of fear.

"I want to understand you, Mata. But I do not think you understand yourself."

He put his hand down, got up, and walked away.

LUTHO BEACH: THE THIRD MONTH IN THE FOURTH YEAR OF THE PRINCIPATE.

The Tiro states, old and new, fell upon one another like squabbling children, and the nobles found themselves in a crowded world filled with newly minted aristocrats.

Kings sat uneasily on their thrones. After all, Zyndu had driven away King Thufi and took the Throne of Cocru for himself because he had the loyalty of the army. The example was tempting to the generals of the other Tiro states, and frightening to their kings.

Mata did nothing to discourage the trend, and coups happened in several places as ambitious generals took the places of their former masters. *Sometimes*, the change was bloodless.

∽ ∾ ∽ ∾

Cocru ships circled around Rui and Dasu, boxing the islands in like a floating wall of wood. The few Dasu ships hid in the harbors, not daring to emerge into the open sea. Kuni Garu made no move to build up a navy to challenge the hegemon. And an airborne invasion was impractical as airships simply did not have that kind of capacity.

The lack of activity after the pamphlets led to whispers that perhaps King Kuni's ambition was simply to have a larger prison within which to stretch his legs. Gradually, discipline on the Cocru ships grew lax. Sailors on the ships spent their endless patrols playing cards and fishing to add a bit more variety to their monotonous diet of stale biscuits.

Sometime the sailors saw great pods of crubens passing under the ships in the sea lanes between Rui and the Big Island. Sighting a cruben was an auspicious occurrence, and most of the sailors were glad. Maybe it was a sign that the gods favored Hegemon Zyndu, and their time away from the comforts of home would soon be over.

On a deserted stretch of Lutho Beach, in the dead of the night, a pod of crubens beached themselves.

One, two, three . . . ten crubens crashed through the waves and laid themselves on the sand, where they would have to wait until high tide to swim free again. The sound of their landing was grinding and metallic, less like living flesh, more like the clanging of weapons tumbling across a stone floor.

Suddenly, the crubens yawned and opened their maws wide. But the jaws kept on opening, opening, until the top half of each cruben's head was pulled so far back that it rested upside down on the creature's back.

From deep within the belly of the scaled whales, hundreds of men spilled out. The soldiers hiding within the mechanical crubens wore the uniform of Dasu. They had been inside the underwater boats for days, and they greedily gulped the fresh salty night air.

Then, quickly, they melted into the shadows of the night to join their comrades, who had set up temporary barracks in caves along the shore. The empty vessels closed their mouths and waited for high tide, when they would dive beneath the waves and go back to Rui to pick up more passengers.

If one looked at the flags they carried, one might have noticed a small change. The whale charging the red field was covered by a layer of blue-black scales, and there was a great horn on its forehead. The ensign of Dasu was now a cruben rising from a sea of blood.

The mechanical crubens—underwater boats—had been the proudest creation of both Luan Zya and Gin Mazoti. While trying to come up with a way to bypass the blockading navy to land an invasion force on the Big Island, Gin had joked that she wished Kuni could summon the crubens again, as he had on that legendary ride to bring down Emperor Erishi.

A twinkle appeared in Luan's eyes. "We don't need to summon the crubens. We can make them."

He reached for Gin's hands, and she let him hold them, taking pleasure at the warmth in her lover's hands.

A boat that could go under water needed to adopt the principles that allowed the airship to adjust buoyancy in a much denser medium. Luan enjoyed the challenge this posed.

The ships were built in secret, in seaside caves on Rui away from the gaze of Zyndu's airships and spies. Plates of thin and strong sword iron were hammered into circular rings around planks of hard ash, much like a cooper puts hoops around staves to make a barrel. These rigid sections were then attached together with short chains to allow the body of the cruben to flex and bend like a living creature. Shark and whale skins were then wrapped around the frame of the body to waterproof the vessels. At the front, a sharpened bowsprit of ironwood served as the cruben's single horn.

Buoyancy tanks along the bottom of the boats would cause the vessels to rise or sink, depending on whether they were filled with water or air pumped in via bellows. The inside of the ships had plenty of room for the crew as well as transported soldiers and goods. The eyes, made of thick crystals, allowed the men inside to see out. Other, smaller portholes were made all along the sides of the boats as well to provide illumination for the dark and dim interior.

The vessels had to look like real crubens from above, from which direction came the most danger of detection. The cosmeticians in Dasu's women's auxiliary corps painted scales onto the smooth skin, and the work was so detailed that no observer, looking down from a naval ship or airship, could tell the reflected light from these artificial scales apart from the real thing.

With the basic plan of the vessel in place, three great difficulties still remained.

One was the fact that water, unlike air, imposed great pressure. No matter how much they tried to waterproof the vessels, they leaked like crazy and would collapse if they dove too deep. This was not fatal, however, as the mechanical crubens only needed to dive under the blockading ships and to hide from airships. Most of the time, the ships would sail near the surface, only diving deeper as the need arose.

Next was the matter of breathing air for the men onboard. Gin, an avid swimmer and diver, learned that some young men in Dasu, in order to observe the beautiful starfish and corals in shallow lagoons, would swim with their heads under water and breathe through straws held in the mouth with the other end poking above the water. Based on this and the behavior of real crubens, she designed a breathing tube. One end stayed inside the vessel, and the other end, attached to a floating buoy, could be let out to peek above the surface of the sea. A bellows could then be used to pump the water out of the tube to let air in, and the resulting spray looked just like the spray from a real cruben's blowhole.

The other matter, that of propulsion, was more difficult to solve. Luan initially tried to have the men inside one of the vessels operate the tail like a giant oar, undulating the tail fin in imitation of nature. But this proved far too exhausting and impractical for a trip that would cover the distance from Rui to the Big Island.

But then Luan remembered one of Cogo's eccentric inventors who had presented a machine that could turn a wheel by means of steam generated from a volcano's heat and a tank of water. Luan generalized the machine's principles. He also had learned, through his years of traveling through the Islands, that the bottom of the ocean between Rui and the Big Island was studded with a range of underwater volcanoes whose peaks rose to near the surface of the sea. The rocks around these volcanic vents were heated so that they glowed red. Luan and Gin trained the crews of the mechanical crubens to hover over these vents, and to operate mechanical arms to scoop up these red-hot rocks into a special tank under the boats.

The rocks caused the water in the tank to boil, and the steam was then drawn through a series of tubes to turn a train of pistons, gears, and cranks connected to the tail fin and the pectoral fins. Engineers inside the mechanical cruben would scoop up enough heated rocks from one vent to power the ship to the next vent. In this way, rising to breathe and diving to pick up more hot rocks, the fleet of underwater boats swam through the ocean like a pod of real crubens. As long as the crubens stuck to paths marked by underwater volcanoes, they could travel for days.

Slowly and in secret, the mechanical fleet transported the Dasu army onto the Big Island.

With the final wave of soldiers safely deposited on the shores of Lutho Beach, Gin Mazoti gave the order.

Lookouts in crow's nests on the ships of North Géfica, Haan, and conquered Rui saw a pod of crubens passing beneath them again. Sailors leaned over the railings to catch sight of the amazing creatures.

But the great beasts slowed as they passed beneath the ships and began to rise to the surface.

Captains shouted frantic orders to maneuver their ships out of the way, but it was too late. Accompanied by explosive cracks and howls of surprise from the Cocru sailors, the mechanical crubens breached the surface, their giant horns smashing holes in the bottoms of the ships, breaking their keels. The panicked ships ran into one another, tangling their oars, and the mechanical crubens dove and rose again, staving them in.

The fleets around Rui were destroyed within a few hours, and all over the sea, survivors clung to the wreckage.

Dasu now ruled the sea from beneath its surface.

Ginpen fell without a single man having to die. King Cosugi saw the massed spears and arrows outside the city walls and surrendered. Marshal Mazoti allowed him to stay in the newly rebuilt palace as a guest of Dasu.

Gin announced that the Dasu army would not bother the occupied population and urged everyone to go on with their lives. At first, the population of Haan was skeptical, but soon grew bolder as the Dasu soldiers really did seem to keep the marshal's promise.

"So you've found a better master," Cosugi said when he saw Luan Zya, unable to keep the bitterness out of his voice.

Luan bowed. "I still serve the people of Haan," he said.

The cruben flags of Dasu whipped in the wind. King Kuni had returned to the Big Island.

# CLOUDS RACE ACROSS THE SKY

CHAPTER FORTY-FIVE

# DASU AND COCRU

WOLF'S PAW AND THE BIG ISLAND:
THE SIXTH MONTH IN THE FOURTH
YEAR OF THE PRINCIPATE.

Mata Zyndu was in Wolf's Paw again.

He did not want to be here, but that old coward, King Dalo of Gan, had given him no choice.

Once Mata had released him back to the island, King Dalo sank into a deep depression. He spent his days watching actors enact legends concerning the ancient splendor and enviable wealth of gleaming Gan's past, and he lamented his own humiliation by the hegemon.

Mocri Zati, one of his generals, grew restless. Emboldened by the example Mata himself had set, he forced King Dalo to abdicate and hand over the Seal of Gan. Dalo put up little resistance. He declared that kingship was not compatible with his temperament and retired to tend to his goldfish ponds.

Thinking Mata preoccupied with the growing problem posed by Kuni Garu, King Mocri immediately began to prepare for war and revolt against the hegemon. Mocri Zati was a famed swordsman himself, but he had been bedridden with an illness during the Battle of Wolf's Paw and thus did not witness Mata's exploits on the field. He had always believed that tales of Mata's valor were exaggerations, and that his victory was due more to corruption within the empire's command ranks than true skill.

To inspire the populace, Mocri announced that he would recover the territories on the Big Island that Mata had taken from Gan. Then he immediately invaded Ogé, administered by King Hoye, the former Gan commander who had joined Mata during the final stages of the Battle of Wolf's Paw and had been rewarded with the little isles for his effort. Hoye was quickly defeated, given that his entire Tiro state had fewer people than the city of Toaza. But Mocri celebrated his victory as though he had already defeated the hegemon himself and paraded in the streets of Toaza for ten days in triumph.

"Mocri is a fool," Torulu Pering said to Mata. "Your real problem is Kuni Garu. Go west, Hegemon, and crush him before he stirs all the other Tiro states against you."

Mata found Pering's meddling annoying. Kuni might have landed on the Big Island, but he only had a toehold in Haan. The three newly created Tiro states in Géfica were all ruled by men who owed their elevation to Mata Zyndu, and they were certainly sufficient to hold back the cowardly Kuni and his girl general. Mocri, on the other hand, was a good fighter and far more dangerous.

In order to keep his world from unraveling, Mata had no choice but to strap on his sword and get back into the saddle. He had no one else he could trust to do the job right. He would deal with Kuni later, after he had pacified the east.

The Tiro states of Dara saw that they had to pick a side. They could either back Mata Zyndu of Cocru, the greatest warrior the world had ever seen, or Kuni Garu of Dasu, the man with a seemingly endless fount of luck.

The King of North Géfica, Théca Kimo, had fought by the side of Mata since the day he killed Huno Krima. Everyone always assumed that he was firmly in Mata's camp.

But before he became a king, before he became a general, before he became a rebel, Théca had been a brawler in Tunoa, a criminal who lived by the tip of his knife. He was sentenced to hard labor for maiming a man. On his face were still frightening tattoos that prison guards had pricked into his skin under the laws of Emperor Mapidéré, so that everyone would always know what he had done. Like Mata, he was a physically imposing man and excelled in battle. But unlike Mata, he never considered himself to be serving a higher ideal.

He understood the culture of the dark alleys and the night streets far better than the formal dance of diplomacy and courtly intrigue. In his view, the life of a noble was no different from that of a petty street criminal. Kuni Garu and Mata Zyndu were like the top bosses of two rival gangs fighting for the control of a city's markets and the rich protection money that merchants paid. And he was merely a lowly subboss caught in the middle.

*You pick the stronger gang or you're lost.*

Théca came to Ginpen in secret to see Kuni Garu. He dressed plainly and did not take any guards. The meeting place was at an old, inconspicuous inn.

When he arrived in the appointed room, he found Kuni lounging in bed with two prostitutes. Théca found this perfectly understandable: It was exactly how he imagined a great crime boss who had everything would act.

Kuni dismissed the women but seemed distracted.

"I believe that Mata Zyndu is the past, while you, Great King Kuni, are the future."

Kuni yawned. He got up and left the room.

Théca didn't know what to make of his reception. He had come to discuss the possibility of an alliance, but Kuni behaved as if he didn't care about him at all.

Cogo Yelu then came in and invited Théca to lunch. Théca was served a cold meal of the coarse and plain fare that the inn had to offer. The eating sticks were misshapen and cheaply made. His unease grew.

Kuni Garu must be treating him this way because he and Marshal Mazoti already had some plot under way to conquer North Géfica. The big boss had figured out a method to take over his territory without including him at all. He was at risk of losing his land and throne, like poor Cosugi, and worse, maybe even his life.

Kuni's coldness was a warning, a last ray of hope.

He begged Prime Minister Yelu to speak to Kuni. Instead of an alliance of equals, now he pleaded to be allowed to submit to Dasu. He was willing to yield up North Géfica and fight for Dasu in exchange for the king's promise of a new domain once the war was over.

Cogo nodded and said that he would do his best.

Once Théca was sent on his way, Cogo and Kuni clasped hands and laughed.

"He swallowed the bait, hook, line, and sinker!" said Kuni.

"Sire, you're a very good actor," said Cogo.

"Never doubt a Zudi gangster."

The dismissive treatment of Théca had been Cogo's idea, but Kuni had put the fine touches on it to exploit what he knew of Théca's history. Sometimes a clever bit of psychology did more wonders than an army.

"Cogo, I'm going to miss you," Kuni said, and he grabbed Cogo by the hands as though they were still in Zudi, where the two often worked late into night and chuckled together at some clever plan for city planning or civil administration that would have bored everyone else.

Cogo Yelu had come to Ginpen to help set up the occupation authority with the aid of the documents he had taken from the Imperial Archives, but now he had to go back to Daye, where he would keep the islands of Dasu and Rui productive and support the war effort on the Big Island.

"I am honored." Cogo paused, moved by the tremor in Kuni's voice. "Know that Mata has only his sword and cudgel, but you have the hearts of all your men."

∽ ∾ ∽ ∾

Once her generals had firmly assumed control of North Géfica, Mazoti sent Théca Kimo—now newly minted as the Duke of Arulugi—to attack King Ponadomu of Amu, confined to the beautiful island of floating cities. Ponadomu was terrified of the hegemon and had refused to even meet with Kuni's messengers.

Mazoti reasoned that the best way to ensure Théca's enthusiasm and loyalty was to send him to secure a new domain for himself; she had to turn her attention to the rest of the Big Island.

Central and South Géfica collapsed before Marshal Mazoti's forces like termite-infested logs before a heavy axe. The two kings, Noda Mi and Doru Solofi, had neglected their own military preparations, thinking Théca would take the brunt of Mazoti's assault. They had no choice now but to flee across the Liru River into Cocru for refuge.

As they crossed, they burned all the ships that they could find in towns along the northern shore of the river, hoping that the river, broad but too shallow for the mechanical crubens, would hold back the Dasu forces. They ordered all remaining ships on the Liru to stay anchored at towns and ports along the southern shore, where garrisons would guard them and make sure they stayed there. While Mi and Solofi kept a fleet of warships at Dimu to help control the Liru, they sent the bulk of the navy—or what was left of it after the devastating attacks by mechanical crubens—to patrol the western coast of Cocru with deep dragnets, hoping thereby to foil another surprise landing by underwater boats.

Mazoti stopped at Dimushi, where she found battle kites, balloons, and airships patrolling the Liru River, vigilant against signs of a Dasu attempt at crossing. Marshal Mazoti tried to construct rafts out of spare bits of lumber—doors, beams from abandoned temples, wagon wheels, even broken furniture—but the surveillance flights by enemy aircraft gave Noda Mi and Doru Solofi ample warning, and they ordered the airships to bombard these construction sites as soon as they noticed the gathering lumber. The few small rafts that Mazoti's men did manage to construct in secret proved too fragile to survive the waves of the Liru and fell apart before even reaching the middle of the river.

Gin Mazoti ordered her own airships to the Liru to engage the defenders. Although the women-crewed Dasu airships were fast and nimble, the Cocru airships benefitted from more battle experience. Dogfights between airships in the sky over the river were cheered on by both sides but proved inconclusive.

Mi and Solofi finally let out a held breath. As Marshal Mazoti had no way to transport her troops across the Liru, the two sides settled down for an indefinite standoff.

Mocri was ferocious. He dug in on Wolf's Paw and made Mata pay dearly for every inch of land he gained. Mata enjoyed the bloody battles against a worthy opponent, but reports from back home made him anxious.

The ever-dishonorable Kuni had reconnected with his old friend, the bandit Puma Yemu—Mata suspected that Jia played a role as well. Once again he was made the "Marquess of Porin" and led his horse thieves, the self-styled "Whirlwind Riders of Dasu," on hit-and-run raids of Mata's convoys and grain transports. Mata despised these tactics, but he was helpless until Mocri's rebellion could be put to rest. He redoubled his efforts, and more blood spilled.

Mata came into the palace in Toaza, which he had taken from Mocri and made into his temporary quarters.

The courtiers whispered among one another, but none dared to approach him.

Mata frowned. "What is it?"

One of them timidly lifted a hand and pointed toward the women's quarter.

Furiously, Mata walked over. One of Mocri's wives must have made a nuisance of herself, perhaps slandering him. He had left the women's quarter untouched when he marched into the palace, but often, he had found out, kindness was repaid unkindly.

As they saw him approach, the women of the palace pointed in the direction he should go and then scattered like frightened rabbits, and so Mata had to open the doors barring his way himself.

Finally, he threw open the door to one of the suites and stopped in the doorway.

Mira was sitting by the wall, embroidering.

It had been months since they had spoken to each other. The courtiers and ladies-in-waiting had not known what to do, uncertain if she had lost his favor. When he left for Wolf's Paw, he had left her behind in Çaruza.

She looked up at him and examined his look of surprise. A smile broke out on her face.

"I see they decided to tell you nothing and let you find out for yourself. Ah, courtiers. They are uncertain if you'll be happy or not to see me, and so this is their clever solution."

Her cheerfulness soothed Mata. She acted as though they had never stopped talking.

"Don't just stand there," she said. "You're blocking the light. Sit down, please. I've come to tell you a few things."

*Something has changed in her,* he realized. *She has made a decision.*

"Are you leaving me?" he blurted out.

As soon as he said it, the question struck him as ridiculous: Why should he care? He had countless women to pick from, and many were far younger and more beautiful. Yet he wanted *her* to like him, to come to his bed of her own free will, to apologize for her impudence and ignorance, and to acknowledge what a great man he was, how lasting a mark he would leave in the world.

The fact of it was that ever since that day, when she had told him what she thought of his glorious deeds, he had been unable to see himself except through her eyes: cruel, unnecessary, inelegant, and trivial.

"No, not at all."

Relieved, he sat down on the cushion next to her.

"The first thing is about my brother," she said.

He waited.

"I used to suffer nightmares where my brother would speak to me, asking about whether you have succeeded in fulfilling the vision that he believed."

Mata's face twitched.

"But lately, the dreams have stopped. Thinking that perhaps his spirit lacked sustenance, I asked a merchant traveling to Pan to burn some incense and make an offering at Mado's grave. He came back and told me that the tablet in front of my brother's grave is the largest in the whole graveyard and that you had ordered the garrison to place fresh chrysanthemums before his altar every day. In fact, you've ordered the same at all the graves of any of the Eight Hundred who had followed you out of Tunoa and died fighting. It's a generous thing you've done."

Mata said nothing.

She put down her hoop. "The second thing is this." She got up, walked to a small traveling trunk in the corner, and came back with a bundle wrapped in cloth.

"What is it?"

She said nothing.

He unwrapped it and stared at the bone dagger that was revealed. He had seen it once before, when it lay next to his uncle's dead body lying in state. Thufi had gravely explained to him that Princess Kikomi, Kindo Marana's lover and assassin, had killed Phin with it.

"Your enemies want to use me to get to you."

Mata stared at her. He did not know how to feel. Was betrayal to be a constant in his life?

"But I am tired of being treated as a tool," she said. "I want to live for myself."

He dropped the dagger on the ground and stumbled out.

Mira continued her embroidery.

Her style grew ever more abstract, more consumed with energy and suggestion than representation of reality. A few bold threads, barely a shadow of an outline, was all she stitched for the figure of Mata against a field of broken lines and chaotic colors, the world that he had put together so carefully falling apart. She stitched radiating starbursts around him—equal parts twirling swords and blooming chrysanthemums. He felt as if he himself were fading in her hands, becoming more legend than reality.

He had each of her embroidered kerchiefs carefully framed and handed them out as rewards for those who pleased him or achieved some deed of merit. His commanders and advisers fought to get a piece of Mira's embroidery, the symbol of the hegemon's esteem. Mira herself seemed amused by this and paid no attention to what happened to her work after she was done.

One day, Mata came back from another bloody day on the battlefield, exhausted with the sight of pain and slaughter and the effort of hacking through bone and sinew. Still dirty with the stench of death, he went directly to Mira's rooms.

Calm as ever, she asked him if he wanted to stay and dine with her. "I'll have my maid draw you a bath. I was thinking of steaming the carp I bought at the market. It's been a while since you've had Tunoa food, hasn't it?"

She did not ask him in a way that was submissive and seductive. She did not ask about his day's exploits on the battlefield or express admiration at his valor or strength. Always, she simply offered him simple things that they might share.

She treated him as a friend, he realized. Not as the Hegemon of the Islands of Dara.

He strode up to her and pulled her to his lips. He could feel her heart fluttering against him like a surprised bird. Her hands, which had been holding the needle and the hoop, dropped to her sides. After a moment, she returned the kiss.

He pulled back and stared into her eyes. She stared back steadily. Other than Kuni Garu, she was the only person who seemed to have no trouble looking into his double pupils.

"I understand you now," she said. "I now know why I could never stitch a proper portrait of you."

"Tell me."

"You are frightened. You are frightened by the legends that have grown up around you, by this shadow of yourself that lives in people's heads. Everyone around you is afraid of you, and so you begin to believe you should be feared. Everyone around you flatters you, and so you begin to believe you should be flattered. Everyone around you betrays you, and so you begin to believe you deserve betrayal. You are cruel not because you want to be, but because you think people expect you to be. You do the things you do, not because you want to, but because you believe the *idea* of Mata Zyndu would want to do them."

Mata shook his head. "You are not making any sense."

"You think the world should be a certain way, and you're disappointed that it does not live up to your vision. But you're also a part of this world, and you fear that your mortal flesh cannot live up to this vision of yourself. So you have constructed for yourself a new image, an image that you think is easier to live up to, an image of cruelty and bloodlust, of death and revenge and injured pride and stained honor. You have erased yourself and replaced *you* with these words, these words copied from old and dead books."

Mata kissed her again. "I don't know what you are talking about."

"But you are not a bad man. You do not have to be afraid. There is passion and compassion in you, but you have locked them away as though they are signs of weakness, of your similarity to other, lesser men. Why do you do this? So what if you leave no mark on the world? What if your work falls apart after your death?

"I was once uncertain whether it was right to love you, when the whole world seemed to quake in fear of you, and a thousand voices told me what was the *right* thing to do. But Mado was right: In all things that matter, faith in the heart is the only measure. But our mortal hearts are small; they are limited in what they can contain. What joy did it give me to hear that a thousand men lived to glory, when my heart grieved only for the loss of my brother? What does it matter if ten thousand men think the man I care for a tyrant, as long as I see him in a different light? Our lives are too brief to worry about the judgment of others, let alone that of history.

"You think my embroidery trivial, and yet all the works of men must be trivial in the fullness of time. There is no need for either of us to be afraid."

And she kissed him back and pulled him into her, and Mata found that he *was* no longer afraid.

A male voice, hard as obsidian and strident as sword striking against shield.

*My brother, it was clever to try to copy the trick of Kindo Marana, but you seem to have done no better. Cruben's Thorn will not taste the blood of another Zyndu.*

Another male voice, filled with the rage of storms.

*The mortals are unreliable as ever.*

A female voice, rasping, distorted, like the air shimmering over lava.

*Stop this nonsense, Kiji. You should be working with me and Fithowéo against the real enemy. Do you really want to see that trickster, the thief of the Immaculate City, win?*

*May both their houses fall.*

Gin Mazoti contemplated the wide expanse of the Liru, and her frustration grew daily.

Constructing a navy would take too long; she needed some way to cross the river, quickly.

Word spread along the Liru that the marshal was offering rich rewards for shipowners in Cocru to defy the hegemon and sail their ships to the northern shore of the river. A few daring merchants took the gamble, but their trading vessels were completely unprepared against airships. Burning wreckage, dead bodies, and the goods the ships had carried—chests of cloth, jars of oil, barrels of food, wine, flour—drifted down the river, bobbing along the surface like so many warnings against others who might think of betraying the hegemon.

Mazoti left the main body of her forces at Dimushi, facing the defenders in Cocru across the wide mouth of the Liru. She journeyed up the river, to Coyeca, a small town where the locals were famous for making earthenware: pots, vases, planters, and so on. These came in all shapes and sizes, some large enough to cook an entire shark in, others suitable only for brewing tea.

She wore a wig and dressed herself as a well-to-do lady from Pan who was here for pleasure, to sightsee and to pick out some suitable furnishings for the new house that would be built to replace the one that Hegemon Zyndu had burned down during the occupation. She browsed through the markets, fondling the earthenware vessels with obvious pleasure.

Dafiro, who was disguised as her servant, observed Marshal Mazoti's actions with puzzlement. She had never shown an ounce of interest in the implements of domesticity before.

Small caravans of merchants began to arrive at Coyeca. They purchased many large pots and planters and jars and amphorae. The workshops of Coyeca were happy for the boost in business. The town had always relied on commerce up and down the Liru, but now that Cocru had sealed its borders and barred all merchant ships from the river, business had slowed to a trickle. These caravans from up north were very welcome.

Then, on a moonless night, the merchants of the various caravans, their servants and footmen, their drivers and errand boys, gathered on the shore of the Liru outside Coyeca. They unloaded the pottery they had purchased and unpacked uniforms and armor from the carriages.

Marshal Mazoti stood before them. She was dressed again in battle gear, and her face was filled with the satisfaction of a plan carried out to perfection. "Gentlemen, I've always said that we must make the most of every advantage we can get. Today, we put that credo into action. Mi and Solofi think they're safe because they destroyed all boats in their desperate retreat across the Liru, but we don't need boats. They think they can catch us whenever we try to build rafts, but we've been buying rafts right under their noses."

She directed the men to stopper and seal the jars, amphorae, pots, and planters. They then tied collections of these air-filled vessels together with strong twine. To increase floatation, she had the soldiers fill their wineskins with air and tie these also to the makeshift rafts.

A Cocru airship drifted over the moonlit Liru. The lookouts leaned outside the gondola, keeping their eyes peeled for any ships or rafts on the surface. They saw bobbing masses of flotsam in the water below—clusters of jars and pots and other containers bumping against one another. Apparently, another greedy merchant had tried to make a run for it to the north with his ship, and a Cocru airship had made quick work of the traitor. It was a pity that perfectly good merchandise had to be ruined.

The airship sailed away.

In the darkness, undetected, the men of Dasu floated across the Liru on pockets of air trapped in kitchenware. The soldiers held on to the rafts with their hands and treaded water with their legs; they wore large pots over their heads to keep up the ruse. A few of the rafts fell apart, and some of the men, unable to swim back to the northern shore, drowned in the crossing. But most of the three hundred soldiers picked by Mazoti for this secret mission made it across safely.

After landing in Cocru, Mazoti's men divided into small squads and made their way west along the river. The squads easily overwhelmed the small garrisons at dozens of river towns and liberated their ships, directing them to sail toward the northern shore of the Liru—the Dasu men did not hesitate to use whatever method of persuasion was most effective with the shipowners.

Even Cocru airships could not stop such a mass exodus.

Mata finally cornered Mocri, and Mocri invited Mata to duel.

From sunrise to sundown, the two matched blow for blow, strike for strike. Sweat poured off their bodies, and their breath became labored. But still Na-aroénna swung through the air like the lobtailing fluke of a cruben, and Mocri's shield met it like the eternal, unyielding sea; Goremaw smashed down like the falling fist of Fithowéo, and Mocri's sword parried it like the hero Iluthan turning aside the jaws of a wolf. When the sun finally sank and the stars blinked into the black-silk sky, Mocri stepped back and held his arms open.

"Hegemon!" His heavy breathing sounded like the gasps of an ancient bellows; his dry tongue could not even form the syllables properly; he stumbled and had to support himself by leaning on his sword. "Have you ever fought a man like me?"

"Never," said Mata. He had never felt so tired, not even during the Battle of Wolf's Paw. But his heart had never felt more joyful. "You're the most skilled opponent I've ever faced." Pity arose in him. "Yield. You have fought well, and I will leave you in charge of Gan if you swear fealty to me."

Mocri smiled. "I am both glad and sorry that we met." And he pulled up his sword, lifted his shield, and came at Mata again.

The stars spun overhead as two great shadows fought in their cold, faint light. Mata's and Mocri's soldiers watched their lords, mesmerized. As their movements grew slower and more deliberate with their exhaustion, the two men seemed to be engaged in a dance rather than a fight. A dance that few mortals had the honor to witness.

Finally, as the sun rose again, Mata's strike with Goremaw broke Mocri's shield, and he took a step forward and thrust Na-aroénna into Mocri's chest.

Mata sheathed the Doubt-Ender and stumbled. Ratho Miro, his personal guard, rushed forward to support him. But Mata shook him off and picked up Mocri's sword. It looked old, battered, unadorned, the edges of the blade full of notches and the handle slick with Mocri's sweat: a weapon fit for a king.

He turned to Ratho. "Rat, you need a better sword, and this weapon deserves to not be buried in obscurity."

Ratho accepted the sword gingerly, overwhelmed by the honor.

"What will you name it?" asked Mata.

"Simplicity," said Ratho.

"Simplicity?"

"Ever since following you, my life has become as clear as the simple songs my mother sang to me as a child. My happiest memories are of that time and this."

Mata laughed. "Well named. Most rare now is our old simplicity."

Back in Toaza, the hegemon ordered that Mocri be given a funeral befitting his station as a king.

Mocri's family would also be spared and continue to be treated as nobles—though they would have to live in Çaruza. Those who fought with Mocri to the end were pardoned. If they would now swear fealty to Mata again, they could even keep their ranks.

Mata's men were confused. They had expected Mata to treat Mocri and his followers harshly, since they had betrayed him.

"Do you understand why?" Mata asked.

Mira was the only one who spoke up in the silence that followed.

"Mocri fought you in the field with no tricks, trusting only that his strength would overcome yours. There was no shame in his loss. He is a hero who lost not because of any fault of his own, but because the gods had decided to put you in the world along with him."

Mata hoped that someday the world would understand him as well as she did.

The Dasu army crossed the Liru in a giant flotilla of captured ships. They found Dimu an empty town.

With memories of their humiliating defeat in Géfica still fresh in their minds, the soldiers of Mi and Solofi had fled as soon as they heard that Marshal Mazoti had landed. She might be only a woman, but she was also a sorceress who could conjure ships out of thin air. What was the point of fighting? Might as well surrender or, even better, desert and find a way to get back to Géfica and be a farmer. Kuni Garu was said to be a good administrator who let the people figure out how to feed themselves without taking everything away in taxes.

Noda Mi and Doru Solofi were preparing to commit suicide in

Dimu when Mazoti entered the city and captured them. She treated them well, in accordance with Kuni's wishes.

Marshal Mazoti continued to march south from the Liru. The Dasu army arrived at Zudi, on the edge of the Porin Plains. The head of the garrison at Zudi, Captain Dosa, had always been thankful to Kuni for sparing his life; he and the elders of the city opened the gates wide and raised the flag of Dasu—begged from the officially licensed cooks of Dasu, with hand-painted scales and horns on the whales to turn them into crubens.

A few loyal men escaped from Zudi and brought news of Dasu's victories to Wolf's Paw. For a long time after hearing their report, Mata sat still on his throne. No one dared to speak up in the tent as the torches flickered and shadows danced across Mata's stony face.

*Torulu Pering was right: I must deal with Kuni Garu once and for all.*

CHAPTER FORTY-SIX

# MATA'S COUNTERATTACK

ZUDI: THE EIGHTH MONTH IN THE FOURTH YEAR OF THE PRINCIPATE.

Kuni's return to Zudi brought tears from his father—who had finally decided that it was time to throw his lot in with the son who would not stop rebelling—and wild jubilation among the people.

To add to the good news, Puma Yemu had managed to rescue Jia and the children right from under the noses of the Cocru troops in a daring raid at Çaruza. The family would finally be reunited in their hometown.

Kuni waited at the city gates from morning until evening, when the torchlights of Puma Yemu's men escorting Jia's carriage finally showed over the horizon.

Toto-*tika* and Rata-*tika* had no memory of their father and shrank back when he held out his arms to them. The little girl clutched Jia's hand while the little boy hung on to Otho Krin's robe. "Who is that man, Uncle Otho?" Toto-*tika* asked before Soto shushed him, and Otho awkwardly backed away.

"Oh, you must be Fa-father," said Rata-*tika*, stumbling over the unfamiliar word.

"The children will warm up to you soon enough," said Soto to Kuni.

The momentary look of pain disappeared from Kuni's face as he bowed deeply to Soto. "The Garu family is in your debt." Soto returned with a deep *jiri*.

Then Kuni turned to Jia. Their embrace at the city gates lasted a long time as the citizens of Zudi clapped and whistled and laughed.

As Kuni repeatedly kissed Jia, he whispered into her ear, "I'm so sorry for everything you've suffered. I know you don't think I understand, but I do. I've chewed on bitter herbs every morning so that I can feel a fraction of what you felt, alone, frightened, surrounded by enemies and trying to raise two children."

Jia, who had always maintained a stoic face in front of the others, finally broke down. She hit Kuni in the chest, hard, a few times, and then pulled him to her in a hungry kiss. Tears and laughter mingled in her face.

Kuni took out of his pocket a small bouquet of dandelions, all wilted.

"They were fresh this morning," he said apologetically.

"There will be new flowers," she said. "Life moves in cycles, like the tide."

"I want us to feel this close, always."

"Then we must treasure the moments we have, for who can predict what tomorrow will bring?"

Kuni nodded, and there were tears on his face too.

The crowd continued to cheer as the couple went on holding each other, swaying slowly in the moonlight.

The reunion of the Garu household continued back in the mayor's house, as joyous as it was awkward. No matter what kind of understanding Kuni and Jia might have shared, they understood that emotions and passions had a way of flowing along channels no one could anticipate.

Kuni introduced Jia and the children to Risana, who was very visibly pregnant. Soto and Otho Krin took the children away to play. Then Kuni seemed to have trouble finding things to say.

Mün Çakri went on and on about the tactical genius of Marshal Mazoti, and Jia politely said "Really!" and "Oh my!" in the appropriate places. After a while, Mün felt Rin Coda pulling on the hem of his robe under the table. He stopped talking. The room became very silent.

"Marshal Mazoti is thinking of planning an invasion of Rima. Mün, Rin, and I have to"—Than Carucono hesitated—"be somewhere else to help her."

The three got up and left, discreetly closing the door behind them. Kuni was alone with his two wives.

"Honored Big Sister," said Risana, "my heart is glad to finally be in your presence."

"I should thank you, Little Sister," Jia said, "for taking care of our husband all this time. His letters never mentioned how beautiful you are."

The two women smiled at each other.

*I can't see.*

Risana paced inside the bedroom that had been designated hers.

Jia's heart had appeared as a solid piece of obsidian to her. She could not tell if she liked her; she could not tell if she hated her; she could not tell if she was sincere; she could not tell if she was trying to insult her.

She didn't know what to do. Others whose hearts were sealed to her sight had only passed through her life. She had never had to live with anyone whose fears and desires she had to guess.

*You've never learned to navigate the darkness, as the rest of us must.*

Jia was glamorous, regal, a woman who had known Kuni when he was but a commoner. About her was the air of someone used to command and servants and wealth. But what was Risana? An entertainer, a woman who had scraped for a living from creating illusions for the amusement of teahouse patrons.

*To delight and to lead.*

The words sounded like a joke to her.

Then she looked into her own heart.

She forced herself to be calm. She would not be afraid. She would not see monsters where there were none.

Wasn't acceptance of the truth about the self her talent? She would accept her limitations and strive to befriend Jia. There must be a voice next to Kuni who spoke for those just like her and her mother, the powerless who yearned for peace. She had come far and carved out a place for herself; Jia could be a powerful ally.

She would stumble through the fog, trusting that no wall would suddenly loom before her.

"Tell me about Lady Risana," Jia said to Rona, Risana's maid.

Jia had cornered the fourteen-year-old girl in the kitchen, where she was trying to prepare a tray of snacks to take up to Risana's room.

"The mistress is very kind," the girl said.

"But how is she with the king? What do they do together?"

The girl blushed.

"No, no. I'm not asking for bedroom gossip, silly girl. I mean what do they talk about?"

"Lady Jia, I don't know much. When they are together, she usually sends me away."

*Well, one thing is for sure, Risana knows how to instill loyalty in her servants.* But Jia had other tricks.

"I hear rumors that King Kuni never laughs when Lady Risana is around," Jia said.

"That's not true!" The girl's tone was indignant. "I hear the king play the coconut lute sometimes after dinner, and the mistress sings. She has a beautiful voice, and sometimes if it's a funny song she laughs, and I hear the king laugh even louder. Other times she sings sad songs, and she cries, and I hear the king cry with her."

"Is it true that Lady Risana is not much of a dancer?"

"Oh no, not at all. She will put on a dress with very long sleeves and loosen her hair. Then she twirls and bends at the waist and leaps into the air, her back arched like a bow. Her sleeves and hair will float and trace out long arcs in the air, like three rainbows in the sky, like the three rivers meandering across the Big Island, like three strands of silk in the wind—"

Jia dismissed her.

In the dark, Jia twisted and turned. Kuni was asleep next to her, snoring loudly as was his wont. She had forgotten about this habit of his. Otho Krin was a quiet sleeper.

She imagined Kuni and Risana together, and despite herself, she was consumed with fury. When they were first married, Kuni and she had shared an easy, joking rapport. But she wasn't much of a singer, and she didn't remember him ever laughing or crying with her the way the maid described him doing with Risana. She did not dance, could never have danced, like Risana. Suddenly she felt the ghost of her vanished youth. Gone was the redheaded girl who had once inspired the future king with a dandelion.

Visions came to her: Risana losing her unborn child; Risana unable to conceive; Risana surrendering the favor of the king. She knew how to make those visions come true: when she had worked out how to cure her own barrenness, she had studied certain herbal recipes that had the opposite effect. As was so often the case in nature, substances tending to opposite effects were bound together; a thin line divided poison from medicine.

She shuddered, revolted and disgusted with herself. It was but a passing moment of weakness, she hoped. No matter how desperate she got, she would never cross that line, for to do so was to give herself up to the maelstrom, to lose herself.

She got up, went to her dresser, and took out the bundle of letters that Kuni had sent her over the years. Without turning on any light, she leafed through them, her fingers tracing the blank surface, remembering the patterns of invisible ink. No matter how busy he was, Kuni always found time to write.

Jia wiped away her tears. She was the mother of Kuni's eldest son, the future crown prince. She would always be his first love, the one who had thrown her lot in with him before he was anybody, the one who believed that he was destined for greatness. She could not really blame him, seeing as she was the one who had told him to take another wife. She had done so to ensure his success, and it was a sacrifice that she would not betray.

Maybe Soto was right. It was silly to make a fetish out of love, and not to accept that love was like food, and each dish had its own flavor. The heart surely had room for more than one.

But she would ask Kuni to name their son, now that Toto-*tika* was four, the age of reason. It was time to secure her place and to prepare for the palace rivalries that were sure to come.

"How about Timu?" said Kuni.

"'The Gentle Ruler'?" said Jia, translating from Classical Ano. She pondered the name. It was regal and proper, of course, being an allusion to Kon Fiji's poem:

*The gentle ruler governs without seeming to govern.*

But she had hoped for something a little more distinctive, something that referenced the boy's wily father and fierce mother. She was about to protest when she remembered the next line in the poem:

*He honors his subjects as he honors his own mother.*

Jia smiled. What better way was there for Kuni to express how he really felt? "It's perfect," she said. "From now on, Toto-*tika* will be known as Prince Timu."

"We might as well name our daughter, too," said Kuni, smiling. "She's a little young, but I think she's brighter than her brother and plenty reasonable now. How about Théra, meaning 'Dissolver of Sorrows'? Though we know her life, like ours, may be full of joy and sorrow, rise and fall, yet perhaps she can dissolve the sad parts and keep on laughing, as her parents have always tried to do."

"Of course," said Jia. "Princess Théra it is."

And her heart was indeed glad.

Mata arrived back on the Big Island to news that his realm was on the edge of collapse. Puma Yemu was making it impossible to safely transport grain anywhere in Cocru. Kuni had settled in Zudi, and rumors flew that he was planning to sweep down to Çaruza any minute. Stories of Marshal Mazoti's victories spooked Mata's men, who believed that she could conjure soldiers from the sky.

Mata did not despair. In fact, he welcomed the news. Ever since the fall of the empire, life had seemed dull to him, to have lost some of its flavor. Mocri was a good opponent, but he did not think big enough. Kuni Garu, on the other hand, was an enemy worthy of his full attention.

The more desperate the situation, the calmer he felt. He would defeat Kuni the way he defeated all his enemies, through strength and honor.

He asked for five thousand of his best riders and requisitioned fifteen thousand horses.

When Marshal Mazoti went north to deal with Rima, she left behind the bulk of the Dasu army at Zudi. Fifty thousand men and tens of thousands of horses, too many to garrison in the city, camped on the Porin Plains. This was a larger army even than the combined forces of Tanno Namen and Kindo Marana at Wolf's Paw. Cogo Yelu, always meticulous and careful, kept the provisions smoothly flowing.

At noon, scouting airships arrived at Zudi with the news that Mata Zyndu and five thousand warriors were riding toward Zudi and would arrive by the afternoon. The main part of Mata Zyndu's army, however, was still in the process of landing at Nokida, on the northern shore of the Itanti Peninsula, returning from Wolf's Paw.

Mata and his five thousand had been riding nonstop for three days, and many of their horses had collapsed from exhaustion.

Kuni's men mustered into orderly formations before the city gates.

Surveying his army from atop the walls, Kuni saw that his troops were not daunted by the prospect of facing the legendary hegemon.

The infantry formed phalanxes, fronted by pikemen to unseat the riders from their horses. To the sides were lines of longbowmen, prepared to launch their deadly missiles long before the riders got close. And in the wings were the cavalry, ready to circle around Mata Zyndu to cut off his retreat.

Kuni's army outnumbered Mata's attackers ten to one.

"Will you speak to the soldiers?" asked Than Carucono.

Kuni shook his head and turned away from the neat formations arrayed in front of him.

"Is something bothering you, Lord Garu? Do you think our preparations inadequate?"

Kuni shook his head again.

"Yet your look . . ." Carucono hesitated. "Forgive me, but I believe you're sad."

"I am thinking of another time," Kuni said. "Perhaps a better time." And he would speak no more.

This would be the day that the mighty hegemon would finally fall.

And then there they were, great clouds of dust and the sound of thousands of horses panting and neighing as they drew near. The five thousand attackers, true to the code of Mata Zyndu, did not deviate from their course as they plowed straight toward the center of Kuni Garu's defensive formation, the densely packed phalanxes of infantry.

The Dasu longbowmen and spearmen unleashed their missiles as the riders got into range, and the sky darkened as clouds of arcing projectiles momentarily obscured the sun. Many of the arrows and spears hit their marks, and some of the riders fell from their horses, lifeless, unmoving. But other riders ignored the arrows that pierced their armor and kept on coming.

Closer and closer they rode. The ground shook. But the armored and masked riders were eerily silent. There were no battle cries. They pushed on relentlessly, fearless of the dense forest of deadly spikes that the pikemen raised in front of the infantry, their shafts braced firmly into the ground, the tips leaning forward, ready to skewer both men and horses by their own momentum.

Like a wave breaking against the craggy shores of fog-shrouded Faça, the riders of Mata Zyndu burst against the phalanxes of Kuni Garu. The air was filled with the screams of dying horses as the pikes impaled them.

Men fell from their steeds. But the horsemen behind them kept on coming, keeping up the pressure. They leapt over their dead comrades or rode roughshod over them, using their bodies as stepping-stones to break through the wall of pikemen. The center of Kuni Garu's formation was slowly pushed back, as the pikemen dropped their weapons and unsheathed their short swords to join the infantry in hand-to-hand combat.

The sides of Kuni Garu's formation of foot soldiers began to envelop and surround the riders like soft dough wrapping around a dollop of stuffing. Kuni's cavalry rode behind the last of Mata's riders and closed the circle. Mata Zyndu had nowhere to go.

Mata faced ten times as many men as he had under his command; the hegemon's valor would not save him. Even if each of his soldiers were a berserker and fought with the strength of three, they would still all leave their bones on the battlefield today. Kuni's men rejoiced and shouted, anticipating victory.

But those closest to the surrounded Cocru riders realized that something was wrong. The men on the horses made no attempt to resist as they closed in. One slash; a rider fell down and did not raise his sword as ten more swords cut into his fallen body.

Kuni's soldiers withdrew their swords and saw no blood. When they flipped the dead body over, they saw why: They had not been fighting a man of Cocru, but a puppet made of straw and cloth.

Everywhere there was confusion and disbelief.

The sun was again momentarily obscured. Kuni's soldiers looked up and saw a fleet of fifty airships flying the colors of Cocru. The airships hovered over Zudi, and soldiers began to jump out of them, their descent slowed by large balloons of silk that the men opened over their heads.

TWO HOURS EARLIER.

Mata was aware of the world around him only faintly, a dim mix of light and sound. He had been riding nonstop for two days and two nights across the plains of Cocru. But he did not feel tired. He found the world distracting: All he needed was to see the narrow path before him, to feel Réfiroa's flesh rise and fall below him, to move his body in harmony. He would arrive at Zudi, and then he would achieve victory or die trying. Nothing else mattered. His life was simple.

But there was an obstacle ahead. Pulling on the reins, he slowed his great black horse for the first time in two days. A fleet of airships hovered before him. One of them had landed right in the path, and Torulu Pering was standing in front of it.

"Without access to Mount Kiji," Pering explained, "the airships have no way to replenish their lift gas. We will not be able to keep our fleet aloft much longer, not unless we begin to salvage some ships to refill others."

Mata nodded. "I intend to win at Zudi today."

"The odds are against you, but there is a way to even the odds."

Mata listened to Pering presenting his plan. And he laughed. He loved the boldness of the idea, the symmetry of it. Unlike Kuni's dirty tricks, Pering's plan had honor, valor, manliness. It was glorious.

∽ ∾ ∽ ∾

As Mata leapt out of the airship and plunged hundreds of feet in a few seconds, his only thought was how like the flight of an eagle this was, this dive toward the ground, toward helpless prey.

And then the air balloon, which Pering had designed, released from his back. With a loud *whump* it opened and caught the air racing past his falling body. Suddenly, he was jerked up and began to descend at a much slower pace.

*And now I am a Mingén falcon.*

He looked up and saw the bright white circle of silk that caught the air. He looked down and saw Zudi's tiny houses and orderly streets and the confused faces of the people looking up at this novel sight.

Mata laughed. While the defenders of Zudi were distracted by straw decoys, he was going to deal death from the air over Zudi, just as he had done once before. Though that seemed a long time ago now, when he and Kuni had fought side by side.

The houses, streets, and faces below grew larger and larger. Mata drew forth Na-aroénna and felt battle-lust course through his veins.

He began his war cries. There would be no doubt this time.

Mata Zyndu's surprise attack from the sky was a complete success. The Cocru soldiers quickly overwhelmed the small garrisons stationed at the city doors and turned the walls of Zudi against the Dasu army.

Since the gates were sealed, the army of fifty thousand outside could only mill around the city's walls helplessly as Mata's men set fire throughout the city and searched for Kuni. Only a few dozen Dasu men managed to make their way back into the city using battle kites—among them Mün Çakri and Than Carucono, who could not bear the thought of abandoning their lord. But this was like trying to put out a fire using teacups, and the Dasu army soon gave up.

Captain Dosa, Mün Çakri, Rin Coda, and Than Carucono rushed

into the mayor's house, where Kuni and his family were staying, with the bad news.

"Sire, Zudi has fallen! Mata's men will be here soon. We have one messenger airship that Marshal Mazoti had left behind for an emergency. It's ready to take off in the courtyard. You must get on it right away."

"I'll hold them off in the streets as long as I can," Captain Dosa said, and left with his soldiers.

Kuni ran around to round up everyone. The messenger airship was small, however, and all the servants would have to be left behind. Kuni's father, Féso Garu, Kuni, Jia, the children, Risana, Soto, Otho, Mün, Rin, and Than climbed aboard. There was hardly enough room left to turn around in, let alone move.

The airship would not take off.

"There's too many of us," Mün said.

"Mata has left me alone all this time, and he'll probably continue to do so. And if I'm going to die anywhere, I'm going to die here, in my home." Féso Garu climbed off despite the protests from Kuni. But the ship still refused to lift.

"We must have forgotten to check the lift gas level earlier," Than said. They heard the clashing of swords and screams from the inhabitants of Zudi in the streets. Mata's men were not far.

Than, Rin, and Mün all got off. The ship remained stubbornly on the ground.

Soto went next. "Mata would never harm me," said Soto. "Don't worry."

Jia and Otho caught each other's eyes for a brief moment. Otho smiled at her and stepped off the ship wordlessly. Jia closed her eyes, her heart pounding.

They both knew that such a day would come. It might be true that a heart has room for more than one love, but in this world, a woman still had to make choices that a man did not have to. Jia looked away.

The ship budged, but settled down on the ground again.

Risana and Jia looked at each other. Risana turned and gave Kuni a kiss and began to walk off the ship. Her movements were slow and difficult due to her very pregnant belly.

"No, no," Jia said. "You go with Kuni and the children. I'll stay with Soto and Otho. I'm used to dealing with Mata. I'll be fine."

Kuni's face became twisted with anxiety and pain. "No, that is not right. Both of you stay on board. *I* will stay and speak with Mata myself."

Everyone protested at this. Mün's voice rang out the loudest. "There's no point to any of this if *you* don't get out. Lord Garu, you must leave so that you can rescue us or avenge us."

Kuni looked at Jia, and then at Risana, then at Jia, then at Risana. Suddenly he turned to the children and knelt down. "Timu and Théra," he said, using their formal names, which he rarely did, "you have to do something brave for me, all right?"

He carried the children to the door of the airship and asked for Soto to come and get them.

"You're insane," shouted Jia. "How can you even think of such a thing?"

"Mata won't harm children," said Kuni. "But no matter what, I can't leave you behind again. There won't be another you, but there can always be more children."

"Jia is right," said Rin Coda. "This is madness." He blocked the door and pushed the children back onto the ship. Kuni continued to shout for Soto and pushed the children out again, and Rin pushed them back in again. Soto stood by and watched expressionlessly.

"Enough of this nonsense," Jia said. She firmly pushed Kuni back into the ship and bent down to kiss the children. Then she turned to Risana. "Little Sister, please take good care of them."

Risana nodded, and Jia resolutely stepped off the ship.

"Mama, Mama!" Timu and Théra cried out, and Risana had to hold them back as Kuni, also teary-eyed, closed the door of the airship.

Now that the ship had only the weight of Kuni, Risana, and the two children to deal with, it rose slowly into the sky. Rin Coda had taken care to drape the ship in black cloth. Pursuers both in the sky and on the ground would have a hard time picking it out against the night sky unless they knew exactly where to look. The ship rose until it was a small shadow against the stars, then turned north, heading toward the safety of Géfica.

For a second, Jia wished she did not always appear so strong, so capable of taking care of herself that Kuni actually believed her.

Soto and Jia stood on one side of the group left behind. Soto gave her a meaningful look and said in a low voice, "That was a nice bit of theater by both you and Kuni back there."

Jia flushed with anger momentarily. "I don't know what you mean."

Soto rolled her eyes. "Kuni made a show of loving both of you equally, to the point where he would give up his children. Since few men would pick their wives over their heirs, he was trying to score some points with you. This would also make a nice story among the people of Dara."

Jia smiled a sad smile. "Kuni was always clever."

"Not as clever as you. By staying behind with me while leaving the children with *her*, you put both of them in your debt. She'll now always think that you saved her life, and Kuni will always feel guilty about your sacrifice. You've laid the foundation for future palace intrigue. This investment may well pay off a hundredfold someday."

"You make both of us sound so calculating and cold," Jia said. "Can't you just attribute our actions to love?"

Soto laughed, and after a while, Jia reluctantly joined in. Truth be told, even Jia wasn't sure why she had done what she did. It wasn't just about jostling for political position with Risana, but it also wasn't purely unselfish. Sometimes it was hard to tell where the performance ended and the real self began—but what was this "real" self other than a set of performances?

Love was a complicated thing, she conceded.

"The only fool I pity here is that girl, Risana. She has no idea who she's dealing with," Soto said.

Their brief moment of merriment was interrupted by the sound of shouting men and clashing swords in the street. The gates to the mayor's house flew open, and a blood-soaked Captain Dosa stumbled in, his body pierced by arrows.

Mata was here.

CHAPTER FORTY-SEVEN

# THE STANDOFF AT LIRU RIVER

DIMU AND DIMUSHI: THE NINTH MONTH IN THE FOURTH YEAR OF THE PRINCIPATE.

Mata Zyndu's surprise victory at Zudi soon entered into the realm of myth all over Dara.

"Each of his men fought with the strength of twenty, and that was how the hegemon defeated a force ten times greater than his."

"Mata Zyndu is Fithowéo incarnate. When he waves his hand, soldiers fall from the sky to fight for him."

"Kuni Garu may have ridden a cruben, but Mata Zyndu eats cruben steaks for dinner."

After Kuni safely escaped to Dimushi, he immediately recalled Marshal Mazoti.

"What's next?" Kuni asked.

"I have to first re-create the army you lost."

Kuni Garu winced at this, but Marshal Mazoti never bothered to sugarcoat things.

"I think most of the troops escaped back to Géfica after the fall of

Zudi, though undoubtedly many deserted. It will take some work to restore morale after the humiliation you suffered, with even Lady Jia taken prisoner. Marquess Yemu's 'noble raiders' are still making trouble for the hegemon in Cocru, though, so he can't invade Géfica until he secures his supply lines."

"What about the other Tiro states?"

"Many of them now think it wiser to side with Mata rather than you. However, Duke Théca Kimo remains firmly in your camp. He has now pacified Arulugi, and his fate obviously depends on your success. He has asked for permission to sweep through both Crescent Island and Écofi, which, given the tiny populations on those islands, will be easy."

"Let him."

"You are not concerned that he might grow too strong and declare independence, like Mocri did in Wolf's Paw?"

"Mata's weakness is that he doesn't trust people, so of course everyone who follows him eventually betrays him. I don't intend to make the same mistake."

Mazoti nodded thoughtfully.

Cocru and Dasu again stood off across the Liru River.

Mata brought to Dimu the prisoners he'd captured in Zudi. In exchange for Kuni's release of Noda Mi and Doru Solofi, Mata agreed to return Mün Çakri, Rin Coda, and Than Carucono. But he kept Kuni's family despite repeated entreaties from Kuni.

Mata decided to press the psychological advantage he had to the fullest. On a large flat-bottomed boat—slow and shallow-drafting and thus not a military threat—he rode into the middle of the Liru and asked Kuni to join him for parley.

Kuni rode out on a flat-bottomed boat of his own. The two sat in formal *mipa rari* on the top decks of their respective vessels, staring at each other across a sliver of river water.

*"Brother."* Mata spat out the word like a curse. "I had hoped to see you in Zudi, but apparently you were too ashamed to see me."

"Brother." Kuni sighed. "I wish we were still friends. This all could have been avoided if you had not been so jealous and full of rage when I entered Pan before you. We could have rebuilt Dara from the ruins of the empire together."

The two sat quietly for a while, contemplating what might have been.

"Yet events have proven my foresight. You're now in rebellion against me."

Kuni shook his head. "It's not you I'm fighting against, but the idea you represent. I mean to re-create the dream of Emperor Mapidéré, but this time I'll do it right. You want to leave the world to be divided between Tiro states, full of endless wars to serve the empty martial glory of the great nobles. I want to end all that and give the common people a chance to live their lives in peace. Mata, don't stand in my way. Abdicate and hand me the seal of the world."

"You're as ambitious as I am, only you dress up your desires with lies. If you really believe your pretty words, why don't we settle our differences in single combat? Let no one else die for our dispute. You and me and our swords will decide our fate. Whoever wins gets to remake this world with his will."

Kuni laughed. "You know me too well to think that I'd agree to something like that. I'm no match for you in a fight, but wars are not won by the strength in one's arms alone."

Mata gestured to his men, and they went inside the ship and brought up a large cutting board.

Kuni stared at it, confused.

They went inside again and brought up a pot large enough to cook a whole shark in. Setting it over a fire in the open-air hearth on top of the deck, they boiled water in it.

Kuni's heart tightened.

They went inside again and brought up a kitchen knife, but it was so large that it was like a giant's axe. A man would have to use both arms to wield it.

Kuni stood up. He wanted to tell Mata to stop.

They went down a final time and brought up a naked man trussed up like a pig. Kuni saw that it was his father, Féso Garu. He had been gagged, and his eyes bulged in fear.

Mata's men laid Féso on the cutting board, and a burly man gripped the oversized kitchen knife and held it over his head like an executioner.

"Kuni, surrender. Or I will cook your father in front of you and eat him."

Blood rushed to Kuni's head, and he almost fainted. But he held on to the railing before him and drove all emotions from his face. He couldn't tell how serious Mata was with this threat. This was just like playing a game of cards during his time as a gangster, except this time, he had much more at stake.

"If you surrender, Kuni, I will allow you to stay in Dasu and Rui, and all your men will be pardoned for their acts of disloyalty to me."

*He's lying,* Kuni thought. *Mata hates betrayal more than anything else. He'll never forgive me or any of my men. If I agree to surrender, all of us will die.*

Kuni sat back and relaxed his legs into *thakrido*. He laughed. "Go ahead, Mata. Cook him. Cook our father."

Mata Zyndu narrowed his eyes. "What?"

"You once called me 'brother,' so my father is also your father. If you want to cook our father today, I won't stop you. Just make sure you save some for me. I'd like a taste too."

"What manner of son are you?"

Kuni focused every ounce of attention to the muscles of his face and his tongue and throat. *Perform!* "Do you think that if I intend to replace you, I would be stopped by the loss of a single life? I invaded Rui when Jia was in your hands; I was prepared to leave my children behind in Zudi; do not underestimate me, for I am as dangerous and ruthless as you. I've seen plenty of men die. Now hurry up and kill him."

Mata stared at Kuni with sorrow. He had staged this execution as a test, and this speech from Kuni had confirmed that he was right to distrust the man, for he was utterly cold, calculating, and without morals. *How could Kuni even believe for a minute that I would kill and eat his father? He has such a low opinion of me only because he's irredeemably corrupt himself.* There were no lines the man wasn't willing to cross; ambition had consumed him. To think that he had once called this man *brother*!

*It's impossible to see into men's hearts.* The last glimmer of hope in his mind died.

Kuni leaned forward, eagerly looking into Mata's eyes. "Cook him! Cook him so I can focus on how to get you into the pot one day."

Mata shook his head. He would demonstrate his moral superiority to Kuni today and shame him with his lack of natural filial sentiments—even if it was doubtful that Kuni had any sense of shame left. That had always been Kuni's problem, utter lack of honor.

Mata ordered the fire extinguished and Féso Garu taken away. "Men ultimately sink to their true stations. You're a heartless thug, Kuni, and the people of Dara will see through your facade."

He sailed back toward Dimu, and behind him, Kuni waited until Mata was out of sight before collapsing to the deck. His clothes were soaked through with sweat, and he felt as though his heart had been pried from him.

Just because Kuni managed to bluff Mata, it didn't mean that Mata's trick wouldn't work on others. Rin Coda immediately suggested that Kuni put Mata's idea to work for himself.

"Several of the Tiro states have agreed to ally themselves with you," said Rin. "It wouldn't hurt to get a little bit of insurance. Also, having those princes and princesses here will give me more opportunities to gather intelligence."

"Ah, Rin," Kuni said, a bitter smile on his face. "Now I wonder if it was a good idea to make you spymaster. You've been hanging around with men comfortable with darker methods for too long."

"Whether the path is well-lit or dark," said Rin, "what matters is that we get there."

Kuni sent out messengers to his allies, saying that he was concerned about the safety of their families. Perhaps, he suggested, it would be best for them to send their families to Dimushi, where the Dasu army could protect them. "With your families by my side, you can continue the fight against the hegemon without worrying about your loved ones."

Reluctantly, the Tiro kings sent their hostages to Kuni.

THE THIRD MONTH OF THE
FIFTH YEAR OF THE PRINCIPATE.

An informal armistice was now in place along the Liru. The people along the river tried to carry on their lives the best they could while living in a war zone that could heat up again at any minute. Merchants and fishing ships cautiously sailed up and down the river. Zones of control and safe passage for civilian vessels had to be negotiated. From time to time, Kuni and Mata sent each other envoys to work out these issues.

One day, a messenger from Mata arrived at the docks of Dimushi, where Luan Zya greeted him.

"Welcome, welcome! You come bearing a message from Master Pering? How is he?"

The messenger, whose name was Luing, was confused. "A message from Master Pering?"

"Oh, of course." Luan Zya looked at him and winked conspiratorially. With a show of nonchalance, he glanced at the two guards the messenger had brought with him. "Too many ears here. May I inquire after the health of the hegemon?"

Luing replayed the comment from Luan in his head again and again. *What did Luan mean about Pering? And why was he so happy to see me?*

Luan brought Luing to the best restaurant in Dimushi, where Luan ordered a lavish lunch of thirty courses, served with eating sticks made from ivory and inlaid with gold. A serving woman came in to light incense burners that filled the room with thick, fragrant smoke.

"It's fashionable to eat Dasu food with smoke," explained Luan. "It cleanses the palate and brings out the flavor of the spices."

The meal went on for hours. Luing felt light-headed and drowsy. After a while, the two guards accompanying Luing seemed to have trouble staying upright.

"They've drunk too much," said Luan, laughing. He summoned servants to bring them downstairs to nap in a private room.

"Now that we are alone, you can feel free to give me the message from Master Pering," Luan Zya said.

"There is no message from Master Pering," Luing said, bewildered. "I'm here on the hegemon's orders to discuss fishing rights around Kidima upriver."

"You are not sent by Torulu Pering?" Luan asked, incredulous.

"No," said Luing.

Luan sighed, shook his head, and rolled his eyes. He then forced himself to smile. "I have no idea what I'm talking about. I think I'm drunk. Forget everything I said today. It must be this herbal mixture I'm taking for my gout—it's making me very confused. Please excuse me . . . I . . . need to go."

He got up and hurried downstairs.

Though the smoke from the incense burners continued to hover in fantastic, shifting shapes—flexing rings, pulsing domes, translucent, billowy bubbles—the air in the room seemed to clear, and Luing felt clarity return to his mind. He thought and thought about the day's events and came to a bold conclusion, like a monstrous shape glimpsed through fog. But he needed more evidence.

Servants came to show Luing to his room in the inn. When Luing asked when he would get to speak with King Kuni's representatives about the matter he came to discuss, the servants replied that they had no idea.

The next day, a minor Dasu functionary named Daco Nir came to see Luing. Daco was rude and cold to Luing, and the negotiations went nowhere. When it came time for lunch, Daco handed a few copper coins to Luing and told him to get some food from the street vendors.

"I don't think we'll make any more progress, right? I'm busy for the rest of the day, so I don't think I can see you off at the pier. Have a safe trip home." Daco disappeared.

Luan Zya, Lady Risana, and "Daco Nir" watched from the window of a warehouse as the small boat of the hegemon's emissary left the docks.

"Your skill is indeed unparalleled," Luan said to Risana. "He saw exactly what you wanted him to see yesterday."

Risana inclined her head in acknowledgment. "You're too kind. It was but a parlor trick." She turned to Rin Coda and smiled. "But look at you! Your face today was so frosty, I could have sworn I heard ice chunks clink in his tea."

"I've had a lot of practice. When I use that expression, people pay me more to get access to the king."

Luan shook his head, and all three laughed.

Luing compared his treatment today with his treatment yesterday. The day before, Luan, Kuni Garu's closest adviser, treated him as an honored guest because he thought Luing was a secret envoy from Torulu Pering. But today this minor bureaucrat dealt with him arrogantly and dismissively because Kuni's men had ascertained that Luing was an ambassador from the hegemon. The facts spoke for themselves.

"Hegemon, don't you see that this is nothing but another trick from Garu?"

Mata regarded the trembling figure of Torulu Pering coldly. He had always found Pering untrustworthy.

The man was not a warrior, but an *adviser*, the sort of man who naturally gravitated toward Kuni Garu, who relied on tricks. He had no appreciation for the nobler virtues that could only be understood in battle. Even though Pering had come up with some good ideas, generally, he was meddlesome and often got in the way. Mata was quite willing to believe that he was secretly in league with Kuni Garu, plotting against him.

"Luan Zya was expecting a message from you. Were you going to offer a detailed listing of my order of battle? Were you going to offer to bribe my officers? Were you going to offer to present Kuni my head on a platter?"

Torulu Pering trembled not from fear, but anger. He had served Mata Zyndu loyally all this time, trying to get him to fight smarter, to be more vigilant against the wily Kuni Garu. Yet Mata was falling for such a simple trick, a trick that a five-year-old would have seen through.

"If you really don't trust me," Pering said, "then please accept my resignation. I would like to go home, to my ancestral farm near Çaruza, and plant yams. I won't serve a lord who cannot tell friend from foe."

"I accept. Go home, old man."

Torulu walked along the road, but his mind was all chaos and his heart in turmoil.

He was consumed with grief and anger at his own failure. He had failed to teach Mata Zyndu to appreciate the value of strategy. He had failed to make him see how dangerous and manipulative Kuni Garu was. He had failed as an adviser. For all his service, in the end, he had only earned the dismissive moniker of "old man."

But Torulu was indeed old, and he was not used to the exertion of journeying far on his own, without a comfortable carriage and a staff of young aides. His stomach ached, and in the heat he felt dizzy, but he was too angry and sorrowful to stop and rest and drink some water. He pressed on.

Men and women rushed by him, telling him to turn around and run. "Bandits are coming!"

Torulu didn't hear them. He was still thinking about what he could have done differently. *Foolish Mata, know that I could have guided you to victory!*

The Whirlwind Riders of Dasu rushed by. Carelessly, casually, one of the passing horsemen slashed out, and Pering stopped feeling sorry for himself, stopped thinking altogether. His head flew through the air.

Luan and Kuni toasted each other on the success of their plot.

"Now Mata has no one to counsel him at all."

Kuni drank, but he felt a gnawing sense of regret. Torulu Pering was a capable man who had saved the rebellion at a critical moment, and he deserved better. Kuni was uneasy about how much blood he was spilling in the pursuit of victory. Did the end always justify the means?

He wished the gods would give him a clear answer.

"There are no clear answers," Luan Zya said.

Kuni realized that he had paused, mid-drink. He laughed weakly and drained the cup.

"To know the future is to have no choice," Luan continued, "to be words fixed on a page by someone else. We can only do what we think is best, trusting that it will all somehow work out."

"I know," Kuni said. "The people think I see a clear path, but I'm stumbling in the dark too."

"Maybe that's what the gods are doing, as well."

CHAPTER FORTY-EIGHT

# THE MARSHAL'S GAMBIT

RIMA AND FAÇA: THE THIRD MONTH OF THE FIFTH YEAR OF THE PRINCIPATE.

As Cocru and Dasu were evenly matched along the Liru, Luan Zya and Gin Mazoti presented a plan to Kuni Garu to shift the strategic balance of power.

Up north, Faça and the reconstituted Rima—which everyone assumed was following Faça's lead—had switched their allegiance between Dasu and Cocru several times and thus avoided being invaded by either. Most recently, they had both declared for Mata, given the lack of recent military success from Kuni.

They could become examples for the other states.

Taking only a small force of five thousand, Marshal Mazoti left Dimushi and marched to the coast of Zathin Gulf, close to Rima. There, she said good-bye to Luan Zya, who put on a disguise and, alone, piloted a small fishing skiff toward fog-shrouded Boama, capital of Faça.

Within the territories of old ring-wooded Rima, Mata Zyndu had created six new Tiro states. After a year of warfare, most of the new

Tiro states were gone, and all the land was now consolidated under the control of Zato Ruthi, who had been one of King Jizu's teachers when he first arrived at the palace in Na Thion. Later, he had immortalized Jizu's sacrifice to save Na Thion from Namen's army in a eulogy that every child in Rima could recite.

The rise of Zato Ruthi was the result of a series of accidents that was unlikely to ever repeat again. He was a scholar through and through, in the mold of someone who preferred neat books to anything in the messy real world.

As a child, rather than playing with friends, Zato memorized all the numbered sayings of the ancient Ano epigrammatist, Ra Oji. As a young man, rather than carousing with friends in bars, he stayed home and read all the commentaries on the ancient Ano moral philosopher Kon Fiji's treatise on an ideal society. Disdaining the civil service examinations because they interfered with the pure contemplation of ideas, he refused to seek gainful employment but journeyed deep into Rima's ancient woods to study in a tiny hut he constructed himself. By the time he was thirty, he was recognized as one of the greatest scholars of ancient philosophy in all of Dara, a rival of Tan Féuji and Lügo Crupo, though he had never studied in the famed academies of Haan.

Tanno Namen spared him when Na Thion fell, and he then traveled between the capitals of the new Tiro states, which Mata Zyndu had created in his beloved old Rima, teaching and lecturing.

As wars destroyed one Tiro state after another, the new conquerors always made a point to seek out Zato to get him to "bless" the new administration as being in harmony with Kon Fiji's moral principles. On some level, Zato Ruthi surely understood that he was being used as a tool of propaganda, but he appreciated the attention that the powerful gave him, and he liked being treated as if his opinion mattered.

The last two Tiro states left in old Rima then went to war, as all along they knew they would. Neither could subdue the other, and as their armies clashed all over Rima, the people suffered.

Then King Shilué of Faça, as was his habit, decided to intervene again in the affairs in Rima and sent his troops to Na Thion to add to the chaos.

As the people of Na Thion suffered yet another military occupation, anger and despair filled the streets. One day, students of the Na Thion Academy took to the streets, demanding that Shilué go home with his foreign army, that the two kings of Rima stop the war, and that the people be left to live in peace.

Idle merchants, who had no business to conduct because of the war; idle farmers, who had no land to till because of the war; and idle workers, who had nothing to do because of the war, joined the students, and mobs of rioters filled the streets. The students led them to the Palace of Na Thion, where Shilué was negotiating with the ambassadors of the two kings of Rima.

The students carried Zato Ruthi on their shoulders, and they hailed him as their leader. "Teacher! Teacher! You've always wanted to build a state in the image of Kon Fiji's ancient virtues. Now's our chance!"

They chanted before the palace, and before he even understood what was happening, Zato Ruthi found himself standing on a makeshift stage in front of the palace, speaking to a crowd of thousands of angry men.

He rehearsed his old themes about the obligations of the ruler toward the ruled, about the importance of restraint and respect and justice and the right to eat, about the need for harmonious relations among all people in a state, and about the injustice of foreign military interference.

It was nothing new, and there was nothing special to the way he spoke, but the crowd roared and clapped, and he felt as though he was being lifted on their voices, on their strength of will. And his words became more fiery in response. He called for the people to tear the palace down, to usher in a more harmonious and just Rima.

Shilué and the ambassadors trembled in the palace, but Shilué shrewdly saw an opportunity. He pressed the two kings of Rima to not only agree to a cease-fire, but to abdicate their thrones and to support Zato Ruthi as the king of a unified new Rima.

"The people have spoken," he said, "and they are not calling for either of your names."

In reality, Shilué thought that Zato, being a mere scholar with no experience at administration, would be an easier puppet to control from Boama than either of the two kings, and he made it clear that Faça's troops were ready to "support the people of Rima and their choice."

Thus did Zato Ruthi become the King of Rima.

Marshal Mazoti called on King Zato to surrender three times. Each time her messengers were rebuffed but returned with earnest letters addressed to Mazoti from Zato:

> *It is known to every child of Dara that all Tiro states are equal, and none can claim lordship over another. King Kuni has breached this principle, which was set forth by the infallible Aruano and approved by the wise Kon Fiji. The hegemon will surely punish King Kuni for these violations of the moral principles governing relations among states.*
>
> *Even worse, King Kuni has made a woman into a soldier and elevated her above men. This is at odds with the principles governing harmonious relations among the sexes that Kon Fiji so eloquently explained centuries ago. Rima hopes that King Kuni will soon recover from his errors and apologize for his mistakes. It is the only way for Dasu to be restored to honor.*

Mazoti rolled her eyes. The words from Zato were as musty and stale as the old books that no one read. Coming from anyone else, the words would have been understood as sarcastic insults, but Mazoti knew that Zato was completely serious. He genuinely believed that there were "moral principles governing relations among states" and didn't see them as the codification of the robber's logic employed by strong states seeking to impose their will on weak ones.

As Mazoti's troops wound their way through tree-canopied Rima, they encountered no resistance. The woodsmen and hunters were told that Kuni Garu's soldiers would leave civilians alone unless they took up arms against them. They stood silently in front of their cottages or moved off the trails as Mazoti's army marched south through the thick forest.

Sometimes a soldier would exchange a knowing smile with a woodsman standing by the side of the trail.

War was fought mostly for the benefit of the nobles, and it was best if it could be fought quickly so as to bother the common people the least. King Kuni at least seemed to honor *that* principle.

The Dasu army came to a small and shallow river about fifty feet wide. It was now spring, and the river, swelled by the melting of winter snow, ran cold and fast. Mazoti could see the defenders of Rima on the other side. They were not stationed at the shore, however, but stood about a mile off.

"Why are they so far off?" one of Mazoti's aides-de-camp asked. "It's not as if they are holding a hill either. There's no tactical advantage to their position."

Mazoti saw the black flags of Rima waving in the distance. The one in the middle was extra large, with golden borders.

"King Zato is with them. That would explain the bizarre location of Rima troops. Kon Fiji wrote in his books that it is not moral to attack an army while it's still fording a river. The defenders must give the attackers enough room to cross the river and set up its formation on the other side so that the fight will be fair."

"Kon Fiji wrote about military tactics?"

"That old fraud wrote about lots of things he knew nothing about. But we should thank him. Since Zato is such a faithful disciple of everything Kon Fiji taught, we'll have a safe crossing."

Five hundred of Mazoti's men crossed over first and set up

defensive lines on the other side of the river, just in case the Rima forces did attack. To avoid being swept away by the swift currents, the rest of the troops linked their arms and held on to one another as they forded the river. At the deepest part of the river, the water covered their chests. Officers and soldiers alike worried that the defenders might decide to charge when the bulk of the Dasu army was still on the north side of the river or in the middle of the crossing. They would be defenseless in the water.

But true to Marshal Mazoti's words, King Zato's men stayed where they were and watched Mazoti's army cross without harassing them.

"Unbelievable," the aide-de-camp said in wonder as the soldiers laid out their gear on the grassy banks to dry. The Rima forces still made no move.

The officers around King Zato were ready to pull their hair out.

"Sire, we must attack now, before Mazoti's troops complete the crossing."

"Nonsense. We outnumber her forces three to one. Besides, she's a woman. Kon Fiji wrote that an army imbued with righteousness would defeat an army steeped in immorality. How can attacking the enemy before they are ready to defend themselves be righteous?"

"Sire, we must attack now, before her men put their armor back on."

"You wish to besmirch the name of our army? What would King Jizu, the Pure-Hearted Ruler, say of your plots? No, we must wait. Besides, look how she's gathering her soldiers into formation! Kon Fiji taught us that when there's a river around, one should never set up the infantry so that the soldiers' backs are against the river because they will have no room to maneuver. We gave them plenty of space to properly form up, yet Mazoti is lining up her men against the shore of the river.

"I wonder if she has ever read the wise books of Kon Fiji or even can read at all. Poor men of Dasu! To be led by an ignorant girl into death is a truly tragic fate!"

∽ ∾ ∽ ∾

"You're taking a page from Mata Zyndu's exploits, aren't you?" Mazoti's aide asked. He glanced back at the tight ranks of men right behind him, all the way back to the shore of the river. There was no room to retreat. The only way to go was forward.

"I've always said that we should make use of every advantage we can find," Gin Mazoti said evenly. "Mata Zyndu had the right idea on Wolf's Paw. Why shouldn't I copy him? Putting your own men into a position where they believe they are dead unless they win is a good tactic—as long as it's not used too often."

They waited, as the forces of Rima finally began to move toward them.

King Zato's soldiers pressed on, hoping to drive Mazoti's five thousand men right into the water. But Mazoti's men dug their heels in and fought with a ferocity that their opponents could not match.

The battle lasted all afternoon, but by the time twilight descended over the banks, Mazoti's smaller force had the definite upper hand.

Finally, King Zato's lines collapsed, and the surviving soldiers of Rima scattered into the woods.

Mazoti wiped the blood from her face and congratulated her soldiers. It was not quite as impressive a victory as Mata Zyndu's at Wolf's Paw, but for Mazoti's men, it was a solid win that felt good after their humiliating defeat at Zudi.

Meanwhile, far to the north, Luan Zya's fishing skiff pulled into the harbor at Boama, capital of Faça.

Faça was a land of craggy coastlines and rugged highlands in the north, where most of the population ranched, and deep valleys and sunny hillsides in the south, where most of the population planted orchards. Fruitful Faça was where one found sheep with the thickest wool, cattle with the fattest shoulders, and apples that were crisp and sweet, with a sun-kissed bite that lingered in the mouth.

The fierce fighters of Faça were as rugged as the terrain. They could move over the highlands faster than horsemen and were skilled at turning the landscape's jagged rocky outcroppings and the capricious, ever-present fog against their enemies. Faça's traditional swordfighting techniques were different from Cocru's but no less effective: They emphasized surprise, unpredictability, and quick footwork.

Faça had rarely been successfully invaded in the past. Mapidéré's conquest of Faça relied on assassinations, plots, and the deaths of many Xana soldiers as they finally overwhelmed the determined defenders through sheer advantage of numbers.

Another invasion of Faça would be costly.

Luan did not want to see Kuni or Gin repeat such a feat with the blood of Dasu, and so he had come to Boama in secret to try to persuade the greedy, crafty, politic King Shilué to surrender.

*If I can.*

The Palace of Boama was built right on the shore, over a cliff plunging into the ocean. Fog drifted through its courtyards and porticoed halls, making the castle seem to float in the clouds.

"King Kuni has always treated his followers with generosity," Luan began. "Have you not heard that he negotiated for the return of his generals, Mün Çakri and Than Carucono, even before he asked for the return of his family? Have you not heard how Théca Kimo is now duke of the three islands of Arulugi, Crescent, and Écofi? Have you not heard how Marquess Puma Yemu, by raiding in the king's name, now has a treasure hoard larger than the treasuries of many Tiro kings? King Kuni rewards those who fight for him."

Shilué sat opposite Luan, carefully chewing oysters and listening without speaking. In the fog-filtered light, the expression on his pale face was unreadable, and his blond hair glowed like a veil.

Luan went on. "But Mata Zyndu has always treated his followers with whim and jealousy. Have you not heard how the hegemon stripped Puma Yemu of his title and land? Have you not heard how he blamed Noda Mi and Doru Solofi for losing Géfica and abused them with words of contempt and mockery until they left him in disgrace? Have you not seen how he hesitated to hand out the seals of power and was sorrowful at having to distribute treasure to men who risked life and limb for him? Mata Zyndu is not a lord you can rely on."

Shilué continued to chew and listen, then he swallowed.

"Théca and Puma are brutes who serve King Kuni by risking their lives," said Shilué. "But what promises can you make to someone civilized, someone who does not wish to die?"

*Ah, he wishes to have all the advantages of surrender without any of the risks*, thought Luan. And he spoke again.

Mazoti pursued the remnants of King Zato's army until they reached another river, this one narrower. King Zato had finally learned his lesson. He set up his defenses right on the southern shore, not giving Mazoti a chance to cross.

"If we can't get to him, we'll make him come to us," Mazoti said.

She directed a few hundred men to sneak through the dark forest in secret. Upstream, they felled some large trees quickly and built a dam to hold back the water, creating a large artificial lake.

As the water downstream slowed to a trickle, Mazoti's men appeared to react with terror. They abandoned their cooking pots and weapons and backed away from the muddy streambed as if in panic.

King Zato gave the order for the Rima army to cross the stream and give chase. "Fithowéo and the spirit of Honored King Jizu must be with us! How else can we explain the sudden, diminished flow? Look at how the men of Dasu flee from our righteous arms! We must cross and punish the invaders."

The Rima commanders said that this might be a trick and asked King Zato to stay behind with half of Rima's forces just in case something went wrong.

But King Zato scoffed. "Kon Fiji taught that when victorious, one should pursue with every soldier to show that there is no fear. A righteous army has no need to fear treachery, for the gods will protect them. If Mazoti is righteous and follows the laws of war, she will give us the courtesy of waiting until we have safely crossed before she attacks, the very same benefit we gave her. If she is not righteous and attacks before we are done crossing, then surely she will lose."

Mazoti waited until about one-third of Rima's forces had crossed the stream and one-third was in the process of crossing. She ordered the trumpeters to give the order for the soldiers upstream to break their dam. The sudden flood washed the soldiers who were still in the streambed away and stranded the other one-third who were still on the southern shore. Then she gave the order for the "retreating" Dasu troops to counterattack. The Rima soldiers who had completed the crossing were quickly captured.

The remaining forces of King Zato fled in terror, and Mazoti dammed up the river again and walked leisurely across.

"You disobeyed the laws of war," King Zato said. He knelt before Marshal Mazoti in the Palace of Na Thion, but his voice was defiant. "Have you ever read the books of Kon Fiji?"

"He had some good things to say about government," Mazoti replied. "But he didn't know anything about how to fight a war."

King Zato shook his head sadly. "You cannot win true victory if you don't follow the laws of war. You are only a woman, after all, and you do not understand the greater principles involved."

"Right," Mazoti said, smiling. She didn't want to execute the old fool. Instead, she sent him to Dimushi, where Kuni Garu might find him entertaining.

Luan Zya came to Na Thion to see Gin Mazoti.

They occupied one of the many bedrooms in the Palace of Na Thion and spent some time *not* discussing the war.

In the morning, Luan congratulated Mazoti for her swift conquest of Rima and then explained that King Shilué of Faça had agreed to surrender.

"How?"

"I talked him into it," said Luan, laughing.

Mazoti did not seem pleased at this news. She sat, deep in thought.

"What's wrong?" Luan asked.

"I've fought for months in Rima, and hundreds, thousands of men had to die before I brought Rima under control. You, on the other hand, captured all of Faça by only wagging your tongue. What will Lord Garu think of our relative merit?"

"Gin, you are not seriously jealous, are you?"

Mazoti said nothing. It always seemed that no matter how hard a woman worked, a man could eclipse her with no effort.

"Gin, I have to head back to Dimushi to advise Lord Garu. Can you go to Boama to formally accept the surrender and provide Shilué with the protection that is his condition?"

Gin Mazoti nodded, and she and Luan kissed and parted ways.

The men of Faça did not put up any fight as Marshal Mazoti and her soldiers marched through the highlands. On Shilué's orders, they were hailed as allies, as the army of Faça's new protector.

In the palace at Boama, King Shilué welcomed Mazoti with an elaborate banquet. Bare-breasted female dancers were brought out to entertain the honored guest, as was customary. Only when the music began did Shilué realize that this might not be the most appropriate way to entertain this particular marshal.

But Mazoti assured him that it was all right. She would enjoy the show as much as any man. King Shilué toasted her and said that he looked forward to working with her in the service of their common lord.

"Shilué, do you confess your sins?"

Shilué was feeling very drunk, so he wasn't quite sure that he had heard the marshal correctly.

"What?"

"Your plot to betray King Kuni," Mazoti said. She unsheathed her sword and killed Shilué on the spot.

As the assembled ministers and generals of Faça stood in shock,

Mazoti's men quickly secured the palace. Outside, the Dasu troops had already seized Boama's gates and harbors.

Mazoti sent a fast messenger airship back to Dimushi with this note:

> *Faça has been conquered. The plan for surrender was a trick Shilué used to fool Luan Zya. He had planned to betray you and defect to Mata Zyndu again. But I saw through the ruse and executed him for treason before he could put the plot into motion.*

She felt a twinge of guilt, but in war, every victory was good, whether against enemies, friends, or lovers.

## CHAPTER FORTY-NINE

# THE TEMPTATION OF GIN MAZOTI

BOAMA: THE FIFTH MONTH IN THE FIFTH YEAR OF THE PRINCIPATE.

Now that Mazoti was in control of both Faça and Rima, as well as tens of thousands of newly surrendered troops, there was a lot of work to do.

People now addressed her as "Queen of Faça and Rima." She had started it as a joke, but then, since no one else seemed to treat it as a joke, she began to think of herself that way.

She put the troops through war exercises, promoted those capable, asked for demonstrations of sword-fighting techniques from veterans. She distributed pensions to the families of soldiers who died fighting for Dasu and for her. She encouraged Rima's bladesmiths with new tax breaks—a trick she had learned from Kuni Garu. She toured the ranches and orchards of Faça, promising the people safety.

It was nice to be queen. Everyone listened to her.

Kuni paced back and forth, unable to stay still for even a moment.

"She's doing a fine job in Boama," Luan Zya said.

"But what about this title?"

"Lord Garu, you know that I cannot speak of her without bias. You must decide what to do about her claim to the thrones of Faça and Rima while she remains Dasu's marshal."

"I need your advice, Luan."

"I can't tell you what to do. We're all stumbling in the dark."

"I don't think what you two do in the dark is 'stumbling,'" Kuni said, giving Luan a look.

Luan Zya spread his hands. "Gin keeps her own counsel, you know that."

"If the hegemon were in my place, he would be marching to Boama right now."

"But you are not Mata Zyndu."

"Yet I wonder if Mata's choice, in this case, would be right."

Lady Risana came into the room. In her arms she carried her new baby. Kuni reached out, and Risana handed the baby to him. Timu and Théra were still awkward with Kuni, as they missed their mother and were not used to their father. The king was thus extra affectionate toward the little boy. The prince, still not formally named, was called Hudo-*tika*.

"If Gin were a man, would you know what to do?" Risana asked as Kuni stopped pacing and played with Hudo-*tika*.

Kuni considered the question. "Maybe. With ambitious men sometimes it's best to let them go as far as they want, so long as they're still helping you. You can't tell how high a kite can fly without being willing to let all the string out. Trust is often better than jealousy as a path to loyalty."

"That's a lesson that Mata Zyndu never learned," Luan Zya said.

"Does the fact that Gin is a woman make any difference?" Risana said. "Gin has always asked simply for the right to play by the same rules as the rest of you."

Kuni nodded. "You have again cleared away the fog in my thoughts. None of us are perfect, yet our imperfections may complement one another and become something grand. I'll congratulate Gin."

"What of her query to send you the Seals of Rima and Faça?" Luan asked.

Kuni tickled Hudo-*tika*, and waved a hand at Luan dismissively. "That query is a test. For me. Tell her to keep them and to take good care of Rima and Faça."

Queen Gin's guards brought to her a bald beggar in a white cape.

"He claims to have important information concerning the hegemon."

"What do you have to tell me, old man?" asked Gin.

"It's for your ears alone."

Gin waved the guards away. But she reached under her desk and grasped the handle of her trusty marshal's sword.

"Speak."

"Every once in a while, the gods send us gifts," the beggar said. "But these gifts are not pure blessings, for the gods have pride and jealousy, the same as mortals. If you refuse a gift from the gods, great misfortune will follow."

Gin laughed. "I grew up in the streets of Dimushi. Do you think I've not heard such speeches from a hundred frauds just like you? All right, how much money do you want? But I don't need you to tell my fortune."

"I'm no fortune-teller."

Gin regarded the beggar more closely. She saw the contrast between his dirty face and his spotless white cape; how he did not really lean on his walking stick; the way his face seemed to flicker between youth and old age in the sunlight filtered through the fog outside the windows of the palace in Boama.

She nodded for him to go on.

"Your Majesty, the Islands of Dara today are divided among three great heroes. Kuni Garu has the west, Mata Zyndu has the south, and you have the north. Garu and Zyndu are deadlocked along the Liru, and neither can gain an inch of advantage over the other. If you aid Garu, Zyndu will lose. If you aid Zyndu, Garu will lose."

"You're very bold."

"Yet if you aid either, in time the victor will turn on you, for great men do not like to be beholden to anyone. Thus, if you aid neither, that may be the most advantageous course for *you*. You now possess the realms of Faça and Rima. There's no reason why you can't conquer Gan and Wolf's Paw as well. At that point, both Garu and Zyndu will have to beg for your support, playing suitor for your regal favor. You can then seize the opportunity to take over all of Dara for yourself, if you like."

Mazoti pictured the Islands of Dara as a giant *cüpa* board. She imagined the stones being placed on the grid, a strategic vision that matched the beggar's words.

"If this is a future you want, you must declare your independence now and sever your allegiance to Kuni Garu. Let the world know that you are your own woman and follow no one's orders but yours."

Mazoti looked at the Seals of Faça and Rima on the small table next to her. There was also a letter from Kuni Garu congratulating her: *Your victories will live on in the annals of Dara forever*.

The beggar was about to go on, but Gin stopped him.

"I must think about what you have said."

Gin went to visit the Temple of Rufizo in Boama. It was built over the site of a hot spring that supposedly had curative powers similar to the Rufizo Falls in eastern Faça.

In front of the giant green jade statue of the healing god, Gin prayed.

"You once came to me to prevent me from going down a path that you judged to be a great harm."

She looked at the white jade dove, Rufizo's *pawi*, carved over the statue's shoulder.

"Speak to me now, and tell me, what is the right road?"

She waited quietly. But the statue made no response.

On the way out of the temple, she dipped her hand into the pool that collected the water from the hot spring. The water was scalding hot, and she could not keep her hand in it for long. But she persisted and held her hand down until the skin blistered and she had to withdraw.

The pain seemed to echo the wounds in her heart that could never be healed: the cries of the children being maimed; the whippings administered by the self-righteous; the humiliation of crawling between the bully's legs; the years of constant fear and terror she was forced to live through because she was small and weak. She clenched her fist: that was why she had to strive, to fight, to display, to achieve. To be safe.

But was that all there was in the world?

The gods were silent and capricious, she thought. She longed to find that doctor who had stopped her at the village in Dasu before she left. She wanted to grab him and shake him until he told her what she needed to hear.

Then, she composed herself and left the temple, nursing her burned hand.

She had to pick her own path, as she always had.

"When I was a nobody, King Kuni treated me as a friend," Gin said to the beggar.

"The friendship of kings is like the promise of a drunkard," said the beggar.

But Gin ignored him. "He shared his food with me and drove me in his carriage. He gave me his sword and elevated me to be the Marshal of Dasu above his other retainers. Kon Fiji always said that men should be willing to die for great lords who recognize their talent. It's no different for a woman. I cannot betray him."

"You think the words of Kon Fiji, that ancient fraud, should govern your actions? We live in a world of swords and blood, not of ideals."

"If one abandons all ideals, then the world will be without substance. Kon Fiji may not have known much about how to win a war, but he did know about the moral way to live."

The beggar shook his head and left.

∽ ∾ ∽ ∾

As Puma Yemu continued to disrupt Mata Zyndu's supply lines in Cocru, Mazoti made steady gains in the east. The Tiro states still loyal to the hegemon lost one battle after another, until she eventually conquered all land east of the Wisoti Mountains, including Wolf's Paw and all the wealthy towns of old Gan.

Théca Kimo was similarly successful in the west. The three islands of Arulugi, Crescent, and Écofi fell to his control, and his ships, supported by the mechanical crubens, menaced the Cocru coast. The airships of Cocru finally lost so much of their lift gas that they could no longer rise into the air, and Kuni Garu sent his fleets of airships on raids to Cocru cities, dropping firebombs or leaflets denouncing Mata Zyndu for his numerous sins.

Mata Zyndu rode across the land putting out one fire after another. Kuni's forces would often steal across the Liru River when Mata was away, only to be driven back when Mata returned. Kuni's army could not stand against Mata in a fair fight, and time and again Kuni had to abandon everything and escape to Dimushi.

The stalemate lasted for three years.

CHAPTER FIFTY

# GLORY OF THE CHRYSANTHEMUM

COCRU: THE ELEVENTH MONTH IN THE EIGHTH YEAR OF THE PRINCIPATE.

Mata's army was finally running out of food. Years of warfare raging across Cocru and his neglect of administration took their toll. Puma Yemu's incessant raids also played a part, and shipping by sea was impossible with Théca Kimo's ships and mechanical crubens blockading Cocru ports.

The soldiers of Cocru resorted to digging for roots and planting their own vegetables, right in the army camps. Desertion was rampant, no matter how inspiring Mata was.

Every day, Mata launched himself into the air over the Liru on a battle kite.

"Kuni Garu, come into the air and fight me!" he shouted.

Kuni Garu never responded.

Instead, Kuni summoned an airship. To Mata's way of thinking, such an act was despicable, like bringing a knife to a wrestling match. But Kuni was not bound by such scruples.

The airship sailed close to the battle kite, and the crew aboard fired arrows at the flying Mata.

Ratho, who was in charge of the crew winching the battle kite, cursed at the perfidy of Kuni Garu. He regretted defending this man at the banquet in Pan. There was no honor in sending archers when the hegemon asked for a fair duel between equals. He could not understand how Kuni Garu's soldiers could bear to serve such a coward. He shouted for his men to winch the kite down.

But Mata shouted at the winch crew to stop. He opened his eyes wide, stared into the eyes of the sharpshooters on the airship deck, and laughed. He laughed and then let out a long, sorrowful, inarticulate howl that seemed the cry of a wolf in pain.

The sharpshooters flinched, and their shots fell wide. They could not bear to look at the lone figure soaring through the sky.

"How many more years must we fight this war?" asked Kuni. "How many more years before I can see Jia?"

His advisers had no wise counsel this time, not even Luan Zya.

Kuni offered to discuss the terms of a permanent peace treaty.

Again, Kuni and Mata rode out to the middle of the Liru River on flat-bottomed boats. They toasted each other.

"To continue this war would only harm the people of Dara. I cannot conquer Cocru, and you cannot move out of it. Can we agree to divide the world in half? All that is south of the Liru and Sonaru Rivers will belong forever to you, and all the rest to me."

Mata chuckled without mirth. "I should have listened to Torulu Pering back in Pan."

"The road both of us have traveled is full of regrets. I would like to call you brother again."

Mata stared at Kuni, and Kuni's face was full of pain. Mata felt a surge of something akin to compassion. Perhaps honor still resided in the hearts of all men, just hidden more deeply in some than others.

He raised his cup to Kuni. "Brother."

~ ~ ~ ~

Mata's march back to Çaruza was long and slow. He had returned Kuni's family to Kuni and granted Puma Yemu safe passage to Géfica if he ceased his raids. His men were tired but happy. The war was finally over.

"Hegemon." Ratho Miro hurried his horse to ride next to Mata. "Kuni Garu never once defeated you in battle. We just had bad luck."

Mata Zyndu nodded. He patted Réfiroa's neck lightly so that he was once again ahead, in the lead, alone.

The reunion of the Garu family was bittersweet.

"Mama!"

Timu, now eight, and Théra, now seven, had always been formal and proper with Kuni. But now they left Risana's side and ran with wild abandon toward Jia, hugging her tightly. Little Hudo-*tika* hung on to his father's robe and looked with curiosity at this new, regal aunt he had never met.

Risana bowed to Jia in *jiri*. "Big Sister, since our parting in Zudi, not a single day has gone by without me and my son thanking you in our prayers. Now that Kuni has you back, Dasu again has a queen, and all is right with the world."

Jia nodded in acknowledgment, a bitter smile on her face.

Lady Soto had also come back with Jia. Kuni was surprised.

"There are families you're born into, and families you make out of those you love," said Soto.

"I am honored," said Kuni, and he bowed to her deeply. "What of Mata?"

"I love my nephew," said Soto. "But his path and mine have diverged too far."

Otho Krin had grown even more gaunt during the years of captivity, but there was also a strength in his eyes Kuni had not seen before. Timu and Théra, still hanging tightly on to Jia, called out to their "Uncle Otho" with a warmth that made Kuni's heart clench.

Then he let out a held breath and smiled. "You have suffered. Thank you."

Otho bowed and backed out of the room with Soto; Risana corralled the children and took them away to play.

Jia and Kuni embraced, both faces covered with tears. The warmth between them was reassuring but also faint, their smells now unfamiliar to each other with the separation of years. It would take time to rekindle that fire that had once warmed their little house in Zudi, that had once blazed into passion in the home outside Çaruza by the sea.

"You have paid a great price for our success," Kuni said.

"As have you," Jia said.

As Luan Zya packed his things to get ready for the retreat, he heard the sound of rustling pages. He looked and saw it was *Gitré Üthu*, the magic book given to him by the old fisherman in Haan.

There was no breeze in the tent.

He walked over: The book lay open to a fresh, blank page. As he stared at it, colorful logograms emerged from the paper like islands rising from the sea.

The logograms told of a fairy tale:

> *Once, two great crubens vied for lordship over the seas, one blue, the other red. The two great scaled whales, being of equal strength, fought for seven days without resolution.*
>
> *Each day, by mutual agreement, as the sun set and as their strength diminished, the two crubens ceased their fight. They slept on two sides of an undersea trench to recover. When the sun rose in the morning, they would be back at it again.*
>
> *On the seventh night, just as the red cruben settled down for rest, a remora attached to him whispered to his host: "Finish him. Finish him. Finish him. When his eyes are closed and his mind in deep slumber, stab him through the heart with your horn. Finish him. Finish him. Finish him."*
>
> *"What kind of counsel is this?" said the red cruben. "Such*

*a path is neither fair nor just. I have come to admire him after so many days of fighting."*

*"I'm attached to you," said the remora. "I live off the detritus that drifts from your maw after you feed. I have traveled the four seas only by dint of your power. If you win, I'll have more to eat, and perhaps I'll puff up and show off my colorful fins to the other fish, but if you lose, I'll just find another great fish to attach to. Though I'll benefit from your victory, I'll not share your dishonor—the memory of the sea is rarely kind to great creatures who blame their moral failing on those who but serve and advise at their pleasure."*

*The cruben was surprised. "So you admit that you risk nothing, and I everything. Why should I listen to you?"*

*"Because I live so low, hanging from your belly, my duty isn't to be your conscience, but to think thoughts you dare not think, devise plans you dare not utter. When you find a great cruben, a lord of the sea, whose scales are shiny, whose hide is smooth, whose muscles bulge with vigor and health, you may be sure that you'll find a great many remoras attached to him gorged on filth. A cruben whose remoras are afraid to get dirty will not live long or find victory."*

*And the red cruben listened to the remora and became the lord of the four seas.*

Luan Zya closed the book and laughed bitterly. Was this how he'd be remembered by history?

Then he recalled the moonlight falling on the ruins in Ginpen and the song of the children of Haan. He remembered the promise he made to his father and felt again the restlessness in his soul.

*The more perfect the ideals, the less ideal the methods.*

Kuni's army pulled back from Dimushi, toward Pan, which Cogo Yelu had rebuilt. Kuni's family had been sent on ahead. The agreement was for both sides to not station troops within fifty miles of the Liru River.

"Have you thought about when we should attack?" Luan asked.

They were riding in Kuni's carriage. The king was reviewing reports of harvests and tax collections and thinking about how to administer his vast new realm now that the war was over. All those old records from the Xana Imperial Archives saved by Cogo Yelu would come in handy, he realized, and he was again thankful for his prime minister's foresight. Luan Zya's question caught him off guard.

"Attack?"

Luan took a deep breath. "You don't really think this peace treaty is the end, do you?"

Kuni looked at him. "The war has gone on long enough. Mata and I, neither of us can overcome the other. I've put my seal on the document. It is done."

"A seal is only a mark on a piece of paper, with exactly as much force as you are willing to give it. The Cocru army has run out of provisions, and now they've scattered across Cocru and let down their guard. We, on the other hand, remain well stocked, thanks to Cogo's efforts. This is the best opportunity to attack them from behind and hit them with everything we have."

"Then I'll be remembered by history as a great betrayer. Mata's accusation against me will be carved in stone, made true by my own act. What you counsel is against all the laws of war. I will have no honor left."

"The judgment of history cannot be ascertained from up close. You see the condemnation of the people of this generation, but you cannot foresee how their descendants will view your deeds in the future. If you do not attack now and end this war, the killing will never stop. In another ten years, or twenty, Dasu and Cocru will again face each other on the battlefield, blood will again stain the Liru River, and the people of Dara will again suffer and die."

Kuni thought of the people of Pan, whom he had abandoned once in the hope of preserving Mata's friendship. Their cries as the streets filled with blood still haunted him in dreams.

"You will have sacrificed the lives of the people for personal honor, an empty word," Luan said. "That seems to me a most selfish act."

"Is there no room for mercy? No sympathy among gods or men?"

"Mercy for your foes, my king, is the same as cruelty to your friends."

"That sort of logic, Luan, could become the salve and loincloth for all tyrants."

"Queen Gin has always argued that if one goes to war, one should do all one can to win. A knife is not malicious merely because it is sharp, and a plot is not evil merely because it is effective. All depends on the wielder. The grace of kings is not the same as the morals governing individuals."

Kuni did not respond.

"If you do not make use of every advantage given to you, the gods will condemn you for your error."

The treaty felt heavy in Kuni's hands. Would the lives of the people feel even heavier?

*I think I wield power,* Kuni thought, *but perhaps it is Power that wields me.*

"Summon Mün Çakri and Than Carucono."

Kuni sighed in resignation and tore the paper into pieces.

In a minute, the pieces had disappeared in the wind, like words spoken and then forgotten.

Mata Zyndu received the news of Kuni Garu's betrayal at Rana Kida, a wall-less town near a hill in the Porin Plains, still miles from Çaruza.

Kuni's army had crossed the Liru, and Théca Kimo's army had landed at Canfin. In the east, Mazoti's men had broken through the defenses in the hills at the southern end of the Wisoti Mountains. Fifty thousand Dasu soldiers and allies were now closing in on Mata.

Mata had already sent the bulk of his army in scattered detachments to garrison the towns all across Cocru, leaving only five thousand riders with him.

"This is just like Wolf's Paw and Zudi," Ratho said. "Though they outnumber us ten to one, we will yet prevail."

"Ah, my brother," Mata whispered. And he tore the treaty in his hand into pieces, scattering them like moths in the chill wind of late autumn.

The Dasu army swept over Cocru, a sickle swinging across fields of wheat. It was winter, and the hard pounding of their horses' hooves could be heard for many miles all around the frozen land. Bypassing the Cocru garrisons in their well-defended cities, Kuni's forces aimed straight for Rana Kida, stretching their supply lines as long as kites straining in a howling gale.

Mata mustered his troops on top of the hill near Rana Kida. Kuni, Théca, and Gin's armies converged and surrounded the hill tightly like the hoops of a barrel. Gin Mazoti was appointed commander-in-chief. This would be her masterpiece, her greatest battle.

Mounts Fithowéo and Kana both erupted, and a snowstorm that was beyond anything in living memory raged over the battlefield. High winds shifted direction from moment to moment, and snow fell in great clumps, mixed with hail. Even the gods seemed to be at war.

Day and night, the hegemon ordered his men to try to break through Gin Mazoti's encirclement, but time and again, Mazoti's troops forced them to retreat back up the hill. The constant snow and whipping wind made it impossible to use airships, and the ground was too frozen to dig deep holes for palisades or other fortifications, so Mazoti had to rely on infantry formations that held Mata back by sheer number of bodies.

When Mata retreated, Mazoti ordered waves of Dasu men to charge up the hill. Always, they were repulsed and left many bodies behind. But Mazoti could afford to lose plenty of bodies. She would not give Zyndu's men a chance to rest, to sleep. She would grind them down.

The temperature dropped further. The Cocru soldiers lacked warm mittens and coats, and their hands stuck to the iron handles of their weapons; they cried out as the skin tore off. They lay down on the frozen ground to try to rest and filled their mouths with handfuls of snow to fight off the pangs of hunger. Many of the horses, having had nothing to eat for days, fell down and were slaughtered for meat.

But there was no talk of surrender anywhere in the Cocru ranks.

"This isn't right, Marshal," said Kuni to Gin in her tent. "Too many soldiers are dying."

For ten days, Mata's men had held the hill, killing five Dasu soldiers for every Cocru rider that fell from his horse.

"There is a time for finesse, and a time for pressing your advantage with numbers," said Gin. "If we do not defeat the hegemon quickly, armies from across Cocru will come to his aid and cut off our supply lines. My tactics may be brutal, but they're working. It has been days since the Cocru men have had anything to eat except dead horses, and most are now wounded. We must press on and not relent."

"But I know how loyal Mata's men are; they'll never surrender. Shall I leave behind as many widows and orphans as Mapidéré as the price of my victory? Even if we win, I will have lost the hearts of the people."

Gin sighed. Kuni's streak of essential kindness was not always militarily convenient, but it was why she served him. "Then what do you propose? We can hardly offer a truce again."

"Lady Risana has an idea."

From the shadows behind Kuni, Risana stepped forward.

When Jia and his father had been seized by the hegemon, Kuni wanted to send Risana and the children to safety in Ginpen, far from the dangers of the front. He could not afford to lose more family. But Risana had insisted that she be allowed to accompany him to the front.

"The women need an advocate," Risana had said.

The women's auxiliary corps created by Gin had contributed greatly to Dasu's rise. Compared to the other armies of Dara, the

Dasu troops ate a healthier diet and kept their armor in better condition, and many Dasu soldiers survived wounds that would have been fatal, thanks to the women's cool heads and steady hands as they applied healing herbs and wielded sewing needles.

But as the war dragged on, Gin was preoccupied by matters in the field and the administration of her own domain, and the women auxiliaries fell into neglect. While the women in Mazoti's air force were treated as exceptional and elite, the auxiliary corps in the army came to be seen as mere support. Some Dasu commanders put in charge of the corps had abused their privilege, denying the women their pay, ignoring their grievances, and even treating them as though they were helpless camp followers instead of part of the army.

"My mother and I both worked for a living," Risana had said. "I can help their voices be heard. What good is my position if I'm not allowed to use it?"

"Marshal," said Risana, "I may know nothing of grand military strategies, but I do know something about the hearts of men. My talent lies in seeing into the tangled thicket of their desires and perhaps picking out a path."

Though Gin respected Risana's wisdom, she was tired and tense, and Risana's words seemed too obscure. "This isn't a matter of parlor tricks and seduction."

"Ah, Marshal, though you have added women to your army, have you ever thought of them as real soldiers?"

Gin narrowed her eyes at Risana but nodded for her to go on.

After she explained her plan, Gin was thoughtful. She paced back and forth in the tent as Kuni and Risana watched. Finally, she looked up. "If this doesn't work, you will have hardened Mata's men so that their resistance will be even more fierce. But it's worth a try. The king will have to speak to them directly."

Through the snow-filled night, Gin, Kuni, and Risana rode to the camp of the women's auxiliary corps. The troops were roused in assembly, and they stared at the three riders with consternation. They trusted Risana, who had done much to improve their conditions. But Kuni and Gin had never come to their camp before.

Gently urging his horse forward a few steps, Kuni spoke, striving to be heard above the howling wind and swirling snow.

"Who among you are from Cocru?"

Hundreds of hands rose up.

"I know many of you joined me after you'd lost your husbands and fathers and sons and brothers in the rebellion and the subsequent wars. We have a chance to end the slaughter tonight, but only if you help."

The women listened, stone-faced, as Kuni explained Lady Risana's plan.

"You will have to face Mata's army unarmed and unescorted," Gin added. "This won't work if they think you're a threat or being forced. If they attack, we will not be able to rescue you. The king and I do not demand this of you, if you think it too dangerous or ill-advised. You must volunteer."

One by one, the women of Cocru stepped forward in the snow, forming a tight phalanx in front of the king, the lady, and the marshal.

Tonight, there was no attack from Mazoti. In fact, Mata Zyndu's scouts reported that the Dasu army had pulled back half a mile, leaving an empty no-man's-land around the hill.

Just before morning, women's voices, carried by the wind, woke Mata in his tent:

*Is it snow that I see falling in the valley?*
*Is it rain that flows over the faces of the children?*
*Oh my sorrow, my sorrow is great.*

*It is not snow that covers the floor of the valley.*
*It is not rain that washes the faces of the children.*
*Oh my sorrow, my sorrow is great.*

*Chrysanthemum petals have filled the floor of the valley.*
*Tears have soaked the faces of the children.*
*Oh my sorrow, my sorrow is great.*

*The warriors, they have died like falling chrysanthemum*
*blossoms.*
*My son, oh my son, he is not coming home from battle.*

Mata stood before his tent. Snow fell against him, and his face was soon wet from the melted flakes.

Ratho Miro rode up the hill and tumbled off the horse in front of Mata. "Hegemon, some women of Cocru are halfway up the hill, singing. Though they're not accompanied by armed escorts, they may be Dasu spies."

Mata now heard male voices taking up the old folk song, known to every child of Cocru.

"Have so many of our men surrendered to Kuni already, that their voices are so loud?" Mata Zyndu asked.

"The men singing are not prisoners," said Ratho, hesitating. "They . . . they are our own troops."

Startled, Mata looked at the small tents around him. Men emerged from them in the predawn darkness. Some wiped their eyes; some began to sing; a few cried openly.

"The women have been singing nonstop for hours," said Ratho Miro. "The commanders told the soldiers to plug up their ears with wax, but they did not obey. Some of the men have walked down to meet the women, looking for those from their home villages to ask for news about their families."

Mata listened without moving.

"Should we order an attack?" asked Ratho. "This . . . tactic from Kuni Garu is beneath contempt."

Mata shook his head. "It's all right. Kuni has already taken the soldiers' hearts. It's too late now."

He reentered his tent, where Mira sat, working on her embroidery.

Mata stepped behind her and saw that she had only a single black thread on the cloth. It twisted and turned in a jagged path around the white field, but there seemed nowhere for it to run. No matter how it moved and feinted, the round edge of the embroidery ring held it in like a caged beast.

"Mira, can you play some music? I don't want to hear the singing."

Mira set down her needle, thread, and cloth, and plucked the strings of a coconut lute. The hegemon clapped his hands to the beat and sang.

*My strength is great enough to pluck up mountains.*
*My spirit is wide enough to cover the sea.*
*Yet the gods do not favor me,*
*My steed has nowhere to gallop.*
*What can I do, my Mira? What can I do?*

A line of tears crawled down Mata's face, and the eyes of all the soldiers standing outside the tent glistened in the torchlight. Ratho reached up and wiped his eyes, hard.

Mira continued to play, and began to sing herself:

*The men of Dasu surround us.*
*The songs of Cocru break our hearts.*
*If only you were a fisherman, my king,*
*And I still a farmer's daughter by the sea.*

Mira stopped playing, but the song seemed to linger in the air as the wind howled outside.

"Kuni is known to be generous with prisoners," Mata said. "When you are captured, make sure to speak of how cruel I've been to you and how you've been mistreated. He'll be good to you."

"All your life, you think everyone betrays you in the end," Mira said. "But it's not true. Not true."

Mira's voice grew faint as she neared the end of her speech. Mata, who was facing away from her, turned around as her voice faded to a whisper. He rushed to her as she collapsed. Her hands held on to the handle of a slim dagger made of bone: the blade of Cruben's Thorn was plunged deep into her heart.

Mata's howl could be heard for miles. It mixed with the singing voices of the men and women of Cocru, and all who heard it shivered involuntarily.

Mata wiped the hot tears off his face and laid Mira's body gently on the ground.

"Ratho, gather all the riders who still wish to follow me. We will break through the encirclement."

It was like Wolf's Paw again, Ratho thought. Eight hundred riders of Cocru rode down the hill like a pack of wolves, and they were halfway through the camps of the dozing Dasu army before alarm sounded, and men rushed to cut them off.

Ratho could feel the familiar battle-lust taking over his body. He no longer felt cold, afraid, or hungry. Despair was gone, replaced by joy at once again riding by the side of his lord, the greatest warrior to have ever ridden through the Islands of Dara.

Did he not once run at the side of Mata Zyndu and defeat the invincible Kindo Marana? Did he not once fall out of the sky next to Mata Zyndu and almost catch the treacherous Kuni Garu in bed? Did he not wield Simplicity, the blade taken by Mata Zyndu from the only opponent who ever made him stumble? *We have not even begun to fight.*

Onward, onward the eight hundred riders of Cocru thundered through the tightly packed fighting men of Dasu. They bashed like a battering ram through flimsy doors. Though riders kept falling off horses behind him, Na-aroénna continued to swing like a sliver of moon through the swirling snow and howling winds, dropping those who dared to stand in his way like weeds before a sickle. Though fewer and fewer stayed by his side, Goremaw continued to strike like the fist of Fithowéo, crushing those who dared to lift their weapons like walnuts under a hammer.

As dawn arrived, Mata finally broke through. Around him, less than one hundred riders were left.

They rode on, toward the south, toward the sea. The swirling snow made everything look the same, every direction identical. Mata was lost.

He stopped at a fork in the roads and knocked on the door of a farmer's house.

"Which way to Çaruza?" he asked.

The old farmer stared at the great man standing in his doorway. There was no question as to the stranger's identity. His height and girth, his double-pupiled eyes. There was no other man in the world like Mata Zyndu.

The old man's two sons had fought and died for the hegemon in his endless wars. The old man was sick of talk of valor and honor, of glory and courage. He just wanted his sons back, strong boys who had worked hard in the fields. Boys who did not understand why they had to die, only that someone told them it was sweet and fitting to do so.

"That way," the old man said, pointing to the left.

Mata Zyndu thanked him and got back on his great black horse. His riders followed.

The old man stood at the door a little longer. He could hear the hoofbeats of the pursuing Dasu army. He closed the door and extinguished the candle on the table.

The road that the old man directed Mata Zyndu to led into a swamp. Many of Mata's men had to jump off their saddles as their horses sank up to their stomachs in the mud, snorting and whinnying in fear and pain.

Mata retraced his steps and rode the other way; only twenty-eight riders now were with him. They could see the torchlights of the pursuing Dasu army.

Mata Zyndu led his men onto a small hill.

"I've lived on the back of a horse for ten years," he said to his men. "I've fought in more than seventy battles and never lost a single one. Everyone who's ever fought me has submitted to me or died. Today, I'm on the run not because I don't know how to fight, but because the gods are jealous of me.

"I'm willing to die, but I'll fight with joy and gladness in my heart first. All of you have followed me this far, and I release you from having to go any farther. Go, and surrender to Kuni Garu. I wish you well."

None of the men moved.

"Then I thank you for your faith in me, and I will show you how a real warrior of Cocru should live. Kuni Garu's men are going to surround us soon, yet I will kill at least one commander, capture one of their flags, and break through their lines. All of you will then know that I die not because I lack skill, but because of fickle fortune."

The pursuing Dasu army arrived and encircled the hill. Mata Zyndu formed his men into a wedge shape, with himself at the head.

"Charge!"

They plowed down the hill, into the thicket of Dasu soldiers. They rode straight at the figure of the Dasu commander, whose eyes widened with fear. But before he could retreat, Mata split him in half from shoulder to belly with one swing of Na-aroénna. Mata's men cheered, and the Dasu soldiers scattered like snowflakes in the wind.

Mata Zyndu pulled back hard on the reins of Réfiroa, and the great black steed reared up on its hind legs. As Mata Zyndu rose high above the surrounding throngs, he let out a loud war cry:

*"Haaaaaiiiii!"*

The cry hung over the battlefield, reverberating against the eardrums of the Dasu soldiers and stunning them into silence. All around him, the men of Dasu backed away, as sheep backed away from a wolf. None dared to meet his piercing eyes.

Mata laughed and rode straight at one of the standard-bearers in the Dasu ranks. He reached out and grabbed the waving cruben banner from the terrified soldier and snapped the pole in half. He threw the battle banner on the ground, and Réfiroa gladly trampled over it.

"Hoo-ah, hoo-ah," his men shouted in unison.

They rode on again, and the frightened Dasu army parted before them like the retreating tide.

As Mata continued south, he counted the men around him: twenty-six. They'd lost only two men.

"What do you think?" he asked.

"It was just as you predicted, Hegemon," Ratho said. Admiration infused his voice.

All of the riders felt as if they had become gods themselves.

Finally, they arrived at the sea. Mata leapt off his horse and saw the dilapidated house nearby. His heart skipped a beat as he recognized it. This was where Jia had stayed for many years right outside Çaruza and where he had once shared drinks with Kuni and held his son in his arms.

Mata Zyndu wiped his eyes. *Cruing ma donothécaü luki né othu*, the Classical Ano poets said. *The past is a country to which one cannot return.*

Ratho came up to him. "We have scoured the coast nearby, and there are no ships except a small fishing boat. Hegemon, please get on it and set sail for Tunoa. We'll stay and hold off Kuni Garu. Tunoa is small, yet it is easily defended and has many men who remember the Zyndu name with fondness. You can recruit a fresh army and come back to avenge us."

Mata Zyndu made no move. He stood in the snow, thinking.

"Hegemon, you must hurry! The pursuers are almost here."

Mata Zyndu leapt off Réfiroa and slapped him hard on his hindquarters. "Poor horse. You've followed me all these years, and I can't bear to see you die. Go, hide, and live a long life."

But Réfiroa refused to leave. He turned his head back to Mata and let out a loud snort. Steamy breath rolled out of his great nostrils like tendrils of smoke. His eyes gazed at Mata with anger.

"I'm sorry, old friend. I was wrong to ask you to do something I would not do myself. You're indeed well matched to me, even unto death."

He turned to face his men, his face full of sorrow. "When I left Tunoa with my uncle and came to the Big Island, eight hundred young men followed me, their heads full of dreams of glory. Yet today, if I return, I will return alone, without even their bones. How I can face their fathers, mothers, wives, sisters, and children? I cannot go home again."

He stood with his men on the beach, Réfiroa by his side, and they watched as the men of Dasu approached.

"Go, go, go!" Dafiro Miro urged his men. "King Kuni has said that whoever catches Mata Zyndu will be awarded ten thousand pieces of gold and given the title of count. Go!"

In the torchlight, the dense ranks of Dasu soldiers formed a semicircle around Mata Zyndu and his twenty-six warriors, the surging sea behind their backs.

All of Mata's soldiers had dismounted, and the horses now stood in a semicircle around their riders, forming a barricade with their heaving bodies. The men stood on the snowy beach, their last arrows nocked in their bows, ready for the final stand.

Mata waved his hand without speaking, and his men let loose with their final volley of arrows. Twenty-six Dasu soldiers fell to the ground. The responding volley was far denser and longer-lasting, and by the time the Dasu soldiers stopped shooting, two more of Mata's men had fallen, along with all their horses.

Réfiroa was on the ground, dozens of arrows sticking out of his great body. He let out a scream that sounded almost human. Around him, most of the other horses were dead, but a few let out piteous screams.

Eyes glistening in the torchlight, Mata walked up to Réfiroa. With a clean, wide sweep of his arm, Na-aroénna swung through the air, and Réfiroa's head, separated from his torso, flew in a long, gentle arc that ended in the distant sea. Mata's soldiers came forward and gave clean deaths to the few other surviving horses as well.

When Mata Zyndu looked up at the Dasu soldiers again, his eyes were clear and dry. He stood with his hands and weapons behind his back, his face full of contempt for these lesser creatures.

The soldiers of Dasu drew their swords, pointed their spears, and tightened their circle. Step by step, they came closer to the legend that was Mata Zyndu.

"Daf!" Ratho cried out. He could see his brother's face in the flickering torchlight. "Daf, it's me, Rat!"

Mata glanced at Ratho. "That's your brother?"

Ratho nodded. "Yes. He picked the wrong side. He serves a lord with no honor."

"Brothers should not take up arms against each other," Mata said. "You've been a great soldier, Rat, the best I've ever seen. Let me give you a final gift. Take my head and make yourself a count."

He lifted Na-aroénna and whispered, "Grandfather and Uncle, I'm sorry. There was never doubt in my heart, but perhaps that is not enough."

With one quick stroke, he severed the arteries in his neck. Blood spurted everywhere and stained the snowy beach. His body remained upright for a moment, then collapsed like a mighty oak cut down.

"Rat, stop!"

But it was too late. Ratho Miro imitated his lord and wiped his own throat with Simplicity. Around him, the other riders of Mata Zyndu also collapsed like great trees.

The men of Dasu rushed in to grab a piece of Mata Zyndu's body and claim the reward. He was torn limb from limb, and ultimately Kuni Garu had to award five soldiers, who each presented a piece of Mata Zyndu's body.

Mata Zyndu's body was sewn together and then buried just outside Çaruza. Kuni Garu gave him the full rites due a princeps, first among the *tiro*.

"The stronger his enemies, the fiercer his heart." Gin Mazoti gave the first eulogy. "Even as his might lessened, his courage grew greater and his mind firmer. Yet when presented with the chance for victory, he would often hesitate from a streak of weak hesitation. Believing himself to be peerless, he listened to no counsel and did not trust his own generals. He conquered; he dominated; he was larger than life. Yet, long ago, he had lost the hearts of the people."

But it was the words of Kuni Garu, who gave the last eulogy, that would be recalled long after: "Though I am declared victorious today, who knows in ten generations whether your name or mine will be the brighter? You died a grace of kings at my hand, but doubt will haunt me till the day I die.

"I saw you soar in the sky when you held Namen back at Zudi, and I bore witness when you slaughtered the innocent in Dimu. I marveled at your courage, nobility, and loyalty, and I shuddered at your cruelty, suspicion, and obstinacy. I laughed as you cradled my infant son outside Çaruza, and I cried as you burned down the Immaculate City. I understood your dedication to the world as you thought it ought to be, and I regret it is not a world that all of us wish to live in. I swallowed bitterness as you refused to call me brother, and I had to do so again to betray you at Rana Kida. I felt closer to you than I did to my brother by blood when the chance for victory seemed remote, yet we could not break bread together in joy in Pan. From the shores of Wolf's Paw to the skies over Zudi, you left in the hearts of the people an indelible image.

"You swept through the world in a tempest of gold. My brother, there will never be another like you in these Islands."

Kuni acted as a pallbearer himself. He covered his face in ashes and wore sackcloth. He walked the casket through the streets until it reached its final resting place. He cried like no one ever remembered seeing him cry.

Blossoming chrysanthemums filled the streets of Çaruza. Their fragrance was so powerful that passing birds steered clear of the city.

As the hegemon's body was about to be lowered into the ground, the sky above the funeral procession was suddenly filled with the beating wings of a flock of giant ravens, both black and white. As they parted like *cüpa* stones sorting themselves by color, Mingén falcons dove toward the procession. The gathered nobles and ministers scattered, abandoning the hegemon's casket next to the gravesite.

Then, the ground around the gravesite exploded like a roiling sea, and a pack of monstrous wolves, each four times as big as a man, emerged. The wolves, ravens, and falcons converged on the casket, and settled around it neatly in rows, like guards preparing for review at a parade.

A furious storm arose: stones tumbled along the ground, trees were uprooted, and a thick cloud of dust obscured everything. In that confusion, all sounds and speech drowned in a sea made of the shrieking of the wind, the howling of wolves, the cawing of ravens, and the shrill, piercing cry of falcons.

The world seemed to return to primordial chaos, and even thought was impossible.

Abruptly, the sound and the fury ceased, and bright sunlight bathed the calm scene left after the destruction. All the animals had disappeared, along with the hegemon's body.

Slowly, the nobles and ministers, prostrate during the brief storm, stood up on unsteady legs, looking around in wonder and confusion.

Cogo Yelu was the first to recover. "How auspicious!" he proclaimed into the stunned silence. "The gods of Dara have together welcomed the hegemon into another realm. We who are left are witnessing the start of a new era of harmonious peace!"

A few other nobles with ears attuned to the shifting currents of politics immediately proclaimed their assent and congratulated Kuni Garu loudly. Others caught on, and a rising tide of praise for King

Kuni soon filled the air, almost as cacophonous as the animals had been.

Kuni looked at Cogo and offered a wan smile. *How can we know the will of the gods?* he mouthed.

Cogo swept his arm at the throng. *It's enough they know yours,* he mouthed.

Lord Garu turned to the crowd and nodded slowly, regal and majestic.

## CHAPTER FIFTY-ONE

# THE CORONATION

DARA: THE FIFTH MONTH IN THE FIRST YEAR
OF THE REIGN OF FOUR PLACID SEAS.

A bald beggar in a white traveling cape walked down a road that wound its way through the sorghum fields.

He emerged into a tiny village with only thirty or so houses: plain, simple, poor. He looked around, picked one at random, and knocked on the door. A boy, about eight, opened the door.

"Could a stranger beg for a bowl of porridge, Young Master?" asked the beggar.

The boy nodded, went away, and soon returned with a bowl of warm porridge. He had even cracked an egg on top.

"Thank you," said the beggar. "Was the harvest good last year?"

The boy looked at the beggar quizzically.

"I've been away," said the beggar. "On the Big Island."

"Ah, that explains it. Your accent tells me you're from Rui, but your question makes you sound from away. No, the harvest was terrible. Kiji was angry, it seems, and there were too many rainstorms last fall on Rui."

The beggar's face fell at this news. "Then it is even more generous of you to share food with a stranger. You're certain your parents will not mind?"

The boy laughed. "There's no need to worry. King Kuni and Prime Minister Yelu ordered grain to be shipped from Géfica, and all of us have plenty to eat."

"You like the king then? Even though he is not from Xana?"

"We no longer speak of Xana," said the boy.

"But that's your country!"

The boy shook his head. "This is Rui, an Island of Dara."

In this remote valley nestled deep in the Damu Mountains, where craggy peaks rose above the clouds like ships drifting in a misty sea, far from the sight and hearing of mortals, the gods of Dara had gathered again.

A simple meal of fruits, nectars, and wild game was laid out on the smooth grass, and the gods reclined or sat around it.

Lutho, Rapa, and Rufizo, the hosts, looked relaxed, joyful, even radiant.

"Of course you look happy," said Fithowéo. "Your favorites won."

"Come, come," said Rufizo. "A new era among the mortals should herald a new era among us as well. Brothers and sisters, let's drink together and heal the discord between us." He lifted a flagon of mead, and Rapa and Lutho followed suit.

"I've always said that we should have been drinking, not fighting," said Tututika, and she lifted her flagon in response.

"I care not one whit whether the mortals fight or don't fight," said Tazu, smirking. "As long as they stay interesting. I enjoyed watching Mata Zyndu make war; I think it will be just as fun to watch Kuni Garu try to keep the peace." He lifted his flagon as well.

But the other three, Fithowéo, Kana, and Kiji, sat stone-faced and made no move.

"Oh, this will be entertaining," said Tazu. "I'm glad I came." He downed his mead without waiting for the others and refilled his flagon.

"The war is over," said Rapa. "Are we to be less openhearted than the mortals?" When she saw no response from the three holdouts, she turned to focus on her twin sister. "Come, Kana-*tika*, how can you say no to me, your other self?"

"Don't play that game with me!" said Kana. "I should never have listened to you when Fithowéo and I went to retrieve Mata's body. 'Oh, sister,' you said, 'let me and Kiji come along. It will be good to have the mortals see all of our *pawi* so that they know how much we all care.'"

"That is indeed all I wanted!" said Rapa. "We may have taken sides in this war, but in the end, we are the gods of all of Dara."

"That may sound pretty," said Fithowéo. "But you *used* Kana and me! You made it seem as if we supported Kuni Garu!"

"Don't forget Kiji," said Kana. "He hates Mata and Kuni equally, and so she made an even bigger fool out of him."

They looked over at Kiji, but the Lord of the Air remained quiet, looking thoughtful.

"You wrong me much," protested Rapa. "In truth, the mortals completely misunderstood the dance I choreographed for our *pawi*. I had meant to show that the gods remained divided—"

"And that was why your ravens and mine were to separate and sort by color," said Kana, finishing her sister's sentence as she used to do.

"Exactly. And then I suggested that Fithowéo's wolves face off against Kiji's falcons so that the mortals wouldn't get the mistaken impression that Kiji had forgiven Mata Zyndu, the Defiler of Mapidéré's Tomb"—Rapa saw that Fithowéo was about to object—"and also the Greatest Warrior of Dara."

"But your plan went wrong," Fithowéo said. "That Cogo Yelu twisted everything and made it appear as if we were all there to show support for Kuni Garu."

"And everyone listened to him!" lamented Kana. "Can't people think for themselves?"

"Our careful signs will be recorded in the annals of Dara only as the misreading of one man," said Fithowéo.

"The mortals have never been good at getting history right," said Tututika. "Ah, my Kikomi." Her blue eyes moistened.

The other gods fell respectfully silent. All remembered the princess who sacrificed everything to save her people, even her own place in history.

Kiji spoke up for the first time. "Little Sister, Kikomi loved Amu as much as Jizu loved Rima or my Namen loved Xana. My heart weeps for her. Will you drink with me?" He lifted his flagon at her. "To the grace of kings, which fit her better than any crown or mortal tribute."

After a moment, Tututika nodded, and the two drank.

Then Kiji said, "Too many have died who loved their land as much as Kikomi, Jizu, and Namen."

Fithowéo and Kana were surprised at this. Of all the gods, Kiji should have been the most angry at how things turned out. The Xana Empire was no more.

But Kiji continued, "Time moves in cycles. The people of Dara were one when they arrived in these Islands, before they divided into the Tiro states. But even then they were of different appearances, indicating that the Ano had been coalesced from many tribes. All the Islands of Dara are now one again, and people may come to love all of Dara as much as they loved their Tiro states. We did promise our mother that we would be the gods of *all* of Dara."

The gods considered this, and the scowls on Fithowéo's and Kana's faces relaxed.

"If the mortals already believe that we have reconciled, we might as well make it a reality. As long as the people of Xana are treated fairly, I'll speak no more of war. But if Kuni should turn out to be other than what he claims to be, I'll not stand by."

"Nor will I," said Fithowéo.

"Nor will any of us," said Rapa and Kana, together.

And the gods drank and ate and conversed of happier things, and they agreed to retire to Arulugi, the Beautiful Island, as Tututika's guests for a few days.

As they left, Lutho and Rapa stayed a little behind the others.

"I noticed that you never spoke while everyone made speeches," said Rapa.

"I had nothing useful to say," said Lutho, smiling.

Rapa lowered her voice, "My tricky brother, suggesting that dance with the *pawi* was a good idea. But how did you know that the mortals would 'misinterpret' it just the way we wanted?"

"I didn't. There was a chance that they could have interpreted it exactly the way you described it today. The mortals are never predictable, that's what makes working with them so hard." He paused and then added, "And so much fun."

"You took a gamble?"

"I prefer to speak of a calculated risk. Pure gambles are more Tazu's thing."

"I think you have spent too much time observing a certain bandit-king."

The voices of the gods faded, and a passing breeze carried some dandelion seeds into the sky over the valley.

All of Kuni's most important advisers and generals were invited to gather in Zudi. The coronation of the new emperor was to occur in a few more weeks. But for now, there was nothing to do but to enjoy the sights of a world at peace and to catch up with old friends.

Rumors spread that Cogo Yelu was building a large estate for himself in Rui. It was so luxurious and extensive that it seemed certain Cogo had been skimming from the Dasu treasury to afford it.

Kuni frowned. Dasu relied on Cogo, now perhaps more than ever. His quick wit in guiding the public opinion after the hegemon's body disappeared was a particular stroke of genius. Sometimes he wondered if Cogo grew impatient with merely advising him . . . in any event, he certainly couldn't afford to have Cogo become complacent.

Kuni invited Cogo to tea.

"We've worked hard to win the hearts of the people," said Kuni. "But let's not lose them carelessly now that success has been achieved."

Cogo immediately apologized and begged forgiveness, but he didn't say what he was apologizing for.

Kuni laughed. "I'm not angry at you, Cogo. I understand that if the water is too clear, we will have no fish. A certain amount of privilege is allowed to those who hold power. But let's keep it reasonable, all right?"

Cogo thanked his lord and seemed to leave in such a state of anxiety that he didn't even finish his tea.

The people whispered to one another what a great lord Kuni Garu was.

As Luan Zya strolled through the streets of Ginpen, he watched and listened: Young scholars earnestly debated philosophy in bars; mothers window-shopped with babies strapped to their backs, chanting the times table or the simpler Ano Classics; the great doors of long-shuttered private academies were open, revealing servants sweeping and washing the floors of lecture halls to prepare them for new students.

He arrived at the site of his ancestral estate. The ruins remained undisturbed, but he saw that wildflowers were blooming in the nooks and crannies of the fallen stones: dandelion, butter-and-eggs, fireweed, columbine, chicory. . . .

He knelt among the broken stones, and the bright sun warmed his face. He closed his eyes and listened, and all around him was the sound of peace.

Then, he went to the Great Temple to Lutho. Stepping through the Great Hall and avoiding the throngs of worshippers, he made his way to the small courtyard behind the temple. There, he looked around and saw that there was a large yellowish rock leaning against one of the trees. It resembled a turtle in its shell.

He knelt down.

"Teacher, I've come because I think my task is done."

He waited patiently, hoping for the old fisherman who had given him *Gitré Üthu*, the book of knowledge, to return. But as the sun set and the moon rose, no one showed up.

He felt a stirring in the bundle on his back. He opened the cloth and took out the magical tome. The pages fluttered open by themselves, filled with notes and diagrams he had recorded over the years, a trail of the peregrinations of his mind. Then the book stopped on the first blank page.

A line of glowing word-squares appeared: *When the cruben breaches, the sensible remora detaches; when the task is done, the wise servant withdraws.*

Luan sat in the darkness for a long time before bowing down to touch his forehead to the ground in front of the book. "Thank you, Teacher."

Another line of text appeared: *You've always known everything in this book; I just had to point them out.*

Then the glowing letters faded, and though Luan Zya waited until the sun rose, nothing more appeared on the empty page.

After visiting the grave of the old dockmaster in the nearby countryside, Queen Gin came to Dimushi.

She stayed in the finest inn in Dimushi with Luan Zya as her guest. They did not emerge from their bedroom for a few days.

One morning, the two decided to take a ride outside the city walls. Gin wrapped herself in a comfortable dress instead of her royal robes, and Luan wore a plain blue scholar's tunic instead of his formal court garb. The two looked like a pair of lovers out for a spring stroll rather than a queen and Dara's prime strategist. They let the reins hang loose and allowed the horses to wander where they would, taking delight in the bright sunlight and warm breeze.

"Have you thought about what's next for you, Gin?" Luan Zya asked.

"Kuni has said that he wants to make me Queen of Géjira after the coronation. Géjira would be far richer than Rima and Faça. It's a good reward."

When there was no response from Luan, Gin turned and saw that his brows were furrowed.

"What?"

Luan spoke slowly. "But you would also have to leave your army behind in Faça and Rima and start all over again in a new place."

Gin laughed. "I'm used to that."

Just then they came upon a few hunters by the side of the road.

"A lot of wild geese?" asked Gin.

"Not a good season," replied one of the hunters. "We've been out for most of the morning and have nothing to show for it. Looks like we'll have to wait until the fall."

Luan and Gin watched as the hunters leashed their hounds, who whimpered unhappily, and wrapped their bows in thick layers of cloth to be stored away until fall. Then the hunters bid them farewell and left.

"You're a marshal," said Luan. "But now there is peace. Do you think you're very different from a hound or bow in the emperor's eyes when all the rabbits have been caught and all the wild geese killed?"

Gin narrowed her eyes. "You think Kuni is sending me to Gan to separate me from officers loyal to me?"

"That is one interpretation."

"But he also told me that I would be allowed to wear my sword to his court, an honor not even allowed to men who have followed him far longer like Mün Çakri or Than Carucono. Why would he tell me this if he suspects me of ambition?"

"Did you refuse this honor?"

"Of course not! I've certainly earned it."

Luan shook his head. "I don't know what Kuni is thinking. But I do know that power changes how a man sees his friends. Cogo understood this before any of us, and he wisely chose to allay Kuni's suspicions by acting the fool. Had he not sullied his own name deliberately, Kuni might have suspected him of trying to pry the hearts of the people away from his master."

"Do you always think of the worst even when well-deserved glory is handed to you?"

"It's the prudent thing to do. Trusting the favor of the powerful is like riding a kite in the wind."

Gin urged her horse to begin a trot. "Speak not to me of prudence. I've lived on the edge of a sword all my life. I'm good at leading soldiers, but Kuni is good at leading generals. My ambition is satisfied with serving a great lord."

"Yet you killed Shilué to pave your rise. Do you truly know your heart? Or how others will see it? If you do not retire when the path is still open to you, you may be forced to fight for your life someday."

Mazoti's face tightened. "I once had the chance to betray Kuni, but I refused it. The world is not only a world of brute force and heartless betrayals. Kuni has nothing to fear from me, and I likewise will not fear him."

They rode back to the city in silence.

There were a few more people that Mazoti needed to see in Dimushi.

First, she asked for Gray Weasel's old gang and the broken children who had once begged for them.

It was not easy to find members of a long-dissolved gang, but the magistrates and constables of Dimushi were eager to please this most powerful of Kuni Garu's new nobles, and eventually, they brought half a dozen men to her in chains.

"These are the only ones we could find," said the senior magistrate. "Even thieves don't do well in wars."

"What about the children?" she asked.

"They"—the senior magistrate dared not meet her gaze—"probably didn't survive."

Mazoti nodded and stared into the distance.

She had the men's hands cut off and their legs broken.

"Look at me," Mazoti said. Her soldiers held up the limp bodies.

The thieves, now barely conscious, struggled to lift their heads. "This is the last face you'll see in your lives."

Then she had their eyes poked out with an iron rod heated in a furnace. The thieves screamed as their flesh sizzled.

"This isn't for me, but those children."

Mazoti had their eardrums pierced as well, so that their own screams would echo in their minds for the rest of their days.

Next was the old laundress who had shared her meal with Mazoti when she was a young girl. It took even longer to find her, but Mazoti sent her soldiers to scour the villages along the Liru River and rounded up all the old women until the right one was found.

The old woman trembled as she was brought to the queen. Mazoti gave her ten thousand gold pieces. "Granny, you helped me when I was a nobody. But the gods do not forget a real act of kindness."

Then came the couple, the followers of Rufizo, who had tried to make her a respectable young lady by hurting her.

Mazoti gave them fifty pieces of silver. "This should be enough to reimburse you for the cost of housing and feeding me for those months. You intended to heal, yet you had no patience for the real hard work of warming the heart of a wounded young girl. Perhaps next time you'll do better."

Finally, Mazoti brought in the bully, the man between whose legs Gin had once crawled.

The man quaked with fear. The tale of what had happened to Gray Weasel's old gang had spread far and wide. He collapsed into a heap of trembling flesh on the floor, not daring to say a word.

Mazoti offered him a seat and asked him to be at ease. "You once humiliated me, but you also taught me that it was important to bear small insults if one wishes to rise high.

"I was once an urchin in these streets, and now I return as a queen. But if I seek only to visit vengeance upon you, then I will be demonstrating that I've learned nothing.

"Let us drink together."

∽ ∾ ∽ ∾

Today would be the last day that Kuni Garu was to be known by his old name. Tomorrow, he would become Emperor Ragin, and the Reign of Four Placid Seas would begin. Eventually, there would be a new palace in Pan, the Harmonious City, a formal coronation, and new rituals and titles. Cogo Yelu had already prepared a thick stack of petitions for Kuni to review: ideas for administering the Dasu Empire and how to make the people's lives better.

But today Kuni would sit in *géüpa* and drink with his old friends as Kuni Garu in Zudi. Wine would flow freely and table manners would be forgotten. Today, anything could be said.

Mün Çakri, First General of the Infantry, Than Carucono, First General of the Cavalry, and Rin Coda, Farsight Secretary (a title he suggested because it sounded better than "Spymaster"), hosted Duke Théca Kimo and Marquess Puma Yemu at a table in the corner, where their rowdy drinking games wouldn't bother the other guests. From time to time, when they argued too loudly about who should be drinking, Kuni had to go over to adjudicate personally.

Next to them was the spirit table, where empty place settings and seats were left for friends and family who did not live to see this day: Naré, Hupé, Muru, Ratho, Captain Dosa, Phin, Mata, Mira, Kikomi . . . From time to time, Kuni and the others came by the table to toast the departed. Though their eyes might be moist, their words were celebratory: Hope was the best way to honor the dead.

The only thing that marred the festive mood was the absence of Dafiro Miro, captain of the palace guards. He had accompanied the body of his brother, Ratho, to their home village near Kiesa for burial, where he vowed to stay in mourning for a year.

Widow Wasu of the Splendid Urn catered the food and drinks; she was offering much more upscale fare these days, thanks to the booming business brought about by visitors curious about Kuni Garu's origins—and Wasu knew to be discreet and only smiled mysteriously when patrons asked her to confirm some legend or other. She was even serving a new drink at the Urn she marketed specifically to scholars—students from around Dara had come to Zudi to study at academies opened by Master Loing's other students; it was too bad that Master Loing had passed away, but surely being taught by the emperor's former classmates was also a measure of honor? A rising tide lifted all boats.

Up on the dais, at the table of honor next to Kuni and his wives, sat Féso Garu, Kuni's father; Kado and Tete Garu, his brother and sister-in-law; and Gilo and Lu Matiza, Jia's parents. The smiles on the faces of the Matizas were a bit strained, but Kuni had been in a forgiving mood, and he hadn't given them a hard time when he came to Zudi. (However, at the beginning of the banquet, he had banged on an empty pot loudly and smiled as Tete blushed furiously.)

Jia kept on raising her cup to Gin Mazoti, Luan Zya, and Cogo Yelu. These three were the most important people in the new Dasu Empire. She seemed to be trying to make up for lost time as she had been absent for years while Risana was here to win their favor.

Soto Zyndu looked at her, and then at Risana, who sat quietly by Kuni, content with his attention alone. Kuni had announced before the banquet that since Risana's son, the young prince known as Hudo-*tika*, had also reached the age of reason, he would be formally named Phyro, meaning "Pearl in the Palm."

Only a few who had studied the Ano Classics in depth understood the obscure allusion. The Cocru patriot and poet Lurusén had once written a poem celebrating the birth of a new prince:

*A son who carries on the legacy of his father*
*Is more precious than a pearl in the palm of a great king.*

Prince Timu's name, Gentle Ruler, had been an allusion to a son's love for his mother, but Phyro's name seemed to indicate Kuni's thoughts on succession. No wonder Jia's face had been stony when the name was announced, though Risana had appeared completely oblivious.

From time to time, the sound of children playing and laughing in the courtyard drifted into the banquet hall.

Soto sighed. Risana was in trouble, and she didn't even know it. Risana thought Kuni's favor alone was enough, but she did not understand that the politics among the wives and children of the emperor would be far more deadly and intricate.

Risana played the coconut lute, and Kuni, drunk and wistful, put down his *kunikin* and began to sing:

> *The wind blows, and clouds race across the sky.*
> *My power sways within the Four Placid Seas.*
> *Now I'm home, my friends and loved ones nearby.*
> *How brief is my respite, how rare this ease?*

Outside, the air was filled with dandelion seeds, drifting like snow in summer.

"I heard you declined the titles of Imperial Scholar and Grand Secretary," said Cogo, as he sat down next to Luan. "So what are you going to do?"

"Oh, I haven't decided yet," Luan said. "Maybe I'll try adapting the machinery in the mechanical crubens into iron horses and oxen; traders and farmers would like that. Maybe I'll travel the Islands in a balloon and make better maps. Maybe I'll go back into the mountains to perfect my stringless kite."

"But you've made up your mind not to stay around the court?"

"There is a time to rise with the cruben, and a time to withdraw."

Cogo smiled and said no more.

Luan looked over at Gin Mazoti. She looked back, smiled, and raised her cup. Luan saw only trust in her eyes, but he could not help but feel a chill as he listened to Kuni's song. *The hunt is over.*

Luan sighed, raised his cup in turn, and drank.

# GLOSSARY

*cruben*: a scaled whale with a single horn protruding from its head; symbol of imperial power.
*cüpa*: a game played with black and white stones on a grid.
*dyran*: a flying fish, symbol of femininity and sign of good fortune. It is covered by rainbow-colored scales and has a sharp beak.
*géüpa*: an informal sitting position where the legs are crossed and folded under the body, with each foot tucked under the opposite thigh.
*jiri*: a woman's bow where the hands are crossed in front of the chest in a gesture of respect.
*kunikin*: a large, three-legged drinking vessel.
*Mingén falcon*: a species of extraordinarily large falcon native to the island of Rui.
*mipa rari*: a formal kneeling position where the back is kept straight and weight is evenly distributed between the knees and toes.
*ogé*: drops of sweat.
*pawi*: animal aspects of the gods of Dara.
*Rénga*: honorific used to address the emperor.
*thakrido*: an extremely informal sitting position where one's legs are stretched out in front; used only with intimates or social inferiors.
*tunoa*: grapes.
*-tika*: suffix expressing endearment among family members.

# NOTES

Mata Zyndu's poem is an adaptation of the late Tang Dynasty "Ode to Chrysanthemum" by Huang Chao ("Huang" is the surname). Huang's story does not have much to do with this book, but it happens to also feature flowers and politics, and so I will tell it briefly here.

Huang, the son of a wealthy salt-smuggling family, wrote his ode in Chang An, capital of Tang Dynasty China, after he failed to place in the Imperial Examinations. The Tang Court favored the peony; praising the chrysanthemum was a political act.

In AD 875, Huang began a rebellion against the corrupt Tang Court, which lived in luxury while the populace suffered under natural disasters and misrule. Five years later, his forces managed to capture Chang An. Surviving historical records indicate that Huang's men slaughtered and preyed upon civilians indiscriminately. Ultimately, his rebellion—though it would accelerate the fall of the Tang Dynasty—failed, and he was betrayed by his followers and killed.

Huang's poem has always been controversial, as is his place in history—in some ways, Kuni and his advisers were too optimistic, as the judgment of history may not be final even a thousand years later.

# ACKNOWLEDGMENTS

This novel benefitted enormously from the critiques and suggestions of my beta-readers: Anatoly Belilovsky, Marty Bonus, Dario Ciriello, Anaea Lay, John P. Murphy, Erica Naone, Emma Osborne, Cindy Pon, Kenneth Schneyer, Alex Shvartsman, and Louis West. I can't thank them enough. Every author should be so lucky as to have such insightful and forgiving friends.

I'm also grateful to my editor, Joe Monti, who believed in this book and helped me shape it to be closer to my vision through a multiyear process, and my agent, Russ Galen, who pried the manuscript out of my hands and found it a great publisher (and dealt with my worries and neurotic questions with unfailing patience). Everyone at Saga Press and Simon & Schuster has been a pleasure to work with, and their patience and good cheer in steering a new author through the book-launch process are very much appreciated.

Finally, the greatest share of credit must go to my wife, Lisa, who came up with the idea for this book with me, read and commented on numerous drafts, and supported me through the ups and downs of the writing process at great personal sacrifice. I hope someday my daughters will be able to read and enjoy this book that consumed so much of their father's time when they were babies.

*For more on the Dandelion Dynasty and Ken Liu's other works, please visit his website at* kenliu.name *and sign up for his mailing list at* kenliu.name/mailing-list.

TURN THE PAGE FOR A SNEAK PEEK AT

# THE WALL OF STORMS

BOOK TWO OF THE DANDELION DYNASTY

# TRUANTS

PAN: THE SECOND MONTH IN THE SIXTH YEAR OF THE REIGN OF FOUR PLACID SEAS.

*Masters and mistresses, lend me your ears.*

*Let my words sketch for you scenes of faith and courage.*

*Dukes, generals, ministers, and maids, everyone parades through this ethereal stage.*

*What is the love of a princess? What are a king's fears?*

*If you lubricate my tongue with drink and enliven my heart with coin, all will be revealed in due course of time. . . .*

The sky was overcast, and the cold wind whipped a few scattered snowflakes through the air. Carriages and pedestrians, with thick coats and fur-lined hats, hurried through the wide avenues of Pan, the Harmonious City, seeking the warmth of home.

Or the comfort of a homely pub like the Three-Legged Jug.

"Kira, isn't it your turn to buy the drinks this time? Everyone knows your husband turns every copper over to you."

"Look who's talking. Your husband doesn't get to sneeze without your permission! But I think today should be Jizan's turn, sister. I heard a wealthy merchant from Gan tipped her five silver pieces last night!"

"Whatever for?"

"She guided the merchant to his favorite mistress's house through a maze of back alleys and managed to elude the spies the merchant's wife sicced on him!"

"Jizan! I had no idea you had such a lucrative skill—"

"Don't listen to Kira's lies! Do I look like I have five silver pieces?"

"You certainly came in here with a wide enough grin. I'd wager you had been handsomely paid for facilitating a one-night marriage—"

"Oh, shush! You make me sound like I'm the greeter at an indigo house—"

"Ha-ha! Why stop at being the greeter? I rather think you have the skills to manage an indigo house, or . . . a scarlet house! I've certainly drooled over some of those boys. How about a little help for a sister in need—"

"—or a *big* help—"

"Can't the two of you get your minds out of the gutter for a minute? Wait . . . Phiphi, I think I heard the coins jangling in your purse when you came in—did you have good luck at sparrow tiles last night?"

"I don't know what you're talking about."

"Aha, I knew it! Your face gives everything away; it's a wonder you can bluff anyone at that game. Listen, if you want Jizan and me to keep our mouths shut in front of your foolish husband about your gaming habit—"

"You featherless pheasant! Don't you dare tell him!"

"It's hard for us to think about keeping secrets when we're so thirsty. How about some of that 'mind-moisturizer,' as they say in the folk operas?"

"Oh, you rotten . . . Fine, the drinks are on me."

"That's a good sister."

"It's just a harmless hobby, but I can't stand the way he mopes around the house and nags when he thinks I'm going to gamble everything away."

"You do seem to have Lord Tazu's favor, I'll grant you that. But good fortune is better when shared!"

"My parents must not have offered enough incense at the Temple of Tututika before I was born for me to end up with you two as my 'friends.' . . ."

Here, inside the Three-Legged Jug, tucked in an out-of-the-way corner of the city, warm rice wine, cold beer, and coconut arrack flowed as freely as the conversation. The fire in the wood-burning stove in the corner crackled and danced, keeping the pub toasty and bathing everything in a warm light. Condensation froze against the glass windows in refined, complex patterns that blurred the view of the outside. Guests sat by threes and fours around low tables in *géüpa*, relaxed and convivial, enjoying small plates of roasted peanuts dipped in taro sauce that sharpened the taste of alcohol.

Ordinarily, an entertainer in this venue could not expect a cessation in the constant murmur of conversation. But gradually, the buzzing of competing voices died out. For now, at least, there was no distinction between merchants' stable boys from Wolf's Paw, scholars' servant girls from Haan, low-level government clerks sneaking away from the office for the afternoon, laborers resting after a morning's honest work, shopkeepers taking a break while their spouses watched the store, maids and matrons out for errands and meeting friends—all were just members of an audience enthralled by the storyteller standing at the center of the tavern.

He took a sip of foamy beer, put the mug down, slapped his hands a few times against his long, draping sleeves, and continued:

*. . . the Hegemon unsheathed Na-aroénna then, and King Mocri stepped back to admire the great sword: the soul-taker, the head-remover, the hope-dasher. Even the moon seemed to lose her luster next to the pure glow of this weapon.*

*"That is a beautiful blade," said King Mocri, champion of Gan. "It surpasses other swords as Consort Mira excels all other women."*

*The Hegemon looked at Mocri contemptuously, his double-pupils glinting. "Do you praise the weapon because you think I hold an unfair advantage? Come, let us switch swords, and I have no doubt I will still defeat you."*

*"Not at all," said Mocri. "I praise the weapon because I believe you know a warrior by his weapon of choice. What is better in life than to meet an opponent truly worthy of your skill?"*

*The Hegemon's face softened. "I wish you had not rebelled, Mocri. . . ."*

In a corner barely illuminated by the glow of the stove, two boys and a girl huddled around a table. Dressed in hempen robes and tunics that were plain but well-made, they appeared to be the children of farmers or perhaps the servants of a well-to-do merchant's family. The older boy was about twelve, fair-skinned and well proportioned. His eyes were gentle and his dark hair, naturally curly, was tied into a single messy bun at the top of his head. Across the table from him was a girl about a year younger, also fair-skinned and curly-haired—though she wore her hair loose and let the strands cascade around her pretty, round face. The corners of her mouth were curled up in a slight smile as she scanned the room with lively eyes shaped like the body of the graceful dyran, taking in everything with avid interest. Next to her was a younger boy about nine, whose complexion was darker and whose hair was straight and black. The older children sat on either side of him, keeping him penned between the table and the wall. The mischievous glint in his roaming eyes and his constant fidgeting offered a hint as to why. The similarity in the shapes of their features suggested they were siblings.

"Isn't this great?" whispered the younger boy. "I bet Master Ruthi still thinks we're imprisoned in our rooms, enduring our punishment."

"Phyro," said the older boy, a slight frown on his face, "you know this is only a temporary reprieve. Tonight, we each still have to write three essays about how Kon Fiji's *Morality* applies to our misbehavior, how youthful energy must be tempered by education, and how—"

"Shhhh—" the girl said. "I'm trying to hear the storyteller! Don't lecture, Timu. You already agreed that there's no difference between playing first and then studying, on the one hand, and studying first and then playing, on the other. It's called 'time-shifting.'"

"I'm beginning to think that this 'time-shifting' idea of yours would be better called 'time-wasting,'" said Timu, the older brother. "You and Phyro were wrong to make jokes about Master Kon Fiji—and I should have been more severe with you. You should accept your punishment gracefully."

"Oh, wait until you find out what Théra and I—*mmf*—"

The girl had clamped a hand over the younger boy's mouth. "Let's not trouble Timu with too much knowledge, right?" Phyro nodded, and Théra let go.

The young boy wiped his mouth. "Your hand is salty! *Ptui!*" Then he turned back to Timu, his older brother. "Since you're so eager to write the essays, Toto-*tika*, I'm happy to yield my share to you so that you can write six instead of three. Your essays are much more to Master Ruthi's taste anyway."

"That's ridiculous! The only reason I agreed to sneak away with you and Théra is because as the eldest, it's my responsibility to look after you, and you promised you would take your punishment later—"

"Elder Brother, I'm shocked!" Phyro put on a serious mien that looked like an exact copy of their strict tutor's when he was about to launch into a scolding lecture. "Is it not written in Sage Kon Fiji's *Tales of Filial Devotion* that the younger brother should offer the choicest specimens in a basket of plums to the elder brother as a token of his respect? Is it also not written that an elder brother should try to protect the younger brother from difficult tasks beyond his ability, since it is the duty of the stronger to defend the weaker? The essays are uncrackable nuts to me, but juicy plums to you. I am trying to live as a good Moralist with my offer. I thought you'd be pleased."

"That is . . . you cannot . . ." Timu was not as practiced at this particular subspecies of the art of debate as his younger brother. His face grew red, and he glared at Phyro. "If only you would direct your cleverness to actual schoolwork."

"You should be happy that Hudo-*tika* has done the assigned

reading for once," said Théra, who had been trying to maintain a straight face as the brothers argued. "Now please be quiet, both of you; I want to hear this."

*. . . slammed Na-aroénna down, and Mocri met it with his ironwood shield, reinforced with cruben scales. It was as if Fithowéo had clashed his spear against Mount Kiji, or if Kana had slammed her fiery fist against the surface of the sea. Better yet, let me chant for you a portrait of that fight:*

*On this side, the champion of Gan, born and bred on Wolf's Paw;*
*On that side, the Hegemon of Dara, last scion of Cocru's marshals.*
*One is the pride of an island's spear-wielding multitudes;*
*The other is Fithowéo, the God of War, incarnate.*
*Will the Doubt-Ender end all doubt as to who is master of Dara?*
*Or will Goremaw finally meet a blood-meal he cannot swallow?*
*Sword is met with sword, cudgel with shield,*
*The ground quakes as dual titans leap, smash, clash, and thump.*
*For nine days and nine nights they fought on that desolate hill,*
*And the gods of Dara gathered over the whale's way to judge the strength of their will. . . .*

As he chanted, the storyteller banged a coconut husk against a large kitchen spoon to simulate the sounds of sword clanging against shield; he leapt about, whipping his long sleeves this way and that to conjure the martial dance of legendary heroes in the flickering firelight of the pub. As his voice rose and fell, urgent one moment, languorous the next, the audience was transported to another time and place.

*. . . After nine days, both the Hegemon and King Mocri were exhausted. After parrying another strike from the Doubt-Ender, Mocri took a step back and stumbled over a rock. He fell, his shield and sword splayed out to the sides. With one more step, the Hegemon would be able to bash in his skull or lop off his head.*

"No!" Phyro couldn't help himself. Timu and Théra, equally absorbed by the tale, didn't shush him.

The storyteller nodded appreciatively at the children, and went on.

*But the Hegemon stayed where he was and waited until Mocri climbed back up, sword and shield at the ready.*

*"Why did you not end it just now?" asked Mocri, his breathing labored.*

*"Because a great man deserves to not have his life end by chance," said the Hegemon, whose breathing was equally labored. "The world may not be fair, but we must strive to make it so."*

*"Hegemon," said Mocri, "I am both glad and sorry to have met you."*

*And they rushed at each other again, with lumbering steps and proud hearts. . . .*

"Now that is the manner of a real hero," whispered Phyro, his tone full of admiration and longing. "Hey, Timu and Théra, you've actually met the Hegemon, haven't you?"

"Yes . . . but that was a long time ago," Timu whispered back. "I don't really remember much except that he was really tall, and those strange eyes of his looked terribly fierce. I remember wondering how strong he must have been to be able to wield that huge sword on his back."

"He sounds like a great man," said Phyro. "Such honor in every action; such grace to his foes. Too bad he and Da could not—"

"Shhhh!" Théra interrupted. "Hudo-*tika,* not so loud! Do you want everyone here to know who we are?"

Phyro might be a rascal to his older brother, but he respected the authority of his older sister. He lowered his voice. "Sorry. He just seems such a brave man. And Mocri, too. I'll have to tell Ada-*tika* all about this hero from her home island. How come Master Ruthi never taught us anything about Mocri?"

"This is just a story," Théra said. "Fighting nonstop for nine days and nine nights—how can you believe that really happened? Think: The storyteller wasn't there, how would he know what the Hegemon and Mocri said?" But seeing the disappointment on her little brother's face, she softened her tone. "If you want to hear real stories about heroes, I'll tell you later about the time Auntie Soto stopped the Hegemon from hurting Mother and us. I was only three then, but I remember it as though it happened yesterday."

Phyro's eyes brightened and he was about to ask for more, but a rough voice broke in.

"I've had just about enough of this ridiculous tale, you insolent fraud!"

The storyteller stopped in midsentence, shocked at this intrusion into his performance. The tavern patrons turned to look at the speaker. Standing next to the stove, the man was tall, barrel-chested, and as muscular as a stevedore. He was easily the largest person in the pub. A jagged scar that started at his left brow and ended at his right cheek gave his face a fearsome aspect, which was only enhanced by the wolf's-teeth necklace that dangled in front of the thick chest hair that peeked out of the loose lapels of his short robe like a patch of fur. Indeed, the yellow teeth that showed between his sneering lips reminded one of a hungry wolf on the prowl.

"How dare you fabricate such stories about that crook Mata Zyndu? He tried to thwart Emperor Ragin's righteous march to the throne and caused much needless suffering and desolation. By praising the despicable tyrant Zyndu, you're denigrating the victory of our wise emperor and casting aspersions upon the character of the Dandelion Throne. These are words of treason."

"Treason? For telling a few stories?" The storyteller was so furious that he started to laugh. "Will you next claim that all folk opera troupes are rebels for enacting the rise and fall of old Tiro dynasties? Or that the wise Emperor Ragin is jealous of shadow puppet plays about Emperor Mapidéré? What a silly man you are!"

The owners of the Three-Legged Jug, a rotund man of short stature and his equally rotund wife, rushed up between the two to play peacemakers. "Masters! Remember this is a humble venue for entertainment and relaxation! No politics, please! We're all here after a hard day's work to share a few drinks and have some fun."

The husband turned to the man with the scarred face and bowed deeply. "Master, I can tell you are a man of hot passions and strong morals. And if the tale has offended, I apologize first. I know Tino here well. Let me assure you he had no intention of insulting the emperor. Why, before he became a storyteller, he fought for Emperor Ragin during the Chrysanthemum-Dandelion War in Haan, when the emperor was only the King of Dasu."

The wife smiled ingratiatingly. "How about a flask of plum wine on the house? If you and Tino drink together, I'm sure you'll forget about this little misunderstanding."

"What makes you think I want to have a drink with *him*?" asked Tino the storyteller, whipping his sleeves contemptuously at Scarface.

The other patrons in the pub shouted in support of the storyteller.

"Sit down, you ignorant oaf!"

"Get out of here if you don't like the story. No one is forcing you to sit and listen!"

"I'll throw you out myself if you keep this up."

Scarface smiled, stuck one of his hands into the lapel of his robe, under the dangling wolf's-teeth necklace, and retrieved a small metal tablet. He waved it around at the patrons and then held it under the nose of the proprietress of the pub. "Do you recognize this?"

She squinted to get a good look. The tablet was about the size of two palms, and two large logograms were carved into it in relief: one was the logogram for *sight*—a stylized eye with a beam coming out of it—and the other was the logogram for *faraway*—composed of the number logogram for "a thousand" modified by a winding path around it. Shocked, the woman stuttered, "You . . . you're with the . . . the, um, the . . ."

Scarface put the tablet away. The cold, mirthless grin on his face grew wider as he scanned the room, daring anyone to hold his gaze. "That's right. I serve Duke Rin Coda, Imperial Farsight Secretary."

The shouting among the patrons died down, and even Tino lost his confident look. Although Scarface looked more like a highwayman than a government official, Duke Coda, who was in charge of Emperor Ragin's spies, was said to run his department in collaboration with the seedier elements of Dara society. It wouldn't be beyond him to rely on someone like Scarface. Even though no one in the pub had ever heard of a storyteller getting in trouble for an embellished tale about the Hegemon, Duke Coda's duties did include ferreting out traitors and dissatisfied former nobles plotting against the emperor. No one wanted to risk challenging the emperor's own trusted eyes.

"Wait—" Phyro was about to speak when Théra grabbed his hand and squeezed it under the table and shook her head at him slowly.

Seeing the timid reactions from everyone present, Scarface nodded with satisfaction. He pushed the owners of the pub aside and strolled up to Tino. "Crafty, disloyal *entertainers* like you are the worst. Just because you fought for the emperor doesn't give you the right to say whatever you want. Now, normally, I would have to take you to the constables for further interrogation"—Tino shrank back in terror—"but I'm in a generous mood today. If you pay a fine of twenty-five pieces of silver and apologize for your errors, I might just let you off with a warning."

Tino glanced at the few coins in the tip bowl on the table and turned back to Scarface. He bowed repeatedly like a chicken pecking at the ground. "Master Farseer, please! That amounts to two week's earnings even when things are going well. I've got an aged mother at home who is ill—"

"Of course you do," said Scarface. "She'll miss you terribly if you are held at the constable station, won't she? A proper interrogation might take days, weeks even; do you understand?"

Tino's face shifted through rage, humiliation, and utter defeat as he reached into the lapel of his robe for his coin purse. The other patrons looked away carefully, not daring to make a sound.

"Don't think the rest of you are getting off so easily, either," said Scarface. "I heard how many of you cheered when he veiled his criticisms of the emperor with that story full of lies. Each of you will have to pay a fine of one silver as an accessory to the crime."

The men and women in the pub looked unhappy, but a few sighed and began reaching for their purses as well.

"Stop."

Scarface looked around for the source of the voice, which was crisp, sharp, and uninflected by fear. A figure stood up from the shadowy corner of the pub and walked into the firelight of the stove, a slight limp in the gait punctuated by the staccato falls of a walking stick.

Though dressed in a scholar's long flowing robes edged in blue silk, the speaker was a woman. About eighteen years of age, she had fair skin and gray eyes that glinted with a steadfastness that belied her youth. The radiating lines of a faint pink scar, like a sketch of a blooming flower, covered her left cheek, and the stem of this flower continued down her neck like the lateral line of a fish, curiously adding a sense of liveliness to her otherwise wan visage. Her hair, a light brown, was tied atop her head in a tight triple scroll-bun. Tassels and knotted strings dangled from her blue sash—a custom of distant northwestern islands in old Xana. Leaning against a wooden walking stick that came up to her eyebrows, she put her right hand on the sword she wore at her waist, the scabbard and hilt looking worn and shabby.

"What do you want?" asked Scarface. But his tone was no longer as arrogant as before. The woman's scroll-bun and her boldness in openly wearing a sword in Pan indicated that she was a scholar who had achieved the rank of *cashima*, a Classical Ano word meaning "practitioner": She had passed the second level of the Imperial examinations.

Emperor Ragin had restored and expanded the civil service examination system long practiced by the Tiro kings and the Xana Empire, turning it into the sole mode of advancement for those with political ambition while eliminating other time-honored paths to obtain valuable administrative posts, such as patronage, purchase, inheritance, or recommendation by trusted nobles. Competition in the examinations was fierce, and the emperor, who had risen to power with the aid of women in powerful posts, had opened the exams to women as well as men. Though women *toko dawiji*—the rank given to those who had passed the Town Examinations, the first level in the exams—were still rare, and women *cashima* even rarer, they were entitled to all the privileges of the status given to their male counterparts. For instance, all *toko dawiji* were exempt from corvée, and the *cashima* had the additional right to be brought before an Imperial magistrate right away when accused of a crime instead of being interrogated by the constables.

"Stop bothering these people," she said calmly. "And you certainly won't be getting a single copper out of me."

Scarface had not expected to find a person of her rank in a dive like the Three-Legged Jug. "Mistress, you don't have to pay the fine, of course. I'm sure you're not a disloyal scoundrel like the rest of these lowlifes."

She shook her head. "I don't believe you work for Duke Coda at all."